FROM THE PAGES
THE ILIAD

Sing, O Goddess, the ruinous wrath of Achilles,
Son of Peleus, the terrible curse that brought
Unnumbered woes upon the Achaeans and hurled
To Hades so many heroic souls, leaving
Their bodies the prey of dogs and carrion birds.   (page 1)

Then Hector spoke between the two armies: "From me,
O Trojans and well-greaved Achaeans, hear the proposal
Of Paris, who began this miserable war. He says
For all other Trojans and men of Achaea to lay
Their excellent arms on the bountiful earth, and that he,
Out here in the middle, will fight with fierce Menelaus
For Helen and all her treasures."   (page 45)

"Think!
O son of Tydeus, think—and shrink! Don't try
To equal the gods in spirit and valor, for the race
Of immortal gods is by no means the same as that
Of earth-treading men!"   (page 83)

"Oh god-nourished Prince,
Our eyes can see nothing but total destruction, and we
Are afraid."   (page 146)

And Cronos' son roused in their hearts an evil
Lust for the din and confusion of war, and down
From the upper air he sent dark dew-drops of blood,
For he was about to hurl down to Hades many
Heroic heads.   (page 177)

"On, you horse-taming Trojans, smash the wall
Of the Argives and hurl on the ships your god-blazing fire!"
          (page 210)

The spear went in beneath Ilioneus' brow
At the base of his eye, forced the eyeball out, passed on
Through the socket and out at the nape of his neck, and Ilioneus
Sank to the ground, stretching out both of his hands.   (page 249)

            "What fills my heart
And soul with so much bitter resentment is simply
That one whose equal I am should want to rob me
And take my prize of prestige for no better reason
Than this, that he has more power."   (page 273)

"Then soon let me die! since I was not there to help
My friend when he died."   (page 320)

      "O Father Zeus, how total is that cruel blindness
You cast upon men!"   (page 342)

      "Hector, I beg you, dear child,
Don't stand there alone and wait for the charge of that man,
Or death at his hands may soon be yours, since he
Is far stronger than you—and a savage!"   (page 379)

      "Show me my bed, now, Achilles,
O nobleman nurtured of Zeus, that we may enjoy
A night of sweet sleep. For never once have my lids
Come together in sleep since my son lost his life at your hands."
                                                (page 435)

THE ILIAD

HOMER

TRANSLATED BY ENNIS REES

WITH AN INTRODUCTION AND NOTES
BY BRUCE M. KING

GEORGE STADE
CONSULTING EDITORIAL DIRECTOR

BARNES & NOBLE CLASSICS
NEW YORK

JB

BARNES & NOBLE CLASSICS
NEW YORK

Published by Barnes & Noble Books
122 Fifth Avenue
New York, NY 10011

www.barnesandnoble.com/classics

It is believed that the *Iliad* was first set down in writing during the eighth century
B.C.E. Ennis Rees's translation first appeared in 1963.

Published in 2005 by Barnes & Noble Classics with new Introduction,
Notes, Biography, Chronology, Inspired By, Comments & Questions,
and For Further Reading.

Introduction, Notes, and For Further Reading
Copyright © 2005 by Bruce M. King.

Translation of the *Iliad*
Copyright © 1963, 2005 by Ennis Rees.

Note on Homer, The World of the *Iliad*,
Inspired by the *Iliad* and the *Odyssey*, and Comments & Questions
Copyright © 2005 by Barnes & Noble, Inc.

The Iliad
ISBN–13: 978-1-59308-232-1
ISBN–10: 1-59308-232-0
LC Control Number 2005929206

Produced and published in conjunction with:
Fine Creative Media, Inc.
322 Eighth Avenue
New York, NY 10001

Michael J. Fine, President and Publisher

Printed in the United States of America

QM

3   5   7   9   10   8   6   4   2

"HOMER"

Scholarly study of the *Iliad* and the *Odyssey* has been shaped by recurring versions of the Homeric Question: Who composed the two epics, and how? Were the two epics composed by a single poet whose comprehensive vision organized the whole, or are they the product of generations of poets working within an oral tradition? Does "Homer" denote an individual, or rather a tradition of bards and a form of poetry that attained prominence throughout Greece? Though the debate has been vituperative and long-lived (its modern formulation dates from F. R. Wolf's *Prolegomena to Homer* of 1795), it has flourished especially in the absence of historical evidence that definitively locates Homer or his poems within a specific time or place. Though there is a profuse and fascinating body of ancient lore about "Homer" and his career, the accounts are multiple and competitive; few cities could resist claiming Homer as their own. Within this vacuum of historical certainty and profusion of lore, scholars and readers have often found a "Homer" who snugly conforms to their interpretation of the poems themselves.

Within contemporary Homeric studies, the researches of Milman Parry and Albert B. Lord have transformed our understanding of the composition of the *Iliad* and the *Odyssey*. Parry confirmed and furthered his initial, text-based studies of Homeric composition (of the late 1920s) by his field research (1933–1935) among the performing oral poets of Yugoslavia. Parry's immersion in the performance culture of practicing bards permitted him to develop a comparative account of Homeric composition-in-performance; recording and analyzing the performances of actual bards allowed him to see how these working singers used the given components of their tradition—repeated epithets, type-scenes, narrative patterns—to improvise a new poem, uniquely fitted to the immediate conditions of its performance and the demands of its particular audience. Parry's work was continued and extended by his student Albert Lord, whose researches in a great variety of performing song cultures broadened and deepened the comparative context within which the Homeric poems might be studied and appreciated. The research of Parry and Lord has offered a model for the composition of the *Iliad* and the *Odyssey* that can account for the entirety of each poem in its present form (there is no need to differentiate between "early" and "late" strata, between interpolation and original—all are equally part of the performance tradition). But their work also decisively challenges the idea that there was a single poet to whose genius each poem (or both poems) can be attributed; in place of a poet of genius, it is an ingenious tradition that emerges.

If we set aside the quest for the one true Homer, we might speak instead of historical stages in the transmission of the *Iliad* and the *Odyssey*, in which the poems moved from a relatively fluid state to an increasingly fixed, textualized form. In this model (brilliantly and controversially developed by Gregory Nagy), the first stage spanned from the early second millennium to the middle of the eighth century B.C.E.— a period of oral transmission and composition-in-performance wholly without written texts. A final stage of Homeric transmission can be dated to about 150 B.C.E., when the scholar Aristarchus of Samothrace, the head of the great library of Alexandria, completed his edition of the Homeric poems, at which point something like a fixed "library edition" of Homer appeared; such an edition no longer presupposes performance. In the 700 years between these two poles, the poems moved from a state of relative fluidity to one of increasing fixity; so, too, the role of the singer moved from one who composed in performance to one who re-performed a poem that was increasingly fixed and that finally, in a late stage, was simply learned by rote and available in written, if not yet authoritative, form.

TABLE OF CONTENTS

THE WORLD OF THE ILIAD

1575– The Mycenaean period takes its name from Mycenae, a city on
1200   mainland Greece that was excavated by Heinrich Schliemann in
B.C.E. 1876 (other great palace-centers have been excavated in Thebes,
Tiryns, and Pylos). While the *Iliad* preserves some fossilized mem-
ories of Mycenaean culture, the poem is not a reliable historical
account of the Mycenaean realm; four and a half centuries separate the formation of our *Iliad* and the legendary past that is the
poem's setting.

1200– The Mycenaean palace kingdoms decline and collapse for reasons
1100   that remain elusive to contemporary historians; according to recent research, the kingdoms may have fallen from strains within
Mycenaean society itself, rather than from invaders. The Fall of
Troy is traditionally dated to 1184.

1100– This period, between the Mycenaean collapse and the first Olympic
776   Games, is traditionally regarded as the "Dark Age" of Greece.
Though some areas—notably Lefkandi on the island of Euboea—
recover and prosper, most Mycenaean centers are abandoned or
greatly diminished in population; trade routes are destroyed, and
material culture reverts to a pre-Mycenaean level. Linear B, the
Mycenaean script, is lost; the heroic poetry that will become our
Iliad and *Odyssey* is transmitted orally.

776–   In the early eighth century, the Greeks adopt a modified Phoenician
179   alphabet. During this period the city-state emerges and prospers,
and a sense of Panhellenic identity takes hold across the separate
Greek states. The existence of the alphabet means the Homeric
poems can be written down, but they are still composed and
transmitted orally.

180–   Aristarchus of Samothrace, while head of the library of Alexandria,
144   produces recensions of the text of the *Iliad* and the *Odyssey*, as well
as commentaries upon those texts. Aristarchus uses a variety of
symbols to query the genuineness of particular verses and the
transmitted order of verses; his goal is to remove corruption and
interpolation from the texts. His versions of the *Iliad* and the
Odyssey, which build upon and modify the work of his teacher
Aristophanes of Byzantium, will be considered by some to be
the first critical editions of Homer.

30–19 The Roman poet Virgil writes the *Aeneid*, with Homer as a model for emulation and transformation

450 With the decline of the Roman Empire, interest in Greek texts and
C.E. in Homer becomes dormant in the West until learning resurges in the Middle Ages.

7th Homeric figures begin to appear in the Arabic tales of Sinbad.
century

1488 The first printed edition of the Greek text of Homer appears.

1598 George Chapman publishes English translations of the *Iliad* and
1615 the *Odyssey*.

1715 Alexander Pope publishes translations of the *Iliad* and the
1726 *Odyssey*.

1788 J. B. G. d'Ansse de Villoison publishes ancient scholarship on the Venetus A manuscript of Homer that remains our richest source for the working methods of ancient Homeric scholars.

1795 Friedrich August Wolf publishes *Prolegomena to Homer*, which inaugurates modern textual scholarship of Homer.

1870 Heinrich Schliemann, a retired German businessman with a passion for the Homeric epics, begins excavations at Troy (Hisarlik).

1933– Based on observations of contemporary verse composition-in-
1935 performance in the Balkans, American scholars Milman Parry and Albert B. Lord present comparative evidence that the Homeric poems were transmitted for many generations by oral bards.

INTRODUCTION

> And as when gusts
> Come many and fast on a day when shrill winds are blowing
> And raising the thick dust on roads up into a swirling
> Huge cloud, so now they clashed in one fierce throng,
> Each man eager to use his sharp bronze on another.
> And the man-wasting battle bristled with lengthy, flesh-rending
> Spears, and eyes were blinded by the blazing of bronze
> From gleaming helmets, new-burnished breastplates, and flashing,
> Resplendent shields, as chaotically on the men came.
>
> (Homer *Iliad* XIII.379–387)

Among the wildly various ancient biographies of Homer—which divergently account for the poet's home-city and date of birth, his poetic works, his blindness or sightedness, his death—the anecdotal compendium entitled *The Contest of Homer and Hesiod* (the bulk of which dates from the beginning of the fourth century B.C.E.) presents an itinerant Homer who wanders from town to town performing his verse. At the funeral games of a Euboean king named Amphidamas, so the story goes, Homer is lured by the promise of a great prize into a contest with the poet Hesiod, who composes in the same verse form as Homer (the dactylic hexameter), but who sings—in his *Works and Days*—not of the hero's battles, but of the farmer's life. At every turn of the ensuing competition in the composition and performance of poetry, Homer decisively bests Hesiod; he is the people's favorite. As a final test of the poets, King Panedes, the arbiter of the contest, asks each to sing his finest passage: Hesiod sings of the farmer's year (*Works and Days* 383–392), while Homer sings—in the passage cited above—of the dazzle of "man-wasting battle," which gleams so bright as to blind the combatants. Upon the completion of Hesiod's and Homer's recitations, the people once again acclaim Homer, but the decisive word belongs to King Panedes (*Contest of Homer and Hesiod* 205–210):

> Full of wonder, the Greeks praised Homer also in this case, and asked that he should be granted victory, because his verses were even better than expected. But the king crowned Hesiod, saying that it was just that the poet who recommended agriculture and peace, rather than the one who described wars and slaughter, should win.

Homer is the favorite of the Greeks, Hesiod of the king; Homer's verses provoke "wonder," Hesiod's provoke considerations of what is "just." King Panedes opts to reward the just, rather than the popular and wondrous. The judgment of King Panedes surely registers the ruler's maxim that if political order is to be maintained, his subjects are better encouraged to hone their farming skills, rather than their acuity in spear-throwing and hand-to-hand combat. But the king's vote—in favor of political concord rather than wonder—perhaps also intimates the unsettling force and appeal of a Homeric poetry that makes vivid not that which is seasonally predictable or politically stable, but that which compels for its very combustibility, for its evocation of desires that might elude the restraints of political order.

In the *Iliad* generally—and in the very verses that the Homer of the *Contest* sings—the wondrous is often a spectacle of violent, chaotic death. Such carnage is scarcely bearable (as the Iliadic passage that Homer sings again exemplifies), especially as it is also a topic of wonder, for the risk and venture of violent death seem also to contain the possibility of a self-making apart from the necessities and regularities of politics and the cultivable fields. Homer's audience—in the *Contest*—wonders at a song that is violent, even transgressive, but that also seems to promise a completion, a fulfillment, greater than what the farmer's life—or the life of the king's subject—can offer. Held in wonder by a poetry that depicts a life apart from, even at odds with, the civilizing, pacifying labor of the fields, Homer's auditors might, indeed, make for restless royal subjects. King Panedes' crowning of Hesiod is neither poetically undiscerning nor politically disinterested (though Homer's advocates might take consolation in the knowledge that Panedes' name was to become proverbial for a powerful man who makes a foolish decision).

In a bravura conclusion to his (losing) performance, Homer imagines a spectator of the very scene he has just narrated: Such an onlooker would be very "hard-hearted" who could look "on that slaughter with joy instead of lament" (XIII.388–389). This is no simple endorsement of the hero's life: The battlefield is a potential site of self-creation through martial strife, but it is also an arena of carnage, within which the combatants themselves can be blinded. Homer's imagined observer of the battle provokes reflection about the "wonder" experienced by his audience—which now includes us as well: The wonder that we experience in listening to Homer would not be possible—or would be possible only for the most hard-hearted of us—if we were "actually" there; it is only when the chaos of battle is shaped and formed by the poet's art that the unbearable becomes a source of pleasure, a wonder. The king would tell us that our unsettled and unsettling desires—which, in Homer, are most manifest on the battlefield—can be assuaged within the political order, by the satisfactions of the ordered, productive life, as exemplified by Hesiod's farmer. The *Iliad*, I would suggest, regards such claims with an astringent skepticism; the wonder that the poet provokes arises from his making into a unity, into a source of pleasure, that which is, in life, fractured, contested, and sometimes unbearable. Our wonder comes from the glimpse of a singularity, a unity of power, a full articulation of desire greater than that permitted in life—or, to put it in somewhat different terms, from a full vision of the unbearable that is consubstantial with death.

Homers

Some say, "there never was such a person as Homer." "No such person as Homer! On the contrary," say others, "there were scores."

— Thomas De Quincey, "Homer and the Homeridae" (1841)

No Homer or many Homers: Both possibilities arise from the difficulty— even the impossibility—of locating a single historical Homer. The texts of the *Iliad* (and the *Odyssey*) that we now read (and translate) have been transmitted to us with none of the signs by which we now recognize an author: There is no self-referential mention of a "Homer" within the epics themselves; there is no single or uncontested account of the occasion and means of first production and transmission; there is no sign or seal that might indicate an "autograph copy" or descent from a singularly privileged source. The ancients themselves attest a discrepant multitude of Homers, born in different cities, traveling to different lands in different eras, even singing different poems (the *Iliad* and the *Odyssey* were not unanimously deemed to be the two sole works of Homer alone until the fourth century B.C.E.—that is, not until after the two poems had been transmitted for some 300 years in a form roughly akin to what we have today and among a multitude of other titles also attributed to Homer). Even Homer's name is a topic of variant and disputatious accounts: One of the ancient lives of Homer, for example, accounts Homer's "real" name to have been Melesigenes and his hometown to have been Cyme, where the local word for "blind" is *homeros*: "Hence, the name Homer gradually replaced Melesigenes on account of his misfortune" (*Vita Herodotea* 162–165)—blindness being one of the few near constants in early accounts of Homer. Melesigenes reappears in another biography of Homer, this time as a citizen of Smyrna, who is sent as a hostage to the rival city of Chios; in this version (recorded by Proclus in the fifth century C.E.), the pun that produces the name plays on the Greek word for "hostage," which is (also) *homeros*: "When he was given as a hostage [*homereian*] to the Chians, he was called Homer" (Proclus, p. 99). And thus in the ancient lives of Homer do etymologies and biographies multiply.

Contemporary scholars have offered an etymology of the Greek *Homeros* that derives the name from an Indo-European (thus pre-Greek) verbal root (*ar-) that means "to fit" or "to join," in the manner that a carpenter (a "joiner," in older English) fits together beams—and especially the beams of a chariot (as discussed in Nagy, *The Best of the Achaeans*; see "For Further Reading"). The name "Homer"—comprised of the elements "together" (Greek *homo-*) and "to fit"—means, then, "he who fits [the song] together." From this perspective, the name "Homer" is generic for the poet's labor, which—like the carpenter's—is a joining together, a crafting, of multiple parts into a single unity, into a single confluence. The English word "harmony" (after the Greek goddess Harmonie) derives from the same root as "Homer"; and the goal of both carpenter and poet is "art," which likewise derives (via Latin *ars*) from the very stem (*ar-) that generates the name "Homer." Indeed, we might finally understand "Homer" to denote the paradigmatic, mythical poet; "Homer" names not an individual singer, but the very idea of the poet.

The traditional semantics that underlie the name of Homer are activated in the poet's description, toward the end of book IV of the *Iliad*, of the death of Simoeisius. This hero, a son of the Trojan river-god, is cut down in battle by the Achaean Ajax; upon Simoeisius' death, the poet offers a startling and haunting simile (IV.557–562):

> . . . [Simoeisius] fell
> To earth in the dust like a smooth black poplar whose branchy top
> Falls in the low grassland of a mighty marsh
> To the gleaming ax of some chariot-maker, who leaves it
> To dry by the banks of a river that he may bend him
> A rim for a beautiful chariot.

Simoeisius, struck down and killed by Ajax' spear, is compared to a felled tree, which will itself be hewed and worked into a chariot-wheel. The unifying craft of the "chariot-maker"—a Greek word derived, again, from the same root as "Homer"—transforms the body of the slain hero into a work of great art. Though Simoeisius is killed in the prime of his youth and upon his very first appearance on the battlefield, his name and fate are now pressed into memory. The simile upon Simoeisius' death presents a visual icon of the poet's work: the transformation of the hero's death into verbal art, the immortalizion of the name in poetry (I will return to this theme below). We might also be reminded of the final lines of Homer's recitation in the *Contest*, for the death of Simoeisius, brutally cut down in his youth, before he might repay his parents' care, is a sight that we could scarcely, if at all, bear, were we its literal onlookers, but that the poet's art transforms into an object—a wheel and a chariot—of splendor and beauty (if also an object that remains, for all its potentially dazzling, even blinding wonder, a vehicle of war).

The multiple Homers of the ancient biographical tradition and the Homer whose name is paradigmatic for the poet and his labor converge upon one fundamental point: Homer belongs to no single city (nor even to one single historical generation), but to many; his art is not local, but—as the etymology of the name Homer intimates—synthetic and, finally, synoptic. Within the *Iliad* (and the *Odyssey*), there are few traces of story-traditions of purely local interest; rather, the *Iliad's* hero-songs, while they provoke intense interest within the widely dispersed cities of Greece, overarch and elude the particularities of local space and time. In this crucial regard, the Homeric poems are Panhellenic; and, as such, the poems, which reach something close to their definitive form in the late eighth and early seventh centuries B.C.E., participate in—and are themselves shaped by—their larger historical moment. For the Greek historical experience of this period is marked by a new and intensified communication among the emergent Greek cities themselves; by the foundation of the Olympic Games, which were open to competitors from throughout the Greek-speaking regions; by the establishment of the great cult site of Apollo at Delphi, whose oracle was open to all and was consulted in matters of dispute between cities; and by the gradual proliferation of the alphabet, itself a technology that might foster further communication within and beyond the walls of a single city. The *Iliad* and the *Odyssey*, in their synthesis—their crafty "joining"—of a set of heroic myths and themes that eludes local or simply aetiological meanings, are themselves preeminent, catalytic signs of this same burgeoning Panhellenism. (See Nagy, *The Best of the Achaeans* and Snodgrass, *Archaic Greece*, for discussions of the centrality of Panhellenism.)

The artful chariot of the simile that follows upon the death of Simoeisius might itself be an emblem of Panhellenism: The story—the fame—of the hero, even of a hero as poignantly short-lived as Simoeisius, is not fixed to a single spot, like a felled tree, but rather, through the craft of the poet-joiner, is set in motion, capable of travel to the borders—and beyond—of a newly expansive Greek culture. And so, too, "Homer," the poet's paradigmatic name, remains open to new etymologies, which will take him far from his place—or places—of origin. The contemporary poet Derek Walcott in his *Omeros*, an epic that relocates the characters and themes of the *Iliad* to the Caribbean island of St. Lucia, offers one of the loveliest of etymologies for the name of Homer:

And O was the conch-shell's invocation, mer was
both mother and sea in our Antillean patois,
os, a grey bone, and the white surf as it crashes
and spreads its sibilant collar on a lace shore.
Omeros was the crunch of dry leaves, and the washes
that echoed from a cave-mouth when the tide has ebbed.

Walcott's etymological play with the name of Homer revivifies the poet
by rehearing and rearticulating the syllables of his name within the local
language—the "patois"—of St. Lucia, though those syllables are themselves long-lived descendants (first by way of Latin, then of French) of
the Greek of Homer. As Walcott's mer washes Homer ashore upon St.
Lucia, ancient meanings are recovered and renewed, even as they are
given contemporary form. And in that sense, the chariot of Simoeisius
remains in motion, as the Iliad—the first work within the Western literary canon—becomes not only Panhellenic but pancultural, inasmuch as
its meanings remain recoverable for present and future poets and readers. This is the ongoing work of the many Homers, as well as of the
poetry for which the name "Homer" is synecdoche: the recovery of the
meaning—ancient and other—of the word.

Poetic Tradition and Its Critique

This book is about Homer. He is our Singer of Tales. Yet, in a larger sense,
he represents all singers of tales from time immemorial and unrecorded
to the present. Our book is about these other singers as well. Each of
them, even the most mediocre, is as much a part of the tradition of oral
epic singing as is Homer, its most talented representative.

—A. B. Lord, "Forward" to The Singer of Tales (1960)

No Homer or many Homers? In contemporary Homeric studies, the
work of Milman Parry and Albert Lord provides an answer: There is
no one Homer because there were generations of Homers who had con-
tinuously sung heroic songs for perhaps a thousand years prior to the
time when the Iliad was first stabilized—around the final quarter of the
eighth century B.C.E.—in a version close to the written form that we now
have. Parry's textual studies in the late 1920s began with the familiar repetition of noun-epithet phrases—for example, "grey-eyed Athene"—and
proceeded to demonstrate that those repetitions were not random, but
systematic. Moreover, such systems of repetition—of formulae, of phrases,
of lines, of typical scenes, of episodes—are characteristic of oral poetries

in general; the oral poet, as he performs, works with the given and re-peated building-blocks, small and large, of his tradition. Parry then con-firmed and expanded his text-based studies by fieldwork, conducted with his student and collaborator Lord, among the performing oral poets—the *guslars*—of Yugoslavia in between 1933 and 1935. Among these still active singers, Parry and Lord recorded—on paper and on an extraordi-nary half-ton of aluminum sound discs—their heroic songs, newly per-formed for the occasion, newly composed without a written text. Each performing bard invokes, reenacts, and distills those performances that have come before, even as he creates a unique and present song, shaped by the particulars of the moment and the occasion—particularly by his keen awareness of his audience and their responses. The bard improvises among the elements of his tradition in the sense that he might reassem-ble or modify the fixed elements of that tradition in especially skillful, often surprising ways. But before the bard can display such heights of skill, he must first master the language of his tradition, as well as its char-acteristic scenes and story-patterns. So, too, in contemplating the *Iliad*, we should speak first of the genius of the tradition that produced it, then—if we wish—of the virtuosity of a poet.

Attention to the traditional language of the bard is crucial not only for the insight that it offers into the workings and transmission of the poetic tradition, but for the access it provides to the poet's generative themes. The formulae, imagery, and type-scenes that recur in Homeric poetry are themselves articulations of the conceptual and thematic well-springs of the bard's song. Repetition—and variation in repetition—is itself a sign of thematic centrality; these are the themes and ideas that the epic has preserved and has, over generations of transmission, distilled to a remarkable degree of concentration. One such recurring image in the *Iliad* is that of the "spring bloom" of the hero, an image both of the hero's exultant battle-strength and of his memorial representation in the bard's song. The *Iliad*'s account of the Trojan warrior Gorgythion presents an especially vivid example of the concentrating power of the poet's tradi-tional language, as the "spring bloom" becomes a synopsis of the war-rior's death and his recompense. Gorgythion makes his entrance upon the battlefield only to be immediately struck down by an arrow from the bow of Teucer—who was, at any rate, aiming for Hector. We hear of Gor-gythion's lineage—he is a son of Priam; then we hear of his death and its poetic transfiguration (VIII.344–345 and 347–350):

> . . . [Teucer] lodged his arrow deep in the breast
> Of peerless Gorgythion . . .
> . . . And now to one side
> Gorgythion drooped his head and heavy helmet:

> He let it fall over like the bloom of a garden poppy
> Heavy with seed and the rains of spring.

Gorgythion steps upon the battlefield only so as to be killed, and of his death the poet makes a simile. The violence of an arrow wound to the neck is elided by an image of unexpected and unsettling beauty: The warrior's severed head is like the bloom of a poppy that has tumbled over because it is overfull of its own life-force. The gore of the battle-field is displaced by an image that precisely articulates the exchange that governs the career of the traditional hero: life for art—and especially, youthful life for epic poetry, for the immortality of the name that is pre-served by the poet. It is the defining claim of the epic bard—indeed, the very premise of his traditional genre—that he will preserve the hero's name and deeds through the medium of epic song, transmitting that name to succeeding generations of singers. But the bard does not im-mortalize the hero's deeds from any point within his life-course, but only from the period of youth that is "spring-bloom," which Homeric Greek calls *hebe*. Though *hebe* can denote the first physical signs of the male transition from youth to maturity, *hebe* is, for the hero, less a spe-cific chronological period of life than it is an attained state of near-divine intensity in which individual superiority, an integrity of body and of action, is visible to all: *Hebe* is that brief moment when the war-rior has "the flower of youth, when the might / Of a man is strongest" (XIII.559–560). And it is precisely this superiority, this force in bloom, that the Homeric hero most possesses at the very moment of his death: The moment of fullest self-creation and self-display is also the moment of death, and it is that same perfection of the hero in an ir-repeatable instant of spectacular, self-consuming force that the bard immortalizes. The simile on Gorgythion's death is a concentrated image and enactment of the "Beautiful Death" and of the logic of heroic com-memoration: Life is exchanged for art; life is perfected in an instant that exhausts mortal life's possibility, but that receives recompense in the immortalizing verses of the bard. (See Loraux, *The Experiences of Tire-sias* and Vernant, *Mortals and Immortals*, for discussions of the "Beautiful Death.")

Both Patroclus and Hector die under the sign of *hebe*; it is, for each, the last word: "His soul flew forth from his body . . . bewailing her lot as one too soon bereft of youth and manly vigor [*hebe*]" (XVI.992–994 and XXII.424–427). Moreover, it is the deaths of Patroclus and Hector (preceded by that of Sarpedon) that structure the final third of the *Iliad* and that make necessary the death of Achilles, which is beyond the end of the *Iliad* but insistently foreshadowed within it. The early death of Achilles is thematic from the *Iliad*'s very first book, where Achilles himself laments to his mother Thetis that she bore him "only to live for a few short years" (I.411). If it is a general description of the epic hero of Homeric tradition that he is to die young for the sake of future fame, Achilles—immediately upon his insulted withdrawal from the Achaean camp and upon suffering the abduction of Briseis—invokes that definition, but now self-consciously, as an explicit conundrum of life and topic for thought. In a sense, his mother's prophecy only makes explicit for Achilles the early death that is the generic requirement of the hero's life; but Achilles, in his rage and disorientation consequent upon the loss of Briseis, now has impulse to think about—and kick against—the fatality that would govern his life. In this thematization of the very stakes of the traditional hero's life (and death), the poet of the *Iliad* reveals the fullest possibilities of his art, which is a preeminently critical art, capable of testing, from the very beginning of the poem, its own generative premises.

This critical exploration of the hero's death-bound fate—of the exchange of youthful life for art—culminates in the passage from book IX that is often called "the choice of Achilles." At this juncture of the plot, Achilles' rage has deepened; the insult of book I has precipitated a general questioning of just what it is that would satisfy heroic desire, if not the gifts, women, and kingships of the world—which Achilles has just declared to be worth no more than "sand and dust" (IX.443). Achilles now elaborates upon his mother's prophecy (IX.471–478):

> My goddess mother, Thetis
> Of the silver feet, tells me I bear two fates
> With me on my way to the grave. If I stay here
> And fight about Troy, I'll never return to my home,
> But men will remember my glory forever. On the other hand,
> If I go back to the precious land of my fathers,
> No glory at all will be mine, but life, long life,
> Will be, and no early death shall ever come on me.

One of the most extraordinary aspects of this speech (as G. Nagy has shown in his *Best of the Achaeans*) is the specificity with which Achilles invokes the epic tradition itself. The phrase "glory forever" translates a formulaic phrase of Indo-European provenance—*aphthiton kleos*—that names the very genre of traditional heroic poetry itself, and that we might translate more literally as "unwithering fame." If the flower in spring bloom, full—and overfull—of its own seed, is a traditional poetic icon of the hero's apotheosis, the bard's work is to make that culminating moment of full bloom and of death—the moment of *hebe*—into verse that is itself "unwithering." The underlying metaphor from nature—the flower that can only, of its own, wither—is transfigured by the cultural work of poetry, such that the evanescence of the bloom is forever captured within the tradition of *aphthiton kleos*, "unwithering fame." Achilles, in contemplating his two choices, explicitly invokes by proper name the epic tradition within which he is himself the central figure; and, in positing an alternative (the long life without glory), he speaks as if he might launch himself out of the very logic and generic requirements of that tradition. Such a rejection will turn out to be, in practice, impossible, but the questions now posed about the recompense offered by the heroic exchange and by the epic's insistent and necessary conjunction of beauty and death remain in motion: If the immortalization promised by epic poetry is insufficient, if the culture's highest achievement is so explicitly bound to death, is this then a cultural order worthy of defense, or within which life itself might flourish? While the Iliadic heroes—Achilles preeminent among them—are doers of ferocious deeds of strength and fortitude upon the battlefield, they also show themselves to be heroes of extraordinarily articulate consciousness; indeed, perhaps the single brake against the blinding ferocity of the battlefield resides in that very consciousness, which the *Iliad* will likewise immortalize in the culminating, contesting, renunciant figure of Achilles.

Homer and the Polis

Finally, and most importantly for our purposes, it seems that Homer lived in a time in which the right of the hero no longer ruled in Greece, and the people's freedom began to be honored . . .

—Giambattista Vico, "On the Discovery of the True Homer" (1744)

Though the *Iliad* does not valorize simply the strength and physical feats of its heroes, the poem does encourage its listeners to imagine the passage from the era of the heroes to that of "present men" as an irreversible loss of vitality, as a fall from exemplarity (XII.481–485):

> And Hector picked up a stone in front of the gate
> And carried it with him, a broad-based, pointed boulder
> That not even two of this generation's strongest
> Could manage to heave on a wagon. Yet Hector easily
> Held it . . .

Compared to the mighty Hector or to any of the other famous heroes arrayed at Troy, the audience of the poet's present, even as it understands itself to be descended from the heroes, is acutely reminded that its descent is a diminution: The ancestors were creators and adventurers; men "such as mortals are now" are but imitators, weak of force and spirit. The era of the heroes is one of origins, of first inventions, of self-creation through adventure, of an ever-regenerative vitalism; the present age is one of insubstantial imitation, of repetition unto exhaustion. And yet, when we turn to the historical record itself, the claims of the epic's mythical history are reversed—or, at least, sharply contested: The culture of the late eighth and seventh centuries B.C.E., the period in which the form and content of the Iliad stabilized, is one of remarkable demographic and geographic expansion, as well as of intellectual, artistic, and political experiment and consolidation.

In the last third of the eighth century, the Greeks took effective control, to their west, of the near coast of Sicily and of the region around the Bay of Naples; to the east (where our literary and archaeological evidence is comparatively meager), colonial settlements were founded along what is now the coast of Turkey and north from the Bosphorus as far as the Danube and the Crimea; in North Africa, the colony of Cyrene was founded around 630 B.C.E., which is also the approximate date for the foundation of Naucratis in the Nile Delta. Within the span of roughly one century, Greeks had come to inhabit the primary points of connection and exchange within the Mediterranean world then known to them as well as those points that connected them to the cultures across their borders. Among these colonies and emporia—to the west, east, and south—a newly flourishing mercantile class plied trade routes along which they offered oil, wine, and luxury goods in return for grain, metals, and slaves. Conjointly with these overseas ventures, a free peasantry was created and strengthened within the city and its territory—a development fostered by the opening of markets abroad and by the spread of chattel slavery. Juridical and economic institutions consonant with the peasantry's interests followed—primarily, the emergence of private alienable property in land and enforceable contracts.

Upon this material foundation, a novel form of political life emerged, characterized by a new inclusivity and relying upon a rotation of political offices among full citizens. The textbook name for these developments is "the rise of the *polis*"—the coming-to-be and flourishing of the Greek city-state. The great scholar J.-P. Vernant has taught us (in his *Origins of Greek Thought*; and see, too, M. Detienne's *Masters of Truth*) to understand the political phenomenon of the *polis* primarily in terms of a transformed relation to speech and its authority. In the palace-kingdoms of the Mycenaean period (c.1450–1200 B.C.E.), rule was held by a divine king—a sovereign who embodied each of the functional classes (priestly, military, and economic) of the society that he ruled and who, in encompassing those different classes, transcended them; the king was thus the principle of social unity, harmoniously conjoining—in his one, divine body—the disparate classes of his society among themselves, as well as within the natural and cosmic realms. As the king orders his society, so too he is himself the juncture of mediation between that society and the transcendent orders. Both nature and the gods respond to the rule of the good king; the king's subjects reap the rewards of their ruler's access to the beneficent regularities of nature and to the favors of the divine. Some remnant of this conception of kingship is evoked in the *Odyssey* in its praise of a king who, "with fear of the gods in his heart . . . upholds justice"; for this king, "the black earth bears barley and wheat, the trees are laden with fruit, the flocks bring forth their young unceasingly, the sea yields fish . . . and the people prosper" (*Odyssey* 19.109–114). Within this order, the speech of the king, sacralized by the king's own proximity to god, is an absolute instrument of power. The commanding word of the king can bear only one, immutable meaning, insusceptible to mortal dispute or human complication. In the word of the divine king, sign and signified are one; the power of the king's word is absolute.

The history of the *polis*, by contrast, can be understood as one of the demystification of speech. As the prerogative of authoritative speech is loosed from the sovereign king, the shape of power is no longer a triangle at the apex of which is god and king, with successive classes (first priests, then warriors) ranged within descending cross-segments, each beneath the other, each further from the divine source of power, and with the great majority (primarily of agricultural laborers) ever subjugated at the triangle's base; rather, in the *polis* the shape of power is the circle, at the center of which is the *agora*, the place of public meeting and adjudication. It is to that center that the members of the community (women and slaves excepted, as usual) convene so as to advocate and mediate their particular claims. Disparate social interests and classes are no longer harmonized in the body of the king, but within a politics of mutual accommodation. Thus, sovereign power came to be the business of each who ventured to the center, where decisions were openly arrived at by public debate among equals; each contestant within the *agora* might experience victory and defeat, but those remain opposite sides of the same relation; neither dominance nor submission is permanent; rather, both are reversible within the deliberative contests of the day to come. In this model, the speech that commands is no longer the ritual word pronounced by the divine king, but an account shaped by a human demand for persuasion and ratified into truth (at least for the day) by the collective assent of the community.

The Future of Achilles

Chaque époque rêve la suivante. [Each era dreams the next.]

—Michelet, "Avenir! Avenir!"

In the first line of the *Iliad*—"Sing, O Goddess"—we learn that speech of divine origin belongs not, or not exclusively, to the king, but to the poet, who begins his monumental work by invoking his goddess, the Muse, whose voice will now merge with his own. In the song that immediately follows upon the invocation, the poet presents the spectacle of kings acting badly—and acting especially badly is Agamemnon, the king who assembled the vast Achaean coalition at Troy and who bears responsibility for the success or failure of the expedition. Within the first few moments of the poem, Agamemnon has insulted a priest of Apollo (by refusing to accept ransom for his daughter) and, in consequence, has brought upon his army a deadly pestilence. In an inversion of the model of the good king, the divine and natural orders punish the impious deeds of Agamemnon, and for the king's outrages, his subjects pay with their lives. At the instigation of Hera, Achilles steps into this breach that Agamemnon has opened within the mutually responsive order of divine and human. Achilles, like Agamemnon, is a "king," as are all the principal Achaean heroes, each of whom leads a contingent of warriors from his home territory. Among these many kings, Agamemnon is *primus inter pares*—"first among equals." The basis of that preeminence is his superior storehouse of gifts for giving and his greater number of ships. Yet, while a rather crude calculation of material goods serves to confer Agamemnon's superior position, his decisions are yet made in consultation with his fellow kings—in a public assembly (as in book I), or in the more restrictive council of peers (as in the beginning of book IX)—and he can be influenced by, even rebuked by, those other kings. Agamemnon's job is to hear and carry out the will of the group; his authority is, in that sense, representative: As a "good king," his actions should embody and unite the will of the collective, but higher than the king is the principle of community itself. Agamemnon's preference for Chryseis to Clytemnestra (I.129–130) is not without a certain poignancy (kingly power, it seems, circumscribes the fulfillment of the king's personal desire), but it can also risk the unity and well-being of the collectivity that he leads.

When Achilles first steps forward, then, he would recall Agamemnon to his proper role as the unifying principle and agent of the martial camp. And Agamemnon does, if grudgingly, assent to the return of the priest's daughter, "if that is the thing to do. / I prefer the men safe and well, not sick and dying" (I.133–134). Thus he acknowledges that the good of the camp supersedes his own preference for the priest's daughter. But Agamemnon then goes one sentence too far: "But you must prepare a prize for me at once. / For me to be the only Argive here / Without some gift of honor would hardly be right!" (I.135–137). As Achilles swiftly points out, there are no undistributed prizes tucked away in storage nor can prizes once distributed be recalled and reapportioned. The dispute now centers upon evaluations of honor: Within the martial camp, "prizes"—the tripods, cauldrons, hunks of metal, and livestock that fill the capacious tents of the Achaeans—are visible signs of a warrior's social standing; and among those prizes, women captured in raids or city-sackings are the topmost signs of a warrior's status among his comrades. Agamemnon's threat to take Briseis from Achilles as a recompense for his loss of Chryseis registers the dilemmatic fact that, within the social economy of the warriors' camp, honor is a finite resource and the totality of the system is zero-sum. In other words, as one man's social standing increases, another's diminishes. In the case of Agamemnon, because he is the king (who is, ideally, representative), a diminution of personal honor is also a threat to the order of the group as a whole; hence, his immediate demand for a compensatory prize upon his acquiescence to the return of Chryseis registers, in addition to personal pique, an assertion of his kingly position. But Achilles immediately and angrily understands that Agamemnon's desire for another token of honor is inevitably a threat to him, as the leading warrior within the camp. The restoration of Agamemnon's honor, if it is to be immediate (as Agamemnon desires), requires a concordant attack upon Achilles' honor and social identity. Though it was Achilles who first spoke forth in defense of the Achaean camp, it is Achilles who will suffer a diminution in social prestige on account of Agamemnon's retaliatory abduction of Briseis; indeed, in Achilles' understanding of what has befallen him that diminution of public standing is absolute, as he will say in book IX, recalling Agamemnon's behavior, he "insulted / Me . . . as though I were some despised / And dishonored outsider" (IX.750–752). It is characteristic of Achilles, here and throughout the *Iliad*, that he is unable to draw limiting distinctions: He is either the greatest of warriors within the camp or he is a disgraced outsider, reduced to the status of a wandering refugee.

The astounding, breakneck speed with which Agamemnon and Achilles take mutual offense, their escalating volleys of insult and contempt, reflect a competitive dynamic within which martial honor is a finite good, but the very volatility of the opening fight also suggests an underlying and ultimately irreconcilable difference between the two men. Agamemnon's claims to authority derive, as previously noted, from his great store of "gifts" (which are never freely given, but always serve to bind recipient to donor), as well as from the number of his ships and, perhaps, from the political centrality of the city of Mycenae, of which Agamemnon seems to have hereditary rule (see the description of his scepter at II.119–128). The inherited status of Agamemnon's rule might be especially suggested by the weakness of his abilities: He is neither the best warrior nor the best leader of men (as will be vividly dramatized for a second time by the episode of the dream, at the opening of book II); thus, in the absence of any apparent qualifications, Agamemnon seems likely to have attained his rule simply by being his father's eldest son. Achilles, on the other hand, is the greatest warrior of the Achaean camp—a claim that no one within (or outside) the camp contests. His superiority as a warrior is three times attributed to the gods in Book I (I.204, I.329, and I.341), and especially to his goddess mother Thetis, who belongs to the Titanic generation that preceded the Olympians. Thus, while Agamemnon's claims are those of (hereditary) position, Achilles' are those of (inborn) prowess; the former has political authority, the latter martial power (we might compare the relation of Hrothgar to Beowulf, Richard II to Bolingbroke, or King Arthur to Lancelot). The conflict between Agamemnon and Achilles, considered at its most general and as it is consistently dramatized over the course of the *Iliad*, is between the necessities of cultural order and the excitations and imperatives of natural ability and desire.

The judgment of King Panedes (in the *Contest of Homer and Hesiod*) is, again, telling: A peaceable—sometimes even a just—political order requires subjects who work within the rhythms and boundaries that are established and emblematized by the seasonal regularity of nature; in contrast, the *Iliad*, with Achilles at its center, provokes within an audience a "wonder" at the spectacle of a particular, irregular, violent, and mortal nature that asserts its own individual claims to justice. Such claims can well devastate the community (as Achilles' withdrawal in book I will devastate the Achaean camp, no less than Apollo's plague did) and so surely fail any test of a justice for which the criterion is a collective equilibrium overseen by the king. Yet, as devastating as Achilles' assertion of his nature will come to be, his rage is initially provoked by a political order that is itself no longer sustaining the life of the community. The rule of the weak king is itself, as has been noted above, a breach of the politico-religious order. Achilles' subsequent assertion of his own primacy, of a nature no longer reconciled to the king's rule, though itself of questionable or unsustainable justice, might well be necessary, if the preference is, *in extremis*, for change rather than death, or, as Achilles says in his first words of the poem, if the Achaeans are to be neither "baffled" in their intent nor killed (I.69). The deadening ossification of traditional social form that leads—as in the case of

Agamemnon's hereditary rule—to the divorce of ability from position provokes a response necessarily unjust from the vantage of collective equilibrium, but no less necessary for that. Just as the ruler's reason is evident in Panedes' preference for Hesiod's verses, so too there is reason in the people's vote for the *Iliad*.

The thematic division between Agamemnon and Achilles over the respective claims of political standing and natural prowess sets the *Iliad* in motion. The quarrel between king and warrior, in its immediate combustibility and headlong acceleration nearly to the point of regicide, is dramatized as a fissure within the Achaean camp that is, from the start, ready to crack—and, crucially, a schism after which the former unities will be irrecoverable. In his description of the staff that confers the right of public speech within the Achaean camp, the poet presents an image of a prior mediation between the claims of the natural and the cultural; it is one mark of the *Iliad*-poet's genius to present that image of unity just as it is being irrevocably destroyed (I.273–278):

> . . . [the staff] which no longer has bud
> Or leaf since it left its stump in the mountains, nor ever
> Grows green again and blooms since the sharp bronze stripped it
> Of foliage and bark, but which now the sons of Achaeans
> Bear in their hands, they who are judges among us
> And uphold the laws of [Zeus] . . .

The icon of the staff presents a foundation story, an aetiology, of political authority within the Achaean camp. The wood of the living, sprouting tree is cut and transformed by human craft into the staff, the possession of which confers the right to authoritative speech—which is to say, to judgment. An ideal relation between the natural and political orders is maintained by the single, balanced staff: The tempering of nature by human skill—and in the service of human ends—becomes the means of political judgment. A foundation for that judgment is preserved through an origin in nature, even as nature is shaped by human craft, becoming itself a work of craft. This idealized concord between nature and culture—a human mediation of an underlying opposition—is permanently sundered in the break between Achilles and Agamemnon. When Achilles simultaneously swears his departure from the Achaean camp and casts down and shatters "the staff with its studs of bright gold" (I.287), the break is irreparable.

The action of the *Iliad* takes place, in a sense, within the disordered space that is created by the casting down of the staff, by the dramatized breakup of an older order of society, with its particular relation between individual and political regime. While the *Iliad* is, at once, a monumental song of praise to the "unwithering fame" of the heroes at Troy—itself a perdurable "proof" of the immortality of the heroes' names—the poem also dramatizes a heroic order that is no longer able to quell the strife that is intrinsic to it. Social contradictions that were previously mediated by the representative rule of the king come now—under the rule of the weak king—to the fore and to the point of permanent rupture. The *Iliad*, then, even as it sings the immortality of its heroes, suggests an end to their imagined era and to the political order that is located there. Indeed, one of the great feats of the *Iliad* is to pose a critique—centered upon the withdrawals and speeches of Achilles—of the heroic order and the possibilities that it offers for mortal happiness. From this point of view, the essential work of the *Iliad* is one of negation—again, the epic is unjust with respect to the old, but potentially beneficent with respect to the future. The old heroic order—for all its blinding beauties and exaltations, for all its aspirant motion toward the realm of the aesthetic—is also revealed as unable to quell strife and its attendant violence, as conducive to no just stability and, finally, as a desolation to its own greatest heroes (as the complaints and career of Achilles will dramatize). To the extent that it thematizes the obsolescence of the old heroic order, the *Iliad* reveals an orientation toward the future; the poem cannot invent the forms that will govern the future, but it can present to the future a kind of *tabula rasa*, upon which the poet's audience might reinscribe new meanings out of the wreckage of the old, upon which the heroes might be reassembled and once again directed toward human ends.

If the warrior order is permanently unmade over the course of the *Iliad*, it is upon the Shield of Achilles (XVIII.540–681) that the poet depicts a collective way of life closer to the historical experience and communal ethos of his late eighth- or seventh-century audience. The Shield is forged by Hephaestus, the god of craft, at the request of Thetis, Achilles' mother. This new and immortal shield replaces Achilles' prior shield, which he had given to his beloved Patroclus, who lost it—along with his life—in combat with Hector, the Trojan prince and defender. In a distillation of pure fury following the death of Patroclus, Achilles has resolved to return to battle to avenge the death of Patroclus, with the full knowledge that his return will necessitate his death at Troy. When the Dawn-goddess delivers the gift of the Shield down from Olympus to Achilles' camp, his companions, upon seeing the images worked upon the Shield, are struck with fear and avert their gaze (XIX.16–18). They cannot look upon the "splendor" of the Shield, for in the depiction of the way of life there—which is that of the poet's own audience—the heroes see their own obsolescence. Achilles, however, gazes long upon the brilliance of the Shield with a combination of adrenal anger and deep pleasure; his eyes gleam back in response, as if themselves afire. The vision that he sees upon the Shield—of a world without heroes, of a world without the relentless martial strife of the Iliad itself—is the source of a renewed, visceral anger for Achilles because it is a world whose possibilities are not meant for him. Yet the vision is also a source of pleasure to him because it is of a world that his own great paroxysm of killing rage in the final quarter of the poem will usher in. In his pleasure at the sight of the Shield, Achilles can, as it were, acknowledge his own role in the foundation of the world to come, even if his role is preeminently one of extraordinary negation: Achilles is the hero whose discontent fully lays bare the failures of the heroic order from the point of view of mortal happiness, while his surpassing strength permits him to make that discontent murderously actual, as he devastates much of the heroic order itself in the final books of the poem. His perfection is such that he is both the culmination and the destruction of the traditional form.

Among the images upon the Shield, it is the depiction of the wedding procession and, in the passage immediately following, of a communal process of adjudication in a case of murder that are foundational for the city-state (XVIII.554–560 and 560–574); both images appear on the second ring of the Shield, in the city at peace. In the wedding procession, the "high-blazing" torches illumine a scene of music and revelry; the sight provokes wonder. The promise of the wedding—which we do not see concluded, but always in motion—is one of social unity, the joining together and mutual strengthening of families within the city. In the Iliad itself, such unity is always in pieces, defended in speech even as it is sundered in action. The Achaean cause at Troy is, of course, the recovery of Helen, whose wedding to Menelaus is overturned by her flight, whether compelled or voluntary, to Troy. The martial expedition to Troy presents itself as a defense of the conjugal union and, by extension, of the social work that the wedding accomplishes—primarily, the joining together of families and the establishment of a new social unit that might, in turn, offer guest-friendship to others and to outsiders, thus creating further links of social exchange and comity. And yet, as Achilles complains with great and piercing sarcasm in book IX, the larger social principle epitomized by the defense of Helen and her marriage has been granted no general applicability, but seems to apply only to Agamemnon and Menelaus (IX.381–388):

> "But why should Argives battle the Trojans? And why
> Has this miserable son of Atreus gathered and led
> This great army here? Wasn't it all for lovely
> Blonde Helen? Can it be that of all mortal men, only

The sons of Atreus love their wives? Not so,
For any real man of good sense both loves and cares for
His own, as I loved her with all of my heart,
Though she was won by my spear."

As it holds for Helen, so too—asserts Achilles—must it hold for Briseis: If the defense of Helen, the daughter of Zeus and the fairest of women, registers a principle that is true for any "man of good sense," that same principle must also be applicable to Briseis, however much her status as captive places her among the lowest ranks of the Achaean camp. Briseis is, as Achilles remorselessly puts it, "won by [his] spear," yet she has come, asserts Achilles, to be one who is beloved, "with all of my heart"—to be, as it were, Achilles' Helen, and so worthy of the same defense. By his own assertion, Achilles' love is transformational: Briseis, who began her captivity in the Achaean camp as a "prize," a sign of the social prestige of Achilles, has become a beloved, no less worthy of defense than Helen, the most illustrious of wives. Indeed, Achilles' defense of Briseis might be a greater defense of the principle of the "man of good sense," in that Achilles fights for the beloved of lowest status rather than of highest. (Achilles' sarcasm surely redoubles in his attribution of this principle befitting men of "good sense" to the sons of Atreus; for we have already seen, in Agamemnon's preference for Chryseis in book I, the extent of his regard for Clytemnestra, while Helen, though not "won by [the] spear" is won by the gift and is accordingly valued by Menelaus.) For Achilles, the abduction of Briseis by Agamemnon is equivalent to the abduction of Helen by Paris; but while Paris shanghaied Helen by stealth (though perhaps with Helen's aid), Agamemnon abducted an unwilling Briseis in public in the very center of the warriors' camp. Moreover, not a single one of Achilles' comrades arose in his defense. The Achaeans thus become, to Achilles in his rage, not men "of good sense," but "worthless" (I.270; literally, "nobodies" in the Greek), no longer deserving of Achilles' protection, no longer entitled to any claims of mutual obligation, which include those of communal defense.

This collective failure to acknowledge Achilles' own claims for Briseis (the refusal to grant that Briseis is as worthy of defense as Helen) is Achilles' initial rationale for his otherwise traitorous desertion of the Achaeans. The Achaeans themselves might well respond that Achilles has not, in fact, married Briseis; her social status is not that of wife, but of concubine. Yet, it bears repeating that, from Achilles' point of view, his own love for Briseis is transformational: The wedding is lacking, but the intensity of his emotion stands and comes to supersede collectively conferred attributions of status. Because Achilles' words are—throughout the *Iliad*—invested with such extraordinary immediacy and because he claims for his words an absolute truth, there is a world-making quality about his speeches—if of a world that would be made to Achilles' desire. The manifesto with which Achilles begins his great speech of rejection in book IX is diagnostic: "The gates of Hades are not more hateful to me / Than a man who hides one thing in his heart and says / Something else" (*Iliad* IX.351–353); as abhorred as death is to life, so the false word is to the true. The truth that Achilles tells is not always—perhaps not even often—the truth that his community acknowledges, but it does concord with his own intertwining of principle and emotion; indeed, the very emotiveness of Achilles' speech becomes itself revelatory of the principles—the truth-claims, the values—that have been lost or covered over in the ceaseless hurly-burly of social exchange and accommodation to power.

Achilles' dilemma, as well as a primary source of the *Iliad*'s thematic force, is that the claims of emotional truth—claims of love or of the values that might underlie all the necessary social transactions—are not those that the Achaean camp (or any political community) has much capacity to acknowledge or formalize. Indeed, to the Achaeans, Achilles has become as unapproachable and as incomprehensible as a wild beast. So protests Ajax, in a passionate burst of frustration at Achilles' refusal of Agamemnon's eventual proffers of reconciliation and, most cuttingly, of the appeals of his comrades: " 'Achilles has filled his proud heart / With savage, inhuman hatred. He has become / A cruel and ruthless man, who cannot remember / The love of his friends and how we idolized him . . . and all / Because of one girl' " (*Iliad* IX.728–731 and 738–739). Ajax' words are as poignant as they are, finally, uncomprehending of his former comrade: Ajax appeals to the paramount value of the warrior camp, the "love"—in Homeric Greek, the *philotes*—of his comrades; it is this love, this masculine camaraderie, that should—on Ajax' account—persist and that should still obligate, even in the face of Agamemnon's outrageousness. For it is *philotes* that not only joins comrade to comrade within the camp, but that, finally, makes the warrior's life worth living. *Philotes* is an active principle of social unity that is both necessary and good.

And Achilles was himself once motivated—prior to his casting down of the staff—by that same ideal of a collective *philotes* to which Ajax now appeals (indeed, of the three speeches of the book IX mission to Achilles, it is Ajax' alone that affects Achilles and that elicits the ultimately fatal concession from Achilles that he will remain at Troy beyond the following morning). For Achilles, with his absolutist turn of mind, the principle, once disgraced, is no longer salvageable: The Achaeans remain "nobodies"; he himself has become an "outsider" (IX.752).

Likewise, Briseis is not, for Achilles, "just one girl" (as Ajax proclaims her). That is, she is not interchangeable with any other sign of male honor (in this regard, Ajax thinks no differently than Agamemnon). Around Briseis—who is, as I've argued above, proclaimed by Achilles to be a beloved, worthy of the same defense as Helen—an alternative pole to that of the warrior's life (and the warrior's "beautiful death") takes imagined form. For Achilles, the return to Phthia, the counter-heroic choice of the long and inglorious life, is conceived in book IX in terms of a marriage and though Achilles speaks of a marriage that his father Peleus will arrange, his own thoughts return repeatedly to Briseis (see again, IX.381–388, cited above). Briseis herself, in one of the most startling and poignant of Homeric speeches, refers to a promised wedding to Achilles in Phthia (XIX.333–339); returning to book I, we see that Achilles forsakes his initial plan simply to return to Phthia (I.193–195) once Agamemnon threatens the abduction of Briseis (I.210–211)—he remains at Troy, then, for her. A marriage with Briseis crystallizes in imagination the life that might await if Achilles were to abandon Troy, if he were to opt for the counter-heroic life. As not "just one girl," but as one who is, by Achilles' account, "fitted to the heart," Briseis—if she were to wed Achilles—augurs the possibility that the social exchanges of the heroic order might yet be working beneficently, that the heroic order itself might be responsive to the desires of its members, perhaps even remediative of the misfortunes of those who, like Briseis, have suffered because of it.

But the wedding of Achilles and Briseis is, of course, a fantasy, persistently articulated even as it is dramatized as impossible. Likewise fantasy is the "choice of Achilles," as he himself formulates it in the central passage from book IX (lines 471–478, discussed above): As the consummate traditional hero, Achilles must eventually find himself back upon the path of "unwithering fame." Yet, the persistent desire to marry Briseis and lead an unheroic life, coupled with the very joylessness (indeed, the extraordinary murderousness) of Achilles' eventual return to battle, suggests a certain vastation of the Homeric hero and of the warrior community he inhabits. Though the form—the necessary plot—of the hero remains, that form has been emptied of choice-worthy content, from the vantage both of individual desire and of communal wellbeing. Though the possibility of Achilles' returning to Phthia was never a "real" choice within the generic requirements of the epic, the opposite pole of immortal fame surely becomes no more choice-worthy for being compulsory. It is, again, a defining quality of the *Iliad*-poet's art to thematize critically—not simply to transmit—the premises of his tradition, and foremost the heroic exchange of life for poetry. As the necessities of the traditional form are dramatized as at increasing odds with the projects of human desire, the inevitable death of the hero comes to seem bound less to the exaltations of art than to the desolations of the spirit. For Achilles, first the loss of Briseis, then the sacrifice of Patroclus: In each case, what is destroyed is the possibility of a love that might be sustained, that might make the heroic world once again meaningful. Such losses might well be reason for abandoning the heroic world.

Just as the wedding procession on the Shield is captured in mid-motion, if joyously directed toward completion, so too the following scene of adjudication is depicted in mid-trial, the outcome of the contention left pointedly unresolved. It is the value of a life that is now debated:

> The men, though, had gone
> To the place of assembly, where two of their number were striving
> To settle a case concerning a murdered man's blood-price.
> The defendant declared his cause to the people and vowed
> He was willing to pay the whole price, but the other refused
> To accept it, and each was eager to have a judge's
> Decision in his behalf. The people were cheering
> Both men, some favoring one and some the other,
> But heralds held all of them back from where in the sacred
> Circle the elders sat on the polished stones,
> Each taking the great-lunged herald's staff when it came
> To him in his turn. With this each elder would come
> To the fore and give his opinion. And in the center
> Two talents of gold were lying, the fee to be given
> To him who uttered the straightest and truest judgment. (XVIII. 560–574)

The murderer is claiming that if the judge were to rule in his favor, he would pay a blood-price to the relatives of the deceased; comparative Near-Eastern texts suggest that in instances where blood-price is a possibility, the murderer is claiming that there were mitigating circumstances. On the other side, the relatives of the murdered man are refusing to accept any blood-price; they are claiming that the murder was aggravated and that they are entitled to blood revenge. In the proposal of the defendant, the payment of the blood-price would serve to save his own life, as well as to maintain the peace of the city as a whole; the kin of the murdered man, in opposition, are claiming that the life of the dead man can be recompensed only by the shedding of the murderer's blood—the honor of the family is preeminent. For the community, the intransigence of the kin raises the destabilizing possibility of the vendetta, in which the collective peace is overmatched by the private, self-perpetuating feuds of particular extended families. The community thus has a pressing, constitutive interest that the kin of the murdered man should accept the blood-price; that is, the kin should accept a form of symbolic substitution—a price—for the person lost. The good that is thus purchased—and the final measure of value—is the unity of the community. The adjudication of murder is, of course, a limit case, but it also crystallizes a version of the social contract, in which each member of the community—like the kin of the murdered man—is asked to accept recompense, denominated in the coin of the community, for the loss of those immediate personal desires—whether for vengeance or for other forms of self-assertion—that are potentially disruptive.

The very inclusion upon the Shield of the trial-scene attests to the historical presence of an institution—the court—that is foundational for the emergent city-state: A place of adjudication is now present, in which conflicting claims might be heard and deliberated upon. Contention need not always end in irremediable, bloody division. In a sense, the staff that was cast down and shattered by Achilles in book I has been re-crafted and is now carried by the civic elders, as each in his turn takes hold of the staff and rises to speak to an approving or disapproving citizenry, who stand arrayed as an audience in an outer circle that surrounds the inner. This image of adjudication concords with the historical shift that I outlined above from the authority of the king to that of the collective citizenry. The speaker's staff has been reassembled out of the pieces of its shattered predecessor, but—in the re-crafting—it has been given new, humanized content, emblematic of a polity that now locates authoritative speech within a communal center rather than upon a single, divinized apex. It is the circle within which the speakers meet that is now "sacred."

We might again, then, propose that the action of the *Iliad* finds dramatic form between the shattered speaker's staff of book I and the reconstituted staff upon the Shield of book XVIII: Achilles' initial casting down of a prior icon of the collective mediation of nature and culture—of the individual and his community—creates the chaotic, charged space (a battlefield real and metaphoric) within which the poem explores the values ascribed to a mortal life: the exchange values (the blood-prices) set by the community, the absolute values set by the self. Upon the Shield itself, the outcome of the trial remains untold: We never learn if the rage of the aggrieved kin of the murdered man is assuaged by acceptance of the blood-price, if the collective good of the community is, thus, acknowledged and the pacifying potential of the court realized. This incompletion perhaps reflects the very newness in the early archaic period of the court as an institution—its still uncertain powers, its potential rather than its fulfillment as yet. But the incompletion of the scene surely also registers the extraordinary emotional and psychological difficulty of subordinating the imperatives of individual principle and desire to the claims of the collectivity. The very intransigence of the desire for revenge, the persistence of the mourner's grief that cannot be assuaged by any blood-price, the crude tyranny of the (necessary) social fiction that one person's life can be recompensed by the substitution of another's—all attest to the difficulty and psychic cost of the subordination of individual aspiration and grief to the collective weal. Human social life is, of course, constituted by ceaseless negotiations of individual passions and communal goods; exchange values are ever determined to better or worse ends. These exchanges can be more or less coercive, more or less devaluing, more or less responsive to the notion that human lives are, finally, neither interchangeable nor mute.

Yet it is in this ceaseless negotiation of value, whether to the better or to the worse end, that a community maintains its equilibrium. The decisive and tragic break arises when one refuses to enter any longer into such exchanges, when such constant re-articulations of value are only a murder of spirit—or are, as Achilles says, as hateful as the gates of Hades (IX.351–353). This is a point about politics but also a point about consciousness. Upon the Shield, the depiction of the scene of adjudication is a wondrous sign of a potentially more humane system of social exchanges, where the collective peace is negotiated by means that offer greater freedom to human speech and reason; the passing of the heroic order makes such a humanized political realm possible. But the incompletion of the adjudication scene might also suggest that even such humane communal advances might not be finally adequate to the consciousness of the individual. The question of the blood-price will always persist, as will those who, to their grief and to our fascination, find the price impossible to set and the loss of value unconscionable:

> For I put a much
> Higher value on life than on all the treasures men say
> Were contained in the rich and populous city of Troy
> Before we sons of the Achaeans came, or,
> For that matter, all the wealth laid up behind
> The marble threshold of the archer god Phoebus Apollo
> In rocky Pytho. For raiding can get a man cattle
> And splendid fat sheep, and barter can get him tripods
> And sorrel horses. But once his soul goes out
> Through the barrier of his teeth, neither raiding nor barter
> Can make it return. (IX.461–471)

Achilles asserts that his own life is beyond value, greater than all the abductable prizes of the world, greater even than the promised compensation of epic poetry. Achilles' assertion of a life beyond value is, from one vantage, a great arrogance and a great delusion: Human beings are social animals and society is comprised not of the sum of individuals, but of the exchanges that transpire between them. The fascination of non-participation can itself be blinding to the values that might be found and made among the speeches and loves of others. But Achilles, for all his arrogance, might remind us that speech is also the private means of constructing an ego, of exploring a consciousness, of determining the values that might underlie the network of signs.

We are ourselves, in the West, the distant heirs of the court and city-state that is prefigured on the Shield of Achilles. And this remains a descent worth reclaiming, if it might still inspirit efforts to expand the circle of political speech beyond that which is depicted upon the Shield. But Achilles, in his assertion of the life beyond value and of the un-compensated absoluteness of death, reminds us of the prices and limits of culture itself. And in that sense, Achilles is also akin to the poet, for it is one of the characteristic works of poetry to recover, impossibly, the values that precede signs and the ways in which individual consciousness is ultimately irremediable, untamable by culture and all its signifying systems.

Bruce M. King earned his B.A., M.A., and Ph.D. from the University of Chicago, and has taught classics and humanities at Columbia University, Reed College, and the University of Chicago. Recently a fellow at the Center for Hellenic Studies, King focuses on archaic and classical Greek literature and philosophy. He is currently a Blegen Research Fellow at Vassar College.

A NOTE ON THE TRANSLATOR

Ennis Rees was born in Newport News, Virginia, in 1925. He graduated from William and Mary and took his M.A. and Ph.D. degrees at Harvard. Before joining the faculty of the University of South Carolina, where he is a Professor of English, he taught at Duke and Princeton. His study, *The Tragedies of George Chapman: Renaissance Ethics in Action*, was published in 1954 by the Harvard University Press, and his verse translation of the *Odyssey* by Random House in 1960. This was followed by the *Iliad* in 1963. Both poems are reprinted in the Library of Liberal Arts published by Bobbs-Merrill. Among the record albums Mr. Rees has made for Spoken Arts are two of selections from his Homer. His *Fables from Aesop* was published by the Oxford University Press in 1966. A book of his poems was published by the University of South Carolina Press in 1964 and his *Selected Poems* in 1973. He has written a number of books of verse especially for children, including *Riddles, Riddles Everywhere, The Songs of Paul Bunyan and Tony Beaver, Tiny Tall Tales, Brer Rabbit and His Tricks, The Little Greek Alphabet Book,* and *Potato Talk.* He and his wife live in Columbia and have three children.

CONTENTS

BOOK I

The Quarrel

Sing, O Goddess, the ruinous wrath of Achilles,
Son of Peleus, the terrible curse that brought
Unnumbered woes upon the Achaeans and hurled
To Hades so many heroic souls, leaving
Their bodies the prey of dogs and carrion birds.
The will of Zeus was done from the moment they quarreled,
Agamemnon, son of Atreus, and godlike Achilles.[1]
    Which of the gods caused two such men to contend?
The son of Zeus and Leto. Deeply incensed
With King Agamemnon for failing to honor Chryses*   10
His priest, Apollo sent a plague on the soldiers,
And many people were dying. Chryses had come
To the swift Achaean ships to ransom his daughter,
And the ransom he bore was boundless. In suppliant hands
On a staff of gold he held the sacred fillet
Of far-darting Apollo, and he made his plea to all
The Achaeans, especially to the two sons of Atreus,[2]
Marshalers of many:
    "O Atreus' sons and you other
Well-greaved Achaeans, may the gods who live on Olympus   20
Allow you to sack the city of Priam† and reach
Your homes in safety. But reverence the son of Zeus,
Apollo who strikes from afar—take this ransom
And return my precious daughter."
    All the other Achaeans
Supported the priest and shouted to reverence him
And accept the splendid ransom. But Atreus' son
Agamemnon was far from pleased. Roughly he sent him
Away with these harsh words:

---

*Chryses, the priest of Apollo, has a daughter named Chryseis; their city is Chryse.
†Priam is the king of Troy, which the Achaeans have now besieged for almost ten years.

30   "Don't let me find you,
Old man, by the hollow ships, neither loitering now
Nor coming back later, or you will find small protection
In the sacred staff and fillet. The girl I will not
Let go! Before that she'll grow old in Argos, far from
Her own native land, working at the loom and sharing
My bed. Now go, old man! and you'll go much safer
If you don't provoke me."
          At this the old priest was afraid
And did as the King bade him do. Without a word
40 He walked off along the shore of the loud-booming sea,
But when he had gone some distance he fervently prayed
To his lord Apollo, whom lovely-haired Leto bore:
          "Hear me, O god of the silver bow, you
That bestride in your power Chryse and sacred Cilla
And mightily rule in Tenedos—O Smintheus, if ever
I built a temple that pleased you, or made burnt-offering
To you of rich thigh-pieces from bulls or goats,
Fulfill this prayer of mine by using your arrows
To make the Danaans* pay for the tears I have shed."[3]
50   Thus he prayed, and Phoebus Apollo heard him.
Down from the peaks of Olympus he came with a heart
Full of wrath and his bow and closed quiver about his shoulders.
The arrows rattled on the back of the angry god
As he moved, and like night he arrived. Then he sat down
Some distance away from the ships and shot the first arrow,
And the silver bow's twang was awesome and chilling indeed.
At first he shot at the mules and flashing-swift dogs,
But then he aimed his bitter shafts at the men
Themselves, and struck! And pyres of the dead were everywhere
60 Constantly burning.
          For nine days the deadly shafts
Of the god sped through the army, but on the tenth day
The white-armed goddess Hera put into the heart
Of Achilles to call the men to the place of assembly,
For it distressed her to see the Danaans dying.
When they were assembled and seated, fleet-footed Achilles
Stood up in their midst, and spoke:
          "Now, O son
Of Atreus, it seems that we shall be baffled and driven

---

*Danaans (and Argives) are Achaeans.

Back home, if indeed we escape with our lives from the war   70
And pestilence too that plague the Achaeans. But come,
Let us consult some prophet or priest, or some reader
Of dreams—for even a dream is from Zeus—someone
Who may be able to tell us why Phoebus Apollo
Rages so fiercely. If it be because of a hecatomb*
Or vow unperformed, perhaps the god will accept
The savor of sacrificed lambs and goats without blemish
And change his mind about plaguing us all this way."

　　When he had spoken and sat down again, up stood
Calchas, son of Thestor, he who was far   80
The best reader of ominous birds, who knew what was
And had been and things that were to be, and who had
By means of the keen prophetic vision given
To him by Apollo guided the Achaean ships
To Ilium. Now, with all good intentions, he addressed
The assembly:
　　"Zeus-loved Achilles, you bid me explain
The wrath of far-smiting Apollo. Therefore I will.
But first you must make up your mind and swear to defend me,
Swear that you'll be both willing and quick with word   90
And hand. For I fear I am going to anger a man
Who rules with might over all the Argives, and from whom
The Achaeans take orders. A king, you know, is always
More lordly when angry at a low-ranking man. Even
If he swallows his wrath at the time, in his heart he nurses it
Still, till he has his revenge. So decide whether you
Will protect me."
　　Then swift Achilles answered him thus:
"Be bold, and tell us what you can of the god's mind and will,
For by Zeus-loved Apollo I swear to you that so long   100
As I live on earth and have my sight, no one
Shall hurt you here by the hollow ships, no one
In the Danaan host, though you mean Agamemnon himself,
Who claims to be far the best of all the Achaeans."
　　At this the peerless prophet took heart, and spoke:
"It's not for a hecatomb or broken vow that he blames us,
But because Agamemnon insulted his priest by not
Accepting the ransom and giving the man his daughter.
Thus the far-smiting god has given us woes,

---

*Literally, a sacrifice of 100 oxen, but often refers to any large animal sacrifice.

110 And will continue to give them. He will not remove
This loathsome plague till we return to her father
His wide-eyed daughter—nor can we accept any ransom—
And we must carry to Chryse a holy hecatomb.
Only then can we hope to change the mind of Apollo."
        When he had spoken and sat down again, the son
Of Atreus, the wide-ruling wager of war Agamemnon,
Stood up in a rage among them. His black heart boiled
With wrath and his eyes were like fire when it blazes. Fixing
Calchas with an evil scowl, he railed at him thus:
120 "Prophet of misery! you've still got your first good thing
To foretell for me. Unhappy events you always
Enjoy predicting, but never yet have you prophesied
Anything pleasant, much less brought it to pass.
And now in the midst of this Danaan meeting you go on
Spouting your oracles, telling the men it's because
Of me that the far-darting god is inflicting these woes
Upon them, because I refused the royal ransom
For the darling daughter of Chryses, since I much prefer
To have her at home with me. I would rather have her,
130 In fact, than Clytemnestra, my wife. For this girl is quite
Her equal, just as tall and good looking, just as
Smart and clever with her hands. Even so, I want
To give the girl back, if that is the thing to do.
I prefer the men safe and well, not sick and dying.
But you must prepare a prize for me at once.
For me to be the only Argive here
Without some gift of honor would hardly be right!
As you can see, my prize is going elsewhere."
        Then Achilles, noble and strong, answered him thus:
140 "Renowned son of Atreus, most covetous of men, how
Can the gallant Achaeans give you a prize? If there
Is some large public treasure, we've yet to learn where it is,
And the plunder we took from the cities we sacked has already
Been divided. Nor can we rightly take these things back
From the people. But you, give up the girl as the god
Demands. We Achaeans will recompense you three
And four times over, if Zeus ever wills that we sack
The well-walled city of Troy."
        And lordly Agamemnon
150 Spoke in reply: "Though you be, O godlike Achilles,
A man of great valor, don't try to outwit me like that,
For I'll not be persuaded or gotten the best of by you!

Do you tell me to give the girl back so that you can keep
What you've got while I sit here with nothing? If the gallant
Achaeans give me a prize to my liking, and equal
To the one I am losing, all right—but if they do not,
Then I myself will come and take your gift
Of honor, or that of Ajax, or I'll seize and bear off
The prize of Odysseus. Wrathful indeed will be
The man to whom I make that visit! But this   160
We can think about later. Right now let us launch a black ship
On the sacred sea, get enough rowers together,
And put on board a hecatomb along with the girl,
The lovely Chryseis herself. And let one of our leaders
Take charge, either Ajax, or Idomeneus, or godly Odysseus,
Or, son of Peleus, you yourself, most dreaded
Of men, that so you may offer gifts and appease
The far-working god."
          Then swift Achilles, scowling
At him, replied: "You greedy-minded shamelessness   170
Incarnate! how can any decent Achaean want to
Take orders from you, to go where you tell him to go
Or battle his best with hostile men? I didn't
Come here to fight because of the Trojan spearmen.[4]
They've never done me any harm, never rustled my cattle
Or horses, or plundered in fertile Phthia a harvest
Of mine, for between here and there lie a great many things—
Shadowy mountains and crashing sea. But we
Came here with you, the incredibly shameless, in an effort
To gratify you! to get satisfaction for Menelaus   180
And you! covetous cur that you are. All this
You turn your back on and choose to forget, and now
You threaten to take my prize of prestige, the gift
I got from the sons of Achaeans and for which I labored
So much. Whenever we warriors sack a populous
Trojan city, my share of the booty is never
Equal to yours. True, I get more, much more,
Than my share of chaotic battle, but when it comes
To dividing the loot, your portion is always far larger
Than mine. Worn out with fighting, I go back to my ships   190
And with me take some pitiful little prize
Allotted to me—little, but mine. Now, though,
I'll go back to Phthia, for I would much rather take all
My beaked ships and go home than stay on here in disgrace
To heap up wealth for you!"

And the king of men
Agamemnon answered him thus: "Go on and run,
If you feel the urge so strongly. I do not beg you
To stay on my account. I've others here
200 Who honor and respect me, including the best of all counselors,
Zeus himself. Of all the god-nurtured leaders,
You are most hateful to me, for strife is always
Dear to your heart, and battles and fighting. And if
You're so full of valor, that's the gift of a god.
So take your ships and your men and go lord it over
The Myrmidons at home. I have no regard for you,
Nor do I care how angry you are. But see now
How you like this. Since Phoebus Apollo is taking
Chryseis from me, I'm returning her with a ship
210 And men of mine—but I myself will come
To your lodge and take your prize, the lovely Briseis,[5]
That once and for all you may know how greatly I
Exceed you in power and excellence, and another man
Will think twice before calling himself my equal and right
In my presence comparing himself with me!"
　　　　He spoke,
And the pain from his words went deep in the son of Peleus,
Rending the heart in his shaggy breast two ways
As to what he should do, whether to draw the sharp sword
220 By his thigh, break up the meeting, and kill the son
Of Atreus, or swallow his rage and control his temper,
While he was thus divided in mind and heart,
With that huge sword of his half drawn from the scabbard,
Pallas Athena came down from the sky, sent
By white-armed Hera, the goddess whose heart held equal
Love and concern for both of the angry men.
Standing behind him, she caught the son of Peleus
By a handful of tawny hair and made herself visible
To him alone, nor could any of the others see her.
230 Astonished, Achilles turned, and as he looked
In the blazing blue eyes of the goddess he knew her at once
For Pallas Athena, and his words came winged with surprise:
　　　　"Why, O daughter of aegis-bearing Zeus, do you come again
Now? Can it be that you wanted to witness the hubris*
And gross overreaching of Atreus' son Agamemnon?

---

*Insolent violence that lessens the honor, the social standing, of another.

Well let me say this, and believe me I mean what I say.
That arrogant pride of his may shortly cost him
His life!"
          And the bright-eyed goddess Athena replied:
"I came down from the sky to help you control   240
Your wrath, if only you will obey, and the goddess
White-armed Hera sent me, for her heart holds equal
Love and concern for both of you. So come,
No fighting, and don't draw your sword. Wound him with words
Instead, and tell him just how it will be. And now
I say this to you, and I too mean what I say.
On account of this arrogant insult, splendid gifts
Worth three times as much as what you may lose will one day
Be given to you. So hold yourself back, and obey us."
          Then Achilles, swift of foot, answered her thus: 250
"No man, O goddess, can ignore the word of two
Such powers, no matter how wrathful his heart may be.
To obey is surely better. The gods hear all
The prayers of him who heeds them."
          He spoke, and restrained
His mighty hand on the silver hilt. Then obeying
The word of Athena he thrust the long blade back into
The scabbard. And the goddess left for Olympus and the palace
Of aegis-bearing Zeus, to mingle with the other gods there.
          And again Achilles, wrathful as ever, spoke violent   260
Words to the son of Atreus: "You drunken sot!
With the greedy eyes of a dog and the heart of a deer!
You never have courage enough to arm yourself
For battle along with the rest of us, or go
With the best Achaeans on a crafty ambush. You'd rather
Die than do either! You much prefer to go
Through this huge camp and seize for yourself the gift
Of anyone here who disagrees with you, you wretched
Devourer of what we win! And truly, the men
You rule are also worthless, or this, O son   270
Of Atreus, would be the last of your arrogant insults.
But I'll make something clear right now, and swear a great oath.
I swear by this staff I hold—which no longer has bud
Or leaf since it left its stump in the mountains, nor ever
Grows green again and blooms since the sharp bronze stripped it
Of foliage and bark, but which now the sons of Achaeans
Bear in their hands, they who are judges among us
And uphold the laws of God—by this staff I swear

A great oath that surely someday a desperate need
280 For Achilles shall come upon all the sons of Achaeans,
Nor will you be able to help them at all, no matter
How grieved you are, when man-killing Hector is cutting them
Down by the dozen. Then, I say, you'll rend
Your heart with wrath and remorse for failing to honor
The best Achaean of all!"
        So saying, Achilles
Dashed to the ground the staff with its studs of bright gold,
And sat down, while opposite him the son of Atreus
Went on venting his rage. Then among them up stood
290 Nestor, the silver-tongued speaker of Pylos, from whose
Lips the words flowed sweeter than honey. Since he
First saw the light, two generations of mortal
Men had come and gone in sacred Pylos,
And now among the third he was the King.
In an effort to help, he addressed the assembly:
        "For shame!
Surely now great grief comes on the land
Of Achaea. But think how glad it would make King Priam
And all of his sons along with the other Trojans
300 To learn of this wrangling between you—you that among
The Danaans stand first in counsel and warfare. But listen
To me. Both of you are younger than I,
And in other days I have campaigned with mightier
Men than you, nor did they ever belittle
Or disregard me. Never since have I seen such warriors,
Nor ever again shall I see such heroes as Peirithous
Was and Dryas, marshaler of men, and Caeneus
And Exadius and Polyphemus, godlike in his might, and that equal
Of the immortal gods, Theseus, son of Aegeus.
310 Of all men reared on earth, these were the strongest.
The strongest, I say, and with the strongest they fought—
With the monstrous mountain Centaurs, and the slaughter they there
Performed was terrible indeed.[6] I came a long way
From distant Pylos and mingled with those very men,
For I came at their summons. And in the war I did
My personal share of the fighting. There are today
No mortals alive on earth who would be fit
To fight with those men. Still, they listened to me
And took my advice. And you too would do better to hearken
320 And heed. You, Agamemnon, are a man of great power,
But don't try taking that girl away. Leave her

Alone, the prize of him to whom the Achaeans
Gave her. And you, O son of Peleus, do not
Presume to pit your might in strife against
A sceptered King, who derives his power from Zeus
And therefore has no common glory. You
Are the son of a goddess and valiant indeed, yet he
Is the mightier man, since he rules over more people.
Check your rage, Atrides—in fact, I beg you
To extinguish this wrath of yours against Achilles,   330
Who in the moil of horrible war is the mightiest
Mainstay we Achaeans have."
          And ruling Agamemnon
Replied: "All that you say, O aged one,
Is just and wise enough, but this man wants
To be higher than anyone else. He wants to rule
Over all—to be King, I tell you, and give orders to all.
Well I know one, at least, who won't take orders
From him! So the immortal gods made him
A mighty spearman—does that give him the right   340
To go around spouting insults?"
          Then the gifted Achilles
Interrupted, saying: "Indeed, for if I yielded
To you in all things, no matter what you commanded,
I would be called a coward and good for nothing.
So boss the others about, but give no more orders
To me! I'm through with doing what you say. And here
Is something else that you will do well to remember.
I will not fight with you or anyone else
For the girl, since you do but take what you gave. But of all   350
That I'll have left by that swift black ship of mine,
I warn you not to take away anything else!
Go on and try, if you like, so that all may learn
I mean business—and see how soon your black blood covers
My spear!"
          When the violent words had all been spoken,
The two men arose and broke up the meeting beside
The Achaean ships. Achilles strode off to his shelters
And well-balanced ships along with Patroclus and all
The rest of his comrades. But the son of Atreus ordered   360
Others to drag a swift ship down into the sea
And he picked out twenty oarsmen. Then they drove on board
For the god the hecatomb of cattle and brought Chryseis
Of the lovely cheeks and put her aboard. And Odysseus,

Resourceful as ever, mounted the deck and took charge.
        When all were embarked and sailing the foamy sea-lanes,
Atreus' son commanded the army to wash,
And they purified themselves in the salt sea-water and offered
To Apollo appeasing hecatombs of bulls and goats
370 By the shore of the unresting sea. And the plentiful smoke
Curled up in the sky and eddying with it the savor.
        While the men were busy with offerings throughout the camp,
Agamemnon proceeded to fulfill his threat to Achilles.
He called his heralds and nimble squires, Talthybius
And Eurybates, and spoke to them thus: "Go to the lodge
Of Peleus' son Achilles, take the hand
Of the beautiful-cheeked Briseis, and bring her to me.
And if he refuses to give her, I myself will go
With more men and take her, which will be far more painful for
            him."
380   With this harsh order he sent them away on their mission,
And they, reluctant, walked off along the beach
Of the desolate sea till they came to the shelters and ships
Of the Myrmidons.* They found Achilles sitting by his lodge
And black ship, nor was he glad to see them. Frozen
With fear and embarrassment, they stood in awe of the Prince,
Unable to speak a word or ask a question.
But he knew very well what they wanted, and spoke to them, saying:
        "Come here, good heralds, and welcome. You bear the words
Of God and men, and my quarrel is not with you,
390 But Agamemnon, who sent you here for the girl Briseis.
So come, god-sprung Patroclus, bring out the girl
And give her to these men to take back with them. And in
That day when I shall be desperately needed to save
The Achaeans from shameful destruction these two shall witness
For me before blissful gods and mortal men
And the stupid King himself. For surely his rage
Will be the ruin of him yet. If he wants his Achaeans to fight
With both success and survivors, he had better try looking
Before as well as behind!"
400   He spoke, and Patroclus
Obeyed his dear friend. He led from the lodge Briseis,
Lovely of face, and gave her to go with the men.
And back they went down the line of Achaean ships

----

*Achaean contingent under Achilles' command.

And with them the unwilling girl. Now Achilles, weeping,
Withdrew from his comrades, and sitting down by himself
On the beach by the silvery surf he looked out over
The wine-dark sea, stretched out his arms, and fervently
Prayed to his own dear mother:
        "Since, O Mother,
You bore me, though only to live for a few short years,   410
Surely Olympian Zeus should have given me honor,
But now that high-thundering god has given me quite
The reverse. For truly the son of Atreus, imperial
Agamemnon, has grossly insulted me. He has robbed me
Of my gift of honor and now he keeps her himself!"
        Thus in tears he spoke, and far down in the sea,
Sitting by her ancient father, his goddess mother
Heard him.[7] And quickly she left the gray sea like a mist
And sank down in front of her weeping son, gently
Caressed him, called him by name, and said: 420
        "My child,
Why are you crying? What sorrow has entered your heart?
Keep it in no longer. Speak out, and share it with me."
        Then moaning, swift-footed Achilles spoke to her thus:
"You know. Why should I tell it to one who already
Knows all about it? We went out to Thebe, the sacred
City of Eëtion, destroyed and plundered it all,
And brought the booty back here. This the sons
Of Achaeans divided fairly among them, and they chose
For the son of Atreus the fair-cheeked daughter of Chryses.   430
But he, as a priest of far-smiting Apollo, came
To the speedy ships of the gallant bronze-clad Achaeans
To ransom his daughter, and the ransom he bore was boundless.
In suppliant hands on a staff of gold he carried
The fillets of far-darting Apollo, and he pleaded with all
The Achaeans, especially with the two sons of Atreus,
Marshalers of many:
        " 'O sons of Atreus and you other
Well-greaved Achaeans, may the gods who live on Olympus
Allow you to sack the city of Priam and reach   440
Your homes in safety. But reverence the son of Zeus,
Apollo who strikes from afar—take this ransom
And return my precious daughter.'
        "All the other Achaeans
Supported the priest and shouted to reverence him
And accept the splendid ransom. But Atreus' son

Agamemnon was far from pleased. Roughly he sent him
Away, threatening him harshly. And back he went,
A very angry old man, and Apollo, who loves him dearly,
450 Sent a shaft of sickness against the Argives.
His arrows flew through the wide Achaean camp,
And more and more people were dying. Then a prophet whom we
Could depend on told us the mind and will of the god
Who smites from afar, and I was the first to suggest
That we try to appease him. At this a great rage gripped
Agamemnon, and he uttered a threat that has now been fulfilled.
For already the quick-eyed Achaeans are taking one girl
To Chryse aboard a swift ship along with gifts
For the god, and heralds have come to my lodge and taken
460 The other, Briseis, my gift from the sons of Achaeans.
But if you really have power, protect your own son.
If you ever did or said anything that gladdened
The heart of Zeus, go now to Olympus and plead
With him. Many times in the halls of my father I have heard you
Glory in telling how you were the only immortal
To help lord Zeus of the dark and lowering sky
And rescue him from shame when other Olympians—
Hera, Poseidon, and Pallas Athena—plotted
To bind him fast. Then, O goddess, you came
470 And untied him, but first with all speed you summoned to lofty
Olympus him of the hundred hands, known as
Briareus to the gods, but Aegaeon to all mankind,
A monster even more powerful than his father Poseidon.
He crouched by the side of Cronos' son, exulting
In his reputation, and the blessed gods were afraid
Of him and made no attempt to bind Zeus again.
Go sit by his side and remind him of this, and embrace
His knees in earnest prayer for him to support
The Trojans, but as for their foes, the Achaeans, may he trap them
480 Between the sterns of their ships and litter the beach
With dead and dying men, that all may share
The reward of their King, and that Atreus' son, imperial
Agamemnon, may know how blind he was to give
No honor at all to the bravest and best of Achaeans!"

     Then Thetis, weeping, replied: "My child, my child,
Why did I raise you to all this misery? I only
Wish that you might have stayed by your ships and escaped
All grief and tears, for the life allotted to you
Is short, not long at all. And now not only

Will you die young, but you have to suffer as well,   490
And more than anyone else. Hence, back home
In our halls, I bore you to a fate most miserable. But I
Will go in person to snowy Olympus and tell
This grievance of yours to Zeus, the lover of lightning,
In hope of his help. Meanwhile, you remain
By the swift seagoing ships, and go on in your wrath
Against the Achaeans and your utter refusal to fight.
For yesterday Zeus departed for the stream of Oceanus*
To attend a feast of the excellent Ethiopians, and all
The other gods went with him. In twelve days he   500
Will be back on Olympus, and then to the brazen-floored palace
Of Zeus I will go, and embrace his knees in prayer.
I believe I shall win him over."
          With this she left him
There on the beach, resentful and brooding on account of
The fair-gowned woman they had forcefully, spitefully
Taken from him. But Odysseus came to Chryse
With the holy hecatomb. Once they were in the deep harbor
They furled the sail and stowed it within the black ship
And lowered the mast by the forestays till quickly they brought it   510
To rest in the crutch. Then with oars they went on and backed her
Into the moorings, threw the anchor-stones from the bow,
Tied her up from the stern, and stepped out themselves
On the shore of the sea. And out of the ship they led
Far-smiting Apollo's hecatomb, and also out
Of the seagoing ship stepped the beautiful daughter of Chryses.
Then able Odysseus led her to the altar
And into the arms of her dear father, saying:
          "O Chryses,
Agamemnon, king of men, sent me to bring you   520
Your daughter, and to offer to Phoebus in behalf of the Danaans
A sacred hecatomb, that we may appease the god
Who has brought upon the Argives great wailing and sorrow."
          With these words he placed her in the arms of her father, and he
With much rejoicing embraced his dear child. For the god
They quickly stood the holy hecatomb in order
About the well-built altar, washed their hands,
And took up the grains of barley. Then Chryses raised
His arms and prayed aloud this prayer for them:

---

*The stream that runs around the flat disk of Earth.

530   "Hear me, O god of the silver bow, you
        That bestride in your power Chryse and sacred Cilla
        And mightily rule in Tenedos—hear as you heard me
        Before when I prayed. You honored me then, and woefully
        Smote the Achaean host. Grant me now
        Another prayer and dispel the deadly disease
        That plagues the Danaans."
                Thus he earnestly prayed
        And Phoebus Apollo heard him. Then, when all
        Had prayed, they sprinkled the grains of barley, drew back
540   The heads of the victims, cut their throats, flayed them,
        And sliced out the thigh-pieces. These they wrapped in thick layers
        Of fat and on them laid still more raw meat.
        All this the old priest burned on the flaming wood,
        And over the meat he sprinkled the sparkling wine,
        While around him the young men held their forks of five tines.
        Now when the thigh-pieces were wholly consumed and all
        Had tasted of the vital parts, they cut up the rest,
        Spitted and roasted it well, and drew it all
        From the spits. Having eaten and drunk as much as they wanted,
550   The young men filled the bowls brimful of wine,
        And then the goblets, first pouring libation drops
        In the goblets of all. Then, for the rest of the day,
        They sang to the god in melodious propitiation,
        The sons of Achaeans hymning far-working Apollo
        With a beautiful paean of praise, and he heard their singing
        With a heart full of joy.
                When the sun went down and darkness
        Came on, they lay down to sleep by the hawsers at the stern
        Of the ship, but as soon as Dawn of the rosy fingers
560   Arrived they put out to sea for the huge Achaean
        Camp. Apollo sent a fast-following wind,
        And when they had set up the mast and spread the white sail,
        The sheet soon bellied before that wind, and the dark waves
        Moaned and hissed about the bow, as the ship
        Cut swiftly through them ever closer to her destination.
        When they came to the huge encampment, they dragged the black ship
        Well up on the beach, forced the large props beneath her,
        And scattered for shelters and ships of their own.
                Meanwhile,
570   Fast Achilles, the god-sprung son of Peleus,
        Remained as wrathful as ever beside his swift ships
        Without once going to the man-enhancing place

Of assembly or into the fighting. He stayed where he was,
Eating his heart out with longing for the battle and war-cry.
　　When the twelfth dawn came, the gods everlasting returned
To Olympus, all together with Zeus in the lead.
Nor did Thetis forget the plea of her son. In the early
Morning she rose from the waves, into the great sky,
And up to Olympus, where she found far-seeing Zeus,
Sitting apart from the others on the highest peak　　　　　　580
Of the craggy mountain. She sank down before him and took hold
Of his knees with her left hand while with her right she held
His chin, and spoke in supplication to her lord God,
The son of Cronos:
　　"O Father Zeus, if ever
Among the immortals any word or deed of mine
Was helpful to you, grant this prayer for me:
Honor my son, who is doomed beyond all others
To an early death. But now the commander-in-chief
Agamemnon has insulted him grossly by taking and keeping　　590
His prize of prestige—an act of arrogant pride!
You at least, O lord of all wisdom, Olympian Zeus,
Give him honor and glory. Increase the might
Of the Trojans and give them the upper hand until
The Achaeans honor my son and glorify him
With repayment."
　　She spoke, but Zeus the cloud-gatherer sat
A long time without one word of reply, while Thetis
Kept on as before, clinging close to his knees, and again
She put her plea: "Tell me now that you'll do this　　　　　600
For me, and promise with a nod of your head, or else,
Since you have nothing to fear, go on and say no.
Then I will be sure how much among all the immortals
I am respected the least."
　　Then greatly disturbed,
Cloud-gathering Zeus replied: "Sorry stuff
When you do anything to cause trouble between Hera and me
And start her to nagging and making me lose my temper.
Already she is constantly making reproaches
In the presence of the other immortals and accusing me　　610
Of helping the Trojans in battle. But now you'd better
Go, before Hera gets suspicious, and I
Will think these things over and bring them to pass. Therefore
I will nod my head to you, that you may be certain,
For of all immortal pledges a nod from me

Is the surest. No word of mine to which I bow
My head may be recalled, or false, or unaccomplished."
　　　So spoke the son of Cronos, and the King's ambrosial
Locks fell forward as he nodded, bowing
620 His iron-dark brows, and huge Olympus quaked.
　　　When these two had made their plans, they parted. The goddess
Sprang from gleaming Olympus into the depths
Of the sea, and Zeus went to his palace. When they saw
The face of their Father, the other gods rose from their seats,
Nor was there one who dared to wait in his chair,
But all stood up before him. Thus there he sat down
On his throne. Then Hera took one look and knew
That he and a goddess had had their heads together—
He and silver-shod Thetis, daughter of the briny
630 Old man of the sea. So at once she spoke these words,
Taunting and sharp, to Zeus, the son of Cronos:
　　　"Now which of the gods, my trickster, has again been plotting
With you? You always enjoy keeping things from me,
Pondering matters in secret and pronouncing upon them,
And you never willingly tell me what you're planning."
　　　Then the Father of gods and men answered her thus:
"Hera, don't ever hope to know all my thoughts.
Many of them you would find very hard and unpleasant,
Even though you are my wife. What it is right
640 For you to hear, no god or man shall know
Before you. But what I plan apart from the gods—
About all such matters you are not to ask or inquire!"
　　　To which the heifer-eyed queenly Hera: "Most dreadful
Son of Cronos, what kind of talk is that!
Truly too often in time gone by I have failed
To ask or inquire, while you went on at your leisure
Plotting whatever you pleased. Now, though, I
Am awfully afraid that the briny old sea-ancient's daughter,
Thetis of the silver feet, has taken you in.
650 For right early this morning she sat with you and embraced
Your knees. And to her, I think, you nodded your head
In a solemn promise to honor Achilles and to slaughter
Many Achaeans beside their ships."
　　　Then Zeus,
God of the storm clouds, replied: "Mysterious goddess!
You think altogether too much! Nor does anything I do
Escape you. But let me assure you there is nothing at all
You can do, except put even more distance between us,

And that will make your existence colder than ever,
Believe me! If what you say is so, then that   660
Must be my will. So quietly take your seat
And do as I tell you, or all the gods on Olympus
Will not be able to help you when I come up
And lay hold of you with my irresistible hands!"

He spoke, and heifer-eyed queenly Hera sat down,
Quietly controlling her temper. But all the heavenly
Gods in the palace of Zeus were troubled. Hephaestus,
The famous artificer, was the first to speak, hoping
To please his mother, Hera of the lovely white arms:

"Truly we'll have a sorry, unbearable life here   670
If you two are going to quarrel on account of mortals
And cause a disturbance among us. There can be no joy
In the splendid feast when such bad things prevail.
So I hereby advise my mother, wise though she is
To try to please our dear Father Zeus, that he
May not rebuke her again and create more chaos
Here at our feast. Why what if the mighty Olympian,
Hurler of lightning, the mightiest god by far,
Should take a notion to strike us all from our seats!
But meekly ask his pardon, and soon the Olympian   680
Will be gracious to us again."

With this he sprang up
And placing the two-handled cup in his dear mother's hand
He spoke to her thus: "Bear up, my mother, and swallow
Your grief, or dear though you are to me I may
Have to watch you beaten and be completely unable,
In spite of my sorrow, to help or console you. For it
Is hard indeed to oppose the Olympian. Once
Before, when I was anxious to help you, he snatched me
Up by the foot and flung me headlong down   690
From the heavenly threshold. All day long I fell
And sank with the setting sun—what little was left
Of me—in Lemnos, where the Sintian people were quick
To come to my aid and take care of me after my fall."[8]

At this the goddess, white-armed Hera, smiled,
And smiling received the cup from her son. Then
He went on from left to right, dipping sweet nectar
From the mixing bowl and pouring for all the others.
And unquenchable laughter broke out mid the blessed gods
As they watched Hephaestus puffing his way through the palace.   700

Thus all day long till the sun went down they feasted,

Nor was there any lack of delight in the banquet
Before them, nor in the gorgeous lyre that Apollo
Played, nor yet in the dulcet Muses, who
Entertained them all with sweet antiphonal song.
    But when the bright sun was gone, they all went home
And to bed, for famous Hephaestus, the great ambidextrous
God, had built with all of his knowledge and art
A palace for each of them. But Olympian Zeus,
710 Lord of the lightning, went up to bed where he always
Lay when delicious sleep was approaching. He lay down
And slept, and beside him Hera of the golden throne.

BOOK II

Trial of the Army and the
Catalogue of Ships

All other gods and mortal wearers of helmets
Plumed with horsehair slept soundly all through the night,
But sweet sleep could not hold Zeus, for in his heart
He was pondering how he might honor Achilles and destroy
Beside the swift ships many other Achaeans. Then
He thought of a plan he preferred, to send a false Dream*
To Atreus' son Agamemnon. So he addressed him
With these winged words:
    "Go quickly, baneful Dream,   10
To the swift Achaean ships, and when you reach
The lodge of Atreus' son Agamemnon tell him
Exactly what I tell you. Tell him to hurry
And arm the long-haired Achaeans, since now he may take
The city of Troy and fill the wide streets with his soldiers.
The immortals who live on Olympus no longer take sides,
For with her pleading Hera has bent them all
To her way of thinking, and now disaster is hanging
Over the Trojans."
    He spoke, the Dream listened, then left   20
And quickly arrived at the swift Achaean ships.
He found Agamemnon, son of Atreus, asleep
In his lodge, deep in ambrosial slumber. The Dream
Stood over his head in the form of Neleus' son Nestor,
Whom Agamemnon respected above all the other
Leading elders. Then, in the likeness of him,
The Dream from heaven spoke thus:
    "You're asleep, O son
Of fiery Atreus, breaker of horses. But to sleep
All night is not good for a man in charge of an army

---

*Homeric dreams regularly divide into the true and the false.

30   And laden with so many cares. Quick, then, pay attention
     To me, for I have a message from Zeus, who far
     Away still has immense concern and pity
     For you. He says that you must go with all speed
     And arm the long-haired Achaeans, since now you may take
     The city of Troy and fill the wide streets with your soldiers.
     The immortals who live on Olympus no longer take sides,
     For with her pleading Hera has bent them all
     To her way of thinking, and now by the will of Zeus
     Disaster is hanging over the Trojans. Keep this
40   In your mind, and when honey-hearted sleep releases you
     Fight forgetfulness off."

            So saying, the Dream
     Departed and left him pondering there on things
     That were not to be. For he really thought he would take
     The city of Priam on that very day, childish
     Fool that he was! completely ignorant of the plan
     And purpose of Zeus, who throughout the terrible battles
     Ahead was yet to bring plenty of pain and groaning
     On Trojans and Danaans both. Then the King awoke
50   With the heavenly voice still sounding around him and sat up
     In bed. Quickly he dressed in a handsome new tunic,
     Threw on his great cloak and beneath his shining feet
     Bound beautiful sandals. Then slinging about his shoulders
     His sword with the studs of bright silver, he grasped the immortal
     Scepter of his fathers and strode out down the line
     Of ships of the bronze-clad Achaeans.

            Just as the light
     Of sacred Dawn appeared to Zeus and the other
     Immortals on lofty Olympus, Agamemnon ordered
60   The heralds to employ their powerful voices and call
     The long-haired Achaeans to the place of assembly. So they gave
     The call, and the men were quick to gather.

            But first
     The commander-in-chief called a meeting of the great-souled elders
     To sit by the ship of Nestor, the Pylos-born King.
     And when they were gathered he spoke and unfolded the definite
     Plan he had formed: "Your attention, friends. To me
     In my sleep a heavenly Dream came through the immortal
     Night, most closely resembling godly Nestor
70   In appearance and stature and build, and standing over
     My head he spoke to me thus:

            " 'You're asleep, O son

Of fiery Atreus, breaker of horses. But to sleep
All night is not good for a man in charge of an army
And laden with so many cares. Quick, then, pay attention
To me, for I have a message from Zeus, who far
Away still has immense concern and pity
For you. He says that you must go with all speed
And arm the long-haired Achaeans, since now you may take
The city of Troy and fill the wide streets with your soldiers.   80
The immortals who live on Olympus no longer take sides,
For with her pleading Hera has bent them all
To her way of thinking, and now by the will of Zeus
Disaster is hanging over the Trojans. Hold this
In your heart.'
        "Then he flew off, and sweet sleep released me.
So come, let us prepare as best we can
The sons of Achaeans for battle. But first it is right
That I should try them with words and bid them flee[1]
With their many-oared ships, though on every side I want all   90
Of you to try to restrain them with words."
        With this
He sat down, and among them up stood Nestor, the King
Of sandy Pylos. He, with all good intentions,
Addressed the elders: "My friends, captains and counselors
Of the Argives, had any of the other Achaeans
Told us this dream, we might have considered it false
And thus ignored it completely. But the man who saw it
Is he who claims first place and greatest worth
By far among the Achaeans. So come, let us do   100
All we can to arm and muster the men."
        He spoke,
And left the council, leading the way, and the other
Sceptered kings got up and followed, obeying
The people's shepherd. The men, meanwhile, were flocking
To the place of assembly. Like thronging bees that pour
From a hollow rock in swarm after swarm, flying
In every direction to cluster on the flowers of spring,
So the numerous companies of men came from the ships
And shelters along the broad beach, troop on troop of them   110
Headed for the place of assembly. And Rumor, the servant
Of Zeus, went blazing among them urging them on.
They met, and their gathering place was filled with confusion.
As the army sat down they made the earth groan beneath them,
And a mighty din went up. Nine shouting heralds

Tried to restrain them, to make them be quiet and listen
To the god-fed kings. At last they got them all seated
And still and quiet in their places. Then King Agamemnon
Stood up among them, holding the scepter which Hephaestus
120   Had made with much labor. Hephaestus gave it to Zeus,
The lordly son of Cronos. Zeus gave it to Hermes,
The speedy slayer of Argus. Lord Hermes gave it
To Pelops, lasher of horses, and Pelops gave it
To Atreus, shepherd of the people. Atreus, dying,
Left it to wealthy Thyestes, owner of many
Flocks, and Thyestes left it to King Agamemnon
To bear throughout his rule over many islands
And all of Argos. He leaned on it now, as he spoke
Among the Argives:
130   "My friends, Danaan heroes
And comrades of Ares, great Zeus, the son of Cronos,
Has bound me now in woeful blindness of spirit,[2]
Heartless god that he is! For long ago
He made me a promise and vowed with a nod of his head
That I should sack the well-walled city of Ilium
Before I went home, but now a vile deceit
Appears in his plans, and he bids me go back in disgrace
To Argos, having lost a great many men. Such,
I suppose, is the pleasure of Zeus, almighty God,
140   Who has toppled the towers of numerous cities and who
Shall continue to topple, since his is the greatest power.
But this is a shameful thing, and shall be so
Even to our children's children, for so large an Achaean
Army to fight a futile war with men
Far fewer than they and still no end in sight!
For if both Achaeans and Trojans should take a notion
To number themselves, and swear a truce with solemn
Oaths and offerings, and if all the householders in Troy
Were then assembled and we Achaeans split up
150   In groups of ten with a single Trojan per group
To pour our wine, then many a squadron of ten
Would lack a Trojan to pour. By even so many,
I think, do we, the sons of Achaeans, outnumber
The natives of Troy. But they have allies from numerous
Cities, spear-brandishing men who greatly frustrate
My earnest desire to sack the fair-lying fortress
Of Ilium. Nine years of mighty Zeus have already
Gone by. Our ships' timbers have rotted and the ropes

Broken, and, I dare say, our wives and young children
Sit home in our halls waiting for us. Yet that   160
Which we came here to do remains completely undone.
But come, all of you do as I say. Let us flee
With our ships to the precious land of our fathers. For we
Can no longer hope to plunder the wide streets of Troy."
    These words caused great commotion throughout the army
In all who were not at the council. And the meeting was moved
Like the rolling high waves of the broad Icarian sea
When down from the lowering clouds of Father Zeus
Wind from the East or South rushes to raise them.
And as tall grain in a field waves wildly under   170
A blast of the hard West Wind and the ears bow down
Before it, so all their great gathering stirred. Then,
With a mighty yell, they broke for the ships in a cloud
Of dust that rose high overhead. They called to each other
To lay hold of the ships and drag them into the bright sea,
And as they cleared the launching-ways and took
The props from under the ships, the huge uproar
Of those home-hungry men went up to heaven itself.
Then indeed the Argives might have returned in spite of
What fate had ordained, if the goddess Hera had not   180
Had a word with Athena, saying:
    "O invincible child
Of Zeus who bears the aegis, alas! Is it thus
That the Argive forces are really going to flee
Over the sea's broad back to the precious land of their fathers?
Flee and leave to Priam and the other Trojans
Their insolent boast, no other than Argive Helen
Herself, for whom so many Achaeans died
Before Troy far from their own dear country? But go now
Throughout the mob of bronze-clad Achaeans and quiet them   190
One and all with your gentle words, and do not
Allow them to launch those curving ships of theirs."
    She spoke, and the blue-eyed goddess Athena did not
Disobey. Down she went darting from the peaks of Olympus
And quickly came to the swift Achaean ships.
There, standing beside his benched black ship,
She found Odysseus, making no effort at all
To lay hands on the vessel, for grief abounding had come
On his heart and soul. Bright-eyed Athena stood close
And spoke to him thus: 200
    "O god-sprung son of Laertes,

Resourceful Odysseus, do all of you really intend
To scramble aboard your many-oared ships and flee
Over the sea's broad back to the precious land of your fathers?
Flee and leave to Priam and the other Trojans
Their insolent boast, no other than Argive Helen
Herself, for whom so many Achaeans died
Before Troy far from their own dear country? But now
Hold back no longer. Go through the Achaean host
210 And quiet them all with your gentle words, and do not
Allow them to launch those curving ships of theirs."

   She spoke, and he knew the voice of the goddess, and set out
At a run, throwing off his cloak, which Eurybates, his Ithacan
Herald and attendant, picked up for him. But he
Went straight to Atreus' son Agamemnon and received
From him the rod of authority, the immortal scepter
Of the great King's royal line, and with this in his hand
He went down the line of ships where the bronze-clad Achaeans
Were thronging.

220   Whenever he met a chieftain or any
Outstanding man, he would come up beside him and try
To calm him with these gentle words: "You're not yourself, sir,
Nor would it become me to threaten you like a coward.
But take your seat, and see that your people are seated,
For you have no idea what Atreus' son
Is thinking. He's only testing us now, but soon
He is likely to smite the sons of Achaeans. Did not
All of us hear what he said at the council? Take care
That he doesn't get angry and punish the sons of Achaeans.
230 Haughty indeed is the spirit of god-nurtured kings.
The honor they have is from Zeus, and Zeus, the lord
Of all wisdom, dearly loves them."

   But whenever he saw
Some man of the people, yelling and screaming for all
He was worth, he would strike him a blow with the scepter and call him
To order thus: "You're out of your senses, man!
Sit down and be still, and pay some attention to the words
Of your betters, you weak, unwarlike fellow, of no
Account in battle or council either! We cannot
240 By any means all be kings here. A host of kings
Is no good at all. So let there be one king only,
One lord and ruler, who has his scepter and right
Of decree from the almighty son of devious Cronos
And so is true king of his people."

Thus king-like himself
He went through the crowd, and the soldiers left their shelters
And ships and hurried back to the place of assembly
With a huge uproar like the rush of surf on a beach
When a wave of the loud-crashing sea breaks and thunders
On a long stretch of shore.   250
Then all the others sat down
And kept quiet. Babbling Thersites[3] alone continued
To raise a racket, he whose mind was full
Of vulgar, disordered words which he used in railing
At kings, not with any good purpose or reason,
But simply to get a laugh from the Argive soldiers.
Of all the men who came to Ilium, he was
By far the ugliest. Bowlegged and lame in one foot,
His shoulders drooped so round that they almost met
In front, and on his head, which came at the top   260
To a rather sharp point, grew a thin and mangy stubble.
Most hateful was he to Achilles and to Odysseus,
For they were the two he usually railed at. But now
He screamed his insults at the man most out of favor,
King Agamemnon, toward whom the indignant Achaeans
Felt wrath and resentment. At him, then, he yelled his abuse:
"Atrides, now what again are you griping about?
And what new demands are you making? Your shelters are bulging
With bronze, and whenever we sack a city you always
Get the choicest booty, including whole bevies   270
Of beautiful women. Can it be that you still want gold,
The ransom some horse-taming Trojan brings out of Troy
To pay for his captured son whom I or some other
Achaean bound and led away? Or would you
Prefer a ripe young lady to sleep with and keep
Shut up somewhere for yourself? Truly, it hardly
Becomes their commander to burden with so many troubles
The sons of Achaeans. O you effeminate fools
And cowards! women, not men, of Achaea! let us
Go home with our ships and leave this fellow to rot   280
With his precious prizes here in the land of Troy,
That he may know once and for all whether we will help him
Or not. And now he has grossly insulted Achilles,
A much better man than himself, by taking and keeping
His prize of prestige—an act of arrogant pride!
But surely the heart of Achilles is not even angry,
Nor does he care one bit, or this, O son

Of Atreus, would be the last of your arrogant insults!"
     Even so Thersites railed at King Agamemnon,
290 Commander-in-chief of the army. But at once the worthy
     Odysseus went up to the fellow and scowling fiercely
     Gave him this harsh reprimand: "Vile Thersites,
     Of words both vulgar and endless, a clear-voiced speaker
     You are, but don't try to argue all by yourself
     With kings. For I think that no more incapable man
     Than you came here with the sons of Atreus under
     The high walls of Troy. I would not advise you, then,
     To take in vain the names of kings in casting
     Insults upon them, nor to always be looking for a chance
300 To go home. None of us here really knows what is going
     To happen, whether the sons of Achaeans shall go back
     In triumph or not. Still you insist on abusing
     Our commander-in-chief Agamemnon, cutting him deeply
     With words on account of the many gifts the Danaan
     Heroes see fit to give him. But I'll tell you this,
     And believe me I mean what I say. If I find you this way
     Again, making a fool of yourself, then
     May the head of Odysseus remain on his shoulders no more,
     Nor may I be called any longer Telemachus' father,
310 If I don't take and strip you, ripping away
     The cloak and tunic that hide your wretched body,
     And send you bawling to the speedy ships, beaten
     From the place of assembly with hard, disgraceful blows!"
          He spoke, and with the scepter struck the man's back
     And shoulders. Thersites cringed and started to cry,
     While a bloody welt swelled up on his back beneath
     The golden scepter. Then he sat down, afraid
     And in pain, and on his face as he wiped his tears
     Was a foolish, forced expression. The Achaeans, vexed
320 Though they were, laughed at him loud and long, and thus
     Would one of them say, with a glance at the man next to him:
          "Good enough! truly Odysseus has done a great many
     Fine things, both as the author of countless good plans
     And as a leader in battle. But of all the deeds
     He has done among the Argives, this is the best
     By far—to squelch this slanderous slinger of insults
     And hush his haranguing! Surely his insolent spirit
     Will never again be stupid enough to make him
     Rail at and criticize kings."
330   So spoke the crowd.

Then city-sacking Odysseus stood up among them
With the scepter still in his hand and beside him, disguised
As a herald, bright-eyed Athena called to the men
For silence, that near and far alike might hear
And take to heart the words of Odysseus, who now,
In an effort to help, addressed the assembly: "O son
Of Atreus, now surely the Achaeans are determined to make
Their King the most despised of all mortal men,
For they refuse to honor the promise they gave you
On the voyage from horse-grazing Argos, that you should not   340
Return until you had sacked the well-walled city
Of Ilium. Now they whine to each other and wail
For home like little children or widowed women.
And truly there's toil enough here to send any man home
Worn out and discouraged. A man will grow impatient
When kept from his wife for only one month, when the storms
Of winter and swollen seas prevent his benched ship
From traveling. But we have been here for nine long years.
Hence, I cannot blame the Achaeans for fretting
Beside their beaked ships. Yet what a disgraceful thing   350
It would be to stay so long and still go home
Empty-handed! Bear up, my friends, and try to hold out
Awhile longer, that we may learn whether Calchas prophesies
Truly or not. For this we well remember,
And all of you whom the fates of death have not
Yet claimed are witnesses still to what happened at Aulis.*
Why now it seems but a day or so ago
That the ships were gathering there, loaded with evils
For Priam and all the Trojans, and around a spring
Of bright water that flowed from the foot of a beautiful plane tree   360
We soldiers were offering on holy altars whole hecatombs
To the immortals. Then all at once a great omen
Appeared—a snake with markings blood-red on his back,
A terrible serpent that Zeus himself sent forth
In the light, glided from under an altar and shot
For the plane tree. Now up on the highest branch, huddled
Beneath the leaves, were the tender, tiny fledglings
Of a mother sparrow, eight of them, and the mother
Made nine. These babies, pitifully cheeping, the snake
Devoured, while the mother fluttered around them screaming   370

---

*Agamemnon initially assembled the entire Achaean fleet at Aulis, in northern Boeotia.

For her precious young. Then coiling himself, the snake
Caught her by the wing as she wheeled and screamed in the air.
But when the beast had swallowed them all, the babies
Along with the mother, God, who brought him to light,
Fixed him where all could see, for the son of Cronos
Turned him to stone right there, and all of us
Stood gaping at what had happened. Then, when that awesome
Portent had thus interrupted the offering of hecatombs
To the immortals, Calchas addressed us and tried
380 To explain the omen, saying:
　　　" 'Why, O long-haired
Achaeans, are you now so quiet? All-knowing Zeus
Has shown a great sign to us, an omen late
In appearance and later still in fulfillment, but a glorious
Omen famous forever. Just as this snake
Swallowed the baby sparrows along with their mother,
Eight of them in all and nine counting her,
Even for so many years we shall fight in the land
Of Troy, but at last in the tenth year we shall take
390 The wide-wayed city.'
　　　　"These were the words of Calchas,
And now all that he foretold is surely
Being brought to pass. So come, you well-greaved Achaeans,
All of you remain here until we take
The great city of Priam."
　　　　At this the Argives raised
A great shout, and about the ships the sound of the shouting
Achaeans loudly resounded as their voices went up
In praise of what sacred Odysseus had said. And then
400 Horse-driving Gerenian Nestor spoke to them thus:
"Incredible! you act like so many squabbling little boys
With no real interest at all in works of war.
What is to become of all our oaths and promises?
Very well, the counsels and plans that we made together
With trusted libations of unmixed wine and faithful
Clasping of hands—let us throw all that in the fire!
For now we do nothing but talk, which does us no good
At all, regardless of how long we wrangle. Therefore,
Son of Atreus, do as you've always done:
410 Hold your purpose firm and unyielding, and lead
The Argives through the heavy fighting ahead. And if
There are one or two plotting traitors among us—men
Who want to see Argos again before we have learned

Whether aegis-great Zeus has promised us truly or not—
Let them die now and plot to no end! For I
Say this, that on the day when the Argives boarded
Their swift-sailing ships to bear death and doom to the Trojans,
Cronos' almighty son gave his word and nod
To us: his lightning flashed on our right, and the signs
He showed were good ones. So let there be no rush   420
To go home, not until every man here has slept
With the wife of some Trojan and been repaid in full
For the struggles and groans endured on Helen's account.
If, however, there be one terribly eager
To set out for home, let him lay hold of his sturdy
Black ship, that here and now with an army for audience
He may meet his death and his doom. But you,
O King, plan wisely yourself and pay some heed
To another. Do not disregard what now I am going
To say. Split up your men, Agamemnon, divide them   430
By tribes and by clans, that clan may succor clan
And tribe bear aid to tribe. If this you do,
And if the Achaeans obey your commands, you will soon
Know the brave from the cowards, which is which among your captains
And in the rank and file, for each company then
Will be on its own in the fight for honor and glory.
And then you will know whether it is divine decree
That prevents you from sacking the city, or the cowardly hearts
Of your men and their ignorance in battle."
        And King Agamemnon   440
Answered him thus: "Once again, old sire, you outspeak
The other sons of Achaeans. O Father Zeus,
Athena, and Apollo, if I had but ten
So truly wise! then the towers of King Priam's city
Would soon be toppled and all laid waste and leveled
Beneath our hands. But Cronos' son Zeus, who bears
The aegis, involves me in futile wranglings and quarrels.
Achilles and I fought over a girl with violent
Words, and I was the one who got angry first.
But if the day ever comes when we two see   450
Eye to eye, then the Trojans' ruin will be delayed
No longer, not for so much as a moment! But for now,
Go eat your meal before we join battle. Sharpen
Your spears and adjust your shields, feed well your fast horses
And thoroughly check your chariots, that throughout the day
We may measure our might in hateful war. Nor will there

Be any let-up at all till night comes on
And parts the furious fighters. The baldric of many
A man-guarding shield shall be wet with sweat on the breast
460 Of its wearer, and about the spear the warrior's hand
Shall grow weary, and the horse of many a driver shall sweat
In streams as he pulls and strains at the polished car.
But whomever I see disposed to loiter beside
The beaked ships apart from the battle, that man shall have
No hope at all of escaping the dogs and the birds!"

　　　He spoke, and the Argives roared like a mighty wave
That the South Wind drives to break on a craggy high coast,
A jutting cliff forever pounded by waves
No matter what wind is blowing. And the men got up
470 And moved out in a hurry, lit fires in their shelters and ate.
Each of them made an offering to one or another
Of the everliving gods and prayed to come out alive
From the toil and moil of Ares. The commander-in-chief
Agamemnon slew a sleek bull of five years to the high
And powerful son of Cronos and sent for the leading
Senior chiefs of all the Achaeans to join him—
Nestor first and King Idomeneus, then both
Ajaxes and Tydeus' son Diomedes, with Odysseus,
Godlike in wisdom, the sixth to be called. Menelaus,
480 Good at the war-cry, needed no call. He knew
The cares his brother bore and came on his own.
They stood round the bull and took up the grains of barley,
And King Agamemnon spoke thus in prayer among them:

　　　"Most great and glorious Zeus, sky-dwelling god
Of the lowering storm clouds, may the sun not set till I
With streaming and furious fire have burned the doors
Of Priam's great hall and reduced his palace to a heap
Of charred and sooty beams, nor may darkness come on
Till I have torn with bronze the tunic on the breast
490 Of Hector, and may his comrades round about him
Fall in the dust and bite the earth by the score!"

　　　Such was his prayer, though Zeus was not ready to grant it.
He accepted the offering but caused an increase of toil
That no man in the world would envy.

　　　　　　When the leaders there
Had prayed, they sprinkled the grains of barley, drew back
The heads of the victims, cut their throats, flayed them,
And sliced out the thigh-pieces. These they wrapped in thick layers

Of fat and on them laid still more raw meat.
All this they burned on split and leafless logs,   500
And piercing with spits heart, liver, and lungs they held them
Over the fire of Hephaestus. Now when the thigh-pieces
Were burned and all had tasted of the vital parts,
They cut up the rest, spitted and roasted it well,
And drew it all from the spits. Then, the work done
And the meal ready, they feasted on the plentiful meat
Abundantly portioned to each. When they had eaten
And drunk as much as they wished, horse-driving Gerenian
Nestor was the first to speak:
    "Most famous son   510
Of Atreus, Agamemnon, king of men, let us
No longer stay here nor put off the work which God
Has laid on our hands. Come then, have the heralds of the bronze-clad
Achaeans go out and give the cry all down
The long lines of ships and call the army together,
And let us go in a body throughout the great camp
Of Achaeans, that we may the sooner stir up in the men
The spirit of blade-keen, furious Ares."
    He spoke,
And his words the commander-in-chief Agamemnon did not   520
Disregard. At once he ordered the heralds to employ
Their powerful voices and call the long-haired Achaeans
To the place of assembly. So they gave the call, and the troops
Were quick to gather. The god-nurtured kings in the council
Of Atreus' son went swiftly marshaling the men,
And among them bright-eyed Athena bearing the priceless
Aegis, immortal and ageless forever, from which
Fluttered a hundred golden tassels, each of them
Perfectly plaited and worth a hundred oxen.
With this she flashed through the host of Achaeans, urging   530
Them on, and in the heart of every man there
She stirred up strength to fight without flagging throughout
The battle. And at once they felt war to be sweeter than any
Return to their dear native land.
    As a great fire flames
On the peaks of a mountain, consuming a boundless forest
And giving a glare one sees from miles away,
So as they came the flash and gleam from their dazzling
And countless bronze went up through the sky to heaven.
    And as the many flocks of winged fowl,   540

Wild geese or cranes or long-necked swans in the Asian
Meadow by the streams of Caÿstrius* fly wheeling about
Exulting in strength of wing and settle always
Onward with clangor and honk, one in front of
Another, making the meadow resound, so out
From the shelters and ships and onto the plain of Scamander
Their many companies poured, and beneath the beat
Of the feet of the men and the horses the earth tremendously
Echoed. And they took their stand in the flowery field
550 Of Scamander, numerous as the leaves and flowers of spring.
        And as the buzzing flies that swarm through the shed
Of a herdsman when spring has come and fresh milk drenches
The pails, even so many were the long-haired Achaeans
Mustering there on the plain for battle against
The people of Troy, all eager to tear them apart.
        And as when goatherds easily single out
Their wide-roaming flocks when they have come in a pasture
Together, so now the leaders on every side
Marshaled their men for battle, and King Agamemnon
560 Among them, his head and eyes like those of Zeus,
The lover of lightning, his waist like the waist of Ares,
His breast like the breast of Poseidon. As a bull stands out
In a herd above all the other cattle, the obvious
Leader of the grazing beeves, so that day Zeus
Made Atreus' son stand out, the one pre-eminent
Man in the forces, the first mid many warriors.
        Tell me now, O Muses,[4] you that have homes
On Olympus—for you are goddesses and in command
Of all knowledge, while all we hear is rumor and we
570 Know nothing at all—say who were the Danaan lords
And leaders. But as for the rest of the army, I could not
Possibly count or name them, not if I had
Ten tongues in as many mouths, an unbreakable voice
And a heart of bronze, unless you Olympian Muses,
Daughters of Zeus of the aegis, chose to help me
Remember all those who came to Ilium. Here, then,
Are the ships' commanders and how many ships there were.
        Peneleos and Leïtus led the Boeotians, along with
Arcesilaus, Clonius, and Prothoënor. Their homes
580 Were in Hyria and stony Aulis, in Schoenus and Scolus

---

*The Caÿstrius (later, Kaüstros) flows into the sea at Ephesus.

And hilly Eteonus, in broad-lawned Mycalessus, Thespeia,
And Graea, and some were from Harma, Eilesium, and Erythrae,
While others held Eleon and Hyle, Peteon, Ocalea,
The well-walled fortress Medeon, Copae, Eutresis,
And dove-haunted Thisbe, Coroneia and grassy Haliartus,
And others held Plataea and the well-built fortress
Of Lower Thebes, Glisas and holy Onchestus
With its splendid grove of Poseidon, Arne of grapes
Rich-clustering, Mideia, sacred Nisa, and Anthedon
The border town. Of these there were fifty ships,   590
And on each came a hundred and twenty young men of Boeotia.

    And those who lived in Aspledon and Orchomenus of the Minyae
Were led by sons of Ares, Ascalaphus and Ialmenus,
Whom the gentle and honored maiden Astyoche bore,
Having gone upstairs in the palace of Azeus' son Actor
And secretly slept with the mighty War-god. With these
The hollow ships drawn up there were thirty in all.

    Schedius and Epistrophus, sons of great-hearted Iphitus
And Naubolus' grandsons, captained the Phocians, who held
Cyparissus and rocky Pytho, sacred Crisa,   600
Daulis, and Panopeus, Hyampolis and Anemoreia,
While others lived by the lovely river Cephisus
And in Lilaea by the springs of Cephisus. Of these
There were forty black ships. And now their leaders were busy
Marshaling the Phocian ranks and preparing the men
For battle hard on the Boeotians' left.

    The leader
Of the Locrian forces was the fleet-footed son of Oïleus,
The lesser Ajax, by no means so much man
As Telamonian Ajax, but the lesser by far. He was slight   610
Of build and the corselet he wore was of linen, but with
The spear he surpassed all Hellenes and Achaeans. His followers
Lived in Cynus, Calliarus, and Opus, in Bessa
And Scarphe and delightful Augeiae, Tarphe and Thronium
And about the waters of Boagrius. With Ajax came forty
Black ships of the Locrians, who live just over the straits
From holy Euboea.

    The fury-breathing Abantes
Came from Euboea itself, where they held Eretria,
Chalcis, and vineyard-rich Histiaea, Cerinthus   620
By the sea and the steep fortress of Dios, and some
Had homes in Carystus and others lived in Styra.
Leader of all was the chief Elephenor, that scion

Of Ares, son of Chalcodon, and commander of the doughty
Abantes, those spirited eager spearmen with hair long
In back, fast men on their feet and quick to thrust
Their good ashen spears through the corselets and breasts of their foes.
They came with their chief Elephenor in forty black ships.
     And there were men from the strong citadel of Athens
630 In the realm of great-hearted Erechtheus, whom long ago
The bountiful earth had borne and Zeus's daughter
Athena reared. She established him in Athens
In her own resplendent shrine, and there, as the years
Roll on, the young Athenians pray for his grace
And favor with sacrificed bulls and rams. Their leader
Was Peteos' son Menestheus, than whom no man
On earth was better when it came to the marshaling of chariots
And shield-bearing men. Nestor alone could rival him
There, since he had been at it for so much longer.
640 And Menestheus came with a company of fifty black ships.
     Ajax led twelve ships from Salamis, and had them
Drawn up on the beach where the forces from Athens were stationed.
     Those who held Argos and high-walled Tiryns were there
And men from Hermione and Asine, towns that embrace
A deep bay, and others from Troezen, viny Epidaurus,
And Eïonae, with young Achaeans from Aegina and Mases—
All led by battle-roaring Diomedes and Sthenelus,
The dear son of renowned Capaneus. And with them as third
In command came godlike Euryalus, King Mecisteus' son
650 And Talaus' grandson. But battle-roaring Diomedes
Was in charge of them all. And of these there were eighty black ships.
     Troops were there from the strong citadel of Mycenae,
Wealthy Corinth, and staunch Cleonae, men
From Orneia, lovely Araethyrea, and Sicyon, where Adrastus
Used to be king, and others who held Hyperesia,
Pellene and high Gonoessa, and who lived around Aegium,
Large Helice, and all up and down Aegialus. Of these
With a hundred ships the commander was King Agamemnon,
Son of Atreus. His men were by far the best
660 And most numerous of all. And as he armed himself
In the gleaming bronze, he stood out among them, the most
World-famous of kings and the most distinguished of warriors,
For he outranked all others, and the unit he led
Was largest by far.
     And there were those with homes
In the rolling country of fair Lacedaemon, in Pharis,

Sparta, and dove-haunted Messe, and those who lived
In Bryseiae and charming Augeiae, and others who held
Amyclae, Laas, and Helus, a citadel close by
The sea, while others lived about Oetylus. All these   670
Were led by King Agamemnon's brother, Menelaus
Of the loud war-cry, with sixty ships, but his forces
Were marshaled and armed as a separate division. And he,
Menelaus the King, went among them, sure of himself
And zealous, stirring up fight in his men, for above
All others he longed to exact full payment for the many
Struggles and groans he had suffered on Helen's account.
      Next came natives of Pylos, delightful Arene,
And Thryum, where Alpheius is forded, men with homes
In firm-founded Aepy and Cyparisseïs, Pteleos,   680
Amphigeneia, Helus, and Dorium, where the Muses
Met Thamyris the Thracian[5] as he came from Oechalia and the
            house
Of Oechalian Eurytus and put an end to his singing.
For he had made the extravagant claim that he
In a singing-match with even the Muses themselves,
Daughters of Zeus of the aegis, would be the winner,
And they in their wrath took from him the gift of song
And made him forget the art of harping. All these
Were led by horse-driving Gerenian Nestor. And ninety
Black ships were drawn up in line on his section of beach.   690
      And there were the men of Arcadia, from below the mountain
Of steep Cyllene by Aepytus' tomb. Some of these
Hand-to-hand fighters had homes in Pheneos and pastoral
Orchomenus, in Rhipe, Stratia, and windy Enispe,
While others lived in Tegea and fair Mantineia,
Stymphalus and Parrhasia. Lord Agapenor, son
Of Ancaeus, was leader of these with sixty ships,
On each of which came many Arcadian warriors,
Skillful in battle. The commander-in-chief himself,
Agamemnon, son of Atreus, had given them   700
The well-decked ships wherein to cleave and cross over
The wine-dark sea, for with nautical matters they had
No concern.
      And there were troops from Buprasium and all
Of beautiful Elis that lies between Hyrmine,
The border town Myrsinus, Alesium, and the looming
Olenian Rock. Four men had charge of these,
And with each came ten swift ships full of Epeans.

Two of the companies were led by Amphimachus and Thalpius,
710 One the son of Cteatus, the other of Eurytus,
And both of the blood of Actor. A third was led
By the son of Amarynceus, the mighty Diores,
And chief of the fourth contingent was godlike Polyxeinus,
King Agasthenes' son and grandson of Augeas.
    Those from Dulichium and the hallowed Echinean Islands
Across the water from Elis were all commanded
By Meges, peer of the War-god and son of the horseman
Phyleus, a god-loved man who quarreled with his father
And went over to live in Dulichium. With Meges came forty
720 Black ships.
    Odysseus commanded the proud Cephallenians,
Holders of Ithaca and Mount Neriton, trembling
With leaves, natives of Crocyleia and rugged Aegilips,
Of Zacynthus and Samos and the mainland across from these islands.
Odysseus, godlike in wisdom, led all of these
And with him came twelve vermilion-cheeked ships.
    And Thoas,
Son of Andraemon, led the Aetolians, soldiers
From Pleuron, Olenus, Pylene, rocky Calydon,
730 And Chalcis close by the sea. For the sons of Oeneus
Were no longer alive, nor was great-hearted Oeneus himself,
And dead was blond Meleager, to whom the Aetolian
Kingship had come. So with Thoas came forty black ships.
    The soldiers from Crete were captained by spear-famed Idomeneus
And came from their homes in Knossos and the well-walled town
Of Gortyn, from the populous cities of Lyctus, Miletus,
Phaestus, Rhytium, and chalk-white gleaming Lycastus,
And the others came from in and around the hundred
Cities of Crete. The entire contingent was led
740 By the famous spearman Idomeneus along with Meriones,
Peer of the slaughtering god of battle. With these
Followed eighty black ships.
    And Tlepolemus, the tall and valiant
Son of Heracles, had come with nine full ships
Of the spirited Rhodians, dwellers in three different parts
Of the island of Rhodes, in Lindos, Ialysus, and chalk-white
Gleaming Cameirus. Spear-famous Tlepolemus led them,
He whom mighty Heracles sired and whose mother
Was Astyocheia, whom Heracles brought from Ephyre
750 And the river Selleïs after laying waste many cities
Of Zeus-fed warrior kings. But Tlepolemus was no sooner

Grown in the fortified palace than he killed his father's
Dear uncle, a scion of Ares, the aging Licymnius.
Then with all speed he built ships, gathered a great host
Of people, and fled overseas, for he was threatened
By the other sons and grandsons of mighty Heracles.
At last in his painful wandering the exile came
To Rhodes, and there in three sections by tribes his people
Settled. And they were loved by Zeus, the ruler
Of gods and men, and prodigious indeed were the riches   760
Cronos' son poured on them.
    Nireus too
Was there with three trim ships from the island of Syme,
Nireus the son of Aglaia and Charopus the King,
Nireus the handsomest man in the Danaan forces
At Troy excepting only the peerless son
Of Peleus. But he was a weakling, and those who came with him
Were few.
    And there were natives of Nisyrus and Crapathus,
Of Casus, the Calydnian Islands, and Eurypylus' city   770
Of Cos—all under Pheidippus and Antiphus, the two sons
Of King Thessalus, whom Heracles sired. And drawn up in the line
With them were thirty hollow ships.
    And now for those
From Pelasgian Argos, men from Alope, Alos,
And Trachis, and those who held Phthia and Hellas, land
Of glamorous women—they were called Myrmidons, Hellenes,
And Achaeans, and fifty full ships of them came with Achilles
As captain. But now they gave no thought to the din
And horror of war, since they had no one to lead them   780
Into the ranks. For the brave, swift-footed Achilles
Lay by his ships in a fit of wrath and resentment
Because of a girl, Briseis of the beautiful hair,
Whom he had won at Lyrnessus when he with much toil
Leveled that city and wasted the walls of Thebe
And struck spear-raging Mynes down, and Epistrophus
Equally fierce, sons of King Euenus,
The son of Selepus. Sorely grieving for her,
Achilles lay idle. But soon he would rise again.
    And there were troops from Phylace and flowery Pyrasus   790
Where Demeter has a grove and temple, from Iton,
Mother of flocks, Antron close by the sea,
And grassy Pteleos. These had been led by warlike
Protesilaus[6] while he was alive, but now

The black earth held him, and his wife was left in Phylace,
Her two cheeks torn in mourning, her husband's house
Half finished. For he had been far the first Achaean
Ashore, but as he leaped from his ship he fell
To a doughty Dardanian. Still, though they longed for their leader,
800 His men were not without a commander. Podarces,
Scion of Ares, marshaled them now, he
The son of Iphiclus, Phylacus' son and the owner
Of many flocks. Podarces was the younger brother
Of magnanimous Protesilaus, who was not only older
But also the better man, warlike and valiant.
So the troops did not lack a commander, though they longed for the
        gifted
Man they had lost. And with him came forty black ships.

        Those who lived by the Boebeian lake in Pherae
And in Boebe, Glaphyrae, and well-settled Iolcus came
810 In eleven ships under Admetus' dear son
Eumelus, whom queenly Alcestis, the loveliest daughter
Of Pelias, bore to her lord.

        The men from Methone
And Thaumacia, from Meliboea and craggy Olizon were led
In seven ships by the skillful bowman Philoctetes,
And fifty oarsmen had come in each ship, all
Fierce men with the bow. But Philoctetes lay in pain
On the island of sacred Lemnos, where the sons of Achaeans
Had left him in anguish from a vicious water-snake's bite.
820 He lay in agony there, nor was it long
Before the Argives beside their ships had cause
To remember King Philoctetes. Still, though they longed
For their leader, his men were not without a commander.
Now they were marshaled by Medon, the bastard son
Whom Rhene bore to Oïleus, taker of towns.

        Those who held Tricca and Ithome of the terraced crags
And Oechalia, the city of Oechalian Eurytus, followed
Two sons of Asclepius, the able physicians Podaleirius
And Machaon. And drawn up with them were thirty hollow ships.
830   And the men from Ormenius and the spring Hypereia, from As-
        terium
And the gleaming towers of Titanus were led by Eurypylus,
The brilliant son of Euaemon. And forty black ships
Followed him.

        Those with homes in Argissa, Gyrtone, and Orthe,
In Elone and the gleaming town Oloösson had

As their leader the furious fighter Polypoetes, son
Of Peirithous, who was sired by immortal Zeus himself.
Glorious Hippodameia bore him to Peirithous
On the very day he got his revenge on the shaggy
Centaurs and drove them from Pelion to the Aethices.   840
But Polypoetes was not their only leader.
He had as his helper Leonteus, scion of Ares
And son of high-hearted Coronus, son of Caenus.
And with them came forty black ships.
    And Gouneus led
From Cyphus two and twenty vessels, and with him
Came the Enienes and the battle-staunch Peraebi,
Who had built their homes round wintry Dodona and lived
On the land about the beautiful stream Titaressus, which pours
Its clear water into the Peneius, but flows on through   850
The darker water of silvery-swirling Peneius
Like so much unmingling oil, for the stream Titaressus
Is a branch of dread Styx, the river of awesome oath.
    Prothous, son of Tenthredon, led the Magnetes,
Who lived about the Peneius and Pelion, trembling
With leaves. Fast Prothous captained them all. And with him
Were forty black ships.[7]
    These were the Danaan lords
And leaders. But tell me, O Muse, who was by far
The best man and which horses were best in the army that followed   860
The sons of Atreus.
    The finest horses by far
Were the mares of Pheres' son Admetus, that his son
Eumelus drove, horses swift as birds,
Of the same color and age, and so equal in height
That a line would be quite level across their backs.
Both of these mares had been reared in Pereia by silver-bowed
Phoebus Apollo, and into battle they carried
The panic of Ares. Much the best of the warriors
Was Telamonian Ajax, but only so long   870
As Achilles continued his wrath. For Achilles was strongest
By far, as were the horses that drew him, the matchless
Son of Peleus. But now he lay mid his beaked
Seagoing ships, withdrawn and full of wrath
For the people's shepherd, Atreus' son Agamemnon,
While along the beach the men of angry Achilles
Amused themselves with the discus, javelin, and bow.
Their horses stood each by his car, munching clover

And marsh-grown parsley, but the officers' chariots stood
880   In their shelters well covered up. And these men longed
For their leader, dear to Ares, and they wandered throughout
The camp and did no fighting.
              But the others marched on
Like a great fire sweeping the plain, and beneath their feet
The earth groaned as it does when raging Zeus hurls lightning
And lashes the land about Typhoeus in the mountains
Of Arima, where they say Typhoeus is sleeping. So now
The earth loudly resounded beneath the beat of their feet
As they went on the double across the groaning plain.
890   Then a messenger came to the Trojans, wind-footed swift Iris,
With a fearful message from Zeus who bears the aegis.
Young men and old alike were gathered in the court
Of King Priam holding assembly when swift-footed Iris
Approached them and spoke. She took the voice of Priam's
Son Polites, who sat on watch for the Trojans
On top of the tomb of old Aesyetes, relying
On speed of foot to bear word whenever the Achaeans
Made a move from the ships. In the likeness of him, fleet Iris
Spoke thus to Priam:
900   "Old sire, you always dote
On endless words come peace or war, but this
Is war unyielding and total! Surely I've been
In a good many battles, but never yet have I seen
So large and splendid an army. And here they come,
Marching across the plain against the city
Like the numberless leaves of the forest or sands of the sea.
Now you most of all, Hector, I urge to do
As I say. Since in this great city of Priam there are many
Allies who come from all over and speak different tongues,
910   Let each of their captains marshal the men of his city
And lead them forth to battle."
              She spoke, and Hector
Knew the voice of the goddess. Quickly he broke up
The meeting, and the men rushed to arms. All the gates were thrown
                    open
And with a tremendous din the army poured out,
Both infantry and horse.
              In front of the city well out
In the open plain is a high mound that men call Thorn Hill,
But immortals call it the tomb of dancing Myrine.

Here both Trojans and allies ordered their ranks.   920
        Bright-helmeted Hector led the Trojans,[8] he
The son of King Priam, and the companies of spear-raging warriors
Marshaled with him were by far the largest and best.
        The Dardanians were led by Anchises' brave son Aeneas,[9]
Whom under Anchises sweet Aphrodite conceived
When the goddess and mortal man made love and slept
Mid the ridges of Ida. Not alone in command, Aeneas
Had help from Antenor's two sons, the very versatile
Fighters Acamas and Archelochus.
        And there were those   930
Who lived in Zeleia below the last foothill of Ida,
A thriving clan of Trojans that drink Aesepus'
Dark water. These were captained by the splendid son
Of Lycaon, Pandarus, whose skill with the bow was a gift
From Apollo himself.
        And those who held Adrasteia
And the land of Apaesus, and the troops from Pityeia and towering
Mount Tereia were led by Adrastus and Amphius,
With corselet of linen, two sons of Percotian Merops,
The world's most skillful prophet, who would not allow   940
His sons to enter the man-wasting war. But they
Would pay no attention, for doom and dark death were leading
Them on.
        And the men who lived round Percote and Practius
And those who held Sestos and Abydos and sacred Arisbe
Were all commanded by Asius, Hyrtacus' son,
A chieftain of warriors—Asius Hyrtacides, whom his glossy
Huge horses had drawn from Arisbe and the river Selleïs.
        Hippothous led the spear-fierce Pelasgian tribes
From the fertile soil of Larissa, he and that offshoot   950
Of Ares, his brother Pylaeus, both sons of Pelasgian
Lethus, son of Teutamus.
        Leading the Thracians
From all along the swift Hellespont were Acamas and heroic
Peirous.
        And the spear-hurling Cicones had as their chief
Euphemus, son of Zeus-nurtured Troezenus and grandson
Of Ceas.
        But Pyraechmes led men of bent bows, the Paeonians
From distant Amydon and the wide-rippling Axius River—   960
Axius, the loveliest river that flows on the face

Of the earth.
      From the Eneti country, home of wild mules,
Came the Paphlagonians with Pylaemenes of the shaggy heart
As leader. These held Cytorus, lived about Sesamon,
And had fine homes by the river Parthenius, and in Cromna,
Aegialus, and high Erythini.
      Odius and Epistrophus
Captained the Halizones from distant Alybe, the source
970 And home of silver.
      Leading the Mysians came Chromis
And Ennomus the augur, who for all his reading of ominous
Birds could not avoid dark doom. He fell
At the hands of Aeacus' grandson, the swift Achilles,
When he in the bed of the river cut down Trojans
And allies alike.
      Phorcys and godlike Ascanius
Commanded the Phrygians, hungry for battle, and led them
To Troy from distant Ascania.
980   And the men of Maeonia
Had two leaders, Mesthles and Antiphus, sons
Of Talaemenes, born of the lake Gygaea. They led
The Maeonians, men from the foot of Mount Tmolus.
      Nastes commanded the Carians, barbarous of speech,*
Men from Miletus and leafy Mount Phthires,
From about the streams of Maeander and the craggy steeps
Of Mycale. These also had two leaders, Amphimachus
And Nastes—Nastes and Amphimachus, the illustrious sons
Of Nomion—but Nastes, childish fool that he was,
990 Went into battle decked out in gold like a girl,
But gold could not help him escape a horrible death
At the hands of Aeacus' grandson, the swift Achilles,
In the bed of the river, and Achilles, fierce and fiery,
Took care of all his gold.
      And the Lycian chiefs
Were Sarpedon and peerless Glaucus, who led their men
From distant Lycia, where the Xanthus eddies and flows.

---

*The Greek *barbaros* indicates that the Carians do not speak Greek.

BOOK III

The Duel of Paris and Menelaus

When each battalion had been drawn up with its captain,
The Trojans advanced with clamor and clang like the noise
Of birds, the clangor of cranes that rises toward heaven
When they flee the storms of winter and floods of beating
Rain and fly with loud cries toward the stream of Oceanus
To offer in battle at dawn terrible slaughter
And death to men of the Pygmies. The Achaeans, however,
Came on with no cries at all, but breathing might
And full of resolve to aid and defend one another.
    As when the South Wind covers the peaks of a mountain   10
With a mist no shepherd loves but that thieves prefer
To night, since through it a man can see but a stone's throw
Ahead, so now from beneath their feet a thick
Dust-cloud arose as swiftly they went on the double
Across the plain.
    When the two advancing armies
Drew near each other, out from the Trojan ranks
Stepped godlike Paris, also called Alexander,*
With a leopard skin on his shoulders along with his sword
And bent bow. Then shaking two bronze-headed spears he challenged   20
The best of the Argives to come out and meet him in grim
And single combat.
    And no sooner did King Menelaus,
The favorite of Ares, catch sight of him there, coming out
Of the crowd and swaggering along with great strides, than he
Was as glad as a starving lion that happens upon
The large carcass of an antlered stag or wild goat and greedily
Gulps away, despite the frantic efforts
Of darting dogs and lusty young hunters. So now
Menelaus rejoiced when first his eyes fell on Prince   30
Alexander, for he thought that vengeance on the sinner was finally

---

*Though both names belong to the poetic tradition, Paris is more frequent.

His. And at once he leaped in full armor from his car
To the ground.

       But when Prince Alexander saw who it was
Who appeared to accept his challenge, his spirit collapsed
And back he shrank mid a crowd of comrades, seeking
To save his life. Like a man who comes on a snake
In a mountain ravine and springs back pale and trembling
And gives the snake plenty of room, so Prince Alexander
40   Feared Atreus' son, and cringing shrank back in the ranks
Of lordly Trojans.

       But Hector saw and tried
To shame him with words of reproach: "Despicable Paris,
Handsome, deceitful, and crazy for women, would you
Had never been born, or had died unmarried! Indeed,
I really wish that you had, since such would have been
Much better than what you are now—an object of scorn
Looked down on by others. Surely the long-haired Achaeans
Will laugh loud and long, saying that a Prince is our champion
50   Because he's good looking, though he be both woefully gutless
And weak. Aren't you the one who rounded up
Your trusty cronies and took off in your seagoing ships
Across the deep to mingle with strangers and bring back
From a distant country a comely, voluptuous woman,
The daughter-in-law of a nation of spear-wielding warriors,
But a cause of terrible harm to your father and city
And all the people—aren't you the strong man who took her,
A joy to your foes and an utter disgrace to yourself?
And can it be that now you refuse to stand up
60   To the fighting Menelaus? You would soon find out what kind
Of fighter he is whose glamorous wife you have.
When you're lying down there in the dust you won't be helped
By that lyre of yours nor the gifts Aphrodite gave you,
Your handsome face and pretty hair. But truly
The Trojans are just as afraid, or you would already
Have paid for all the evil you've done—paid
By donning that tunic of stone which rocks from their hands
Would have furnished!"

       And godlike Alexander replied: "Hector,
70   You chide me no more than is right and not a bit more
Than you should. Yours is a tireless heart, and unyielding,
Like an ax that serves the blow of a skillful shipwright
As he sends it down through a log to shape a ship's timber.
So the heart in your breast bears all before it, but do not

Reproach me for the winsome gifts of golden Aphrodite.
The gods give wonderful gifts no man can choose   ·
For himself, and such are not to be scorned or discarded.
But now, if you really insist on my doing battle
With Ares-loved Menelaus, have all other Trojans
And men of Achaea sit down, and put us together   80
Out there in the middle to fight for Helen and all
Her treasures. And whoever is stronger and wins, let him take
Both wealth and woman and carry them home, while you others
Swear oaths of faith and friendship and solemnize all
With sacrifice, that you may remain in the fertile land
Of Troy, and they return to their thoroughbred horses
And beautiful women in Achaea and grassy Argos."
     Then Hector rejoiced, and stepping out between
The two armies he gripped his spear by the middle and held
The Trojan line back till all were seated. Meanwhile,   90
The long-haired Achaeans kept trying to strike him with arrows
And stones, but now the king of men Agamemnon
Raised his voice in command:
     "Enough, Argives!
No more shooting, you men of Achaea! for it seems
That bright-helmeted Hector has something to say."
     He spoke,
And they ceased their shooting and hurling and quickly grew quiet.
Then Hector spoke between the two armies: "From me,
O Trojans and well-greaved Achaeans, hear the proposal   100
Of Paris, who began this miserable war. He says
For all other Trojans and men of Achaea to lay
Their excellent arms on the bountiful earth, and that he,
Out here in the middle, will fight with fierce Menelaus
For Helen and all her treasures. And whoever is stronger
And wins, let him take both wealth and woman and carry them
Home, while we others swear oaths of faith and friendship
And solemnize all with sacrifice."
     So Hector, and no one
Answered a word till among them out spoke Menelaus   110
Of the fierce battle-scream: "Hear also me, as one
Whose heart has borne more pain than any of yours.
Now I think that Trojans and Argives should part,
Since you have already suffered sorrows enough
Because of my quarrel, which Alexander began.
For one of us two, death and doom are allotted.
So let one of us die, and you others part

With all speed. But first bring two lambs, a white ram and black ewe
For Earth and the Sun, and we'll bring another for Zeus.
120 And some of you go for the powerful Priam, that he too
May swear and sacrifice, for he has haughty, unscrupulous
Sons, and we do not want any proud overreacher
To spoil the oaths we swear in God's name. The hearts
Of young men are often unstable, but whenever an old man
Is present, he thinks of the future as well as the past,
And so both parties benefit greatly."
        He spoke,
And both sides rejoiced, hoping to cease their miserable
Fighting. They reined their chariots back in the ranks,
Stepped down, and took off their armor, which they laid on the
130   ground
Beside them with not much space between. And Hector
Sent two heralds to bring the lambs from the city
As fast as they could and to summon King Priam, while ruling
Agamemnon dispatched Talthybius to the hollow ships
With orders to bring a lamb, and he did not ignore
His royal commander.
        Meanwhile Iris arrived
With a message for white-armed Helen, and she came in the likeness
Of her sister-in-law Laodice, the loveliest daughter
140 Of Priam and the wife of lord Helicaon, son
Of Antenor. Helen she found in the hall, weaving
A web of double width and of iridescent
Purple. And in it she wove not a few of the battles
That the horse-breaking Trojans and bronze-clad Achaeans had suffered
At the hands of Ares on her account.[1] Standing
Close by her side, nimble Iris spoke to her, saying:
        "Come, my dear, that you may see an incredible
Thing that the horse-breaking Trojans and bronze-clad Achaeans
Have done. They who but lately were eager to clash
150 On the plain and tearfully tear each other to pieces
Have now called off the battle and are sitting quietly
Out there, leaning back on their shields, with their long spears fixed
In the ground beside them. But Paris and fierce Menelaus
Are to use their long spears to fight each other for you,
And you will be called the dear wife of whichever one wins."
        These words of the goddess aroused in the heart of Helen
An irresistible yearning for her former husband,
Her city, and parents. Quickly she veiled herself
In shining white linen, and softly crying hurriedly

Left her chamber, not by herself but attended   160
By two of her handmaids, Aethra, daughter of Pittheus,
And heifer-eyed Clymene. And quickly they came in sight
Of the Scaean Gates.
      There in the council of Priam
Sat the elders of Priam's people, Panthous and Thymoetes,
Clytius, Lampus, and Hicetaon, scion of Ares,
And two other men of wisdom, Ucalegon and Antenor.
Too old for battle, these elders were excellent speakers,
And now they sat on the wall like forest cicadas
That sit on a tree and sing with their lily voices.   170
Even so, the leaders of Troy sat on the turreted
Wall, and when they saw Helen approaching spoke softly
One to another in these words winged with wonder:
      "Surely no one could blame either side for suffering
So much and so long for such a woman, for she
In appearance is terribly like an immortal goddess!
But still, though lovely she is, let her go home
With the ships and not be left here as a curse to both us
And our children."
      So they, but Priam spoke to her, saying: 180
"Come here, dear child, and sit before me, that you
May see your former husband, your kinsfolk and friends.
I certainly don't blame you. The gods alone
Are to blame for hurling upon me this tearful war
With Achaeans. But tell me the name of yonder huge
Achaean, that chieftain so valiant and tall. To be sure
There are others at least a head taller than he, but never
Have I laid eyes on a man so truly handsome
And regal. That man has the look of a ruler, of one
Who is King indeed."   190
      And glamorous Helen replied:
"You I regard with respect and reverence, you
My own dear father-in-law. But now I wish
It had been my good fortune to die when I came here
With your son, deserting my marriage chamber and daughter
So precious, my blood relations and circle of charming
Friends. But that wasn't to be. Instead, I weep out
My life little by little. Now though, I will answer
Your question. Yonder Achaean is Atreus' son,[2]
Great Agamemnon, a high-ranking King and mighty   200
Spearman. And as sure as ever there was such a man
He was once the brother-in-law of bitch-hearted me."

She spoke, and the old man marveled, saying: "O happy
Son of Atreus, born lucky, god-blessed man,
How very many young men of Achaea are under
Your rule! I journeyed once to the viny land
Of Phrygia where I saw huge hosts of Phrygian warriors
With their glancing-swift horses, the armies of Otreus and royal
Mygdon, encamped along the banks of the river Sangarius.
210 And I was an ally of theirs and numbered among them
That day when the man-matching Amazons came. But not even
They were so numerous as are the quick-eyed Achaeans."
     Next the old man noticed Odysseus, and said:
"Come, dear child, tell me who that man is too.
He's a good head shorter than Atreus' son Agamemnon
But broader through shoulders and chest. His armor lies
On the bountiful earth while he goes up and down
Through the ranks like the leading ram in a herd. To me
That's what he is like, a wooly ram that paces
220 His way through a truly large flock of silvery-white sheep."
     And Zeus-born Helen answered again: "That
Is the son of Laertes, resourceful Odysseus, who was raised
In rocky Ithaca. He's a cunning and clever man,
Both wily and wise."
     Then the grave Antenor answered
Her thus: "What you say, my lady, is true indeed.
For some time ago the brilliant Odysseus was here
With Ares' own Menelaus to confer about you,
And I was their host.* I welcomed them in my halls
230 And got to know what they look like and how they think.
Whenever they mixed in a meeting with Trojans, Menelaus
Stood head and shoulders above Odysseus, but when
They were seated Odysseus was the more majestic. And when
They stood before all to weave the words of wise counsel,
Menelaus' words were few, but fluently uttered,
Clear, and to the point. Though the younger man,
He was surely no rambler or bungler with words. But whenever
Resourceful Odysseus got up, he would stand looking down,
His eyes fixed hard on the ground, nor would he gesture
240 At all with the staff he held. He would hold it rigid,
Like a man who wasn't all there. You would, in fact,
Have thought him a sullen and foolish fellow. But when

---

*Antenor remembers a first diplomatic mission to recover Helen.

He spoke, that great voice of his poured out of his chest
In words like the snowflakes of winter, and then no other
Mortal could in debate contend with Odysseus.
Nor did we care any longer how he looked."

Then the old man, noticing Ajax, asked: "And who
Is that other manly Achaean, the one so tall
And knightly, whose head and broad shoulders tower above
The Argives?"   250

And exquisite Helen of the flowing gowns:
"That's the enormous Ajax, a very fortress
Of Achaean valor. And over there Idomeneus
Stands like a god mid the men and captains of Crete.
Many times, on journeys from Crete, he stayed at our house,
And my warrior lord, Menelaus, welcomed him warmly.
And now I see many other quick-eyed Achaeans
Whom I know well enough and could name, but two of their
          martial
Commanders I cannot see, horse-mastering Castor
And Pollux, good in a fist-fight, my own blood brothers,   260
For all of us had the same mother. Either they didn't come
With the men from dear Lacedaemon, or else they came
All the way in their seagoing ships but are now too ashamed
To mingle with others in battle on account of the vile
And insulting things the soldiers say about me."

Thus Helen, but they already lay in the close
Embrace of the life-giving earth back home in Lacedaemon,
Their own dear country.

Meanwhile, the heralds were bringing
Through town the holy offerings whereby to swear   270
The faithful oaths of a truce—two lambs and a goatskin
Bottle of heart-warming wine, fruit of the soil.
And the herald Idaeus, bearing a gleaming bowl
And golden cups, came up and aroused old Priam,
Saying:

"Come, O son of Laomedon, the chiefs ·
Of the horse-breaking Trojans and bronze-clad Achaeans want you
Down on the plain to join with them in sacrifice
And in swearing the faithful oaths of a truce. Prince Paris,
Though, and fierce Menelaus are to take their long spears   280
And fight a duel for the woman, and to the winner
Will go both woman and wealth, while the rest of us
Swear oaths of faith and friendship and solemnize all
With sacrifice, that we may remain in the fertile land

Of Troy, and they return to their thoroughbred horses
And beautiful women in Achaea and grassy Argos."
        At this the old King shuddered, but told his companions
To yoke the horses, which quickly they did. Then Priam
Mounted the ornate car and drew back on the reins
290 While Antenor got up beside him, and off they drove
The fast horses through the Scaean Gates and on to the plain.
        When they reached the waiting armies, they stepped from the car
To the bountiful earth and strode out to a spot midway
Between the Trojan and Achaean hosts. At once
The king of men Agamemnon and resourceful Odysseus
Arose, and the stately heralds brought out the offerings
For the holy oaths of peace, mixed wine in the bowl,
And over the hands of the kings poured water. And the son
Of Atreus drew the knife that always hung
300 Beside his great scabbard and from the heads of the lambs
He cut hair, which the heralds gave out to the chieftains of the Trojans
And Achaeans alike. Then there in the midst of all
Agamemnon lifted his arms and prayed aloud:
        "O Father Zeus, ruling from Ida, most great
And glorious lord, and you, all-hearing, all-seeing
Sun, and you, O Earth and Rivers, and you
Infernal powers that punish the shades of men
Who here swear falsely, I pray to all of you now
To witness and then watch over these faithful oaths.
310 If Menelaus goes down before Alexander,
Let him keep Helen and all her treasures, and we
Will depart in our seagoing vessels. But if Menelaus
Of the tawny hair shall slay Alexander, then let
The Trojans return both Helen and all of her wealth
And make to the Argives whatever further repayment
Seems adequate and right, some ample repayment that men
Yet to be will remember. However, if Priam and the sons
Of Priam should refuse this repayment, then I will fight on
To win it and remain in this land till I see the end
320 Of our war."
        He spoke, and drawing the ruthless bronze
Across the throats of the lambs he laid them down
On the ground, jerking and gasping for breath, the bronze
Having taken their strength. Then from the bowl they took wine
In the cups and poured it out in libation with prayers
To the gods everlasting. And thus would some Achaean
Or one of the Trojans pray:

"Most great and glorious
Zeus and you other immortal gods, may the brains
Of those who first violate these oaths be poured out   330
On earth as now this wine is poured, theirs
And their children's too, and may others possess their wives."
        So they prayed, but Zeus was not yet ready
To give them the peace they desired. Then ancient Priam,
Descended of Dardanus, spoke thus among them: "Hear me,
You Trojans and well-greaved Achaeans. I am now going back
To windy Ilium, since I'm certain I could not endure
The sight of my own dear son in battle with fierce
Menelaus. But Zeus, I think, and the other immortals
Already know which one is to die and meet   340
His end in the duel."
        So spoke the sacred King.
Then, having put the lambs in his chariot, he mounted
The ornate car and drew back on the reins while Antenor
Got up beside him. And back to Troy they went.
But Hector, son of Priam, and godly Odysseus
Marked off a space for the duel, then shook a couple
Of pebbles in a bronze and leather helmet to see
Which man would be first to hurl his bronze spear. And the people,
Praying, lifted their hands to the gods, and thus   350
Would some Achaean or one of the Trojans say:
        "O Father Zeus, ruling from Ida, most great
And glorious lord, grant that he who brought
These troubles upon us—whichever one of these two—
May die and go down to the house of Hades, but to us
Grant peace and faithful oaths of friendship."
        So they,
And the huge bright-helmeted Hector, turning his own eyes
Away, shook the lots, and quickly the pebble of Paris
Leaped out of the helmet. Then the soldiers sat down in rows   360
Close to their inlaid armor and high-stepping horses,
While handsome Paris, lord of the lovely blonde Helen,
Put on his beautiful armor.[3] First he covered
His shins with greaves, fair greaves with ankle-clasps of silver.
Next, about his chest he put the breastplate
Of his brother Lycaon and adjusted the straps of it well,
And from his shoulders he slung his bronze sword with the studs
Of bright silver along with his large and solid shield.
Then on his noble head he put a strong helmet
With horsehair plume defiantly waving above him,   370

And in his hand he took a doughty spear
That fitted his grip to perfection. And the grim Menelaus
Likewise donned his equipment.
　　　　Having armed themselves
On either side of the throng, they stalked out into
The space between the two armies, and as they glared
At each other with terrible fierceness, amazement fell
On horse-taming Trojans and well-greaved Achaeans alike.
And they came to a halt not far apart in the marked-off
380　Space and stood there angrily shaking their spears
At each other. First Paris hurled his long-shadowing spear
And struck the round shield of Atreus' son. But instead
Of the bronze tearing on through, the point was turned
By the sturdy buckler. Then Atreus' son Menelaus
Got ready to throw, praying thus to Father Zeus:
　　　　"Lord God, help me to punish Prince Alexander,
Him who wronged me in the beginning. Slay him
By means of me, that many a man as yet
Unborn may shudder to wrong a host who has offered
390　Him friendship."
　　　　With this he drew back his long-shadowing spear
And hurled it, and he struck the round shield of Priam's son.
The great spear tore through the gleaming shield and on
Through the beautiful breastplate and tunic too, but Paris
Twisted in time to avoid dark death as the spear
Went by at his side. Then Atreus' son whipped out
His sword with the studs of bright silver, and raising it high
Overhead he brought it down hard on the metal horn
Of his enemy's helmet. But on it his bright sword shattered
400　Into three or four pieces and flew from his hand. Menelaus
Groaned, and glancing up at broad heaven he cried:
　　　　"O Father Zeus, no other god is more ruthless
Than you! Here I thought I had surely got
Full payment from foul Alexander, but now my sword
Is broken and gone and I've thrown my spear and missed."
　　　　So saying, he sprang upon him and grabbed his helmet
By the horsehair crest. Then flinging him down and whirling him
Round, he started to drag Paris off toward the line
Of well-greaved Achaeans, and the tightly-drawn strap of his helmet,
410　The thong of richly wrought ox-hide, began to crease
His soft throat and choke him. And now Menelaus would surely
Have dragged him off and won unspeakable glory,
If Zeus's daughter, fair Aphrodite, had not been

Sharply watching. She broke the strap, though cut
From the hide of a slaughtered ox, and the powerful hand
Of the hero shot forward with an empty helmet. Spinning,
He tossed it among the well-greaved Achaeans, and his loyal
Friends retrieved it. And he charged his foe once again,
Eager to pierce him through with a sharp bronze spear.
But then Aphrodite whirled Paris away with the ease   420
Of deity working, enclosed him in cloud, and set him
Down in his own high-vaulted and perfumed bedroom.
Then she went to get Helen, whom she found on the lofty
Turreted wall in a crowd of Trojan women.
Taking the likeness of a very old woman, a worker
In wool and a long-time favorite of Helen's who had carded
Fine fleece for her before she left Lacedaemon,
Bright Aphrodite took hold of her nectar-sweet gown,
Pulled it gently, and spoke:
        "Let's go. Paris   430
Says to come home. For he is there in the bedroom,
Stretched out on the inlaid bed, a man well dressed
And radiantly handsome. So far from thinking him one
Just back from a duel, you'd think he was on his way
To a dance, or already there and resting."
        These words
Stirred Helen's heart, but when she noticed the graceful
Neck, delectable breasts, and sparkling eyes
Of the goddess, she answered her in amazement, saying:
"Mysterious deity! why are you trying to trick me?   440
Now that King Menelaus has gotten the best
Of royal Paris and is ready to take despicable
Me back home again, now doubtless you want
To lead me further on to some populous city
Of Phrygia or pleasant Maeonia where lives another
Masculine favorite of yours. So now you come here
With your slyness. But you, go sit by his side yourself.
Forget you're a goddess and never again go back
To Olympus, but stay and make yourself utterly wretched
Caring for him till he makes you his wife—or slave!   450
But I won't be shameless enough to return to his bed.
All the women in Troy would blame me, and my misery
Is already boundless."
        Then fair Aphrodite got angry
And spoke to her thus: "Don't provoke me, you obstinate wretch,
Or I might become spiteful and leave you, and come to despise you

As much as I now exceedingly love you. I might even
Create in Trojans and Danaans both a hatred
So grievous that you would die in the conflict between them,
460 A terrible fate!"
          She spoke, and Zeus-born Helen
Was afraid. Quietly she gathered her shining white gown
About her and left unnoticed by the Trojan women.
She followed where the goddess led.
          Now when they reached
Alexander's richly wrought home, the handmaids turned
To their chores, but their lovely mistress went straight to the high-
                    ceilinged
Bedroom, where Aphrodite, adorer of smiles,
Got a seat for her and set it before Alexander.
470 Then Helen, the daughter of aegis-bearing Zeus, sat down,
And looking off to one side she began to rebuke
Her husband:
          "So, you are back from the battle. Would you
Had died there, slain by that powerful man, my former
Lord! And you are the one who used to brag
About how much stronger you were than fierce Menelaus,
Stronger with your hands and better than he with your spear.
Well go ahead and call him back out to fight you
Again. But no, I wouldn't really advise you
480 To be so mad as to fight with tawny Menelaus,
Lest you find yourself down and his sharp spear clean through you!"
          And Paris replied: "This, my dear, is no time
For nagging. Menelaus, with the help of Athena, has won
This bout, that's true, but another time I'll conquer
Him. For we have gods on our side too!
But come, let's enjoy ourselves in bed, making love
With each other, for never before have I felt so full
Of desire—not even when I first took you from fair
Lacedaemon, and sailing away in my seagoing ships
490 Made love with you in bed on the island of Cranaë.
But now even more I love you and feel myself
In the grip of sweet desire."
          So saying, he drew her
To him, and she unresisting joined him in bed.
But while those two lay making love at home
On the inlaid corded bed, Menelaus raged
Through the ranks like some wild beast, searching all over
For Prince Alexander. Nor could the Trojans nor any

Of their famous allies point out to fierce Menelaus
Where handsome Alexander was, and no man there   500
Would have hid him for reasons of friendship, since dark death itself
Was not more hateful than he to all of those warriors.
Then the king of men Agamemnon spoke out among them:
    "Hear me, O Trojans, Dardanians, allies. It appears
Without question that victory has gone to the favorite of Ares,
King Menelaus. So relinquish Argive Helen
And all that goes with her by way of treasure, and make
Some ample repayment that men yet to be will remember."
    So spoke Atrides, and all the Achaeans applauded.

BOOK IV

Agamemnon's Inspection of the Army

Meanwhile, the gods were enthroned on the golden floor
In council with Zeus. Graceful Hebe* poured nectar
For them, and as they looked out on the city of Troy
They drank to each other from goblets of gold. But Zeus
At once began trying to irritate Hera, sarcastically
Saying:

"Menelaus has two divine helpers, a couple
Of goddesses, Argive Hera and mighty Athena,
The defender of many. But both of them sit up here
10 Enjoying themselves, while light-o'-love Aphrodite,
That hustling, giggling goddess, goes constantly
To the side of her favorite and makes the fates keep their distance.
Just now she saved him again, when he thought sure
He was done for. Even so, the victory has gone to the favorite
Of Ares, King Menelaus, and now we must make
A decision, whether again to renew evil war
And the blood-chilling din of battle, or to bring the armies
Together in friendship. If we all agree on peace,
King Priam's city survives as a town still fit
20 To live in, and fierce Menelaus takes Argive Helen
Home."

At first his words got murmurs only
From Athena and Hera, who sat by each other contriving
Disasters for Trojans. Then Athena kept quiet and said nothing,
Though seized by savage anger at Father Zeus.
But the breast of Hera could not contain her rage,
And she railed at him thus:

"Most dreadful son of Cronos,
What kind of talk is that! Just how do you plan
30 To ruin all I've done and utterly waste the sweating
Toil I suffered when I exhausted my horses

---

*Hebe is the goddess of youth and the Olympian wine steward.

In gathering those Achaeans to ruin both Priam
And all of his sons? Do as you like, but don't
Suppose for one moment that all of us like what you do!"
      Then angry indeed, cloud-gathering Zeus replied:
"Strange, implacable goddess! how many horrible
Wrongs can Priam and his sons have done you to make you
So frantically fierce in your rage to destroy and level
Their mighty stronghold?[1] Perhaps if you went within
The gates and high walls and ate old Priam raw   40
Along with his sons and all the rest of the Trojans,
Your wrath might find some relief. Well do as you please
About Troy, but don't bring this point up again to cause
More quarreling between us. And here's something else you'll do well
To remember. When it comes my turn to be eager for the ruin
Of some city where favorites of yours are living, don't make
A move to stand in the path of my anger! Give me
My way, since now of my own accord I am giving
You yours, though still with an unwilling heart. For under
The sun and starry sky there is no earthly city   50
I care for more than holy Troy, nor any
Mortals whom I regard with more pleasure than Priam
And the people of Priam, him of the good ashen spear.
Never yet has my altar in Troy been bare of an ample
Feast, libations of wine and savory burnt-offerings,
The gifts we claim as our due."
      Then the heifer-eyed Queen
Of the gods replied: "The cities I care for most
Are three—Argos, Sparta, and wide-wayed Mycenae.*
But whenever you come to hate them, destroy away   60
At your pleasure. I'll not stand up for them, nor will I
Resent or begrudge what you do. And what good would it do
If I did get resentful and tried to prevent their destruction,
Since you are so very much stronger? But surely the work
I do should also amount to something. I too
Am divine and from the same stock as yourself. For I
In two respects am the most honored daughter of Cronos,
Crooked in counsel, in that I am the eldest and also
Your wife, you being King of all the immortals.
But now let us yield to each other, me to you   70
And you to me, and the other immortal gods

---

*Hera's cult was prominent in these three Peloponnesian cities.

Will do as we do. And now tell Athena to enter
The noisy throng of Achaeans and Trojans and find
Some way of making the Trojans break their oaths
Of truce by an act of violence against the triumphant,
Exulting Achaeans."
          So she, and the Father of gods
And men by no means ignored her.[2] At once he spoke
To Athena with these winged words: "Hurry on into
80 The gathered hosts of Achaeans and Trojans and find
Some way of making the Trojans break their oaths
Of truce by an act of violence against the triumphant,
Exulting Achaeans."
          So saying, he started Athena,
Who needed no urging, and down she went darting from the peaks
Of Olympus. Like a shooting star that the son of crooked
Cronos sends with a long trail of fire as a sign
To sailors at sea or a huge encampment of soldiers,
So Pallas Athena shot down to earth right into
90 The midst of innumerable men, and all who saw
Were astonished, both horse-breaking Trojans and bronze-clad
                    Achaeans.
Then one would glance at the man next to him, and say:
          "Surely again, now, horrible war and the screaming
Chaos of battle are coming upon us, either that,
Or peace is ours by decree of Zeus, who has
All wars in his keeping and decides when men will fight."
          Thus Achaeans and Trojans spoke to each other. Athena,
Meanwhile, entered the Trojan host as a man,
The powerful spearman Laodocus, son of Antenor,
100 To find the princely Pandarus if she could.
And she found that son of Lycaon, the matchless and mighty
Pandarus, standing amid the stalwart ranks
Of shield-bearing men who had followed him there from the streams
Of Aesepus. She approached and spoke with these winged words:
          "Shrewd son of Lycaon, listen to me. I dare you
To shoot a quick arrow at yonder fierce Menelaus!
Think what fame and favor you'd win from the whole
Trojan army, but especially from Prince Paris. When it came
To the giving of splendid gifts, he would surely be far
110 More generous to you than to anyone else, if now
He should see Menelaus, the warlike son of Atreus,
Brought down by an arrow of yours and then laid out
On a grievous funeral pyre. So come, let fly

At yonder illustrious King and promise Apollo,
Your light-born Lycian god, the famous archer,
That when you return to your own hometown of sacred
Zeleia you will offer to him a glorious hecatomb
Of first-born, excellent lambs."
     So spoke Athena,
And persuaded the mind of a mindless fool. He quickly   120
Unwrapped his burnished bow, made from the horns
Of a leaping wild antelope that he himself had shot
From a place of ambush as the beast stepped down from a rock,
Striking it full in the chest and sending it back
In a heap on the slab. Its horns grew sixteen hands high,
And these a craftsman had worked and fitted together,
Burnished well, and tipped with curving gold.
Resting one end on the ground, he strung the great weapon
And laid it carefully down, while his valiant companions
Held up their shields before him so that the warlike   130
Sons of Achaeans would not interfere with the shooting
Of fierce Menelaus, Atreus' battling son.
Next he lifted the lid of his quiver and drew out
A feathered arrow fraught with dark pains, a new one
That had never been shot. Deftly he fitted this bitter
Shaft to the ox-hide string and promised Apollo,
His light-born Lycian god, the famous archer,
That when he returned to his own hometown of sacred
Zeleia he would offer to him a glorious hecatomb
Of first-born, excellent lambs. And he drew the notched arrow   140
And ox-hide string all the way back to his chest
Till the iron head touched the bow and the bow itself
Was bent in a circle. Then he shot with a clanging twang
Of the mighty weapon as the resonant string sang out
And the sharp-headed shaft went winging its way, eager
To fly mid the enemy ranks.
     But ah, Menelaus,
The blissful immortal gods did not forget you,
And especially mindful was Zeus's daughter Athena,
The bringer of booty, who stood before you and quickly   150
Deflected the sharp-pointed shaft. She brushed it away
From the flesh of the King as a mother brushes a fly
From her baby sweetly sleeping, and the goddess herself
Guided it where his golden belt buckles joined
And the halves of his breastplate met. So the keen arrow struck
Where the richly wrought belt was buckled and cut right through

And on through the beautiful breastplate and heavily armored
Kilt, which he wore for just such protection and which did
The most to help him, yet even through this the arrow
160 Pierced, wounding him slightly, and the cloud-black blood
Ran out from the shallow cut.
        As when some Maeonian
Or Carian woman stains with crimson dye
A horse's ivory cheek-piece, that later lies
In store and though many a horseman covets it keenly
Remains where it is to enhance the horse of a king
And thrill his driver, so now, Menelaus, your thighs
Were stained with the flowing blood, your handsome huge thighs,
Your calves, and ankles beneath.
170   When he saw the dark blood
Running down from the wound, the commander-in-chief
          Agamemnon
Shuddered, as also shuddered Ares' own
Menelaus. But when he saw that the arrowhead's barbs
And binding of sinew were still outside the flesh,
The spirit returned to his breast. But King Agamemnon,
Loudly moaning and holding Menelaus's hand,
Spoke thus among his men, who all around him
Re-echoed his moans:
       "O my dear brother, it seems
180 I've accomplished only your death in swearing this solemn
Oath and setting you out before the Achaeans
To fight the Trojans alone, since now they have managed
To shoot you and so have insulted our sacred swearing!
Even so, an oath is an oath, and by no means taken
In vain with the blood of lambs, holy libations
Of unmixed wine, and the faithful clasping of hands.
For even though the Olympian fulfills it not
At the moment, still he fulfills it sooner or later.
And then the price of atonement is heavy indeed,
190 For then men pay with their heads, their wives, and their children.
And this my heart and soul are utterly sure of—
That sooner or later the day of destruction shall come
For holy Troy and Priam and all the people
Of Priam of the good ashen spear. Then high-throned Zeus,
The sky-dwelling son of Cronos, shall rise in wrath
At this treacherous deed and shake his dark and terrible
Aegis over the Trojans. Don't think all this
Won't happen. But O Menelaus, what awful misery

Will surely be mine if you die and fulfill your destiny
Now! For then the Achaeans will immediately want   200
To go home, back to thirsty Argos, where I
Should return in utter disgrace, and leave to Priam
And the other Trojans their insolent boast, no other
Than Argive Helen herself. And here in the dirt
Of Troy your bones shall rot while the task undertaken
By you remains unfinished. Then some Trojan,
Proud and triumphant, will dance on the tomb of great
Menelaus, and shout:
" 'May such be the way Agamemnon
Always wreaks his wrath, as now he came here   210
With a host of Achaeans only to leave in defeat
And go back to his own precious country with empty ships
And no superb Menelaus!'
          "But on the day
When any man shall so vaunt, may the wide earth then
Engulf me!"
          But tawny Menelaus reassured him, saying:
"Don't worry, and whatever you do don't alarm the army.
The head of the shaft is fixed in nothing vital.
It was all but stopped by my flashing belt and leather   220
Protector and the armored kilt beneath them, the one
Well plated by workers in bronze."
          And King Agamemnon
Answered him thus: "May it be as you say, my dear
Menelaus. But a surgeon shall search the wound and treat it
With proper ointments to take away the dark pains."
          Then he spoke thus to the high-born herald Talthybius:
"Go, Talthybius, as fast as you can, and fetch
Machaon, son of the peerless physician Asclepius,
To see warlike Menelaus, whom some skillful archer,   230
Some Trojan or Lycian bowman, has struck with an arrow,
Covering himself with glory, but us with nothing
But sorrow."
          This order the herald was quick to obey,
And he ran through the ranks looking this way and that for the
          martial
Machaon, whom he found on his feet mid the stalwart ranks
Of shield-bearing soldiers who had followed him there from the
          grassy
Fields of Tricca, land of fine horses. He approached him
And spoke with these winged words:

240   "Come, O son
           Of Asclepius. Great Agamemnon calls you to see
           The warlike King Menelaus, whom some skillful archer,
           Some Trojan or Lycian bowman, has struck with an arrow,
           Covering himself with glory, but us with nothing
           But sorrow."
                    These words startled Machaon, and the two of them
           Hurried through the huge crowd of Achaeans. When they reached
           The spot where tawny Menelaus lay wounded, surrounded
           By all the chieftains, the divinely able Machaon
250   Stepped into their midst and quickly extracted the arrow
           From where the belt was buckled, breaking back
           The keen barbs as he drew out the head. He loosened the flashing
           Belt and leather protector and the armored kilt
           Beneath them, the one well plated by workers in bronze,
           And examined the wound which the bitter arrow had made.
           Then he sucked out the blood and ably applied
           Soothing ointments which once the affable Cheiron had given
           His father.
                    But while they were busy with King Menelaus
260   Of the great battle-scream, the shield-bearing Trojan forces
           Began to advance, and again the Achaean warriors
           Put on their armor and did their best to recover
           Some stomach for fighting.
                    You would not then have found
           The great Agamemnon napping,[3] or cringing with fear
           And reluctance to fight, but still exceedingly eager
           For the man-enhancing battle. He left his horses
           And bronze-bright car in the care of his squire Eurymedon,
           Ptolemy's son, Peiraeus's grandson, who held
270   In check his snorting charges. But first he gave him
           Strict orders to have the chariot near in case
           His legs should grow tired as he toured and re-ordered the ranks.
           Then off through the host he strode, and whenever he saw
           Any swiftly-drawn Danaans up and eager for action
           He would stop and encourage them thus:
                    "Argives, don't relax
           Your impetuous valor one whit, for Father Zeus
           Will be no helper of liars! Vultures shall surely
           Devour the tender flesh of those who first
280   Went back on their word and violently broke the truce,
           And when we have plundered their city, their beloved wives
           And little children shall go with us in our ships!"

But whenever he saw any hesitant men, shrinking
From horrible war, he would stop and fiercely rebuke them:
"Disgraceful Argives! brave with the bow alone,
Have you no shame? Why are you standing here
In a daze, like fawns that exhaust themselves by running
Across a wide plain and then just stand there, stupid
And still, too lacking in spirit to move? So here
You stand in a trance instead of preparing to fight!   290
Can it be that you're waiting for Trojans to threaten your ships
Where their sterns are drawn up on the beach of the foaming sea,
That then you may know whether Zeus will stretch out his hand
And save you?"
          Thus, as he ranged through the crowded ranks
Issuing orders, he came to where the Cretans
Were arming themselves about their excellent leader
Idomeneus, who stood formidable as any wild boar
Mid the foremost champions, while Meriones speeded the arming
Of ranks in the rear. The commander-in-chief Agamemnon   300
Rejoiced at their zeal, and spoke at once to their leader
With these friendly words:
          "Idomeneus, you I respect
Above all other swiftly-drawn Danaans, in war
And works of peace, and at the royal feast
When a bowl of the elders' flaming wine is mixed
For the Argive chiefs. Then the other long-haired Achaeans
Drink their allotted share, but your cup stands
Ever full, like mine, that you may drink whenever
You have a mind to. But on into battle, fully   310
The man you've always claimed to be!"
          And Idomeneus,
Leader of Cretans, replied: "Atrides, surely
To you I will be a loyal comrade, as in
The beginning I gave my promise and pledge I would be.
But urge on the rest of the long-haired Achaeans, that quickly
We may join battle now that the Trojans have broken
Their oath. Death and mourning shall surely be theirs
Who first went back on their word and promise of peace!"
          He spoke, and Atreus' son, now greatly pleased,   320
Strode on through the host till he came to where the two Ajaxes
Stood armed, with an ominous cloud of infantrymen
Behind them. As when from some high crag a goatherd
Sees a far cloud blowing in from over the deep
Before the roaring West Wind, a cloud that brings

The huge hurricane and seems to him blacker than pitch
As he shudders and drives his herd in a cave, so now
The crowded ranks of god-fed, lusty young fighters
Moved with the two Ajaxes into the fury
330 Of war—dark battalions, and everywhere bristling
With shields and spears. As he looked at them, the heart
Of King Agamemnon grew gladder still, and the words
He spoke to their leaders came winged with hearty praise:
        "I give no orders to you, my brave Ajaxes,
Commanders of Argives clad in bronze. It would hardly
Be right to do so. For you yourselves do all
That is needed to fire up your men and fill them with fight.
O Father Zeus, Athena, and Apollo, if only
I found such spirit in the hearts of all my men!
340 Then the towers of King Priam's city would soon be toppled
And all laid waste and leveled beneath our hands."
        With this he left them there and went on to others.
And he came to where Nestor, the eloquent speaker from Pylos,
Was haranguing his men and marshaling them under their leaders—
The powerful Pelagon, Alastor, and Chromius, lordly
Haemon and the people's shepherd Bias. First came
His charioteers, and to the rear, as a wall
Of defense, he had stationed crack troops of infantrymen.
And between these contingents he had driven the weaklings and cowards,
350 That they might be forced to fight in spite of themselves.
At the moment he was instructing his charioteers,
Bidding them hold their horses in check and not
To go rushing ahead in the mob, old Nestor saying:
        "May no man here allow his own good opinion
Of his horsemanship and manly prowess to send him charging
Out front apart from the others to fight the Trojans
Alone, nor will any giving of ground make a one
Of you any stronger! Wait till we all get close,
Then engage the car of a foe and swiftly thrust home
360 With your spear. These tactics are much the best. Such
Was the disciplined spirit that enabled the heroes of old
To lay waste walls and cities!"
        Thus the old one
Drew on his knowledge of battles fought long ago
To advise and inspire his men. Agamemnon rejoiced
As he watched him in action, and to him spoke these winged words:
"Old sire, I only wish that your limbs and bodily
Vigor might still keep pace with your wonderful spirit!

But evil old age that comes to all lies heavy
Upon you. Would that you might change years with one   370
Of our lusty young spearmen!"
                    To which replied horse-driving
Gerenian Nestor: "Son of Atreus, I too
Am tempted to wish that I were the man I was
On the day I cut down huge Ereuthalion. But the gods
Never grant men all things at once. As then I was young,
So now old age is upon me. Even so, I shall stay
With my charioteers, rightly fulfilling the office
Of age by giving them orders and good advice.
I'll leave the wielding of spears to younger men   380
Who trust the might of their brawn."
                    He spoke, and Atrides
Moved on as confidence grew within him. Then
He saw Peteos' son, horse-lashing Menestheus, standing
Mid the Athenians, masters at raising the war-cry,
And not far away resourceful Odysseus, standing
Mid the strong Cephallenians. None of them made any move
To advance, since Achaean battalions and horse-breaking Trojans
Had just begun to get under way and no one
There with Odysseus had heard the war-cry. So they stood   390
Where they were and waited for some other thick wall of
                    Achaeans
To charge on the Trojans and start the battle. This calmness
Of theirs made a poor impression on King Agamemnon,
And now his words came winged with bitter harshness:
       "O son of royal Peteos, nurtured of Zeus,
And you the champion of treacherous tricks who first
Looks out for himself, why are you cringing back here,
Fearful and waiting for others? It would seem that you two
Should fight in the very front rank and throw yourselves
In the midst of blazing battle. For surely you're always   400
The first to respond when I send out a call to the feast
And we Achaeans prepare a fine meal for the chiefs.
I've noticed that then you sit and eat roast meat
With a wonderful zest and drink uncounted cups
Of honey-sweet wine. But now you would gladly loiter
Back here and look on though ten great Achaean battalions
Fought with the ruthless bronze in front of you!"
       Then, with an angry scowl, resourceful Odysseus
Replied: "Son of Atreus, what words are these that just
Got by the barrier of your teeth! What   410

Do you mean by saying that we don't do our part
In waging keen war with the horse-taming Trojans? You'll see,
If you bother to look, the father of Prince Telemachus
Mixing it up with the front-rank fighters of Troy.
The words you speak are nothing but so much wind!"
    When he saw how angry Odysseus was, great
Agamemnon smiled and took back all he had said:
"O god-sprung son of Laertes, resourceful Odysseus,
I did not mean to overly criticize you
420 Or give you commands, for I know your heart is full
Of gentle wisdom, since surely you and I
Think very much alike. So come now, all this
We'll make up to each other later, and if any hard words
Have been spoken, may the gods themselves see to it that nothing
Ever comes of them."
    With this he left them there
And went on to others, till he found the son of Tydeus,
Bold Diomedes, standing among the horses
And sturdy chariots, and by him stood Capaneus' son
430 Sthenelus. The sight of Diomedes also just standing
Angered Agamemnon again, and the words he spoke
Came winged with reproach:
    "Confound it! You son of the fiery
Horse-taming Tydeus, why are you cringing back here
Staring at the other brave companies, true bulwarks of battle?
Surely Tydeus never did any cringing,
But fought in the blaze of war well out in front
Of his friends, as all who saw him toiling in battle
Will tell you. He, they say, was the best of warriors.
440 I never met him myself, nor even so much as
Saw him, though it's true he came to Mycenae once—
As a guest, not a foe—and with him came Prince Polyneices.[4]
They were looking for strong reinforcements, since they at that time
Were laying siege to the holy walls of Thebes.
They made their plea for famous allies, and the men
Of Mycenae were going to give them what they required
When Zeus changed their minds by causing unfavorable signs
To appear. They left and went on their way till they came
To the grassy meadows of the reedy river Asopus.
450 From there the Achaeans sent Tydeus forth on a mission
To Thebes. Upon his arrival he found the many
Descendants of Cadmus feasting together in the palace
Of Prince Eteocles. Your father was a stranger there

And all alone mid many Cadmeans, but the gallant
Horseman Tydeus was so far from being afraid
That he challenged them all to athletic games, and there,
With the gracious help of Athena, he beat them all—
A defeat which did not set well with the horse-racing Cadmeans.
So as he returned from their city they laid an ambush
Of fifty strong men commanded by Maeon, son   460
Of Haemon, and Autophonus' son, battle-staunch Polyphontes.
But they all came to grief and a shameful end at the hands
Of Tydeus, who slew them all—all but Maeon.
Him he sent home, obeying signs from the gods.
Even such was Aetolian Tydeus. But the son he sired
Is not like his father in battle, though more than his equal
When it comes to the making of speeches in the place of assembly!"

   Strong Diomedes said nothing at all in reply,
Respecting reproof from the honored King. But Sthenelus,
Son of illustrious Capaneus, answered him thus: 470
"Atrides, don't lie! You know very well what the truth is.
We claim to be much better men than our fathers,
For we were the ones who succeeded in taking Thebes
Of the seven gates, and we did it with fewer men
And against a more strongly fortified city. We put
Our trust in the heavenly portents and the help of Zeus,
Whereas our fathers died on account of their own
Presumption and folly! So don't compare our merits
With theirs."[5]

   At this the strong Diomedes, glaring   480
At Sthenelus, said: "Quiet, my friend, and do
As I say. I surely don't blame our commander-in-chief
Agamemnon for stirring up fight in the well-greaved Achaeans,
For he is the one who stands to win the most glory
If we Achaeans destroy the Trojans and sacred
Ilium falls, just as he stands to suffer
The most if we go down in defeat. Come, man,
Concentrate now on nothing but furious fighting!"

   So saying, he leaped in full armor from his car to the ground,
And the startling ringing and clashing of bronze on the breast   490
Of the agile chief was enough to give pause and trembling
To any man however brave.

   As when a great surf
Of the sea pounds and resounds on an echoing beach,
Wave after wave coming in with the driving West Wind,
Waves that gather and swell far out on the deep

To break at last and thunder on the shore, curling
And rising around the big rocks and abundantly spewing
Their briny foam, so now the Danaans moved
500 Rank after rank into battle, and the captains did
All the shouting, commanding their disciplined men, who might
Have been dumb for all the talking they did, as fearing
Their leaders they went ahead by the thousands in their inlaid
Flashing armor. But as for the Trojans, they sounded
Like a vast flock of ewes that stand and wait in the yard
Of a wealthy man to give their white milk and incessantly
Bleat as they hear the cries of their lambs. Even such
Was the clamor that rose throughout the Trojans' great host,
For they shouted their orders in no one language, but men
510 From many lands cried out in a jangling of tongues.
These were impelled by Ares, the Achaeans by bright-eyed
Athena, and all were driven by Panic and Rout
And raging Hatred, implacable comrade and sister
Of murdering Ares. She comes to little at first,
But continues to rise till though her feet tread earth
Her head knocks very heaven. It was she who now
Spread dire discord among them as she went throughout
Both armies augmenting the groans of men.
        For now
520 The two forces met with a fearful din of spears
And bossed shields clashing in a fierce and furious melee
Of bronze-breasted fighters. And there the screams of the dying
Were mingled with cries of triumph as blood flowed over
The earth. As when two winter torrents flow down
From great mountain springs to mingle their turbulent floods
Where the two streams meet and thunder on down a deep gorge,
And the shepherd far off in the mountains hears the roar,
So now as the two armies clashed in the fury of battle
A terrible roar of toil and shouting arose.
530   Then Antilochus first took care of one of the Trojans,
A valiant man fully armed mid the foremost fighters,
Echepolus, son of Thalysius. Him he caught
With his spear on the horn of his helmet crested with horsehair
And drove the bronze point through the bone of his forehead.
Darkness enveloped his eyes, and he fell as a tower
Falls in the raging conflict. Then lord Elephenor,
Chalcodon's son and chief of the doughty Abantes,
Seized his feet as he fell and started to drag him
From under the hurtling spears, eager to strip off

His armor. But soon indeed his effort ended. 540
For as he was dragging the body, a Trojan chief,
High-hearted Agenor, saw him and drove the bronze point
Of his spear in his enemy's side, which as he stooped
Was uncovered by shield. His limbs relaxed as spirit
Left him, and over his body Achaeans and Trojans
Savagely battled each other. Like so many wolves
They sprang, and man staggered man as they fought for the corpse.
  Then Telamonian Ajax killed the son
Of Anthemion, the manly youth Simoeisius,* born
By the banks of Simoeis on a day when his mother was journeying 550
Down from Mount Ida, where she had gone with her parents
To take a look at their flocks, which is why they called him
Simoeisius. But for his upbringing he never repaid
His dear parents, since now his life was cut short by the spear
Of spirited Ajax. As the youth came on in front
Of the others he got the bronze in his chest beside
The right nipple. On through his shoulder it went, and he fell
To earth in the dust like a smooth black poplar whose branchy top
Falls in the low grassland of a mighty marsh
To the gleaming ax of some chariot-maker, who leaves it 560
To dry by the banks of a river that he may bend him
A rim for a beautiful chariot. Even such was the fall
Of Anthemion's son Simoeisius, brought down by Zeus-born
Ajax, who now became the target of Antiphus,
Son of Priam. He, his breastplate flashing,
Hurled his sharp spear through the crowd, and missing Ajax
Struck in the groin Odysseus' good friend Leucus
As he was dragging the body away to one side—
He lost his grip and fell face down on the corpse.
  The killing of Leucus greatly enraged Odysseus. 570
Clad in flaming bronze, he plunged through his own
Front ranks and coming up close to the enemy line
Glared fiercely about him and hurled his bright spear, and before him
The Trojans fell back. And not in vain he threw,
For he hit King Priam's bastard son Democoön,
Who had come from Abydos, leaving his string of swift horses.
Enraged at the death of his comrade, Odysseus sent
The keen bronze point of his spear in at one temple
And out at the other, and darkness enveloped his eyes

---

*Simoeisius is named after the Trojan river upon whose banks he was born.

580 As he fell with a thud and his armor clanged about him.
Then the foremost Trojan fighters and glorious Hector
Gave ground, and the yelling Argives dragged off the bodies
And charged much further on.
        Now Apollo, indignant,
Looked down from Pergamus,* stronghold of Troy, and shouted
Thus to the Trojans: "Hold fast! you horse-taming Trojans.
In lust for battle don't be outdone by the Argives.
Their bodies aren't made of stone or iron, nor can they
Resist the flesh-cleaving bronze. And besides, Achilles
590 Is no longer fighting. The son of fair-haired Thetis
Is back at the ships coddling his soul-searing wrath!"
        So spoke the dread god from the fortified hill of Troy.
But Athena Tritogeneia, the glorious daughter
Of Zeus, was at work among the Achaeans, constantly
Urging them on and increasing their courage wherever
She saw them yielding.
        Then Amarynceus' son,
The Epean Diores, was caught in the toils of fate.
For the Thracian leader Peiros, Imbrasus son
600 From Aenus, struck him a blow with a cruel and jagged
Stone on the right leg over the ankle, tearing
The sinews and utterly crushing the bones. And he fell
On his back in the dust, stretching out both of his hands
To his dear comrades and gasping his life away.
Then Peiros, who threw the stone, ran in with his spear
And ripped him across the navel, and all his guts
Gushed out on the ground as darkness came over his eyes.
        But as that ally of Troy sprang back from the corpse,
Aetolian Thoas threw his spear and caught him
610 In the chest just over the nipple, lodging the bronze
In his lung. Then he ran up and pulled the great spear
From his chest, and drawing his sword slashed open his belly
In turn, leaving him lifeless. But Thoas got
No bronze from the corpse at his feet, for around him the comrades
Of Peiros, Thracian fighters who wear their hair tufted
On top, stood firm with long spears in their hands, and though
He was huge and mighty and fearful, they made him reel
And fall back before them. Thus the two captains lay stretched
In the dust together, Peiros, the leader of Thracians,

---

*Pergamus is the highest point, the acropolis, of Troy.

And Diores of bronze-clad Epeans, and about their bodies   620
Numerous others were slain.
     It was hardly a battle
For any man to make light of, though he entered it fresh
And hand in hand with Athena whirled through it all
Unwounded by flying spear or thrust of keen blade,
Protected by her from the hail of hurtling bronze.
That day a tremendous mass of Achaeans and Trojans
Alike were stretched side by side face down in the dust.

BOOK V

The Valiant Deeds of Diomedes

Now Pallas Athena gave courage and manly prowess
To Tydeus' son Diomedes, that he might distinguish
Himself mid all the Argives and win great glory.
She caused his helmet and shield to blaze with tireless
Flame, like that bright star of late summer that rises
From bathing in the stream of Oceanus and outshines all
The others. Such was the fire she made flame out
From this man's head and shoulders, and she sent him into
The thickest part of the battle.[1]

10   Among the Trojans
Lived one by the name of Dares, a wealthy and worthy
Priest of Hephaestus, and he had two warrior sons,
Phegeus and Idaeus, skillful in battle. Now these
Drove out from the rest of the host to meet Diomedes,
Who charged along on foot. As soon as they
Were well within range of the oncoming chief, Phegeus
Flung his long-shadowing spear, and the point of it narrowly
Missed the left shoulder of Tydeus's son, who came on
With the bronze as before. And not in vain did his spear
20 Fly from his hand. For he landed it square in the chest
Of Phegeus between the nipples and knocked him from the chariot.
And Idaeus sprang back, leaving the ornate car,
But did not dare bestride the corpse of his brother.
In fact, he himself would not have evaded black fate
If Hephaestus had not been his guard and wrapped him in night
To save him, that his old priest their father might not
Be utterly wretched with grief. Then the stout-hearted son
Of Tydeus drove off their horses and gave them to comrades
Of his to lead back to the hollow ships.

30   When the Trojans
Saw the two sons of Dares, one running away,
The other dead by his car, their hearts recoiled.
And bright-eyed Athena, taking the hand of rash Ares,
Spoke to him thus: "Ares, Ares, ruiner

Of men, you blood-stained stormer of walls, may we not
Leave the Achaeans and Trojans to fight this out
For themselves? Father Zeus will grant glory to whichever side
He wishes, but let us avoid his wrath by removing
Ourselves right now."
So saying, she led the fierce War-god   40
From battle and made him sit down on the sandy bank
Of Scamander. Then the Trojans were routed by the Danaan fighters,
And each of their captains killed his man. First,
The king of men Agamemnon tumbled great Odius,
Chief of the Halizones, out of his chariot.
He had been first to wheel in retreat, but just
As he turned, Agamemnon planted a spear in his back
Between the shoulders and drove it out through his chest.
And he fell to the ground with a thud and a clashing of armor.

    And Idomeneus slew the son of Maeonian Borus,   50
The warrior Phaestus from fertile Tarne. Idomeneus,
Famed as a spearman, thrust his long lance clean through
His right shoulder just as he mounted his car. Phaestus
Fell to the ground, as hateful darkness seized him,
And the squires of Idomeneus stripped the corpse of its armor.

    Then Atreus' son Menelaus with his sharp spear
Took care of Scamandrius, Strophius' son, the skillful
Hunter whom Artemis herself had taught to hit
All the wild creatures that feed in the mountain forest.
But arrow-scattering Artemis was no good at all   60
To her protégé now, nor was his exceptional skill
At long-distance shooting. For Atreus' son Menelaus
Struck him in the back as he fled, and drove his spear in
Between the shoulders and out through his chest. And
         Scamandrius
Fell on his face, as on him his armor rang.

    And Meriones killed the son of Tecton and grandson
Of Harmon, the builder Phereclus, who could make all manner
Of intricate things with his hands. It was he who had built
For Paris those shapely ships, the beginning of ills,   70
That became a curse to all Trojans including himself,
Who had no idea what the immortal gods had decreed.
When Meriones, giving chase, caught up with him,
He lunged with his spear, and the point went in the right buttock,
Under the bone, and into the bladder beneath.
Then Phereclus fell to his knees with a scream, and death
Came over him there.

Then Meges slew Pedaeus,
Antenor's bastard son, whom, to please
80 Her husband, his godly wife Theano had reared
Like one of her own. Phyleus' son Meges, renowned
As a spearman, drew near and hurled his sharp lance through the nape
Of this man's neck. The point cut off his tongue
At the root and lodged between his teeth, and Pedaeus
Fell in the dust and bit the cold bronze.
        And Eurypylus,
Son of Euaemon, killed the splendid Hypsenor,
Son of high-hearted Dolopion, who was made priest
Of the river Scamander and honored like a god by the people
90 Of Troy. As Hypsenor fled before him, Eurypylus,
Glorious son of Euaemon, slashed with his sword
And lopped his heavy arm off. Streaming blood
It fell to the ground, and purple death came down
On the eyes of Hypsenor as powerful fate embraced him.
        So they toiled in the huge confusion of battle.
But as for Diomedes, you could not have told which side
He was on, Achaean or Trojan. For across the plain
He raged like a swollen winter torrent that swiftly
Sweeps the embankments away, tight dikes and the walls
100 Of fruitful vineyards, as the rain of Zeus drives it on,
And many a man's fine work goes down in destruction
Before it. So now the thick Trojan battalions were routed
By Tydeus' son, nor could they for all their great numbers
Stand up to him.
        But the son of Lycaon, Prince Pandarus,
No sooner caught sight of him raging across the plain
With the Trojan battalions running in rout than he bent
His curved bow, took careful aim, and sent a sharp shaft
Through the right shoulder-guard of his armor, spattering blood
110 On his breastplate. Then the glorious son of Lycaon loudly,
Triumphantly shouted:
        "About! you spirited Trojans,
You charioteers. The best Achaean they've got
Is badly hit, nor will he last long with that
Grim shaft in his shoulder, if God's own son Apollo
Truly blessed my setting forth from Lycia!"
        So Pandarus boasted, but strong Diomedes was not
Undone by the flying arrow. Falling back
To his horses and car, he spoke to Sthenelus thus:

"Quick! good son of Capaneus. Get down from that car 120
And pull this keen shaft from my shoulder."
    And Sthenelus leaped
To the ground beside him and pulled the swift arrow point-first
Through his shoulder, and blood spurted up through the weave of his
          tunic.
Then battle-roaring Diomedes prayed: "Hear me,
O unwearied child of Zeus who bears the aegis.
If ever you cared for my father and stood by his side
In the blaze of battle, care now, Athena, no less
For me. Bring within range of my spear the wretch
Who shot me before I saw him and now loudly brags 130
That I haven't much longer to live in the sun's bright light."
    Hearing his earnest prayer, Pallas Athena
Quickly renewed his vigor, and once again
He felt light on his feet and strong. Then standing beside him
She spoke these winged words: "You're ready now,
Diomedes, and eager to battle the Trojans, for I
Have filled your heart with the untrembling might of your father,
The great shield-wielding warrior, Tydeus the horseman.
And I have removed the mist with which your eyes
Were darkened, that now with ease you may distinguish 140
The god from the man. Do not, then, fight with any
Immortal power that may come here to try you,
Save only Zeus's daughter, fair Aphrodite.
If she should enter the battle, give her a thrust
With your keen-cutting bronze!"
    So saying, blue-eyed Athena
Went her way, and Tydeus' son returned
To the fight mid the foremost champions. And though before
His heart had been eager for battle with Trojans, now
He was seized with fury three times as great, like that 150
Which comes on a lion some shepherd has wounded but failed
To kill while guarding his fleecy sheep on an outlying
Farm: he hurts the beast just enough to enrage him
As he leaps over the wall of the yard, then hides
Amid the buildings instead of pursuing him further,
While the frantic sheep are driven pell-mell about
And huddled together in clumps and the furious lion
Takes the high fence at a bound and is back in the fields.
Even such was the rage of strong Diomedes as now
He clashed with the Trojans. 160

He first took on Astynous
And the people's shepherd Hypeiron. Hurling his spear
He struck the one just over the nipple. Then bringing
His huge sword down on the collarbone of the other
He sheared his shoulder clean off from the neck and back.
Their bodies he left where they fell and rushed in pursuit
Of Abas and Polyidus, sons of Eurydamas,
An aged reader of dreams. But those two never
Again brought dreams for their old sire to interpret,
170 For strong Diomedes slew them. Then he charged
The cherished sons of Phaenops, Xanthus and Thoön.
Their father was old and feeble, and he begot
No other son to leave his property to.
There Diomedes cut both of them down, taking
Their sweet lives away and leaving their father with nothing
But grief and pain. For never again did he welcome them
Home from battle, and their kinsmen divided his wealth.
    Next he encountered two sons of Dardanian Priam,
Echemmon and Chromius, riding in a chariot together.
180 As a lion springs in among cattle and breaks the neck
Of an ox or heifer grazing in a glade of the forest,
So Tydeus' son knocked both of these from their chariot,
Which they were loath to leave, and stripping off
Their armor he gave the horses to comrades of his
To drive to the ships.
        But Aeneas saw him ruining
The ranks and made his way through the fight mid a tumult
Of hurtling spears to find the princely Pandarus
If he could. When he found that matchless and mighty
190 Son of Lycaon, he went up to him and said:
"Pandarus, where now are your bow and winged arrows
For which you're so famous? We have no archer to equal you
Here, nor is there any in Lycia who claims
To be better. So come, lift up your hands and pray
To Zeus, then take a shaft and let it fly
At yonder man, whoever he is, that has brought
Not a few of our best men down and done much harm
To the Trojans. I fear he may be some wrathful god,
Angry with Trojans because of neglected offerings.
200 The wrath of a god is hard for mortals to bear."
        Then the glorious son of Lycaon answered him thus:
"Aeneas, wise counselor of bronze-clad Trojans, to me
He looks very like Diomedes, for I know his shield

And crested helmet, and those are his horses too.
Still, I don't really know: he may be a god!
And even if he's the man I think he is,
The fiery son of Tydeus, he doesn't rage
Through the ranks that way without the help of a god.
Surely some cloud-wrapped immortal stood by him today
And deflected the flying shaft with which I hit him.   210
For hit him I did, upon the right shoulder, with a shaft
That went right through the plate of his armor. I thought
At the time I had sent him to Hades for sure, but I
Was wrong—truly he must be some wrathful god!
And here I am with neither horses nor car,
Though at home in the care of my father Lycaon are eleven
Lovely new chariots covered with robes, and standing
By each, a pair of fine horses munch wheat and white barley.
Back in the palace, before I left for the war,
The aged spearman, my father Lycaon, told me   220
Again and again to take a car and horses,
That I might mount and so lead the Trojan fighters
In mighty battles. But I like a fool wouldn't listen.
I wanted to spare the horses, afraid that here
In a crowd so large, there wouldn't be fodder enough,
And they had always had more than enough to eat.
So I came on foot to Ilium, relying on my bow,
Which hasn't, however, been very much help. For today
I have shot at two Kings, Diomedes and Menelaus, and on both
I scored hits and drew blood. But all I really accomplished   230
Was to make them fight more fiercely than ever. So that
Was a sad day for me when I took my bent bow from its peg
And set out with my men for beautiful Ilium, bringing
Much joy to the brilliant Hector. But if I ever
Get back and lay eyes once again on my own native land,
My dear wife, and lofty huge palace, then any man
Who wishes may cut my head clean off if I,
With my own hands, don't break this bow in two
And throw it all in the blazing fire. For it
To me is worthless as wind!"   240
          Then Aeneas, leader
Of Trojans, answered him thus: "Don't talk that way.
But surely it's true that things won't really improve
Till we take horses and car and confront the man
With other weapons. So come, get up in my chariot,
That you may see what the horses of Tros are like.[2]

They're equally fast pursuing or fleeing, and should Zeus
Again grant victory to Tydeus' son Diomedes
They'll get the two of us safely back to the city.
250 Come then, you take the lash and glossy reins
And I'll be the one to dismount and do the fighting,
Or you can do that and I will handle the horses."

     And the glorious son of Lycaon replied: "You manage
The reins yourself, Aeneas, and drive your own horses.
In case we do have to flee Diomedes they'll surely
Run better before the curved car with someone they know
At the reins. I wouldn't want them to panic and balk
And refuse to take us out of the battle for lack of
Your voice to urge them. For then the son of spirited
260 Tydeus would charge and kill us both and drive off
Your solid-hoofed horses. No, you drive your own chariot
And pair, and I'll take him on with a sharp-pointed spear."

     So saying, they mounted the ornate car and fiercely
Drove the swift horses against Diomedes. And Sthenelus,
Son of Capaneus, saw them and quickly spoke
To the son of Tydeus these words winged with warning:
"Diomedes, dear friend, here come two mighty men
Of measureless strength bearing down at a gallop upon us
And eager to fight you! One is the skillful bowman
270 Pandarus, who says he's the son of Lycaon, and with him
Rides Aeneas, who claims Anchises for father
And Aphrodite for mother. But come, let us
Fall back in the chariot. I beg you to stop this raging
Mid front-line fighters before you too fall a victim."

     Then strong Diomedes, darkly scowling, replied:
"Don't talk to me of retreating, since you haven't, I think,
A chance to persuade me. It's not in my blood to skulk
And run from a fight—my spirit remains unshaken!
I haven't the slightest desire to get in that chariot,
280 But just as I am, on foot, I'll go to meet them:
Pallas Athena will not allow me to quail!
And as for those two, one of them may get away,
But their swift horses will never take both of them back!
And another thing I'll say for you to remember.
If fertile-minded Athena grants me the glory
Of slaying them both, hold our swift horses here,
Drawing the reins back taut and making them fast
To the chariot's handrail. Then put all you've got in a dash
For Aeneas's horses and drive them away from the Trojans

And into the host of well-greaved Achaeans. For they   290
Are descended from those very horses that far-seeing Zeus
Gave Tros by way of repayment for carrying off
His dear son Ganymede, since of all horses on whom
The dawn broke and the bright sun shone, they were the best.
Later when King Laomedon owned the breed,
His royal kinsman Anchises stole a strain
By putting his mares to them without permission.
And by those mares six colts were foaled in his stables,
Four of which he kept himself and reared
At the manger, but the other two he gave Aeneas,   300
The same two masters of rout he's driving now!
Could we but capture those two, great indeed
Would be our glory."
          While they were talking thus,
Their attackers came up at a gallop, and Pandarus
Loudly called out: "You fiery, stout-hearted son
Of lordly Tydeus, I see you survived that bitter
Swift arrow of mine. Well now I intend to try
My luck with a spear!"
          So saying, he drew back and hurled   310
His long-shadowing lance and struck Diomedes' shield.
All the way through it the bronze point tore, but stopped
At his breastplate. Then Pandarus, son of Lycaon, shouted
In triumph: "Right through the belly! Nor can you last long
After that—but to me you have given tremendous glory!"
          And strong Diomedes, fearless as ever, replied:
"No hit at all! You missed me completely. But the two
Of you will not, I think, get out of this fight
Till one or the other has fallen and glutted with blood
The battling Ares, him of the tough hide shield!"   320
          With this he let fly, and Athena guided his spear.
The stubborn bronze went in between the man's nose
And eye, then tore through his teeth, cut off his tongue
At the root, and came out at the base of his chin. He crashed
From the car, as his armor all bright and flashing rang
About him and the nimble horses shied. And there
His strength was undone, and the spirit of Pandarus left him.
          But Aeneas leaped down with shield and long spear, afraid
The Achaeans might drag off the body, which now he bestrode
With the confident spirit and strength of a lion. Yelling   330
His terrible war-cry, he gripped his spear and round shield,
Ready to kill whoever might come against him.

But Diomedes picked up a huge stone, one
That no two men of today could even lift
But that he picked up with one hand and easily threw.
The rugged boulder struck the hip of Aeneas
Where the thigh-bone turns in its socket, which men call the cup,
Ripping the skin and tendons away and crushing
The cup completely. The hero then dropped to one knee,
340 Supporting himself with one great hand on the ground
Till darkness enveloped his eyes.
      And now Aeneas,
King of men, would surely have died, if the daughter
Of Zeus had not been sharply watching, Aphrodite
His mother, who lay with his father Anchises while he
Was out with the cattle. She threw her white arms about
Her dear son and drew over him for protection a fold
Of her radiant gown, lest one of the swiftly-drawn Danaans
Rob him of life by hurling a spear through his chest.
350   Now while she was bearing her darling son from the battle,
Sthenelus did not forget the careful instructions
That Diomedes of the great war-cry had given
To him. He held their solid-hoofed horses apart
From the crashing waves of conflict, drawing the reins back
Taut and making them fast to the chariot's handrail.
Then he dashed for Aeneas's mane-tossing horses
And drove them away from the Trojans and into the host
Of well-greaved Achaeans, where he gave them to his dear friend
Deïpylus, the man he respected and cared for most
360 Among men his age, since the two of them thought alike.
Bidding him drive the horses to the hollow ships,
He leaped in his chariot, seized the glossy reins,
And galloped their hard-hoofed horses in search of Diomedes.
      He, meanwhile, had gone with the ruthless bronze
In hot pursuit of Cyprian Aphrodite,
Knowing that she was a cowardly goddess and not
One of those like Athena, or Enyo, sacker of cities,
Who turn the tide of mortal conflict. Chasing her
Through the huge crowd, the son of spirited Tydeus
370 Caught up with her and lunged with his spear, slightly
Wounding her tender hand. The keen bronze pierced
Her ambrosial gown, woven for her by the Graces
Themselves, and went into her flesh at the lower part
Of her palm. And out flowed the goddess's immortal blood,
The ichor that flows in such divine beings as she,

For they eat no bread and drink no flaming wine:
Hence they are bloodless and called immortals. She screamed
And dropped her son, whom Phoebus Apollo took
In his arms and wrapped in a cloud of darkness, lest one
Of the swiftly-drawn Danaans rob him of life by hurling   380
A spear through his chest. Then battle-roaring Diomedes
Shouted in triumph:
           "Keep your distance, O daughter
Of Zeus, from war and the blaze of battle! Aren't you
Content with seducing feeble women? If you
Insist on frequenting the fight, believe me you'll learn
To shudder at the very name of war, no matter
How far from battle you may be when you hear it!"
           At this, Aphrodite withdrew, deeply distraught
And frantic with pain, her fair skin stained with blood.   390
But wind-footed Iris guided her out of the tumult
To where, on the left of the fighting, the impetuous Ares
Sat, his sharp spear propped on a cloud and his pair
Of swift horses at hand. And she fell on her knees and begged
For her dear brother's horses with halters of gold:
           "Help me,
Sweet brother, and give me your horses, that I may get home
To those on Olympus, for I am in terrible pain
Where the son of Tydeus struck me—a mortal man,
Who now would fight Father Zeus himself!"   400
           She pleaded,
And Ares gave her the horses with halters of gold.
She got in the chariot, her heart still greatly distressed,
And Iris, mounting beside her, caught up the reins
And lashed the horses, who not unwilling took off
At a gallop. Quickly they came to steep Olympus,
Home of the gods, and there wind-footed swift Iris
Stopped and unharnessed the horses, then threw down before them
Ambrosial fodder. But fair Aphrodite sank down
At the knees of her mother Dione, who put her arms   410
Around her daughter and tenderly stroked her, saying:
           "Who of the heavenly gods, dear child, has badly
Mistreated you now, as though you had done something wrong
Where everybody could see?"
           To which Aphrodite,
Adorer of smiles, replied: "High-hearted Diomedes,
The son of Tydeus—he struck me! and all because
I was bearing from battle my own dear son Aeneas,

By far the most precious of mortals to me. For that
420 Dreadful war is no longer between just Achaeans and Trojans.
O no, now the Danaans fight with immortals too!"
      And the gracious goddess Dione answered her thus:
"Bear up, my child, and endure your suffering bravely.
Many of us with homes on Olympus have also
Suffered from men in the course of our mutual efforts
To hurt one another. So Ares suffered greatly
When those young giants, Otus and strong Ephialtes,*
The sons of Aloeus, bound him in painful, unbreakable
Chains and kept him tied up for thirteen months
430 In a great bronze jar. And bloodthirsty Ares would surely
Have died there if the lovely Eëriboea, stepmother
To the sons of Aloeus, had not brought word to Hermes,
Who managed by stealth to free the War-god, though he
By this time was all but undone by his torturing chains.
And Hera certainly suffered when the brutal Heracles,
Whom some thought the son of Amphitryon, pierced her right breast
With a three-barbed arrow. For a while her pain was unquenchable!
And even huge Hades has suffered no less than the others,
He too from a bitter arrow, when the same irreverent
440 Heracles—who was really the son of aegis-great Zeus—
Shot him there mid the dead at his own grim gate
And left him in anguish. Full of misery and darting
Pains, he journeyed up here to lofty Olympus,
For the shaft had gone deep in his solid shoulder, and his might
Was ebbing away. But Paeëon, our skillful physician,
Applied some pain-killing ointments and healed his wound,
For Hades, of course, has nothing mortal about him—
A rash and violent man that Heracles, one
Who cared so little what evil he wrought that he
450 Didn't scruple to vex the Olympian gods with his arrows!
And now, my child, the bright-eyed goddess Athena
Has enabled this man to injure you—fool
That the son of Tydeus most certainly is, since he
Doesn't know in his heart that one who contends with immortals
Lives a very short life, nor does he return from the sad
Conflagration of war to gather his little children
About his knees and hear them call him father.

---

*The giants would attack the gods by heaping Mount Ossa on Olympus, and then Mount Pelion on Ossa.

So Tydeus' son had better be careful, no matter
How mighty he is, or some immortal more able
Than you may enter the fight against him! Let him   460
Beware, if he doesn't want his own gallant wife,
Adrastus' thoughtful daughter Aegialeia,
To waken her household with wails for her dear but missing
Husband, the best of Achaeans, horse-taming Diomedes!"[3]
    So saying, she wiped the ichor from the goddess's hand
With both of hers. The wound was healed, and the pains
So burdensome left her. Now Athena and Hera, who sat
Looking on, took the occasion to irritate Zeus,
The son of Cronos, and the bright-eyed goddess Athena
Spoke up among them with these sarcastic words: 470
    "Father Zeus, I hope what I say won't make you too angry,
But surely your Cyprian daughter has been persuading
Some other Achaean woman to run off with one
Of her darling Trojans. I guess it was while caressing
That very same fair-gowned female that she scratched her dainty
Hand—no doubt on the lady's golden brooch-pin."
    These words got a smile from the Father of gods and men,
And calling golden Aphrodite he spoke to her thus:
"Warfare, my child, is not your concern. So mind
Your own affairs and the sweet love-making of marriage,   480
And leave all these things to Athena and rushing Ares."
    Such was their talk, but meanwhile Diomedes, screaming
His war-cry, charged on the stricken Aeneas, knowing
Quite well that Apollo himself was holding his arms
Above him. Still, he had no awe, not even
Of that great god, but was just as eager as ever
To kill Aeneas and strip off his splendid armor.
Thrice he charged him, raging to kill, and thrice
Apollo beat back his bright shield. But when like a demon
He charged a fourth time, then with a terrible cry   490
Far-working Apollo spoke to him thus:
    "Think!
O son of Tydeus, think—and shrink! Don't try
To equal the gods in spirit and valor, for the race
Of immortal gods is by no means the same as that
Of earth-treading men!"
    At this, Diomedes fell back
A little, avoiding the wrath of far-darting Apollo,
Who then took Aeneas up out of the crowd and into
His temple on sacred Pergamus, stronghold of Troy.   500

There, in that great holy of holies, Leto
And the archer Artemis healed his wound and restored
His strength completely. Meanwhile, Apollo of the silver
Bow fashioned a phantom in Aeneas's likeness,
Armor and all, and over this ghostly deception
The Trojans and valiant Achaeans struck out at the breasts
Of each other, belaboring the circular bull's-hide bucklers
And the lighter fluttering shields. Then Phoebus Apollo
Spoke thus to the violent War-god:
510   "Ares, Ares,
Ruiner of men, you blood-stained stormer of walls,
Won't you go into the battle and withdraw this man
Diomedes, who now would fight Father Zeus himself?
He's already wounded Cyprian Aphrodite
On the lower part of her palm and charged down on me
Like a demon!"
            So saying, Apollo sat down on the top
Of Troy's fortified hill, and the murderous Ares
Entered the ranks of the Trojans and urged them on
520 In the form of swift Acamas, leader of Thracians, calling out
Thus to the god-fed sons of Priam: "O sons
Of a god-gifted King, how long will you let the Achaeans
Go on slaying your men, till they actually storm
The sturdy gates of your city? There lies a man
Whom we honored like godly Hector himself—Aeneas,
The son of great-hearted Anchises. But come, let us save
Our noble comrade from out the roaring tumult!"
            At this they all became bolder, and Sarpedon harshly
Rebuked godly Hector, saying: "Hector, where now
530 Is the courage that used to be yours? And you said you could hold
This city alone, with no other help than that
Of your brothers and brothers-in-law, that you didn't need
Any troops or allies. Well where are your brothers now?
Cringing and cowering like dogs round a lion! And we
Are the ones who do the fighting, we, the allies
Among you. Even such am I, from far-off Lycia
By the eddying waters of Xanthus, where I left my dear wife
And baby boy, and the countless possessions that many
A covetous fellow would like to have for his own.
540 Still I encourage the Lycians, and always I'm willing
To take on my man, though here there is nothing of mine
That Achaeans might drive or carry away. But you
Just stand around, not even urging your men

To buckle down and defend their own wives. Look out,
My friend, or you and yours will soon be caught
Like so many fish in an all-ensnaring net
And become the prey and booty of those who hate you,
Who very soon now will sack your teeming city!
All this should be your concern both night and day,
And you above all should plead with the leaders of these   550
Your world-famous allies to hold their ground without flinching.
Then no one would ever harshly rebuke you this way."
    Sarpedon's taunt bit deep in the heart of Hector.
At once he leaped fully armed from his car to the ground,
And brandishing two sharp spears he ranged through the ranks
Arousing new spirit in the routed men. They spun
And faced the Achaeans, a solid wall of steadfast
Argive resistance. And even as the winnowing wind
Whitens with chaff all those on the strong threshing-floors
When golden-haired Demeter separates grain from chaff   560
And the chaff piles up in heaps of white, so now
The Achaeans grew white in the swirling dust that went up
From the beating feet of the horses and men, clouding
The all-bronze sky as they clashed in battle again
And the drivers wheeled in their cars.
    Then the Trojan warriors
Struck out straight ahead with all of their might, and Ares,
Everywhere raging, enveloped the battle in darkness
To help the Trojans. Thus he fulfilled the command
Of Apollo, Phoebus of the golden sword, who seeing   570
Athena leave the battle bade him repair
The Trojan morale, for it was she who had made
The Achaeans so mighty. And Apollo himself sent down
From his opulent temple the people's shepherd Aeneas,
Filling his heart with strength. So Aeneas rejoined
His comrades, and they rejoiced to see him returning
Alive and well and as splendidly valiant as ever,
Though then they were far too busy to ask any questions,
One and all embroiled in the battle stirred up
By him of the silver bow with the eager help   580
Of man-maiming Ares and raging, implacable Hatred.
    And the two Ajaxes, Odysseus, and strong Diomedes
Sparked the fight of the Danaans, though they of themselves
Refused to give way before the Trojans' violent
Assaults. They held their own like the motionless clouds
That on a still day Zeus stands on the mountain peaks

When the North Wind sleeps along with all other hard blasts
That scatter the shadowy clouds with their shrill blowing.
So the Danaan troops steadfastly resisted the Trojans
590 With no retreating. And King Agamemnon strode up
And down in the melee bawling these words of command:
        "Be men, my friends, and stout of heart! Fear nothing
In this great clash but dishonor before each other.
Of men who shun dishonor, more are saved
Than slain, but flight is a poor defense and wins
No glory of any kind!"
        He spoke, and mightily
Hurling his spear he struck a front-line fighter,
A comrade of noble Aeneas, Pergasus' son
600 Deïcoön, whom the Trojans regarded as highly as the royal
Sons of Priam, since he was always quick
To fight his man in the foremost rank of battle.
The spear of King Agamemnon struck his shield,
And the keen bronze cut its way through, went on through his belt
And deep in his belly. Deïcoön thudded to earth,
And on him his armor rang.
        Then Aeneas slew
Two Danaan champions, Crethon and Orsilochus, the sons
Of Diocles, a man of very great substance who lived in
610 Well-fortified Pherae and claimed descent from the river
Alpheius, whose wide stream rolls through the Pylian country.
The first Orsilochus, King over thousands, was sired
By this River, and he begot magnanimous Diocles,
Whose sons were the twins Crethon and the second Orsilochus,
Trained and versatile warriors. In the prime of young manhood
Both of them went with the black Argive ships to Ilium,
Known for its horses, seeking to win satisfaction
For Atreus' sons Menelaus and King Agamemnon,
But now enshrouding death put an end to their lives.
620 Like them two lions grow up on the peaks of a mountain,
Reared by their dam in the bush of a tangled forest,
Cubs that mature to be killers of cattle and wooly
Plump sheep, farm-wrecking marauders till they themselves
Fall victims to men's piercing bronze. Even so these two
Lost their lives at the hands of Aeneas and crashed to the ground
Like lofty pines.
        Warlike King Menelaus
Pitied their fall, and through the front-line fighters
He rushed, armored in gleaming bronze and shaking

His lance. For Ares himself had aroused his spirit,   630
That he too might fall at the hands of Aeneas. But Antilochus,
Son of great-hearted Nestor, saw him, and deeply
Afraid that the people's shepherd might come to grief
And so destroy all they had toiled for, he rushed
Through the front-line fighters to join him. When Antilochus
          reached
Menelaus, he and Aeneas were squaring off
With their whetted spears, spoiling to battle each other.
But Aeneas, though fast on his feet, when staunchly confronted
By two such attackers, did not attempt to hold out.
So together they dragged off their dead, rich Diocles' sons,   640
And laid the unfortunate pair in the arms of Achaeans.
Then turning back, they fought once again at the front.
     Together they took on Pylaemenes, peer of Ares
And chief of the bold Paphlagonian troops. Menelaus,
Renowned as a spearman, caught the man standing still
And in at the collarbone hurled his lance, while Antilochus
Threw at his driver and squire, the valiant Mydon,
Atymnius' son, and struck him hard with a stone
On the point of his elbow just as he turned the solid-hoofed
Horses. The ivory-decked reins fell in the dust,   650
And Antilochus sprang and drove his sword through the temple
Of Mydon, who gasping lurched from the well-made car
And pitched headfirst to the ground in a place of deep sand.
He went in past head and shoulders and stuck where he was
Till his horses trampled him down and into the dust.
Then Antilochus whipped them away, an Achaean prize.
     Across the ranks this action caught Hector's attention,
And fiercely he charged down upon them with a terrible scream
And whole battalions of Trojans behind him, all
Led on by Ares and powerful Enyo, mistress   660
Of misery and the shameless turmoil of battle. Wielding
A monstrous spear, grim Ares charged with Hector,
Now pulling ahead, now dropping behind.
     When he saw
The ferocious War-god, Diomedes' blood ran cold,
And even that great battle-roarer felt suddenly helpless,
As that man feels who crossing wide country stops
In dismay at a river rushing seaward, takes
One look at the seething white water, and quickly steps back
Quite hopeless. So now Diomedes gave ground, shouting thus   670
To the men around him:

"Look there! my friends. It's very
Clear why we've always marveled at the great Hector's valor
And skill with a spear, for always beside him a god goes,
Warding off death, as Ares yonder runs
By his side in the form of a mortal man. But all of
You now, fall back! keeping your faces turned
Toward the Trojans. Don't be so mad in your rage as to fight
Against gods!"

680   But the Trojans by now were upon them, and Hector
Cut down a couple of trained and aggressive fighters,
Menesthes and Anchialus, both in one car. But the huge
Telamonian Ajax pitied their fall, and coming up
Close to their bodies he hurled his spear into Amphius,
Selagus' son, a wealthy chief from Paesus,
A man of many rich harvests. But fate had made him
An ally of Priam and the sons of Priam. And now
Telamonian Ajax hurled his long-shadowing lance
Through the belt of this leader and lodged it deep in his belly.

690   He fell with a thud, and the fiery Ajax rushed in
To strip off the armor, his great shield catching many
Of the gleaming sharp spears that the Trojans rained upon him.
Bracing one foot on the body, he pulled out his spear,
But the Trojan bronze was flying so thick that he
Was unable to strip the fine armor off the man's shoulders,
And he feared the stubborn defense of the spirited warriors,
Who many and brave closed in with their lances. Though Ajax
Was tall and burly and lordly, they made him reel back
And retreat.

700   Thus they labored in the terrible struggle,
And now irresistible fate sent Heracles' son
Tlepolemus, valiant and huge, against Sarpedon,
Son of Zeus. And when they had come within range
Of each other—the son and grandson of sky-clouding Zeus—
Tlepolemus shouted:

"Sarpedon, counselor of Lycians,
What is it that drives so unwarlike a man as yourself
To skulk about in a battle? They're liars indeed
Who say you're the son of aegis-great Zeus, since you
710   Are no man at all compared with his genuine sons
Of the good old days! You take, for instance, bold Heracles,
My own staunch lion-hearted father. He came here to Troy
One time for the mares of Laomedon, with only six ships
And a force much smaller than ours to say the least.

Even so, he leveled the city of Troy and plundered
Her streets.[4] But you have the heart of a coward, and daily
Your people diminish. And now, believe me, your coming
From Lycia will never be any defense for the Trojans,
No matter how mighty you are, for I myself
Will conquer you once and for all and send you down   720
Through the gates of Hades!"

      And Sarpedon, leader of Lycians,
Answered him thus: "Tlepolemus, truly your father
Did sack this holy city, but only because
Of the folly of haughty Laomedon, who insulted Heracles
In return for well-doing and refused to give him the mares
For which he had journeyed so far. But you, I think,
Shall meet your death and dark fate right here at my hands.
Sprawling beneath my spear, you shall give glory
To me, and your miserable soul to horse-famous Hades!"   730

      Sarpedon had no sooner spoken than Tlepolemus drew back
His spear, and both the long lances shot at one time
From their hands. Sarpedon's caught him full in the neck
And the hard point passed clean through, as the blackness of night
Came down, eclipsing his eyes. And the lance of Tlepolemus
Pierced the left thigh of Sarpedon, and the point tore madly
Through, grazing the bone. But still his Father
Kept death at a distance.

      Then the noble comrades of godlike
Sarpedon bore him away from the fighting, heavily   740
Trailing the long ashen spear from his thigh, for such
Was their haste and toil as they labored in battle to help him
That no man thought to draw out the lance and get him
Up on his feet.

      On their side the well-greaved Achaeans
Carried Tlepolemus out of the fighting, and the spirit
Of brilliant, enduring Odysseus was filled with rage
At the sight. In heart and soul he pondered whether he
Should pursue Sarpedon, son of loud-thundering Zeus,
Or go on killing his Lycian subjects. But since   750
It was not the lot of gallant Odysseus to kill
With keen bronze the god-sprung King, Athena turned
His attention to Lycians more lowly. And there his bronze
Took fatal hold of Coeranus, Alastor, and Chromius,
Alcandrus and Halius, Noëmon and Prytanis. Nor would
The worthy Odysseus have ceased very soon his killing
Of Lycians if great bright-helmeted Hector had not

Been quick to notice the slaughter. Fully armed
In flaming bronze, he rushed through the foremost ranks,
760 His strong hands loaded with panic for Danaan troops.
Sarpedon, son of Zeus, was more than glad
At his coming, and pitifully spoke to him thus:
          "O Hector,
Don't allow me to lie here and become a prey
Of the Danaans. Do what you can to keep them off.
Since it isn't likely I'll ever return to delight
My dear wife and baby boy in my own native land,
At least let me die in your city instead of out here
On the plain!"
770   Bright-helmeted Hector made no reply
But flashed on by him, determined to thrust back the Argives
And kill as many as possible. But the loyal comrades
Of godlike Sarpedon laid him beneath a beautiful
Oak tree, sacred to Zeus who bears the aegis,
And powerful Pelagon, a good friend of his, pushed
The ashen spear from his thigh. Then all grew misty
And consciousness left him. But soon he revived, as the North Wind
Breathed upon him and brought to life again
The spirit he had so painfully gasped away.
780   Now before the onset of Ares and bronze-clad Hector
The Argives neither turned and made a break for the ships
Nor could they hold out in the fight, but kept backing back,
Once they had heard that Ares was helping the Trojans.
Then who was the first and who was the last to be slain
And stripped by Priam's son Hector and brazen Ares?
Prince Teuthras was first, and then horse-lashing Orestes,
The Aetolian spearman Trechus, Oenomaus, and Helenus,
Son of Oenops, and rich bright-belted Oresbius,
Who back at his home in Hyle by Lake Cephisis
790 Had carefully watched his wealth, while close around him
Lived other Boeotians on land exceedingly rich.
          When the white-armed goddess Hera noticed this slaughter
Of Argives in the furious struggle, at once she spoke
To Athena with these winged words: "O invincible child
Of Zeus who bears the aegis,[5] surely our promise
To King Menelaus, that Troy's thick walls should fall
To him before he went home, will amount to nothing
If we let murderous Ares go on raging
This way. But come, let the two of us also make up
800 Our minds to show our spirit and valor!"

She spoke,
And the blue-eyed goddess Athena was equally willing.
So honored Hera, daughter of mighty Cronos,
Began to harness the horses with bridles of gold.
And Hebe, without hesitation, knocked the wheels
Of eight bronze spokes about the iron axle, projecting
On either side of the car. These wheels are of gold
Everlasting, with bronze outer rims, a wonder to see,
Their silver hubs on either side revolving.
The body is plaited with straps of gold and silver,   810
And running around above it is a double railing.
Now on the end of the chariot's silver shaft
Queen Hera bound the beautiful yoke of gold
And to it attached the golden breast-bands. Then eager
For war and the cries of battle, she led the fleet horses
Beneath the fair yoke.
        And Athena, daughter of aegis-great
Zeus, on the floor of her Father's palace, shed
The soft robe that she herself had made and embroidered,
Put on instead the tunic of stormy Zeus,   820
And armed herself for tearful war. About
Her shoulders she slung the terrible tasseled aegis
Encircled with Fear, inwrought with Hatred and Force
And the chilling War-charge, and crowned with the head of that
            horrible
Monster the Gorgon, most dread and awful emblem
Of aegis-great Zeus. And about her temples she put
Her golden helmet, four-horned and double-crested,
And richly engraved with figures of fighting men
From a hundred cities. Then she, the child of an almighty
Father, mounted the flaming car, gripping   830
The heavy huge spear with which she conquers whole armies
That have enraged her.
        Hera gave the horses a flick
With the lash, and the gates of heaven groaned on their hinges,
The self-opening gates which are kept by the Seasons, who have
In their keeping Olympus and all the wide sky, and who open
Or close the thick clouds as they see fit. On
Through the gates they drove their impatient horses, and found
Great Zeus sitting aloof from the other gods
On the highest peak of many-ridged Mount Olympus.   840
Then the white-armed goddess Hera pulled up the horses
And questioned Cronos' son thus, the lord most exalted:

"O Father Zeus, aren't you indignant at Ares
For this wanton violence of his, killing so many
Splendid Achaeans for no good reason at all?
I grieve for them greatly, but Cyprian Aphrodite
And silver-bowed Phoebus Apollo just loll around
Amusing themselves, having set this maniac on,
This raging monster completely oblivious of rules!
850 But Father Zeus, will you be angry at me
If I beat all the fight out of Ares and chase him from battle?"
         And Zeus of the gathering storm made this reply:
"No, be off. But send spoil-driving Athena
Against him. She's had the most practice at making him twinge!"
         He spoke, and the white-armed goddess Hera was glad
To obey. She lashed the horses, and they not at all
Unwilling, flew on between earth and the starry sky.
As far as a man can see who sits on a crag
And looks out over the wine-blue water and into
860 The hazy distance, so far at every bound
Gallop the gods' high-whinnying horses. But when
They reached the rivers of Troy, where the Simoeis joins
The Scamander, the white-armed goddess Hera pulled up
And unharnessed the horses and hid them both in thick mist,
While Simoeis caused to grow up ambrosia for them
To graze on. Then the goddesses made for the battle, quick stepping
Like two running doves, so eager were they to aid
The fighting men of Argos.
         When they reached the spot
870 Where most of the leaders were milling around horse-breaking
Strong Diomedes, pacing about like so many
Ravenous lions or wild inexhaustible boars,
The white-armed goddess Hera shouted thus,
Assuming the form of stout-hearted Stentor, whose great
Brazen voice has all the volume of fifty men shouting:
         "For shame, you miserable Argives, men only outwardly
Brave! While valiant Achilles took part in the fighting,
The men of Troy would not so much as come out
The Dardanian Gates, so deathly afraid were they
880 Of his heavy spear, but now far out from the city
They fight well-nigh at the hollow ships!"
         Her words
Encouraged them all. And the goddess Athena, her blue eyes
Blazing, sprang to the side of King Diomedes.
She found him beside his horses and car, cooling

The shoulder wound he had got from Pandarus' arrow,
For beneath the wide strap of his circular shield, the sweat
Was making it sting, and his throbbing arm was all
But worn out. So now he was lifting the baldric and wiping
Away the dark and clotted blood. Then laying   890
A hand on the yoke of his horses, the goddess spoke thus:
        "Not much like Tydeus is the son he begot! For Tydeus
Was little in build, but very large in battle.
Why even when I would not let him fight and show off
His prowess—that time he went on a mission to Thebes,
Alone mid many Cadmeans, and I explicitly
Told him to peacefully feast in their halls—even then
His old unquenchable spirit inspired him to challenge
And easily beat in every event the young athletes
Of Thebes, with me ever present and helping of course.   900
And surely no less I stand by you and protect you,
And urge you to battle the Trojans with all the spirit
You have. But now you're either exhausted from too many
Charges, or heartless terror has hold of you.
In that case, you are no son of Tydeus, the flame-hearted
Son of Oeneus!"
        Then strong Diomedes replied:
"I know you, goddess, the daughter of aegis-great Zeus.
Hence I'll speak to you gladly and cover up nothing.
No heartless terror has hold of me, nor shrinking   910
Of any kind. I'm merely mindful of orders
From you, not to contend with any immortal
Save only Zeus's daughter Aphrodite. You said
If she should enter the battle to give her a thrust
With my keen-cutting bronze! That's why I've now retreated
And ordered the other Argives to congregate here.
For that is Ares out there, I'm very sure,
Dominating the fighting!"
        And blue-eyed Athena:
"Tydeus' son Diomedes, delight of my heart,   920
Forget what I said and put your faith in my presence.
Have no fear of Ares or any immortal,
But drive at him now with your solid-hoofed horses. Close in
And strike him hard. You need not have awe of Ares,
That raving double-dealer, that curse made only
For evil! Why lately he talked with Hera and me
And promised us both he would fight the Trojans and help
The Argives. But now he's forgotten all that and falsely

Supports the Trojans!"

930   So saying, she reached out her hand
And jerked Sthenelus from the car to the ground. He quickly
Got out of the way as the eager goddess and brave
Diomedes stepped up in the car, and beneath the weight
Of that grim goddess and the prince of fighters the axle
Of oak creaked loudly. Then Pallas Athena caught up
The lash and the reins and galloped the solid-hoofed horses
At Ares, who spattered with blood was busy stripping
The bronze from gigantic Periphas, best of Aetolians
And glorious son of Ochesius.

940   Athena put on
Her helmet of darkness, that brawny Ares might not
Be able to see her. But now he saw Diomedes,
And ruinous Ares left the gigantic Periphas
Lying where he had undone him and fiercely charged
Diomedes, breaker of horses. When they closed with each other,
Ares lunged over yoke and reins to plant
His bronze spear in the foe, but the bright-eyed goddess Athena
Deflected the spear with her hand and flipped it away
From the car. Then strong Diomedes drove his spear

950 At the War-god, and Pallas Athena caused it to pierce
His armored kilt and tear the white flesh of his belly.
There he made his blow tell, and drew out the spear.
Then brazen Ares bellowed as loud as nine
Or ten thousand men who scream as they clash in battle.
And Achaeans and Trojans all trembled with fear, so terribly
Bellowed the bloodthirsty War-god. And as a tornado
Turns in the darkening sky when late on a hot
Summer day a gusty wind comes up, so now
To Tydeus' son Diomedes brazen Ares

960 Appeared, as upward he went through the clouds on his way
To broad heaven.

      Quickly he came to steep Olympus,
Home of the gods, and bitter at heart he sat down
By Zeus, displaying the immortal blood that poured
From his wound, and wailing out these words winged with resentment:
"O Father Zeus, aren't you indignant at all that
Wanton violence? Whenever we gods try helping
Men, we always end by hurting each other.
And now we are all at odds with you, for you

970 Are the Father of that insane and cursed virgin
Who cares for nothing but evil! All other gods

On Olympus obey and bow down to you, every one
Of us. But at her you never lash out with word
Or deed. Instead, you set her on, and just
Because the pestilent wretch is a child of yours.
Now she's encouraged proud Diomedes to take out
His rage on immortal gods. He's already wounded
Cyprian Aphrodite on the lower part
Of her palm and charged down on me like a demon! If I
Weren't fast on my feet, I'd have been there no telling how long,   980
All tangled up in the heaps of gory corpses.
Either that, or the blows I'd have got from his bronze would have
                    left me
A weakling forever!"
          Then fiercely scowling, Zeus
Of the gathering storm spoke thus: "Don't whine at me,
You renegade! To me you're the most despicable god
On Olympus, since always you're eager for strife and fighting
And war. You have the same overbearing spirit,
Hard and unyielding, as your mother Hera, and her
I can scarcely control with words alone. She,   990
I dare say, is the cause of your present pain. But I
Can't let you suffer this way any longer, for you too
Are my child, offspring of my wife. But had you been born
To some other immortal and become the plague you are now,
Long since you'd have found yourself lower than the battered sons
Of Uranus!"*
          He spoke, and told Paeëon to help him.
So the gods' physician applied some pain-killing ointments
And healed the wound, for Ares, of course, has nothing
Mortal about him. As fast as juice of the fig   1000
Curdles the thin white milk a man mixes and stirs,
Even so quickly Paeëon closed up the wound
Of impetuous Ares. And Hebe bathed him, and dressed him
In pleasing and comfortable clothes. Then Ares sat down
By Cronos' son Zeus, his same old vainglorious self.
          Now Argive Hera and Athena, defender of many,
Returned to the palace of almighty Zeus, having forced
Man-murdering Ares to stop his slaughter of mortals.

---

*Zeus refers to Cronos and the other Titans, who are imprisoned in Tartarus, the deep-
est level of the Underworld.

BOOK VI

Hector and Andromache

Thus the Achaeans and Trojans were left to themselves
In the awesome confusion of war, and the tumult surged
Now here, now there on the plain as the warriors hurled
At each other their bronze-headed spears, between the waters
Of Simoeis and the holy river Scamander.

Telamonian Ajax, bulwark of Achaeans, was first
To break the Trojan ranks and bring new light
To his comrades. This he did by downing the chief
Of Thracians, the tall brave Acamas, Eussorus' son.
10 His spear went in at the horn of his helmet, thickly
Crested with horsehair, and pierced the bone of his forehead,
And darkness enveloped his eyes.

Then Diomedes,
Roaring his chilling war-cry, killed Teuthras' son Axylus,
A rich and lovable man from splendid Arisbe,
Where he lived in a house by the road and welcomed all comers.
But now not one of his many friends was there
To meet his assailant and keep off dismal destruction.
Instead, Diomedes robbed him of life, along with
20 His squire Calesius, then at the reins of his car.
Together they entered the subterranean halls.

Dresus and Opheltius fell to the bronze of Euryalus,
Who then went on in pursuit of Aesepus and Pedasus.
These were the sons of the Naiad nymph Abarbarea
And peerless Bucolion, haughty Laomedon's first-born
Son, the child of a dark and secret affair.
While out with his sheep, Bucolion lay with the nymph,
Who conceived and bore twin sons. These now fell
To Mecisteus' son Euryalus, who undid the might
30 Of their marvelous limbs and stripped their shoulders of armor.

And battle-staunch Polypoetes brought Astyalus
Down, while Odysseus felled Percotian Pidytes,
And Teucer the brave Aretaon. And Ablerus died
On the gleaming spear of Nestor's son Antilochus,

And the king of men Agamemnon accounted for Elatus,
Whose home was in hilly Pedasus near the banks
Of the rolling river Satnioeis. And battling Leïtus
Laid fleeing Phylacus low, and Eurypylus killed
Melanthius.

    Meanwhile, battle-roaring Menelaus   40
Took Adrastus alive. For his two horses, panicking
Over the plain, ran foul of a tamarisk bush,
Broke off the shaft at the curving car, and continued
Their bolt for the city as part of the general stampede.
But their master spun from the car and fell on his face
In the dust by one of the wheels. And there above him
Stood King Menelaus, his long spear casting a shadow.
Then clutching the knees of his captor,[1] Adrastus pleaded:

    "Alive! O son of Atreus, take me alive!
And an ample ransom is yours. Stored in the mansion   50
Of my rich father are many treasures, bronze
And gold and highly wrought iron. Of these my father
Would gladly give you a ransom past counting, if he
Should hear that I am alive at the ships of Achaea."

    Thus he tried to persuade Menelaus, and he
Was just on the point of letting his squire lead
The man off to the swift Argive ships, when King Agamemnon
Ran up with this loud rebuke: "Soft Menelaus!
What do you care for the Trojans? Did they do you
Any favors that time they stayed in your home? Let none   60
Of them escape unholy destruction from us—
Not even the baby in his mother's belly! No,
Not even him, but let all Trojans utterly
Perish, unmourned, unburied, and leaving no trace!"

    These words made sense to his brother, so fierce Menelaus,
With a thrust of his hand, shoved the hero Adrastus away,
And powerful King Agamemnon jabbed a spear
In his side and flopped him down on his back, then planted
A heel on his chest and jerked the ashen spear out.

    Now Nestor yelled to the Argive soldiers: "My friends,   70
Danaan heroes and comrades of Ares, let no man
Drop behind, greedy to pounce on the spoils
And go to the ships with the heaviest load of loot!
But keep on killing men. Then at your ease
You can strip the armor from a whole plain full of corpses!"

    At this they fought even harder. And now the fiery
Achaeans would surely have driven the terrified Trojans

Back up into Troy, if Priam's son Helenus, much
Their best reader of ominous birds, had not found Aeneas
80 And Hector and said to them; "You two are the best men
We have, and always bear the brunt of the fighting
And do far more than your share of the thinking, which is why
I plead with you now to make a stand right here!
Go through the ranks and rally the men and keep them
Away from the gates, or believe me they won't stop running
Till they give their pursuers the pleasure of seeing them drop
In the arms of their women. But once you have rallied the army,
I'm sure we'll be able to hold out here against
The Danaan forces. No matter how worn-out and weary
90 We are, we have to hold out and we will! But Hector,
You go to the city and speak to our mother. Tell her
To gather the noble women and go to the temple
Of bright-eyed Athena high on the fortified hill.
And let her take with her the finest, most flowing robe
In the palace, the one she prefers to all others. Then,
When the holy doors have been opened by means of the key,
Let her lay the robe on the knees of fair-haired Athena
And promise to sacrifice there in her temple twelve yearling
Heifers untouched by the goad, if only the goddess
100 Will pity our town, our wives and little children,
And keep Diomedes away from holy Troy,
Tydeus' son Diomedes, that brutal spearman
And powerful master of rout who has, I think,
Shown clearly that he is the strongest Achaean of all.
We were never so much afraid of Achilles himself,
Though he is a leader of fighting men and the son,
They say, of a goddess. But this Diomedes raves
With a furious vengeance! When it comes to brute force, he has
No real competition."
110   He spoke, and Hector was glad
To accept the advice of his brother, the gifted seer.
At once he leaped fully armed from his car to the ground,
And brandishing two sharp spears he ranged through the ranks
Arousing new spirit in the horrible rout. They spun
And faced the Achaeans, who soon fell back before them
And ceased their killing. They thought some immortal had come
From the starry sky and enabled the fighting Trojans
Thus to rally. Then Hector called out to the host:
        "You gallant Trojans and famous allies, be men,
120 My friends, and show the stuff you're made of, while I

Go into Ilium and bid Our wives and counseling
Elders pray to the gods and promise them hecatombs."
    So saying, bright-helmeted Hector left for the city,
And the black hide rim of his center-bossed shield knocked neck
And ankles as swiftly he strode.
    Now Glaucus, son
Of Hippolochus, and Tydeus' son Diomedes rode out
In the middle between the two armies, both men eager
To fight. When they came within range Diomedes, loud
At the war-cry, shouted first: "Who are you, big man,   130
Who among mortals? Never before have I seen you
In man-enhancing battle, but now you dare
To come out so far beyond all the others and await
My long-shadowing spear, though they are unhappy indeed
Whose children oppose me! But if you are some immortal
Come down from the sky, I will not fight you, nor
Any other heavenly god. Not even the son
Of Dryas, brawny Lycurgus,[2] lived long after strife
With celestials—he who drove the Maenad nurses
Of mad Dionysus running down holy Mount Nysa.   140
He took an ox-goad to them, and beneath his flailing
They dropped their ivy wands, and Dionysus himself
Fled and plunged in the sea, where he with the waves
Far above him cringed in the bosom of Thetis, trembling
With dread at the threatening screams of Lycurgus. For this
The leisurely gods all hated that man, and Zeus
Struck him blind, nor did he live long after that, so fiercely
Despised was he by all the immortals. I, then,
Have no desire to fight with the blessed gods.
But if you're a man, sustained by fruit of the earth,   150
Keep coming on, that you may be caught all the sooner
In the terrible toils of death!"
    Then Hippolochus' son,
Great Glaucus, answered him thus: "Magnanimous Diomedes,
Why do you ask who I am? The frail generations
Of men have scarcely more lineage than leaves. Wind blows
The leaves to earth in the fall, but springtime comes
And the forest blooms: so one generation of men
Gives way to another.[3] But if you really would hear
Who I am, listen and learn what many know   160
Already. In the heart of horse-pasturing Argos is the city
Ephyre, where Sisyphus ruled, Sisyphus, son
Of Aeolus and the slyest of men. He begot

The first Glaucus, whose son was the flawless Bellerophon. Him
The gods made handsome and showered with masculine charm.
But Proetus the King plotted evil against him, and since
His might was much greater, drove him from the Argive country.
For Zeus had brought all Argos under the scepter
Of Proetus, whose wrath began this way. Anteia,
170   His beautiful wife, lusted madly to lie with Bellerophon[4]
In secret love, but she could in no way seduce
That princely, prudent young man. Hence, she made up
A lie and told it thus to her husband the King:
'If you don't want to die, O Proetus, kill Bellerophon.
Though I wouldn't let him, he did his best to seduce me.'
At this the King was seized with rage, but since
His soul recoiled from murdering a guest, he sent him
To Lycia instead, where Anteia's father was King.
And grievous credentials he gave the young man to take with him,
180   A folded tablet wherein lord Proetus had written
Many pernicious and fatal signs, which he bade
Bellerophon show to the Lycian King—who would then
Contrive his death.
          "So he, with the gods' unfailing
Protection, journeyed to Lycia, and when he reached
That wide land and the flowing Xanthus, the King made him welcome
And heartily entertained him for all of nine days
With as many sacrificed oxen. But when, on the tenth
Dim morning, rose-fingered Dawn appeared, the King
190   At last got around to asking about the credentials
His guest may have brought from Proetus his son-in-law.
Then, having seen the murderous signs, he began
By bidding Bellerophon kill the ferocious Chimaera,
A female demoniac monster of strictly inhuman
Descent, with the head of a lion, the tail of a serpent,
And the body of a monstrous goat, and blasting forth flame
At every terrible breath. But putting his faith
In the portents of heaven, Bellerophon killed her. Next
He fought the redoubtable Solymi, who according to him
200   Were the roughest fighters he ever encountered. And thirdly
He slew the man-matching Amazons. But around him, as he
Returned, the King wove another thick plot. He sent
The best troops in all Lycia to lay an ambush for him,
But not one man returned to his home, for all
Were destroyed by flawless Bellerophon. Then, when at last
The King knew that his guest was of godly descent, he prevailed

Upon him to stay in Lycia, gave him his daughter
In marriage, and equally shared all royal honor
With him. And the Lycians laid out an estate for him
Greater than any other, acres of orchard   210
And plowland for him to enjoy.
          "And the Princess bore
To honored Bellerophon three children in all: Isander,
Hippolochus, and Laodameia, who lay with Zeus
The contriver and became the mother of godlike Sarpedon,
Our bronze-clad leader of Lycians. But when Bellerophon,
Even he, found all the gods in hatred
Against him, he roamed alone the Aleian Plain,
Consuming his soul and avoiding all human tracks.[5]
His son Isander was killed by war-hungry Ares   220
While fighting the powerful Solymi, and Artemis, she
Of the golden reins, wrathfully slew his daughter.
That left Hippolochus, who fathered me, and from him
I claim to be sprung. He sent me to Troy with many
Stern reminders to always be bravest and best
Above all others, and not to disgrace the house
Of my fathers, by far the noblest in Ephyre
Or the ample land of Lycia. Such is my lineage
And the blood I claim to be of."
          This speech delighted   230
Diomedes, the great battle-roarer. Planting his spear
In the bountiful earth, he spoke these friendly words
To the people's shepherd Glaucus: "Surely our families
Have an old tradition of friendship. For once my grandfather
Oeneus entertained yours, the flawless Bellerophon,
And kept him a guest in his palace for twenty days.
And they gave each other exquisite gifts of friendship.
Oeneus gave a brilliant red war-belt, and Bellerophon
A golden two-handled cup, which I left at home
When I came here. But I don't remember my father Tydeus,   240
Since I was too small when he set out for Thebes,
Where he died with the other fighting Achaeans. So now
You have a good friend in the middle of Argos, and I one
In Lycia, if ever I visit your people's country.
Let us, then, strictly avoid the spears of each other,
No matter how thick the melee. For me there are plenty
Of Trojans and famous allies to slay, whomever
God grants and I overtake, and for you there are all
The Achaeans you can manage to kill. Therefore, my friend,

250 Let us exchange our armor, that both sides may know
     Of the old family friendship we claim from the time our grandfathers
     Feasted together."
              Having so spoken, they leaped
     From their chariots, shook hands, and swore their faith to each other.
     But Cronos' son Zeus took the wits from Glaucus completely,
     For to Tydeus' son Diomedes he gave golden armor
     For bronze, or a hundred oxen for nine.[6]
              When Hector
     Got to the Scaean Gates* and the oak tree, the daughters
260 And wives of the Trojans came flocking about him, anxiously
     Asking of sons and brothers, friends and husbands.
     But Hector bade them go pray to the gods, to each
     Of the gods in turn, for mourning hung over many.
              On he strode to the gorgeous palace of Priam
     With gleaming stone colonnades. Within the court
     Were fifty adjoining chambers of polished stone,
     Wherein the sons of Priam slept with the wives
     They had courted and won. And for his daughters, across
     From these were twelve more chambers adjoining and built
270 Of well-polished stone, wherein the sons-in-law
     Of Priam slept with their honored, desirable wives.
              Now Hector's mother, the gracious Hecuba, came out
     To meet him, and with her Laodice, her loveliest daughter.
     She took her son by the hand and spoke to him thus:
     "My child, why have you left the hard fighting and come here
     To us? Surely the sons of the cursed Achaeans
     Have worn you out in this battle around our city
     And you have decided to lift your hands to Zeus
     In earnest prayer from high on top of the citadel.
280 But wait till I bring you honey-sweet wine, that first
     You may pour a libation to Zeus and the other immortals
     And refresh yourself too, if you will. Wine greatly increases
     The strength of a weary man, as you now are weary
     From defending your friends."
              But the tall bright-helmeted Hector
     Answered her thus: "Bring me no heart-soothing wine,
     Good mother. It might unnerve me and make me forget
     My spirit and strength. And besides, with hands unwashed
     I stand in awe of pouring to Zeus a libation

---

*The Scaean Gates of Troy face the battlefield and are a regular observation point.

Of flaming wine, nor should a man ever pray   290
To the stormy son of Cronos when all bespattered
With blood and gore. But gather the noble women
And go to the temple of victory-bringing Athena.
Go with offerings to burn on her altar and the finest,
Most flowing robe you have in the palace, the one
You prefer to all others. Lay this on the knees of Athena,
The lovely-haired goddess, and promise to sacrifice there
In her temple twelve yearling heifers untouched by the goad,
If only she will pity our town, our wives
And little children, and keep Diomedes away   300
From holy Troy, Tydeus' son Diomedes,
That brutal spearman and powerful master of rout.
Go, then, to the shrine of the spoil-driving goddess Athena,
And I will go to call Paris, if the man will listen
To me. Would earth might open and swallow him now,
For he was reared by the mighty Olympian to bring
Great pain to magnanimous Priam, to the sons of Priam,
And to all the other Trojans. The sight of Paris
Headed for Hades might make me think my heart
Had forgotten its misery."   310
        He spoke and Hecuba went
To the hall and told her handmaids to go through the city
And gather the noble women. But she herself
Went down to the fragrant chamber wherein she kept
Her richly wrought robes, made and embroidered by women
Of Sidon whom royal Paris brought in his ships
To Troy on the same sea-voyage from which he returned
With high-born Helen.* Now Hecuba took the most flowing
And richly embroidered of all and carried it with her,
A gift for Athena. It lay beneath all the others,   320
But now like a star it glittered. Then off she went,
And many were the noble women who hurried along
In her train.
        When they reached Athena's temple on top
Of the fortified hill, the doors were opened for them
By Theano, lovely of face, the daughter of Cisseus
And wife of Antenor. For she was Athena's priestess,
Made such by will of the Trojans. Then all of them raised
The sacred cry and lifted their hands to Athena,

---

*Paris and Helen seem to have sailed to Troy by way of Phoenicia.

330 And lovely Theano laid the robe on the knees
    Of the fair-haired goddess and made their vows in prayer
    To almighty Zeus's daughter:
            "O saver of cities,
    Great Athena, of goddesses most resplendent,
    Splinter the spear of fierce Diomedes and grant
    That he himself may fall face down in the dust
    Well out from the Scaean Gates, and we will sacrifice
    Here and now in your temple twelve yearling heifers
    Untouched by the goad, praying for you to take pity
340 On Troy and the Trojans' wives and little children."
            Thus she prayed to Zeus's unheeding daughter,
    Pallas Athena deaf to their plea. But Hector,
    Meanwhile, went to the house of handsome Paris,
    The beautiful palace that he himself had built
    With the most skillful craftsmen in the fertile land of Troy.
    These had made him a bedroom, a hall, and a courtyard
    High in the citadel close to the mansions of Priam
    And Hector, the valiant god-cherished Hector, who swinging
    A sixteen-foot spear now entered the house of his brother,
350 And always before him the spearhead of bronze shone brightly
    And the ring of gold that held it. Paris he found
    In the bedroom, shuffling his gorgeous armor, handling
    His breastplate, shield, and bent bow, while Helen of Argos
    Sat in the midst of her maids instructing them all
    In their marvelous handwork. Then Hector spoke to him roughly,
    Shaming him thus:
            "Unaccountable man! your sulking
    This way is not very pretty, believe me! Your people
    Are fighting and dying about the steep wall of the city,
360 And it is solely on your unhappy account
    That the roaring battle blazes. Why you yourself
    Would quarrel with any shirker you saw holding back
    From the horrible fighting. But up! Or the city itself
    Will soon be fiercely blazing!"
            And Prince Alexander
    Replied: "Hector, you chide me no more than is right,
    And not a bit more than you should. But do calm down
    And listen to me. It's not on account of resentment
    Against the Trojans that I sit here in my chamber,
370 Not really. It's just that I felt like indulging my sorrow.
    Already my wife, in her own winsome way, has endeavored
    To change my mind and talk me back out on the field.

And I myself have decided to go: a man
Can't always lose. But have a seat. I'm putting
My armor on now. Or go ahead if you wish
And I will follow. I think I'll be able to catch up
With you."
      Since now bright-helmeted Hector said nothing,
Helen spoke to him sweetly: "Believe me, dear brother,
Cold and troublesome bitch that I am, I heartily   380
Wish that some malevolent storm had whirled me
Away on the very same day my mother bore me,
Far away to some wild mountain or into
The waves of the loud-booming sea, where I might have died
Before any of this ever happened. But since the gods
Ordained these horrors, I also wish I had been
The wife of a better man, one who was sensitive
To insult and blame from his fellows. The heart of my husband
Is wavering and weak, nor will it ever be firm—
A fault, I think, for which he will pay! But now,   390
My brother, come here and sit down in this chair, for you
Above all others have burdened your spirit with toil
Because of bitch-hearted me and the willful blindness
Of Paris, whom Zeus decreed a miserable doom for,
That men in days to come might have a song."
      Then tall bright-helmeted Hector: "You're kind
To ask me to sit, Helen, but don't. I cannot accept.
Already my spirit is spoiling to fight for the Trojans,
Who always miss me keenly when I am not
On the field. But try to hurry this husband of yours,   400
And may he himself make haste and catch up with me
Before I leave the city. Meanwhile, I want
To go home and briefly look in on my servants and family,
The wife I love and my baby son, whom I
May never, for all I know, come back to again,
Since any time the gods may hurl me down
Beneath the hands of Achaeans."
      So saying, Hector
Left them, his helmet flashing, and quickly arrived
At his comfortable home. But there he did not find   410
His white-armed wife Andromache. She, with the baby
And one of her pretty-robed women, had gone to stand
On the wall, and there she was now, weeping and frantically
Anxious. When Hector saw that his excellent wife
Was out, he stopped on the threshold and spoke to the maids:

"Tell me truly, women. Where did Andromache go
When she left the house? Is she visiting one of my elegant
Sisters or sisters-in-law, or has she gone
To the shrine of Athena, where the other fair-braided women
420 Of Troy are making their vows to the awesome goddess?"
       Then the busy housekeeper answered him thus: "Hector,
To tell the truth you so urgently ask for, your wife
Has not gone to see any one of your elegant sisters
Or sisters-in-law, nor has she gone to the shrine
Of Athena, where the other fair-braided women of Troy
Are making their vows to the awesome goddess. She heard
The Trojans were yielding to the powerful men of Achaea
And ran from the house toward the great city wall like a woman
Half out of her senses, and the nurse took the baby and followed."
430   The housekeeper spoke, and Hector rushed from the palace
And back through the well-laid streets the way he had come,
Striding down through the great city. But just as he got
To the Scaean Gates, through which he intended to pass
On his way to the plain, his wife came running to meet him,
His gifted wife Andromache, daughter of hearty
Eëtion, who lived at the foot of wooded Mount Placus
In Hypoplacian Thebe and ruled the men
Of Cilicia. His daughter it was whom Hector had married,
And now she met her helmeted husband, and with her
440 The nurse came holding the child, great Hector's dear son,
A laughing baby fair as any bright star.
His father called him Scamandrius,* but others Astyanax,
Or Lord of the City, with reference to his tall father
On whom alone the safety of all depended.
Hector smiled at the sight of his son, but Andromache
Fairly grew to his arm, and weeping spoke thus:
       "Ah, Hector, possessed by a demon, your might as a fighter
Will be the death of you yet. Nor do you pity
Your baby boy and my unfortunate self,
450 So soon to be your widow, for any time now
The Achaeans will gang up and kill you, I know. But I
Would be better off in my grave, were I to lose you,
For once you have met your fate, never again
Can there be any warmth in my life, nor anything else

---

*Hector named his son after the principal river of Troy, the Scamander.

But pain. I have no father, no lady mother.
My father was killed by fierce Achilles when he
So utterly sacked the Cilicians' teeming city,
High-gated Thebe. He killed Eëtion, yes,
But even his spirit recoiled at stripping that King
Of his armor. So him he burned in his richly wrought bronze   460
And heaped a high barrow above him, and all about it
The mountain nymphs, daughters of Zeus of the aegis,
Planted elm trees. And the seven brothers I had
At home went down to Hades the very same day,
For right in the midst of their shuffling cattle and silvery
White sheep, quick-footed Achilles killed them all.
But here he brought my mother the Queen, torn
From below our wooded Mount Placus along with the rest
Of the spoils. Then having extorted a ransom past counting,
He let her go to her father's house where she died   470
A victim of arrow-scattering Artemis. So you,
My Hector, are father and mother to me, and brother
And manly husband. Have pity, then, and stay
Right here on the wall, or truly your son will soon
Be an orphan, your wife a miserable widow. And order
The army to make a stand at the fig tree, where the city
Is best assaulted and the wall most easily scaled.[7]
Three times already their bravest men have charged there,
Led by the two Ajaxes, world-famous Idomeneus,
Atreus' sons, and strong Diomedes—all   480
Kept trying to get at us there, as if some knowing
Seer had told them our weakness, or they themselves
Had guessed it."
              Then great bright-helmeted Hector replied:
"I too, my dear, have all these things on my mind.
But how could I face the men of Troy, or their wives
Of the trailing gowns, if I were to skulk like a coward[8]
And stay away from the battle? Nor does my own spirit
Urge me to do so, since I have learned to be valiant
Always and fight mid the foremost champions of Troy,   490
To win and uphold the King my father's glory
As well as my own. For this one thing in heart
And soul I know: the day of ruin shall surely
Come for holy Troy, for Priam and all
The people of Priam, who wielded the good ashen spear.
But when I think of the suffering the Trojans will have to

Endure, of Hecuba's grief and that of King Priam,
And of my many brave brothers who shall on that day
Go down in the dust, slain by those who hate them,
500 I am not troubled so deeply as at the thought
Of your grief when some bronze-clad Achaean leads you off
Weeping and puts an end to your freedom. Then
In Argos you'll weave at the loom of somebody else
And carry water for her from the spring Messeïs
Or Hypereia, unwillingly always, but forced
To do as you're told. Then someone, seeing your tears,
Will say: 'Look there at the wife of Hector, the best
In battle of all the horse-taming Trojans in the war
We fought about Ilium!' So then will someone remark.
510 And stabbing new grief will surely be yours to think
Of losing that man who could have held off the day
Of your bondage. But I'd much rather be dead, with earth
Heaped high above me, than hear your screams as warriors
Drag you away to a life of slavery!"

     So saying,
Resplendent Hector reached out to take his son,
But the baby cried and clung to the fair-belted nurse,
Afraid of the way his own father looked, with all
That bronze and the horsehair crest dreadfully waving
520 On top of his helmet. This made them both laugh, his father
And lady mother, and quickly resplendent Hector
Took off his helmet and laid the dazzling thing down.
Then he took the baby and kissed him, bounced him a bit
In his arms, and prayed this prayer to all of the gods:

     "O Zeus and you other immortals, grant that my son
May be, like myself, outstanding among the Trojans,
As strong as I and as brave, and a mighty ruler
Of Ilium. And may it be said of him someday, as home
He comes from battle, 'There goes a much better man
530 Than his father.' Let him be bearing the blood-stained bronze
Of an enemy slain, and may he rejoice the heart
Of his mother."

     He prayed, and placed the child in the arms
Of his wife, and she held him close in her fragrant bosom,
Laughing and crying at once. Seeing her so,
Her husband felt deep compassion, and gently caressed her,
Saying: "Poor haunted one, do not be overly
Anxious. No man in the world can hurl me to Hades

Before my appointed time comes. And no man, valiant
Or vile, can escape his fate ordained, once he's been   540
Born. So go to the house and keep yourself busy
With the loom and spindle, and see that your maids are busy.
War is for men, my dear, for all men here
In Ilium, but most of all for me."

      So saying,
Resplendent Hector picked up his helmet with the horsehair
Plume, and his dear wife started for home, shedding
Big tears and often looking behind her. But soon
She arrived at the comfortable home of man-killing Hector
And found her numerous maids inside. Her coming   550
Made all of them join her in wailing lament for Hector.
So there in his house they mourned for Hector still living,
For none of them thought he would ever return, once
He fell into the violent hands of Achaeans.

      Now Paris
Did not linger long in his palace, but trusting his swiftness
Of foot he donned his elaborate bronze and set out.
As when a horse at the manger eats his fill
Of barley, breaks his halter, and thunders away
On the plain, eager to splash in the rippling river—   560
He throws back his head, and his mane streams over his shoulders
As he exults in his splendor and gallops full speed
For the grazing grounds of mares—so Priam's son Paris
Strode down from the citadel heights, laughing aloud
To himself and bright as the sun in his glittering armor.
Rapidly walking, he quickly caught up with his brother,
Brave Hector, just on the point of turning away
From where he had talked with his wife. Then handsome Paris
Spoke first:

      "Surely, old fellow, I've held you back,   570
And you so anxious to get there. I took too long,
I know, and wasn't as fast as you told me to be."

      And Hector, his helmet flashing, made this reply:
"My playful brother, no right-thinking man would belittle
Your prowess in battle. You're brave enough when you want
To be, but only too often you let yourself go
And don't seem to care. That attitude pains me deeply,
Nor does it help when I hear the Trojan fighters
Insulting you right and left, the men who suffer
Hard battle on your account. But come, let us go.   580

We'll make all this up to each other yet, if only
Zeus grants us the power to rid our Trojan land
Of the well-greaved Achaeans. Then we shall mix in our halls
The bowl of deliverance to the heavenly gods everlasting."

BOOK VII

The Duel of Hector and Ajax

So saying, resplendent Hector rushed out through the gates
And with him his brother Paris, both of them eager
At heart for fighting and war. As a god-sent wind
Is welcome to longing seamen, exhausted from beating
The deep with their oars of polished pine, their limbs
Already leaden, so now to the longing Trojans
These two appeared.
    Then Paris cut down Menesthius,
King Areïthous' son, whose home was in Arne,
Where he had been born to Areïthous surnamed the Maceman   10
And heifer-eyed Phylomedusa. And Hector's sharp spear
Loosened the limbs of Eïoneus, striking the man
On the neck right under the rim of his strong bronze helmet.
And Glaucus, leader of Lycians and son of Hippolochus,
Hurled his spear through the furious moil at Iphinous,
Dexius' son, and caught him deep in the shoulder
Just as he sprang on the car behind his fast horses.
He fell to the ground, his strength completely destroyed.
    But when the goddess Athena noticed this slaughter
Of Argives there in the thick of the struggle, her blue eyes   20
Blazed, and down she went darting from the peaks of Olympus
To holy Troy. Then Apollo on Pergamus looked down
And saw her, and eager for Trojans to win he sprang down
To meet her. The deities met at the oak tree, and the son
Of Zeus, lord Apollo, spoke first:
              "Why, O daughter
Of almighty God, does your great spirit impel you
Once more in such hot haste from Olympus? Is it
To throw your power on the Danaan side and give
The victory to them? since surely you have no compassion   30
At all for dying Trojans. But if you will let yourself
Listen to me, all will turn out for the best.
Let us now put an end to this day's fiery battle.
Later the war will go on till you deathless goddesses

111

Get the dear wish of your hearts and Ilium falls
For your favorites to plunder and waste.
          And the blue-eyed goddess
Athena answered him thus: "Far-worker, so be it.
With this very thought in mind I came down here
40   From Olympus to the midst of Achaeans and Trojans. But tell me,
How do you intend to stop these fighting men?"
          And Zeus's son, lord Apollo, replied: "Let us rouse
The bold heart of horse-breaking Hector on the very good chance
That he will then challenge the Danaan chiefs for a man
To meet him in the awesome grim fire of single combat.
That challenge the bronze-greaved Achaeans will be too proud
To ignore. They'll send out a man to fight noble Hector."
          He spoke, and the bright-eyed goddess Athena approved.
And Helenus, dear son of Priam, knew in his heart
50   This favored plan of the plotting gods. So he came up
To Hector and said: "O son of Priam, Hector
Divinely wise, consider these words from your brother.
Make all other Trojans sit down and all the Achaeans,
Then challenge the best man they've got to come out and fight
With you in the awesome grim fire of single combat.
As yet it isn't your fate to overtake doom
And die. This I heard from the gods everlasting."
          At these words Hector rejoiced, and going into
The midst of the battle he gripped his spear by the middle
60   And held the Trojan line back till all were seated.
And King Agamemnon seated the well-greaved Achaeans.
Athena and bright-bowed Apollo in the likeness of vultures
Sat high on the oak of aegis-great Zeus, their Father,
Delightedly watching the men sitting close in their ranks,
The battalions bristling with spears and helmets and shields.
And as the West Wind rises and darkens the deep
With ripples, so stirred on the plain the seated ranks
Of Achaeans and Trojans. Then Hector walked out between
The two armies, and spoke:
70   "Your attention, O Trojans and well-greaved
Achaeans, that I may say what now my heart urges.
Zeus who looks down from on high has not seen fit
To fulfill the oaths we so earnestly swore. He cruelly
Postpones the final decision till either you Argives
Conquer the high walls of Troy or fall in defeat
By your seagoing ships. But you that are champions and chieftains
Among the united Achaeans, whichever one

Whose heart now urges him on to fight with Prince Hector,
Let him come out of the crowd and be your champion.
And these conditions I hereby proclaim with Zeus   80
As our witness. If your man slays me with the long sharp point
Of his bronze, let him strip off my armor and carry it back
To the hollow ships, but let him give up my body
To be taken home, that the men and women of Troy
May duly burn it. And if Apollo gives me
The glory of slaying the man you send out, I'll strip off
His armor, carry it into the city, and hang it
Up on the temple of lord far-smiting Apollo,
But I will release his corpse to be taken back
To the well-decked ships, that you, the long-haired Achaeans,   90
May give him all due funeral rites and build a high barrow
For him beside the wide Hellespont. Then one of these days
Somebody, as he goes by in his many-oared ship
On the wine-blue sea, will point toward shore and say:
'There rises the barrow of one who died long ago,
A champion whom glorious Hector battled and slew.'
Thus indeed somebody will say, and so men's memory
Of me and my glory will not be destroyed."[1]

      He spoke,
And an awful hush fell on the Achaeans, one   100
And all ashamed to refuse, but afraid to accept.
At last Menelaus stood up and spoke, harshly
Rebuking the men and inwardly groaning: "Well now,
You braggarts, women, not men, of Achaea! surely
We'll have a disgrace on our heads to end all disgraces
If now no Danaan goes to meet Hector! May all
Of you rot and go back to mud, you that just sit here
Utterly gutless and infamous! I'll arm and go
Against him myself. The immortal gods on high
Hold all the strings of victory."   110

      So saying, he started
To don his fine armor. And now, Menelaus, life
For you would have ended out there at the hands of Hector,
A mightier man by far, had not the kings
Of Achaea leaped to their feet and held you back.
And great Agamemnon himself seized the right hand
Of his brother, and said:

      "You're mad! Zeus-fed Menelaus.
This folly of yours is completely uncalled for. Swallow
Your pride and back down. Why should you want to fight   120

A match with one so much better than you? Nor are you
Alone in dreading Priam's son Hector. Why this
Is one chief whom even Achilles shudders to meet
In the hero-enhancing battle, and he is far stronger
Than you. So go sit down with your people and friends.
The Achaeans shall find someone else to be their champion
Today. Fearless though Hector may be and greedy
For battle, he will I assure you be glad to sit down,
That is if he ever escapes the awesome grim fire
130 Of this hard fight he has asked for."
     So spoke Agamemnon,
And changed the mind of his brother. Menelaus obeyed,
For he knew the truth when he heard it, and happy squires
Were quick to remove the bronze from his shoulders. Then Nestor
Arose and spoke to the Argives:
     "What a disgrace!
Now indeed great grief has come on Achaea. Think how
The knightly old Peleus would groan, that worthy counselor
Of Myrmidons, that eloquent speaker, who questioned me once
140 In his palace and asked with great pleasure concerning the birth
And lineage of all the Argives. If he should hear
That now those very same men, one and all, were cringing
At Hector, surely he'd lift his arms many times
In fervent pleas to the immortal gods that his soul
Might leave his limbs and enter the house of Hades.
O Father Zeus, Athena, and Apollo, if only
I were as young as when[2] the Pylians met
The Arcadians, fierce with their spears, by the rapid waters
Of Celadon and fought with them in front of the walls
150 Of Pheia about the streams of Iardanus. Then out strode
Their godlike champion, huge Ereuthalion, wearing
The armor of King Areïthous, brave Areïthous
Surnamed the Maceman and so referred to by others,
Both men and their fair-belted wives. For he did not fight
With bow or long spear, but broke up the ranks with an iron
Battle-mace. And it was by cunning, not might, that Lycurgus
Killed him, in a narrow pass where there wasn't room
To swing his iron mace with the usual speed. Before
He was ready, Lycurgus was on him, and thrusting his spear
160 Through the Maceman's belly he hurled him backwards to earth.
And Lycurgus stripped off the armor which the fallen man
Had been given by brazen Ares, and he himself wore it
Thereafter amid the turmoil of battle. But when

Lycurgus grew old in his halls, he gave the armor
To Ereuthalion, his comrade and squire. And he
Had it on that day when he challenged our bravest and best.
But all of them shook with terror, nor would anyone go
Against him. But my perdurable spirit gave me
The daring to fight him, though I was the youngest man there.
So fight him I did, and Athena gave me the glory.   170
He was the hugest and mightiest man that I
Ever slew, and seemed to sprawl all over the field.
If only I were that young again and as sure
Of my brawn, then soon enough bright-helmeted Hector
Would have a fight on his hands. But you the chieftains
Of all the Achaeans, not one of you has spirit enough
To go against Hector and meet him in single combat!"

    The old man's rebuke brought nine men in all to their feet.
Far the first to arise was the king of men Agamemnon,
Followed by strong Diomedes, son of Tydeus,   180
And both Ajaxes, furious valor incarnate,
And after these Idomeneus and Idomeneus' comrade
Meriones, peer of the slaughtering god of battles,
And after these Eurypylus, splendid son
Of Euaemon, Andraemon's son Thoas, and keen Odysseus.
All were willing to fight great Hector. But now
Horse-driving Gerenian Nestor addressed them again:

    "You'll have to cast lots to see who the chosen will be.
For he shall profit the well-greaved Achaeans and greatly
Enhance his own soul as well, if indeed he survives   190
The awesome grim fire of single combat."

    He spoke,
And each of them put his mark on a pebble and dropped
The lot in the helmet of Atreus' son Agamemnon.
Meanwhile the army all prayed, lifting their hands
To the gods. And thus would one say, looking up to broad heaven:

    "O Father Zeus, let it be Ajax, please,
Or Tydeus' son Diomedes, or the great commander
Himself, Agamemnon, lord of golden Mycenae."

    So prayed the men, and when horse-driving Gerenian   200
Nestor shook the helmet, out leaped the lot
They wanted most, that of the greater Ajax.
This a herald took round through the host from left
To right and showed it to all the Achaean chieftains.
None of them knew it, and each of them said so. But when
He reached the man who had marked it and dropped it in,

Then glorious Ajax held out his hand and the herald
Gave him the lot. One look at the mark and Ajax
Knew it was his. Then heartily glad, he dropped
210 The pebble and said:
        "My friends, the lot is surely
Mine, and glad I am that it is, for I
Believe I shall conquer excellent Hector. But come,
While I am donning my war-gear, spend the time praying
To Cronos' son Zeus, silently now to yourselves,
So that the Trojans won't know what you're doing—or pray
Aloud if you like, since we are afraid of no one!
Not by force shall any man beat and rout me,
Nor for that matter by skill, since surely not
220 For nothing was I in Salamis born and brought up."
        He spoke, and again the Achaeans prayed to Lord Zeus,
The son of Cronos. And thus, looking up to broad heaven,
Would one of them say: "O Father Zeus, most great,
Most glorious lord, give victory to Ajax and splendid
Renown, but if you also love Hector, if
You care for him too, grant equal power and glory
To both."
        While they were praying, Ajax put on
His glittering bronze. Then fully armed, he charged
230 To the fight as fiercely as monstrous Ares enters
A battle of armies that Zeus has made clash in the fury
Of heart-eating hatred. So now gigantic Ajax,
Bulwark of Achaeans, charged out with the grimmest of smiles
On his face, and shaking his lance that cast the long shadow
He rushed to meet his opponent. And the Argives thrilled
With joy at the sight, but there was no Trojan whose legs
Did not tremble, and Hector's own heart began to leap
In his breast. But he who had issued that confident challenge
Had no hope at all of running, or losing himself
240 In the crowd behind him. So on Ajax came, bearing
His shield like a tower, his seven layers of bull's-hide
Fronted with bronze, made with much labor for him
By Tychius, best of workers in leather. At home
In Hyle he had made that flashing shield, using
The hides of seven great bulls and hammering on
An eighth strong layer of bronze. This shield Telamonian
Ajax held before him as he came up close
To Hector and threatened him thus:

"Now, Hector, you'll know
Face to face what sort of Danaan leaders there are   250
Besides lion-hearted, man-mauling Achilles. He lies
Mid his beaked seagoing ships withdrawn in his wrath
Against our commander-in-chief Agamemnon. But still
There is no lack of men to stand up against you. Many
Were eager to do so. But go ahead and begin!"
    Then tall bright-helmeted Hector answered him thus:
"Zeus-sprung Telamonian Ajax, I know that you captain
Your company, but do not treat me like some puny boy
Or some unwarlike woman. My knowledge of fighting
And slaughter is great, and I am skillful indeed   260
At wielding to left and to right my seasoned hide shield,
At handling tough hide as only a good warrior can.
And I am expert at darting in deep among
The fast horses and cars, and surely in hand-to-hand fighting
You'll find me agile as any at dancing the dance
Of fiery Ares. But I have no wish to strike
Such a man as yourself without a fair warning. All out
In the open, then, I'll cut you down if I can!"
    With this he poised his long-shadowing spear and hurled it,
Striking Ajax's dread seven-hide shield on the single   270
Layer of bronze, the eighth and outermost thickness.
On through six layers of leather the stubborn bronze cut,
But stopped in the seventh. Then kingly Ajax hurled
His long-shadowing spear and struck the round shield of Hector.
The great spear cut through the gleaming buckler and on
Through the beautiful breastplate and tunic too, but Hector
Twisted in time to avoid black death as the spear
Went by at his side. Then both at once drew out
Their long spears and fell on each other like ravenous lions
Or wild inexhaustible boars. And Hector lunged   280
With his spear, hitting the center of Ajax's shield,
But instead of piercing it through, the point turned back
On the bronze. And Ajax ended the charge with one
Of his own, but his spear pierced clean through Hector's shield
And went on to cut a considerable gash in his neck,
From which the dark blood gushed. Even so, bright-helmeted
Hector did not give up in the fight, but stepping
Back he seized with his powerful hand a nearby
Stone, black, jagged, and huge, and bounced it hard
Off the boss of Ajax's dread seven-hide shield with a clang   290

Of the bronze. But Ajax, lifting a much larger stone,
Swung it and hurled it with measureless might, and the boulder,
Big as a mill-stone, crumpled the buckler of Hector
And stretched him out on the ground with the shield crushed in
On his chest. But Apollo raised him at once. And now
The two would have closed and cut at each other with swords,
If two wise heralds, word-bearers for God and men,
Had not put a stop to the fight. They came from each side,
From the Trojans, Idaeus, from the bronze-clad Achaeans,
    Talthybius,
300 And held their staves between the two fighters. Then
The herald Idaeus, a man of ample discretion,
Spoke to them thus:
   "No more, brave sons. Let the match
Be over. Zeus of the gathering storm loves both
Of you, and all of us know what splendid spearmen
You are. Moreover, night is already upon us,
And men do well to heed the demands of darkness."
   To which Telamonian Ajax replied: "Idaeus,
Tell Hector to say these things, for he was the one
310 Who so proudly challenged all our best men. Let us first
Hear from him. Whatever he says is all right with me."
   And tall bright-helmeted Hector spoke to him thus:
"Ajax, since God gave you stature and strength and shrewdness
As well, and since you are far the best spearman among
The Achaeans, let us call off this blazing hot battle
And fight no more today. Another day
We'll go at each other till God says who wins and gives
The victory to whichever side he chooses. Now night
Is already upon us, and men do well to heed
320 The demands of darkness. Then all the Achaeans will surely
Rejoice at their ships, your comrades and kin most of all,
And the Trojan men and their wives of the trailing gowns
Will surely be glad on my account throughout
King Priam's great city, and they will enter the presence
Of the holy gods to offer thanksgiving for me.
But now let us each give the other some glorious gift,
That Achaeans and Trojans alike may say: 'They fought
A fierce match in heart-eating hatred, but then made up
With each other and parted friends.' "
330   He spoke, and stepping
Forward he gave him his sword with the studs of silver
Along with the scabbard and well-cut baldric, and Ajax

Gave his brilliant red war-belt. So they turned back,[3]
One to the host of Achaeans, the other to the thankful
Trojans, happy indeed at the sight of Hector
Returning alive and whole, surviving the fury
Of Ajax and his invincible hands. Back
To the city they escorted their leader, scarcely believing
That he was still safe. The well-greaved Achaeans, meanwhile,
Exulting in Ajax's victory, conducted their hero   340
To King Agamemnon.

       When they arrived at the lodges
Of Atreus' son, the commander-in-chief Agamemnon
Slaughtered a bull of five years to almighty Zeus.
This offering they flayed and dressed and skillfully butchered,
Cutting the carcass into small pieces, which meat
They spitted and roasted well, and drew it all
From the spits. When they had done what was needed and the meal
Was ready, they feasted, nor was there a man who lacked
A fair portion. And Atreus' son, wide-ruling Agamemnon,   350
Honored Ajax with cuts from the choice long chine.
When they had eaten and drunk as much as they wanted,
The old one stood up and wove wise counsel for them,
The ancient Nestor, whose wisdom had won out before.
Now he, in an effort to help, spoke out among them:

       "Atreus' son and you other Achaean leaders,
A woeful number of long-haired Achaeans lie dead
On the plain. Slashing Ares has darkened the earth
With their blood all about fair-flowing Scamander, and their souls
Have descended to Hades. Hence, at dawn tomorrow,   360
Let a truce be called, and we will go with our oxen
And mules and cart the corpses back here, that we
May burn them not far from the ships and see that the bones
Of the dead are kept to be given their children at home
By those of us who return to the land of our fathers.[4]
Then over the pyre let us build a huge barrow, a single
Tomb for all, heaping it up from the plain
And quickly extending it out into turreted walls,
Lofty ramparts for us and our ships. And let us
Build strong-locking gates through which to drive chariots, and all   370
Along outside we must dig a deep ditch as another
Defense against troops and chariots of the lordly Trojans
If ever they storm us here at the camp."

       He spoke,
And the kings all agreed. Meanwhile, the Trojans were gathered

High on the fortified hill of Troy in an awesomely
Turbulent throng before the doors of King Priam.
And first to get their attention was grave Antenor,
Saying: "Hear me, you Trojans, Dardanians, allies,
380   Hear what my heart commands me to speak. Come now,
Let us give Helen of Argos and all the wealth
That goes with her back to the sons of Atreus, trusting
They'll take her and go. For now we fight after breaking
The oaths we so faithfully swore. Hence, I have
No hope that anything good will happen to us
So long as we do not return her."

    Antenor no sooner
Sat down than up rose the handsome Prince Paris, lord
Of lovely blonde Helen, and the words of his answer came winged
390   With displeasure: "Antenor, that speech was not to my liking.
You certainly know how to give better counsel than that.
But if you are really in earnest, then surely the gods
Have addled your brains. But now I will speak my mind
To this meeting of horse-taming Trojans and make myself perfectly
Clear: my wife I will not give up! But the treasure
I brought home from Argos, all that I would like to give back,
And to it I'll add some costly things of my own."

    When he had spoken and taken his seat, Dardanian
Priam, godlike in wisdom, stood up among them.
400   Then, with benevolent purpose, he spoke to them all:
"Hear me, you Trojans, Dardanians, allies, hear
What my heart commands me to speak. Go take your supper
Throughout the city as usual, still mounting guard
And every man sharply alert. But tomorrow at dawn
Let Idaeus go down to the hollow ships and announce
To Atreus' sons, Agamemnon and Menelaus, the decision
Of royal Paris, who started this quarrel between us.
And furthermore let him inquire, in accord with good sense,
Whether they are willing to stop high-screaming war
410   Till we have burned our dead. Then the fight shall continue
Till God says who wins and gives the victory to whichever
Side he chooses."

    He spoke, and they gladly obeyed him,
Taking their supper by companies throughout the host,
And at dawn Idaeus went down to the hollow ships,
Where he found the Danaan comrades of Ares assembled
Around the stern of King Agamemnon's ship.
And the mighty-lunged herald strode into their midst and spoke:

"Atrides, and all other princes of peoples Achaean,
Priam and all of his high-ranking leaders have sent me   420
To tell you—if it pleases you, sirs, to hear my message—
The decision of royal Paris, who started this quarrel
Between us. The shiploads of treasure he brought home to Troy—
Would he had died first!—all that he wants to give back
And says he will add some costly things of his own.
But the wedded wife of illustrious King Menelaus
He will not give up, though the other Trojans urge him
To do so. And further they bade me inquire whether you
Are willing to stop high-screaming war till we
Have burned our dead. Then the fight shall continue till God says   430
Who wins and gives the victory to whichever side
He chooses."
        At this a long hush fell over them all.
But at last battle-roaring Diomedes spoke out among them:
"Let no man now accept such treasure from Paris,
Nor take Helen back. The merest baby can see
That the Trojans are already caught in the net of destruction!"
        He spoke, and the sons of Achaeans all shouted approval
Of what Diomedes, master of horses, had said.
Then King Agamemnon spoke thus to the Trojan herald: 440
"Idaeus, you've already heard the Achaeans' decision
And how they answer your speech, and their good pleasure
Is also mine. But concerning the dead, of course
I will not refuse your request to burn the bodies:
No man should begrudge dead bodies the swift consolation
Of fire. So to this burial truce of ours
Let Zeus be witness, Hera's loud-thundering lord."
        So saying, he lifted his scepter to all of the gods,
And Idaeus went back to sacred Ilium. There
The men of Troy and Dardania too had met   450
In one body to wait for Idaeus, who came and stood
In their midst and told them his message. Then quickly they got
                themselves
Ready, some to bring in the dead, others
To go after wood. And across the plain the Argives
Hurried from the well-timbered ships, some to bring in
The dead, others to go after wood.
        Now the Sun
Was just striking the fields, as he rose from the gliding deep stream
Of Oceanus and into the sky, when the two parties met
On the plain. And hard indeed it was to know   460

Their own dead. But they with water washed blood and gore
Away and lifted the bodies into the wagons,
Shedding hot tears as they worked—but quietly, since Priam
Would not permit any wailing. Silently, then,
But grieving inside, they piled the corpses high
On the pyre, and having burned them in flaming fire
Returned to holy Troy. And across from them
The well-greaved Achaeans, heart-stricken, piled corpses high
On the pyre, and having burned them in flaming fire
470 Returned to the hollow ships.
      The next day, just
Before light, as darkness began to give way to dawn,
A picked working force of Achaeans met at the pyre
And over it built a huge barrow, a single tomb
For all, heaping it up from the plain and extending
It out into turreted walls, lofty ramparts
For them and their ships. And then they built strong-locking gates
Through which to drive chariots. And all along outside
They dug a trench both wide and deep, and in it
480 They planted sharp stakes.
      While thus the long-haired Achaeans
Were toiling, the gods were sitting with lightning-lord Zeus
And marveling at the great effort of bronze-clad Achaeans.
Earth-shaking Poseidon spoke first: "O Father Zeus,
What mortal now on the boundless earth will still
Declare to the gods his mind and purpose? Don't
You see that the long-haired Achaeans have built a wall
In front of their ships with a trench all along outside it,
But to the gods have offered no glorious hecatombs?
490 Surely word of that wall will spread as far
As young Dawn scatters her light, and all will forget
The wall that I and Phoebus Apollo labored
To build for the warrior Laomedon, King of Troy."
      Then greatly vexed, cloud-gathering Zeus replied:
"Ah me, you mighty embracer and shaker of earth,
What have you said! Some other god far weaker
Than you in hand and spirit might possibly fear
This notion of theirs. But you—why it's your renown
That shall spread as far as young Dawn scatters her light.
500 So come, when the long-haired Achaeans have gone with their ships
To their own dear country, break up the wall with your waves
And sweep it all far out in the brine. Leave nothing

Behind on that wide beach but the covering sand.
Thus you may surely demolish the Achaeans' great wall."
       While they were talking, the Achaeans worked on, and the sun
Went down on the finished ramparts. Then the weary men
Slew oxen and ate by their lodges. And many ships
With cargoes of wine were drawn up there from Lemnos,
Ships dispatched by Jason's son Euneus,
Borne by Hypsipyle to Jason, the people's shepherd.   510
For Atreus' sons, Agamemnon and Menelaus, Euneus
Had sent as a gift a thousand measures of wine.
And the other long-haired Achaeans bought wine from the ships
In exchange for bronze and gleaming iron, for hides,
Live cattle, and slaves, and they made a rich feast for themselves.
Through most of the night the long-haired Achaeans caroused,
As did the Trojans and their allies in the city.
And all through the night contriving Zeus planned evil
For them, awesomely crashing his thunder. And each of them
Turned a pale olive with fear and from their cups   520
Poured wine on the ground, nor was there a man who dared
To drink without a libation to almighty Zeus,
The son of Cronos. At last they went to bed,
And each of them received the gift of sleep.

BOOK VIII

The Weakening Achaeans

As crocus-clad Dawn was scattering light over earth,
Zeus who exults in the thunder gathered the gods
On the highest peak of craggy Olympus and spoke
To them thus, with all the immortals keenly attentive:
"Hear me, you gods and goddesses too, that I
May say what now my spirit desires. Let none
Of you deities, male or female, cross me in this
I command, but all of you gladly obey me, that I
May quickly conclude these works of war. Whichever
10 Of you I see apart from the others, trying
To give your support to Trojans or Danaans either,
Him I shall smite and disgrace, and back he shall come
To Olympus, or I shall seize and hurl him down deep
In the gloomy abyss of Tartarus, the deepest pit
In all the earth, far down to the iron gates
And threshold of bronze, as deep below Hades as sky
Is high above earth!* Then he will know how far
My power surpasses the power of all other gods.
But come, divinities, try for yourselves, that all
20 Of you may know. Hang a golden chain from the sky
And all of you gods and goddesses too take hold
Of that chain and pull. Even so, you would not be able
To drag great Zeus, the powerful wisdom most high,
From heaven to earth, no matter how hard you pulled.
But if I should take a good notion to pull on that chain,
Then up would come all of you along with the earth
And sea, whereupon I would make the chain fast to a crag
Of Olympus and leave you all hanging high in the air!
That's how much stronger I am than you gods and all
        mortals."[1]

---

*The four levels of the Homeric cosmos, in descending order, are Aether, Sky, Hades, and Tartarus. Olympus is between Aether and Sky; Earth is between Sky and Hades.

He spoke, and the others sat utterly silent, in awe 30
At his words, for he had spoken with masterful force.
But finally blue-eyed Athena answered him thus:
"Our Father, son of Cronos, ruling high
Above all other rulers, we know very well
How strong and unyielding you are. Even so, we feel sorry
For the Danaan spearmen, who now shall die and come
To a miserable end. Of course we'll do as you say
And stay out of the fighting, but still we will help the Argives
With good advice, that all may not perish because of
Your wrath." 40
Then Zeus, god of gales, smiled at his daughter
And said: "Why so grim, my Tritogeneia?
Dear child, I was not altogether in earnest in what
I said, and surely I want to be gentle with you."
So saying, he harnessed his brazen-hoofed horses, fast-flying
Steeds with manes of streaming gold. And the garments
He wore were of gold, as was the well-wrought whip
He held in his hand as he mounted the car and lashed
The horses ahead. And they, not at all unwilling,
Flew on between earth and the starry sky. He went 50
To well-watered Mount Ida, mother of wilderness creatures,
To Gargarus peak, where he has a grove and temple
And altar fragrant with incense. There the Father
Of men and gods pulled up and unharnessed his horses
And hid them both in thick mist, but he himself
Sat mid the beetling crags looking out on the city
Of Troy and the long dark line of Achaean ships.
And now the long-haired Achaeans ate quickly and put on
Their armor, and opposite them the men of Troy
Dressed for battle throughout the city. Fewer 60
They were than the Argives, but in their pressing need
All the more eager to fight for their children and wives.
Then all the gates were thrown open, and with a tremendous
Din the army poured out, both infantry and horse.
And now the two forces met with a knocking of spears
And bossed shields clashing in a fierce and furious uproar
Of bronze-breasted fighters. And there the screams of the dying
Were mingled with cries of triumph, and blood flowed over
The earth.
Now all morning long, as the sacred daylight 70
Grew brighter, the missiles of both sides struck home, and the
    warriors

Fell. But when the Sun-god bestrode mid-heaven,
The Father lifted his golden scales and in them
Placed two lots of grievous and leveling death,
One for the horse-taming Trojans, for the bronze-clad Achaeans
The other. Then he took hold of the middle and lifted
The scales, and the fatal day for Achaeans sank down
And their fates rested on all-feeding earth, while those
Of the Trojans were raised toward heaven's expanse. And now
80 Zeus uttered a great crash of thunder and hurled a huge bolt
Of lightning down into the host of Achaeans. At this
They were stricken with awe, and olive-pale panic gripped all of them
Hard.
       Then neither Idomeneus nor Agamemnon
Had heart enough to hold his ground, nor did
Those comrades of Ares, the two Ajaxes. Only
Gerenian Nestor, Achaea's old sentinel, stayed
Where he was, not at all that he wanted to, but a trace-horse
Of his was badly wounded. Handsome Prince Paris,
90 Lord of lovely blonde Helen, had driven an arrow
Deep in the horse's brain, striking him right
Where the mane begins on top of the head, the deadliest
Spot of all. In agony, lunging and leaping
And rearing high with the bronze, the horse had entangled
The team, and the old one had leaped from the car with his sword
And was hacking away at the traces. But now the fast horses
Of Hector came on through the rout with a very bold man
Behind them, brave Hector himself. And now the old one's
Life would have ended if battle-roaring Diomedes
100 Had not been sharply alert. He saw the trouble
And shouted with all of his might to Odysseus for help:
       "Zeus-sprung son of Laertes, resourceful Odysseus,
Where are you going so fast with your back to the battle
Mid all the rest of the cowards? Watch out as you run,
Or someone will plant a spear in your back. But stop
And hold your ground, that we may thrust this wild man
Away from old Nestor!"
       Diomedes yelled, but the worthy
Long-suffering Odysseus paid him no heed as he
110 Shot past toward the hollow ships. Thus all alone
Diomedes confronted the foremost fighters, taking
His stand in front of the horses of Neleus' son Nestor
And speaking thus to the old one in these winged words:
       "Old sire, surely young warriors strain your endurance.

Your strength is not what it was now that old age
Lies heavy upon you, your squire is a puny fellow,
And surely your horses are out of the running. So come,
Get up in my chariot here, that you may see
What the horses of Tros are like. They're equally fast
Pursuing or fleeing, these mighty masters of rout   120
I lately took from Aeneas. Let both of our squires
Look after your horses, while we go galloping on
Against the horse-taming Trojans, that Hector too
May learn how madly this spear of mine leaps from my hand!"
      Such were his words, and horse-driving Gerenian Nestor
Agreed. So the squires, brave Sthenelus and gentle Eurymedon,
Took charge of the horses, and the old King mounted the car
With Diomedes.[2] Then Nestor took hold of the glossy reins
And lashed the horses ahead, and on they went
At a gallop directly for Hector, whose chariot came   130
Straight at them. In close, Diomedes threw, missed Hector,
But struck his squire on the breast by the nipple, Eniopeus,
Holding the reins, the son of high-hearted Thebaeus.
He plunged from the chariot, causing the quick-footed horses
To shy, and there his spirit and strength were undone.
And the heart of Hector was crowded with terrible pain
For his charioteer. Even so, he left him stretched out
Where he fell, and went off, greatly grieved for his comrade, in search
Of another bold driver. Nor were his horses for long
Without such a master, for quickly he came on the brave   140
Archeptolemus, Iphitus' son, and making him mount
Behind the fast horses he put the reins in his hands.
      Then ruinous, irreparable damage would soon have been done
To the Trojans, and they would all have been penned up in Troy
Like so many lambs, if the Father of gods and men
Had not been sharply watching. He thundered with a terrible
Crashing and hurled a dazzling white lightning-bolt,
Hurled it to earth before Diomedes' team,
Where it burst in an awesome flare of fuming sulphur,
Terrifying the horses and making them balk and back up   150
The car. And the heart of Nestor was also afraid
As he dropped the reins and spoke thus to Diomedes:
      "Come now,
Turn your solid-hoofed horses and flee. Don't
You see that power from God is not yours today?
Zeus has given that glory to Hector there,
But another day great Cronos' son will give it

To us, if he pleases. No man can thwart God's will
In any way. No matter how mighty the man,
160 God is stronger by far."
                Then Diomedes,
The fierce battle-roarer, answered him thus: "Surely,
Old sire, all that you say is true enough.
But terrible pain torments my soul when I think
How Hector will someday say in a gathering of Trojans:
'Diomedes, driven before me, fled to the ships.'
So someday he'll boast—but first let the wide earth open
For me!"
                To which horse-driving Gerenian Nestor:
170 "Ah now, you son of flame-hearted Tydeus, what
Are you saying! Hector may call you coward and weakling,
But who of the Trojans or their Dardanian allies
Will ever believe him? Certainly not the wives
Of the spirited, shield-bearing fighters of Troy, women
Whose lusty young husbands you have hurled in the dust."
                So saying, he turned the solid-hoofed horses and joined
The general rout, and now the Trojans and Hector,
Awesomely screaming, rained their groan-fraught missiles
Upon them, and tall bright-helmeted Hector loudly
180 Shouted in triumph:
                "You above all, Diomedes,
The swiftly-drawn Danaans honored with a special seat
At the feast, choice cuts, and an ever-full cup. But now
They will surely despise you as a man more woman than warrior!
Run, you pampered doll! You'll never scale
Our city walls through any yielding of mine,
Nor carry our women away in your ships. I'll make you
A feeble ghost long before that ever happens!"
                He spoke, and Tydeus' son was torn two ways,
190 Whether to wheel his horses and meet him head on,
Or not. Three times he hovered in heart and soul
On the point of turning, and three times Zeus the planner
Thundered from the range of Ida, giving a sign
To the Trojans that he was on their side and victory was theirs.
Then Hector loudly encouraged his fighting comrades:
                "You Trojans and Lycians and dueling Dardanians, now,
My friends, be men, and filled with furious boldness!
I know that Zeus has willingly nodded assent
And given the victory and very great glory to me,
200 But death and defeat to the Danaans, fools that they are

To have built those miserable walls, weak and scarcely
Worth noticing. Those ramparts will never withstand our onslaught,
Believe me, and lightly our horses shall leap the dug ditch.
But when at last I stand mid the hollow ships,
Make sure that we are provided with blazing fire,
That I may burn the ships and slay the men
Beside them, that I may slaughter, I say, the Argives,
All of them choking and falling around in the smoke!"

    So saying, he shouted these words to his horses: "Xanthus,
And you Podargus, and Aethon, and glossy Lampus,   210
Now is your time to repay me for all the good care
You've had at the hands of Andromache, great-hearted Eëtion's
Daughter, who fed you so often on sweet-hearted wheat
And poured good wine in your water for you to drink
Whenever your spirits bade—fed you, in fact,
Before she did me, and I am her own loving husband.
So gallop ahead in pursuit, that we may take
Nestor's shield, that solid gold buckler, gold arm-rods and all,
Famous from earth to heaven, and that we may strip
Horse-breaking Diomedes' richly wrought breastplate off,   220
A piece laboriously fashioned by Hephaestus himself.
If we could only account for those two, then
I might hope to drive the Achaeans away in their ships
This very night!"

    His vaunting aroused the resentment
Of queenly Hera, who made all lofty Olympus
Quake as she stirred on her throne. Then she spoke thus
To the great god Poseidon: "Ah me, you far-reaching shaker
Of shores, not even the heart in your breast has pity
For the Danaans dying. Yet they honor you with many   230
Delightful gifts at Helice and at Aegae.
Grant, then, the victory to them. For if all of us
Who support the Danaans willed to hurl back the Trojans
And hold back loud-thundering Zeus, then surely he'd sit
In a miserable mood down there all alone on Mount Ida!"

    Greatly disturbed, earth-shaking Poseidon replied:
"Heedless, word-slinging Hera, what are you saying!
Surely I would not be willing to join with the others
And fight against Cronos' son Zeus, since he is so very much
Stronger than we are."   240

    While thus the two of them talked,
Priam's son Hector, now that Zeus gave him glory,
Penned up the Achaeans, shield-bearing warriors, horses

And all, in the space from the deep-ditched wall to the ships
Drawn up on the beach. And now would Hector have put
The torch to their shapely vessels, if queenly Hera
Had not inspired Agamemnon to try with all speed
To rally the jostling Achaeans. Bearing his great
Crimson cloak over one thick arm, he went past lodges
250 And ships to the huge black hull of Odysseus' vessel,
Which stood drawn up in the middle within shouting distance
Of both ends of the line, where Ajax, Telamon's son,
And Achilles had their lodges, for such was their trust
In manly valor and the strength of their hands that they
Had drawn up their ships at the furthermost ends. From the deck
Agamemnon shouted as loud as he could, calling out
Thus to the Danaans:

     "For shame, you miserable Argives,
Men only outwardly brave, where now are your brags
260 That we are the men most valiant, the hollow vaunts
You made in Lemnos* while gorging yourselves with meat
Of high-horned cattle and guzzling great bowls brimful
Of wine, each of you boasting that you would stand up
In battle to a hundred, no two hundred, Trojans! But now
We're no match for even one Hector, who very soon
Will put his bright torch to our ships. O Father Zeus,
Was there ever another of high-ruling kings whose soul,
Like mine, you blinded with folly and whose great glory
You seized? Still I am sure that I passed in my ship
270 No exquisite altar of yours on my lamentable
Way here without a burnt-offering to you of the fat
And thighs of bulls, so eager was I to sack
The thick-walled city of Troy. But please grant this
I ask of you now, O Zeus, and let us at least
Escape with our lives. Do not allow the Trojans
Thus to destroy us all."

     He prayed, and the Father
Had pity on the weeping King and, nodding, gave him
A sign that his people should live and not he destroyed.
280 At that very moment he sent an eagle, surest
Of winged omens, his talons clutching a fawn,
The young of a swift-running doe. And beside the exquisite

---

*On the way to Troy, the Achaeans stopped at Lemnos, where they abandoned Philoctetes
(the hero of Sophocles' eponymous tragedy).

Altar of Zeus he let the fawn fall, right where
The Achaeans sacrificed offerings to the almighty Father,
Source of all omens. Then they, when they saw that the bird
Was from Zeus, sprang once again at the Trojans and quickly
Regained their lust for battle.

     But no man there
Of the Danaans, though they were many, could claim he beat
Diomedes across the trench in his swiftly-drawn car   290
To clash in close fighting. For Tydeus' son was far
The first to bring down a helmeted Trojan warrior,
Phradmon's son Agelaus. He was just reining
His horses around getting ready to run, but as
He wheeled, Diomedes planted a spear in his back
Midway of the shoulders and drove it on out through his chest.
He pitched from the car, and on him his armor rang.

     Behind Diomedes came Atreus' sons, Agamemnon
And Menelaus, and both Ajaxes, furious valor
Incarnate, Idomeneus next and Idomeneus' comrade   300
Meriones, peer of the slaughtering god of battles,
And after these Eurypylus, splendid son
Of Euaemon, and Teucer came ninth, stringing his supple
Bent bow, and took his position behind the huge shield
Of Ajax, son of Telamon. And Ajax would move
His shield to one side while Teucer looked for a target
In the enemy throng, shot, and brought his man down
No longer alive. Then Teucer would quickly take cover
With Ajax again, like a child that runs to his mother,
And Ajax would hide him completely behind his bright shield.   310

     Who then was first of the Trojans that matchless Teucer
Laid low? Orsilochus first, Ormenus next,
Then Ophelestes and Daetor, Chromius and Prince Lycophontes,
Polyaemon's son Amopaon and Melanippus.
All these in quick succession Teucer stretched out
On the all-feeding earth. And the king of men Agamemnon
Rejoiced to see him wrecking the Trojan battalions
With that mighty bow of his, and coming up to him
He said:

     "Beloved Telamonian Teucer, captain   320
Of many, keep up the good shooting and surely you'll be
A light to the Danaans and to your father Telamon,
Who brought you up from a baby, and though you were
A bastard son cherished you dearly and gave you
The best of care at home in his palace. Now

Give him great glory through you, far away though he is.
And this I will promise to you and surely perform:
If aegis-great Zeus and Athena grant me the sacking
Of firm-founded Ilium, I will hand over to you,
330 First after myself, some splendid prize of prestige,
A tripod, perhaps, or a chariot and pair, or a woman
To share your bed."

      Then matchless Teucer replied:
"Most famous Atrides, why urge me on when I
Am already so eager? Believe me, I fight as long as
I'm able, and ever since we turned them toward Ilium,
Ever since then I have crouched here and brought men down
With my bow. Eight of my long-barbed arrows are fixed
In the flesh of fast and lusty young fighters, though yonder
340 Mad dog I cannot hit."

      But he was determined
To bring Hector down, and so let another shaft fly
From the string directly at him. Again, however,
He missed, but lodged his arrow deep in the breast
Of peerless Gorgythion, Priam's brave son, borne
By a wife from Aesyme, the beautiful Castianeira,
A woman made like a goddess. And now to one side
Gorgythion drooped his head and heavy helmet:
He let it fall over like the bloom of a garden poppy
350 Heavy with seed and the rains of spring.

      But Teucer,
Determined to bring Hector down, let another shaft fly
From the string directly at him. Again, however,
He missed, for Apollo himself deflected the arrow.
But Hector's bold driver Archeptolemus, eagerly charging,
Received the shaft in his breast by the nipple and plunged
From the chariot, causing the quick-footed horses to shy,
And there his spirit and strength were undone. And the heart
Of Hector was crowded with terrible pain at the death
360 Of his driver. But he, though greatly grieved for his friend,
Bade his brother Cebriones, close at hand,
To take the reins of the horses, and Cebriones heard him
And did what he said. But Hector himself, wildly screaming,
Leaped from his gleaming car to the ground, and seizing
A hand-filling stone rushed straight at Teucer, determined
To strike him. Now Teucer had taken a bitter shaft
From the quiver and laid it upon the bowstring, and had just

Drawn it back to his shoulder when charging bright-helmeted
          Hector
Came down hard with the stone on that most mortal spot
Where the collarbone separates neck and chest. There   370
He dealt him a furious blow with the jagged stone,
Breaking the bowstring and numbing his hand to the wrist.
And Teucer, dropping the bow, fell to his knees.
But Ajax saw his brother fall and ran
And stood over him, using his shield as a cover.
Then two loyal comrades, Echius' son Mecisteus
And noble Alastor, lifted their friend and carried him,
Heavily groaning, back to the hollow ships.
          Now again the Olympian roused the Trojans to rally,
And fiercely they hurled the Achaeans straight back to their own   380
Deep trench. And Hector, reveling in martial prowess,
Led the hard charge. As a quick-footed hound pursues
A wild boar or a lion, snapping at him from behind
At buttock or flank and warily watching for the beast
To turn, so Hector pressed hard on the long-haired Achaeans,
Constantly killing the hindmost as all of them fled
In the general rout. But when they had scrambled through trench
And sharp stakes and many had died at the hands of the Trojans,
They came to a halt beside their ships, and calling
For help to one another each of them lifted   390
His arms in loud and fervent prayer to all
Of the gods. But Hector kept wheeling his mane-tossing horses
This way and that, and surely his eyes were as fierce
As those of the Gorgon or man-maiming Ares himself.
          Watching them die, the white-armed goddess Hera
Pitied her favorites and spoke at once to Athena
In these words winged with compassion: "Ah me, you daughter
Of Zeus of the aegis, shall we two lack all concern
For Danaans dying in this late hour of pain?
Now they'll surely fulfill a miserable fate   400
And fatally fall before the charge of one man,
Priam's son Hector, who rages beyond their control
And who has already done many quite horrible things."
          And the bright-eyed goddess Athena answered her, saying:
"I heartily wish the spirit and strength of this man
Would be destroyed there in the land of his fathers
Beneath the hands of the Argives! But my own Father
Also rages with evil intent, that cruel

And constant old sinner who thwarts my deepest desires.
410 Now he doesn't remember how I on many
Occasions rescued his son when he was worn out
By the labors Eurystheus had him perform.* All Heracles
Had to do was cry out to heaven, and Zeus
Would send me down to help and defend him. But if
My heart had only foreseen all this the time
Eurytheus sent him to gate-guarding Hades to bring
Out of Erebus the loathed Death-god's hound,† then never
Would he have recrossed the high-banked waters of Styx.
Surely Zeus hates me now, but he has fulfilled
420 The wishes of Thetis, who kissed his knees and took hold of
His chin with her hand, pleading with him to honor
Town-taking Achilles. But just as surely the day
Will come when again he will call me his blue-eyed darling.
So harness our solid-hoofed horses while I go into
The palace of aegis-bearing Zeus and put on my armor,
That I may find out how glad bright-helmeted Hector
Will be when he sees me appear in the fighting ranks
Of battle. Truly the muscle and fat of many
A Trojan will glut the dogs and carrion birds
430 Beside the Achaean ships!"
      So she spoke,
And the white-armed Queen of the gods was equally willing.
So honored Hera, daughter of mighty Cronos,
Harnessed the gold-bridled horses. And Athena, daughter
Of Zeus, on the floor of her Father's palace, shed
The soft robe that she herself had made and embroidered,
Put on instead the tunic of stormy Zeus,
And armed herself for tearful war. Then she,
God's daughter, mounted the flaming car, gripping
440 The heavy huge spear with which she conquers whole armies
That have enraged her. Hera gave the horses a flick
With the lash, and the gates of heaven groaned on their hinges,
The self-opening gates which are kept by the Seasons, who have
In their keeping Olympus and all the wide sky, and who open
And close the thick clouds as they see fit. So on
Through the gates they drove their now impatient horses.

---

*Heracles was enslaved to Eurystheus as punishment for killing his own wife and children.
†Cerberus is the multiheaded "hound" that guards the entrance to Hades.

But Father Zeus caught sight of them from Ida
And terrible rage welled up within him. At once
He sent golden-winged Iris to bear the two goddesses word:
"Fly swiftly, quick Iris, and turn those two back. Don't let them   450
Encounter me face to face, for the sequel of such
A conflict would not be very pleasant. And this
I declare, and truly I'll do what I say. I'll cripple
Their horses and knock both goddesses out of their chariot,
Which car I will smash into pieces. Nor will they recover
For ten circling years from the wounds my lightning will give them.
Then she of the blazing blue eyes will know what it is
To fight her own Father. With Hera I'm not so indignant
And angry, since I am quite used to her opposition
In everything I say do."   460
          So spoke the Father,
And storm-footed Iris swiftly flew off with the message,
Leaving the range of Ida for lofty Olympus.
There at the marvelous gates of the deep-creviced mountain
She met the two goddesses, stopped them, and thus delivered
The message of Zeus:
          "Where to in such a hurry?
How can the hearts within you so foolishly rage?
Cronos' son Zeus will not allow you to help
The Argives. Now he threatens you thus, and surely   470
He'll do what he says. He says he will cripple your horses
And knock the two of you out of your chariot, which car
He will smash into pieces. Nor will you recover for ten
Circling years from the wounds his lightning will give you. Then you,
Blue-eyes, will know what it is to fight your own Father.
With Hera he's not so indignant and angry, since he
Is quite used to her opposition in everything
He says do. But you are most brazen, Athena, bitch-hearted
And shameless, if you really dare to raise your great spear
Against Zeus."   480
          Having so spoken, quick-footed Iris
Flew off. And Hera turned to Athena, saying:
"O child of aegis-great Zeus, no longer will I
Allow us to go against God in battle for the sake
Of mere mortals. Let mortals live and die as they will,
And now let Zeus ponder those plans of his and judge
Between Trojans and Danaans wholly as he sees fit."
With this she turned back her solid-hoofed horses. And the Seasons
Unyoked the mane-tossing steeds, tied them at mangers

490 Filled with ambrosia, and tilted the car against
     The gleaming wall by the gates. Then the goddesses, hurt
     And resentful, took their places on golden thrones
     Mid the other immortal powers.
                    Father Zeus, meanwhile,
     Mounted his well-running car and hurried his horses
     From Ida to Mount Olympus, where he entered the session
     Of gods. Poseidon, famed shaker of shores, unharnessed
     His brother's horses, put his car on its stand, and covered it
     All with a cloth. And far-seeing Zeus sat down
500 On his golden throne, while beneath his feet huge Olympus
     Quaked. Only Athena and Hera sat apart
     From the Father, and only they said nothing at all
     By way of greeting or question. But the heart of Zeus
     Knew very well what the goddesses thought, and he spoke
     To them thus:
              "Why so unhappy, Athena and Hera?
     Surely you haven't exhausted yourselves in battle,
     Where men win glory, ruining the Trojans whom you
     So dreadfully hate. No matter what I undertake,
510 All the gods on Olympus could never dissuade me,
     For such is my spirit and such my invincible hands.
     But trembling seized the glorious limbs of you two
     Before you had even so much as a glimpse of the fighting
     And horrors of war. But let me remind you of what
     Would surely have happened if the two of you hadn't turned back.
     I would have blasted you both with a charge of lightning
     So great that you would have had no chariot left
     In which to come back to Olympus, where the immortal gods
     Abide."
520   At first his words got murmurs only
     From Athena and Hera, who sat by each other contriving
     Disasters for Trojans. Then Athena kept quiet and said nothing,
     Though seized by savage anger at Father Zeus.
     But the breast of Hera could not contain her rage,
     And she railed at him thus:
                    "Most dreadful son of Cronos,
     What kind of talk is that! We know very well
     How almighty strong you are. Even so, we feel sorry
     For the Danaan spearmen, who now shall die and come
530 To a miserable end. Of course we'll do as you say
     And stay out of the fighting, but still we will help the Argives

With good advice, that all may not perish because of
Your wrath."
　　Then Zeus of the gathering gale replied:
"Tomorrow at dawn, O heifer-eyed mighty Hera,
You'll see, if you deign to behold, the truly mighty
Son of Cronos wrecking still further the ample
Ranks of Argive spearmen. For massive Hector
Shall not stop fighting till swift Achilles himself
Arises beside his ships, and that will not be　　　　　　　　540
Till all are fiercely contending in deadly close quarters
At the sterns of the ships about the corpse of Patroclus.[3]
Such is heaven's decree. And I don't care
At all how angry you get, nor how far away
You go in your sulking. Go to the bottom of earth
And sea for all I care, down where Iapetus
And Cronos sit in the depths of gloomy Tartarus,
Unrelieved by light from the Sun-god Hyperion
And unrefreshed by any breeze that blows.*
Go on, if you wish, and see how much I'm disturbed　　550
By your miserable wrath and resentment. For nothing that lives
Is more bitch-hearted than you!"
　　　　So spoke great Zeus,
But white-armed Hera had nothing to say in reply.
Then the smoldering sun dropped into the stream of Oceanus
And drew black night across the grain-giving earth.
Unhappy indeed were the Trojans to see the light sink,
But to the frantic Achaeans the darkness was welcome,
The night thrice earnestly prayed for.
　　　　Then glorious Hector　　　　　　　　　560
Called the Trojans together and led them apart
From the ships, assembling them all by the swirling river
In an open space clear of corpses. Down they stepped
From their cars to the ground to hear what god-loved Prince
　　　　　Hector
Wanted to tell them. He held a sixteen-foot spear
In his hand, while over his head the bronze point blazed
And the ring of gold that held it. And now he leaned
On the spear and spoke these words to the Trojans:

---

*Zeus invokes the dread fates of his prior opponents, who now languish in the lowest
depths.

"Your attention,
570 Trojans, Dardanians, allies. Just now I thought
That we would destroy the ships and all the Achaeans
Before going back to windy Ilium. But darkness
Fell too soon. That most of all has now
Saved the Argives along with their ships on the surf-beaten shore.
So let us give in to black night and make preparations
For supper. Loose from the cars your mane-tossing horses
And throw some fodder before them. Then go with all speed
To the city for oxen and splendid fat sheep. Get sweet-hearted
Wine and bread from your houses, and gather much wood,
580 That all through the night till early dawn we may
Have fires sufficient to light up heaven itself.
That way we'll prevent the long-haired Achaeans from making
A try by night to run for home in their ships
Over the sea's broad back. Let them not at their leisure
Board the ships, nor leave without a battle.
See to it that many a man takes home a shaft
To remember us by, an arrow or keen-headed spear
Lodged in his back as he makes a leap for the deck
Of his ship. So others may live in terror of bringing
590 Sad war on the horse-breaking Trojans. And let our heralds,
Beloved of Zeus, call out through the city for all
The young lads and gray-templed elders to spend this night
On the god-built walls, and tell our wives to kindle
Great fires at home in their halls, that careful watch
May be kept to prevent a raid on the city while we
Are out here. So be it, my great-hearted friends, as I have
Just said. But enough of good counsel for now. Tomorrow
At dawn I'll have more to say to you, the horse-breaking
Trojans. And now I hopefully pray to Zeus
600 And the other gods that we may drive from our land
Those fate-driven dogs, who came in their death-borne black hulls
Long ago. And we too must keep a close watch tonight,
Guarding ourselves, but just before dawn let us put on
Our armor and throw our whole strength into keen-bladed war
At the hollow ships. Then I'll find out whether Tydeus'
Son, the strong Diomedes, will force me back
From the ships to the wall, or whether I'll bring him down
With the bronze and bear off his blood-stained armor. Tomorrow
He'll know how able his valor is to withstand
610 The chilling onrush of my spear. He'll lie, I dare say,
Mid the fallen foremost fighters, undone by a thrust

Of the bronze, and many a comrade of his will lie
Stretched out around him at sunrise tomorrow. I only
Wish that I were as sure of being immortal
And ageless throughout all days to come, like Athena
And Phoebus Apollo, as I am certain that daylight
Tomorrow will bring disaster on all of the Argives!"
    So Hector harangued them, and all of them shouted approval.
Then they unharnessed their sweating horses and tethered
Them with the reins, each man beside his own car.   620
And with all speed they led from the city oxen
And splendid fat sheep, brought sweet-hearted wine and bread
From their houses, and gathered great heaps of wood. Then
To the gods they offered complete hecatombs, and the breezes
Wafted the savor up from the plain into heaven,
But from that fragrance the blissful gods abstained.
They would not partake at all, so hateful to them
Were sacred Ilium, Priam, and the people of Priam,
Great King of the good ashen spear.
    So the confident Trojans   630
Waited all night in their companies, and many indeed
Were the watchfires burning. As when the stars shine out
Round the gleaming moon on a fair, still night when all
The high peaks and headlands and forest glades are easy
To see, so open then is the sky, so clear
The infinite air, and the shepherd's heart is made glad
By the countless stars overhead—even so many
That night seemed the fires of the Trojans bivouacked before Troy
Between the ships and the river Xanthus. The plain
Was lit with a thousand fires, and in the light   640
Of each blaze sat fifty men, while by their chariots
Stood their fine horses, munching a mixture of wheat
And white barley and waiting for Dawn of the beautiful throne.

BOOK IX

Agamemnon's Offers to Achilles

While thus the Trojans kept watch, the Achaeans were gripped
With awesome Panic, companion of freezing Fear,
And all their leaders were filled with unbearable grief.
As the fish-full sea is stirred by a storm when hard winds
Quickly arise and blow from the North and West
Directly from Thrace, raising dark foam-crested billows
And strewing the beaches with seaweed, so now the hearts
Of Achaeans were stirred.
      But Atreus' son Agamemnon,
10 Deeply despairing, went up and down through the host
Commanding the clear-voiced heralds to call each man
By name to the place of assembly, to call without shouting,
And he himself worked with the heralds. At last they sat
In assembly, troubled and grieving, and King Agamemnon
Stood up to speak, weeping like a spring whose dark streams
Trickle down the rocky face of a cliff. Even so,
And heavily sighing, he addressed the Argives thus:
      "My friends, captains and counselors of the Argives,
Almighty Zeus, the son of crooked Cronos,
20 Has bound me now in woeful blindness of spirit,
Heartless god that he is! For long ago
He made me a promise and vowed with a nod of his head
That I should sack the well-walled city of Ilium
Before I went home, but now a vile deceit
Appears in his plans, and he bids me go back in disgrace
To Argos, having lost a great many men. Such,
I suppose, is the pleasure of Zeus, almighty God,
Who has toppled the towers of numerous cities and who
Shall continue to topple, since his is the greatest power.[1]
30 So come, all of you do as I say. Let us flee
With our ships to the precious land of our fathers. For we
Can no longer hope to plunder the wide streets of Troy."
      He spoke, and the grieving sons of Achaeans sat
A long time in silence, till finally strong Diomedes,

He of the fierce battle-scream, spoke out among them:
"Son of Atreus, with you and your folly, O King,
I'll be the first to contend in the privileged place
Of assembly, here where speech is respected. Do not, then,
Be angry at me and my words. You, after all,
Amid the Danaans slandered my valor first,   **40**
Saying that I was weak and unwarlike.* Nor is there
A single Argive, young or old, who isn't
Aware that you spoke so to me. But you are the one
Whom the son of Cronos, crooked in counsel, uncertainly
Endowed: he gave you the scepter, yes, and with it
The highest honor, but courage he did not grant you,
And courage is far the most kingly virtue of all.
Strange man, do you really believe that the sons of Achaeans
Have hearts as weak and unwarlike as you imply?
But if your own heart is anxious to go, go on!   **50**
You know the way, and the whole huge fleet that followed you
Here from Mycenae still stands drawn up by the sea.
But the other long-haired Achaeans will stay till Ilium
Falls. And if they also should flee in their ships
To the precious land of their fathers, we two, Sthenelus
And I, will surely fight on till Troy is ours,
For we came here with the blessing of almighty God."

    He spoke, and all the sons of Achaeans shouted
Approval, applauding the words of brave Diomedes,
Breaker of horses. Then knightly old Nestor stood up   **60**
And spoke out among them: "Son of Tydeus, you
Are the strongest of men in battle and surely the best
Of all our young men in council. No Achaean would scorn
The speech you just made or contradict what you said.
Even so, there is more that badly needs saying. It's true
That you're still a young man, quite young enough to be
My youngest son. Still your words of reproof
To the kings of Argos were prudent and utterly right.
But now let an older man speak and complete your good counsel.
Nor is there a man who will scorn what I say, not even   **70**
King Agamemnon. Friendless, lawless, and homeless
Is he who enjoys the horror of blood-chilling strife
Among his own people. But now let us yield to black night
And make preparations for supper. Let sentinels take

---

*Agamemnon's abuse of Diomedes is described beginning at IV.433.

Their positions beyond the wall along the deep ditch.
This I say to the young men only. Then you,
Agamemnon, make the first move, since you are highest
In royal rank, and give a feast for the chieftains,
As is but fitting and right. Your lodges are full
80 Of wine brought daily to you in Achaean ships
From Thrace across the wide water, and you, as ruler
Of many, have means to receive us as only a great king
Can. Then you may take his advice who speaks
Most wisely in our discussion. And surely all
The Achaeans are sorely in need of advice, of practical
Good advice, now that our foes are lighting
Their many fires so close to the ships. Who
Among us rejoices in that? Believe me, this night
Will determine the ruin or salvation of all our great army!"
90   He spoke, and they, quite attentive, did as he said.
The armor-clad sentries went out on the double, commanded
By Nestor's son Thrasymedes, shepherd of the people,
Ascalaphus and Ialmenus, sons of Ares, and Meriones,
Aphareus, Deïpyrus, and able Lycomedes, son
Of Creon. These captains of the guard were seven in all,
And with each of them marched a hundred young warriors armed
With long spears. They all went out and took their posts
Midway between trench and wall, and there they lit fires
And each prepared his own supper.
100   But King Agamemnon
Led the whole body of chieftains to a royal feast
In his lodge, where all their hearts could wish for was theirs.
They fell to feasting and enjoyed the good things before them.
But when they had eaten and drunk as much as they wanted,
The old one stood up and wove wise counsel for them,
The ancient Nestor, whose wisdom had won out before.
Now he, in an effort to help, spoke out among them:
     "Renowned Atrides, king of men Agamemnon,
From beginning to end my remarks are especially for you.
110 For you are King over many, and Zeus himself
Has given the scepter to you and entrusted you
With the laws, that you might rule wisely and well. Hence you
Above all should speak your counsel and listen to that
Of others, listen and also abide by the good
Advice you get. You, of course, will finally
Have to decide on anything we may suggest.
So now I will speak what seems to me best, nor will

Another find any better suggestion than this
I have had in my mind for some time, since the day when you,
O Zeus-sprung mighty chief, took the girl Briseis   120
From the lodge of angry Achilles and went your own
Heedless way completely against our will. I myself
Did all I could to change your mind, but you
Gave in to your pride and insulted our mightiest man,
Whom even the gods do not fail to honor. You took
And kept his prize of prestige. But still it is not
Too late for us to consider how we may make up
For all that and how we may win his good will again
With friendly gifts and gentle words of entreaty."
    And thus the commander-in-chief Agamemnon replied: 130
"Old sire, you speak of my folly with perfect truth.
I acted blindly,[2] and I don't for a moment deny it.
A man whom Zeus loves in his heart and honors, as surely
He honors this man, while beating the rest of us down,
Is worth any number of regular uninspired armies.
But since I did give in to my miserable pride,
And since I did act with such folly and lack of foresight,
I now would like very much to make amends
And give the man gifts of limitless value. Here
In the midst of you all I will name the glorious tokens: 140
Seven tripods untouched by the fire, ten talents
Of gold and twenty bright cauldrons, along with twelve
Strong prize-taking horses, swift winners of many a race.
By no means lacking in treasure or precious gold
Would be that man whose wealth was as great as the prizes
These solid-hoofed horses have won me. And I will give him
Seven fair women of Lesbos, skillful weavers
Of matchless work, women I personally chose
From the spoil when he himself took well-fortified Lesbos,
The loveliest women the world has to offer. I'll give him   150
These seven, and with them the daughter of Briseus, the girl
I took away. And I will swear a great oath
That never once have I slept or made love with her,
As men and women so naturally do. All
Of these things shall be his at once, and if the immortals
Grant us the sack of Priam's great city, let him
Be present when we Achaeans are dividing the spoil,
That he may fill his ship full of gold and bronze,
And let him choose twenty women, the fairest in Troy
After Argive Helen herself. And if we return   160

To Achaean Argos, rich udder of earth, he
Shall be my own son-in-law, nor will I treat
My beloved and richly reared son Orestes any better.
I have at home in my solid-built palace three daughters:
Chrysothemis, Laodice, and Iphianassa. Of these
He may take the bride of his choice to the house of Peleus,
And I will not only forego all wedding gifts
From him, but will myself give a dowry far larger
Than any man yet has sent with a daughter. And I
170   Will give seven populous cities to him: Cardamyle,
Enope, grassy Hire, and hallowed Pherae,
Antheia, deep in meadows, lovely Aepeia,
And Pedasus, rich in vineyards. They're all near the sea
On the lower coast of sandy Pylos, and those
Who live there are wealthy in cattle and sheep, men
Who will honor him like a god and give him fine gifts,
And under his scepter they'll do as he says and prosper
Immensely. All of these gifts are his, if only
He'll stop being angry. And let him stop—Hades,
180   You know, is hard and implacable, and so he's the god
All mortals hate most! Let him give in to me,
For I am higher in royal rank, and besides
I'm an older man."

           Then the horseman, Gerenian Nestor,
Answered him thus: "Most famous son of Atreus,
King of men Agamemnon, no man would despise
These gifts of yours to kingly Achilles. So come,
Let us choose men and send them at once to the lodge
Of Peleus' great son. Or rather, let those I select
190   Be willing to go. First, then, I single out Phoenix,
Dear to Zeus, and with him the powerful Ajax
And brilliant Odysseus, and let these three be attended
By two of our heralds, Odius and Eurybates. But first
Bring water for the washing of hands, and call for holy
Silence, that we may pray to Cronos' son Zeus
For mercy in this our trouble."

           He spoke, and his words
Were pleasing to all. Quickly the heralds poured water
Over their hands, and the young men filled the bowls
200   Brimful of wine, and then the goblets, first pouring
Libation drops in the goblets of all. But when
They had made libations and drunk as much as they wished,
They left the lodge of Atreus' son Agamemnon.

And the horseman, Gerenian Nestor, with an earnest glance
At each, but especially at Odysseus, urgently
Ordered them all to do their best in persuading
The peerless son of Peleus.

    So off they went
Along the beach of the surf-booming sea, with many
A prayer to Poseidon, god who holds and shakes   210
The earth, that they might easily change the great heart
Of Aeacus' grandson Achilles. Now when they came
To the lodges and ships of the Myrmidons, there they found him
Soothing his soul with a resonant lyre, exquisitely
Wrought and carved, with a bridge of solid silver,
Part of the loot he had taken when he himself sacked
Eëtion's city.³ With this he was pleasantly passing
The time, as to it he sang of warriors' fame,
Alone but for Patroclus, who sat across
From his friend quietly awaiting the end of his song.   220
But now the envoys approached with shrewd Odysseus
Leading the way, and stood in the great man's presence.
And he, astonished, leaped up with the lyre in his hand,
And also Patroclus, seeing the men, got up
From his seat. Then swift Achilles greeted them, saying:

    "Welcome, my friends, for such you truly are.
Very great is our need of each other. Even in anger
You are to me the dearest of all the Achaeans."

    So saying, noble Achilles led them in
And gave them all chairs with coverings of purple, and at once   230
He spoke thus to Patroclus: "Set out a larger bowl,
You son of Menoetius, and mix us a livelier drink.
Then fill a cup for each of these men, for these
Are my dearest friends who sit here under my roof."

    At this Patroclus got busy. He moved a great block
Out into the firelight, and on it he laid the chines
Of a sheep and fat goat along with that of a huge,
Well-larded hog. And the driver Automedon held them
While noble Achilles carved. Expertly he cut up
The meat and put it on spits, and godlike Patroclus   240
Built up the fire. Then, when the flame had died down,
He spread the hot coals and laid the meat above them,
Resting the spits in holders and sprinkling the cuts
With holy salt. And when he had roasted the meat
And heaped it on platters, Patroclus put beautiful baskets
Of bread on the table, while Achilles gave helpings of meat.

Then he sat down by the wall across from Odysseus
And told his comrade Patroclus to sacrifice meat
To the gods, and Patroclus threw the gods' share in the fire.
250 And they all helped themselves to the good things before them, eating
And drinking as much as they wanted. Then Ajax nodded
To Phoenix. But Odysseus caught the signal, and filling
A cup with wine he pledged Achilles thus:
        "Here's to you, Achilles. We have no lack of fine food,
Either in the lodge of Atreus' son Agamemnon
Or here in yours. This has indeed been a wonderful
Meal. But we are not really concerned with food,
However delicious, for now, O god-nourished Prince,
Our eyes can see nothing but total destruction, and we
260 Are afraid. Unless you come back in all of your might,
We can as easily lose the benched ships as save them.
Not far from the ships and wall the confident Trojans
And their far-famed allies have made their camp
And kindled innumerable fires throughout the battalions.
They no longer think that we can keep them from falling
Upon our black ships. Great Zeus encourages them
With lightning-bolts on the right, and Hector exulting
In martial prowess rages like mad, trusting
In Zeus, but quite regardless of all other gods
270 To say nothing of men. Irresistible madness has made him
Her own. He prays for the speedy arrival of sacred
Young Dawn, and swears he will hew the high horns from the sterns
Of our ships and burn the hulls with ravenous fire,
Killing Achaeans reeling around in the smoke.
Such is the terrible fear in my heart, that the gods
May make his threats good and our fate be to die in the land
Of Troy so far from rich Argos where thoroughbreds graze.
But up, if now at last you are willing to enter
The horrible din of battling Trojans and save
280 The hard-pressed Achaeans. Otherwise, you too will suffer,
Nor is there any real help for evil done.
But come, before it's too late, and think how you
May help the Danaans and ward the evil day off.
Surely, old friend, your father Peleus was talking
To you the day he sent you from Phthia and home
To King Agamemnon, saying:
            " 'My son, if it be
Their wish, Athena and Hera will make you strong,
But you will have to restrain your own proud spirit.

Good will is always best. And should you find yourself   290
Caught in a ruinous quarrel, be reconciled quickly,
That Argives young and old may respect you still more.'[4]
    "Even so the old one bade you, but you have forgotten.
Still, though, it isn't too late for you to renounce
Your heart-eating wrath. And if you will, Agamemnon
Offers these adequate gifts, which I will enumerate
Now, if you will but listen. Here then are the tokens
That in his lodge Agamemnon promised to give you:
Seven tripods untouched by the fire, ten talents
Of gold and twenty bright cauldrons, along with twelve   300
Strong prize-taking horses, swift winners of many a race.
By no means lacking in treasure or precious gold
Would be that man whose wealth was as great as the prizes
These solid-hoofed horses have won him. And he will give you
Seven fair women of Lesbos, skillful weavers
Of matchless work, women he personally chose
From the spoil when you yourself took well-fortified Lesbos,
The loveliest women the world has to offer. He'll give you
These seven, and with them the daughter of Briseus, the girl
He took away. And he will swear a great oath   310
That never once has he slept or made love with her,
As men and women so naturally do. All
Of these things shall be yours at once, and if the immortals
Grant us the sack of Priam's great city, then you
Be present when we Achaeans are dividing the spoil,
That you may fill your ships full of gold and bronze,
And you may choose twenty women, the fairest in Troy
After Argive Helen herself. And if we return
To Achaean Argos, rich udder of earth, you
Shall be his own son-in-law, nor will he treat   320
His beloved and richly reared son Orestes any better.
He has at home in his solid-built palace three daughters:
Chrysothemis, Laodice, and Iphianassa. Of these
You may take the bride of your choice to the house of Peleus,
And he will not only forego all wedding gifts
From you, but will himself give a dowry far larger
Than any man yet has sent with a daughter. And he
Will give seven populous cities to you: Cardamyle,
Enope, grassy Hire, and hallowed Pherae,
Antheia, deep in meadows, lovely Aepeia,   330
And Pedasus, rich in vineyards. They're all near the sea
On the lower coast of sandy Pylos, and those

Who live there are wealthy in cattle and sheep, men
Who will honor you like a god and give you fine gifts,
And under your scepter they'll do as you say and prosper
Immensely. All of these gifts are yours, if only
You'll stop being angry.⁵ But if your heart is still full
Of hatred for Atreus' son, for him and his gifts,
Then at least have pity on the other united Achaeans
340 Now on the verge of total defeat. They will surely
Hold you in highest honor and glorify you
Like a god. For now you may take great Hector himself,
Since he in his self-destroying rage would come
Right up to you. He no longer thinks that our ships
Brought any man here to equal his prowess in war."
        Then Achilles, swift of foot, answered him thus:
"O god-sprung son of Laertes, resourceful Odysseus,
Regardless of persons, I have to say what I think
And what shall indeed come to pass. Don't sit here with me,
350 Coaxing and wheedling, first one and then the other.
For the gates of Hades are not more hateful to me
Than a man who hides one thing in his heart and says
Something else. I, then, will say what seems to me best.⁶
Atreus' son Agamemnon will not, I think,
Persuade me, nor the other Danaans either, since now
I know there were never to be any thanks at all
For my ceaseless efforts against the foe. He
Who lolls in his lodge has equal reward with him
Who fights on the field, coward and hero are honored
360 Alike, and death comes just as surely to the soldier
Who labors much as it does to the unmanly sluggard.
And what do I have to show for the pains my heart suffered,
Forever risking my life in battle? You've seen
A bird that brings in her bill whatever food
She can find to sustain her unfledged babies, while she
Herself most miserably goes without. Even so,
I've watched through many a sleepless night and fought
My way through many a bloody day, and all
For the sake of a woman. I've sailed in my ships to twelve
370 Well-garrisoned cities and plundered them all, and eleven
Others, I say, I've stormed and taken by land
Throughout the fertile Troad. Much marvelous booty
I took from them all, treasure I brought and gave
To Atreus' son Agamemnon. And he, having stayed
In camp beside his swift ships, would take what I won

And dole out a little, but most he would keep for himself.
Some he gave as prizes to princes and kings,
And they still have them untouched. But from me—and only
From me—he has taken and kept the bride I adored.

"Well let him sleep with her now and enjoy himself.   380
But why should Argives battle the Trojans? And why
Has this miserable son of Atreus gathered and led
This great army here? Wasn't it all for lovely
Blonde Helen? Can it be that of all mortal men, only
The sons of Atreus love their wives? Not so,
For any real man of good sense both loves and cares for
His own, as I loved her with all of my heart,
Though she was won by my spear. So now that he's played
Me false and taken my prize from my arms, let him
Not try me again. I know him too well, and now   390
He shall not persuade me.

"But you, Odysseus, let him
Make plans with you and the other chieftains to keep
The ruinous fire away from the ships. Surely
He's done a great deal without assistance from me.
He's built a wall and dug a ditch all around it,
A deep wide ditch bristling with sharp-pointed stakes.
Still, though, he hasn't been able to cope with the strength
Of man-killing Hector, who had no stomach for fighting
Out from the wall so long as I was in battle   400
Among the Achaeans. Then he would venture only
So far as the Scaean Gates and the oak tree. There
He awaited me once in single combat, and there
He just barely escaped my charge with his life. But now
That I am no longer inclined to battle great Hector,
Tomorrow I'll make an offering to Zeus and all
Of the gods, then launch my ships on the sea and load them
Down with treasure. Tomorrow at daybreak, then,
If you care to look out on the fish-full Hellespont water,
You'll see my ships pulling out from shore and in them   410
Men eager to row. Then, if the mighty Earthshaker
Grants me good sailing, I'll reach the rich soil of Phthia
On the third day out. Treasures uncounted I left there
To make my unfortunate way to this land, and still
More treasure I'll take home from here, gold, red bronze,
And fair-belted women, along with a plentiful store
Of gray iron—all wealth allotted to me. Even so,
My prize has been taken from me by the arrogant lord

Who gave it, King Agamemnon, son of Atreus.
420 So go and tell him all I've told you, and say it
Out loud in assembly before all the other Achaeans,
That they may also be angry, and warned. For he
In his utter meanness of spirit may even now
Be planning to cheat someone else of the Danaan fighters.
Yet he lacks the courage to so much as look at me
Face to face, greedy and shameless dog that he is!
I'll take no counsel with him, nor will I assist him
In fighting. For he has been utterly unfair to me,
Grievously sinning against me. Not again will I let him
430 Trick me with words. Of that he has done quite enough.
So let him be damned as he himself wishes, for Zeus
The contriver has robbed him of all good sense.
        "I hate
And despise his proffered gifts, nor do I value
The man himself worth a straw. Not if he gave me
Ten times all he has now, or twenty times,
And added to that every bit of the wealth that enters
Orchomenus or Egyptian Thebes—and in that city
Of a hundred gates, through each of which two hundred men
440 With horses and cars sally forth, more treasure is stored
In the houses of men than anywhere else in the world—
Not if he gave me gifts as numberless quite
As sand and dust, still Agamemnon could not
Prevail any more on my soul till he himself
Has personally paid for all of the insult and pain
That gnaws at my heart.
        "Nor will I take as my bride
Any daughter of Atreus' son Agamemnon, not
If she rivaled in beauty golden Aphrodite herself,
450 Or bright-eyed Athena in skill at handwork. Still
I would not marry any daughter of his. Let
The man choose some other Achaean, someone more
Like himself and more kingly than I. For if the gods keep me
And see me home safely, Peleus himself, I dare say,
Will find me a suitable wife. There is no shortage
Of Achaean girls throughout both Hellas and Phthia,
Daughters of chieftains in charge of protecting the cities.
From these I can have the beloved wife of my choice.
At home my proud heart very often desired to woo
460 And win some excellent wife, and enjoy life
With the wealth old Peleus won me. For I put a much

Higher value on life than on all the treasures men say
Were contained in the rich and populous city of Troy
Before we sons of Achaeans came, or,
For that matter, all the wealth laid up behind
The marble threshold of the archer god Phoebus Apollo
In rocky Pytho. For raiding can get a man cattle
And splendid fat sheep, and barter can get him tripods
And sorrel horses. But once his soul goes out
Through the barrier of his teeth, neither raiding nor barter   470
Can make it return. My goddess mother, Thetis
Of the silver feet, tells me I bear two fates
With me on my way to the grave. If I stay here
And fight about Troy, I'll never return to my home,
But men will remember my glory forever. On the other hand,
If I go back to the precious land of my fathers,
No glory at all will be mine, but life, long life,
Will be, and no early death shall ever come on me.
        "Yes, and I would advise you others also
To set sail for home, since now you no longer have hopes   480
Of taking steep Ilium. For loud-thundering Zeus holds out
A mighty arm above her and greatly inspirits
Her people. So go and perform the honored office
Of senior chiefs by giving my answer to all
The kings of Achaea, that they may devise some better
Plan than this to save the Achaean army
And hollow ships, for now their appeal to me
Has done them no good, because of the wrath I still have.
Phoenix, though, can spend the night here with us,
That he may go in the morning with me and the ships   490
Back to my own dear country, that is if he wants to.
I'll surely not force him to go."
        Such was his answer,
And all of them sat in silence, stunned by the force
Of his bitter refusal. At last, old Phoenix, driver
Of horses, spoke out among them, the tears streaming down
His face, so deeply he feared for the ships of Achaea:
"Resplendent Achilles, if you really mean to return,
And are so wrathful at heart that you have no wish
At all to keep the fierce fire away from the ships,   500
How could I stay here without you, dear child? The knightly
Old Peleus made me your guardian,[7] then sent us both
From Phthia to King Agamemnon, you a mere child
With no experience then of horrible war

Or of speaking in council where men win distinction. So Peleus
Sent me along to be your instructor in all
Of these things, that you might be an effective speaker
As well as a man of action. Hence, dear child,
I have no wish at all to stay here without you,
510 Not even if God himself should promise to strip me
Of age and make me as strong as I was on the day
I first left Hellas, land of glamorous women.
I fled from a quarrel with Ormenus' son, my father
Amyntor, who hated me on account of a fair-haired
Mistress whom he adored, thereby disgracing
His wife, my mother. So she was always begging me
Close at my knees to lie with the girl myself
And make her despise the old man. But I had no sooner
Done what my mother wished, than my father knew
520 What had happened and fearfully cursed me, calling out
On the dreaded Furies* for them to prevent my ever
Having a son of my own to take on my lap.
And the underworld powers, Hades and awesome Persephone,
Made his curse good, whereat I decided to use
My keen bronze and kill the old man, but some immortal
Restrained my rage, reminding me of public
Opinion and what the Achaeans would say of a man
Who killed his own father. But then my heart was too restless
To stay any longer at home with my hostile sire,
530 Though friends and kinsfolk did all they could to keep me
There in the palace. Daily they slaughtered many
Fine sheep and shuffling sleek cattle, and many fat swine
They singed and stretched out above the flame of Hephaestus,
Feasting and drinking much wine from the old man's jars.
All night long for nine nights they camped about me,
Taking turns at standing watch and feeding
The fires, one out in the front colonnade of the well-walled
Courtyard, the other up in the portico, right
In front of my bedroom door. But during the tenth
540 Dark night, I burst through the tightly closed doors of my chamber
And easily leaped the wall of the courtyard, nor was I
Seen by any of the guards or women servants.
Then I fled far away through the open fields

---

*The Furies—or Erinyes—are guardians of oaths and curses; they are especially sensitive
to the disrespect of parents.

Of Hellas to fertile Phthia, mother of flocks,
And the house of King Peleus. And warmly he took me in
And loved me quite as a wealthy father loves
His only son and heir. He made me rich
And the ruler of many subjects, and I went to live
On the furthest border of Phthia as lord over all
The Dolopians.   550
        "Since that time, O godlike Achilles,
I've loved you deeply and done all I could to make you
What you are. For you would go in to meals
With no one else but me, nor would you eat
Even then until I had taken you up on my lap
And cut you your fill of juicy meat and held
The wine to your lips. Many indeed were the times
When you, like the difficult baby you were, spluttered
The wine right back all over my tunic. Thus
I worked very hard for you and put up with a lot,   560
Since I knew very well that the gods were never to give me
A son of my own. So you, O godlike Achilles,
I tried to raise as my son, that someday you
Might save me from ruin and a sad, unseemly end.
        "Therefore, Achilles, master your pride. Relentlessness
Doesn't become you. Even the gods can yield,[8]
And theirs is surely superior majesty, honor,
And power. Yet they are appeased by offerings burned
On their altars, by humble prayers, reverent libations,
And the savory smoke that goes up to them when some   570
Poor supplicant sinner has foolishly broken their laws.
For Prayers are the daughters of almighty Zeus, and they always
Come limping along behind Sin, sad creatures with wrinkled
Skin and downcast eyes. Sin, however,
Is lusty and swift, and so outdistances them,
Arriving first all over the world and doing
Her damage to men, while Prayers come halting after
And try to heal the wounds of Sin. Now he
Who reveres these daughters of Zeus when they approach,
That man they greatly bless, and when he prays   580
They heed him. But if a man stubbornly turns from them
In refusal and sends them away, they go and pray
To Cronos' son Zeus that Sin may follow that man
Till he too falls and pays the full price for his pride.
So you, Achilles, be careful to reverence these daughters
Of God, who continue to bend the wills of all

Right-thinking men. For if Atreus' son were still
In his furious rage instead of offering you gifts
With promises of still more, I surely would not
590   Advise you to throw off your wrath and help the Argives,
No matter how desperate they were. But now he offers you
Many fine gifts with a pledge of more hereafter,
And besides he sends these envoys, choosing the most
Outstanding men in the whole Achaean army
And those whom you hold dearest of all the Argives.
Do not, then, scorn their coming to you and what
They have said, though before they came here no man could blame
Your wrath and resentment.
          "We've all heard similar stories
600   About the old heroes,[9] men who allowed fierce anger
To come upon them, but yielded to gifts and entreaty.
I'm thinking now of something that happened a long time
Ago, a crucial event of no recent occurrence,
And I will tell you, since we are all friends, how it was.
The Curetes once were fighting the staunch Aetolians
Around the walls of their city, beautiful Calydon,
And men on both sides were dying, the Aetolians bravely
Defending their town, the Curetes striving to sack it.
For on the Aetolians golden-throned Artemis had sent
610   A great evil, she being angry at Oeneus their King
For neglecting to offer her harvest first-fruits from his orchard.
All the other gods reveled on whole hecatombs from him,
While she alone, great Zeus's own daughter, got no
Sacrifice at all. He either forgot her completely,
Or thought he had done what he had not: great blindness of soul
Was surely upon him. So the goddess of flying arrows,
Deeply offended, sent against Oeneus a huge
And ferocious wild boar that flashed his white tusks and tore up
The King's great orchard, doing much damage, as fiercely
620   He rooted up many a large apple tree and laid it
Out on the ground—roots, sweet blossoms, and all.
But Oeneus' son Meleager killed the great boar,
Though not without gathering hunters and hounds from many
Strong cities. No meager force of mortals could ever
Have cut the beast down, so truly enormous he was,
And many were the men he heaped on the sad funeral pyre.
Then Artemis caused a savage and noisy quarrel
Over the spoils, a fight between the Curetes

And great-souled Aetolians, both sides eager to take
The huge head and shaggy hide as trophies.   630
  "Now just
So long as Prince Meleager, dear to the War-god,
Fought for his people, the Curetes steadily lost,
Unable to hold their own outside the walls
Of the city, though many the men they had brought there. But then
Wrath seized Meleager, wrath that swells the hearts
Of others too, no matter how wise they may be.
Meleager quarreled with his own dear mother Althaea,
Daughter of Thestius, King of the brave Curetes,
And sullenly lay at home beside his young wife,   640
The fair Cleopatra, child of Euenus' daughter,
Trim-ankled Marpessa, and Idas, the strongest man
Of his time, Idas who drew his powerful bow
Against lord Phoebus Apollo himself, when fighting
The god for the trim-ankled maid Marpessa. Later,
At home, he and Marpessa called their daughter
Halcyone, thinking of how like the halcyon bird
Her mother had mournfully cried when the far-working god
Snatched her away—their daughter whom all others called
Cleopatra.   650
  "And now by her side Meleager lay,
Indulging his wrath and resentment because of the curses
His mother called down upon him out of fierce grief
For her brother Meleager had slain. She fell on her knees
And beat with her hands on the all-feeding earth, streaking
Her bosom with tears and praying to the infernal powers,
To Hades and awesome Persephone, begging them both
To kill her son. And the Fury that stalks through the mist,
She of the ruthless heart, heard her from Erebus.
  "Soon the Curetes were raising a din at the gates   660
And storming the walls with a battering, thunderous noise.
Then the Aetolian elders besought Meleager
To come out and ward off the foe. They sent as envoys
To him the godly high priests of the city and promised
To give him a splendid reward. He could take, they said,
His choice of fifty acres from the richest part
Of the fair Calydonian plain, half to be
In vineyard land, half in land for plowing.
And often his knightly old father begged him to help.
He stood outside the high-roofed room of his son   670

And shook the well-bolted doors, fervently pleading.
His sisters and queenly mother kept after him too,
But to them his refusal was firmer than ever. Even
His friends, those who were dearest and truest of all,
Even they could not change his mind. But when the Curetes
Were scaling the walls, firing the city, and raining
Their missiles down hard on the room of Prince Meleager,
At last his fair-belted wife came to him in tears
And vividly pictured for him the horrors that people
680 Suffer when enemies take their town, reminding
Him of the men all slaughtered, of the city reduced
To ashes, of children and fair-belted women dragged off
By the foe. Her lurid account stirred Meleager's
Soul to the point where he went out and donned
His flashing armor.[10] Thus he did what his own heart
Wanted and kept the Aetolians safe from the evil
Day. But they thereafter gave him none
Of the many and gracious gifts they had earlier offered.
He saved the people, but late, and so got nothing
690 For what he did.
        "But you, my friend, don't let
This happen to you. Think otherwise, and don't allow
Some demon to harden your heart as his was. To save
The ships already burning will surely be
Much harder. Come then, while gifts and honor are yours
For the mere accepting, and then you'll live as a god
Among the Achaeans. But if, too late for gifts,
You enter the man-ruining war, you may indeed
Drive our enemies back, but the honor we offer you now
700 Will be no longer the same."
        Then swift Achilles
Answered: "Phoenix, my god-sprung good old father,
What do I care for this honor you offer? I'm honored
Enough, I think, by Zeus himself, and the favor
He shows me will keep me here by the curving ships
So long as there's breath in my body and strength in my limbs.
And here's something else I'll say for you to remember.
Don't try to confuse me with grieving and weeping, hoping
That I'll do the pleasure of Atreus' son Agamemnon.
710 It hardly becomes you to care for that man at all,
Lest my love for you be changed into hatred. It would be
Much better, I think, for you to oppose whoever
Hurts me. Take half of my kingdom, Phoenix, and half

Of my royal prestige, but the message I've given these others
To bear shall surely remain unchanged. Meanwhile,
Stay here with me and sleep on an excellent bed.
Then tomorrow at dawn we'll make up our minds whether we
Should go back to our own or stay where we are."[11]

    So saying,
He nodded his brow at Patroclus to start making up   720
A well-covered bed for Phoenix, that all of the others
Might quickly decide to leave. But Ajax, the godlike
Son of Telamon, spoke out among them, saying:
"God-sprung son of Laertes, resourceful Odysseus,
Let us go now, since surely our mission has failed
And we are obliged to tell the results, however
Unpleasant, to the Danaan chiefs, who must be sitting up
Waiting for us. Achilles has filled his proud heart
With savage, inhuman hatred. He has become
A cruel and ruthless man, who cannot remember   730
The love of his friends and how we idolized him
Like nobody else among the black ships. Incredibly
Pitiless man! Why others accept recompense
From one who has murdered a brother or even a son,
And the killer who pays the blood-price in full stays on
In his land, while the kinsman's revengeful proud spirit is checked
By the wealth he receives. But to you, Achilles, the gods
Have given a heart both evil and changeless, and all
Because of one girl. And here we have offered you seven
Of the loveliest girls there are, and a great deal more   740
Besides. So come, be gracious and remember that we
Are your guests. And here beneath your roof we have come
Representing all of the Danaans, and still we would like
Very much to remain your nearest and dearest friends
Among the whole host of Achaeans."

    And swift Achilles
Answered him thus: "O god-sprung ruler of many,
Telamonian Ajax, I almost agree with all
That you say, but my heart swells with bitter rage
Whenever I think how Atreus' son insulted   750
Me mid the Argives, as though I were some despised
And dishonored outsider. So go and deliver my message,
For I will not fight again in any man's bloody
War till wise-hearted Priam's son, great Hector,
Reaches the Myrmidon lodges and ships, killing
Argives all the way, and puts his torch to the hulls.

But Hector, however hungry for war he may be,
Will stop his advance, I think, when he reaches my lodge
And looming black vessel!"[12]
760   He spoke, and each of them took
A two-handled cup, poured a libation, and left,
Walking back down the long line of ships with Odysseus striding
Ahead. But Patroclus at once instructed his men
And the women servants to make up a well-covered bed
For Phoenix and quickly they did as he said, spreading
The frame with fleeces and blanket and smooth linen sheet.
On this the old one lay down and waited for bright Dawn
To come. But Achilles slept in one corner of the spacious,
Strongly built lodge and with him a woman, one
770   Whom he had brought from Lesbos, the pretty Diomeda,
Daughter of Phorbas. And Patroclus lay down on a bed
In the opposite corner with fair-gowned Iphis beside him,
A girl given him by kingly Achilles when he
Laid Scyrus waste, Enyeus' steep citadel.
        Now when the envoys got back and entered the lodge
Of Atreus' son, the kings of Achaea stood up
All around them, raising their cups of gold and asking them
Questions. But surely most urgent of all was the king
Of men Agamemnon, asking: "Come now, most worthy
780   Odysseus, great glory of all the Achaeans, tell me
If he is willing to ward off fierce fire from the ships,
Or did he refuse you because his great heart still seethes
With bitter resentment?"
        And noble, long-suffering Odysseus:
"Most famous Atrides, commander-in-chief Agamemnon,
Achilles has no intentions at all of quenching
His wrath and resentment. Now, in fact, he is filled
With more rage than ever, and says he will have no part
Of you or your gifts. And you he advises to meet
790   With the Argives and make some plan for saving the ships
And Achaea's army. As for himself, he threatens
To launch at dawn his well-benched, graceful ships.
And he says he would counsel the other Achaeans also
To set sail for home, since now you no longer have hopes
Of taking steep Ilium. For loud-thundering Zeus holds out
A mighty arm above her and greatly inspirits
Her people. These were his very words, and here
Are the men who went with me, Ajax and two wise heralds,
To confirm what I say. But the old man Phoenix will spend the night

There. Achilles urged him to stay, that tomorrow   800
The old one may go with him and his ships back to
His own dear country, that is if he wants to. He says
He'll not force him to go."
        Thus bluntly Odysseus reported,
And the grieving kings of Achaea sat a long time,
Stunned and silent, till finally strong Diomedes,
He of the great battle-scream, spoke out among them:
"Most famous Atrides, commander-in-chief Agamemnon,
Would you had never pleaded at all with Peleus'
Peerless son, or offered him all those gifts.   810
He's haughty enough with no help from us, but now
You have made him more haughty than ever. Hence we've no choice
But to leave him alone, to go or stay as he wishes.
He'll not fight again till the heart in his breast says fight,
Or until some god sets him on. But come, let all of us
Do as I say and go to our beds, now that
We've taken our fill of the meat and wine men need
To keep up their strength and courage. But you, O King,
As soon as fair Dawn of the rosy fingers appears,
Marshal your soldiers and horses in front of the ships   820
And urge them to battle. Then fight in the front rank yourself."
        The kings all had praise for these words from brave Diomedes,
Breaker of horses. They poured their libations and went
To their lodges, where each received the sweet gift of sleep.

BOOK X

The Night Adventure

Beside their ships all other kings of Achaea
Slumbered throughout the night, fast in the soft bonds
Of sleep, but no sweet sleep held the people's shepherd,
Atreus' son Agamemnon, so worried was he
By the many problems of war.[1] As when the husband
Of lovely-haired Hera splits the sky with his lightning,
Foretelling some storm of rain unspeakably heavy,
Or hail, or snow that covers the plowlands, or else
Foretelling the start of ravenous wide-gaping war,
10   Even so, from deep in his breast, groans tore the trembling
And fearful heart of King Agamemnon. Whenever
He looked toward the Trojan plain, he marveled at all
The many fires that burned before Troy, and at
The sound of flutes and pipes and the hubbub of men.
But then, when he looked toward the ships and troops of Achaea,
He pulled his hair out by the roots in fervent pleas
To high-dwelling Zeus, and greatly his proud heart groaned.
At last he thought of a plan he preferred, to go first
Of all to Neleus' son Nestor and work out some scheme
20   With him for warding off ruin from the Danaan army.
So he got up and put on his tunic, and on
His shining feet bound beautiful sandals, then threw
Round his shoulders the tawny-red skin of a lion, a fiery
Huge pelt that reached all the way to his feet. So clad,
He picked up his spear and went out.
           And King Menelaus
Likewise lay wakeful, fearful and trembling lest ruin
Should come on the Argives who for his sake had crossed
The wide water, their hearts resolved on making fierce war.
30   About his broad shoulders he slung the spotted skin
Of a leopard, put on his helmet of bronze, and took up
A spear in his powerful hand. Then he went out
To rouse his brother, the mighty commander-in-chief
Of all the Argives, honored by them like a god.

He found him covering his shoulders with exquisite armor
Close by the stern of his ship, and glad indeed
Was King Agamemnon to see him. But the first to speak
Was he of the great battle-scream, Menelaus, saying:
"Why, my brother, why are you arming now?
Are you going to wake up some comrade of yours to spy   40
On the Trojans? I very much fear you'll find nobody
Willing to undertake that, to go out alone
Through the dead of night and spy on hostile warriors.
Such work requires an extremely brave-hearted man!"
    And powerful King Agamemnon answered him thus:
"You and I both, my god-nurtured brother, have need
Of advice sufficiently shrewd to deliver the Argives
And save the ships, now that Zeus has changed
His mind and looks with far greater favor on offerings
From Hector than he does on any from us. For I   50
Have never seen, nor heard another man tell of,
A warrior doing in only one day so much
Sheer damage as god-loved Hector alone has done
To the sons of Achaeans, he that was born of neither
Goddess nor god. Still the huge devastation
That man has wrought on the Argives will live in the minds
Of Achaeans for many generations to come. But go now
And run with all speed down the line of ships and call to us
Ajax and kingly Idomeneus. Meanwhile, I'll go
And rouse Nestor to see if he will be willing to go out   60
And speak to the stalwart company of sentries and put them
More on the alert. They'll pay more attention to him
Than to anyone else, for his own son Thrasymedes
Captains the guard with Idomeneus' squire Meriones.
We put those two in command of the whole detachment."
    And battle-roaring Menelaus answered by asking:
"But what do you have in mind for me to do then,
After I give them your message? Shall I wait for you there
With them, or fully give them your word and run back
To rejoin you?"   70
    Then the king of men Agamemnon replied:
"Stay there, or as we go we might possibly miss
Each other, for paths through the camp are many. But call out
Loudly wherever you go and wake up the men,
Being careful to call each man by the lineage and name
Of his father. Don't be too proud to labor and give
Each man his due of respect. We too must toil—

Especially we. For from the time we were born
Zeus laid out for us a heavy allotment of sorrow."

80   He spoke, and dispatched his brother with these explicit
Instructions. But he himself went off after Nestor,
The people's shepherd, and found him lying outside
His lodge on a comfortable bed by the stern of his ship
With richly wrought armor beside him—his shield, two spears,
And a gleaming helmet. And there lay the glinting war-belt
With which the old one girded himself whenever,
Unyielding to painful old age, he put on his armor
And led his troops into man-eating battle. Now
He lifted his head, and raising himself on an elbow
90   Questioned Atrides thus:

"Who goes there alone
By the ships, roaming the camp through the darkness of night
While other people are sleeping? What are you looking for,
Man—some mule of yours, or one of your friends?
Don't come any closer until you declare who you are
And what it is you're after!"

Then great Agamemnon
Answered: "Neleus' son Nestor, pride of all
The Achaeans, surely you know Agamemnon, son
100   Of Atreus, me whom Zeus gives painful labor
Beyond all others, constant suffering and toil
So long as I'm able to breathe and move my limbs.
I'm up and abroad because sweet sleep refuses
To come on my lids, so worried am I about
The war and woes of Achaeans. I'm terrified now
At the danger we face, nor can I make up my mind
What to do, as sadly I waver. My heart pounds so hard
It almost leaps from my breast, and my powerful legs
Tremble and knock beneath me. But if you are willing
110   To help, since you too are sleepless, come, let us go
To the sentries and see that they have not forgotten their guard
And yielded to drowsy fatigue. We can brook no sleeping
Out there. The enemy camps hard by, and for all
We know they are planning a night attack right now!"

Then horse-handling Gerenian Nestor replied:
"Most famous Atrides, commander-in-chief Agamemnon,
Zeus the contriver will surely not fulfill for Hector
All that he hopes for. In fact, if Achilles changes
His mind and rids himself of miserable rage,
120   I dare say Hector will find himself caught in toils

More grievous than ours. Of course I'll go with you, but let us
Get others up too—Diomedes, famed as a spearman,
Odysseus and Ajax the swift, and sturdy Meges,
Son of Phyleus. And it would be well for someone
To go for the godlike Ajax, Telamon's son,
And King Idomeneus, whose ships are furthest away
And not at all close. But much as I love and respect
Menelaus, and though you'll probably be angry with me,
I will not conceal what I think about his sleeping
And leaving this labor to you. He should be up   130
And working among the leaders, urging them on
To do their best. For the need is desperate that now
Has come on us all!"

    And the king of men Agamemnon
Answered him thus: "Old sire, some other time
I'll tell you myself to chide him. He's often remiss
And idle, not that he's lazy or fearful or foolish,
But simply because he's always looking to me
And waiting to follow my lead. But tonight he was up
Before even I was, and came to me. Hence   140
I've already sent him for those you just mentioned. So come,
Let us go. We shall find them outside the gates of the camp
Among the sentries, for there I told them to gather."

    And knightly Gerenian Nestor answered him, saying:
"If Menelaus keeps that up, no man of the Argives
Will ever resent his urging him on, or refuse
To obey his orders."

    So saying, he put on his tunic
And on his shining feet bound beautiful sandals,
And around him he buckled a large crimson cloak, downy soft   150
And of double thickness. Then he took up a sturdy
Bronze-pointed spear and strode off down through the ships
Of the bronze-clad Achaeans.

    Now first to be wakened by him
Was Odysseus, godlike in wisdom. The old one's voice
Rang in his ears and out from his lodge he came,
Answering thus: "Why do you roam our encampment
Of ships through the dead of night by yourselves? What urgent
Need is upon you?"

    And knightly old Nestor replied: 160
"Zeus-born son of Laertes, resourceful Odysseus,
Don't blame us for this. You know what unspeakable grief
Overwhelms the Achaeans. But come on with us, that we

May wake someone else, whoever can help us most
In deciding this night on whether to fight as before
Or board our ships and flee."
          At this the shrewd
Odysseus went back in his lodge, slung round his shoulders
A richly wrought shield, and followed his friends. Soon
170 They came to Tydeus' son Diomedes. They found him
Outside his lodge lying beside his war-gear,
While all around him his comrades were sleeping, their heads
On their shields and the butt-end spikes of their spears driven into
The ground. Thus the bronze points reflected the firelight
And shone far out through the night like the lightning-flashes
Of Father Zeus. The heroic Diomedes was also
Asleep, with his head resting on a lustrous soft rug
And the hide of a field-ranging ox beneath him.
          The knightly
180 Old Nestor approached, and rousing the chief with a touch
Of his foot, berated him thus to his face: "Wake up,
You son of Tydeus. Are you going to lie there snoring
All night? Or haven't you heard that the Trojans are camped
Just up the plain from us and the ships. Believe me,
The space between us is far too small for comfort!"
          At this, Diomedes sprang up from his sleep and answered
In these winged words: "You're a hard one, old sire, and never
Rest from your toiling. But are there no younger sons
Of Achaeans who might be up and rousing the kings
190 Throughout our sleeping host? Truly, old sire,
There is no keeping up with you!"
          And knightly old Nestor
Replied: "You speak as you should, my friend. I have
Matchless sons myself, and there are many others, any one
Of whom could go and rouse the chieftains. But now
Without doubt a desperate need overwhelms the Achaeans,
Whose fate uncertainly stands on a razor's edge,
Balanced between a chance to go on living
And sheer, most miserable ruin! But go, if you really
200 Feel sorry for me, and rouse up Ajax the swift
And Phyleus' son Meges, for indeed you are younger than I am."
          So brave Diomedes threw round his shoulders the skin
Of a lion, a fiery huge pelt that reached all the way
To his feet, then seized his spear and took off. Having roused
The two leaders, he brought them back where the others were
          waiting.

Now when they came to the sentries outside the walls,
They caught no chief of the guard asleep at his post,
But all were armed and alert. As dogs keep restless
Watch about a yard full of sheep, sleepless
Indeed when they hear some ferocious wild beast come crashing   210
His way through the wooded hills with baying hounds
And shouting men at his back, so no sweet sleep
Came on the lids of the sentries as they kept watch
Throughout that evil night. They kept their faces
Turned toward the plain, awake to the slightest sound
Of advancing Trojans.
      Seeing them so, old Nestor
Was glad, and spoke these words winged with encouragement:
"Continue, dear sons, thus sharply on the alert,
Unless you would like to make our enemies happy."   220
      So saying, he quickly strode out through the trench, followed
By all the Argive chieftains who had been called
To the council and by Meriones and Nestor's staunch son
Thrasymedes, whom they had invited to join in their planning.
They left the deep trench and sat down together on ground
That was open and clear of corpses, the very spot
Huge Hector had been when night came upon him and he
Had turned back from his slaughter of Argives. There they sat
Discussing their plight till Nestor addressed them, saying:
      "My friends, is there no one here with sufficient faith   230
In his own bold spirit to go mid the arrogant Trojans,
Thus to catch and cut down some straggler of theirs?
Or he might even hear what the Trojans are planning, whether they
Want to stay where they are so close to the ships, or would rather
Go back to the city again now that they've won
Their victory. If any man found out all this and returned
To us unharmed, his fame would be great among men
All over the sky-covered world. For each of the kings
Who captain the ships will give to him, as a mark
Of matchless distinction, a solid black ewe and suckling   240
Lamb, and he will always be honored at feasts
And royal banquets."
      He spoke, but no one else
Said a word till battle-roaring Diomedes spoke
To them thus: "Nestor, my heart and proud spirit urge me
To enter the camp of the hostile, hovering Trojans.
However, if some other man would go with me, there would be
More comfort and confident strength. When two go together,

One at least can look forward and see the advantage,
250 Whereas if a man by himself discerns anything,
Still he is likely to hesitate sadly and make
Disastrous mistakes."
     So spoke Diomedes, and many
Volunteered to go with him. The two Ajaxes, comrades
Of Ares, said they would go, as did Meriones
And Nestor's son Thrasymedes. Spear-famed Menelaus,
Son of Atreus, also was willing, and Odysseus,
He of the patient but ever-adventuring heart,
Was eager to slip in among the huge host of Trojans.
260 Then the king of men Agamemnon spoke to them thus:
     "My dear Diomedes, choose whom you will to go with you,
But choose the best of these who so eagerly offer
Themselves. Don't let your respect for person and rank
Influence your choice so that you leave the better man
Here and go with one not so good. Now is
No time to consider one's lineage or more royal station."
     This he spoke out of fear, terrified lest
His tawny-haired brother Menelaus be chosen. Then again
Diomedes spoke out among them: "If you really want me
270 To choose a companion myself, how could I forget
Godlike Odysseus, whose heart and manly spirit
Are eager and ready beyond the daring of others
When it comes to dangerous toil of any kind—
And Pallas Athena adores him. If he will go with me,
The two of us might go through flaming fire
And come back alive, for no one else can think
So quickly and well."
     To which long-suffering Odysseus:
"Diomedes, don't overly praise or blame me. You're talking
280 To Argives, and they know well what I am. But come,
Let us start, for now it is late and dawn is already
Near. See, the stars have moved on in their courses
And the night is more than two-thirds gone. All
We have left is the waning third watch."
     He spoke, and both men
Received their dread weapons. Battle-staunch Thrasymedes
Gave a two-edged sword to Tydeus' son—since his own
He had left at the ship—and with it a shield. Then he put
On his head a helmet of bull's-hide, hornless and crestless,
290 A leather casque of the sort often worn by lusty
Young fighters. Meanwhile, Meriones gave Odysseus

A bow, quiver, and sword, and set on his head
A helmet of hide, reinforced inside with tightly
Stretched thongs and a lining of felt, while around it outside
Were skillfully fixed the white teeth of a tusk-flashing boar.
This helmet Autolycus* stole in Eleon, he
Having broken into the thick-walled wealthy palace
Of Ormenus' son Amyntor, the father of Phoenix.
And Autolycus gave it to strong Amphidamas, King
Of Cythera, who took it into Scandeia, his harbor   300
At home, and King Amphidamas gave the toothed helmet
As a guest-gift to Molus, and Molus passed it on
To his son Meriones to take with him and wear.
And now it protected the head of brilliant Odysseus.
    When the two had received their dread weapons, they left the
        kings
And went on their way. And Pallas Athena sent an omen
For them, a heron hard by on the right, and though
The night was too dark for the bird to be seen, they heard
Its cry, and Odysseus, glad at the bird-sign, offered
This prayer to Athena: "Hear me, O child of aegis-great   310
Zeus, you that stand by me in all of my labors
And constantly watch over me, love me now
As never before, and grant that we may return
To the ships, having covered ourselves with glory by some
Great work of war to fill the Trojans with sorrow."
    Then battle-roaring Diomedes prayed his prayer
To Athena, saying: "Now, O unwearied child
Of Zeus, hear also me, and go with me now
As once you went with glorious Tydeus my father
Into the city of Thebes, where he had been sent   320
By the bronze-clad Achaeans with a message of honeyed words
For the Theban descendants of Cadmus. But on his way back,
He and you, fair goddess, did fearfully bloody work
Against that ambush of Thebans, for you were eager
To stand by his side.† So now be equally willing,
I pray, to go by my side and guard me. And I
Will offer to you a sleek yearling heifer, broad-browed
And unbroken, never yet in any man's yoke. Such a beast,
With horns wrapped in gold, will I sacrifice to you."

---

*Autolycus ("Wolfman") is Odysseus' thievish maternal grandfather; see *Odyssey* 19.
†For Tydeus' exploits, see IV.450 and V.893.

330   Such were their prayers, and Pallas Athena heard them.
Then, having prayed to great Zeus's daughter, they paced
Along through the blackness of night like two mighty lions,
Picking their way through the carnage and gore, through the blood-
                    stained
Corpses and weapons of war.
              Nor did Hector allow
The lordly Trojans much sleep. He called a meeting
Of all the leaders, those who were captains and counselors
Of the Trojans, and when they had gathered he spoke
To them and unfolded the plan he had made, saying:
340   "Who now will take on and do, for a very great gift,
This work I want done? Truly that man's reward
Shall be ample and sure. For I will give him a chariot
Drawn by the best two neck-arching horses we capture
Tomorrow among the swift ships of Achaea. These
Shall be his in addition to all the glory he'll win,
Whoever is daring enough to go in close
To the fast-faring ships and find out whether they have
The usual guard, or whether our beaten foes
Are far too terribly weary to watch through the night
350   And already are planning to flee."
              For a time his words
Got no response. But among the Trojans there
Was a man called Dolon,* the son of a sacred herald,
Eumedes, and rich in bronze and gold. Now Dolon
Was not at all handsome, but he was an excellent runner,
And the only brother to sisters five in all.
These are the words he spoke in the midst of the gathering:
              "Hector, my heart and proud spirit impel me to go
In close to the fast-faring ships and learn all I can.
360   But first I would like you to take this staff, lift it up
And swear to me that you really will make me a present
Of Achilles' ornate bronze-bright car and the horses
That draw that matchless man. And I will not
Be useless to you as a scout, nor will I disappoint you.
For I will go straight through the enemy camp to the vessel
Of King Agamemnon, where, I dare say, the leaders
Will be in council, deciding on whether to fight
Or board their ships and flee."

---

*The name Dolon means "Sneaky" or "Tricky."

He spoke, and Hector,
Receiving the speaker's staff, swore to Dolon   370
This oath: "Now may Hera's bolt-crashing lord, great Zeus
Himself, be my witness that no other Trojan shall mount
Behind those horses. You alone, I say, shall glory
In them from tomorrow on."
　　　　Even such was his oath,
Empty and vain, but enough to get Dolon started.
Quickly he slung his curved bow round his shoulders along with
The pelt of a great gray wolf. Then he put on his head
A ferret-skin cap,[2] seized a sharp spear, and left
His own camp for the enemy ships, but from those ships   380
He was never to come with any tidings for Hector.
Once out beyond the huge crowd of horses and men,
He ran swiftly on, but Zeus-sprung Odysseus saw him
Approaching and spoke these words to the friend at his side:
　　　　"There, Diomedes, some Trojan is coming from camp,
Either to spy on our ships or to strip a few corpses—
I do not know which. Let's let him get by us a little
And then we'll rush out and seize him. And if he outruns us,
Be sure to give chase, threatening him with your spear,
And drive him in toward the ships, away from his camp.   390
Thus he'll not escape us and break for the city."
　　　　At once they lay down mid the corpses just off the place
Where Dolon would pass, and he unsuspecting ran swiftly
By them. But when he had gone about the length
Of a mule-plowed furrow—and mules are better than oxen
At drawing the jointed plow through deep new ground—
Then the two gave chase, and he, when he heard their footsteps
Pounding behind him, stopped still in his tracks, hoping
With all of his heart that they were friends whom Hector
Had sent from the Trojans to call him back from his mission.   400
But when they got a spear-cast away and closer,
He knew they were hostile and set out again, this time
At top speed, with his enemies swiftly, fiercely pursuing.
And as when a brace of razor-fanged good hunting hounds
Race through the woods, pressing hard on a doe or hare
That flees and screams before them, so now Diomedes
And city-sacking Odysseus cut Dolon off
From the Trojan host and pursued him relentlessly hard.
But when, as he sped toward the ships, he had come almost
To the sentries, Athena gave Tydeus' son a new   410
Burst of strength, that none of the other bronze-clad Achaeans

Might strike Dolon down and boast to have dealt the first blow.
So powerful lord Diomedes, poising his spear,
Drew close to him, and shouted:
    "Halt! or I
Will bring you down with my spear, nor will you live long,
I think, once I get hold of you!"
    So saying,
He hurled his spear, but purposely missed, throwing
420 The gleaming shaft sufficiently high for the point
To pass above his right shoulder and fix itself
In the ground. The terrified Dolon froze in his tracks
And turned a pale olive with fear, and there he stood
With gibbering tongue and chattering teeth till both
Of his mighty pursuers came panting up and caught
His hands. Then starting to weep he spoke to them thus:
    "Alive, take me alive! and I will ransom
Myself, for at home I have great stores of bronze
And gold and highly wrought iron. Of these my father
430 Would gladly give you a ransom past counting, if he
Should hear that I am alive at the Argive ships."
    And shrewd Odysseus answered: "Cheer up, and don't even
Think about dying. But answer my questions, and tell me
The truth. Where were you going, headed away
From your camp and toward the ships, running along
Through the darkness of night when other mortals are sleeping?
Did you intend to strip a few corpses, or did Hector
Send you down to the hollow ships as a spy?
Or could it be that you came at your own heart's urging?"
440   Then Dolon, with legs that shook beneath him, replied:
"Hector beguiled me with foolhardy hopes. He promised
To give me the solid-hoofed horses and bronze-bright car
Of proud Achilles, son of Peleus, if I
Would go as he bade, close to the enemy, through
The blackness of quick-coming night and spy on the ships,
To see if they have the usual guard, or whether
Our beaten foes are far too terribly weary
To watch through the night and already are planning to flee."
    Then smiling at him, resourceful Odysseus answered:
450 "Surely your heart was set on a very great prize,
The horses of fire-souled Achilles. But no mere mortal
Can well control those horses. Only Achilles
Can, for he is the son of an immortal mother.
But come, answer my questions, and tell me the truth.

Where, when you left camp, was the army's commander
Hector? Where is his war-gear lying, and where
Are his horses? How are all the sentries disposed,
And where are the companies sleeping? And what are the Trojans
Planning among themselves—to stay where they are,
So close to the ships, or to go back into the city   460
Now that they've won their victory?"

    Then Dolon, son
Of Eumedes, spoke to him thus: "Believe me, I'll answer
Your questions truly. Hector, with all his advisers,
Is holding a council of war out by the tomb
Of sacred Ilus, away from all the confusion.
And as for the sentries you ask about, my lord,
No special detail has been posted to guard and protect
The camp. But by each fire of the sleeping Trojans,
Those who must are up and alert, and they   470
Call others to guard when the watches change. But all
Our many and far-called allies are asleep, for they leave
Guard-duty to Trojans, since none of their children or wives
Is here and in danger."

    And wily Odysseus replied:
"How, then, do the allies sleep, right in among
The horse-breaking Trojans or somewhere apart? Tell me
Exactly, since I want to know in full detail."

    And Eumedes' son answered him thus: "Again
I will tell you the truth. There toward the sea lie the Carians   480
And crook-bowed Paeonian archers, and near them the Leleges,
Caucones, and the valiant Pelasgians, whereas the Lycians
And hard-charging Mysians, the horse-borne Phrygian fighters
And chariot-armed Maeonians lie on the ground
Allotted to them over there toward Thymbra.
But why do you ask me all these details? If you're
Really eager to raid the Trojan host, there
On the very verge of the camp, apart from the others,
Sleep the Thracians, newly arrived, and among them
Their King, Rhesus,[3] son of Eïoneus. His   490
Are the biggest and best-looking horses that I've ever seen,
Whiter than snow and swift as the wind. And his chariot
Gleams with inlaid silver and gold, and he brought
With him huge pieces of golden armor, a truly
Incredible sight. No mortal man should ever
Wear such stuff, fit only for immortal gods.
But take me now to the fast-faring ships, or tie me

Up tight and leave me here. Then go and see
For yourselves whether I have spoken the truth or not."
500   But scowling at him, fierce Diomedes replied:
"Now that you, Dolon, are in our hands, don't set
Your heart on escape, though the information you've brought us
Is good. For if we let you go now, you'll surely
Come back to our swift ships, either to spy
On us or fight man to man. But if at my hands
You lose your life now, you'll never be any trouble
To Argives again!"
        He spoke, and Dolon reached up
To take hold of his beard and plead,* but huge Diomedes
510 Lashed out with his sword and brought it down on the neck
Of the Trojan, severing both of the sinews, and right
In the midst of a word his head rolled down in the dust.
Then they took off his ferret-skin cap and the gray wolf-skin
And stripped him of supple curved bow and long spear, and royal
Odysseus took these in his hand, held them up high
To booty-bringing Athena, and prayed to her, saying:
        "Rejoice, O goddess, in these, for you are the first,
Of all the Olympian immortals, to whom we will offer.
Now guide us on to the horses and sleeping soldiers
520 Of Thrace."
        So saying, Odysseus hung up the spoils
On a tamarisk bush and marked it well with handfuls
Of reeds and leafy tamarisk branches, that they
Might not miss the place as they returned through the darkness
Of fast-falling night. Then on they went through the blood-stained
Corpses and war-gear, till soon they reached the contingent
Of Thracian fighters. All were sleeping, overcome
By fatigue, and their excellent armor lay by them there
On the ground, neatly stacked in three rows, and each man's yoke
530 Of horses stood beside him. Rhesus the King
Slept in the midst, and close beside him stood
His fast horses, tied by the reins to the front handrail
Of his chariot. Him Odysseus was first to see,
And pointing him out to strong Diomedes, he said:
        "There, Diomedes, that's the man, and there
Are the horses that Dolon, whom we just killed, referred to.
But come, give all you've got! It isn't like you

---

*On supplication, see endnote 1 to book VI.

To stand there armed and idle. Untie the horses—
Or start killing men, and I will take care of the horses."

He spoke, and into the heart of King Diomedes   540
Bright-eyed Athena breathed might, and he laid about him,
Killing men right and left, and from them came grim sounds
Of groaning as they were struck with the sword, and the ground
Ran red with their blood. Like a lion that comes on an unguarded
Flock of sheep or goats and springs in among them
With heart set on slaughter, so now the son of Tydeus
Slashed about mid the Thracian troops till twelve
Of them lay dead. And those whom Tydeus' son smote
With the sword, Odysseus, coming behind, would seize
By the foot and drag aside, endeavoring to clear   550
The way for the silver-maned horses, that as yet were unused to
War and might easily panic at treading on corpses.
Rhesus the King was the thirteenth man whom Tydeus' son
Robbed of honey-sweet life. He lay there dreaming
And breathing hard, for his dream had taken the form
Of stern Diomedes, grandson of Oeneus, such being
The will of Athena.

Meanwhile, steady Odysseus
Untied the solid-hoofed horses and used the reins
To bind them together, then drove them clear of the crowd,   560
Using his bow for a whip, for he had not thought
To take the bright lash from its place in the colorful car.
Once clear, he whistled to let Diomedes know.

But that grim King was lingering amid the carnage,
Pondering what deed would be most dog-daring to do,
Whether he should take the chariot, wherein the inlaid
Armor lay, and draw it off by the shaft,
Or pick it up high and carry it off that way,
Or whether it might be still more audacious to go on
And kill more Thracians. But while he debated thus   570
With himself, the goddess Athena stood by him and said:

"You great-hearted son of Tydeus, concentrate now
On getting back to the hollow ships, or you may
Go there pursued by the wrathful Trojans, whom another
God may very soon arouse!"

She spoke,
And he knew the goddess's voice. Then quickly he left
And leaped on one of the horses that now Odysseus
Whipped with his bow, and off they went at a gallop
Toward the fast-faring ships of Achaea.   580

Now Apollo, armed
With the silver bow, was not unaware of Athena's
Attention to Tydeus' son Diomedes, and the god,
In rage against her, entered the huge Trojan camp
And awakened a prominent Thracian, the counselor Hippocoön,
A valiant kinsman of Rhesus. He sprang up from sleep,
And seeing the empty place where the King's fast horses
Had stood and the dying men still gasping and choking
Amid the hideous carnage, he groaned and called
590 His dear royal kinsman by name. And the Trojans rushed up
With unspeakable noise and confusion, and there they stood staring
At the gruesome sight, the terrible work that the two spies
Had done before they went back to the hollow ships.

Now when the two Argives came to the spot where they
Had killed Hector's spy, Zeus-loved Odysseus pulled up
The galloping horses, and Tydeus' son leaped down
And handed up to his friend the bloody spoils
Of Dolon, then mounted once more. And Odysseus whipped
The horses, and off they flew at a gallop again
600 Toward the hollow ships of Achaea, willingly bearing
The two eager men. And Nestor, the first to hear hoof-beats,
Spoke to his comrades, saying:

"My friends, captains
And counselors of the Argives, I may be mistaken,
But still my heart would swear that I hear the hoof-beats
Of galloping horses. If only Odysseus and brave
Diomedes have already driven away from the Trojans
Some solid-hoofed chargers! But I am terribly fearful
That now our two best men have got themselves
610 Into perilous trouble with a pack of war-screaming Trojans."

The old one was still speaking when up rode the two men in
        question.
They leaped to the ground, and joyfully all of the others
Welcomed them warmly with hand-clasps and words of praise.
Horse-driving Gerenian Nestor questioned them first:
"Come now, O much-praised Odysseus, great glory of all
The Achaeans, tell me how you two took these horses.
Did they really come from among the great throng of Trojans,
Or did you get them from some god you met? Believe me,
They're wonderfully like two rays of brilliant sunlight!
620 Old Warrior though I am, I constantly mix
With the Trojans in battle, nor do I loiter at all
By the hollow ships. Even so, I've yet to see

Or even so much as imagine such horses as these!
I do think they came to you from a god you met.
After all, you're both beloved by stormy Zeus
And the daughter of that strong aegis-great God, the maidenly
Blue-eyed Athena."
    To which resourceful Odysseus:
"Neleus' son Nestor, great glory of all the Achaeans,
A god that willed it might easily give still better   630
Horses than these, for the gods are far abler than men.
But these, old friend, about which you ask, are horses
Just in from Thrace, and brave Diomedes killed
Their master the King and twelve of his greatest warriors.
All told, we accounted for fourteen men, including
A scout we killed near the ships, a man sent out
By Hector and the other insolent Trojans to spy
On our camp."
    So saying, Odysseus drove the fine horses
On through the trench, and he, exultantly laughing,   640
Came on behind, and with him followed the other
Rejoicing Achaeans. When they reached the strongly-built lodge
Of Diomedes, they used the well-cut reins to tie
The horses beside Diomedes' own swift steeds
That stood at the manger munching the honey-sweet grain.
But Odysseus stowed in the stern of the ship the bloody
Equipment of Dolon, till they could make ready a gift
For Athena. Then both of them waded out into the sea
And washed all the sweat from their shins and necks and thighs.
And when the surf had cleansed their skin and greatly   650
Refreshed their spirits, they stepped into well-polished baths.
Then, having bathed and rubbed themselves richly with oil,
They sat down to supper, and dipping sweet wine from a full
Mixing-bowl, they poured to Athena their sacred libations.

BOOK XI

The Valiant Deeds of Agamemnon

As Dawn arose from beside her lord Tithonus
That she might bring light to gods and mortal men,
Zeus sent the harsh goddess Strife down to the swift ships
Of the battered Achaeans, holding in both of her hands
The banner of war. She took a strategic stand
High on the huge black hull of Odysseus' vessel,
Which stood drawn up in the middle within shouting distance
Of both ends of the line, where Ajax, Telamon's son,
And Achilles had their lodges, for such was their trust
10 In manly valor and the strength of their hands that they
Had drawn up their ships at the furthermost ends. From here
Strife shouted a loud and terrible war-scream, which stirred
The hearts of all the Achaeans to struggle and fight
Without ceasing.[1] And at once they felt war to be sweeter than any
Return to their dear native land.
     And King Agamemnon
Shouted commands for the Argives to dress for battle,
And he himself put on the gleaming bronze.
First he covered his shins with greaves, fair greaves
20 With ankle-clasps of silver. Next, about his chest,
He put the breastplate given to him by Cinyras,
King of Cyprus. For he had heard the wide-spread
News that Achaeans were soon to set sail for Troy,
And so had graciously sent the breastplate for King
Agamemnon to wear and enjoy. Inlaid upon it
Were ten dark bands of blue lapis, twelve of gold,
And twenty of shining tin, and three blue-lapis
Serpents arched up toward the neck on either side,
Like the rainbows that Cronos' son hangs in the clouds as signs
30 For mortal men. And about his shoulders he slung
His sword, flashing with studs and straps of gold
And sheathed in a silver scabbard. Then he took up
His warlike, richly wrought shield, man-covering and splendid

To see. For inlaid upon it were ten bright circles
Of bronze and twenty bosses of shining tin
Surrounding a central boss of blue lapis. And set
In the lapis, the awesome head of the Gorgon glared grimly
Forth, flanked by the figures of Panic and Rout.
From this great shield hung a baldric of glittering silver
Whereon a blue-lapis, three-headed serpent writhed.   40
And on his head he put a helmet, four-horned
And double-crested, with plume of horsehair defiantly
Waving above him. He also took up two sturdy
Spears, keenly pointed with bronze, and far up into
The sky the bright bronze flashed. And now, to honor
The King of golden Mycenae, Athena and Hera
Thundered.
      Then each of the charioteers ordered
His driver to draw his team up in an orderly line
At the trench, but they themselves in full armor went swiftly   50
Forward on foot, and their wild, unquenchable cry
Went up in the dawn. Thus they formed their line
At the trench, and behind them at some little distance their drivers
Followed. And Cronos' son roused in their hearts an evil
Lust for the din and confusion of war, and down
From the upper air he sent dark dew-drops of blood,
For he was about to hurl down to Hades many
Heroic heads.
      And up the plain from them,
The Trojans fell in about great Hector and peerless   60
Polydamas, Aeneas, whom Trojans honored quite
Like a god, and the three brave sons of Antenor—Polybus,
Noble Agenor, and the youthful Acamas, handsome
As any immortal. And Hector, round shield on his arm,
Stood out mid the foremost fighters. Like a baleful star
That brilliantly gleams through a break in the overcast sky,
Only to vanish soon behind the dark clouds,
So Hector would now appear in the front rank of champions,
Then amid the last lines, giving them orders.
And all in brilliant bronze, he flashed like the lightning   70
Of Father Zeus of the aegis.
      And as when reapers
Start from opposite sides of a wealthy man's field
Of wheat or barley and work in toward each other
Cutting their swathes, so that thick and fast fall the handfuls

Of grain, so now Achaeans and Trojans charged
And cut each other down, nor did either side think
Of ruinous retreat, equally matched as they were
And ferocious as so many wolves. And Hatred, fierce goddess
80 Of groans, rejoiced as she watched them, for she alone
Of the gods was with them there in the slaughter. The others
Were quietly relaxing at home on Olympus, where each
Has a beautiful mansion built mid the mountain crags.
And most of them were incensed with Cronos' son Zeus,
God of the lowering sky, because he willed
To give the victory to Trojans. But the Father, unperturbed,
Sat aloof from the others, glorying in his power
As he looked down on the city of Troy and the ships
Of Achaea, on the lightning-like flashes of bronze, and on
90 The killers and killed.
             Now while it was morning and sacred
Daylight grew brighter, the missiles of both sides struck home,
And the warriors fell. But at that hour when a woodcutter
Takes his meal in the shady glen of a mountain,
When his arms are tired from felling tall trees and desire
For food and sweet wine comes over his weary spirit,
Right then the valorous Danaans, hailing each other
Throughout the ranks, broke the Trojan battalions.
And first Agamemnon charged through and cut down the fighter
100 Bienor, marshaler of men, and after Bienor
His comrade horse-lashing Oïleus. That warrior sprang
From his car and faced Agamemnon, but as he rushed straight
At the King, Agamemnon's keen spear caught him full in the forehead,
Nor was the point stopped by his bronze-heavy helmet. Straight
             through
Both bronze and bone it tore and spattered his brains
About the helmet's inside. Thus he overcame the furious
Charge of Oïleus.
             Then the king of men Agamemnon
Stripped these two of their tunics and left them lying
110 With their bare chests white in the sun, and on he went
To kill two children of Priam, Isus and Antiphus,
One a bastard and one a legitimate son,
Both riding now in the same bright car, with Isus
The bastard handling the reins and illustrious Antiphus
Standing beside him. Once, as these two were watching
Their sheep on the lower slopes of Mount Ida, Achilles

Had captured them both and bound them fast with pliant
Branches of willow, and then set them free for a ransom.
But now the son of Atreus, wide-ruling Agamemnon,
Speared Isus full in the chest above the nipple   120
And toppled Antiphus out of the car with a fierce
Sword-blow by the ear. Then quickly he stripped them both
Of their beautiful armor, and recognized both, for he
Had seen them before, when Achilles, fast on his feet,
Brought them from Ida. And as a lion comes
On the bed of a swift-running doe and easily crushes
The tender life from her fawns, tearing at them
With strong teeth, and the mother, though near, can do nothing to
          help them,
Since she too is seized with terrible trembling and swiftly
Goes bounding away through the dense brushwood of the forest,   130
Running and sweating before the much-dreaded force
Of the powerful beast: even so, not one of the Trojans
Was able to save these two, Isus and Antiphus,
Since they themselves were fleeing before the Argives.
          Next he killed Peisander and the resolute Hippolochus.
They were the sons of cunning Antimachus, whose lust
For splendid gifts of Paris's gold made him
Most fervent of all in opposing the movement to give
Helen back to tawny-haired Menelaus. Now powerful
Agamemnon caught his two sons in one car, which both   140
Were vainly trying to manage, for the glossy reins
Had slipped from their hands, and their two-horse team was panicking
Over the plain. Like a lion Agamemnon rushed them,
And they, while still in the chariot, pleaded thus:
          "Alive, O son of Atreus, take us alive!
And an ample ransom is yours. Stored in the mansion
Of wealthy Antimachus are many treasures, bronze
And gold and highly wrought iron. Of these our father
Would gladly give you a ransom past counting, if he
Should hear that we are alive at the ships of Achaea."   150
          Such were their tearful, pitiful words, but not
At all pleasing were those they heard in reply: "If you
Are really the sons of cunning Antimachus, the man
Who once in a Trojan assembly, when King Menelaus
And godlike Odysseus had come to Troy on a mission,
Suggested they kill Menelaus right there, rather than
Let him go back among the Achaeans, now surely

You both shall pay in full for the infamous act
Of your father!"*
160 Then jabbing his spear in the chest of Peisander,
He hurled him down on his back in the dirt. But Hippolochus
Leaped from the car, and the King killed him on foot.
Then lopping off arms and head, he rolled him away
Like a log through the jostling ranks.
    Leaving these two
Where they lay, he rushed with other well-greaved Achaeans
To where the Trojan battalions were now in full
Retreat. And as they helplessly fled, footmen
Killed footmen and horsemen killed horsemen, and dust rose up
170 From the plain as their chargers thundered along and Argives
Killed with the bronze. And powerful Agamemnon, constantly
Killing, rushed on in pursuit, calling out to his men.
As dense brushwood in a forest collapses at once
Before the onslaught of furious fire that a whirling
Wind spreads quickly throughout the timber, so now
Fell Trojan heads before the fierce charge of King
Agamemnon, and many were the neck-arching horses that rattled
Their riderless cars through the blood-wet lanes of battle,
Leaving their masterful drivers stretched out on the ground,
180 Far dearer now to vultures than to their wives.
  Zeus drew Hector out of that cloud of missiles
And dust, away from the blood and killing and turmoil,
But powerful Agamemnon kept on in pursuit, screaming
His cry to the Danaans. And the Trojan host fled fast
On the open plain, thundering past the wild fig tree,
Frantically trying to reach the city, with the screaming
Son of Atreus always pursuing and constantly
Fouling his huge, invincible hands with carnage
And gore. But when they reached the Scaean Gates
190 And the oak tree, the Trojans halted to wait for their comrades
Who still remained on the open plain, where they
Were driven in rout like cattle attacked by a lion—
The beast comes on them in the dead of night and scatters
Them all, but one of them he marks for certain
Death, and seizing her neck in his powerful jaws
He snaps it, then gulps her entrails and laps his fill

---

*The mission of Menelaus and Odysseus to Troy has been previously mentioned at III.226–229.

Of her blood. So King Agamemnon scattered the Trojans,
Constantly killing the hindmost as they fled.
Thus, as he raged with his spear around and before him,
Many a Trojan fell from his car face down   200
In the dust or flat on his back beneath the hands
Of Atrides. But when he had almost reached the steep wall
Of the city, then at last the Father of men and gods,
With thunderbolt firmly in hand, came down from the sky
And sat on the heights of well-watered Ida. And now
He dispatched with a message golden-winged Iris, saying:
        "Fly swiftly, quick Iris, and speak these words to Hector.
So long as he sees the commander-in-chief Agamemnon
Raging amid the foremost and mowing men down
By the dozen, so long let him give ground with orders   210
For all the others to keep the enemy busy,
Fiercely resisting. But when Agamemnon, wounded
By spear or arrow, leaps on his car, then I
Will grant Hector might to cut men down till he comes
To the well-timbered ships, steadily killing till the sun
Goes down and powerful darkness arrives."
        He spoke,
And wind-footed Iris did not disobey, but swiftly
Flew down from the range of Ida to sacred Ilium.
She found wise Priam's noble son Hector standing   220
Mid horses and cars in his own well-jointed chariot,
And swift-footed Iris stood by him, and said:
        "Hector,
Son of Priam and peer of Zeus in counsel,
Zeus, our Father, has sent me to you with these words.
So long as you see the commander-in-chief Agamemnon
Raging amid the foremost and mowing men down
By the dozen, so long you are to give ground with orders
For all the others to keep the enemy busy,
Fiercely resisting. But when Agamemnon, wounded   230
By spear or arrow, leaps on his car, then Zeus
Will grant you might to cut men down till you come
To the well-timbered ships, steadily killing till the sun
Goes down and powerful darkness arrives."
        When Iris
Had spoken the message, she flew swiftly off. But Hector,
Fully armed, leaped from his car to the ground,
And brandishing two sharp spears he ranged through the ranks
Arousing new spirit in the routed men. They spun

240 And faced the Achaeans, who now re-formed their ranks
To oppose them. Thus the armies clashed, and still
Agamemnon rushed forward in front of them all, eager
To fight the first man.
        Now tell me, O Muses, you
That have homes on Olympus, who first came against Agamemnon,
Whether one of the Trojans or one of their famous allies.
It was Antenor's son Iphidamas, a man
Both brawny and brave. He had been raised in fertile
Thrace, mother of flocks, at the home of his grandfather
250 Cisseus, sire of his pretty mother Theano.
And when he grew up a splendid young man, Cisseus
Attempted to keep him there by giving him one
Of his daughters to marry. But he was no sooner a bridegroom
Than word reached him of Achaeans at Troy, and off
He went with a company of twelve beaked ships. These graceful
Vessels he left at Percote and came on by land
To Troy, where now he faced in single combat
Atreus' son Agamemnon. And as they charged
Each other, the spear of Atrides glanced off to one side,
260 But Iphidamas, putting his trust in the might of his beefy
Arm, landed his hard-lunging thrust on the war-belt
Just beneath the King's breastplate. Still he failed
To pierce the all-glinting belt, for the point of his spear
No sooner struck the silver than it was bent back
Like lead. Then the wide-ruling lord Agamemnon, fierce
As a lion enraged, seized the spear of Iphidamas
And jerked it out of his hand, then loosed his limbs
With a sword-blow deep in the neck. Even so, Iphidamas
Fell and slept the bronze sleep, a hapless young man,
270 Aiding his people far away from his bride,
The girl for whom he had given so much but never
Enjoyed at all. And truly he had given much:
A hundred head of fine cattle with a promise of one thousand
Sheep and goats to come, for such were herded
For him in tremendous numbers. Now Agamemnon
Stripped him and strode off toward the Achaean ranks
Bearing his exquisite armor.
        But when the outstanding
Warrior Coön, eldest son of Antenor,
280 Saw his dear brother fall, great sorrow dimmed
His eyes, and coming up from the side, unseen
By King Agamemnon, he jabbed the point of his gleaming

Spear clean through the commander's forearm, just
Below the elbow. At this the high King shuddered,
But so far from quitting the fight, he gripped his spear
Of wind-toughened wood and fiercely sprang upon Coön.
Now Coön had seized the foot of his father's son
Iphidamas, and frantically he was dragging his brother
Away and calling for help to all the bravest.
But as he was dragging him into the throng, Agamemnon   290
Unstrung the man with a thrust of smooth-shafted bronze
Beneath his bossed shield. Then standing beside him he lopped off
His head right over the corpse of Iphidamas. There then,
At the hands of royal Atrides, the sons of Antenor
Filled up their measure of fate and journeyed down
To the house of Hades.
          Now just so long as the blood
Welled warm from his wound, Agamemnon raged through the enemy
Ranks, hacking and thrusting and throwing huge rocks.
But when the blood stopped and the wound got dry, keen pangs   300
Of anguish came on the mighty Atrides. Like the searing
Arrows of pain that shoot through a woman in labor,
The piercing pangs sent on by the Eileithyiae,
The labor-inducing daughters of Hera, who have
Such pain in their keeping, even such were the sharp and bitter
Pangs that racked Agamemnon now.[2] Heavyhearted,
He leaped on his car and bade his driver make
For the hollow ships, but as he left he yelled
A far-carrying cry, and shouted these words to the Danaans:
          "O friends, captains and counselors of the Argives,   310
Ward off from our seagoing ships the grievous turmoil
Of battle, for Zeus in his wisdom has not allowed me
To fight throughout this day against the Trojans."
          His driver lashed the mane-tossing horses, and they,
Not at all unwilling, galloped away toward the ships.
With breasts foam-flecked and bellies sprinkled with dust,
They bore from battle the weary and wounded King.
          When Hector saw Agamemnon leaving, he shouted
As loud as he could to the Trojans and their Lycian allies:
"You Trojans and Lycians and dueling Dardanians, now,   320
My friends, be men, and filled with furious boldness!
Their best man is gone, and Cronos' son Zeus has given
Great glory to me. But drive your solid-hoofed horses
Straight and hard at the powerful Danaan host,
That you may win the higher glory yet!"

These words encouraged and strengthened all of his men.
For with all the heart of a hunter who sets his snarling,
Gleaming-toothed hounds on a savage wild boar or a lion,
Priam's son Hector, the peer of man-maiming Ares,
330 Urged on the spirited Trojans. And he himself,
Greatly courageous, charged out from the foremost rank
And fell on the fight like a high-howling gale that rushes
Down from the heights and lashes the violet sea.

Then who was the first and who was the last to be slain
And stripped by Priam's son Hector, now that Zeus
Gave victory to him? Asaeus was first, then Autonous,
Opites, Opheltius, and Dolops, son of Clytius,
Agelaus, Aesymnus, Orus, and the resolute Hipponous.
These were the Danaan leaders he slew. Then
340 He fell on the rank and file with all the force
Of a hurricane gale that blows from the West, clearing
The sky of white clouds which the rapid South Wind has collected,
A baffling blow that drives on many a swollen,
Rolling billow and fills the air with droplets
Of spray—even so very numerous now
Were the Argive heads laid low by raging Hector.

And now irreparable ruin would have wrecked the Achaeans
And they in full flight would have flung themselves on the ships,
If Odysseus had not called out to strong Diomedes:
350 "O Tydeus' son, what causes us thus to forget
Our furious valor? But come, my friend, and make
A stand by my side, for it would surely disgrace us
If now bright-helmeted Hector captured the ships!"

And mighty Diomedes replied: "Of course I will stand
And resist, but I don't think we'll do a great deal of good,
Since cloud-gathering Zeus has obviously willed to give
The victory to Trojans."

So saying, he knocked Thymbraeus
Out of his chariot, striking him with his spear
360 Beneath the left nipple, and Odysseus took care of that
Great chieftain's driver, the godlike Molion. These
They left where they fell, having put an end to their fighting.
And now they turned and fought their way through the ranks,
Wreaking much ruin all around them, quite like a couple
Of vicious wild boars that whirl on the hounds behind them.
So now they turned on the Trojans again and fiercely
Cut them down, thus giving their fellow Achaeans
Some chance to catch their breath in their flight before Hector.

The first car taken by strong Diomedes held
Two lords in their land, the sons of Percotian Merops,   370
The world's most skillful prophet, who would not allow
His sons to enter the man-wasting war. But they
Would pay no attention, for doom and dark death were leading
Them on. Now Tydeus' son, famed as a spearman, robbed them
Of spirit and life and stripped off their marvelous war-gear,
While Odysseus slaughtered and stripped Hippodamas and
          Hypeirochus.
     Then Cronos' son Zeus, as he looked down from Ida,
Evened the killing between the straining forces.
King Diomedes thrust his spear in the hip
Of Paeon's heroic son, the raging Agastrophus,   380
On whom great blindness of soul had surely come,
For he had no horses nearby behind which to flee.
He had left them far back with his squire and plunged on ahead
Mid the foremost fighters till now he lost his dear life.
But across the ranks keen Hector saw what had happened,
And fiercely he charged down upon them with a terrible scream
And whole battalions of Trojans behind him. Diomedes,
The great battle-roarer, shuddered to see him coming,
And immediately spoke to Odysseus close by:
     "Much trouble,   390
Odysseus, is rolling our way in the person of yonder
Huge Hector! But come, let us stand where we are and beat
The man back."
     With this he poised his long-shadowing spear
And hurled it, and so far from missing his mark, he struck
Hector hard on top of his triple-thick helmet, where bronze
Turned bronze aside, leaving his handsome head whole,
The spear-point foiled by the crested, glittering helmet,
A gift from Phoebus Apollo. Quickly Hector
Reeled back a long way in the crowd, then dropped to one knee,   400
Supporting himself with one great hand on the ground
Till darkness enveloped his eyes. But while Diomedes
Went after his spear far through the foremost fighters
To where it had fallen to earth, Hector revived,
And springing up on his car drove further back
In the battling throng, thus escaping black fate.
And strong Diomedes charged up with his spear, and shouted
After him thus:
     "Again, you dog, you've managed
To get away with your life, though this time just barely!   410

Once more you have Phoebus Apollo to thank, to whom
You must be careful to pray before you come
Within even the sound of hurtling spears. Well,
Believe me, I'll finish you yet—the next time we meet,
If only some god will also look out for me.
Right now I'll take my rage out on your friends, whomever
I happen to come on!"
      He shouted, and went back to strip
The man he last slew, spear-famous Agastrophus, son
420 Of Paeon. But Paris, the lord of lovely blonde Helen,
Drew his bow against Diomedes, half hid
As he aimed by the pillar on the man-made barrow of Ilus,
The descendant of Dardanus and ancient elder. Diomedes
The King was busily stripping the all-glinting breastplate
From mighty Agastrophus, taking the shield from his shoulders
And removing his heavy helmet, when Paris drew back
The string and shot. Nor did the arrow fly
From his hand in vain, for it cleanly pierced the sole
Of Diomedes' right foot, and pinned him fast to the ground.
430 Then gleefully laughing, Paris sprang out from the pillar
And boastingly yelled:
      "Aha! you're hit! That surely
Was no idle shot. I only wish I had sunk
A shaft in the pit of your belly and stopped you for good!
Then the Trojans could all have relaxed a bit, since now
They tremble before you like bleating goats at a lion."
      And strong Diomedes, fearless as ever, replied:
"You foul-fighting cowardly bowman and gaper at girls,
With your pretty hair fresh out of curlers! if only you'd come out
440 In armor and fight like a man, you'd see how worthless
To you that bow and fistful of arrows would be!
Now there you are bragging at scratching the sole of my foot.
I think no more of it than if some woman or silly
Child had slapped me, for the dart of a no-good weakling
Is puny and dull. But the man I so much as touch
With the weapon I wield knows very well, as he dies,
How keen it is! His fatherless children grieve,
And the cheeks of his wife are torn in her weeping and wailing,
While he but reddens the earth with his blood, and rots,
450 With far fewer women than vultures flocking around him!"
      He spoke, and spear-famed Odysseus came up and stood
Before him, while Diomedes sat down and painfully
Pulled from his foot the swift-flying arrow. Heavyhearted,

He leaped on his car and bade his driver make
For the hollow ships.
    Now that renowned spearman Odysseus
Faced the foe all alone, since no other Argive
Had courage enough to stay by his side. Deeply troubled,
He spoke to his own great heart:[3] "Ah miserable me,
What is to become of me now! To run in fear   460
Of that mob would be a great evil, but to stay here and let them
Catch me alone would be even worse, now that Zeus
Has utterly routed all of the other Danaans.
But why do I argue thus with myself? I know
All too well that those who run from a fight are cowards
And that whoever does best in a battle must firmly
Stand his ground, whether he be the one who is struck
Or whether he strike another."
    While he so pondered
In mind and heart, the companies of shield-bearing Trojans   470
Hemmed him in, surrounding their own destruction.
And just as hounds and lusty young hunters close in
On a boar, and then withstand his blood-chilling charge
From the depths of his thicket-lair, noisily whetting
His tushes and gnashing his crooked jaws, so now
The Trojans rushed in on Zeus-loved Odysseus. And first
He stabbed flawless Deïopites, lunging at him
With his well-sharpened spear and coming down with it deep
Into the man's shoulder. Then he killed Thoön and Ennomus.
And as Chersidamas sprang from his car, he thrust   480
His spear beneath his bossed shield and into his navel,
Stretching him out in the dust, where he clawed the dirt
With his hand. Leaving these where they fell, he jabbed
His bronze into Charops, Hippasus' son and full brother
Of wealthy Socus, a godlike man, who now
Rushed in to defend his own. He came right up
To Odysseus, took his stand, and spoke to him thus:
    "Much-praised Odysseus, insatiably wily and eager
For toilsome action, today you'll either kill two
Of Hippasus' sons and boast how you cut down and stripped   490
Such a pair, or else beneath my spear you yourself
Shall give up the ghost and die!"
    So saying, he plunged
His ponderous spear clean through the shining round shield
Of Odysseus, and on through his richly wrought breastplate it tore
To rip all the flesh away from the great fighter's side,

Though Pallas Athena did not allow it to puncture
His entrails. Odysseus knew the wound was not mortal,
But now he gave ground, and spoke these words to Socus:
500   "You wretch, surely sheer ruin is rushing upon you!
You've ended this action of mine against the Trojans,
But here and now, believe me, you'll be overtaken
By death and dark fate. Sprawling beneath my spear,
You shall give glory to me, and your miserable soul
To horse-famous Hades!"
            He spoke, and just as Socus
Turned to run, he planted a spear in his back
Between the shoulders and drove it out through his chest.
He fell to the ground with a thud, and worthy Odysseus
510   Exulted over him, saying: "Ah Socus, son
Of flame-hearted Hippasus, breaker of horses, death
After all was too quick for you, nor could you writhe out
From beneath it. Poor wretch, your father and lady mother
Shall never close those corpse's eyes of yours,
But carrion birds shall pick the flesh from your bones,
Flocking and flapping about you. Whereas, if I die,
The noble Achaeans will surely bury me
With all due funeral rites."[4]
            So saying, he pulled
520   From his flesh and bossed shield keen Socus's ponderous spear,
And the blood gushed out, whereat his heart grew sick.
But when the spirited Trojans saw the blood
Of Odysseus, a cry went up throughout the throng,
And all together they rushed him. And now he gave ground
And called to his comrades for help. Three times he called
As loud as he could, and three times warlike Menelaus
Heard him. Then at once he spoke thus to Ajax nearby:
            "O god-sprung Ajax, Telamon's son and ruler
Of many, just then there rang in my ears the cry
530   Of steadfast Odysseus. He sounded as though the Trojans
Had cut him off alone in the huge confusion
And so were getting the best of him. But come,
Let us make our way through the toiling tangle of men,
For surely we had better help him. I fear that he
All alone, great warrior though he is, may suffer
Some harm from the Trojans. The Danaans then would miss
The man greatly."
            With this he led the way, and godlike
Ajax followed. Then soon they found Zeus-loved Odysseus,

And Trojans fiercely beset him on every side   540
Like so many tawny jackals that dart in about
A high-horned stag in the mountains, one that some hunter
Has struck with an arrow—swiftly he bounds away,
So long as the blood flows warm and his knees remain nimble,
But when at last the deeply lodged arrow subdues him,
The ravenous jackals tear him apart in a shadowy
Glen of the mountains, till God sends against them a murderous,
Plundering lion that scatters the jackals and tears
At the prey himself. So now the Trojans, many
And strong, charged fiercely in on Odysseus, wily   550
And wise. And he, lunging desperately out with his spear,
Kept off the ruthless day of his doom, till Ajax
Came up, bearing his shield like a tower, and stood
By his side, thus quickly scattering Trojans in every
Direction. And warlike King Menelaus led Odysseus
Out through the crowd, supporting him by the arm,
Till a squire drove up Menelaus's horses and car.

       But Ajax sprang at the Trojans and soon accounted for
Doryclus, bastard son of King Priam, then felled
With rapid spear-thrusts Pandocus and Lysander,   560
Pyrasus and Pylartes. And as when a river
In winter flood, swollen by rain from Zeus,
Rushes down from mountains to plain, bearing on
In its course to the sea innumerable dead oaks and pines
Along with tons of mud and debris, so now
Resplendent Ajax stormed recklessly over the plain,
Demolishing horses and men.

       Hector, meanwhile,
Knew nothing of this, for he was fighting on the far
Left fringe of battle by the banks of the river Scamander,   570
Where most thickly men's heads were falling and the cries
Of warring men went up in one constant roar
About the great Nestor and martial Idomeneus. With these
Hector was dallying somewhat roughly and wrecking
Their youthful battalions. But the noble Achaeans would still
Not at all have given way, if Paris, the lord
Of lovely-haired Helen, had not put an end to the valiant
Deeds of the leader and surgeon Machaon, sinking
A three-barbed arrow deep in the chieftain's right shoulder.
Then the fury-breathing Achaeans were greatly afraid,   580
Lest Trojans should cut him down in the fickle turns
Of battle. And quickly Idomeneus spoke to King Nestor:

"Neleus' son Nestor, great glory of all the Achaeans,
Up on your chariot, quick! and with you take wounded
Machaon. Then drive your solid-hoofed horses as fast as
You can to the ships. For one good physician is worth
A battalion when it comes to cutting out arrows and spreading on
Healing ointments."

    He spoke, and the aged horseman,
590 Gerenian Nestor, did as he said. At once
He mounted his car, and Machaon stepped up beside him.
Then Nestor lashed the horses, and off at a gallop
They flew to the hollow ships, willing to go
And eager to get there.

    Now Cebriones, driving for Hector,
Noticed the Trojans retreating, and spoke to his brother,
Saying: "Hector, while we two are dallying here
On the fringe of hateful battle, other Trojans
Are there being routed and ruined, both horses and men.
600 And the cause of all that chaos is Ajax, son
Of Telamon. I know him surely by that wide shield
About his shoulders. But come, let us drive our horses
And car over there, where most of all both horsemen
And footmen, clashing in evil strife, are cutting
Each other down and filling the air with their loud,
Unquenchable cries."

    So saying, he raised the lash
And brought it down on the mane-tossing horses, that swiftly
Took off at the very first sound of the whistling whip
610 And rapidly drew the light car through fighting Achaeans
And Trojans, trampling on corpses and shields. And the axle
Below and handrails above were all splashed and bespattered
With blood from the hooves of the horses and metal rims
Of the wheels. And Hector, hotly eager to crash
Through the man-mingling throng and break the Trojan retreat,
Brought evil confusion into the Danaan ranks,
And little indeed was the rest he gave his great lance.
Hacking and thrusting and throwing huge rocks, he raged
Through the enemy host, but avoided a clash with huge
620 Telamonian Ajax.

    Finally, Father Zeus,
Looking down from on high, made Ajax afraid. He stood
Bewildered, then swung his sevenfold bull's-hide shield
On his back and turned to retreat, like a wild beast at bay
Anxiously glancing at all those about him and slowly,

Step by step, giving way—like a tawny lion
That dogs and farmhands, watching all night to protect
Their fat oxen, drive from a cattle-yard. The flesh-hungry lion
Charges right in, only to be driven back
By a rain of spears and blazing torches, hurled   630
At him by brawny bold arms. Still eager, he has to
Retreat, and slinks off at dawn disappointed. So Ajax,
Sullen at heart, gave way to the Trojans, greatly
Reluctant, since much he feared for the ships of Achaea.
He went, in fact, like a balky and stubborn ass
That gets the better of boys and enters a field
Of tall grain, where staunchly he eats his fill regardless
Of countless cudgels the puny boys break on his back
Before, at last, they drive him forth. Even so,
The spirited Trojans and their far-called, many allies   640
Hung on the heels of Telamonian Ajax, constantly
Smiting his shield with their spears. And he would resummon
His furious valor, wheel, and beat back the ranks
Of horse-breaking Trojans, then turn again and resume
His deliberate retreat. Thus he contended, and barred
Them all from the ships, making himself a bulwark
Between the Achaeans and Trojans. And some of the spears
That brawny bold arms hurled at him rushed eagerly on
To embed themselves in the great shield of Ajax, but many
Failed and fell short and fixed themselves in the earth,   650
Unable to gain their glut of the warrior's flesh.

    But now Eurypylus, glorious son of Euaemon,
Saw how Ajax labored beneath a skyful
Of spears, and coming up he took a stand
By his side and hurled his own bright lance, striking
A chieftain, Phausius' son Apisaon, in the liver
Under the midriff, thus suddenly causing his knees
To buckle. Quickly Eurypylus leaped upon him
And started to strip his shoulders of armor, but handsome
Prince Paris saw what he was doing and sank an arrow   660
Into the right thigh of Eurypylus. The shaft broke off
In the wound, and his leg dragged heavy with pain, as he,
Avoiding death, shrank back to take cover with men
Of his company, but shouting thus to the Danaan host:

    "Turn! my friends, you that lead and counsel
The Argives. Then hold your ground, that you may ward off
The ruthless day from our spear-belabored Ajax!
He has small chance, I think, of escaping alive

From out the screaming tumult. So come now, face
670   The Trojans and make a stand about great Ajax,
      Son of Telamon."
            So spoke the stricken Eurypylus,
      And those about him crouched low, with shields sloping back
      To their shoulders and spears held high and ready. Ajax
      Came to them, turned, and staunchly faced the foe.
            The deadly fighting raged on like a roaring conflagration.
      But meanwhile the sweat-lathered mares of Neleus' breed
      Drew Nestor off the field, and with him Machaon,
      The people's shepherd. And foot-flashing, noble Achilles
680   Saw them leave, for he was watching the grievous
      Toil and tearful rout of battle from high
      On the stern of his sea-monster ship.
            At once he called down
      To his comrade Patroclus, who heard, and looking like Ares
      Came out of the lodge—thus marking the start of evil
      For him.⁵ Then the valiant son of Menoetius spoke first:
      "Why do you call me, Achilles? What is it you want?"
            And swift Achilles replied: "Great son of Menoetius,
      You so dear to my heart, now I believe
690   The Achaeans will really abase themselves at my knees,
      Praying for me to help them, for truly their need
      Is desperate and not to be borne. But go now, my god-loved
      Patroclus, and find out from Nestor what man he brings wounded
      From battle. From behind he looks just like Machaon, son
      Of Asclepius, but the eager horses shot by me so fast
      I didn't see the man's face."
            He spoke, and Patroclus
      Obeyed his dear friend. Off he went at a run
      Past the lodges and ships of Achaeans.
700   When Nestor arrived
      At his lodge with the wounded Machaon, they both stepped down
      On the all-feeding earth, and the old one's squire Eurymedon
      Unhitched the horses, while the warriors stood on the beach
      In the breeze to dry the sweat from their tunics. Then
      They went into the lodge and sat down on reclining chairs,
      And skilled Hecamede, she of the beautiful braids,
      Mixed them a drink. Old Nestor had gotten the girl,
      Daughter of hearty Arsinous, when Tenedos fell
      To Achilles. The Achaeans had picked her for him as reward
710   For his always superior counsel. First she drew up

A table before them, a polished and beautiful piece
With feet of blue lapis, and on it she set a bronze saucer
Whereon was an onion to go with their drink, and beside it
She put yellow honey and meal of sacred white barley.
By these she placed an exquisite cup that the old one
Had brought from home. Studded with rivets of gold,
It had two handles on either side, about which
Two pairs of golden doves were sipping, while below
Were circular bases at bottom and top of the stem.
And though it was no small thing to raise that full cup   720
From the table, old Nestor could lift it with ease. Now in it
The girl like a goddess mixed them a drink, with honey
And Pramnian wine, on which with a grater of bronze
She grated some goat's-milk cheese and lastly sprinkled
White barley. Then, when the mixing was done, she asked them
To drink. And having quenched their burning thirst,
They fell to amusing each other with stories, when suddenly
There in the door stood the godlike man Patroclus.
At sight of him the old one quickly got up
From his gleaming chair, led him in by the hand, and told him   730
To sit. But Patroclus firmly refused to, saying:

      "I cannot, O god-fed ancient, nor will you persuade me.
Respected and feared is the man who sent me to learn
Who it is you bring here wounded. But since I now see
For myself that it is my lord Machaon, I'll take
The word back to Achilles. You know very well, O godlike
Ancient sir, how irritable he is,
A man who might quickly blame even one who is blameless."

      Then horse-driving Gerenian Nestor spoke thus:
"Why this concern on the part of Achilles for wounded   740
Sons of Achaeans? He has no idea what grief
The whole army is in. For now our bravest men,
Stricken by arrows or spear-thrusts, lie at the ships.
Strong Diomedes, Tydeus' son, has been hit,
And both spear-famous Odysseus and King Agamemnon
Have suffered disabling spear-wounds. And now Machaon,
Whom, I've just brought from the field, has also been hit
By a painful bolt from the bowstring. But Achilles, great man
That he is, neither cares for nor pities the Danaan people.
Can it be that he'll wait till our swift ships here on the beach   750
Go up in smoke and we ourselves die by the dozen?
For I no longer have limbs so supple and strong

As surely I did in the old days. If only I were
As young and my strength as unyielding as once[6] when trouble
Arose between the Epeans and us concerning
The rustling of cattle, when I by way of reprisal
Was taking cattle in Elis and slew Itymoneus,
Valorous son of Hypeirochus. While he fought
Mid the foremost, defending his cattle, a spear from my hand
760   Laid him low, and the rustics around him all fled for their lives.
Great indeed was the booty we rounded up there on the plain:
Some fifty herds of cattle with as many sheepflocks,
As many droves of swine and as many herds
Of wide-roaming goats, along with a hundred and fifty
Sorrel horses, all mares, and many of them
With colts at the teat. All these we drove by night
To Neleian Pylos and into the city, and Neleus
Rejoiced at the great success such an untried stripling
As I had had on the raid. And at dawn the heralds
770   Proclaimed loud and clear for all those to gather who then
From sacred Elis had anything coming to them.
And the Pylian leaders all came and divided the spoils,
For to many of us in Pylos the Epeans owed wealth,
Since we were at that time both few and downtrodden. The brutish
And powerful Heracles had come in the years before
And cruelly oppressed us, killing our bravest and best.
Twelve were the sons of Neleus the blameless, but of these
Only I was still alive. Hence the Epeans,
Bronze-clad and presumptuous of heart, were wickedly plotting
780   And working evil against us. But now old Neleus
Selected a whole herd of cattle along with a huge flock
Of sheep, three hundred in all and their shepherds with them.
For great was the debt owed him in sacred Elis—
Especially for four fine horses, prize-winning steeds
That had gone to the games with a car to race for the tripod.
But King Augeas had kept them there and sent back
Their vexed and horseless driver with words of insult
For Neleus. Both act and insult had angered the old one
Greatly, and now he chose reprisal past telling.
790   And what was left he gave to the people, that none
Might go without a just share.
          "Thus we divided
The spoils, and then throughout the city made offerings
To the gods. But on the third day the Epeans gathered

Their forces of many men and solid-hoofed horses,
And among them the two Moliones* put on their armor,
Though they as yet were little more than boys
With no great knowledge of furious fighting. Quickly
They came and laid siege to the citadel Thryoessa,
An outlying hilltop town on the river Alpheius   800
Down near the coast of sandy Pylos. This town
They were eager to pillage and plunder, and about the hill
They filled the plain with their men. But Athena shot down
From Olympus by night and alerted our forces for battle,
And those she gathered in sandy Pylos were not
Loath to fight. They were indeed eager, and I among them,
But Neleus had hidden my horses, since he thought I
Had not yet acquired much prowess in serious warfare.
Even so, with the help of Athena, I on foot
Proved first in the fight, even among the horsemen.   810
        "Our forces formed where the river Minyeius flows into
The sea at Arene. There the Pylian horsemen
Awaited bright Dawn while many companies of infantry
Poured in behind them. Pushing on in full armor, we reached
By noon the next day the hallowed stream of Alpheius.
There we sacrificed splendid victims to Zeus,
The exalted and mighty, a bull apiece to Poseidon
And Alpheius, god of the river, but a herd-fattened heifer
To blue-eyed Athena. Then we ate supper in companies
Throughout the host and lay down on the banks of the river   820
To sleep, each man still clad in his war-gear.
        "Meanwhile,
The great-souled Epeans, encircling the city, stood ready
And eager to sack it. But now intervened a mighty
Work of the War-god, for when the bright Sun arose
Over earth, we made our prayers to Zeus and Athena
And moved to attack. And in the great clash of Epeans
And Pylians, I was the first to kill a man
And take his solid-hoofed horses—the spearman Mulius.
He was the son-in-law of Augeas, the husband   830
Of his eldest daughter, tawny-tressed Agamede,
Whose knowledge of herbs and potions was truly world-wide.

---

*The Moliones are elsewhere represented as "Siamese twins"; they reappear in another
of Nestor's reminiscences ("the two sons of Actor"), at XXIII.738.

With a cast of my bronze-headed spear I broke his charge
And toppled him down in the dust, then leaped on his chariot
And fought mid the foremost champions. But when the haughty
Epeans saw the man fall, their captain of horse
And bravest in battle, they scattered on every side,
As I swept down like a black hurricane and overtook
Fifty chariots, and two men from each took the dirt
840 In their teeth, all spear-victims of mine! And now
I'd have wrecked the careers of the two Moliones, supposedly
Sons of Actor, had not their real father, Poseidon,
The wide-ruling shaker of shores, saved them from battle
By hiding them both in a thick cloud of mist. Then Zeus
Gave great power to the Pylian fighters, and far across
The wide plain we pursued the Epeans, constantly killing
Their men and collecting the armor, till at last we came
To the fertile wheat fields of Buprasium, the Olenian Rock,
And a place called Alesium Hill. There Athena turned back
850 Our forces, and leaving I slew the last man. The Pylians
Drove their fast horses from Buprasium back to Pylos,
And all gave thanks and great glory to Zeus among gods
And to Nestor bravest of men.
          "That was the kind
Of warrior I was, just as sure as I ever was one!
But Achilles would like to enjoy his valor alone,
Though surely the man will later most terribly grieve
For his own people destroyed. Ah, my boy,
How well I remember the charge Menoetius laid on you
860 The day he sent you from Phthia to King Agamemnon.
We two were there with you, I and worthy Odysseus,
And there in the house we heard his instructions to you.
For we had come to the fair-lying palace of Peleus
Recruiting soldiers throughout many-feeding Achaea.
Inside with Achilles we found your father Menoetius,
And you, while out in the courtyard the knightly old Peleus
Was burning to bolt-hurling Zeus the fat thigh-slabs
Of a bull, and from a gold cup in his hand he was pouring
Libations of sparkling wine to go with the sacred
870 And flaming meat. Menoetius and you were busily
Carving the beef when we two appeared in the porch.
The surprised Achilles sprang up, led us in by the hand,
And told us to sit, then set before us refreshment
Befitting strangers. And when we had greatly enjoyed
The food and drink he served us, I spoke out first,

Inviting Achilles and you to come with us.
And since you were both quite willing to do so, your fathers
Gave much instruction to you. Old Peleus urged
His son Achilles to always be bravest and best,
But Menoetius, son of Actor, counseled you thus: 880
    " 'My son, Achilles is nobler in birth than you are
And far more gifted with martial prowess, but you
Are the elder, and so should instruct, counsel, and guide him.
And he will do well to heed the advice you give him.'*
    "Thus your old father gave you a charge—but one
That you have forgotten. Even now, though, go speak
To the fiery Achilles and see if he'll listen. Who knows
But that with God's help your persuasion may still prevail?
The advice of a friend is frequently most effective.
But if his heart is set on escaping some dire word   890
From Zeus, revealed to him by his goddess mother,
Let him send you at the head of the Myrmidon host,[7]
That you may be a light of hope to the Danaans.
And let him give you his splendid armor to wear
Into war, that the Trojans may take you for him and quickly
Withdraw from the fighting. Then the battling, war-worn sons
Of Achaeans may have a chance to catch their breath—
Such chances in battle are few—and you that are fresh
May easily drive, with little more than your war-screams,
The exhausted Trojans away from the ships and the shelters   900
And back toward the city."
    He spoke, and his words stirred the heart
In the breast of Patroclus, who left now to run down the long
        line
Of ships to Achilles, Aeacus' grandson. But when
He came at a run to the ships of godlike Odysseus,
Where he and his men had their place of assembly and judgment
And where they had built the gods' altars, there he was met
By Eurypylus, Zeus-sprung son of Euaemon, pierced
In the thigh by an arrow and painfully limping from battle.
The sweat streamed down from his head and shoulders, and from   910
His deep wound the dark blood oozed, but still his mind
Remained clear. Seeing him so, the gallant Patroclus
Felt pity for him, and his words came winged with foreboding:

---

*Nestor now recalls, at greater length, the parting scene in Phthia that Odysseus had also
recalled at IX.284–292. (See also endnote 4 to book IX).

"O miserable leaders and lords of the Danaan people,
Were you, then, doomed to fall so far from home
And loved ones, here where the swift dogs of Troy may gulp
Their glut of your glistening fat? But come, tell me this,
O god-nurtured hero Eurypylus. Have the Achaeans
A chance to somehow hold back monstrous Hector, or will they
920   Now die beneath his great spear?"
          Then the stricken Eurypylus:
"No longer, O Zeus-sprung Patroclus, will there be any
Defense of Achaeans, who soon will be frantically climbing
Aboard the black ships. For surely all those who have been
Our bravest lie at the ships disabled by Trojan
Arrows or spear-thrusts, while the enemy's strength continues
To grow. But me at least you can help. Lead me
Now to my black ship, cut the keen bronze
From my thigh, and wash the dark blood away with warm water.
930   Then put some soothing salve on the wound, some healing
Excellent thing men say you learned from Achilles,
Who had it from Cheiron, most civil and righteous of Centaurs.
For of our physicians, Machaon and Podaleirius,
One I believe lies mid the lodges wounded
And in need of a skillful surgeon himself, while the other
Is out on the plain withstanding the Trojans' hard charge."
          And the stalwart son of Menoetius answered him thus:
"How can these things be? But what shall we do, Eurypylus?
I'm on my way to fiery Achilles with word
940   From Gerenian Nestor, Achaea's old sentinel. Still,
I will not desert you so nearly exhausted."
          So saying,
He put his arm round the great leader's waist and helped him
Back to his lodge, where his squire at sight of them
Piled oxhides thick on the earthen floor. On these
Patroclus stretched the man out, and with a knife
Removed the keen-cutting bronze from his thigh, and washed
The dark blood away with warm water. And when he had crushed
A root in his hands he applied it well to the wound—
950   A pungent, pain-killing root that ended his pangs.
Then the bleeding stopped and the wound began to dry.

BOOK XII

The Storming of the Wall

While valiant Patroclus was tending the stricken Eurypylus
There in the shelter, the Argives and Trojans were clashing
In furious melee, nor were die Danaan ditch
And the wide wall behind it long destined to keep off the foe.
They had built the wall and trenched all along it to keep
In safety their swift-sailing ships and enormous spoils,
But they had neglected to sacrifice glorious hecatombs
To the immortals. Hence it was built without
The good will of the gods, and so could not long endure.
So long as life lasted in Hector and wrath in Achilles,   10
And royal Priam's city remained unsacked,
The Achaeans' great wall stood firm. But when all the best
Of the Trojans were dead and many of the Argives too—
Though some of their bravest survived—and the city of Priam
Was sacked in the tenth long year, and the Argives had left
In their ships for their own dear country, then Poseidon
In counsel with lord Apollo decided to wreck
The great wall by bringing against it the united force
Of all the rivers that flow from the range of Ida
Seaward—the waters of Rhesus, Caresus, Heptaporus,   20
Rhodius, Granicus, Aesepus, along with the streams
Of sacred Scamander and Simoeis, by whose banks
Many a bull's-hide shield and helmet had splashed
In the mud along with many a half-divine mortal
Of that renowned generation—all of these rivers
Apollo made to flow out at one mouth and drove
For nine days their churning torrent against the great wall,
While Zeus continued to rain, that he might all the sooner
Flood the wall with salt sea. And Poseidon, creator
Of earthquakes, holding his trident, directed the onrush   30
Of waters and washed out to sea the log and stone
Foundations laid by the laboring Achaeans, then smoothly
Leveled all beside the strong Hellespont stream.
When the wall was demolished, again he covered the wide beach

With sand and turned the rivers back into the channels
Where they before had poured their bright-flowing streams.[1]
      These things Poseidon and Apollo were someday to do.
But now a roaring battle blazed at the well-built
Wall, and the wooden beams of the towers resounded
40   Beneath the missiles, as the Argives were cowed by the lash
Of Zeus and penned up and held by the hollow ships.
There they huddled in terror of Hector, that mighty
Master of rout, who raged like a howling gale.
As a wild boar or lion, exulting in strength, wheels
On hounds and hunters, who form a wall against him
And rain their javelins down, while onward his stout heart
Comes, unafraid and persistent until his own courage
Kills him—again and again he wheels about
And tries the line of spearmen, and wherever he charges
50   The line gives way—so Hector raged through the throng
Urging his comrades to cross the Achaean trench.
But the quick-hoofed horses balked there, frightened and shrilly
Neighing on the very lip of the trench, for it
Was too wide to leap or easily drive across,
Since the banks overhung on either side, and along
The top toward the wall the sons of Achaeans had planted
A row of sharp stakes, close-set and tall, to keep off
The foe. No horse could easily drag a car,
However well-rolling, through those defenses. The footmen,
60   Though, were eager to try them, and Polydamas came up
To daring Hector and spoke to him and the others:[2]
      "O leaders of Trojans and Trojan allies, any
Attempt to drive our fast horses across this deep ditch
Would surely be senseless. The crossing would be indeed hard,
For the ditch is bristling with sharp-pointed stakes and not far
Beyond them looms the Achaean wall. That space
Over there is so narrow that horsemen could wage no war
Without great hurt to themselves. But if high-crashing Zeus
Is really determined to aid the Trojans and ruin
70   Our foes in his wrath, then I too of course would like
Nothing more than that the Achaeans, unsung and nameless,
Might perish here far from Argos. But if they should rally
And drive us back from the ships and into the ditch,
Then not one of us would ever get out alive,
Not even a man to tell our story in Troy.
But come, let all of us do as I say. Let us leave
Our horses here at the trench with our squires, while we

In full armor cross over on foot with Hector before us.
Then the Achaeans will not be able to stem
Our advance, if they are truly bound fast in the fatal   80
Bonds of destruction."
   Such was the prudent advice
Of Polydamas, a plan well pleasing to Hector, who clad
In his bronze leaped down at once from his car to the ground.
And the other Trojans, seeing Prince Hector afoot,
Broke their chariot ranks and likewise leaped down.
Then each of them ordered his driver to hold back the horses
Quietly there at the trench, but they themselves
Split up and formed five ordered battalions, marshaled
Behind their chieftains.   90
   The largest and bravest battalion
Fell in behind Hector and peerless Polydamas, all men
Most eager to breach the wall and fight their way
To the hollow ships, and with them Cebriones went
As third in command, for Hector had left with his car
A less able man. The second battalion was led
By Paris along with Agenor and Alcathous,
And the third by two sons of Priam, Helenus and godlike
Deïphobus, with the warrior Asius third in command—
Asius, Hyrtacus' son, whom his glossy huge horses   100
Had drawn from Arisbe where flows the river Selleïs.
And leading the fourth battalion was the valorous son
Of Anchises, Aeneas himself, and with him served
Two versatile fighting men, Antenor's sons Acamas
And Archelochus. And Troy's renowned allies were led
By Sarpedon, who chose as his captains Glaucus and battle-fierce
Asteropaeus, whom next to himself he deemed
The best men, for he was the finest soldier among them.
When all had been marshaled with shield touching bull's-hide shield,
They ferociously made for the Danaan troops, nor did   110
They feel that they could be kept from hurling themselves
Upon the black ships.
   Then all the Trojans and all
Their far-famed allies adopted the plan of peerless
Polydamas—all but Asius, Hyrtacus' son.
That leader of men had no intention of leaving
His horses there with his rein-holding squire. But still
In his chariot he approached the swift ships, childish
Fool that he was! for never would he escape
The dire fates and go back from the ships to windy Troy   120

Triumphant, exulting in horses and car. Instead,
Cursed fate enshrouded the man by the spear of lordly
Idomeneus, son of Deucalion. On he drove
Toward the long left flank of the ships, heading his horses
And car for a bridge over which the Achaeans were accustomed
To drive as they returned from the plain. Asius
Got across and found that the doors were not shut
Nor the long bar yet in its place. The Achaeans were holding
Them open, hoping to save some comrade of theirs
130 Who might still be fleeing from battle and trying to make
The ships. Right over the bridge he drove with his screaming
Squadron behind him, nor did they feel that Achaeans
Could keep them from hurling themselves upon the black ships—
Fools one and all! For there at the gates they found
Two men of superlative prowess, spirited sons
Of spear-hurling Lapithae, Peirithous' son Polypoetes
The strong and Leonteus, the peer of man-maiming Ares.
These two were planted in front of the gaping high gate
As firmly fixed in their stance as a couple of oaks
140 In the mountains, high-crested giants with ground-gripping roots
Great and long, abiding both wind and rain throughout
Innumerable days. So now these two, with faith
In their powerful arms, awaited, firm and unflinching,
The fierce onslaught of mighty Asius. And on
He came with his followers straight for the well-built gate,
All of them screaming their terrible war-cries and raising
Their hard leather shields about their leaders—King Asius,
Iamenus and Orestes, and Adamas, Asius' son,
And Thoön and Oenomaus. The Lapithae inside the wall
150 Had been urging the well-greaved Achaeans to fight in defense
Of the ships, but when they saw troops charging down on the wall
And the panicking Danaans fleeing with screams of terror,
These two rushed out in front of the gate like a pair
Of wild boars in the mountains, ferocious beasts that await
The clamorous onset of men and dogs, charging out
To either side, crushing and rooting up saplings
And vines with a gnashing and clashing and grinding of tusks,
Till finally spears deprive them of spirit. Even so
The bright bronze grated and clanged on the breasts of these two
160 As they were struck hard glancing blows while facing the foe
And keenly contending, trusting their strength and the army
Of comrades above them. For men on the well-built ramparts
Kept hurling down stones in defense of their lives, their shelters,

And fast-faring ships. And the stones came down like flakes
Of snow when a blizzard wind buffets the lowering clouds
And drifts the snow deep on the all-feeding earth, the huge stones
Hurtling through air from the powerful hands of Achaeans
And Trojans too, and harsh was the grating and clanging
As rocks big as millstones struck helmets and studded shields.
Then Asius, Hyrtacus' son, smote his thighs   170
And spoke thus, painfully groaning in great consternation:
    "So you, Father Zeus, have also become an utterly
Lie-loving god! For surely you led roe to think
The Achaeans would be no match for our mighty strength
And invincible hands. But they are like quick-waisted wasps
Or bees that build their nest in a hollow close by
A rocky path, and that stay and fight against hunters
In stubborn defense of their young. So now these men,
Though only two, will not give ground at the gate
Nor cease their slaying till they themselves be slain!"   180
    He spoke, but his words left the mind of Zeus unchanged,
For still he willed to give the glory to Hector.
    Meanwhile, others at other gates were battling,
And hard indeed it would be for me, even though
I were a god, to tell the tale of what happened,
For all along the great wall the god-inspired fire
Of stones kept up, as the sore-beset Argives were forced
To defend their ships. And all the gods who supported
The struggling Danaans deeply grieved in their hearts.
    And the two Lapithae fought on in the blazing battle.   190
Strong Polypoetes, Peirithous' son, let fly
His spear and struck the bronze-cheeked helmet of Damasus.
On through the bronze and bone beneath went the point
And spattered the helmet inside with the warrior's brains,
Thus stopping Damasus' furious charge. Then
Polypoetes went on to account for Pylon and Ormenus.
Meanwhile Leonteus, scion of Ares, aimed
His spear at Hippomachus, son of Antimachus, hurled it
And brought the man down, striking him full on the war-belt.
Next he drew his sharp sword from its sheath and sprang   200
Through the crowd to kill in close fight Antiphates, thrusting him
Back on the ground, after which Leonteus went on
To Iamenus, Menon, Orestes, all of whom
He stretched out on the bountiful earth.
        While the Lapithae stripped
From the dead their glittering armor, the young men who followed

Polydamas and Hector, they who formed the largest
And bravest battalion and were most eager to breach
The wall and put their fire to the ships, these
210 Still stood in conflict and doubt at the brink of the trench.
For as they were going to cross, an ominous bird
Had appeared to them, a high-haunting eagle that flew
By the host on the left with a blood-crimson snake in his talons,
A monstrous serpent alive and writhing, with plenty
Of fight left in him. Doubling up he struck
At his captor's breast and neck till the burning pangs
Forced the eagle to let the snake go, and it fell in the midst
Of the troops at the trench. Then with a scream the eagle
Flew down the wind and away, while the Trojans shuddered
220 At sight of the writhing snake, a glistening omen
From Zeus of the aegis. Then again Polydamas came up
To bold Hector and offered advice:
        "Hector, somehow
You always rebuke me when I in assembly say
What I think, no matter how good my counsel may be,
Since never never should any man of the people
Contradict you in council or on the field,
Or do anything but uphold and increase your command.
But now once again I intend to speak my mind,
230 As it seems to me I should. Let us, then, not
Advance to fight for the Danaan ships. For now
I know what will happen to us, if this is a truly
Ominous bird, this high-haunting eagle that came
Just as we were eager to cross, flying by on the left
With a blood-crimson snake in his talons, a monstrous, writhing
Serpent that he let fall before he could reach
His own nest and ravenous young. Thus it shall happen
To us, though we do by our great strength break through
The Achaean gates and wall and force the foe back—
240 Even so we ourselves shall return from the ships, retracing
Our steps in no very orderly fashion, and leaving
Innumerable Trojans behind, killed by the bronze
Of Achaeans defending their ships. Such would any
Good soothsayer say who knew the truth about omens
And so had the people's trust."
        With an angry scowl
Bright-helmeted Hector replied: "Polydamas, truly
This last speech of yours I do not find very pleasing.
You certainly know how to give better counsel than that.

But if you are really in earnest, then surely the gods   250
Have addled your brains, since now you bid us forget
The message of mightily-thundering Zeus, who made me
A promise which he confirmed with a nod of his head.*
But you would have us obey these long-winged birds,
About which I could not care less, regardless of whether
They fly to the right toward morning and sunrise, or
To the left toward the murky gloom of twilight. Let us
Obey the counsels of almighty God, of Zeus
Who is King over all, mortals and immortals too.
One omen only is best—to fight for one's homeland!   260
But why are you so afraid of blazing battle
And warfare? For even if all the rest of us fell
At the ships of the Argives, still there would be no danger
Of death for you, since you have no battle-staunch heart
Or warlike spirit at all. However, if now
You hold back from the fiery struggle or try to persuade
Any other Trojan to do so, quickly you'll die
Beneath the force of my spear!"
        So saying, brave Hector
Led the advance and all his men followed, screaming   270
Their unearthly war-cries. And bolt-hurling Zeus stirred up
From the mountains of Ida a blasting hard wind that bore
The dust in billows straight at the ships. Thus
He confused the Achaeans still more, and guaranteed glory
To Trojans and Hector. Trusting in such signs from Zeus
And in their own might, they did their best to break
The Achaean's great wall. They tore down towers and breastworks
And pried up beams that buttressed the battlements—all
In their efforts to breach the Achaean wall. But not
Even now did the Danaans give way before them, but quickly   280
They closed the gaps with barriers made of bull's-hide
And threw from behind them at those who came at the wall.
        The two Ajaxes ranged all along the ramparts
Arousing the strength of Achaeans and urging them on.
They harshly berated whomever they saw disposed
To give up and retreat, but others they cheered with words
Of encouragement, saying: "O friends, you Argive princes,
Officers, commoners, all are by no means equal
In war, but now there is plenty of work for all,

---

*Hector is thinking of Zeus' promise, as relayed by Iris at XI.212–216.

290 As surely you already know. Therefore let no man
Turn toward the ships away from the cries of the foe,
But keep facing forward and urging each other on,
That Olympian Zeus, lord and lover of lightning,
May give us the power to stem this assault and drive
Our foes back to the city."

    So shouted the two Ajaxes,
Arousing Achaean resistance. And as snowflakes fall thick
On a winter day when all-planning Zeus displays
His missiles to men, as he lulls every wind and continues
300 To snow until he has covered the high mountain peaks
And jutting lofty headlands, the clover fields
And fertile plowlands of men, and all the harbors
And shores of the gray sea are white, as the heavy snowstorm
From Zeus wraps all but the beating waves: even so
The stones from both sides flew thick, many falling on Trojans,
Many upon the Achaeans, and as they hurled
At each other, the screaming and thudding resounded all up
And down the great wall.

    But not even now would the Trojans
310 And glorious Hector have broken through gate and long bar
If Zeus the contriver had not sent his son Sarpedon
Against the Argive troops, like a lion against
Fat cattle. Quickly he swung his round shield to the front—
His gorgeous buckler of beaten bronze that a smith
Had hammered out and backed with many a bull's-hide,
All fastened together with stitches of golden wire
Running around the circumference. With this before him
And brandishing two long lances, he charged like a lion
Of the mountains, a meat-starved beast whose ferocious spirit
320 Sends him right into the close-barred fold for a try
At the sheep. And though he lands amid shepherds with spears
And dogs watching over the sheep, still he is loath
To leave the pens before he has made his attack,
And either he springs on the flock and seizes a victim,
Or he himself is struck mid the foremost defenders
By a spear from someone's quick hand. Even so the spirit
Of godlike Sarpedon made him feel eager to charge
Full speed at the wall and break his way through the battlements.
Hence he spoke thus to Glaucus, son of Hippolochus:

330   "Glaucus, why is it that we above all are honored
With royal seats, choice cuts, and ever-full cups
In Lycia, and gazed on by all as though we were gods?[3]

And why do we hold and enjoy that huge estate
On the banks of Xanthus, those acres of excellent orchard
And fertile wheat-bearing fields? Surely it best
Becomes us to fight mid the foremost and throw ourselves
In the blaze of battle, that many a bronze-breasted Lycian
May say:
    " 'Surely the lords of Lycia are no
Inglorious men, our Kings, who feast on fat sheep   340
And drink the choice mellow wine. But they are truly
Powerful warriors, men who always fight
Up front with the foremost champions of Lycia.'
    "Ah,
My friend, if we had only to turn from this battle
To make ourselves deathless and ageless forever, neither
Would I myself fight mid the foremost, nor would I urge you
To take part in the man-enhancing struggle. But now,
Since countless fates of inescapable death surround us
Here and always, let us go forward and fight,   350
That we may give glory to someone, or win it ourselves."
    He spoke, and Glaucus did not turn heedless away,
But both of them charged straight onward, heading the great host
Of Lycians. At sight of them coming, Menestheus, son
Of Peteos, shuddered, for they were directing all
Their destruction at his high part of the wall. Hoping
To see some chief who might save his comrades from ruin,
Menestheus looked up and down the Achaean wall,
And not far off he saw the two Ajaxes,
Hungry for battle, and standing there with them, just back   360
From his lodge, was Teucer. But it was impossible now
For him to make himself heard, so great was the din
That went up to heaven of hard-beaten shields and helmets,
Crested with horsehair, and battered gates, for all
The doors had been closed and now the foe fought before them
To crash their way through and enter. Quickly Menestheus
Dispatched the herald Thoötes:
    "Go, my noble
Thoötes, run call Telamonian Ajax, or rather
Call both Ajaxes, for that would be far best of all   370
In our present desperate condition. Here, bearing down
On us hard, come the fierce Lycian leaders, men who have always
Proved themselves mighty in battle. But if there too
The toil and tumult of war have arisen, at least
Let the brave Telamonian Ajax come, and with him

Teucer, the expert bowman."
    So he spoke,
And the listening herald did not disobey him, but went
At a run by the wall of the bronze-clad Achaeans till soon
380 He approached the two Ajaxes and thus delivered
His message: "O leaders of bronze-breasted Argives, Menestheus,
Fostered of Zeus, appeals for your help—though it be
But briefly given—to stem a terrible onslaught.
Both of you now would surely be far best of all
In our present desperate condition. There, bearing down
On them hard, come the fierce Lycian leaders, men who have always
Proved themselves mighty in battle. But if here too
The toil and tumult of war have arisen, at least
Let the brave Telamonian Ajax come, and with him
390 Teucer, the expert bowman."
    Thoötes spoke thus,
And huge Telamonian Ajax did not ignore him.
At once he spoke winged words to the son of Oïleus:
"Ajax, you and strong Lycomedes stand
Your ground firmly and urge the Danaans here to fight fiercely.
I will go and face the foe with Menestheus,
And come back here as soon as I've done what I can."
    With this Telamonian Ajax went on his way,
And with him his half-brother Teucer, both of them sons
400 Of one father, and with them Pandion carried the curved bow
Of Teucer. Rushing along within the wall,
They came to the bastion of great-souled Menestheus. To men
Under pressure they came, for the enemy now were swarming
Upon the battlements, warriors like a black whirlwind,
The powerful Lycian counselors and kings. They clashed
Head on in the tumult, and the screams of battle rose high.
    Ajax, Telamon's son, was first to kill
His man, the intrepid Epicles, a friend of Sarpedon,
Striking him down with a craggy huge rock that lay
410 On top of the wall within the battlements. Not
Without great effort could a man of our generation,
No matter how young or strong, so much as lift it
With both of his hands, but Ajax raised it up high
And hurled it down, smashing the four-horned helmet
And crushing the skull of Epicles, who pitched from the wall
Like a diver, as spirit took leave of his bones. And Teucer
Struck Glaucus, the stalwart son of Hippolochus, wounding
His uncovered arm with an arrow as hotly he rushed up

The ramparts and Teucer shot from the top. His shaft
Took the fight out of Glaucus, and furtively he leaped down   420
From the wall, that no Achaean might see he was wounded
And make a brag over him. But Sarpedon soon knew,
And great was his grief at the absence of Glaucus, though still
He fought hard as ever. With a well-aimed thrust he embedded
His spear in Alcmaon, son of Thestor, and when
He withdrew it Alcmaon came with it, falling face down
With a ringing of ornate bronze. Then Sarpedon laid hold
Of the breastwork with both of his powerful hands, and pulled,
And a long length of battlement fell. He thus bared the top
Of the Argive wall and made a passage for many.   430
      But now both Ajax and Teucer came at him at once.
Teucer glanced a shaft hard off the gleaming baldric
That crossed his chest and held his man-guarding shield,
As Zeus kept death from his son Sarpedon, that he
Might not fall by the sterns of the ships. And Ajax sprang
At him and lunged with his spear, but the point did not pierce
His shield, though he made him reel in his charge. And now
He fell back a bit from the top, but not altogether,
Since still his heart had hopes of glory. Turning,
He called to his godlike people: 440
      "O Lycians, where now
Is your furious war-charge? No matter how strong I may be,
I can't very well break through the wall all alone
And beat a path to the ships. After me, then,
And the more of you the better!"
      He shouted, and they,
In fear of rebuke, pressed forward on either side
Of their brave King and giver of counsel, and the Argives
Opposite them reinforced their battalions behind
The great wall. And now a still hotter struggle ensued.   450
For the powerful Lycians could not break their way through
The Danaan wall and beat a path to the ships,
Nor could the Danaan spearmen thrust them back
From the wall once they had won a position upon it.
But as two men with measuring-rods in hand
Contend with each other from either side of a fence
Where their two fields come together, and bitterly fight
In a narrow space for a just allotment of land,
So now the battlements held them apart as over
The top they smote the bull's-hide bucklers in front of   460
Their chests, the circular shields and fluttering targets.

And many were cut by thrusts of the ruthless bronze,
Not only when anyone turned his back in the fight,
But many were wounded clean through the shield itself.
All down the line the towers and battlements glistened
With flowing blood from men of both sides, Achaeans
And Trojans alike. But still the Achaeans staunchly
Held their ground. As a careful widow that wearily
Spins for a living balances weight and wool
470 In either pan of the scales, making them equal,
That she may earn some paltry support for her children,
So equally now their raging battle was drawn,
Till Zeus gave the higher glory to Priam's son Hector,
The first man to plunge inside the Achaeans' wide wall,
First shouting thus to the horde of Trojans behind him:
        "On, you horse-taming Trojans, smash the wall
Of the Argives and hurl on the ships your god-blazing fire!"
        Thus he urged all of them on, and they giving ear
Charged in one body straight at the wall and started
480 To climb the ramparts with sharp-pointed spears in their hands.
And Hector picked up a stone in front of the gate
And carried it with him, a broad-based, pointed boulder
That not even two of this generation's strongest
Could manage to heave on a wagon. Yet Hector easily
Held it alone, since now crooked Cronos' son Zeus
Made the stone light for him. As a shepherd lightly
Picks up with one hand and carries the fleece of a ram,
Scarcely aware of the weight, so Hector easily
Lifted the boulder and bore it straight on at the thick
490 And tight-fitting doors of the gate, high double-doors
With two crossbars inside well locked by a bolt
In the middle. Charging in close, he took a firm stance
And hurled the stone at the doors, planting his feet
Well apart to insure the force of his blow. And the stone
Crashed into the middle, broke off the hinges, and fell
Inside, as the great gate groaned and the bars gave way
And the doors flew apart beneath the force of the boulder.
Then glorious Hector sprang in, his stern face dark
As fast-falling night. But his bronze shone ghastly about him,
500 And in his hands he held two spears, nor could
Anyone but a god have held the man back, when once
He had plunged through the gate with his eyes so fiercely flaming.
Whirling about in the crowd, he called the Trojans

To scale the wall, and again they heeded his urging.
Quickly many climbed over the top while others
Poured in through the strongly wrought gate. And the Danaans fled
In fear mid the hollow ships, and the screams were unceasing.

BOOK XIII

Fighting Among the Ships

Now when Zeus had sent Hector and many Trojans charging
Down on the ships, he left the two armies there
In the toil and tears of unceasing struggle, while he
Averted his shining eyes and looked far out
On the lands of the horse-handling Thracians, the close-fighting
         Mysians,
The august Hippemolgi, drinkers of mares' milk, and the Abii,
Justest of men. The Father no longer turned
His shining eyes toward Troy, for he had no hint
In his heart that any immortal would dare come down
10   To strengthen either the Trojan or Danaan forces.[1]
      But lordly Poseidon, shaker of shores, was not
For a moment unwatchful from where on the highest peak
Of well-wooded Samothrace* he sat rapt at the sight
Of raging battle, for from his position there
He could clearly see all Ida, the city of Priam,
And the ships of Achaeans. There he sat, after he
Had emerged from the sea, and he had compassion on all
The Achaeans now overcome by the Trojans, but against
Almighty Zeus he seethed with bitter resentment.
20   Soon he strode swiftly down the precipitous slope,
And the towering mountains and the trees of the forest trembled
Beneath the immortal feet of Poseidon. Quickly
He took three mighty strides, and with the fourth
He reached his goal at Aegae, where built in the depths
Of the sea he has his famous home, a palace
Golden and gleaming, enduring forever. Once there
He hitched to his car his brazen-hoofed horses, fast-flying
Steeds with manes of streaming gold. And the garments
He wore were of gold, as was the well-wrought whip
30   He held in his hand as he mounted the car and drove out

---

*From Troy, the peak of Samothrace is visible to the northwest, beyond "craggy Imbros."

Over the waves. And the beasts that live in the sea*
Came up from the depths on all sides and gambolled beneath him,
Acknowledging him as their King, and the sea itself,
Rejoicing, parted and made way before him. And the chariot's
Axle was dry, as swiftly his far-bounding horses
Bore Poseidon toward the Achaean ships.
    Midway between Tenedos and craggy Imbros
There is a huge cave in the depths of the sea, and here
The mighty creator of earthquakes pulled up and unharnessed
His horses and threw down before them ambrosial fodder 40
To munch on. Then he put hobbles of gold on their feet,
Hobbles that could not be broken or shaken loose,
That his pair might stay where they were until their master
Returned. Then off he went to the camp of Achaeans.
    There the massed Trojans, like flame or hurricane wind,
Were rushing on with Priam's son Hector, roaring
And screaming their war-cries, and hoping that they would soon take
The Achaean ships and kill all the bravest beside them.
But now Poseidon, embracer and shaker of earth,
Emerged from the brine, determined to urge on the Argives. 50
Taking the form and tireless voice of Calchas,
He spoke first of all to the two Ajaxes, who were
Already eager for action:
    "If you two will only
Be mindful of might and not at all of chill fear,
You'll save the Achaean army. Nowhere else
In the fight do I dread the powerful Trojans. Though many
Have scaled the great wall, the well-greaved Achaeans will hold them
All back. Only here am I really afraid of what
Might happen to us, here where yonder madman 60
Leads on like furious fire, Hector, who falsely
Claims Zeus as his father. But may some god inspire
You both to firmly stand your ground here and to bid
The others do likewise. Thus you may drive him back
From the fast-faring ships, no matter how eager he is,
And even though the mighty Olympian himself
Is urging him on."
    So saying, the kingly embracer
And shaker of shores touched both of them with his staff
And filled them with valorous heart, and their arms and legs 70

---

*The gambolling beasts of the sea are dolphins.

He made feel rested and light. Then he took off
Like a swift-winged hawk that rising hangs high in the sky
Above a tall thrust of rock before swooping over
The plain in pursuit of some other bird. Even so
Earthshaking Poseidon darted away. Quick Ajax,
Son of Oïleus, was first aware of the god,
And now he spoke thus to Ajax, son of Telamon:

  "Ajax, one of the gods from Olympus, appearing
To us in the form of our prophet, tells us to fight
80 By the ships. For that was surely not Calchas, our seer
And reader of bird-signs. I glimpsed his feet and legs
As he left, and knew him at once for a god, since even
The gods are sometimes easily known. And now
The heart in my breast feels more than ever eager
For struggle and conflict, and now my feet below
And hands above are madly desirous of battle!"

  Then Ajax, son of Telamon, answered him thus:
"Even so my own invincible hands are restlessly
Gripping my spear, my spirit is hot, and the feet
90 Beneath me are more than ready to charge. Right now
I would like nothing better than meeting in single combat
Priam's son Hector, the always eager to fight."

  While the two Ajaxes were talking thus to each other,
Exulting in battle-joy that a god had put
In their hearts, earth-girdling Poseidon was in the rear
Arousing disheartened Achaeans, who there mid the swift-sailing
Ships were attempting to get back their courage. Their limbs
Were leaden from hours of fearful toil, and now
Their hearts were filled with terror at sight of the horde
100 Of Trojans that had already scaled the great wall.
As they saw these advancing, they wept in cringing despair,
But the mighty creator of earthquakes went easily in
Among them and set them on to form once again
Their stalwart battalions. He came first of all to Teucer
And Leïtus, with whom were the warriors Peneleos, Thoas,
And Deïpyrus, as well as Meriones and Antilochus, those masterful
Raisers of war-cry. To them he spoke these winged words:

  "For shame, you Argives, acting like so many babies!
Your prowess, I thought, would save our ships from the Trojans.
110 But if now you cringe from miserable war, then surely
The day of defeat has dawned for the Argives. Who
Would believe it! this wonder before my eyes, this terrible
Thing I never imagined could happen—the Trojans

Charging our vessels! Why they have always been
Like timorous, panicky deer that fearfully wander
The woodland till they, unresisting and weak, fall prey
To jackals and panthers and wolves. So until now
The Trojans have had no slightest desire to stand
And face the spirit and might of Achaeans, not even
For one brief moment. But here they are now, far   120
From the city, waging their war at the hollow ships,
And this all because of our leader's ignoble deed
And a pusillanimous people, who since they are striving
With him had rather die mid the fast-faring ships
Than fight to protect them. But even though the warlike
Son of Atreus, powerful King Agamemnon,
Is to blame for it all, he having insulted
The quick-footed son of Peleus, still we ourselves
Cannot afford to be shirkers in battle. Let us,
In fact, quickly make up for his evil. The hearts   130
Of heroes are able to heal. Nor can you excuse
Any longer your lack of furious valor, you
The Achaeans' bravest and best. I wouldn't quarrel
With some wretched fellow who couldn't do any better,
But my heart seethes with blame at sight of you here.
O you slackers, soon you shall see what greater pain
Cowardice causes! But come, let each one of you
Fill his heart with shame and blame for himself,
For now the battle has grown to be truly tremendous.
Screaming Hector, mighty as ever, has smashed   140
His way through gate and long bars and carries his war
Right in toward the ships!"
          So saying, earth-girdling Poseidon
Stirred the Achaeans to rally their powerful ranks
About the two Ajaxes, nor could host-urging Athena
Nor Ares himself have come among them and failed
To honor their might. For there picked men of the bravest
Awaited the charge of the Trojans and noble Hector,
Forming against them a spear-bristling wall. So close
The Achaeans stood to each other that shield pressed on shield,   150
Helmet on helmet, and man on man, so close
That the horsehair plumes on the bright-horned helmets
                    brushed
Each other with every nod of a head, and spears
Were crossed as brave hands brandished them forward. All minds
Were fixed on the battle, for which they were ready and eager.

Unswervingly on came the Trojans, massed and mighty
With Hector before them, great Hector plunging ahead
Like a ruthless, death-bearing boulder that bounds down the slope
Of a mountain when a wintry, rain-swollen river washes it
160 Loose with a flooding of water and sends it headlong
Bouncing and flying—high in the air it leaps
Through the echoing forest, crashing its way through all
Before it until it reaches the level plain,
Where at last it loses its force and rolls to a stop.[2]
So for a while Prince Hector ferociously threatened
To kill his way through to the sea past shelters and ships
Of Achaeans, but when that warrior came to collide
With the serried battalions, there his onslaught was halted.
The sons of Achaeans met him with thrusting swords
170 And double-barbed spears and made him reel and fall back,
Screaming thus to the army of fighters behind him:
        "You Trojans and Lycians and dueling Dardanians, hold
With me here! This wall of Achaeans will not keep me back
For long. They'll yield before my spear, believe me,
If truly the greatest of gods drives me on, the bolt-crashing
Husband of Hera!"
        So Hector encouraged the Trojans,
And out strode his brother Deïphobus, holding his round shield
Before him and quickly advancing. But at him Meriones
180 Aimed a bright spear, nor did he miss his mark.
He struck the round shield, but instead of piercing the bull's-hide
The long shaft broke at the socket, as Deïphobus quickly
Held from him the bull's-hide buckler, fearing the spear
Of fiery Meriones, who now shrank back in a crowd
Of his friends, frustrated and angry at breaking his spear
And failing to fell his man. Off he went
Past shelters and ships of Achaeans to fetch a long lance
He had left in his lodge.
        But the others fought on with loud,
190 Unquenchable cries. And Teucer, Telamon's son,
Was first to bring a man down, the spearman Imbrius,
Son of many-horsed Mentor. Before the sons
Of Achaeans came, Imbrius lived in Pedaeum
And had as his wife a bastard daughter of Priam,
Medesicasta. But when the Danaans came
In their swiftly maneuverable ships, he went back to Troy,
Where he was great mid the Trojans, and lived in the house
Of Priam, who honored him equally with his own children.

This was he whom Teucer jabbed under the ear
With a thrust of his lengthy javelin, then drew the point out. 200
And Imbrius fell like an ash that grows on top
Of a far-seen towering mountain till someone's bronze
Brings it down and its fresh green foliage strikes earth. Even so
He fell, and about him rang his elaborate armor.
Then Teucer rushed eagerly forward to strip the man
Of his war-gear, but Hector met his advance with a cast
Of his glittering spear. But Teucer, looking straight at him,
Just managed to dodge the hurtling bronze, which embedded
Itself in the chest of charging Amphimachus, son
Of Actorian Cteatus. And Amphimachus crashed to the ground 210
With a clanging of brazen war-gear. Then Hector rushed out
To tear from the fallen Achaean his head-hugging helmet,
But Telamonian Ajax lunged with his spear
At the charging Hector, failing however to find
His flesh behind so much grim bronze. But he struck
The boss of his shield such a powerful blow that Hector
Reeled back from the corpses, and Achaeans bore both of
        them off.
The Athenian chieftains, Stichius and noble Menestheus,
Carried Amphimachus into the host of Achaeans,
While both Ajaxes, raging with furious fight, 220
Bore off the Trojan Imbrius. Just as two lions
Seize a goat from a pack of razor-fanged hounds
And carry it off through dense underbrush, holding it
High in their jaws, so now the two helmeted Ajaxes
Held Imbrius high and stripped off his bronze. Then Ajax,
Son of Oïleus, angry and grieved for Amphimachus,
Hacked the head from Imbrius' tender neck
And sent it spinning away like a ball, to drop
In the dust at the feet of Hector.
      The heart of Poseidon 230
Seethed with rage when his grandson Amphimachus fell
In the awesome encounter, and off he went by the shelters
And ships to stir up Achaeans and make still more trouble
For Trojans. And then he met spear-famous Idomeneus.
He had been with a comrade whose knee the keen bronze
Had recently wounded. His men had carried him in,
And Idomeneus, now that he had instructed the surgeons,
Was on his way to his lodge before going back
To the battle, for which he still was eager. Taking
The voice of Andraemon's son Thoas, King of Aetolians 240

In Pleuron and sheer Calydon and honored by them
Like a god, lordly earth-shaking Poseidon spoke
To him thus:
        "Idomeneus, counselor of Cretans, where now
Are the threats that sons of Achaeans used to hurl
At the Trojans?"
        To which Idomeneus, leader of Cretans:
"So far as I know, O Thoas, no one of us
Is to blame. All of us here are experienced fighters,
250   And not a man of us shrinks from evil war
Because he is gripped by cowardly fear. I am forced
To believe that it must be the pleasure of Cronos' son Zeus,
The high and the mighty, that we Achaeans should die here
Far from Argos, forever unsung and unknown.
But Thoas, you have consistently been a staunchly
Foe-fighting man and a splendid urger of others
Whenever you've seen men about to retreat. So do not
Give up now, but call your encouragement out
To every man you can."
260   And Poseidon, shaker
Of shores, replied: "Idomeneus, never may he
Who willingly shrinks from this fight today return home
From Troy, but here may that man become the delight
Of ravenous dogs. But go, get your gear and come on.
Now we must hurry and do what we can together.
For there is a prowess in union even of weaklings,
And we two have what it takes to fight with the bravest."
        So saying, the great god rejoined the toiling men,
And Idomeneus went to his well-built lodge, put on
270   His exquisite armor, caught up a couple of spears,
And headed back for the field like a bolt of lightning
That Cronos' son Zeus takes up in his hand and hurls
From gleaming Olympus, a far-seen bolt that dazzles
Across the sky as a fiery sign to mortals.
So flashed the bronze about the breast of Idomeneus
As he ran. But while he was still near his lodge,
He met his able comrade and squire Meriones
On his way to fetch a bronze-headed spear,[3]
And stalwart Idomeneus spoke to him, saying:
280   "Meriones,
Son of Molus, fast on your feet and the dearest
Of all my comrades, why do you come here now,
Leaving the fierce and fiery struggle? Can you

Be wounded, weak and in pain from the point of some arrow?
Or do you come after me with a message? No need,
Since I, at least, am already eager—to fight,
Not sit in my lodge!"
    And Meriones, getting his drift:
"Idomeneus, counseling lord of bronze-armored Cretans,
I am on my way for a spear, if perhaps   290
You have one left in your lodge. Just now I shattered
The one I had on the shield of haughty Deïphobus."
    To which Idomeneus, King of the Cretans, replied:
"If spears are your wish, whether one or twenty, you'll find them
Propped in my lodge against the bright entrance wall,
Spears I have taken from Trojans I've slain, since I
Do not care for fighting the foe at a distance. Hence
I have spears and bossed shields, helmets and flashing breastplates."
    Then gravely Meriones answered: "I too am supplied
With plenty of Trojan spoils, but they are all stored   300
In my lodge and black ship and none of them now are near.
For believe me, I too am not remiss in courage,
And when the battle-strife breaks out I always
Take my stand mid the very foremost men
In the hero-enhancing battle. Some other Achaean
Might very well be unaware of my prowess,
But surely, I think, you know me much better than that."
    And then Idomeneus, King of the Cretans, replied:
"What need is there for you to speak of these things?
I do indeed know how valiant a man you are,   310
As would be seen if now all the bravest of us
Were counted off by the ships for an ambush, wherein
A man's valor is soonest discerned and the cowards set off
From the brave. For the coward's face changes color, nor can
His spirit sustain him. He cannot keep still, but crouching
He nervously shifts his weight from foot to foot,
And his heart pounds hard as he broods on the imminent fates
Of death, and his teeth continue to chatter. But the brave man
Keeps his color, nor is he overly fearful
When once he has taken his place in the warriors' ambush.   320
That man's only prayer is quickly to clash
In the awesome flames of fight. Not, I say,
At the picking of such a party would any man scorn
Your courage or the might of your hands. And should you in toil
Of war be hit by arrow or spear, it would not
Be from behind, but as you were charging ahead

To dally a bit with the foremost you would receive
The bitter shaft in belly or breast. Come then,
Let us no longer loiter here nor talk
330   Any more like two little boys, or someone may lose
All patience with us. Go on to my lodge and get
A strong spear for yourself."
          He spoke, and Meriones, peer
Of the hurtling War-god, quickly took from the lodge
A bronze-pointed spear, and immensely eager for battle
Followed Idomeneus. As murdering Ares enters
A battle with Rout, his mighty and fearless son
Before whom even the bravest retreat—these two
Put on their armor and go out from Thrace to join
340   The Ephyri or the great-hearted Phlegyes, both of whose pleas
They never grant, but always give the glory
To one side or the other—even like that pair of gods
Did Meriones and Idomeneus, leaders of men, go forth
Into battle helmeted well in blazing bronze.
And now Meriones spoke to Idomeneus, saying:
          "Son of Deucalion, where are you most inclined
To enter the battle? On the right of the host,
Straight up the center, or shall we go in on the left,
Where surely, I think, the long-haired Achaeans are failing
350   Most in the fight?"
          And again Idomeneus, King
Of the Cretans, replied: "The ships in the center have others
To guard them, the two Ajaxes and Teucer, the best
Of our bowmen and also good in hand-to-hand combat.
They will give Priam's son Hector more than his fill
Of fighting, no matter how eager and mighty he is!
Hard indeed he will find it, rage as he will,
To master the spirit and dauntless strength of those men
And then set fire to the ships, unless great Zeus
360   Himself should hurl a blazing firebrand down
Among the swift vessels. For huge Telamonian Ajax
Will never yield to any mere mortal who eats
The grain of Demeter and can be quelled by cleaving
Bronze or a heavy rock. Not even before
Rank-smashing Achilles would Telamon's son give way,
At least in hand-to-hand fighting, for no man can vie
With Achilles when it comes to swiftness of foot. But let us
Do as you have suggested and head for the host
On the left, that we may find out right away whether we

Shall win glory ourselves or give it now to another."   370
     He spoke, and Meriones, peer of the rapid War-god,
Led the way toward the left of the battle, where Idomeneus
Wanted to enter.
     As soon as the Trojans sighted
Idomeneus, surging in like a flame, him
And his squire armored in ornate bronze, they shouted
One to another through the great melee and all charged
At him together, and now by the sterns of the ships
Loud strife and clashing arose. And as when gusts
Come many and fast on a day when shrill winds are blowing   380
And raising the thick dust on roads up into a swirling
Huge cloud, so now they clashed in one fierce throng,
Each man eager to use his sharp bronze on another.
And the man-wasting battle bristled with lengthy, flesh-rending
Spears, and eyes were blinded by the blazing of bronze
From gleaming helmets, new-burnished breastplates, and flashing,
Resplendent shields, as chaotically on the men came.
Hard-hearted indeed would that man have been who could
Have looked on that slaughter with joy instead of lament.
     Thus two mighty sons of Cronos pitted their power   390
Against each other, creating horrible pain
For heroic mortals. Zeus wanted Hector and his side
To win—just enough to give glory to foot-swift Achilles,
For Zeus had no wish at all that the host of Achaeans
Should die there at Troy. He wanted only to glorify
Thetis along with her brave-hearted son. But Poseidon
Stole furtively forth from the gray salt-sea, and going
Among the Argives urged them on, for he
Was deeply indignant at Zeus and filled with resentment
Because he was helping the Trojans conquer the Argives.   400
Both gods came of one stock and lineage, though Zeus
Was the elder and richer in wisdom. Hence Poseidon
Would openly not aid the Argives, but furtively went
Through the host in the form of a man, seeking thus to arouse them.
Then each god took an end of strong strife's rope
In that all-leveling and evil war, and between
Both armies they tugged on the taut, unbreakable bond
Till the knees of many a warrior loosened in death.
     Now Idomeneus, although his hair was graying,
Called to the Danaan troops, and charging right into   410
The horde of Trojans he turned their advance to retreat.
For he killed one of their proudest allies, Othryoneus

Of Cabesus, a relative stranger in Troy,
Who had but recently followed the rumor of war
And come. This man had asked in marriage the loveliest
Daughter of Priam, Cassandra herself. But instead
Of rich gifts of wooing, he had promised to do a great deed—
To drive the stubborn sons of Achaeans away
From the land of Troy. And the ancient Priam promised
420 To give him the girl, confirming his word with a nod
Of his head. Then trusting in this, Othryoneus fought
For the Trojans. But now Idomeneus aimed his bright spear
At him and caught him full in the belly as he
Came swaggering on, uselessly clad in a breastplate
Of bronze. He thudded to earth, and thus Idomeneus
Vauntingly mocked him:
            "Othryoneus, my most hearty
Congratulations on your engagement to marry
Dardanian Priam's daughter—that is if you really
430 Deliver all that you promised the man. We too,
You know, would promise as much as he did and keep
Our word exactly. We would, in fact, be delighted
To give you the loveliest daughter of King Agamemnon,
Bringing her here from Argos for you to make her
Your wife—if only you'd join up with us and sack
The populous city of Troy. But say, come now
With us to the seagoing ships that we may make terms
And arrange for the wedding. You'll find us no churls when it comes
To the price for a bride."
440   So taunting his victim, warlike
Idomeneus started to drag him off by the foot
Through the terrible struggle, but Asius came to help
His comrade Othryoneus. He came on foot in front of
His chariot, which his driver kept so close behind him
That always the horses' breath was hot on his shoulders.
Asius came very eager to cut down Idomeneus,
Who, however, was too quick for him and hurled
His spear in at the throat just under the chin and drove
The bronze clean through, so that Asius fell as an oak
450 Or poplar or lofty pine falls when men in the mountains
Cut them down with keen axes to furnish timber
For ships. So now, in front of his horses and car,
The groaning Asius lay stretched out, clutching
At the bloody dust. And his driver, stricken with panic,
Lost his wits completely, nor did he dare

To turn back the horses and so escape the hands
Of the Argives. Then battle-staunch Antilochus, son
Of magnanimous Nestor, aimed at him with his spear
And hurled it hard through his middle, missing the useless
Breastplate of bronze and fixing it full in his belly.   460
Gasping he fell from the sturdy car, and Antilochus
Drove the horses away from the Trojans and into
The hands of well-greaved Achaeans.
      Then Deïphobus,
Bitterly grieving for Asius dead, came up
Very close to Idomeneus and hurled his glittering spear.
But Idomeneus, looking straight at him, avoided the hurtling
Bronze, for he hid himself behind his round shield,
His buckler well wrought with bull's-hide and flashing bronze
And fitted with two arm-rods. Behind it he crouched   470
While the spear flew over, stridently grazing the rim.
But not in vain did Deïphobus let the lance fly
From his powerful hand, for he struck Hippasus' son,
The people's shepherd Hypsenor, in the liver
Under the midriff, and immediately unstrung his knees.
And Deïphobus fiercely exulted, loudly boasting:
      "Not unavenged, I think, good Asius lies.
Now he'll be glad on his way to the house of Hades,
The strongest gate-guarder of all, for I have provided
A traveling companion for him!"   480
      Such was his vaunt,
Which grieved the Argives and most of all aroused
The spirit of flame-hearted Antilochus. And he, in spite of
His sorrow, did not neglect his dear friend, but ran
And stood over him, using his shield as a cover.
Then two loyal comrades, Echius' son Mecisteus
And noble Alastor, lifted Hypsenor and carried him,
Heavily groaning, back to the hollow ships.
      But Idomeneus mightily raged with no pause at all,
Constantly eager to shroud some Trojan in blackness   490
Of night, or to go down himself in keeping off death
From the men of Achaea. The next man he killed was strong
Aesyetes' god-nurtured son, heroic Alcathous.
He was a son-in-law of Anchises, married
To that lord's eldest daughter, Hippodameia,
Whose father and lady mother at home in their hall
Had doted on her their darling, for she surpassed
All other girls her age in beauty, skill,

And good sense, and so the best man in the wide realm of Troy
500 Had made her his wife—the man whom lordly Poseidon
Now destroyed beneath the spear of Idomeneus.
For the god bewitched his bright eyes and so paralyzed
His powerful legs that Alcathous found it impossible
Either to run to the rear or dodge to one side.
But he was standing still as a pillar or high
Leafy tree when the raging Idomeneus thrust his spear
Deep into his chest, cleaving his coat of bronze
That had till then kept death away from his body,
But which now gave a dull clang as through it the spear cut.
510 And Alcathous thudded to earth with the spear fixed
In his heart, that beating yet caused the butt-end to quiver
Till finally hulking Ares stilled its fury.
And Idomeneus fiercely exulted, loudly boasting:
    "I say, Deïphobus, you that saw fit to brag so,
Shall we now call it quits—three dead men
For one—or would you, mad sir, care to come on
And face me alone, that you may discover what manner
Of Zeus-sprung King has come here? For our line is
From Zeus, who first begot Minos to be the ruler
520 Of Crete, and Minos begot the flawless Deucalion,
Who then begot me, the King of many men
In broad Crete. And now my ships have brought me here
As a curse to you and your father King Priam, and to all
Of the other Trojans."
            Now Deïphobus could not decide
What to do, whether to go back and get some comrade
Of his, some great-souled Trojan to help him, or whether
To try it alone. But pondering gave him the answer—
Namely, to go for Aeneas. Him he found standing
530 In back of the battle, for Aeneas was always angry
At royal Priam[4] because he paid him no honor
Among the people, great man though he certainly was.
Now Deïphobus came up close and his words came winged
With telling entreaty:
            "Aeneas, counselor of Trojans,
Now there is great need of you to help in the fight
For your brother-in-law Alcathous. If you care
At all for your sister's husband, come with me now
To rescue his corpse. He, after all, was the one
540 Who brought you up at home from the time you were little,
And he, I say, has fallen to spear-famed Idomeneus!"

These words stirred the heart in the breast of Aeneas,
Who hungry for battle went at once for Idomeneus.
He, however, did not flee in his fear
Like some pampered boy, but stood his ground like a boar
Hard-pressed in the mountains, one that trusts in his strength
And awaits the clamoring throng that comes against him
At bay in a lonely place. He bristles his back
Up high and fire flames from his eyes as he whets
His tushes and impatiently waits for his chance at the dogs   550
And men. So now Idomeneus stood and faced
Cry-answering Aeneas, but he did bellow back to his comrades
For help, looking to Ascalaphus, Aphareus, and Deïpyrus,
As well as Meriones and Antilochus, masters of war-cry.
To these he spoke winged words, urging them thus:
        "Come here, my friends, and help one standing alone,
For deeply I fear the swiftly-charging Aeneas,
Now coming at me. Great is his power to kill men
In battle, and his is the flower of youth, when the might
Of a man is strongest. Were we of equal age   560
And in our present mood, then the outcome would be
More uncertain, and either of us might win a great victory."
        He spoke, and they with one accord closed in
And stood by Idomeneus, close together and sloping
Their shields to their shoulders. And Aeneas on his side called
To his comrades, looking for help to Deïphobus, Paris,
And noble Agenor, who like him were leaders
Of Trojans. And after them came the troops, as sheep
Follow after the ram from pasture to where they drink,
And their shepherd rejoices to see them. Even so, the heart   570
Of Aeneas was glad when he saw the host behind him.
        Then over Alcathous' corpse they clashed with long spears,
And the bronze on their breasts rang grimly as through the crowd
They aimed at each other. And more than all the rest
Two fiercely battling peers of the War-god, Aeneas
And Idomeneus, lusted to cleave each other's flesh
With the ruthless bronze. Aeneas made the first cast,
But Idomeneus, looking straight at him, avoided the spear,
The hurtling bronze of Aeneas that vainly flew
From his powerful hand and quivering stuck in the ground.   580
Then Idomeneus threw and pierced the gut of Oenomaus,
Cutting a gash in his armor, through which his entrails
Oozed. He fell in the dust and clawed the ground.
And Idomeneus wrenched his long-shadowing spear from the corpse,

But so belabored was he by missiles he could not
Remain to strip from his victim's shoulders the exquisite
Armor. For he was no longer fast in a charge,
Neither able quickly to follow a cast of his own
Nor nimbly avoid another's. And since his speed
590 Was no longer such as to take him safely from battle,
He mixed in hand-to-hand fighting and kept off death
At close quarters. Now, as step by step he withdrew,
Deïphobus hurled his bright spear at him, for always,
Remembering his taunts, he hated Idomeneus. Again,
However, he missed, but sent his huge shaft through the shoulder
Of Ares' son Ascalaphus, bringing him down
In the dust, where dying he clutched at the ground. But as yet
Huge-hulking, bellowing Ares was not aware
That his son had gone down in the mighty struggle. For he sat
600 On the highest peak of Olympus beneath golden clouds,
Where he along with the other immortal gods
Was kept from the war by the will of almighty Zeus.
        Now over Ascalaphus fighting men rushed together,
And Deïphobus tore the bright helmet off the still head.
But Meriones, peer of swift Ares, sprang at Deïphobus,
Stabbing the Trojan's upper arm with his spear,
And the plumed bronze fell from his hand and clanged on the
                ground.
Then again Meriones sprang, swooping in like a vulture,
Jerked the huge spear from the arm of Deïphobus, and quickly
610 Shrank back mid a crowd of comrades. And Polites took
His brother Deïphobus round the waist with both arms
And got him out of the horrible conflict, back
To where his fast horses stood waiting for him with their driver
And ornate car. These bore him off to the city,
Faint with pain and heavily groaning, and the dark blood
Dripped from his new-wounded arm.
                But the others fought on
With loud, unquenchable cries. Then Aeneas, leaping
At Aphareus, son of Caletor, plunged his sharp spear
620 Deep into his throat, and the man's head fell to one side
As he crumpled up beneath his helmet and shield,
And heartbreaking death engulfed him. And Nestor's son
Antilochus, watching his chance sprang out at Thoön
Just as he turned and slashed his back with a spear,
Completely cutting the vein that runs up the back
To the neck. This he severed, and Thoön fell

On his back in the dust, stretching up both of his hands
To his dear friends. But Antilochus leaped upon him
And started to strip his shoulders of armor, cautiously
Looking from side to side. For he was soon   630
Surrounded by Trojans fiercely thrusting their spears
At his all-glinting shield. They failed, however, to pierce
The huge piece, nor did they so much as scratch his flesh
With the ruthless bronze they wielded. For Poseidon, shaker
Of shores, completely protected the son of King Nestor,
Even though he was belabored with many keen missiles.
Nor did Antilochus try to flee from the foe,
But ranged among them constantly wielding his spear
And eager to cast at some Trojan, or to charge in close
And clash hand to hand. But as he drew back to throw   640
Through the melee, Adamas, son of Asius, seeing
Him so, charged in from nearby and plunged his sharp bronze
At Antilochus' shield. Poseidon, however, god
With the blue-black hair, destroyed the force of the spear-point,
Begrudging that bronze the life of Nestor's brave son.
Half of the shaft stuck there in the shield like a fire-hardened
Stake, while the rest of it lay on the ground. And Adamas,
Shunning destruction, shrank back mid a crowd of comrades.
But Meriones came at him hotly and hurled his spear in
Between his privates and navel, where Ares is cruelest   650
To suffering mortals. Deeply he planted it there,
And Adamas leaned toward the shaft, writhing about it
Like a stubborn bull that herdsmen rope in the hills
And drag away resisting. So Adamas twisted
And writhed for a while, but not very long—just
Till the warring Meriones came and wrenched the spear
From his gut. Then darkness enveloped his eyes.
         And Helenus,
Son of Priam, swinging a huge Thracian sword,
Came down on Deïpyrus' temple, splitting his helmet   660
And ripping it off to the ground, where it rolled mid the feet
Of the fighters till some Achaean retrieved it. And the pit-black
Darkness of death came down on Deïpyrus, quickly
Eclipsing his eyes.
         Then Atreus' son Menelaus
Was gripped with grief for his fellow Achaean, so he,
The great battle-roarer, boldly stalked out, threatening
Heroic Prince Helenus, Atrides drawing his spear back
Even as Helenus bent the horns of his bow.

670 Thus both at one instant let fly, the one with an arrow
     Swift from the bowstring, the other with keen-pointed spear.
     And the son of Priam landed his shaft on the breast
     Of King Menelaus, but the painful point glanced off
     The bronze of his breastplate. As the black-skinned beans or chickpeas
     Along a large threshing floor leap from the flat
     Wide winnowing-fan, tossed up by a rapidly shoveling
     Winnower before a gusty shrill wind, so now
     The keen arrow glanced from the bronze of famed Menelaus
     And sped on its way. But he, the great battle-roarer,
680 Threw and struck Prince Helenus full on the hand
     Wherein he was holding his polished weapon, and the bronze point
     Tore through his flesh and into the bow. Then Helenus,
     Shunning destruction, shrank back mid a crowd of comrades,
     Dangling his hand and dragging the ashen shaft.
     And great-souled Agenor drew the spear from his hand
     And wrapped the wound with a strip of twisted sheep's wool,
     Making a sling of the fine-woven stuff, which the squire
     Of the people's shepherd Agenor carried for him.
           Now Peisander charged straight at illustrious King Menelaus,
690 But an evil fate was leading him on to his death—
     His death at your hands, Menelaus, there in the awesome
     Heat of battle. But as they came close to each other,
     Atreus' son Menelaus missed, his spear
     Turning off to one side. Peisander, however, struck
     With his bronze on the other's wide shield, which stopped the point
     From piercing clean through, and the shaft broke off at the socket.
     Even so, Peisander rejoiced and still had high hopes
     Of winning. But Atreus' son whipped out his sword
     With the studs of silver and sprang at Peisander, who brought
700 From behind his shield a splendid bronze battle-ax
     Set on a lengthy handle of well-polished olive.
     At once they came at each other. And Peisander hacked
     Menelaus on the horn of his helmet, a little below
     The horsehair plume, but Atrides caught his opponent
     Squarely between the eyes, crunching the bones in
     Loudly and dropping both bloody eyes in the dust
     At his feet. Doubling up, Peisander fell, and Menelaus
     Planted a foot on his chest and stripped him of armor,
     Exultantly saying:
710   "Surely in just this condition
     Will all you insufferable Trojans leave the ships
     Of the swiftly-drawn Danaans, you that are always so hungry

For the horrible screams of battle. Nor have you any
Shortage at all of other most shameful disgraces—
Such, for instance, as that you heaped on me,
You men like so many filthy bitches! you
That had no fear in your hearts of the harsh wrath of Zeus,
Hospitality's high-thundering god, who some day will sack
Completely your steep citadel. For you abducted
My wife, who had I am sure welcomed you warmly,   720
And taking much treasure to boot you wantonly sailed
Away. And now you would like nothing better than throwing
Your terrible fire on the seagoing ships of heroic
Achaeans, whom surely you'd like to destroy one and all.
But you will be stopped, believe me, no matter how spoiling
For blood you may be—O Father Zeus, they say
You vastly surpass all men and gods in wisdom,
Yet from you all of these horrors come!
Even now you are favoring proud and evil men,
Trojans who always presume and whose spirit is blindly   730
Wanton and wicked, nor do they ever get half
Enough of evil, all-leveling war. Men get
Their fill of all things, of sleep and love, sweet song
And flawless dancing, and most men like these things
Much better than war. Only Trojans are always
Thirsty for blood!"
        So saying, Menelaus the blameless
Stripped the corpse of its bloody armor and gave it
To comrades of his, and he himself went back
And mixed with the front-line champions. At once Harpalion,   740
King Pylaemenes' son, charged down upon him,
He who followed his dear sire to Troy to fight
In the war but never returned to the land of his fathers.
Closing in quickly, he plunged his spear at the center
Of King Menelaus's shield, but did not succeed
In driving the bronze clean through. Back he shrank
Mid a crowd of comrades, shunning destruction and nervously
Glancing about him, lest someone should get to his flesh
With the bronze. But as Harpalion headed for cover,
Meriones shot at him a bronze-pointed arrow   750
And struck him on the right buttock. The point passed under
The bone and into his bladder, and Harpalion sank
In the arms of his friends, where soon he breathed forth his life
And lay stretched out in the dust like a worm, while his blood
Ran darkly forth, soaking the ground. The brave

Paphlagonians did all they could. Then putting him
In a chariot, some of them took him to sacred Ilium,
Grieving, and among them went his weeping father.
Nor for his dead son was any blood-price ever paid.*
760   But the death of this man infuriated Prince Paris,
For Harpalion had once been his host among the numerous
Paphlagonians. Hence, in anger for him,
He shot a bronze-headed shaft. Now there from his home
In Corinth was a son of the seer Polyidus, a certain
Euchenor, both wealthy and good. This man had boarded
His ship with very full knowledge of his deadly fate,
For often his noble old sire Polyidus had told him
That he must either die of a horrible illness
At home, or among the ships of Achaea be killed
770 By the Trojans.† Therefore, he went to the war, avoiding
The onerous fine he would else have had to pay
And also escaping the pain of hateful disease.
Now Paris struck him just under the jawbone and ear,
And at once the spirit took leave of his limbs, and he
Was seized by abhorrent darkness.
                So here the fight raged
Like blazing fire. But Zeus-loved Hector had not
Been informed and had no idea that there on the left
Of the ships the Argives were rapidly killing his men.
780 The Argives, in fact, very nearly won a great victory,
So huge was the might of Poseidon, embracer and shaker
Of earth, who kept inspiring the Argives and adding
His strength to theirs. Hector, then, still fought
At the point where first he had crashed in the gate and sprung
Within the wide wall, smashing the close-drawn ranks
Of shield-bearing Danaans, there where the ships of Ajax
And Protesilaus were hauled up high on the beach
Of the briny gray sea. At this point the wall was lower
Than anywhere else, and here the melee of men
790 And Danaan horses was most chaotic of all.
                And the warriors here, the Boeotians and long-robed Ionians,
The Locrians, Phthians, and splendid Epeans, had all
They could do to stem noble Hector's attack on the ships,
Nor were they able to thrust him back from themselves,

---

*"In peace, sons bury fathers; in war fathers bury sons" (Herodotus' *Histories* 1.87).
†Euchenor's choice of fates resembles that of Achilles: home or Troy.

As onward the great Prince came like flaming fire.
Here too were picked Athenians led by their chieftain
Peteos' son Menestheus, followed by Pheidas,
Stichius, and able Bias. The Epeans were headed
By Phyleus' son Meges, Amphion, and Dracius, while the
        Phthians
Fought behind Medon and unretreating Podarces.   800
This Medon was King Oïleus' bastard and thereby
A brother of Ajax, but since he had killed a kinsman
Of his stepmother Eriopis, wife of Oïleus,
He lived far from home in Phylace. And Podarces, the other
Brave leader, was Iphiclus' son and the grandson of Phylacus.
These two in full armor fought in front of the spirited
Phthians, who with the Boeotians fought in defense
Of the ships. But the lawful son of Oïleus, Ajax
The swift, would not for an instant leave the side
Of Ajax, son of Telamon. Quite like a pair   810
Of wine-red oxen that strain with equal heart
To draw the strong plow through fallow earth, as the sweat
Streams up from about the base of their horns and they
Toil on down the furrow, held no further apart
Than the polished yoke holds them, till they have cut through to
        the edge
Of the field, so now the two Ajaxes stood and fought
By each other's side. Behind Telamonian Ajax
Came many a brave band of comrades, who always took
His shield whenever his sweat-drenched limbs grew weary.
But after the great-hearted son of Oïleus came none   820
Of his Locrian troops, for none of them relished close combat,
Since they had no bronze-plated helmets, plumed thickly with
        horsehair,
Nor any round shields or ashen spears, but trusting
In bows and slings of well-twisted sheep's wool, they followed
Oïleus' son to Ilium. Rapidly shooting
With these, they broke the Trojan battalions. So those
Up front, clad in their richly wrought armor, fought
With the Trojans and brazen-helmeted Hector, while these,
The Locrian bowmen, shot from behind unnoticed,
But with their arrows they took all fight from the Trojans   830
And threw them into confusion.
    The Trojans then
Would miserably have retreated, leaving the ships
And making for windy Troy, had Polydamas not

Again come up to brave Hector, and said: "Hector,
Surely you find it hard to accept the advice
Of another. Because God gave you pre-eminent prowess
In war, you want to believe that you're also supreme
In wisdom and counsel, but you cannot possibly take
840 All things on yourself. For to one man God gives prowess
In war, to another in dancing, or playing the lyre
And singing. And in another man far-seeing Zeus
Puts an excellent mind, much to the profit of many,
Whom his quick thinking frequently saves from ruin,
As surely he knows better than anyone else.
Hence I will speak and say what seems to me best.
Around you burns a ring of blazing war,
But the spirited Trojans who got past the wall are some
Of them standing apart though fully armed, while others
850 Are scattered among the ships where always outnumbered
They're fighting. But come, fall back and call in all
Our best men. Then we can think of all possible plans
And together decide what to do, whether to fall
On the many-oared ships, if God should will that we win,
Or else to withdraw from the ships without further harm
To ourselves. Frankly I fear the Achaeans may yet
Pay us back for what we did to them yesterday, for they
Have one at the ships who never gets battle enough,
And who, I think, will not much longer keep
860 So completely out of the fighting."
            Polydamas spoke,
And Hector, pleased with such counsel, leaped down and replied
In these winged words: "Polydamas, keep here with you
All our best men, while I go yonder and face
The fighting. I'll come back as soon as I've given my orders."[5]
        So saying, he left, his bronze as glittering bright
As a snowy mountain, and shouting instructions he ran
Through the army of Trojans and Trojan allies. And they
All made for the genial Polydamas, Panthous' son,
870 When they heard the orders of Hector. But he sped on
Through the foremost champions, seeking Deïphobus and mighty
Prince Helenus, and Adamas, son of Asius, and Asius,
Son of Hyrtacus, hoping that he might find them.
But he found none of them both alive and unwounded,
For two were stretched out by the sterns of Achaean ships,
Felled by Argive hands, and the others were back

In the city, wounded by spears at close range and long.
One, though, he soon discovered there on the left
Of the tearful struggle, Prince Paris, the lord of lovely
Blonde Helen, cheering his comrades and urging them on   880
In the fight. Coming up to him, Hector spoke these harsh words:
        "Foul Paris! most handsome, girl-crazy seducer, where,
If you will, are Deïphobus and mighty Prince Helenus, and
                Adamas,
Son of Asius, and Asius, son of Hyrtacus?
And where, I say, is Othryoneus? Now steep Troy
Is utterly lost, and now total ruin is utterly
Certain for you!"
        Then the handsome Paris replied:
"Hector, now you are blaming an innocent man.
At some other time I may have left a battle,   890
But not today. My mother bore even me
Not wholly a coward. For ever since you sent
Your men into battle against the ships, we
Have held our ground here and ceaselessly dallied our bit
With the Danaan forces. Our friends, of whom you inquire,
Are dead, except Deïphobus and mighty Prince Helenus,
And both of them have withdrawn with arm-wounds received
From long spears. Cronos' son Zeus kept death from those two.
But on! Lead us wherever your heart and soul
Say go, and we will eagerly come on behind you,   900
Nor shall we, I think, be any way lacking in valor
So long as our strength holds out. Once that is gone,
No man can fight, no matter how eager he is."
        So saying, Prince Paris persuaded the mind of his brother,
And they made straight for the place where the din of battle
Was greatest, about Cebriones and peerless Polydamas,
And Phalces, Orthaeus, godlike Polyphetes, and Palmys,
And Hippotion's sons Ascanius and Morys, who had come
The morning before from fertile Ascania, sent
As relief for their fellows, and now Zeus impelled them to fight.   910
And on they came with the force of perilous winds
That rush down hard on the sea before the thunder
Of Father Zeus and stir up the brine with incredible
Roaring, raising up numerous foaming waves
In the swell of the surging and loud-crashing sea, high-curled
And white, billow on billow one after the other.
So the Trojans, massed in formation, rank

Upon rank and blazing with bronze, followed their chieftains.
Priam's son Hector led all the rest, he
920 The equal of man-ruining Ares. Before him he held
His round shield, thick with hides and heavy bronze plate
Hammered on it, and about his temples his bronze helmet swayed.
Striding out here and there, he tried the Achaeans' battalions,
Seeing if anywhere one of them would give way
Before his shield-covered charge. But he was unable
To quell the Achaean spirit, and Ajax, coming
Ahead with long strides, was first to challenge him, saying:
      "Madman! come closer. Why are you trying so vainly
To frighten the Argives? Believe me, we are not at all
930 Unskillful in battle, and only by Zeus's rough scourge
Have we been so whipped. You, I suppose, would still like
To plunder our ships, but know that we too have hands
That are quick to defend what is ours. In fact, we have
A much better chance to take and plunder your populous
City. And as for yourself, I say the day nears
When you in full flight shall pray to Father Zeus
And the other immortals to make your mane-tossing horses
Faster than falcons, as on toward the city they bear you
Beating up dust from the plain."
940   As he spoke, a bird
Flew by on the right, a high-flying eagle, whereat
The Achaeans cried out, made brave by the ominous bird-sign.
But shining Hector replied: "Ajax, you word-bungling,
Bellowing fool! what now have you said! I only
Wish that I all my life were as surely the son
Of aegis-great Zeus and queenly Hera and so
Were honored as Athena and Apollo are, as surely
Today holds evil for every one of the Argives!
And with them you too will be killed, if you have the courage
950 To stand and await my long spear, which soon shall bite deep
Through your lily-white skin. And you with your fat and your flesh
Shall glut the dogs and carrion birds of Troy
When you have gone down among the ships of Achaea!"*
      He spoke, and led the charge, and after him came
His men with an unbelievable roar, which the host
Behind them took up. And the Argives opposite them

---

*Compare the end of the single combat at VII.334 (also see endnote 3 to book VII); the contest of Hector and Ajax is rejoined at XIV.454.

Replied with their screams of battle, nor did they forget
Their courage and war-skill, but stood and awaited the charge
Of the bravest Trojans. And the two armies' cries went up
Through the air to the ray-bright, splendid aether of Zeus.* 960

---

*Though the cries of the armies ascend to the aether, Zeus' attention remains averted.

BOOK XIV

The Tricking of Zeus

The cries of battle were not unheard by Nestor,
Though at his wine,[1] and his words to Asclepius' son
Came winged with concern: "Think, my noble Machaon,
What we had best do. By the ships the cries of lusty
Young fighters grow constantly louder. But you, now, sit
Where you are and drink the bright wine, until Hecamede,
She of the beautiful braids, heats a warm bath
For you and washes the clotted blood from your wound.
I will go out at once to where I can see
10   How the fighting progresses."
          So saying, he took the thick shield
Of his horse-breaking son Thrasymedes. All gleaming with bronze,
It lay in the lodge, for the son had taken the shield
Of his father. And now, picking up a strong spear, sharp-pointed
With bronze, the old one stepped out of the lodge and immediately
Saw a disgraceful sight, the great wall breached
And the Argives in chaotic flight before the high-hearted
Trojans. And as the huge sea stirs darkly, heaving
With silent swell foretelling the onset of swift
20   Shrill winds, while the waves roll on in no certain direction
Till some steady gale from Zeus comes down and determines
Their course, even so the old King pondered, his mind
Divided two ways, whether he should charge into the mass
Of swiftly-drawn Danaans, or go for Atreus' son
Agamemnon, high King of the host. And as he pondered,
One way seemed better, to go for the son of Atreus.
Meanwhile, the others were fighting and killing each other,
And loudly the stubborn bronze rang about their bodies
As they smote each other with swords and two-pointed spears.
30   But Nestor now was met by the god-fostered kings
As they made their way up through the ships, those whom the bronze
Had wounded—Tydeus' son Diomedes, Odysseus,
And Atreus' son Agamemnon. Far from the fighting
Their ships were drawn up on the beach in the very first row

Beside the gray sea, and the wall had been built beyond those
Drawn furthest up on the plain. For the beach, though wide,
Could not begin to hold all the vessels, and the warriors,
Cramped for space, had drawn the ships up in rows
That covered the whole wide shore between the two headlands.
The kings, therefore, together and using their spears   40
For support, were headed inland to get a good view
Of the screaming struggle, and their mood was one of depression.
But when they saw old Nestor, their spirits sank lower
Still, and lord Agamemnon spoke to him thus:
    "O Neleus' son Nestor, great glory of all the Achaeans,
Why have you left the man-wasting war and come here?
I fear huge Hector may yet live up to his word,
The threats he laid upon us when once he spoke
Among the Trojans, saying that he would never
Return from the ships to Ilium till he had sent them   50
All up in flames and slaughtered us as well.
Such were his words, and now they are coming true.
O shame! for surely the other well-greaved Achaeans
Have filled their hearts with resentment against me, just
As Achilles did, and now they are all refusing
To fight by the drawn-up ships."
    And Gerenian Nestor:
"Yes truly, these things have now come to pass, and now
Disaster is on us, nor could great Zeus himself,
He who thunders on high, make anything else   60
Occur. For the wide wall is down, the unbreachable bulwark
We trusted as sure protection for both the ships
And ourselves, and now amid the swift ships the battle
Goes ceaselessly on, nor can you tell, no matter
How hard you look, from which side the Achaeans are being
Driven in rout, so completely confused is the slaughter
As up to the sky the battle-roar rises. But come,
Let us consider what we had best do—if thinking
Can help at all now. But this much is certain, that none
Of you here should enter the battle, since no wounded man   70
Is any good in a fight."
    Then again Agamemnon,
King of men, replied: "Nestor, since they
Are fighting now beside the sterns of the ships,
And the well-made wall and trench have failed, on which
The Danaans labored so hard in the hope they would be
An impassable bulwark protecting the ships and ourselves,

I'm forced to believe that it must be the pleasure of Zeus,
The high and the mighty, that we Achaeans should die here
80 Far from Argos, forever unsung and unknown.
This I felt when he was helping the Danaans
Heartily, and now I know it is so, for he
Is glorifying our foes like blissful gods
And binding the strength of our mighty hands completely.
But come, let everyone do as I order. Take
All the ships drawn up in the first row hard by the sea
And drag them well out on the sparkling brine and moor them
With anchor-stones until divine night shall arrive—
If indeed the Trojans will cease their attack for her sake—
90 And then we may drag down all the rest of the ships.
For surely one cannot be blamed for shunning sheer ruin,
Though it be by night. Far better to flee and escape
Than stay and be taken."[2]

      Then, with a scowl of disgust,
Resourceful Odysseus replied: "O son of Atreus,
What words are these that pass the guard of your teeth!
Accursed and ruinous man that you are, would you
Were heading some army of miserable cowards and not
The commander of us, to whom great Zeus has given
100 The task, from youth to old age, to fight and wind up
Each horrible war till each of us withers away.
Can it be that you're really so eager to leave untaken
The wide streets of Troy, for which we have suffered so much?
Be silent, then, lest another Achaean should hear
These words that no man possessed by his senses should ever
Give voice to, much less a sceptered King, the ruler
Of many, these Argive hosts who look to you
For their orders. But obviously you have no sense at all
To have given this order in the midst of a screaming battle,
110 To have us drag down to the sea our well-decked ships,
And so give the Trojans, who even now are the victors,
An even more wonderful chance of wiping us out
Completely! For once the ships are drawn down to the sea,
The Achaeans will surely no longer hold out in the battle,
But constantly looking behind them, they'll soon have no heart
For fighting. Then, O leader of hosts, your plan
Will destroy us all!"

      And again the commander-in-chief
Agamemnon replied: "Odysseus, truly your words
120 Of harsh reproach hurt me deeply, but I am not bidding

The sons of Achaeans to drag their ships down to the sea
Against their will. So now I would like to hear—
From young or old—some better counsel than mine.
Right now such counsel would be more than welcome to me."
　　　Among them then spoke battle-roaring Diomedes,
Saying: "That man is nearby, nor will you have to
Look for him long, provided you all are willing
To listen and not be resentful and angry toward me
Because I'm the youngest man here. I too declare
That I am the son of a noble, valiant father,   130
Tydeus, whom now in Thebes the heaped earth covers.
For Portheus sired three marvelous sons—Agrius,
Melas, and thirdly my own father's father, Oeneus
The horseman, who lived, as did the others, in Pleuron
And steep Calydon and outdid them all in prowess.
He stayed on there, but my father his son went wandering
And settled in Argos, for such, I believe, was the will
Of Zeus and the other immortals. And there he married
A daughter of King Adrastus and lived as a wealthy
Man, in a splendid house with more than enough   140
Rich wheat fields, many fine orchards of fruit trees, and plenty
Of sheep and cattle. And with his spear my father
Excelled all other Achaeans. But surely you must have
Heard all these things, and so you know I speak truly.
Hence you cannot despise any worth-while counsel
Of mine on grounds that I am the son of a coward
And weakling. So come, let us go as we must to the battle,
Wounded men though we are. There we can hold
Ourselves back from the fiery fighting and out of range
Of the missiles, and that way receive no second wound,   150
But there we can urge on the others and send into battle
Those who indulge their spiteful spirits and stand
Apart from the melee."
　　　He spoke, and they listened closely,
Then obeyed him, setting out with the king
Of men Agamemnon leading the way.
　　　Now Poseidon,
The famous shaker of shores, had not missed any
Of this, and taking the form of an aged man
He went along with the chiefs, gripped the right hand   160
Of Atreus' son Agamemnon, and spoke winged words:
"Atrides, surely now the ruthless heart
Of Achilles rejoices within him as he looks out

On the slaughter and rout of Achaeans, utterly stupid
Fool that he is. But may God yet cast him down,
And may he die in his folly! With you, though, O King,
The happy gods are not altogether angry.
Even yet you shall see the wide plain dim with dust
As the captains and counselors of the Trojans beat
170 A retreat to the city from these your shelters and ships."
　　　　So saying, Poseidon, speeding off over the plain,
Gave out a great shout as loud as the cries of nine
Or ten thousand men embroiled in the War-god's chaos
Of battle. Even such was the shout that the lordly Earthshaker
Gave out from his breast, inspiring the heart of every
Achaean with truly great power to fight and wage war
Without ceasing.
　　　　Now Hera, she of the golden throne,
From high on a peak of Olympus saw how Poseidon
180 Busied himself in the man-enhancing battle,
And joyfully knew him at once for her and her husband's
Own brother. But also she saw Zeus, where he sat
On the highest peak of well-watered Ida, and hatred
Welled up in her heart. And then she considered, the heifer-eyed
Queenly Hera, how she might best trick the wits
Of aegis-great Zeus.[3] And this is the plan she preferred—
To make herself sweetly seductive and go to Mount Ida,
Tempting him thus to lie with her and make love,
That she might steep his lids and cunning mind
190 In soothing and subtle sleep. So off she went
To the bedroom her dear son Hephaestus had fashioned for her,
Hanging thick doors from the door-posts and fitting them well
With a secret lock that no other god could open.
Having entered and closed the bright doors, she began by taking
Ambrosia and cleansing her exquisite body, then rubbed herself
Richly with oil, ambrosial, soft, and fragrant,
Which when it is used in Zeus's brazen-floored palace
Sweetens both heaven and earth with its fragrance. With this
She rubbed her desirable body, then combed her hair
200 And plaited bright beautiful braids, ambrosial, which she
Let fall from her fair immortal head. Next
She put on a gown perfumed with ambrosia, one made
And richly embroidered for her by Athena herself.
This she pinned about her breasts with beautiful
Brooches of gold, and fastened around her waist
A belt, from which a hundred tassels fluttered,

And in her pierced lobes she put a fine pair of earrings,
Glowing and graceful three-drop clusters. And high
On her head she fixed a veil, as shimmering white
As sunlight, and on her shining feet bound beautiful   210
Sandals. Now when she had thus prepared her body
With all this enchantment, she left the bedroom and called
Aphrodite, getting her well apart from the other
Immortals, and saying:
      "Will you now listen to me,
Dear child, and do me a favor? Or will you refuse
What I ask because, while you help the Trojans, I help
The Danaans, for which your heart is resentful, I know?"

      To which Aphrodite, daughter of Zeus: "Hera,
Honored goddess and daughter of mighty Cronos,   220
Say what you have in mind, and if it can
Be done and done by me then my heart says do it."

      And slyly Queen Hera replied: "Give to me now, then,
Love and desire,[4] the powers with which you subdue
All immortal gods as well as all death-destined men.
For I am on my way to the very ends
Of the all-feeding earth to visit Oceanus, source
Of all the immortals, and Tethys our mother, both of whom
Nurtured and cherished me at home in their halls,
Having taken me from Rhea* when all-seeing Zeus   230
Thrust Cronos down beneath earth and the unresting sea.
I am going to visit them both and put an end
To their incessant quarreling, for truly now
It has been a long time since they went to bed and made love,
Since each avoids the other and both hearts seethe
With bitter resentment. If I with words could change
The way those two feel and get them to go back to bed
And make love with each other, they would surely adore me
And honor me highly forever."
      Again Aphrodite,   240
Adorer of smiles, replied: "I cannot, of course,
Refuse you, nor would it be right for me to, since you
Sleep close in the arms of Zeus, our greatest and best."

      So saying, she loosed from about her breasts an artfully
Handworked sash whereon were depicted all sorts

---

*Rhea is Hera's (and Zeus') mother; Hera is kept safe in remote Oceanus while Zeus is battling Cronos.

Of erotic allurements—love and desire and words
So seductively sweet they would turn the head of anyone,
Even the wise. Laying this in her hands, she said:
     "Take now this sash and tuck it deep in your bosom.
250 Richly embroidered upon it is all lovers need,
And with it, believe me, you won't come back unsuccessful,
No matter what your heart may desire."
     So spoke
Aphrodite, and heifer-eyed queenly Hera smiled,
And smiling she tucked the sash in the fold of her bosom.
     Then Aphrodite, daughter of Zeus, went home,
But Hera went darting down from high on a peak
Of Olympus, touched at Pieria and lovely Emathia,
Then sped across the topmost snowy peaks
260 Of the horse-handling Thracians, nor once grazed the ground with
           her feet.
At Athos she left the land and swiftly skimmed
The billowing sea till she came to Lemnos, the city
Of godlike King Thoas. There she found Sleep, brother
Of Death, clung fast to his hand, and spoke to him thus:
     "O Sleep, lord of all gods as well as all men,
If ever you paid any heed to my words, please do
What I ask of you now, and I will always be
Extremely grateful to you. Lull to sleep the shining,
Brow-shaded eyes of Zeus, as soon as I've lain
270 With him and made love, and I will give you fine gifts,
Including a gorgeous throne of immortal gold,
Which my son Hephaestus, the lame ambidextrous god,
Shall skillfully fashion for you, with a foot-rest below
On which you may rest your shining feet when you dine."
     And soothing Sleep replied: "Hera, great goddess,
Daughter of powerful Cronos, any other of the gods
Everlasting I might put to sleep with no compunctions
At all, even the stream of the river Oceanus,
Whom the gods are all from, but Cronos' son Zeus
280 I will not come near, nor will I lull him to sleep
Unless he himself says do so. For I have already
Learned my lesson from a task you once gave me when Heracles,
Zeus's high-hearted son, set sail from Ilium
After he'd sacked and leveled the Trojans' city.
Then I beguiled the wits of Zeus of the aegis
And drifted my sweetness around him, since you were determined
To do his son harm, having stirred up blasts of dangerous

Winds that swept huge Heracles off across
The open sea to the populous island of Cos,
Far away from his friends. And Zeus awoke in a rage   290
And hurled the gods all about his great house, looking
For me above all, and he would have flung me clean
Out of sight, from heaven into the deep sea, if Night
Had not saved me, she who masters both gods and men.
To her I came asking help, and Zeus, in spite of
His fury, stopped his pursuit, for he had awe
Of doing whatever swift Night disliked. And now
You want me to do this other impossible thing."[5]
        To which the heifer-eyed queenly Hera: "Sleep,
Why let your mind dwell on such miserable things? Do you   300
Imagine that all-seeing Zeus will ever support
The Trojans with anything like the fury he felt
On account of Heracles, his own son? But come now,
Do as I ask, and I'll give to you in marriage
One of the fresh young Graces, Pasithea, her
Whom you've always yearned for."
        She spoke, and Sleep, now happy,
Answered her thus: "Come, then, and swear to me
By the fateful water of Styx, taking hold with one hand
Of the bountiful earth and of the bright sea with the other,   310
That all of the gods below with Cronos may witness
This promise of yours* to give me one of the fresh
Young Graces, Pasithea, her whom I've always longed for."
        Such were his words, and the white-armed goddess Hera
Did not disregard him, but swore the oath he demanded,
Invoking by name each one of the gods called Titans
That lurk in the depths below Tartarus. Then, having ended
Her oath, she and Sleep, enclosed in thick mist, sped over
The cities of Lemnos and Imbros and swiftly flew
On their way. At Lectum they first left the sea, then came   320
To well-watered Mount Ida, mother of wilderness creatures,
As they flew on above the dry land with the tree-tops
Trembling beneath them. And now, before Zeus saw him,
Sleep flew up into a tall pine tree, the tallest
That grew on Mount Ida, shooting up through the mist
Into the clear aether above. There he perched,
Well hidden amid thick branches of pine, in the form

---

*Hera must swear by powers greater and older than herself.

Of a mountain songbird, one that the gods call chalcis,
But men cymindis.

330   Hera, though, swiftly approached
The heights of Gargarus, peak of lofty Ida,
And cloud-gathering Zeus laid eyes upon her. He no sooner
Did so than love encompassed his keen-plotting heart,
As on that day when first they went to bed
And made love together, without their dear parents' knowledge.*
So now he stood up before her and spoke to her, saying:
          "Hera, what is it you so much desire, that thus
You have come down here from Olympus? And where are the horses
And car you usually drive?"

340   And cunningly Hera
Replied: "I am on my way to the very ends
Of the all-feeding earth to visit Oceanus, source
Of all the immortals, and Tethys our mother, both of whom
Nurtured and cherished me at home in their halls.
I am going to visit them both and put an end
To their incessant quarreling, for truly now
It has been a long time since they went to bed and made love,
Since each avoids the other and both hearts seethe
With bitter resentment. And my horses stand at the foot

350 Of well-watered Ida, horses to draw me over
Both solid land and the sea. But now I have come
Down here from Olympus, since you might get angry with me
If I without a word should leave for the house
Of deep-flowing Oceanus."
          And Zeus, collector of clouds,
Replied: "Hera, later on you may go there—but come,
Let the two of us now lie down right here and enjoy
Ourselves making love. For never before did desire
For either goddess or woman so overwhelm

360 The heart in my breast—not even when I loved the wife
Of Ixion, who bore me Peirithous, peer of the gods
In counsel, nor when I loved the trim-ankled Danaë,
Acrisius' daughter, who gave birth to Perseus, the most
Distinguished of men, nor when I loved the daughter
Of far-famed Phoenix, who bore me Minos and godlike

---

*According to Callimachus (frag. 48), the secret and incestuous liaison of Zeus and Hera lasted three centuries.

Rhadamanthus, nor when I loved Semele, or Alcmene in Thebes,
Alcmene who bore me a son, strong-hearted Heracles,
While Semele bore Dionysus, delighter of mortals,
Nor when I loved Queen Demeter, with the beautiful braids,
Or glorious Leto, or hitherto yourself—   370
As now I love you and feel more strongly than ever
The grip of delicious desire."
    Then, still trying
To trick him, Queen Hera spoke thus: "Most dreadful son
Of Cronos, what are you saying! What would happen
If now we did as you wish and lay down up here
Making love on the heights of Mount Ida, where all is wide open
To view, and one of the gods everlasting should see us
Asleep and go tell the tale to all of the other
Immortals? Then, believe me, I could not get up   380
And go back to your house, I'd be so ashamed and embarrassed.
But if you really would like to, if that's what your heart
Now desires, why you have a bedroom, you know, one fashioned
For you by your own dear son Hephaestus, who hung
Thick doors from the door-posts. Let us go there and lie down,
Since bed is what you desire."
    Then Zeus of the gathering
Clouds spoke thus: "Hera, have no fear
That anyone, god or man, shall see what we do,
For I shall conceal us well with a thick golden cloud.   390
Through it not even the Sun could see us, though his
By far is the brightest light of all."
    So saying,
Cronos' son Zeus caught his wife in his arms, and under them
Sacred earth made tender new grass grow up,
And dewy clover, crocus, and hyacinth, thick
And softly luxuriant, holding them up off the ground.
There they lay down, completely concealed by a fair
Golden cloud, from which fell drops of glistening dew.
    Then peacefully slumbered the Father on Gargarus peak,   400
By love and sleep overcome, still holding his wife
In his arms. But sweet Sleep flew off to the ships of the Argives
To tell the embracer and shaker of earth. Coming up
To him close, he spoke winged words: "With all of your heart,
Poseidon, add your strength to the Danaans' and give them
Glory, if only briefly, while Zeus yet sleeps,
For Hera has subtly seduced him to lie with her

And make love, and I have drifted soft slumber about him."
    He spoke, and took off for the famous nations of men,
410 But he stirred Poseidon to give still more help to the Danaans.
Quickly he sprang mid the foremost and loudly shouted:
"Argives, can it be that you're really willing to yield
The victory again to Priam's son Hector, to have him
Capture the fleet and cover himself with glory?
He himself boasts that thus it shall be, since Achilles
Remains mid the hollow ships with a heart full of bitter
Resentment. But Achilles we won't miss too much, if only
We do our best to support one another. So come,
Let everyone do as I say. Let us put on the largest
420 And best shields we have in the host and cover our heads
With all-gleaming helmets and take in our hands the longest
Spears—and charge! I myself will go in the lead,
Nor will Priam's son Hector be able to hold his ground long,
Believe me, no matter how great his fury. Whoever
Considers himself a battle-staunch fighter, but has
A small shield on his shoulder, let him give it to someone weaker
And arm himself with one of the larger shields."
    He spoke, and all of them gladly agreed. And the kings,
Though wounded, marshaled the men, even Tydeus' son
430 Diomedes, Odysseus, and Atreus' son Agamemnon.
These went through the army and made the men exchange war-gear,
And the good men donned the good armor, while the worse fighters
        put on
The worse. Having covered their bodies in blazing-bright bronze,
They charged ahead with mighty shore-shaking Poseidon
In the lead, and in his strong hand he held
An awesome long sword—a blade like a flash of lightning—
Which no man may so much as touch in horrible war,
A dreadful weapon which all men shrink from in terror.
And opposite them resplendent Hector marshaled
440 The forces of Troy. And truly the tension of terrible
Hatred was drawn to the point of breaking, by Poseidon,
God of the blue-black hair, and glorious Hector,
Who lent his strength to the Trojans, while the great god aided
The Argives. As the two armies clashed with a mighty hubbub
Of war-cries, the surf surged up to the shelters and ships
Of the Argives. But neither the crashing thunder of billows
That break on the beach, driven in from the deep by hard-blowing
Blasts of North Wind, nor the roar of raging fire
When it leaps to wither the forest in the deep ravines

Of a mountain, nor the shriek of the wind in the high-foliaged oaks   450
When it howls in its fury the loudest, is so very loud
As the chilling screams of battle that came from Achaeans
And Trojans alike as now they charged at each other.
    Resplendent Hector led off by hurling a spear
At Ajax, Telamon's son, who then was turned
Full toward him, nor did he miss his man, but struck him
Where the two baldrics—one of his shield and one
Of his silver-nailed sword—were stretched across his chest,
And they protected his tender flesh. And Hector
Was angry because the swift shaft had flown in vain   460
From his hand, and back he shrank in a crowd of his comrades,
Seeking to save his life. But as he withdrew,
Great Ajax, Telamon's son, struck him hard
With a stone, one of the many used to prop
The swift ships, but rolling now among the feet
Of the fighters. Lifting it high in the air, he struck
Hector hard on the chest, above the shield-rim and close by
The neck, and the blow spun Hector around like a top
And caused him to stagger in circles. And as when a huge oak
Falls, uprooted by lightning from Zeus our Father—   470
An awesome, sulphureous bolt that takes the courage
From anyone standing nearby and watching—even so
Great Hector crashed to the dusty earth.[6] His second spear
Dropped from his hand, and quickly he crumpled up
Beneath his helmet and shield, as about his body
The elaborate bronze rang loudly.
    Then sons of Achaeans,
Hurling their spears and fiercely screaming their war-cries,
Ran up with the hope of dragging him off, but not
One man of them managed to wound the commander-in-chief   480
Of the Trojans with either a thrust or a cast, for the bravest
Surrounded their leader and guarded him well—Polydamas,
Aeneas, and noble Agenor, Sarpedon, King
Of the Lycians, and blameless Glaucus, and there not one
Of the others was oblivious of him and his plight, but all
Held out their round shields before him. And his friends took him up
In their arms and carried him out of the toilsome fight
Till they came where his swift horses waited, standing with driver
And ornate car at the rear of the battle and tumult.
These drew him, heavily groaning, back toward the city.   490
But when they came to the ford of swirling Xanthus,
The fair-flowing river whose Father is immortal Zeus,

The comrades of Hector lifted him from the chariot,
Stretched him out on the ground, and over him splashed
Cool water. At this he came to and looked up, and kneeling
He vomited clots of dark blood. Then back he sank
To the ground, and darkness like that of black night enveloped
His eyes, for still the blow was too much for his spirit.
    Now when the Argives saw Hector withdrawing, they charged
500 The Trojans with even more zest and keenly recalled
Their prowess in battle. Then far the first to draw blood
Was Ajax, son of Oïleus, who wounded Satnius,
Springing at him with his sharp-headed spear, even Enops'
Son, whom a flawless Naiad nymph conceived
To Enops while he was tending his herd by the banks
Of Satnioeis. Springing at him, the spear-famous son
Of Oïleus wounded him deep in the side, and Satnius
Writhed to the ground, as about him the Trojans and Danaans
Clashed in strenuous struggle. To help him then
510 Came fiercely spear-wielding Polydamas, Panthous' son,
And casting he struck the right shoulder of Prothoënor,
Son of Areïlycus, and all the way through his shoulder
The heavy spear tore its way, and down in the dust
Prothoënor fell, in agony gripping a handful
Of dirt. And Polydamas cruelly exulted, boasting
As loud as he could:
    "Aha! once more, I believe,
A spear has not leaped in vain from the powerful hand
Of Panthous' son. For one of the Argives has kindly
520 Received it deep in his flesh, and now, I think,
He can lean on it for a staff, as down he hobbles
To Hades' house!"
    He shouted, boasting, and deeply
Disturbed the Argives, especially the fiery heart
Of great Telamonian Ajax, who was nearest the man
When he fell. Quickly he hurled his bright spear as the boaster
Drew back, but Polydamas dodged to one side and thus
Avoided dark death. The spear was received, however,
By Archelochus, son of Antenor, for the gods had decreed
530 He should die. Him the spear struck at the place where head
And neck come together, on the top vertebra of the spine,
And severed both sinews. Far sooner then his head
And mouth and nose reached earth as he fell than did
His shins and knees. And Ajax called out in turn
To peerless Polydamas:

"Consider, Polydamas, and tell me
Frankly if this was not a worthy one
To be slain in requital for Prothoënor. He seemed
No coward to me, nor at all ignobly descended,
But more like a brother of strong horse-breaking Antenor,   540
Or maybe even a son. Surely the family
Resemblance is striking indeed!"

    He spoke, well aware
Who it was he had killed, and grief gripped the hearts of the Trojans.
Then Acamas came and bestrode his brother Archelochus,
And felled with a thrust of his spear Boeotian Promachus,
Who had hold of the feet and was trying to drag
From beneath him Archelochus' corpse. And over him Acamas
Loudly, terribly vaunted:

    "You Argive cowardly   550
Bowmen, insatiate lovers of talking big,
Not for Trojans alone shall there be labor
And sorrow, but you too shall just as wretchedly die!
See how your Promachus sleeps, overcome by my spear,
That my brother's blood-price may not long remain unpaid.
This is why a man prays for a kinsman at home to survive him,
For one to avenge his death and ward off disgrace."

    Thus he called, and his boasting pained the Argives,
Especially the spirit of fiery Peneleos. He rushed upon
Acamas, who, however, did not hold fast   560
Against Prince Peneleos' onslaught. Peneleos' thrust
Struck Ilioneus, the only son his mother bore Phorbas,
Rich in flocks, the man whom Hermes loved most
Of all the Trojans and so gave great wealth to him.
The spear went in beneath Ilioneus' brow
At the base of his eye, forced the eyeball out, passed on
Through the socket and out at the nape of his neck, and Ilioneus
Sank to the ground, stretching out both of his hands.
But Peneleos drew his sharp sword and brought it down hard
On the dying man's neck, and the helmeted head, with the great spear   570
Still through the eye, dropped to the ground. And Peneleos
Held it up high like the head of a poppy, showing it
Thus to the Trojans and, boasting, exultantly shouted:

    "I say, O Trojans, go tell the dear father and mother
Of lordly Ilioneus to wail for him in their halls,
In payment for Promachus' life, Alegenor's son,
Whose wife will never rejoice in her loved husband's
Coming, when we young men of Achaea go home

In our ships at last from this your land of Troy."
580   At these words trembling took hold of the knees of all Trojans,
And each of them frantically glanced about in search of
Some way to escape dire death.
         Now tell me, O Muses,
You that have homes on Olympus, which Achaean
Was the first to carry off bloody armor as spoils
When once the famed shaker of earth had turned the course
Of battle. The first was surely Ajax, son
Of Telamon. He struck down Hyrtius, son of Gyrtius
And chief of the brave-hearted Mysians. Antilochus stripped
590 The bronze from Phalces and Mermerus, Meriones cut down
Morys and Hippotion, and Teucer accounted for Prothoön
And Periphetes. Then Atreus' son Menelaus
Thrust his spear deep in the side of the people's lord
Hyperenor, and the cleaving bronze made way for the entrails
To ooze through. His life throbbed out at the spear-stabbed wound,
And darkness came down on his eyes. But Ajax the runner,
Swift son of Oïleus, caught and killed most of all,
For no other could equal his speed in pursuit, when Zeus
Put panic in soldiers and turned them to headlong retreat.

BOOK XV

The Achaeans Desperate

When the Trojans had scrambled through trench and sharp
        stakes, and many
Had died at the hands of the Danaans, terrified still
They came to a halt beside their chariots, their faces
A ghastly pale olive with fear. And Zeus woke up
Where he lay beside golden-throned Hera, high on a peak
Of Mount Ida. At once he sprang up and saw what was happening,
Trojans chaotically fleeing and Argives pursuing,
With lord Poseidon among them. And then he saw Hector
Stretched on the plain with his comrades sitting around him,
Great Hector gasping for breath, half conscious, and vomiting   10
Blood, for it was by no means the feeblest Achaean
Of all who had dealt him the blow. Seeing him thus,
The Father of gods and men felt compassion for him,
And sternly scowling at Hera he spoke to her, saying:
    "Hera, impossible goddess! surely your own
Evil tricks have put noble Hector out of the action
And driven the host in retreat. Truly I do not
Know but that you shall yet be the first to reap
The fruits of your miserable malice and plotting—when I
Put stripes on you with a whip! Can it be that you've really   20
Forgotten when I hung you high with an anvil suspended
From each of your ankles and a band of unbreakable gold
About your wrists? And you hung far up in the air
Among the clouds, and the gods throughout high Olympus,
Though greatly indignant, were none of them able to get
Close to you and release you. And any of them I got hold of
I seized and hurled from my threshold, so that when he reached earth
He just lay there too weak to move. Even so, my heart
Still hurt for godlike Heracles, whom you, in league
With the blasting North Wind, had sent in accord with your evil   30
Contriving far over the barren and unresting sea
To the populous island of Cos. Him I brought back
From there, safe to horse-pasturing Argos, though only

After his toils had been many and painful. Of this
I remind you once more to put an end to your wiles
And make you see how little real good it does you
To come here apart from the other immortals and subtly
Seduce me to lie with you and make love."[1]
     At this
40 The heifer-eyed queenly Hera shuddered, and answered
In these winged words: "Now then, to this let earth
Be my witness and broad heaven above and the tumbledown waters
Of subterranean Styx—which to the gods
Is the oath most great and terrible—and your own divine head
And the marriage bed of us both, by which I would never
Swear falsely, that it is by no will of mine that Poseidon,
Creator of earthquakes, does damage to Trojans and Hector
And nothing but good for their foes.[2] I think that he saw
The Achaeans worn out and despairing beside their vessels
50 And pitied them so much that his own soul urged him and told him
To help. But to you, O god of the gathering storm,
I say I myself would counsel Poseidon to go
Wherever you told him to go."
     She spoke, and the Father
Of gods and men smiled, and answered in these winged words:
"If truly, O heifer-eyed queenly Hera, our thoughts
Hereafter agree, as you sit among the immortals,
Then surely Poseidon will bend his mind to ours,
Regardless of how disinclined he may be. So if
60 You are frank and sincere in what you have said, go now
To the family of gods and send Iris here along with
Bow-famous Apollo, that she may go mid the host
Of bronze-clad Achaeans and bid lord Poseidon drop out
Of the fight and go home. And Phoebus Apollo must rouse up
Hector to action again, breathing strength back into
His body and making him quickly forget the pains
That are now unnerving his spirit. Then let Apollo
Put cowardly panic in all the Achaeans and hurl them
Back in headlong retreat on the many-oared ships
70 Of Peleus' son Achilles, who then will rouse up
His comrade Patroclus. Him resplendent Hector
Will kill with his spear in full view of Troy, but only
After Patroclus has slain many other young men,
Including my own noble son Sarpedon. And Achilles
The kingly, raging in wrath for Patroclus, shall end
The life of Hector, from which time I'll cause a constant

Retreat of the Trojans away from the ships till at last
The Achaeans shall take steep Troy with the help of a plan
From Athena. Until then, though, I will not cease my anger,
Nor will I allow any other immortal to help   80
The Danaans, not till Achilles has had his desire
Fulfilled, as I at first promised and bowed my head
In assent on the day the goddess Thetis embraced
My knees, pleading with me to honor her son,
Achilles, taker of towns."[3]
  He spoke, and the white-armed
Goddess Hera did not disobey him, but went
From the mountains of Ida to the heights of lofty Olympus.
And quick as the thoughts of a much-traveled man who often
Wishes himself here or there, remembering richly   90
And thinking, "I wish I were this place, or that": even
So swiftly Queen Hera eagerly flew till she came
To steep Olympus and found the immortal gods
Together in Zeus's palace. At sight of her there
They all sprang up and pledged her with cups of welcome.
But she passed all of them by save pretty Themis,*
Whose cup she accepted, for Themis was first to run up
And greet her, speaking to her these winged words:
  "Hera, why do you come here like one distraught?
Surely the son of Cronos has frightened you badly,   100
And he your own husband!"
  Then Hera, the white-armed goddess,
Replied: "Do not ask me to go into that, divine Themis.
You yourself know what kind of spirit he has,
How haughty, harsh, and unyielding. But go take your place
And begin for the gods the abundant feast in these halls,
And then you shall certainly hear, along with all
Of the other immortals, what evil things Zeus declares
He will do. My news will not, I believe, make everyone
Equally glad, whether mortals or gods, if indeed   110
There is anyone now who can dine in anything like
A good mood!"
  So saying, Queen Hera sat down, and wrath
Arose in all of the gods throughout the great hall
Of Zeus. And Hera laughed with her lips, but the frown
Froze hard on her forehead above the dark brows, as vexed

---

*A principal role of the goddess Themis is to preside over divine assemblies.

With them all she spoke out among them: "Fools! how childish
And thoughtless we were to vent our rage against Zeus.
Yet truly we're still just as eager to go up to him
120 And thwart his will, either by words or by force.
But he sits apart and gives no one here so much as
A second thought, so sure he is that his power
And strength are supreme among the immortals. Therefore,
Take with patience whatever bad things he sends you.
Already, I think, keen pain has been fashioned for Ares,
Since his own son, to him the dearest of men,
Has fallen in battle, Ascalaphus, he whom huge Ares
Claims as his own."*

    So she, and Ares slapped
130 His brawny big thighs with the flat of his hands, and angrily
Spoke out, crying: "Do not now blame me,
O you that have homes on Olympus, if I go down
To the ships of Achaea and take revenge on the Trojans
For killing my son, even though my fate be to fall
A victim of Zeus's bright bolt, and to lie mid the dead
Stretched out in the blood and the dust."

    He spoke, and at once
Gave orders to Panic and Rout to harness his horses,
While he put on his all-shining armor. Then greater,
140 More miserable wrath and resentment would surely have been
Stirred up between Zeus and the other immortals, if Athena
Had not been seized with fear for them all. Leaving
The chair she sat in, she shot through the door and removed
The helmet from Ares' head and the shield from his shoulders.
Then taking the bronze-headed spear from his powerful hand,
She stood it aside and thus rebuked the impulsive,
Furious War-god:

    "You stupid, maniacal fool!
Yes you will be utterly ruined. Surely you have ears
150 To hear with, but now all your sense and self-control
Have left you. Didn't you hear what the white-armed goddess
Hera just said, she who has newly returned
From Olympian Zeus? And now do you really wish
To bring all these woes on yourself, and so, grieving still,
Be forced back up to Olympus, having sowed the seeds
Of many great evils for all the rest of us here?

---

*Ascalaphus was killed by Deïphobus at XIII.595–597.

For Zeus will leave the Achaeans and high-hearted Trojans
At once and come straight here to Olympus to punish
Us all, and he, believe me, will lay violent hands
On each of us here, on the innocent and guilty alike.   160
Therefore I bid you forget this wrath for your son.
For many more powerful men than he in force
And might of hand have long before this been slain,
And many others will die hereafter. The offspring
Of mortals can hardly all be kept safe, regardless
Of what their lineage may be."
       So saying, she made
Impetuous Ares sit down again in his chair.
Then Hera requested Apollo and Iris, the immortal
Gods' messenger, to go with her from the hall, and once   170
Outside she came to the point in these winged words:
"Zeus says for you both to go with all speed to Mount Ida.
When you have arrived and looked on his face, carry out
Whatever he then may urge and command you to do."
       Having thus delivered her message, Queen Hera returned
To her throne, but Apollo and Iris took off at once
And flew on their way. When they came to well-watered Ida,
Mother of wilderness creatures, they found far-thundering
Zeus, where he sat on the summit of Gargarus peak,
While about him wreathed a cloud of fragrant mist.   180
Then the two of them stood in the presence of Zeus, collector
Of clouds, and he was by no means displeased to see them,
For they had promptly obeyed the words of his wife.
And first to Iris he spoke in these winged words:
       "Fly swiftly, quick Iris, and carry this message in full
To lord Poseidon, and see that you do not speak falsely.
Tell him to leave the battle at once, and either
Rejoin the family of gods, or shroud himself deep
In his own sacred sea. And if he will pay no attention
To these words of mine, but chooses instead to ignore them,   190
Let him consider in mind and heart whether he
Will be able to stand against an attack by me,
Regardless of how great his strength. For I declare myself
Much his better in might, and the elder besides,
Though he thinks nothing of calling himself the equal
Of Zeus, whom all of the other immortals regard
With an awesome deep dread."
       He spoke, and wing-footed Iris
Did not disobey, but swiftly flew down from the range

200   Of Ida to sacred Ilium. And as when snow
      Or freezing hail falls fast from the clouds, driven on
      By hard blasts of the sky-born North Wind, even so swiftly
      Quick Iris flew eagerly down, and coming up close
      To the world-renowned shaker of shores, she spoke to him thus:
          "O blue-haired embracer of earth, I come here to you
      With a message from Zeus, who bears the aegis. He says
      For you to leave the battle at once, and either
      Rejoin the family of gods, or shroud yourself deep
      In your own sacred sea. And if you will pay no attention
210   To these words of his, but choose instead to ignore them,
      He threatens to come here at once and pit his might
      Against yours in an all-out fight. But he warns you to keep yourself
      Well out of reach of his hands, for he declares himself
      Much your better in might, and the elder besides,
      Though you think nothing of calling yourself the equal
      Of Zeus, whom all of the other immortals regard
      With an awesome deep dread."
                  Then fiercely indignant, the world-renowned
      Shaker of shores spoke thus: "Outrageous, outrageous!
220   Truly a haughty and arrogant message, no matter
      How strong he may be, if he really thinks he can force one
      Equal in honor with him to do as he wishes.
      For we are the sons of Cronos and Rhea—Zeus,
      Myself, and the third is Hades, King of the nether
      Dead. And the world is divided three ways among us,
      And each has his own domain. When the lots were shaken,
      I won the gray sea as my home and realm forever,
      And Hades won the deep nether gloom, while Zeus
      Was allotted broad heaven, the clouds and clear upper air,
230   But the earth and lofty Olympus are common to all.
      Therefore I refuse to do as Zeus says I should.
      Let him abide in peace in his third of the world,
      No matter how strong he may be. And let him stop trying
      To scare me with threats of superior might, as though
      He thought me some cowardly weakling. For him it would be
      Far better to hurl his blustering threats at his own
      Sons and daughters, those he sired himself, who have
      No choice in the matter, but have to do as he bids."
                  To which wind-footed swift Iris replied: "Can it be,
240   O blue-haired embracer of earth, that you really wish me
      To go back to Zeus with this answer so hostile and harsh?
      But since the great are never rigid, will you

At all change your mind? The Furies, you know, always
Favor the elder."
    And again earth-shaking Poseidon:
"Divine Iris, your point is well taken, and surely it is
A fine thing when a messenger speaks with such understanding.
But still most bitter resentment comes over my heart
And soul whenever Zeus hurls harsh words at another
His peer in every respect and to whom has fallen   250
An equal share. For now, though, I yield, in spite of
My deep indignation. But let me add this, a threat
Straight out of my wrath—if ever apart from me
And the spoil-driving goddess Athena, and Hera, Hermes,
And lord Hephaestus, Zeus shall decide to spare
Steep Troy and not lay it waste, nor give the Argives
Great power, then truly the rancorous breach between us
Will not be subject to healing!"[4]
    So saying, the Earthshaker
Left the Achaean ranks and shrouded himself   260
In the sea, and sorely those warring heroes missed him.
    Then Zeus, who gathers the clouds, spoke thus to Apollo:
"Go now, dear Phoebus, straight to bright-helmeted Hector,
For now the embracer and shaker of earth has entered
His sacred sea, avoiding our ruinous wrath.
Had he not, others too would have heard of our feud, even
Those nether gods in the gloomy world about Cronos.
But this way is better far for me, as well as
Himself, that he should have yielded to my strong hands
In spite of his bitter resentment, since not without sweat   270
Would the issue have been decided. But you take up
The tasseled aegis and shake it wildly above
The warring Achaeans to stir up panic among them.
And then, far-smiter, take care of glorious Hector
And waken huge might in him until the Achaeans
Shall come in their flight to the ships and the Hellespont stream.
From that time on I myself will decide what things
Must be said and done to give the Achaeans new wind
And respite from war."
    He spoke, and Apollo did not fail   280
To heed the words of his Father, but darted down
From the mountains of Ida with all the speed of a falcon,
Killer of doves and swiftest of birds. He found
Prince Hector, son of wise-hearted Priam, no longer
Sprawled out on the ground, but now sitting up, since from

The moment Zeus willed to revive him he had begun
To regain his great heart and to know his comrades about him,
And so his gasping and sweating had finally ceased.
Far-working Apollo came up to him close and spoke thus:
290   "Hector, son of Priam, why are you sitting
Apart here, weak and unable to rise? Can it be
That some great pain has recently overwhelmed you?"
    Bright-helmeted Hector weakly answered him, saying:
"Which of the gods, O mightiest one, are you?
Aren't you aware that back at the sterns of the ships,
As I was killing his comrades, fierce-screaming Ajax
Struck me hard on the chest with a stone and took
All the fight from my furious spirit? Indeed, I thought
That surely I'd see the dead and Hades' house
300 This very day, when once I had breathed my last."
    Then lordly far-working Apollo replied: "Be strong,
For strong indeed is the helper whom Zeus has sent down
From Ida to stand by your side and assist you, even I,
Phoebus Apollo, god of the golden sword,
Who have always protected both you and your steep citadel.
But up now, and order your numerous charioteers
To drive their fast horses straight for the hollow ships,
And I will go in the lead and level the way
For the horses and cars, and also I'll turn back in flight
310 The fighting Achaeans."
    So saying, Apollo inspired
The Trojan commander-in-chief with powerful strength.
As when a horse at the manger eats his fill
Of barley, breaks his halter, and thunders away
On the plain, eager to splash in the rippling river—
He throws back his head, and his mane streams over his shoulders
As he exults in his splendor and gallops full speed
For the grazing ground of mares—so Hector, once
He had heard the god's voice, ran hard through the Trojan ranks
320 Urging on his charioteers. And as when farm-hands
And dogs pursue a horned stag or wild goat and lose
Their quarry among the sheer rocks or in the dark woods,
And suddenly then a bearded lion, aroused
By their cries, appears in their path, and they quickly forget
Their ardor and, turning, take to their heels, so now
The Danaans thronged in pursuit of the Trojans, constantly
Thrusting at them with swords and two-pointed spears,
But once they saw Hector ranging the ranks they were all

Unmanned by terror, and their hearts sank down to their heels.
    Then Thoas, son of Andraemon, spoke out among them.   330
He was by far the most gifted of all the Aetolians,
Skillful in hurling the lance and just as good
In hand-to-hand combat, nor were there many Achaeans
Who could defeat him when in the place of assembly
The young men strove in debate. Now he, in an effort
To help, spoke to them, saying:
    "Amazing! this is
A truly great marvel my eyes behold—huge Hector,
Risen again, somehow escaping the fates.
Surely we all were hoping that Hector had died   340
At the hands of Ajax, son of Telamon. Now, though,
Some god has saved and delivered the man, who has
Already relaxed the limbs of many a Danaan,
Nor has he, I think, ended his slaughter yet,
Since he would not be out there as the eager champion
Of Troy if bolt-crashing Zeus had not so willed it.
But come, let everyone do as I say. Let most
Of the army go back to the ships, but we who claim
To be bravest and best, let us make a stand against him
And hold him off with our outheld, thrusting spears.   350
No matter how hot his fury, I do not believe
He has the courage to charge headlong into
Such a band of Danaans."
    With this, having listened closely,
They gladly agreed. Then those who rallied round Ajax
And King Idomeneus and Teucer, Meriones, and Meges,
Peer of the War-god, braced themselves for the clash,
Calling out to the other champions to come and face
The oncoming Hector and army of Trojans, while behind them
Most of the men made their way back to the ships.   360
    And the Trojans came on in close-ordered ranks with Hector
Rapidly striding before, while ahead of him
Went Phoebus Apollo, his shoulders wreathed in mist,
Bearing the awesome tasseled aegis, gleaming
And grim, that Hephaestus the smith had given to Zeus
To awaken panic in warriors. Apollo bore this
In his hands as he went at the head of the host.
    And the Argives
Stood still in close-ordered ranks, awaiting the clash,
And the piercing war-scream went up from both sides, as arrows   370
Leaped from the bow-strings and many a spear, hurled hard

By some brawny arm, sank home in the flesh of a fast-fighting
Youthful warrior, while many another stuck up
In the ground midway, nor ever reached the white flesh
For which it so lusted. Now just as long as Apollo
Held the aegis motionless in his hands,
The shafts of both sides hit their marks and fighters kept falling.
But when he glared straight in the horse-loving Danaans' faces
And shook the dread aegis, while shouting fiercely at them,
380   Then their hearts quailed in their breasts, and quickly they lost
Their impetuous valor. Like a herd of cattle or large flock
Of sheep stampeded at night in the murky darkness
By two wild beasts that suddenly spring out at them
And find no herdsman nearby, so now the Achaeans
Lost their nerve and fled, for Apollo filled them
With panic, that he might give glory to Hector and the Trojans.
       Then, as the Argives scattered, the Trojans cut them down
Singly. Hector killed Stichius and Arcesilaus,
The first a trusted companion of great-souled Menestheus,
390   The other a captain of bronze-clad Boeotians. And Aeneas
Boldly cut down and stripped both Medon and Iasus.
This Medon was King Oïleus' bastard and thereby
The brother of Ajax, but since he had killed a kinsman
Of his stepmother Eriopis, wife of Oïleus,
He lived far from home in Phylace. And Iasus served
As a captain among the Athenians, he the son
Of Sphelus and grandson of Bucolus. And Polydamas killed
Mecisteus, while in the first charge Polites laid Echius
Low, and noble Agenor accounted for Clonius.
400   Meanwhile, Paris struck down Deïochus, trying
To flee mid the foremost fighters, hitting him hard
At the base of the shoulder and driving the bronze clean through.
       Now while they were stripping the war-gear from these, the
                     Achaeans
Were scrambling this way and that through the trench and sharp
                     stakes,
Forced to take cover behind their wide wall. Then Hector
Called out to the Trojans: "Let the bloody spoils be
And charge on the ships! Anyone I see holding back
Over here, away from the vessels, I'll kill on the spot,
Nor shall his kin, neither men nor women, give him
410   His due funeral fire later on, but dogs shall rip up
His body in front of our city!"

So saying, he brought
The lash down on his horses and sent a great shout ringing all
Up and down the ranks of the Trojans, and they, returning
His cry, drove onward with him in the midst of incredible
Clamor. Going before them, Phoebus Apollo
Easily bridged the deep trench by kicking the banks down
Into the middle, thus building a causeway across,
A way long and wide, as wide, in fact, as a strong man
Testing his strength can hurl a javelin. Over this   420
They streamed, rank after rank, with Apollo still
Before them, sternly bearing the awesome aegis.
And he with great ease knocked down a long length of the Argive
Wall, as when a small boy at play by the sea
Scatters the mansion of sand that he with much pleasure
Has built, gleefully knocking it down with his hands
And his feet. With equal ease, O powerful Phoebus,
You undid the Achaeans' hard toil and filled them with panic.[5]

Then the Danaans halted beside their ships, and calling
For help to one another each of them lifted   430
His arms in loud and fervent prayer to all
Of the gods. But surely Gerenian Nestor prayed hardest,
He the Achaeans' old sentinel, lifting his hands
To the starry sky and praying:
          "O Father Zeus,
If ever a man of us back in wheat-wealthy Argos
Burned to you fat pieces of thigh from bull
Or ram while making a prayer for his safe return
Which then you promised, nodding your head in assent,
Remember those offerings now and ward off from us,   440
O Olympian, the ruthless day of our doom, nor allow
The Achaeans thus to be overwhelmed by the Trojans."

Such was his prayer, and Zeus the contriver, hearing
The words of Neleus' aged son, mightily
Thundered. But when the Trojans heard the loud clap
Of aegis-great Zeus, they felt more warlike than ever
And charged harder still on the Argives. As when a huge wave
Of the far-journeyed sea, driven on by the force of the wind,
Best raiser of waves, washes over the side of a ship,
So now the war-screaming Trojans poured over the ruins   450
Of the rampart, driving their chariots up to the sterns
Of the ships, where they fought in close combat with two-pointed
          spears—

Still in their cars, though now the Achaeans had climbed
High up on the decks of the drawn-up black ships, and from there
They were fighting with long-jointed, bronze-headed pikes that lay
At hand on the ships to be used in battles at sea.

    Now Patroclus, so long as Achaeans and Trojans fought
Round the wall away from the ships, sat in the lodge
Of kindly Eurypylus, cheering him up with talk
460 And applying ointments to his severe wound to deaden
The piercing dark pangs. But when he saw troops pouring in
Through the wall and the panicking Danaans fleeing with screams
Of terror, he groaned aloud and slapped his thighs
With the flat of his hands,[6] sadly, anxiously saying:

    "Eurypylus, I cannot stay with you here any longer,
Great though your need surely is. For now a huge fight
Is upon us. Let your squire, then, take care of you here, while I
Run back to Achilles and urge him to enter the battle.
Who knows but that with God's help my persuasion may work?
470 The advice of a friend is frequently most effective."

    While he was still speaking, he started out for Achilles.
Meanwhile, the other Achaeans staunchly fought back
At the charging soldiers, but though the Trojans were fewer,
They could not drive them back from the vessels, nor could
The Trojans break through the Danaan ranks and get in
Among the shelters and ships. The line of battle
Was drawn so even it made one think of the line
A skillful carpenter, taught in his craft by Athena
Herself, uses to cut a ship's timber straight.
480 So evenly then the two warring sides were strained.

    Others were fighting round various ships, but Hector
Singled out flashing-bright Ajax, and these two fought
For one ship, nor could huge Hector drive Ajax back
And set the ship on fire, nor could Ajax thrust
Hector back, since a god drove him on. But Ajax threw
His spear and pierced the chest of Caletor, Clytius'
Son, as he was coming with fire for the ship,
And Caletor thudded to earth, dropping the torch
From his hand. Then Hector, seeing his cousin prone
490 In the dust before the black ship, called out to the Trojans
And Lycians:

    "You Trojans and Lycians and dueling Dardanians,
Whatever you do, yield no ground now in this
Our time of great need, but rescue Clytius' son
Before the Achaeans strip off his armor, now that

He lies in the dust before the long line of ships."
    So saying, he hurled his bright spear at Ajax, and missed,
But Lycophron, son of Mastor, a comrade-in-arms
Who lived with Ajax, since he in sacred Cythera
Had murdered a man—him the piercing bronze   500
Of Hector struck on the head just over the ear
As he stood on the deck with Ajax, and down in the dust
He toppled from high on the stern of the ship, and his limbs
Relaxed in death. Shuddering, Ajax called thus
To his brother:
    "Teucer, old friend, truly now
We have lost a trusted companion, Mastor's brave son,
Whom since the day he came to us from Cythera
We've honored at home in our halls as much as we have
Our own parents. Now huge-hearted Hector has killed him.   510
    Where, then,
Are those quick-killing arrows of yours and the bow you received
From Phoebus Apollo?"
    He called, and Teucer, hearing,
Took his bent bow and quiver of arrows and hurried
To take his stand beside Ajax, and at once he began
To shower his shafts on the Trojans. The first man he hit
Was Cleitus, Peisenor's glorious son and the squire
Of Polydamas, lordly son of Panthous. Cleitus
Was busily reining his horses, trying to drive them   520
Where Trojan battalions were in the most trouble, thereby
Winning the thanks of Hector and all the Trojans.
But swiftly indeed he met with disaster, an evil
That no one, however zealous, could then have kept from him.
For the groan-fraught arrow pierced the back of his neck,
And Cleitus pitched from the chariot, causing the horses
To shy and run off, rattling the empty car.
But their master, princely Polydamas, quickly saw
What had happened and was first to get hold of the horses. He
        turned them
Over to Astynous, son of Protiaon, giving him   530
Careful instructions to hold them nearby, while keeping
A sharp eye on him at the front. Then he went and rejoined
The first rank of champions.
    Now Teucer took another shaft out,
This one to shoot at bronze-helmeted Hector, and he
Right then would have ended the fight by the ships of Achaea,
If only his bolt had gone true and ended the life

Of Hector raging in battle. But Teucer was not
Unobserved by the keen mind of Zeus, who protected Hector
540 And took that glory from Teucer. For just as he drew
His flawless bow against Hector, Zeus broke the strong-twisted
String, and the bronze-weighted arrow flipped off to one side
As the big bow dropped from his hand. Shuddering, Teucer
Spoke thus to his brother:
        "Now confound it all! surely
Some god is utterly thwarting our efforts in battle,
For now he has knocked the bow from my hand, having broken
A new-twisted string that I myself tightly bound on
This morning, that it might bear well the many shafts
550 I then intended to shoot."
        And Telamon's son,
Great Ajax, replied: "So be it, brother. You let
Your bow and thick-flying arrows lie where they are,
Since now some god, begrudging success to the Danaans,
Has undone their strength. But take a long spear in your hand
And a shield on your shoulder, and while you are battling the foe
Do all you can to encourage the rest of our men.
The Trojans may have the upper hand now, but let us
Remember our furious prowess and not allow them
560 To capture without a hard struggle our well-oared vessels."
        At this, Teucer ran and put the bow in his lodge.
Then around his shoulders he hung a hide shield of four layers,
And on his noble head he put a strong helmet
With horsehair plume defiantly waving above him,
And then, picking up a strong spear sharp-pointed with bronze,
He ran at full speed and resumed his stand beside Ajax.
        When Hector saw that the arrows of Teucer had failed,
He called to the Trojans and Lycians, loudly shouting:
"You Trojans and Lycians and dueling Dardanians, now,
570 My friends, be men, and filled with furious boldness
Here at the hollow ships! For truly my eyes
Have just seen how Zeus brought to nothing the arrows of one
Who ranks very high. Quite easy it is to tell
Whose side Zeus is on, since he gives glory to some
And fails to help others, in fact takes their might away,
And now he takes strength from the Argives and helps us instead.
Charge, then, in close ranks at the ships, and if any of you
Stops an arrow or spear and so overtakes
His death and doom today, why then let him die!
580 To die in defense of one's country is not ignoble.

And that man's wife and children, as well as his house
And allotment of land, will then be safe and free
From all harm—if only the Argives have gone in their ships
To their own dear native land!"
    Hector's words made them fight
Even harder. And Ajax, opposite him, called
To his comrades, shouting: "For shame! you Argives. Now
It is certain that either we ourselves die, or else
Save our lives by driving this imminent evil back
From the ships. Or do you suppose that once these vessels   590
Are taken by yonder bright-helmeted Hector you all
Will then be able to walk your way back to the precious
Land of your fathers? Do you not hear how Hector,
Raging to burn the ships, urges on his whole army?
Believe me, it's not a dance he's inviting them to,
But a battle! Nor have we any way wiser or better
Than this—to try our might against theirs in hand-to-hand
Combat. Far better to find out at once whether we here
Are destined to live or die than to have our lives uselessly
Squeezed drop by drop from our bodies against these black ships   600
By men worse than we in this most miserable struggle!"
    With this he inspired the Argives also to fight
Even harder. Then Hector killed Perimedes' son Schedius,
Leader of Phocians, and Ajax cut down an infantry
Captain, Laodamas, splendid son of Antenor.
Polydamas laid low and stripped Cyllenian Otus,
A friend of Phyleus' son Meges and a chief of the proud
Epeans. And Meges, seeing, lunged at Polydamas,
Who, however, caused him to miss by writhing
Out from beneath him, for Apollo did not see fit   610
For Panthous' son Polydamas to be overcome
In that front rank of champions. But Meges' spear
Sank deep in the chest of Croesmus, who no sooner crashed
To the ground than Meges was on him stripping his shoulders
Of armor. But at once the great spearman Dolops leaped
Upon him, Dolops the bravest offspring of Lampus,
Son of Laomedon. He it was, a man
Well schooled in furious fighting, who charged in close
And stabbed his spear clean through the center of Meges' shield,
But his thickly wrought breastplate saved him, the curved one of   620
        bronze
That he always wore. For his father Phyleus had brought it
Home from Ephyre, where flows the river Selleïs

And where Euphetes, King of his people, had made him
A present of it, that he might wear it in battle,
A guard against furious foemen. And now it kept death
From the body of Meges his son, who countered by thrusting
His keen-cutting spear at Dolops' helmeted head.
Striking the socket on top of his bronze-plated head-gear,
He shore off the horsehair plume, which fell in the dust,
630 Still bright with its dye of fresh scarlet. But Dolops, yet hoping
To win, stood his ground and fought on, oblivious
Of fierce Menelaus who now came up from behind
And hurled his spear. And the bronze went in at the shoulder
Of Dolops and madly tore on through his breast. Reeling,
He pitched face down in the dust, and both Menelaus
And Meges hurried to strip from his shoulders his war-gear
Plated with bronze.
          But Hector called out to his kinsmen,
A shout intended for them one and all, but first
640 He rebuked Hicetaon's son, the strong Melanippus.
He, while the foe was still far away, had lived
In Percote and fed his lumbering cattle there.
But when the graceful ships of the Danaans came,
He went back to Troy, where he lived a high-ranking man
In the house of Priam, who treated him quite as well
As he did his own children. Now Hector called him by name
And chided him thus:
          "Are we then to give up this way,
Melanippus? Has your heart no feeling at all for your kinsman
650 There in the dust? Don't you see what they're doing with the brazen
War-gear of Dolops? But on! For the long-distance fighting
Is over. Now we must clash hand to hand in a fight
To the finish—either we kill them, or they take our city
And utterly wipe out her people!"
          So saying, he led
And the other, godlike, followed. Meanwhile, the great
Telamonian Ajax spurred on the Argives, shouting:
"Be men, my friends, and stout of heart! Fear nothing
In this great struggle but dishonor before each other.
660 Of men who shun dishonor, more are saved
Than slain, but flight is a poor defense and wins
No glory of any kind!"
          He spoke, and though
The men were already eager to fight for their lives,
They took his words to heart and fenced in the ships

With a wall of bright bronze. And Zeus continued to strengthen
The Trojan attack. Then King Menelaus, the loud
Battle-roarer, thus exhorted Antilochus:
  "No other
Man we have, Antilochus, is younger than you, 670
Nor more fleet-footed than you, nor as valiant as you
In battle. Go on, then—charge out there and lay
Some Trojan man low!"
      So saying, he quickly drew back
Himself, but stirred up Antilochus, son of Nestor.
He quickly sprang out in front of the foremost fighters,
Glared fiercely about him, and hurled his bright spear, and before
            him
The Trojans fell back. And not in vain he threw,
But struck Hicetaon's son, the proud Melanippus,
Just as he entered the battle, full on the breast 680
By the nipple, sending him thunderously down and covering
His eyes with darkness. Antilochus, then, leaped upon him,
Quick as a hound that springs on a wounded fawn,
One some hunter has happened to hit, relaxing
His limbs in death, as swiftly he sprang from his bed.
Even so nimbly on you, Melanippus, leaped Antilochus,
Staunch in battle, eager to strip off your armor.
Brave Hector, however, was not unaware of the action,
And swiftly he charged through the fighting to meet Antilochus,
Who, though fast as a fighter, would not await him, 690
But fled like a frightened wild beast, one that has killed
A hound or a herdsman tending his cattle, and flees
Before a great crowd of angry men can gather.
So now retreated Antilochus, son of Nestor,
Followed by inhuman screams and a shower of groan-fraught
Missiles. Nor did he turn and stand till he reached
The company of comrades.
          Now the Trojans, like so many ravenous
Lions, charged at the ships, fulfilling the promise
Of Zeus, who continued to heighten their power and weaken 700
The hearts of the Argives, depriving them of sweet glory,
While keenly inciting the Trojans. For Zeus had decreed
In his heart to give the glory to Hector, that he
At last might hurl on the beaked black ships his god-blazing,
Tireless fire, thereby fulfilling completely
The brazen request of Thetis. So Zeus the planner
Was waiting to see the glare from a flaming ship,

For then henceforth he would cause a Trojan retreat
From the ships and give the Danaans glorious victory.[7]
710   With all this in mind, he was driving on at the hollow
Ships bold Priam's son Hector, a man already
Quite eager. But now he raged like spear-wielding Ares,
Fierce as a fire on the mountains, burning the brush
And trees of a thickly grown forest. Foam formed round his mouth,
His eyes blazed madly beneath his lowering brows,
And the shining helmet about his temples shook awesomely
As he fought. For Zeus of the bright upper air was himself
His protector, pledged to glorify him alone
Mid so many other warriors. For he would not live long,
720 Since Pallas Athena* was rapidly bringing closer
The day of his doom, when he would go down forever
Beneath the huge strength of Peleus' son Achilles.
Now, though, bold Hector was eager to break the Achaean
Ranks, charging fiercely at them wherever he saw
The most men and the most splendid armor. But he, in spite of
His ardor, could not break through, for they held close together,
Tight and firm as a wall, solid and strong
As a huge beetling cliff close by the gray sea, a bulwark
Of stone that takes unshaken the many hard blasts
730 Of screaming wind and the blows from the swollen big waves
That boom against it. So the Danaans, unretreating,
Stood fast against the Trojans.
          Then Hector, shining like fire
All over, sprang at the line of men and fell on them
Hard, like a towering, wind-swollen wave that under
The clouds rolls swiftly along to crash on a ship,
And the decks for a while disappear under foaming sea-water,
While the dread blast roars in the sail and the hearts of the sailors
Quake in their terror at thus escaping death
740 By so very little. Even so the hearts of Achaeans
Went all to pieces with fear. For Hector fell
On their ranks like a hugely ferocious lion that springs
Mid a great herd of cattle grazing their fill in a low-lying
Meadow—the herdsman with them is one who has never
Learned how to deal with a fierce wild beast that has just
Undone a sleek heifer. He goes with the herd, but either
Up front or behind, while the lion leaps in at the middle,

---

*Athena is the patron goddess of the Achaean victory.

Kills a fine cow, and stampedes all of the others.
So now the Achaeans were thoroughly routed by Hector
And Father Zeus, miraculously, for Hector killed   750
But one man—Periphetes, Copreus' dear son from Mycenae,
A man far better than Copreus his father, he
Who had frequently gone with orders from cruel King Eurystheus
To powerful Heracles. Surely his son Periphetes
Was better in every way, in fleetness of foot,
In fighting, and also in brains, for he was one
Of the keenest men in Mycenae. And he it was
Who enabled Hector to win and cover himself
With glory, for turning he tripped on the rim of his foot-reaching
Shield, his wall against spears, but now it served only   760
To trip him and send him down on his back, while about
His temples his helmet horribly rang. This attracted
The notice of Hector, who ran and standing above him
Transfixed his breast with a spear, right in among
His horrified comrades, who did him no good at all,
For they too were frozen with terrible fear of great Hector.

    Soon the Achaeans fell back, taking cover behind
The first line of ships, but the Trojans poured in upon them
And forced them to give still further ground, but they stopped
At the first line of shelters, where all remained in a body,   770
Instead of scattering throughout the camp, for they constantly
Yelled at each other, and shame held them fast, and fear.
But most of all Gerenian Nestor, old sentinel
Of Achaea, besought each man by his parents, pleading:

    "Be men, my friends, and don't be disgraced in the eyes
Of others. Remember, each of you, children and wife
And possessions, and your parents living or dead. For the sake
Of those who are absent, I beg you to make a strong stand
And not to turn tail and flee!"

    So saying, he strengthened   780
The spirit and might of all, and Athena cleared
From before them a murky thick cloud of amazing darkness,
So that daylight shone brightly, as well from the side of evil,
All-leveling battle as from that where the other ships lay.
Then all saw war-screaming Hector along with his men,
Both those who stood in the rear, inactive, and those
Who fought by the swift-running ships.

    But now it no longer
Seemed good to the soul of magnanimous Ajax to stay
At the shelters where huddled the rest of the sons of Achaeans.   790

He much preferred to stride up and down the decks
Of the ships, wielding a long battle-pike for fighting
At sea, jointed with rings and thirty-three feet
In length. And like a trick-rider who harnesses four
Fine horses, carefully picked, and gallops toward
A great city, over a plain down a well-traveled road
Where many people, both men and women, marvel
At his performance as he continues to leap
From horse to horse while onward they fly, so Ajax,
800   Now, kept leaping from deck to deck of the ships,
And always his voice went up to the sky, as he
With terrible shouts cried out to the Danaans to defend
Their shelters and ships. Nor was Hector content to stay
Mid the throng of bronze-breasted Trojans, but as a flashing
Gold eagle plunges ferociously down on a flock
Of wild birds that feed by the bank of a river—whether geese
Or cranes or long-necked swans—so Hector charged straight
For a dark-prowed ship, and the huge hand of Zeus thrust him on
From behind, as that god also aroused the rest
810   Of Hector's fierce army.
               So again a shrill battle took place
Beside the ships, a fight so slashingly fought
That you would have said they faced each other fresh
And unwearied. But the two struggling sides did not think alike.
The Achaeans knew they were trapped and felt doom was sure,
While the Trojans hoped in their hearts to burn the ships
And destroy the Achaean army. Then Hector grasped
The stern-horn of a brine-skimming, beautiful seagoing ship,
That had brought brave Protesilaus to Troy, though it never
820   Carried him home to his own dear country again.
Now around his ship the Achaeans and Trojans were cutting
Each other down in close combat, since they no longer
Threw lances or shot whizzing arrows. But standing up close
In stubborn oneness of spirit they hacked at each other
With keen battle-axes and hatchets, and slashed away
With huge swords and two-pointed spears. And many indeed
Were the splendid dark-hilted blades that littered the ground,
Some falling from warriors' hands, some cut from their shoulders,
As fiercely they fought, flooding the black earth with blood.
830   Now Hector, once he had seized the ship by the stern,
Would not let go the high horn he gripped, and thus
He called to the Trojans: "Bring fire, and with it your voices
All raised at once in the war-cry. For Zeus now gives us

A day worth all the rest—to take the ships
That came here to Troy against the will of the gods
And brought us innumerable woes, woes we suffered
On account of the cowardly elders, who when I was eager
To fight at the ships, held me and all the rest back.
But if far-seeing Zeus then blunted our wits,
Now of himself he urges and orders us on!"   840
    At this they sprang at the Argives harder than ever.
But Ajax no longer remained where he was, for missiles
Rained down all around him. Expecting death any moment,
He little by little retreated on the seven-foot bridge
Amidships, leaving the deck of the well-balanced vessel.
There he stood watch, and kept from the ship any Trojan
Who tried to burn it with unwearied fire, and always
His awesome voice called out to the Danaan troops:
    "O friends, heroic comrades of Ares, be men,
Dear friends, and remember your strength in the war-charge. Can it be   850
That we think we have reinforcements behind us, or some
Stronger wall to keep off destruction? Believe me, there is
No walled town nearby, wherein we might find reinforcements
And so, defending ourselves, succeed in reversing
The fortunes of war. No indeed! we are here on the plain
Of bronze-breasted Trojans, with nothing behind us but water!
Survival lies in the strength of our hands, not
In compassion shown toward the Trojans."
    He shouted, and all
The while kept thrusting madly away at the foe   860
With his keen-cutting spear. Whoever would charge at the hollow
Ships with a blazing torch in his hand, striving
To win praise from Hector, urging them on, for that man
Ajax waited and wounded him soon with a thrust
Of his lengthy sea-pike. That bronze he embedded in twelve
Trojan warriors, wounding them there in front of the ships.

BOOK XVI

The Death of Patroclus

While they were warring around the benched ships, Patroclus
Came up to Achilles, Prince of his people, and standing
Beside him shed hot tears, weeping like a spring
Whose dark streams trickle down the rocky face of a cliff.[1]
And noble Achilles, a warrior fast on his feet,
Had compassion on him, and spoke in these winged words:
  "Why are you weeping, Patroclus, like some little girl
That runs along by her mother and begs to be
Taken up, clutching her dress, holding her back,
10 And looking tearfully up at her till at last
She is taken up? Like that little girl, Patroclus,
You shed these big tears. Have you something to say to the Myrmidons,
Or to me myself? Have you alone heard some late news
From Phthia? Surely men say that Menoetius, son
Of Actor, still lives, as does King Peleus,* Aeacus'
Son, at home among his Myrmidons. Were either
Of those two dead, then indeed we would greatly grieve.
Or is your sorrow for Argives, now being slaughtered
Beside the dark hulls on account of their own overreaching?
20 Keep it in no longer. Speak out, and share it with me."
  Then heavily sighing, the horseman Patroclus replied:
"O Peleus' son Achilles, far strongest of all
The Achaeans, do not mock or blame me for this,
So awesome now is the terrible pain in which
The Achaeans are toiling. For now our bravest men,
Stricken by arrows or spear-thrusts, lie at the ships.
Strong Diomedes, Tydeus' son, has been hit,
And both spear-famous Odysseus and King Agamemnon
Have suffered disabling spear-wounds, and Eurypylus too
30 Is out with an arrow deep in his thigh, and about these

---

*Menoetius and Peleus are the fathers, respectively, of Patroclus and Achilles; see
IX.284–292 and XI.878–884 for the fathers' parting words in Phthia.

Our surgeons of many drugs are busy, trying
To help them. But what, Achilles, can anyone do
With you? May wrath like that you cherish never
Lay hold of me, O man perversely courageous!
What profit will men yet to be have from you, if now
You refuse to keep from the Argives shameful destruction?
O creature without compassion, surely you are
No son of Thetis and knightly Peleus. Only
The gray salt-sea and the beetling cliffs of stone
Could have brought into being a creature so harsh and unfeeling!   40
But if your heart is set on escaping some dire word
From Zeus, revealed to you by your goddess mother,[2]
Then send me forth now at the head of the Myrmidon host,
That I may be a light of hope to the Danaans.
And let me strap on my shoulders that armor of yours,
That the zealous Trojans may take me for you and quickly
Withdraw from the fighting. Then the battling, war-worn sons
Of Achaeans may have a chance to catch their breath—
Such chances in battle are few—and we who are fresh
May easily drive, with little more than our war-screams,   50
The exhausted Trojans away from the ships and the shelters
And back toward the city."

     Such was his plea, poor childish
Fool that he was, for it was his own hard death
And doom for which he pleaded.

     Then greatly disturbed,
Quick-charging Achilles spoke thus: "Ah, my Zeus-sprung
Patroclus, what are you saying! I don't give a straw
For anyone's fateful foretelling—none that I know of,
That is—nor has my goddess mother brought to me   60
Any such word from Zeus.[3] What fills my heart
And soul with so much bitter resentment is simply
That one whose equal I am should want to rob me
And take my prize of prestige for no better reason
Than this, that he has more power. This indeed bitterly
Rankles, after all I have done and suffered for him!
That girl the sons of Achaeans picked out as a prize
For me, since I had sacked a walled town and made her
Mine with my spear. Then Atreus' son Agamemnon,
Our great and lordly commander, snatches her back   70
From my arms as though I were some lowly, contemptible tramp.

     "Well, what's done is done. I will not, it seems,
Be filled with fierce anger forever, though I said I would not

Change my mind till the fighters were screaming about my own
     vessels.[4]
So now put my famous armor about your shoulders
And lead into battle the fight-loving Myrmidons, if truly
A dark cloud of Trojans has settled about the black ships,
Leaving the Argives little space and nothing
Behind them by way of support but the surf-beaten shore

80   Of the sea. I suppose the whole town of Troy has poured out
Against them, fearless as can be, since now they no longer
See the shining front of my helmet glaring
Nearby. If only King Agamemnon treated
Me well, very soon those Trojans would run for their city
And fill all the gullies with corpses on their way,
Whereas now they have brought their attack right into our camp.
For the spear of Tydeus' son Diomedes rages
No longer to keep off death from the Danaans, nor as yet
Have I heard the voice of Atreus' son Agamemnon,

90   Bawling orders from his hated head. But the shouts
Of slaughtering Hector crash round about me, as he
Continues to urge on the Trojans, who fill the plain
With their own mighty cries, as they horribly scourge the Achaeans.
     "Go, then, Patroclus, fall on them hard and save
The ships from destruction, lest the Trojans really burn them
And their blazing fire rob all of us of our precious,
Longed-for return. But pay close attention to this
Most important part of my counsel, that you may win
For me great honor and glory from all of the Danaans,

100 Making them bring back to me that exquisite girl
And give in addition splendid gifts. When you
Have driven the Trojans away from the ships, come back.
And if Hera's loud-crashing lord should give you a chance
To win great glory, even so do not fight without me
The war-loving Trojans, since that would do my reputation
No good! Do not, I tell you, get carried away
In the heat of conflict and slaughter and so lead the men
Toward the city. For one of the gods everlasting may decide
To descend from Olympus and fight against you—Apollo,

110 For instance, who works from afar and dearly loves
All Trojans. Come back, then, when once you have saved the vessels,
And let the others go fighting across the plain.
O Father Zeus, Athena, and Apollo, how very
Deeply I wish the death of every Trojan
Who lives in the world, and of every Argive too,

That just myself and Patroclus might live and alone
Succeed in reducing this tower-crowned, sacred city
To rubble and dust!"[5]
    While thus they spoke to each other,
Ajax, belabored with missiles, no longer stood firm.   120
For the will of Zeus and the lordly bronze-hurling Trojans
Were too much for him. The flashing helmet he wore
About his temples constantly rang with the terrible
Blows that steadily fell on the well-wrought plates
Of bronze, and his strong left shoulder grew numb from always
Firmly holding his sun-glinting shield. Nor were they
Able to knock it aside, no matter how hard
They threw. But now he was painfully panting, and the sweat
Streamed down all over his body, since he had not even
A moment to catch his breath, and danger on danger   130
Shot in from every side.
    O tell me now, Muses,
You that have homes on Olympus, how fire first fell
On the Argive ships.
    Bold Hector charged in at Ajax,
And swinging his huge sword hard he shore off the point
Of the long ashen spear, so that now Telamonian Ajax
Stood foolishly shaking a pointless pike, while well
Away to one side the bronze point bounced and lay still.
Then Ajax shuddered from deep in his breast, as his great heart   140
Knew the work of immortal gods and had
To admit that high-crashing Zeus was willing a victory
For Trojans and rendering vain whatever he tried
To do in the fight. So at last brave Ajax fell back
From the fierce fall of missiles, and the Trojans threw untiring fire
On the graceful ship. At once unquenchable flame
Streamed over the hull.
    As the hungry fire swirled round the stern
Of the ship, Achilles slapped his huge thighs* and spoke
To Patroclus, saying: "Up now, Zeus-sprung Patroclus,   150
Commander of horsemen. Now for certain I see
At the ships the rush of high-roaring fire. Don't allow them
Thus to destroy the vessels and cut off our only
Escape. On with that armor, then, faster! while I
Go muster the men."

---

*For the gesture of thigh-slapping, see endnote 6 to book XV.

      Such were his words, and Patroclus
Put on the glittering bronze.[6] First he covered
His shins with greaves, fair greaves with ankle-clasps of silver.
Next, about his chest he carefully strapped
160 The richly wrought breastplate of Aeacus' grandson Achilles,
A gorgeous piece that sparkled and shone like the stars.
And from his shoulders he slung the bronze sword with the bright
        studs
Of silver along with the shield both wide and thick.
Then on his noble head he put a strong helmet
With horsehair plume defiantly waving above him,
And last he took up two long sturdy spears that fitted
His grip to perfection. But the spear of peerless Achilles
He left where it was, a huge spear, heavy and long.
No Achaean fighter could wield it but mighty Achilles
170 Himself, this strong spear of ash that Cheiron the Centaur
Had given to Peleus, Achilles' dear father. It came
From the peak of Mount Pelion, and was meant to bring death to
        the foe.

      Then Patroclus ordered Automedon quickly to harness
The horses. For next to rank-smashing Achilles, he cared for
Automedon most, and he of all drivers was surest
To stay close at hand, awaiting his call in the melee.
So Automedon yoked Achilles' fast horses, Xanthus
And Balius, swift as the blasting gales. For the West Wind
Had sired them on the stormy filly Podarge, as she grazed
180 In a field by the stream of Oceanus. And in the side-traces
He put the perfect horse Pedasus, that Achilles had won
When he took Eëtion's city, and Pedasus, though
But a mortal steed, kept up with the immortal pair.

      Meanwhile, Achilles strode mid the shelters, giving all
Of his Myrmidons orders to arm, after which they rushed out
Like so many flesh-rending wolves, great beasts unspeakably
Savage—wolves that have killed a huge horned stag
In the mountains and gorged themselves on his flesh till the jaws
Of all are dripping with blood, and off the pack runs
190 To lap with their slender lean tongues from a spring of dark water,
Belching up scarlet gore and still quite ferocious,
Though now their bellies are bulging. Even so the Myrmidon
Captains and counselors rushed to form round Patroclus,
The noble dear friend of their leader. And Achilles himself,
Resembling the War-god, stood in the midst of all,
Urging on charioteers and shield-bearing soldiers.

God-loved Achilles led fifty swift ships to Troy,
And on the benches in each came fifty men,
His comrades. And he had appointed five trusted commanders,
While he himself ruled mightily over all.   200
The first battalion was led by Menesthius, him
Of the bright-glinting breastplate, the son of Spercheius, god
Of the Zeus-fed river. His mother, a daughter of Peleus,
The fair Polydora, had lain with untiring Spercheius
And borne him Menesthius, who, however, took
The surname of Borus, Perieres' son, who gave
Gifts of wooing past counting and publicly married the girl.
The next battalion was led by warlike Eudorus,
A god's child born of a maiden, Phylas' daughter
Polymele, the exquisite dancer. Powerful Hermes,   210
Slayer of Argus, saw her dancing in the chorus
Of Artemis, goddess of golden shafts and the echoing
Shouts of the chase. Soon he went up to her room
And secretly lay with her, and she bore to Hermes
The helper a splendid son, Eudorus, swift
Of foot and quick as a fighter. But when at last
The goddess of childbirth, labor-inducing Eileithyia,
Had brought him forth to the light and he had seen
The rays of the sun, then the strong and fiery Echecles,
Son of Actor, took Polymele home   220
As his wife, having given innumerable gifts of wooing,
And Eudorus was left with his grandfather Phylas, who raised him
And tenderly loved him, quite as if he had been
His own son. And the third battalion was led by Peisander,
Maemalus' son, a warlike man expert
As a spearman, surpassed in such fighting by no other Myrmidon
Save Patroclus, the comrade of Peleus' great son.
And the knightly old Phoenix captained the fourth contingent,
And Alcimedon the fifth, he the faultless son
Of Laerces. When at last Achilles had martialed them all   230
With their leaders, battalion by separate battalion, he laid
This stern charge upon them, saying:
        "Myrmidons, let no man
Forget the many harsh threats that you here with me
Beside the swift ships throughout all the time of my wrath
Have hurled at the Trojans, each one of you chiding me thus:
'O hard son of Peleus, surely, O pitiless one,
Your mother nursed you on gall, not milk, since now
You hold your unwilling comrades here at the ships.

240 But come, let us all return home in our seagoing vessels,
     If thus disabling is this evil wrath that has so
     Encompassed your heart.' So you would often gather
     And babble such stuff at me. Well now you have
     Before you a truly great chance for warlike deeds,
     Of which you have been so exceedingly avid. Go then,
     With hearts full of valor, and show the Trojans your prowess."
          So saying, he put still more courage in all of the men,
     And the ranks as they listened drew even closer together.
     Like the close-fitting stones a man lays in building the wall
250 Of a lofty house, a wall to keep out the wind,
     So now their helmets and brightly bossed shields were together,
     The Myrmidons standing so close that shield pressed on shield,
     Helmet on helmet, and man on man, so close
     That the horsehair plumes on the bright-horned helmets brushed
     Each other with every nod of a head. And out
     Before all, arrayed in full armor, were two fierce warriors,
     Patroclus and Automedon, both equally eager to fight
     In the Myrmidon van.
          But Achilles went into his lodge
260 And lifted the lid of a beautiful inlaid chest
     That his mother Thetis, silvery-footed, had put
     On his ship for him to carry along, having filled it
     Full with tunics and wind-warding cloaks and fleecy
     Warm blankets. There too he kept a fair-beaten cup,
     From which no other man drank the bright wine, nor would
     Achilles pour libations from it to any god
     Other than Zeus the Father. Taking this cup
     From the chest, he cleansed it with sulphur and rinsed it well
     In pure running water, then washed his hands and ladled
270 A cup of the sparkling wine. Nor was he unnoticed
     By Zeus, strong lover of thunder and lightning, as he
     Stood out in the forecourt's center and poured forth the wine,
     Looking to heaven, and praying:
          "Lord Zeus, Dodonaean,
     Pelasgian, you that dwell in the distance, ruling wintry
     Dodona, where your prophets the Selloi live, priests
     Who go with feet unwashed and who sleep on the ground—
     Hear as you heard me before when I prayed. You honored me
     Then, and woefully smote the Achaean host.
280 Grant me now another prayer, for though
     I myself will stay at the ships, I am sending my friend
     Into battle along with the Myrmidon troops. With him,

O far-seeing Zeus, send glory. Make strong and courageous
The heart in his breast, that Hector too may know
Whether my dear comrade can fight his own battles, or whether
His hands invincibly rage only when I too
Enter the toil and tumult of Ares. But when
He has driven the chaotic fighting away from the ships,
I pray let him come back to these swift ships and me,
Completely unharmed and with all of his armor intact,   290
And with him bring back his close-fighting Myrmidon comrades."[7]
    Such was his prayer, and Zeus the contriver heard him,
And the Father granted him part, and part he denied.
That Patroclus should beat the battling men from the ships
He granted, but refused to grant his safe return
From the fight.
    Now Achilles, when he had poured the libation
And made his prayer to Father Zeus, re-entered
His lodge and put the cup back in the chest. Then
He came out and stood in front of the door, for still   300
His heart was eager to witness the awesome clash
Of Achaeans and Trojans.
    Meanwhile, the bronze-armored men
Marched on with noble Patroclus, till fiercely they charged
And hurled themselves on the Trojans. Like wasps that nest
At the wayside and are forever tormented by boys,
Who stir them up and make them a menace to many,
So that when some traveler, going by, unwittingly
Stirs them again, out they swarm in their fury
Of heart to fight in defense of their young, so now   310
With heart and spirit like theirs the Myrmidons fell
On the Trojans, and unquenchable cries went up. But the voice
Of valiant Patroclus was heard over all, shouting:
    "Myrmidon comrades of Peleus' son Achilles,
Be men, my friends, and remember your powerful prowess,
That you may win honor for Peleus' son, your Prince,
Who by the ships is far the best of the Argives,
As you are his able and excellent close-fighting comrades.
Strike hard, I say, that Atreus' son, imperial
Agamemnon, may know how blind he was to give   320
No honor at all to the bravest and best of Achaeans!"
    These words inspired them with courage, and as they fell
All at once on the Trojan troops, the ships re-echoed
Their terrible war-cries. And when the Trojans caught sight
Of stalwart Patroclus, of him and his comrade Automedon,

Both blazing in war-gear of bronze, the heart of each man
Was disturbed, and all their battalions were shaken, for now
They thought that Achilles the quick had renounced his wrath
At the ships and chosen to help once again. So each
330 Of the Trojans frantically glanced about in search of
Some way to escape dire death.
      Then Patroclus was first
To hurl a bright lance straight at the mass of men
That moiled round the stern of the ship of Protesilaus.
His victim was bold Pyraechmes, the chief who had led
The horse-drawn Paeonians out of Amydon, where flows
The wide-rippling Axius. He struck his right shoulder, knocking him
Back in the dust with a groan, and about him his comrades
Were routed, for when he killed their superlative leader
340 Patroclus roused panic in all the fighting Paeonians.
Thus he beat them back from the ships and extinguished
The roaring flames, then left the half-burnt vessel
Behind as the war-screaming Danaans poured through the gaps
Between ships with fierce-yelling Trojans retreating before them.
As when lightning-gathering Zeus rifts a dark cloud
That enshrouds the crest of a towering mountain, revealing
All peaks, high headlands, and even ravines, as the light
Breaks through from the infinite aether, even such was the moment
Of respite enjoyed by the Danaans when they had extinguished
350 The ravenous fire. But still the battle went on,
For the Trojans had not yet been turned to headlong retreat
From the ships by the battle-lusty Achaeans, but always
They tried to resist them, and only fell back when they had to.
      Then man accounted for man in the scattered fight
As the battle chieftains paired off. First brave Patroclus
Drove his sharp bronze clean through Areïlycus' thigh,
Just as he turned, and the spear broke the bone and hurled him
Face down on the earth. And fierce Menelaus thrust
His spear deep into the breast of Thoas, where his flesh
360 Was uncovered by shield, and relaxed his limbs in death.
And Phyleus' son Meges kept his eyes fixed on Amphiclus
Ferociously charging, and proved too quick for him
With a stab in the leg's thickest part, where sinew and muscle
Were ripped and cut round the point of the spear, so that darkness
Eclipsed his bright eyes. Then one of the sons of Nestor,
Antilochus, jabbed his keen bronze at Atymnius and drove
The spear through his side, pitching him prone. But Maris,
His brother, rushed in a rage at Antilochus and stood

In front of the corpse. Prince Thrasymedes, however,
Another of Nestor's sons, was too quick for him,   370
And well before Maris could thrust, Thrasymedes pierced
His shoulder and shore the arm muscles away and completely
Shattered the bone, felling the man with a crash
And covering his eyes with darkness. Thus brothers overcame
Brothers, who now descended to Erebus, two brave
Lycian friends of Sarpedon and spear-throwing sons of Amisodarus,
Who raised the raging Chimaera, the ruin of so many.
And Ajax, son of Oïleus, charged Cleobulus
Caught still alive in a tangle of warring men,
And there he undid his strength by a blow on the neck   380
With his dark-hilted sword, whereat the whole blade was left smoking
With blood, as purple death came down on his eyes
And powerful fate embraced him. Then Peneleos and Lycon,
Each missing the other with spear-casts, charged together
With swords. And Lycon came down very hard on the horn
Of the other's plumed helmet and broke his blade off at the hilt,
But Peneleos sank his sword deep in his enemy's neck
Just under the ear, and all but cut off his head,
It hanging by nothing but skin, and the limbs of Lycon
Were loosed. And Meriones swiftly caught up with Acamas   390
And thrust his bronze into that leader's right shoulder
At the moment he mounted his car, hurling him hard
To the ground, where everything went black. Then Idomeneus
Drove his ruthless bronze straight through the mouth
Of Erymas and on beneath the man's brain, splitting
Apart the white bones and knocking his teeth out. Both eyes
Filled with blood, and gaping he spurted and sprayed more blood
Through nostrils and mouth, till death's black cloud enclosed him.
        Thus each of these Danaan leaders killed his man.
As ravenous wolves spring out on terrified lambs   400
Or kids, when the flocks, through the fault of some careless shepherd,
Are scattered about in the mountains, so now the Danaans
Sprang on the Trojans, who no longer thought of their furious
War-charge, but only of screaming retreat.
        And Ajax
The great was constantly eager to hurl his spear
At huge bronze-helmeted Hector, but he, in his knowledge
Of fighting, kept his broad shoulders well covered with shield
Of enduring bull's-hide and always stayed on the alert
For whistling arrows and whizzing spears. He knew,   410
Of course, that the tide of battle was turning, but still

He stood fast in an effort to save his faithful comrades.
And as when Zeus overcasts the earth with storm
And clouds go forth from Olympus throughout the bright sky,
Even so the terrified screams of battle and rout
Arose from the Argive ships, nor was it with any
Small semblance of order that those harried Trojans retreated.
And Hector himself, with full armor on, now abandoned
The troops he had led, drawn away behind his fast horses,
420 While other less fortunate Trojans struggled to get
Through the deep-dug ditch. There many a pair of galloping,
Car-drawing horses broke off the shaft at the base
And left the car of their master.
          And Patroclus was hot
In pursuit, calling savagely out to the Danaans and intending
The Trojans no good, who now in the screaming terror
Of rout retraced their tracks on the plain, their broken
Battalions stampeding beneath a huge cover of dust
That spread out under the clouds as the hard-hoofed horses
430 Ran at full speed away from the shelters and ships
And back toward the city of Troy. And Patroclus, yelling
His war-scream, directed his horses wherever he saw
The thickest rout of retreating men, and they
Kept going down beneath his chariot's axles,
Pitching headlong from cars that overturned
With clatter and clang. And the deathless swift horses of Peleus,
Those glossy gifts of the gods, bore brave Patroclus
Over the ditch at a bound, hurtling on
After Hector, whom always Patroclus was eager to strike,
440 But his horses too were swift and kept him ahead.
As when on an autumn day Zeus darkens the earth
With storm clouds and sends the gale-driven rain beating down,
He being in wrath against men for crooked decrees
They have made in the heat of assembly, driving out justice
And giving no thought to the vengeance of gods, and all
Their rivers flood over in spate, washing great gullies
In every hillside, as down from the mountains they roar
To the dark-blue sea, wrecking the farmers' tilled fields:
Even so awesome and deafening now was the roar
450 Of Trojan horses galloping on toward the city.
          But when Patroclus had headed off the retreat,
He turned the leading battalions back toward the ships,
Nor would he allow them, in spite of their frenzy, to get
Within the town walls. And there in the space between ships

And the river and high wall of Troy, he rode in among them
And killed right and left, thus taking his vengeance for many
Dead comrades. The first to fall was Pronous, pierced
With a cast of Patroclus' bright spear, hitting deep in the chest
At a spot uncovered by shield, and his limbs relaxed
In death as he crashed to the ground. Next he charged down   460
On Enops' son Thestor, who huddled and cringed in his chariot,
Terrified out of his wits and no longer holding
The reins. Patroclus approached and jabbed his spear
Through this man's right jaw and on through his teeth. Then
                gripping
The shaft he hoisted him over the rail and out of
The car, as a man out on a projection of rock,
Angling with line and glittering hook, hauls in
A huge fish from the sea. Even so Patroclus heaved Thestor,
Impaled on the glittering bronze, up out of the car
And flopped him down on his face, and life took leave   470
Of him as he fell. Then, as Erylaus ran at him,
He struck him full on the head with a stone, splitting
His skull within the deep helmet and dropping him prone
In the dust, where heartbreaking death engulfed him. And then,
One after the other, he fought with Erymas, Amphoterus,
And Epaltes, Damastor's son Tlepolemus, Echius,
Pyris, and Ipheus, Euippus, and Argeas' son
Polymelus, and each of them he stretched out in death
On the bountiful earth.
        But when Sarpedon saw   480
His godlike comrades, Lycians with unbelted tunics,
Being thus overwhelmed by Patroclus, son of Menoetius,
He shouted these words of reproach: "For shame, O Lycians,
Disgraceful! and where are you off to, running so swiftly?
Now I myself will confront this man and find out
Who he is who proves so vastly too much for you all,
Having loosed the knees of many excellent warriors
And done the Trojans much damage."
        So saying, he sprang
Fully armed from his car to the ground. And Patroclus, opposite   490
Him, saw and did likewise. And now, like a pair
Of crook-clawed, bent-beaked vultures that fight with harsh screams
High up on a rock, these two charged screaming together.
And Zeus, the son of devious Cronos, saw them
And felt compassion, and thus he spoke to Hera,
His sister and wife:

"Ah, miserable me! since the man
I love most, Sarpedon my son, is fated to die
At the hands of Patroclus, son of Menoetius. And now
500 As I ponder I cannot decide whether I shall snatch him
Up yet alive and set him down far away
From weeping war in the rich land of Lycia, or whether
Now I shall let him go down at the hands of Patroclus."
        And heifer-eyed regal Hera answered him thus:
"Most dreadful son of Cronos, what are you saying!
Can it be that you really wish to deliver a mortal,
One long fore-destined by fate, from dolorous death?
Well do as you like, but don't suppose for one moment
That all of us like what you do! And here's something else
510 You'll do well to remember. If you do send Sarpedon alive
To his home, don't be surprised when some other god
Wishes to take his own dear son away
From the horrible conflict. For fighting around the great city
Of Priam are many sons of the gods, and you
Will surely stir up fierce resentment among the immortals.[8]
But if the man is really so dear to your heart,
And if you are really so deeply grieved at his fate,
Why go ahead and allow him to fall and die
At the hands of Patroclus down there in the bloody encounter.
520 Then, when his years are over and his soul gone forever,
Send Death and care-lulling Sleep, that they may bear him
Away to the wide land of Lycia. There his brothers
And kinsfolk will give him the dead's due rites, a proper
Entombment, with mound and memorial pillar."
        She spoke,
Nor was she ignored by the Father of men and gods.
Yet he wept a shower of bloody tears on earth
In honor of his dear son, whom Patroclus was soon
To kill in the fertile land of the Trojans, far away
530 From his own dear country.
        Now as they came within range,
Patroclus threw and hit Thrasymelus, the able
Squire of Sarpedon, the spear going deep in his gut
And loosing his limbs forever. But Sarpedon's bright spear
Missed its mark and struck the right shoulder of the trace-horse
                Pedasus,
Who frantically whinnied as down in the dust he thudded.
Choking, he gasped out his life, and his spirit took flight.
But the other two horses shied apart, creaking

The yoke and tangling the reins, while the trace-horse lay dead
In the dust. Then spear-famed Automedon found what to do.　　540
Whipping out his long sword from beside his big thigh, he leaped
To the ground and quickly cut the horse loose, and the other two
Came together and pulled at the yoke once more,
As again the two warriors charged in heart-eating hatred.
　　　　But again Sarpedon's bright spear missed its mark, and the
　　　　　　　point
Hurtled over Patroclus' left shoulder without even grazing
The flesh. Then Patroclus in turn came on with the bronze,
And not at all vainly did that spear fly from his hand,
For it struck where the midriff encloses the quick-throbbing heart.
And Sarpedon fell as an oak or poplar or lofty pine　　550
Falls when men in the mountains cut them down
With keen axes to furnish timber for ships. So now,
In front of his horses and car, Sarpedon lay groaning,
Stretched out on the earth and clutching at the bloody dust.
And as when a lion brings down a glossy red bull,
Springing into the midst of the shuffling cattle, and the fiery bull
Struggles and bellows as he dies in the jaws of his foe,
Even so did the leader of shield-bearing Lycians gasp out
Defiance in death at the hands of Patroclus, calling out
Thus in his throes on the name of his cherished comrade:　　560
　　　"Good Glaucus, great fighting man among men, now truly
Your skill with the spear and boldness in battle are needed!
Now, if indeed you are eager to fight, let war,
Evil war be the chief desire of your heart. But first
Go up and down through the Lycian host and urge
All the leaders to fight for Sarpedon, and then put your own
Bright bronze into action, fighting in my defense.
For if now the Achaeans strip me of armor out here
In front of the drawn-up ships, I shall be a disgrace
To you and a hanging down of the head for as long a　　570
You live. So come, hold your ground like a man, and urge on
All of the others."
　　　As thus he spoke, dark death.
Came over his eyes and nostrils alike. Then Patroclus,
Planting a foot on his chest, jerked the spear from his flesh,
And the midriff followed the spearhead, so that he drew out
Together his keen-cutting bronze and the warrior's soul.
Meanwhile, the Myrmidons held Sarpedon's hard-snorting
Horses, who panicked and reared, now that their car
Was left empty.　　580

When he heard the cry of Sarpedon, the heart
Of Glaucus was filled with unspeakable grief, since he
Was unable to succor his friend. He caught and gripped
His arm hard, for his wound still throbbed with pain, the wound
That Teucer, keeping off death from his comrades, had made
With an arrow as Glaucus charged the high wall. Then praying,
He made this plea to Apollo, who strikes from afar:
    "O listen, my lord, to me, you that roam
Through the rich land of Lycia or else here in Troy, and can
590 Everywhere well hear a mortal in pain, such a mortal
As now Glaucus is. For I am sorely afflicted
With this grievous wound, and the sharp pangs shoot through my arm,
Nor will it stop bleeding. My shoulder above it is heavy
And aching, and I am no longer able to grip
My spear firmly or go out and fight with the foe. And now
The bravest of men is dead, Sarpedon himself,
The son of Zeus, who would not protect his own child.
But you, my lord, heal this terrible wound—
Lull the pain and give me strength, that I
600 May encourage my Lycian comrades to fight for Sarpedon
And that I myself may battle about the body
Of him now fallen and dead."
       Thus he prayed,
And Phoebus Apollo heard him. At once he relieved
His sharp pain, staunched the flow of dark blood that ran
From the horrible wound, and put in his heart new courage.
And Glaucus knew what had happened and deeply rejoiced
That the great god Apollo had answered his prayer so promptly.
First he ranged up and down throughout all the Lycians,
610 Exhorting the leaders to fight for their fallen chief,
And then he strode rapidly into the Trojan troops
To Panthous' son Polydamas and noble Agenor,
And on to Aeneas and bronze-armored Hector, by whom
He stood and spoke, and his words came winged with entreaty:
    "Hector, now surely you altogether neglect
Your allies, men who are fighting and dying on your
Account, far from their friends and the land of their fathers.
Even so, you don't care to help them. Now low lies Sarpedon,
High leader of shield-bearing Lycians, he that ruled Lycia
620 With justice and strength. Him brazen Ares has dashed
In the dust beneath the spear of Patroclus. But come,
My friends, go with me, and share my fear of the shame
That will be if the Myrmidons strip off his armor and do

Vile things to his corpse, they being in terrible wrath
For Danaans dead, men whom we killed with our spears
Here at the ships."

At these words the Trojans were seized
With grief overwhelming, unbearable sorrow, for Sarpedon
Had long been a pillar of strength to their city, though he
Was no native of Troy. For with him came many men,   630
And of them all he was the greatest in battle.
So the Trojans charged straight at the Danaans, eager for slaughter,
And Hector led the attack, in wrath for Sarpedon.
But shaggy-hearted Patroclus urged on the Achaeans,
Savagely shouting thus to the two Ajaxes,
Who scarcely needed his urging:

"Be fierce, you two,
In fighting the foe! Be the men you've always been
Among fighters, or even more deadly. Low lies Sarpedon,
The first man to breach the Achaean wall. Let us charge, then,   640
And strip his shoulders of armor and do vile things
To his corpse, and let us cut down with the ruthless bronze
Any man of his comrades who makes an attempt to defend him."

He spoke, but they were already eager for action.
And when both sides had ordered and strengthened their forces,
Trojans and Lycians opposing Achaeans and Myrmidons,
They clashed with-awesome screams and strident ringing
Of armor to fight for the body of him now fallen.
And to make the battle-toil even more baneful, Zeus spread
Murderous darkness all over the bloody encounter.   650

At first the Trojans thrust back the quick-eyed Achaeans,
For down went a man by no means the worst of the Myrmidons,
Namely the son of spirited Agacles, shining
Epeigeus, who once had ruled over pleasant Budeum,
Till having killed a noble near kinsman of his
He came as a suppliant straight to king Peleus and Thetis
Of the silver feet, and they had sent him to Troy
Along with rank-smashing Achilles, that he too might fight
The Trojans. Now just as he laid his hands on the corpse,
Resplendent Hector came down on his head with a stone,   660
Splitting his skull within the thick helmet and dropping him
Prone in the dust as heartbreaking death engulfed him.
Then grief for his slaughtered comrade came over Patroclus,
And he charged through the front rank of warriors fast as a hawk
In flight, when the swift bird drives before him the jackdaws
And starlings. Even so straight, O Patroclus, commander

Of horsemen, you charged on the Lycians and Trojans, wrathful
At heart on account of your comrade slain. And he struck
Ithaemenes' dearly loved son Sthenelaus hard
670 On the neck with a stone, tearing the tendons away.
Then the front-fighting champions and glorious Hector fell back.
        They fell back as far as a lengthy javelin flies
When a man in a contest or life-wrecking battle tests
His might in a distance throw. So far and no farther
The Trojans retreated before the charging Achaeans.
Glaucus, brave leader of shield-bearing Lycians, was first
To whirl round, and whirling he brought down magnanimous Bathycles,
Chalcon's dear son, whose home was in Hellas, where thriving
He had been one of the wealthiest Myrmidon lords.
680 Turning suddenly on him as he was about to catch up,
Strong Glaucus pierced his chest with a spear and sent him
Crashing to earth. And heavy grief came over
The hearts of Achaeans at the fall of so splendid a man,
But the Trojans rejoicing, with courage renewed, quickly rallied
About the dead Myrmidon.
        Nor did the Achaeans give up,
But still came on straight at the foe. Then Meriones
Killed a helmeted Trojan, Onetor's bold son
Laogonus, a priest of Idaean Zeus, one honored
690 Like a god by the people. Him Meriones pierced
Beneath the jaw and ear, and quickly his spirit took leave
Of his limbs and abhorrent darkness seized him. Aeneas
Now hurled his bronze at Meriones, hoping to hit him
As on he came under cover of shield. But Meriones,
Looking straight at him, avoided the bronze by ducking
Forward, and Aeneas' long lance, flying vainly forth
From his powerful hand, embedded itself in the ground
Behind its intended victim, where the butt-end quivered
Till finally hulking Ares stilled its fury.
700   Aeneas, then, shouted in anger: "Meriones, surely
You are an agile dancer, but if my spear
Had found its mark your dancing days would have ended,
I think, forever!"
        To which spear-famous Meriones:
"Very hard it would be, Aeneas, strong though you are,
To quench the life of every man who confronts you.
You too, I suppose, are mortal. Hence if I cast
And vitally wound you with my keen bronze, very quickly,
In spite of your strength and the faith you have in your hands,

You would give glory to me and your miserable soul   710
To horse-famous Hades!"

      He vaunted, but valiant Patroclus
Rebuked him, saying: "Meriones, why would a brave
Fighting man like yourself make such a speech? Good friend,
Our insults will never drive any of those Trojans back
From the body. Their own bloody corpses will litter the ground
Far sooner. Victory in battle still lies in the might
Of our hands, while words are for men in council. Hence
As a soldier it does not become you to multiply words,
But only and always to fight!"   720

      So saying, he led
And the other, godlike, followed. And as when a thudding
And crashing goes up from mountain ravines where woodsmen
Are felling tall trees, and the din is heard in the distance,
So now about them a loud noise arose from the much trampled
Earth, a clanging of bronze and hammered hide shields,
As they smote each other with swords and two-pointed spears.
Nor could the best eyes in the world have still recognized
Sarpedon, so thick was the covering of missiles, blood
And dust that lay on his body from head to foot.   730
And warriors thronged round the corpse as numerous quite
As flies that drone through a dairy when spring has come
And fresh milk drenches the foaming full vessels and pails.
Even so, they swarmed round the corpse.

      Meanwhile, Zeus
Never once turned his eyes away from the horrible struggle,
But kept looking down on the fighters, pondering much
In his heart concerning the death of Patroclus, whether there
In the battle Prince Hector should hew him down with the bronze
And strip his shoulders of armor, or whether for still   740
More men he should cause to increase the terrible toil
Of war. And as he pondered, one way seemed better,
To let the brave friend of Achilles once again drive
Toward the city the Trojan troops and bronze-armored Hector,
And thus take many more lives.

      So first he made Hector
Afraid and, panicking, he leaped up on his car
And wheeled round to run, calling out on the rest of the Trojans
To follow and flee, for Hector saw clearly which way
Zeus' sacred balance was tipping. And the mighty Lycians   750
No longer stood fast, but all of them ran in retreat,
Having seen their King lying dead with a spear in his heart,

Dead in a huge heap of dead, for many had fallen
Upon him as Zeus strained taut the horrible strife.
      Then from Sarpedon's shoulders the Achaeans stripped off
The glittering bronze, which valiant Patroclus gave
To his comrades to carry back to the hollow ships.
And now to Apollo cloud-gathering Zeus spoke thus:
      "Up if you will, loved Phoebus, and go lift Sarpedon
760 From under that hailing of spears and wipe from his body
The cloud-black blood. Then carry him far away
And wash him well in the silvery rills of a river,
Anoint his flesh with ambrosia, and clothe him all
In the fragrant garments of gods. Having done as I ask you,
Give him to Sleep and Death, the swift twin brothers,
To carry, that they may quickly set him down
In the fertile wide land of Lycia. There his brothers
And kinsfolk will give him the dead's due rites, a proper
Entombment, with mound and memorial pillar."[9]
770   He spoke,
And Apollo did not disregard the voice of his Father,
But down he came from the mountains of Ida and entered
The grim confusion of fighting. Quickly he lifted
Sarpedon from under the hailing of spears, and when
He had carried him far away from ruinous war,
He washed him well in the silvery rills of a river,
Anointed his flesh with ambrosia, and clothed him all
In the fragrant garments of gods. Having done these things,
He gave him to Sleep and Death, the swift twin brothers,
780 To carry, and very quickly they set him down
In the fertile wide land of Lycia.
      Then Patroclus, calling
Commands to the horses and to Automedon, drove
In pursuit of the Trojans and Lycians, blind foolhardy child
That he was! For had he obeyed the careful orders
Of Peleus' son Achilles, he surely would then
Have escaped the miserable doom of murky death.
But always God's will is stronger by far than man's.
Great Zeus can make the bravest fighter retreat.
790 And easily keep him from winning, especially when
He inspires another to fight like fury against him.
And now it was surely Zeus who filled with blind force
The spirit of gallant Patroclus.
      Then who was the first
And who was the last you slew and stripped, O Patroclus,

That day when the gods invited you deathwards? Adrastus
Was first, then Autonous and Echeclus, and Megas' son Perimus,
Epistor, and Melanippus, followed by Elasus, Mulius,
And Pylartes. From these he took life away, and all
The others decided to flee.   800
      Then indeed would the sons
Of Achaeans, led on by raging Patroclus, have taken
Tall-gated Troy, for all around him Patroclus
Killed with his spear. But Phoebus Apollo stood firm
On the well-built wall, intending destruction for him,
But only good for the Trojans. Three times Patroclus
Sprang up on an angle of that lofty wall, and three times
Apollo battered him back[10] by dint of blows
From his own deathless hands, striking hard against the bright
        shield.
But when like a demon he charged a fourth time, then   810
With a terrible cry Apollo spoke these winged words:
      "Fall back! Zeus-descended Patroclus. It is not fated
That by your spear this town of the gifted Trojans
Shall be laid waste, nor even by that of Achilles,
A man far better than you!"
      Before the dread voice
Patroclus fell back a long way, avoiding the wrath
Of far-darting Apollo.
      Meanwhile, Hector was holding
His solid-hoofed horses in check at the Scaean Gates,   820
Unable to make up his mind whether he should drive
Once again out into the hubbub of battle, or whether
Now he should order the Trojan troops to gather
Within the thick wall. As he pondered, divided, Apollo
Came up to him there in the guise of a man young and strong,
Even Asius, horse-breaking Hector's uncle, own brother
Of Hecuba and son of Dymas, whose home was in Phrygia
Close by the river Sangarius. Looking exactly
Like him, Apollo, son of Zeus, spoke thus
To the Trojan chieftain: 830
      "Why is it, Hector, that you
Are no longer fighting? Such idleness hardly becomes you!
Were I as much stronger as I am weaker than you,
You would soon regret this drawing away from the battle.
But come, drive out at Patroclus these strong-hoofed horses
Of yours, and see if Apollo will grant you the glory
Of bringing that great fighter down."

So saying, the god
Re-entered the tumult of toiling mortals. And Hector,
840 Resplendent, gave orders to fiery Cebriones to lash
The team into battle. Meanwhile, Apollo, back
In the turmoil of slaughter, spread mid the slashing Argives
Evil confusion and gave the glory to Trojans
And Hector. But Hector, ignoring all other Danaans,
Did not attempt to kill any of them, but drove
His strong-hoofed horses straight and fast at Patroclus,
Who opposite him leaped down from his car to the ground
With a spear in his left hand, while with his right he caught up
A hand-fitting stone, jagged and sparkling. Then,
850 With no long awe of Hector, he hurled it with all
Of his weight in the throw, nor did he hurl in vain,
For the sharp stone hit Hector's driver Cebriones, bastard
Son of world-famous Priam, hit him squarely
Between the eyes as he held the reins of the horses,
Bashing the bone in, bringing both of his brows together
And dropping his eyes in the dust below his feet.
And like a diver he pitched from the well-made car
As life took leave of his bones forever. Then,
O horseman Patroclus, you shouted these mocking words:
860   "Aha! what a fine acrobat that warrior is!
What a really superb somersault! Truly, if he
Were out on the fish-full sea, he could bring up bushels
Of oysters, no matter how rough the water, leaping in
From the deck of his ship as now he turns flips from his
                    chariot
Here on the plain. I had no idea they had
Such performers in Troy!"[11]
                    With this he charged at the fallen
Cebriones with a spring like that of a wounded lion,
A beast undone by his own fierce heart, that gets
870 A spear in the chest while raiding a cattle-pen.
Even so on Cebriones, O Patroclus, you sprang
In your fury. And opposite him huge Hector leaped down
From his car to the ground, and the pair squared off to fight
For the corpse, quite like a couple of lions that high
Mid the peaks of a mountain contend for a slaughtered stag,
Both equally hungry and savage of heart. So now
For Cebriones those two masters of combat, Patroclus,
Son of Menoetius, and all-shining Hector, were eager
To gash each other's flesh with the pitiless bronze.

But Hector had hold of the corpse by the head and would not   880
Let go, and Patroclus held fast to one foot, while around them
The others, Trojans and Danaans, pitted their powers
In battle. And as the East Wind and the South compete
With each other at tossing the trees in a thick-wooded glen
Of the mountains, a forest of beech and ash and smooth-barked
Cornel trees, the long boughs of which strike against one another
With a fearful noise of knocking and breaking branches,
So now the Achaeans and Trojans clashed man to man
And struck deadly blows left and right, nor would either side think
Of disastrous retreat. All around Cebriones' body   890
Keen-pointed spears stuck up in the earth, and the ground
Fairly bristled with feathered arrows that eagerly sprang
From the bowstrings. And many huge stones bashed into the shields
As the warriors battled about him. But Cebriones lay
In the swirling dust, forgetful of chariot-skill,
Though mighty even in death.

      Now as long as the Sun
Climbed up toward mid-heaven, the missiles of both sides struck
        home,
And the warriors fell. But when he turned toward the time
When oxen are loosed from the yoke,* then the Achaeans,   900
In a manner surpassing their lot and power, proved stronger.
Dragging Cebriones from under the missiles
And away from the screaming Trojans, they stripped his shoulders
Of armor, but Patroclus returned for more fierce fighting.
Ferociously now he charged on the Trojans. Three times
This peer of the fast-fighting War-god sprang at the foe,
Yelling his blood-chilling cry, and three times he slaughtered
Nine men. But when like a demon he charged a fourth time,
Then at last, O Patroclus, the end of your life came in sight.†
For there in the mighty struggle Apollo came at you,   910
An awesome grim god indeed! And he was unseen
By Patroclus as on through the turmoil he came in a thick
Cloud of mist. Then standing behind him, Apollo struck
His back and broad shoulders hard with the flat of his hand,
Whirling the eyes of Patroclus. Off came his high-crested
Helmet and rolled with a clang mid the horses' feet,

---

*Oxen are unyoked when the day is two-thirds done; the sun's descent bodes Patroclus'
final hour.
†See XVI.806–809, with endnote 10, for the triple charge.

And the plumes were smirched with blood and dust. Never
Before had this been allowed, to foul with dust
That horsehair-crested helmet, for always before
920 It guarded the head and handsome brow of the son
Of a goddess, Achilles himself. But now Zeus allowed it
To come into Hector's possession, that he might wear it
The little while he yet had to live on earth.
And in Patroclus' hands the long-shadowing, bronze-pointed
Spear, though huge and heavy and strong, was broken
To pieces, and from his shoulders the tasseled shield
With its baldric fell in the dust, as lord Apollo,
Son of Zeus, stripped off his breastplate. Then,
His mind dazed and his splendid body unable to move,
930 He stood in a stupor, till a young Dardanian struck him
Between the shoulders with a short spear-cast from behind,
Even Panthous' son Euphorbus, he who surpassed
All fighters his age as a spearman, horseman, and runner,
And who had already hurled twenty warriors down
From their cars at this his first time with a chariot, fighting
In actual combat. He it was, O knightly
Patroclus, who first got his bronze in your flesh. But when
You remained on your feet, he jerked the ash spear from your
            body
And lost himself in the throng. For Euphorbus had no
940 Intention of facing Patroclus in that fiery fight,
Completely unarmed though he was.

        Now Patroclus, stunned
And weak from the blow of Apollo and wound of the spear,
Fell back mid a crowd of his comrades, avoiding sure death.
But Hector, aware that great-souled Patroclus was wounded
And drawing back, charged down on him through the ranks
And drove his bronze-headed spear clean through his lower
Belly and back, and Patroclus fell with a dull,
Disheartening thud, filling the host of Achaeans
950 With horror and grief. As a lion at last gets the best
Of a weariless boar, when the two most savagely fight
Mid the peaks of a mountain for one small pool of water
Which both are thirsty to drink from—the wheezing, obstreperous
Boar fights hard, but the lion is stronger and wins—
So now from Menoetius' brave son, after he had himself
Slain many, Priam's son Hector took the life,
Standing right by him and thrusting him through with his spear.
Then he spoke these words, harsh and winged with vaunting:

"Patroclus, you thought, I suppose, that you would level
Our city, then take all freedom away from the women   960
Of Troy and carry them back in your ships to your own
Dear country, poor infantile fool that you are! In defense
Of those women Hector's fast horses go galloping forth
To the fight, where I surpass with the spear all other
War-loving Trojans, I that keep from my people
The hard day of doom. As for you, vultures shall pick
Your bones right here. Ah miserable wretch! not even
Achilles, for all his great prowess, could help you, he
That remained in the camp, but gave you careful instruction,
I'm sure, saying, as forth you sallied: 'Do not   970
Come back to these hollow ships, O Patroclus, commander
Of horsemen, until you have torn the tunic on murderous
Hector's breast and soaked it red with his blood!'
Ah yes, I can hear him saying it now, and you
Were the miserable fool he persuaded!"
          Then very feebly,
O dying Patroclus, you answered him thus: "For this time,
Hector, make your high vaunt, for Cronos' son Zeus
And Apollo have given you victory, though they themselves
Are the ones who broke me and stripped my shoulders of armor.   980
Not twenty Hectors could ever have done it, but all
Would surely have died on this plain beneath my long spear.
Pernicious fate in the form of Apollo slew me,
And a man named Euphorbus—while Hector came third in my
          slaying.[12]
And here's something else that you will do well to remember:
Namely, that you yourself are not very long
For this life, since death and powerful fate are standing
Beside you even now, and they will surely
See to it that you go down in death at the hands
Of mighty Achilles, Aeacus' matchless grandson."   990
          As thus he spoke, the final end arrived,
And his soul flew forth from his body and journeyed to Hades,
Bewailing her lot as one too soon bereft
Of youth and manly vigor. And now to the corpse
Of his foe, all-shining Hector spoke thus:
          "Patroclus,
Why do you prophesy my sheer ruin? Who knows
But that Achilles, though son of fair-haired Thetis,
May first lose his life to me and become a spear-victim
Of mine?"   1000

So saying, he put one foot on the corpse
And wrenched the bronze head from the wound, shoving the body
Back from the spear. And at once he took off with the weapon
In pursuit of Automedon, godlike squire of Achilles
The swift, for Hector was eager to bring him down too.
But the horses Automedon drove kept him ahead,
The deathless swift horses of Peleus, bright gifts of the gods.

BOOK XVII

The Valiant Deeds of Menelaus

Now King Menelaus, beloved of Ares, saw
That in the hot struggle Trojans had slain Patroclus,
And armored in flaming bronze he charged through the front rank
Of fighters and took his stand, bestriding the corpse
Of his comrade, as over her first-born calf a cow stands
Plaintively lowing. So now tawny-haired Menelaus
Stood over Patroclus, holding his spear and round shield
At the ready, raging to kill whoever might come
Against him.
     And Panthous' son Euphorbus, he   10
Of the tough ashen spear, was also well aware
That peerless Patroclus had fallen, and coming up close
He spoke these words to Ares-loved Menelaus:
"Atrides, nurtured of Zeus, commander of armies,
Fall back and leave the body and leave, I say,
The bloody war-gear. For none before me of the Trojans
And their far-famed allies got a spear in Patroclus
In this huge battle. Therefore, allow me to finish
My triumph and win great renown in the city of Troy,
Or I with one throw will deprive you of honey-sweet life!"   20
    Then deeply angered, tawny Menelaus replied:
"Great God almighty! how poor a thing arrogance is!
Of course no leopard or lion or even ferocious
Wild boar, most mighty and savage of beasts, has anything
Like the fierce spirit of Panthous' sons, men
Of the tough ashen spear. Maybe so, but the strong Hyperenor,*
Panthous' horse-breaking son, got very little
From his short life, once he had made light of my prowess
And stood up against me, thinking that I was the weakest
Of Danaan warriors. It was not, I say, on feet   30
Of his own that he went back to gladden the heart

---

*Menelaus killed Hyperenor at XIV.592–596.

Of his darling wife and delight his excellent parents.
Nor will I fail to undo your strength, Euphorbus,
If now you stay and confront me. But I myself warn you
Not to do so, but lose yourself in the crowd
Before you suffer disaster. Once it occurs,
It will be too late for you not to play the fool!"

He spoke, but words brought only this from Euphorbus:
"Now indeed, O god-fed King Menelaus, you shall pay
40   Every jot of the price for my brother, about whose death
It seems you're still bragging. And truly you are the blackguard
Who widowed his bride, withdrawn in her new bridal chamber,
And heaped indescribable anguish and grief on his parents.
But now I've a chance to soften their sorrow, if only
I bring your head and bloody armor and toss them
Proudly in Panthous' hands and in those of his wife,
The beautiful Phrontis. But on with the fight! It will not
Take long to decide it and see whose strength will be first
To give in."

50   So saying, he stabbed the round shield. But instead
Of the bronze tearing on through, the point was turned
By the sturdy buckler. Then Atreus' son Menelaus
Lunged with his spear, praying to Father Zeus.
And as Euphorbus fell back, he plunged his bronze in
At the pit of his throat, with faith in his beefy hand
And all of his weight behind it, and the point passed clean
Through Euphorbus' soft neck, sending him crashing to earth
With a ringing of armor about him. Warm blood now ran through
His hair, which had been like the hair of the Graces, braided
60   And bound with silver and gold and gathered in
As a wasp is. And like a lusty young olive tree
That a man tries to grow in a lonely place, where water
Plentifully burbles, a slender flourishing sapling
That sways with all of the breezes that blow and puts out
Lovely white blossoms, till all at once a hurricane
Comes and tearing it up from its trench lays it out
Undone on the earth, even such was Euphorbus, he
Of the tough ashen spear, whom Atreus' son Menelaus
Stretched out in death and started to strip of his armor.

70   And as when a mountain-bred lion with trust in his brawn
Springs on the choicest heifer in all of a grazing
Herd and snaps her neck in his powerful jaws,
Then gulps her entrails and laps his fill of her blood,
While at a safe distance around him the hounds and herdsmen

Raise a great racket but lack the courage to come
Any nearer, since olive-pale fear grips all of them hard,
So now not one of the Trojans dared go and face
Renowned Menelaus. Hence quite simply would he
Have carried away the glorious gear of Euphorbus,
If Phoebus Apollo had not begrudged him the spoils,   80
And so, in the form of Mentes, a leader among
The Cicones, stirred up huge Hector against him, approaching
That peer of the fast-fighting War-god and speaking to him
In these winged words:

    "Hector, you race after what
You can never attain, the horses of fire-souled Achilles.
Besides, no mere mortal can well control those horses.
Only Achilles can, for he is the son
Of an immortal mother. Meanwhile, warlike Menelaus
Stands over Patroclus and has already cut down   90
The best of the Trojans, Panthous' son Euphorbus,
Whose furious war-charge has now been ended forever!"

    So saying, the god re-entered the tumult of mortals.
But Hector's heart was packed with darkest torment,
As he looked across the ranks and quickly spotted
King Menelaus stripping the glorious war-gear
From dead Euphorbus, stretched out on the ground with blood
Still running down from the horrible spear-wound. Then Hector
Strode out through the foremost fighters, armored in flaming
Bronze and screaming his awesome war-cry, a man   100
Like the flame of Hephaestus, not easily quenched. Nor did
Menelaus fail to hear that heart-piercing cry,
And now deeply troubled he spoke to his own great heart:

    "Ah miserable me! if I should leave behind me
This exquisite bronze and Patroclus too, who lies here
Fallen in my behalf, then surely every
Danaan fighter who sees me will show his contempt.
But if, upholding my honor, I stand all alone
To do battle with Hector and other Trojans, I'm afraid
They'll surround me, their many against my one, for now   110
Bright-helmeted Hector is leading all of the Trojans
This way. Why, then, do I argue thus with myself?
Any man at all who insists on fighting another
Whom God himself sponsors, quickly brings on his head
A great wave of woe. Therefore, no Danaan fighter
Who sees me fall back before Hector will blame me one bit,
Since surely Hector's strength comes directly from God.

Even so, if only I might find powerful Ajax,
Good at the shrill battle-scream, we two could turn
120 And regain our stomach for fighting, even though we did it
In God's despite, still hoping and trying to win
For Peleus' son Achilles the corpse of his friend.
So something, at least, would be saved."[1]
              While he so pondered
In mind and heart, the Trojan troops came on
With Hector leading. And now Menelaus retreated,
Leaving the corpse and turning from side to side,
Like a bearded lion that dogs and angry men
Drive from a cattle-pen, hurling their spears and shouting
130 Till his heart so valiant before soon freezes with fear,
And reluctantly he goes forth, leaving the farmyard.
So now from Patroclus went tawny Menelaus. But when
He reached the mass of his men, he turned and stood,
Looking all over for great Telamonian Ajax.
Quickly he saw him on the far left flank of the battle,
Cheering his men and urging them on in the fight,
For Phoebus Apollo had filled them with panic. Menelaus
Took off at a run and soon he came up to him, saying:
              "Ajax, good friend, come with me, and let the two of us
140 Hurry to fight for the dead Patroclus, that we
May at least carry back his corpse to Achilles—his naked
Corpse, for already bright-helmeted Hector has taken
The armor!"
              These words deeply stirred huge flame-hearted Ajax,
Who rapidly strode away through the front rank of champions
With tawny Menelaus beside him. Now Hector had finished
The stripping of dead Patroclus and was at that moment
Dragging the corpse to where he could cut off the head
With his keen-bladed bronze and give the trunk to the lean dogs
150 Of Troy. But when Ajax approached him, bearing his shield
Like a tower, Hector fell back, merged with his men,
And leaped on his chariot. First, though, he gave the exquisite
Armor to comrades of his, that they might carry it
Into the city to be his most glorious trophy.
Meanwhile, Ajax stood over Patroclus, covering
Him with his huge broad shield, bestriding him there
Like a lioness over her cubs, one that hunters
Have met as through the forest she leads her litter,
And that, in the pride of her power, lowers her brows
160 Till her eyes are mere slits as she awaits their attack.

Even so, great Ajax bestrode heroic Patroclus,
And by him stood Atreus' son Menelaus, who,
Though the War-god's favorite, was seething with still-growing sorrow.
    Then Glaucus, Hippolochus' son and leader of Lycians,
Scowled darkly at Hector and harshly berated him thus:
"Hector, your looks are surely impressive enough,
But a fight finds you wanting. It seems that your great reputation
Belongs to one who is really a cowardly turntail!
Just ask yourself how you intend to save your city
And home with no other help than that provided   170
By native-born Trojans. For at least not one of the Lycians
Will fight any longer to save your town from the Danaans,
Since now we know there were never to be any thanks
At all for our ceaseless efforts against the foe.
For how, O stone-hearted one, how in the heat
Of battle would you ever help any ordinary soldier
When here you have left Sarpedon, your guest and your friend,
To be the Argives' victim and spoil? And Sarpedon
Was one to whom you owed much, both your whole city
And you, though now you lack the courage to keep   180
The dogs from his body. Therefore, if the Lycians will listen
To me, we'll all go home and leave your city
To certain and utter destruction. But if only there were
In the Trojans that dauntless, unshakable valor that should
Possess men who labor and fight in defense of their country,
Then we right quickly would drag Patroclus to Ilium.
And if we should do so, haling his body from battle
And into King Priam's great city, the Argives would soon
Return the splendid war-gear of Sarpedon, and then
We would bring into Ilium his body too. For the man   190
About whom we fight was the friend of a very great soldier,
By far the best of all Argives here with the ships
And the leader of truly superior close-fighting troops.
But you most lamentably lacked what it takes to stand
Face to face with huge-hearted Ajax and look him straight
In the eyes and do battle with him in the fiery midst
Of war-screaming men, for he is much stronger than you!"[2]
    Then scowling at him, bright-helmeted Hector replied:
"Glaucus, why would such a man as you are say anything
So uncalled for? Truly, good friend, I thought you   200
The wisest of all who live in rich-landed Lycia.
But now I would not give a straw for your understanding,
Since you have accused me of running from monstrous Ajax.

Believe me, I'm not one who shudders at bloody battle
Nor at thundering horses. But always God's will is stronger
By far than man's. Aegis-great Zeus can make
The bravest fighter retreat and easily keep him
From winning, especially when he inspires another
To fight like fury against him. So come, my friend,
210 Go by my side and observe my prowess in battle.
Just see throughout this whole day if ever I act
Like the coward you call me, or if instead I don't stop
Many Danaans, eager for war though they be, from fighting
To win dead Patroclus."
     So saying, he sent a great cry
Ringing out to the Trojans, shouting: "You Trojans and Lycians
And dueling Dardanians, now, my friends, be men,
And filled with furious boldness! while I put on
The bright armor of matchless Achilles, the splendid war-gear
220 I took from stalwart Patroclus once I had slain him."
     So saying, Hector, his bronze helmet flashing, left
The fiery conflict, and rapidly running he soon
Caught up with his comrades, who had not yet got very far
Toward town with Achilles' famous and exquisite armor.
Then standing apart from the tearful struggle, he changed
His war-gear, giving his own to the fight-loving Trojans
To carry to sacred Ilium, and putting on
The immortal bronze of Peleus' son Achilles,
Armor the heavenly gods had given his father
230 And that he, when old, had given his son, who never
Lived to be old in the armor he had from his father.[3]
     Now when from far off cloud-gathering Zeus saw Hector
Donning the war-gear of Peleus' godlike son,
He shook his head and spoke to his own heart thus:
"Ah wretched mortal! you have no thoughts at all
Of death, though death draws very near you. Instead,
You are donning the immortal armor of a most valiant man,
Before whom you're not the only one who trembles,
You that have killed his brave and lovable friend
240 And ignobly taken his war-gear. For a while, however,
I'll give you great martial force, in return for which
You must forfeit your sweet home-coming from battle. Never
Will your Andromache take from the hands of her husband
The glorious armor of Peleus' son Achilles."
     He spoke, then bowing his iron-dark brows he made
The armor fit well on the body of Hector, into whom

Now came the spirit of Ares, the grim god of slaughter,
And his limbs were renewed from within with spirit and vigor.
Then he went back to his famous allies, roaring
His powerful war-cry, and all of them saw him there   250
Resplendently clad in the bronze of huge-hearted Achilles.
Going up and down among them, he cheered and encouraged
Each man he could—Mesthles and Glaucus and Medon,
Thersilochus, Asteropaeus, Deisenor, and Phorcys,
Hippothous, Chromius, and Ennomus, reader of bird-signs—
All these he encouraged, speaking to them winged words:
     "Listen, you unnumbered nations of neighboring allies.
I did not call you men here from your native cities
Merely to swell the army of Troy, but that
You might willingly save the Trojans' children and wives   260
From these warmongering Achaeans. For this reason only
I've all but exhausted the goods of my people that you
Might have food and presents and a daily renewal of spirit.
Therefore let every last man of you here charge straight
At the enemy, heedless of whether you live or die—
For such is the game of battle. And whoever forces
Ajax to yield and drags Patroclus, dead
Though he is, into the midst of horse-breaking Trojans,
With that man I'll split the spoils half and half, and his glory
Shall be as mine is!"   270
     He ended, and all of them rushed
Headlong on the Danaans, holding their spears up high
And eagerly hopeful of dragging the corpse of Patroclus
From beneath the great Ajax, poor childish fools that they were!
For truly over that corpse he was to take
The lives of many in that attack. But now
Even Ajax spoke thus to battle-roaring Atrides:
     "O god-fed good Menelaus, I no longer think
That even we two can back out off this fight by ourselves.
Nor am I by any means so much concerned for the corpse   280
Of Patroclus, that soon shall glut the dogs and birds
Of the Trojans, as now I am for the safety of my head
And yours. For yonder comes glowering Hector, a terribly
Dark cloud of war enshrouding us all, and we two
Especially are sure to die—unless, my friend,
You can call to the other Danaan chiefs and make
Someone hear!"
     He spoke, and battle-roaring Menelaus
Did not ignore him, but shouted a far-piercing cry

290 To the chiefs: "O friends, captains and counselors
    Of the Argives, you that drink the community wine
    With Atreus' sons Menelaus and King Agamemnon
    And issue orders to your respective commands—
    All you that receive your rank and honor from Zeus—
    I cannot now easily pick you separately out,
    So hotly blazes the huge strife of battle.
    But now let each of you come on the double, with no
    Special summons from me, and with you bring fierce indignation
    Lest the poor corpse of Patroclus soon become
300 The delight of Trojan dogs."
            Then the son of Oïleus,
    Ajax the racer, heard every word, and he
    Was the first to come running through the hot fighting, and
                    Idomeneus
    Followed and Idomeneus' comrade Meriones, that peer
    Of the slaughtering War-god. But as for the others who came
    To support those Achaeans, who has the mind to recall them
    And name all the names?
            Then the Trojans, with Hector leading,
    Charged all together. And as when a gigantic wave
310 Roars in at the mouth of some Zeus-fed river, opposing
    The flow, and the headlands resound on either side
    As the salt-sea booms against them, so now with a din
    As great the clamoring Trojans came on. But now
    The Achaeans stood round the corpse of Patroclus, firm
    And unflinching, united in purpose and walled about
    With bronze shields. And Cronos' son Zeus shed a heavy mantle
    Of mist down over their bright-flashing helmets, for Patroclus,
    While he was alive and the friend of Achilles, had never
    Been disliked by Zeus, and now he hated to see
320 His body become the delight of his enemies' dogs.[4]
    Hence Zeus aroused his comrades in defense.
            But at first the Trojans dislodged the quick-eyed Achaeans,
    Who left the corpse and shrank back in fear, but not
    One man did the eager Trojans lay low with their spears,
    For they turned their efforts to dragging the corpse away.
    The Achaeans, however, did not stay back very long,
    For Ajax rallied them quickly—Ajax, who
    In form and fighting surpassed all the Danaan chiefs
    But the peerless son of Peleus. Straight through the front rank
330 Of fighters he burst with the furious might of a foaming

Wild boar that wheels at bay in some glade of the mountains
And easily scatters the hounds and lusty young hunters.
Thus great Telamon's son, the illustrious Ajax,
Charged mid the Trojan battalions and scattered them quickly,
Though they had taken their stand round Patroclus, fiercely
Determined to drag him into their city and so
Win the glory themselves.

    Already Hippothous, splendid
Son of Pelasgian Lethus, was dragging the corpse
Through the melee, having bound his baldric about one ankle   340
In his eager effort to please the Trojans and Hector.
But swiftly indeed he met with disaster, an evil
That no one, however zealous, could then have kept from him.
For Ajax came darting in through the crowd and plunged
A spear through his bronze-cheeked helmet, and the headpiece crested
With horsehair was split round the point, and Hippothous' blood-
        mingled
Brains spurted out from the wound and ran down along
The socket and shaft of the weapon. Right there his strength
Was dissolved, and letting the foot of great-souled Patroclus
Fall to the ground, he fell very quickly himself,   350
Face down on the corpse, far away from loamy Larissa.
And for his careful upbringing he never repaid
His dear parents, since now his life was cut short by the spear
Of spirited Ajax.

    Then Hector met his advance
With a cast of his own bright spear. But Ajax, looking
Straight at him, just managed to dodge the hurtling bronze,
Which flew on to lodge in Schedius, magnanimous Iphitus'
Son and best by far of the Phocians, one
Who lived in a mansion as lord over many at Panopeus,   360
World-renowned. Hector's spear hit him squarely just under
The collarbone, tore on through, and came out at the base
Of his shoulder. And royal Schedius clanged to the ground
With a clashing of brazen war-gear. Then Ajax in turn
Killed flame-hearted Phorcys, son of Phaenops, striking him
Full in the gut as he boldly bestrode Hippothous.
The bronze cut a gash in his armor, through which his entrails
Oozed, and Phorcys, falling full length in the dust,
Clawed at the earth. Then glorious Hector and the foremost
Trojan fighters gave ground, and the yelling Argives   370
Dragged off the bodies of Phorcys and Hippothous and stripped

Their shoulders of armor.
     And now the fiery Achaeans
Would surely have driven the weary, terrified Trojans
Back up into Troy, and so by dint of sheer force
And power have won more glory than Zeus intended,
If Phoebus Apollo himself had not roused Aeneas,
Appearing to him in the form of his old father's herald,
Periphas, Epytus' son, a kindly man
380 Who had served long and well in the house of Anchises. Looking
Exactly like him, Apollo, son of Zeus,
Came up to Aeneas and spoke:
     "How in the world,
Aeneas, would you ever defend steep Troy if God
Were against you? as indeed I have seen others do, putting
Their faith in their own manly prowess and that of their fellows
And holding their realm in defiance of Zeus himself.
But here Zeus clearly wills the victory for us
Far more than he does for the Danaans, yet you are much
390 Too afraid to do any real fighting!"
     He spoke, and Aeneas
Looked on his face and knew him at once for Apollo,
The god who strikes from afar, and lifting his voice
He shouted to Hector and all of the others, saying:
"O leaders of Trojans and Trojan allies, what
A disgrace it will be if now these fiery Achaeans
Drive the terrified Trojans back up into Troy!
But truly a god just stood by my side and assured me
That all-knowing Zeus is still on our side in the battle.
400 So let us charge straight for the Danaans and make all the trouble
We can for them as they struggle to get to the ships
With the body of dead Patroclus."
     With this he sprang
Far out in front of the first-line champions and stood,
And the Trojans rallied and turned to face the Achaeans.
Then with a thrust of his spear Aeneas brought down
Leocritus, son of Arisbas and excellent comrade
Of Lycomedes. And as he fell Lycomedes,
Dear to the War-god, felt pity for him, and coming
410 In close he hurled his bright spear and struck Apisaon,
Hippasus' son and the people's lord, in the liver
Under the midriff, thus suddenly causing his knees
To buckle—Apisaon from fertile Paeonia, who next to
Asteropaeus surpassed all the rest of his people

In fighting. And as he fell this Asteropaeus,
Dear to the War-god, felt pity for him and fiercely
Charged in to battle the Danaans. He, however,
Charged in vain, for he met a wall of bronze shields
Bristling with spears, long lances held by the chieftains
Who stood round the corpse of Patroclus. For Ajax was busy   420
Among them shouting orders, instructing them strictly
To hold their ground, with none either falling back
Or boldly fighting in front of the other Achaeans,
But all, he said, should stand fast by the body and fight
Hand to hand.
    Such were the commands of gigantic Ajax,
And quickly the earth was empurpled with blood as the dead
Fell thick and fast, the Trojan dead and the dead
Of their proud allies, and the dead of the Danaans too,
For they fought no bloodless encounter, though of them far fewer   430
Were falling, since always they tried in the melee to keep death
Away from each other.
    Thus war's holocaust blazed on,
Nor would you have thought either sun or moon were shining,
So thick was the dark cloud of mist that enshrouded the struggle
Of all the great fighters who fought round Menoetius' dead son.
But the other Trojans and well-greaved Achaeans fought
In relative comfort beneath a clear sky, from which
The piercing rays of the sun shone down upon them,
And no cloud could be seen above either the plain or the mountains.   440
These fought at intervals, resting from time to time
And standing apart far enough to avoid the groan-fraught
Shafts of the foe. Those leaders around the body,
However, were greatly distressed by the fog and the fighting
And suffered much from the weight of their pitiless bronze.
Two chiefs were not there, Antilochus and Thrasymedes,
For they did not know that flawless Patroclus was dead.
They thought he was still alive and fighting the Trojans
Up front. Meanwhile, they fought in another part
Of the field, looking out to avoid both death and panic   450
Among their companions, as Nestor had told them to do
When he sent them away from the black-hulled vessels and forth
Into battle.
    So all day long their hard hatred raged,
And the knees and legs and face of each man, the arms
And the eyes, incessantly streamed with the sweat of their toil,
As the two armies fought round swift Achilles' dead friend.

And as when a man gives a large bull's-hide to his people
For stretching, one already drenched in fat, and they
460 Stand apart in a circle and pull away at the sides
Till its own moisture goes and the fat sinks in, many men
Tugging with all of their might to stretch it as taut
As they can, so now all around they were tugging away
At the corpse, with neither side making much gain, though still
Their hearts were full of hope, the Trojans eager
To drag the body to Troy, the Achaeans pulling
Toward the hollow ships. And around the corpse the struggle
Grew savagely wild, as on the strong champions fought,
Nor could even host-urging Ares nor Pallas Athena
470 Have seen them so and made light of their efforts, no matter
How spiteful those deities were.

     Even such was the toil
Of evil war that Zeus strained taut that day
Over dead Patroclus. Nor as yet did godlike Achilles
Have any knowledge at all of Patroclus' death,
For the fighting went on beneath the Trojan wall
Far away from the swift-running ships. Hence Achilles had
No idea what had happened, but thought his friend would surely
Return alive after he had pressed eagerly on
480 To the very gates of Troy. He knew that Patroclus
Would not sack the city without him, nor with him either,*
For often his goddess mother had told him in private
What almighty Zeus was planning. Now, however,
She did not let him know of the monstrous thing that had
     happened,
That now his most precious friend had been destroyed.

     Meanwhile, round the dead body the fighters continued
To clash, constantly killing with sharp-pointed spears.
And thus would one of the bronze-clad Achaeans shout:
"O friends, it would scarcely be to our credit for us
490 To go back to the hollow ships without the body.
Far better for us if at once the black earth would engulf us
All, if now we're to give these horse-taming Trojans
The glory of dragging Patroclus to their city!"

     And likewise one of the spirited Trojans would yell:
"O friends, though all of us here be destined to die

---

*Achilles had thought that he and Patroclus would not sack Troy together; see XVIII.12–13
(with endnote) and XIX.371–374.

By this body, yet let not a man of us shrink one foot
From the fighting!"
　　　Thus they would cry to encourage and strengthen
Each other as on they fought. And the iron din
Went up through empty air to the burnished bronze sky.   500
But apart from the battle Achilles' horses were weeping,
And had been so since first they learned that their fighter
Had gone down dead in the dust at the murderous hands
Of Hector. Surely Automedon, stalwart son
Of Diores, had done all he could to move them, laying on
Many hard blows with his flying swift lash and alternately
Coaxing and cursing for all he was worth. But the pair
Refused to go back to the ships and the broad Hellespont,
Nor would they go into battle among the Achaeans.
Instead, they stood with the ornate car, still   510
As a pillar of stone on the grave of some dead man or woman,
Bowing their heads to the ground.[5] And their hot tears
Fell on the earth as they mourned for Patroclus, and both
Their luxuriant manes were dirtied with dust as they streamed
From under the yoke-pad on either side of the yoke.
And as they wept, Zeus saw and felt compassion.
Shaking his head he spoke to his own heart thus:
　　　"Poor wretches! why did we give you to Peleus the King,
A mortal, while you are immortal and ageless? Was it
That you too might suffer the woes of unhappy men?   520
For of all the creatures that breathe and move on earth,
I know there is none more utterly wretched than man.
At any rate Priam's son Hector shall never mount up
In your colorful car, since that I will not allow.
Is it not quite enough that he wears Achilles' armor
And makes his vain boast about it? But now I'll put
New strength in your hearts and legs that you may carry
Automedon safely from war to the hollow ships.
For I shall give more glory still to the Trojans,
Urging them on until they have driven the Argives   530
Back to the well-timbered ships, steadily killing
Till the sun goes down and powerful darkness arrives."
　　　So saying, he breathed noble ardor into the horses,
And shaking the dust from their manes they took off at a gallop
And drew the swift car mid the moil of Achaeans and Trojans.
And Automedon fought behind them, though greatly grieved
For his friend Patroclus, swooping in with the car
Like a vulture that falls on a large flock of geese. Rapidly

He would dash in through the huge chaos of battle,
540 Then rapidly flee. But fast though he went in the sacred
Car, it was more than one man could do to handle
Both spear and horses at once, so Automedon slew
Not a single man as in and out he charged.
But at last a comrade noticed his actions, Alcimedon,
Son of Laerces and grandson of Haemon, and standing
Behind the chariot he spoke to him thus:
          "What god,
Automedon, has so deluded your excellent mind
That now you fight in this manner amid the Trojans—
550 Up front and completely alone? For your fighter and friend
Is dead, and the armor he wore is now on the shoulders
Of Hector, who glories in wearing the famous bronze
Of Achilles."
          And Automedon, son of Diores: "What man,
Alcimedon, equals you at holding and driving
Immortal horses? No one but Patroclus, godlike
In skill, was as good, and now death's doom has engulfed him.
Come then, you take the lash and glossy reins
And I'll be the one to dismount and do the fighting."
560   He spoke, and Alcimedon sprang on the battle-swift car
And caught up the lash and reins as Automedon leaped
To the ground. Then shining Hector noticed them there
And quickly spoke thus to Aeneas nearby: "O counselor
Of bronze-breasted Trojans, yonder I see the two horses
Of Aeacus' grandson Achilles appearing in battle
With two really puny charioteers. If you
Are willing, I'm sure we can capture that fine pair of chargers,
Since those two weaklings with them will never stand up
To us and fight man to man."
570   Such were his words,
And Anchises' brave son agreed. Then they charged straight ahead,
Their shoulders protected by shields of bull's-hide, well-tanned
And tough and covered with plenty of hammered-on bronze.
And with them went godlike Aretus and Chromius too,
And all of them went full of hope to kill the two men
And drive off the neck-arching horses—poor infantile fools
That they were! For not without shedding blood of their own
Were they to get back from Automedon. He now made his prayer
To Father Zeus, and within him his dark-seething heart
580 Was infused with spirit and power. Then he spoke thus
To his trusted companion Alcimedon:

"Come now, good friend,
And don't hold those horses too far away, but let me
Feel their hot breath on my back as I fight. For truly
I don't think that Priam's son Hector will run out of fury
Until, having killed both of us, he springs up behind
Achilles' mane-tossing horses and routs the ranks
Of the Argive warriors, unless he himself should fall
Mid the foremost."

    So saying, he called to the two Ajaxes   590
And King Menelaus: "You Ajaxes both, leaders
Of Argives, and you, Menelaus, come now! Leave the corpse
With those who are bravest to hold their ground and keep off
The enemy ranks, and keep off from us, the yet living,
The pitiless day of our doom. For now charging down
On us hard through the tear-fraught toil come Aeneas and Hector,
The bravest of Trojans. The outcome lies in the lap
Of the gods. So here goes my cast, and may Zeus determine
The issue of all."

    With this, he drew back his long-shadowing   600
Spear and hurling it struck the round shield of Aretus,
And the keen bronze cut its way through, went on through his belt
And deep in his belly. And as when a powerful man
Comes down hard with a keen-cutting ax on the head
Of a field-ranging ox just back of the horns and cuts
Clean through the bone, causing the beast to lurch forward
And fall, so now Aretus sprang forward, then fell
On his back, and the quivering, razor-keen spear in his guts
Unstrung his limbs. Then Hector hurled his bright spear
At Automedon, who looking straight at him avoided the bronze   610
By ducking forward, and Hector's long lance embedded
Itself in the ground behind its intended victim,
Where the butt-end quivered till finally hulking Ares
Stilled its fury. And now the two would have closed
And cut at each other with swords, if the two Ajaxes
Had not intervened, for when they answered the call
Of their comrade and came through the melee, fear seized Aeneas
And Hector and godlike Chromius, and back they fell,
Leaving dead Aretus stretched out on the earth. And Automedon,
Peer of the fast-fighting War-god, stripped off the armor   620
And made his boast, exulting:

    "Surely I've got
Some small satisfaction now for the death of Patroclus,
Though this man I've killed cannot be compared with him."

So saying, he picked up the bloody war-gear, and placing it
In the chariot he mounted, his feet and hands
Smeared with blood, like a lion fresh from devouring a bull.

And again the hard struggle, tearful and grim, was strained
Inhumanly taut above the corpse of Patroclus,
630 And Pallas Athena came down from the sky and augmented
The strife. For loud-thundering Zeus, whose purpose was
                                changing,
Had sent her to urge on the Danaans. As when Zeus arches
An ominous rainbow across the sky as a portent
Of war or chilling storm that makes men on earth
Stop work and bothers the flocks, so now Athena,
Shrouding herself in a lurid cloud, entered
The Danaan host and incited the heart of each man.
The first she encouraged was strong Menelaus, he being
Nearby. Assuming the form and weariless voice
640 Of Phoenix, she spoke to him thus:
                              "To you, for sure,
Menelaus, head-hanging shame will come, if the faithful
Friend of haughty Achilles be ripped by swift dogs
Beneath the Trojan wall. So hold your ground
With all of your might and urge on all of the others!"

Then King Menelaus, he of the shrill battle-scream,
Replied: "Phoenix, old sire, my ancient-born friend,
If only Athena would give me strength and keep off
The raining missiles, I surely would like nothing better
650 Than this defense of Patroclus' body, for deeply
His death has pierced my very heart. But Hector
Rages like furious fire and doesn't let up
At all with his deadly havocking bronze. Obviously
Zeus has decided to give the glory to him."

At this the blue eyes of Athena blazed with delight,
Since in his appeal he had mentioned her first of all gods.
And she put strength in his shoulders and legs and infused
His heart with the daring persistency of a fly,
That always comes back for more no matter how often
660 It be brushed away from one's skin, so dauntless is it
In stinging and so very fond of man's blood. With such
Bold daring as that she filled his dark-seething heart,
And standing over Patroclus he hurled his bright spear.
Now among the Trojans was one both wealthy and brave,
Podes, son of Eëtion, and he was the favorite
Of Hector, a man with whom he had shared very many

Fine dinners. Him tawny-haired Menelaus pierced
With his bronze through war-belt and belly, just as he started
To flee, and brought him down with a thunderous crash.
And Atreus' son Menelaus quickly dragged   670
The dead body away from the Trojans and into the ranks
Of his own good comrades.

    Then Phoebus Apollo came up
To Hector and urged him on, in the form of Phaenops,
Asius' son from Abydos, whom Hector preferred
Over all of his guests from abroad. Looking exactly
Like him, far-working Apollo spoke thus: "How can you,
Hector, expect any man of Achaea to fear you
At all after this—this blenching before Menelaus
Who often has proved a puny spearman indeed?   680
But now with no one to help him he's drawn a dead body
Away from the Trojans for good—the body of your
Noble favorite, a champion surpassing champions—yes Podes,
Son of Eëtion!"

    He spoke, and a black cloud of grief
Descended on Hector, who rapidly strode through the front rank
Of fighters, clad in his high-burnished bronze. And Zeus
Took up the terrible tasseled aegis and shook it
All awesomely gleaming, and over Mount Ida he gathered
The storm clouds and filled the sky with thunder and lightning,   690
Thus signaling victory for Trojans, rout for Achaeans.

    The first to begin the retreat was Boeotian Peneleos.
For as he stood fast, ever facing the foe, he received
A wound on top of his shoulder, as Polydamas' spear-point
Cut through to the bone, for he it was that had cast
From not far away. And Hector in man-to-man combat
Put Leïtus, son of Alectryon, out of the action
By jabbing his bronze in the brave Boeotian's wrist,
And Leïtus, anxiously looking around him, shrank
From the fighting, since now he no longer felt sure of his grip   700
On the spear as he sought to battle the Trojans. But as Hector
Went after Leïtus, Idomeneus threw and struck him
A blow on the breastplate close by the nipple, causing
A scream to go up from the Trojans as that long spear-shaft
Broke in the socket. Then Hector hurled his bright bronze
At Idomeneus, son of Deucalion, standing now
In a car, and just barely missed him. He struck, though, Coeranus,
Meriones' comrade and driver who came with him
From the fortified city of Lyctus. For Idomeneus had come

710 From the well-balanced ships on foot, and would surely have fallen
     A glorious triumph for Trojans if Coeranus had not
     Come up very fast with the flying-hoofed horses. He came
     To Idomeneus then as a light of deliverance and kept
     From him the ruthless day of his death, though he
     Himself lost life at the hands of murderous Hector.
     His spear went in beneath bold Coeranus' ear
     And jaw, uprooting his teeth and splitting his tongue.
     Coeranus pitched from the car and let the reins fall
     To the ground. But quickly Meriones gathered them up,
720 Handed them to Idomeneus, and spoke to him, saying:
          "The lash now! and use it well until you get back
     To the swift-running ships. You yourself know very well
     That we no longer have any chance in this fight."

          He spoke, and Idomeneus lashed the mane-tossing horses
     Back to the hollow ships, for fear had fallen
     Upon him.
          Nor did Menelaus and huge-hearted Ajax
     Fail to see that Zeus was giving the victory
     To Trojans, and great Telamonian Ajax spoke thus:
730 "Now confound it all! any man, however foolish,
     Can see whose side Zeus is on. For the Trojans let no missile
     Fly that doesn't strike home, no matter who hurls it,
     Whether brave captain or coward—Zeus guides them all
     To their marks, while all of our shafts fall vainly to earth.
     But come, let us think for ourselves and find the best way
     To rescue this body and please our dear friends by returning
     Ourselves, for our comrades behind us must be in great fear
     As they look out at us and lose all hope that the fury
     Of slaughtering Hector and his invincible hands
740 Will be stopped before he falls on the black-hulled vessels.
     If only some comrade of ours would carry word
     With all speed to Peleus' son Achilles, who,
     I believe, has not even heard the horrible news
     That his dearest friend is dead. But I can see
     No Achaean fit for the mission, so thick is the dark
     Cloud of mist enshrouding us all, both men and horses.
     O Father Zeus, deliver the sons of Achaeans
     From this great darkness. Clear the air and enable
     Our eyes to see. If kill us you must, then kill us,
750 O lord, in the light."
          Such was his plea, and the Father,
     Pitying him as he wept, quickly dispersed

The dark cloud of mist, and the sun shone brightly on all
As the whole battlefield was clearly revealed. Then Ajax
Said this to battle-roaring Menelaus:
        "Look about now,
God-fed Menelaus, and see if Antilochus, son
Of magnanimous Nestor, is still alive. If so,
Instruct him to run with all speed to fiery Achilles
With word that his most precious friend has been destroyed."   760
        Menelaus did not ignore him, but went like a lion
Leaving a cattle-yard, one exhausted from harassing
Dogs and farmhands, who watch all night to protect
Their fat oxen and drive him away. The flesh-hungry lion
Charges right in, only to be driven back
By a rain of spears and blazing torches, hurled
At him by brawny bold arms, Still hungry, he has to
Retreat, and slinks off at dawn disappointed. So now
Menelaus, unwilling at heart, went away from Patroclus,
Greatly reluctant, since much he feared that Achaeans   770
In painful rout would leave the body a prey
For the foeman. Hence he exhorted both Ajaxes
And Meriones, fervently saying:
        "Both of you Ajaxes,
Leaders of Argives, and you, Meriones, remember
How lovable luckless Patroclus was, for he
Knew how to be kind to all those about him, before
Death's doom engulfed him."
        So saying, tawny Menelaus
Took off, searching the plain like an eagle, the bird   780
That men say possesses the sharpest eyesight of all
Winged creatures that fly under heaven, that sees from on high
Even the fleet-footed hare as he huddles beneath
Some leafy bush—even on him the fierce eagle
Falls and catching him kills him at once. So now,
O King Menelaus, your bright eyes roamed through the moil
Of your numerous troops in search of old Nestor's son
Still alive. Soon then he saw him far on the left,
Cheering his men and urging them on in the fight.
Approaching him there, tawny Menelaus spoke thus: 790
        "God-nurtured Antilochus, come here to me, that you
May learn what horrible thing has happened, something
I deeply wish never had. You see, I'm sure,
How God is rolling a great wave of woe on the Argives
And giving the victory to Trojans. And now the best

Of Achaeans is dead, Patroclus himself, and the Danaans
Terribly miss him. But you now, run with all speed
To the ships and tell Achilles what I have told you.
If he loses no time, he may yet bring to his ship
800   The still whole corpse of his friend—the naked corpse,
Since huge bright-helmeted Hector is already wearing
His armor."

      At this, Antilochus paled with horror.*
He stood for a while quite speechless, his eyes full of tears
And his sobs all choked up within him. He did not, however,
Neglect Menelaus' command, but set out on the run,
Having given his bronze to his matchless driver Laodocus,
Who close beside him was wheeling his solid-hoofed horses.
      Then weeping he ran from the field of fighting to tell
810   The cruel word to Achilles. Nor was your spirit disposed,
O King Menelaus, to stay and assist the battered
Friends of Antilochus, men of Pylos who missed him
Greatly. Instead, Menelaus sent Prince Thrasymedes
To help them and hurried to stand once again by the corpse
Of Patroclus. There with the two Ajaxes he spoke
To them, saying:
      "I've sent out a man to the fast-faring ships
On his way to fleet-footed Achilles, not that I have
The slightest idea that Achilles will come and do battle,
820   No matter how great his hatred for royal Hector.
For how can he fight the Trojans without any armor?
But come, let us think for ourselves and find the best way
To get out of here with the body and get ourselves out
Alive from this perilous moil of war-screaming Trojans."
      And great Telamonian Ajax replied: "All
That you say is quite right, most illustrious King Menelaus.
So quickly now, you and Meriones stoop and shoulder
The body and bear it out of the fighting, while we two
Behind you, alike in soul as we are in name,
830   Fight off the Trojans and royal Hector, even we,
The two Ajaxes, who many a time have stood
By each other and fought in the face of mad-slashing Ares."
      At this the two powerful warriors stooped and quickly
Shouldered the body, whereat the throng of Trojans

---

*Antilochus' ignorance of Patroclus' death is explained at XVII.446–447; Antilochus is
fighting in a distant part of the battle.

Behind them shouted in protest. And straight upon them
The fierce Trojans charged, like hounds that dart in front of
Young hunters straight on a stricken wild boar, lusting
To rip him apart till the great beast, trusting in brawn,
Wheels and confronts them, sending them back on their haunches
And off in all directions. Even so the Trojans   840
Came on in a pack, repeatedly thrusting with swords
And two-pointed spears, but whenever the Ajaxes turned
And stood against them, their faces paled with fear
And no man dared to charge in and fight for the dead.

    As the two chiefs labored to bear the body quickly
From battle and to the hollow-hulled vessels, a war-charge
Wild as blazing fire was hurled against them,
An onset hot as a huge conflagration that suddenly
Comes on a city and, fiercely flaming, collapses
The homes as a high wind keeps it roaring. Even so   850
After them the Trojans came on with a constant hubbub
Of horses and spearmen. And as when two mules pull hard
On either side of a log or a long ship-timber
To drag it down a rugged trail from the mountains
And, straining, both are well nigh overcome with the pain
And sweat of their toil, so now Menelaus and mighty
Meriones labored to bear the body quickly
From battle. And always behind them the two Ajaxes
Held off the foe as a ridge does flooding waters—
Some wooded ridge that happens to lie across   860
A whole plain and so holds back the cruel streams
Of powerful rivers, turning their currents to wander
The plain and remaining unbroken no matter how mighty
The force of the flood. Even so, the two Ajaxes
Held off the onrush of Trojans, who, however,
Kept coming, led by Aeneas, son of Anchises,
And bronze-blazing Hector. And as a cloud of starlings
Or jackdaws scream for their lives and flee when they see
A hawk falling toward them with certain death for small birds,
So now before Hector and slashing Aeneas the nimble   870
Achaeans fled screaming in fear for their lives, having lost
All stomach for fighting. And many fine pieces of armor
Fell in and about the trench as the Danaans fled,
And there was no respite at all from horrible war.[6]

BOOK XVIII

The Shield of Achilles

While thus on the plain war's holocaust blazed, Antilochus,
Fast on his feet, arrived with his news for Achilles.
He found him in front of his high-horned vessels, anxiously
Brooding on what had now come to pass, deeply troubled
And speaking thus to his own great-hearted self:
　"Ah miserable me! how is it that now once more
The Achaeans are driven in panic across the plain
And back to the ships? O let it not be that the gods
Have wrought for my soul that ghastly evil foretold
10　To me once by my mother, who said that while I yet lived
The Myrmidon's bravest and best would leave the light
Of the sun beneath the hands of the Trojans! Truly,
Gallant Patroclus must now be dead.[1] O foolhardy
Comrade of mine! Surely I gave him strict orders
To come back here to the ships as soon as the fierce fire
Was out, and not to pit his powers against
Those of Hector."
　As thus he worried in mind and heart,
Antilochus, shedding hot tears, came up and reported
20　The miserable message: "What pain is mine, O son
Of wise-hearted Peleus, that I have to tell you such horrible
News, of a thing I wish deeply had never occurred.
Patroclus has fallen, and round his corpse they are fighting—
His naked corpse, for huge bright-helmeted Hector
Is already wearing your armor!"
　At this a black cloud
Of grief enveloped Achilles, and taking a dark
Double-handful of soot he poured it over his head,
Defiling his handsome face and fragrant tunic
30　With filthy black ashes. Then he dropped down full length
In the dust, mighty even in grief, and with his
Own hands he befouled and tore at his hair. And the women
Whom he and Patroclus had taken as booty shrieked
In anguish of heart and ran out of doors to sink

Round the form of their flame-hearted master and beat their breasts
With their hands, while Antilochus, weeping and moaning, held
The hands of heart-grieved Achilles, for fear that he might
Draw a blade and cut his own throat.[2]
  Then awesome indeed
Were the groans and shrieks of Achilles, and though she sat deep   40
In the sea beside her old sire, his goddess mother
Heard him. At once she took up the wail, and the goddesses
Crowded around her, all of the daughters of Nereus
That live with their father deep in the salt-water sea.
Glauce was there and Thaleia and with them Cymodoce,
Speio, Nesaea, Thoë, and heifer-eyed Halia,
Limnoreia, Cymothoë, and Actaea,
Iaera, Amphithoë, Melite, and Agaue,
Doto and Proto, Dynamene and Pherousa,
Dexamene, Callianeira, and Amphinome,   50
Doris, Panope, and world-renowned Galatea,
Nemertes and Apseudes and Callianassa,
And Clymene with Ianeira and Ianassa,
Maera, Orithyia, and fair-braided Amathea,
And all the other daughters of Nereus that live
In the depths of the sea. With these was the silvery cave crowded,
And all of them beat their breasts in lament, as Thetis,
Who led their wailing, cried out among them, saying:
  "Hear me, O Nereids, sisters of mine, that all
Of you may know what pain there is in my heart.   60
Ah wretched me! the miserable mother of valor
And woe, for I bore a matchless heroic son
To be the best of all warriors. When I had tenderly
Reared him, as one would a seedling he plants in a rich
Orchard plot, and watched him shoot up like a sturdy young tree,
I sent him off with the big-beaked ships to Troy,
That he might do battle with Trojans. But never again
Shall I welcome him home to the house of Peleus. Yet
He must suffer so long as he lives in the light of the sun,
Nor can I help him at all by going to him.   70
Go I will, though, that I may see my dear child
And hear what grief has come on him while he has held back
From battle and bloodshed."
  So saying, she left the cave,
And the weeping nymphs went with her, cleaving the waves
Of the sea till they came to the loamy rich land of the Trojans.
Then one by one they came up on the beach where thickly

The Myrmidon ships were drawn up around fast Achilles.
And his divine mother came to where he lay groaning,
80 Uttered a shrill cry of grief herself, and taking
His head in her hands spoke these words winged with compassion:
       "My child, why are you crying? What sorrow has entered
Your heart? Speak out to me now and hide it no longer.
Surely you've got what you wanted from Zeus, since you prayed
With uplifted hands that all of the sons of Achaeans
Should be huddled up at the sterns of their ships and suffer
Disgraceful defeat because of their great need for you."
       Then heavily sighing, fast-footed Achilles replied:
"My mother, it's true the Olympian has answered my prayers,
90 But what good to me is all that when my dearest friend
Is dead, Patroclus, the man I loved and respected
Above all other comrades, as much indeed
As I do my own self? Now I have lost him, and Hector,
Who killed him, has stripped off that beautiful armor, huge
And incredibly bright, a present the gods gave Peleus
The same day they gave you to him in marriage. Would you
Had stayed where you were mid the deathless nymphs of the sea
And that Peleus had taken a mortal woman for bride.
But now you too will have measureless grief, you
100 For the death of your son, whom never again will you
Welcome home. For my heart bids me no longer to live
Among men, unless first of all I am able to take
Hector's life with my spear in requital for that of Patroclus,
Whom he made his booty and spoil."
       Then again tearful Thetis
Spoke to her son: "If you, my child, do
As you say, then surely you too will soon die, for soon
After Hector's death your own will certainly come."
       Then greatly moved, fast-footed Achilles replied:
110 "Then soon let me die! since I was not there to help
My friend when he died.[3] He fell very far from the land
Of his fathers, and needed me with him to keep off destruction.
So now, since I shall never return to my own
Precious country, and since I was no help at all to Patroclus,
Nor to my many other friends whom Hector
Has slaughtered, with me sitting here by the ships just so much
Useless weight to burden the earth, me,
Who am unsurpassed as a fighter, though not as a talker,
By any man now alive mid the bronze-clad Achaeans—

O how I wish all strife would die among gods   120
And men and with it anger, that causes the wisest
To sulk and storm, resentment that is more delicious
Than trickling honey and spreads like smoke in the hearts
Of mortals, as mine most surely did when King
Agamemnon provoked me. Well, what's done is done.
Now we must conquer the anger within us—because
We must. And I will enter the battle in search of
Hector, the man who killed my most precious friend,
And as for my own fate, certainly I'll accept that
Whenever Zeus wills to fulfill it, Zeus and the other   130
Immortal gods. For not even powerful Heracles
Kept death away, though he was surely the favorite
Of Cronos' son Zeus the almighty. Even he succumbed
To fate and the grim resentment of Hera. And so
I too shall lie still in death, if a similar fate
Has been fashioned for me. But now I intend to win
Splendid fame, and now because of me will many
Of Troy's women and many deep-breasted Dardanians
Wipe with both hands the tears from their tender cheeks
As sob follows grief-laden sob, for I will have made them   140
Know what it means for me to be present in battle.[4]
Don't try, then, to keep me from fighting because of your love
For me. You will not succeed!"
      Then the goddess Thetis,
She of the silvery feet, spoke thus: "Surely,
My child, it is no evil thing to help your comrades
Survive the bloody dangers of war. But now
Your fine armor is held by the Trojans, your gleaming bronze war-gear.
Bronze-loving Hector, in fact, exultantly wears it
About his own shoulders, though he'll not enjoy it long,   150
Since now his own death is near. So hold yourself back
From the turmoil of Ares until you see me returning,
And in the morning I will return with exquisite
Armor from lord Hephaestus himself."
      With this
She turned from her son and spoke to her sea-born sisters:
"All of you, now, plunge into the sea's broad bosom
And go to the halls of our father, the briny old man
Of the sea, and make your report to him of all this.
I must be off to the famous craftsman Hephaestus   160
On lofty Olympus to see if he'll make for my son

Some marvelous, all-shining armor."
        She spoke, and her sisters
The sea nymphs quickly vanished amid the salt waves,
But the goddess Thetis, she of the silvery feet,
Went up to Olympus, that she might bring glorious armor
For her precious son.
        While her feet were taking her there,
The screaming Achaeans fled before man-killing Hector
170 And came to the ships and the Hellespont. Nor could the well-greaved
Achaeans draw forth Patroclus, the friend of Achilles,
From under the raining missiles, for again the men
And horses of Troy came up to the body, led by
Priam's son Hector with fury like that of fire.
Three times resplendent Hector seized the corpse
By the feet and loudly called out to the Trojans, so eager
Was he to drag it away, and all three times
The two Ajaxes, fired with unquenchable courage, beat him
Back from the body. But Hector remained unshaken
180 In his resolution, and either he charged at them
Through the tumult, or stood his ground and called to his men,
But he never once yielded so much as a foot. For the Ajaxes
Had no more success in frightening Hector
Away from the corpse than field-dwelling shepherds who try
To drive from a carcass a tawny and starving lion.
And now would Hector have hauled off the body and won
Unspeakable glory had not wind-footed swift Iris
Sped down from Olympus with word for Achilles to arm
For the battle. She came in obedience to Hera, without
190 The knowledge of Zeus and the other immortals, and standing
Close to Achilles she spoke to him these winged words:
        "On your feet! son of Peleus, most dreaded of men. Go rescue
Patroclus, on whose account a grim battle is raging
In front of the ships. There men are slaughtering men,
The Achaeans defending the corpse of your friend, while the Trojans
Charge in to drag it away to windy Ilium.
Blazing Hector is fiercest of all in his efforts
To haul off the corpse, and his urge is to hack off the head
From the tender neck and fix it high up on a stake
200 Of the wall. On your feet, then, and lie here no longer! Let shame
Fill your heart, lest soon the poor corpse of Patroclus become
The delight of Trojan dogs—your shame and disgrace,
If that corpse should come to your hands at all mutilated
By Trojans!"

Then quick Achilles answered her thus:
"Divine Iris, which of the gods sent you here with this message?"
        And again wind-footed swift Iris: "Hera sent me,
The illustrious wife of high-throned Zeus, who has
No knowledge at all of my coming down, nor does
Any other immortal that dwells on snowy Olympus."   210
        To which Achilles replied: "But how should I go
Into battle when they out there are holding my armor?
And my dear mother forbade me to arm myself
Till she gets back from Hephaestus with splendid war-gear
For me. I'm aware of no man's armor that I
Could use, except the big shield of Telamonian Ajax,
And he, I'm sure, is using that piece himself
Mid the foremost fighters, where he rages hotly, wielding
His spear in defense of dead Patroclus."
        And again   220
Wind-footed swift Iris: "We know very well who has
Your armor. But go to the trench as you are and show
Yourself to the Trojans that they may be so appalled
By the sight that they will stop fighting. Then the war-worn son
Of Achaeans may have a chance to catch their breath.
Such chances in battle are few."
        When thus she had spoken,
Fast-footed Iris took off. Then Zeus-loved Achilles
Got up, and about his great shoulders Athena flung
The bright-tasseled aegis,⁵ and round his head the fair goddess   230
Drifted a golden mist, from which she made blaze
A high-flaming fire. And as when smoke billows up
From a distant island-city beleaguered by foes,
And the soldiers defend it throughout the day from the walls
Of their town till at last the sun sets and the signal fires, many
And large, send their glare high up in the sky, that men
On neighboring islands may see and come in their ships
To ward off destruction, so now from the head of Achilles
The blaze went up toward heaven.
        Striding out from the wall,   240
He took his stand by the trench, though he did not join
The Achaean troops, since he had respect for his mother's
Strict command. He stood there and shouted, while out
On the plain Athena joined her voice with his, and he caused
Unspeakable chaos among the Trojans. His voice
Rang out as piercingly clear as the scream of a trumpet
When soul-wrecking foes are attacking a city. And when

They heard Achilles' brazen voice, the hearts
Of the Trojans were stunned with surprise, and even the mane-tossing
250 Horses sensed fear in the air and turned back their cars
In panic. And their drivers were terrified when they saw
The unwearying fire blaze up with such awesome glare
Above the head of great-souled Achilles, for the bright-eyed
Goddess Athena made the flames rise. Three times
Across the trench great Achilles mightily shouted,
And three times the Trojans and their world-famous allies
Were thrown into chaos. And there twelve men of their bravest
Were killed by the cars and spears of their own fellow soldiers.
     Meanwhile, the thankful Achaeans dragged Patroclus
260 From under the missiles and lifted him onto a litter,
While round him followed his dear mourning friends, and with them
Went fast Achilles, shedding hot tears, as now
He looked down on his faithful friend, torn by the mangling
Bronze and borne on a litter. He had sent him with horses
And car into battle, but never again did he welcome him
Back from the fighting.
          Then heifer-eyed queenly Hera
Sent the unwearying Sun on his way to the stream
Of Oceanus. So at last the Sun, though reluctant,
270 Went down, and the brave Achaeans had rest from the cruel
Strife of that all-leveling and evil war.
          And opposite them the Trojans, drawn back from the harsh
Encounter, unyoked from the cars their fast-running horses
And met in assembly before even thinking of supper.
And they stood all during the meeting, since no one there
Cared to sit, so anxious were they at the coming forth
Of Achilles, who had for so long stayed out of the fighting.
Then thoughtful Polydamas,* Panthous' son, spoke first,
For he alone looked before as well as behind.
280 He was a comrade of Hector—both had been born
On the selfsame night—and he was as gifted in speech
As Hector in battle. Now, in an effort to help,
He spoke to them thus:
          "Consider closely, my friends.
My own advice, since we are so far from the wall,
Is that all of us now should go back to the city, instead of

---

*See endnote 2 to book XII, about Polydamas.

Awaiting bright Dawn out here on the plain by the ships.
So long as Achilles held back because of his wrath
Against King Agamemnon, the Achaeans were easier men
To fight, and I too was glad to spend the night out   290
By the shapely ships in the hope that we might soon take them.
But now I am deeply afraid of quick-charging Achilles,
A man of so mighty a spirit that he will be
Unwilling to fight in the midst of the plain, where both
The Achaeans and Trojans have suffered the War-god's fury.
Now he will aim his attack at the city itself—
And at our wives! Let us, then, go back there ourselves,
For believe me, I know what will happen. Right now divine night
Has delayed fast-footed Achilles. But if in the morning
He puts on some armor and comes out to find us still here,   300
I tell you a great many men shall get well acquainted
With him. That man who escapes to holy Troy
Will be very glad that he did, but the dogs and the vultures
Shall feast on innumerable Trojans—may I never hear
How many! If, however, we do as I say,
Even though we dislike to, we'll concentrate our forces
In the meeting place of the city, which is well protected
By walls with their strong, smooth-timbered gates, high
And well-barred. Then, at the first sign of Dawn, we'll arm
And take our stand on the walls, so that if Achilles   310
Wishes to leave the ships and fight against us
For the city, so much the worse for him! He'll go back
Again to the ships, having worn out his neck-arching horses
With galloping back and forth in front of the walls.
He won't have the courage to break his way in and pillage
The town. Before that, he will himself be devoured
By the flashing-swift dogs of Troy!"
             Then scowling at him,
Bright-helmeted Hector replied: "Polydamas, this counsel
Of yours, that we should go back and be penned up again   320
In the city, is most distasteful to me. Can it be
That you haven't had quite enough of being shut up
In those walls? There was a time when men were accustomed
To tell of King Priam's city, so famous it was
For its stores of bronze and gold. But now its exquisite
Treasures are gone from the homes, and countless fine things
Have been sold into Phrygia and into lovely Maeonia,
Since great Zeus became angry with us. And now

When at last that almighty god, the son of devious
330 Cronos, has given me victory beside the ships
And enabled me thus to coop the Achaeans up close
By the sea, you, like a fool, advise the host
To retreat. I command you to cease such folly, nor will
So much as one man pay attention to you.
I'll see to that! But come, let all of us now
Do as I say. Go take your supper by companies
Throughout the host, and don't neglect to stand watch
And all of you stay alert. And if any Trojan
Is overly worried about his possessions, let him
340 Collect them and turn them over for public consumption.
Better for our own people to profit from them
Than for the Achaeans to. But at the first sign
Of Dawn, let us launch a keen-slashing attack on the ships.
And if Achilles is really there to fight us,
It will indeed be so much the worse for him!
I surely will not run from him nor away from the horrors
Of battle, but face to face I'll oppose him and see
Who wins the great victory, he or I. The War-god
Is partial to none, and often he who would kill
350 Is the one who gets killed!"

        Thus Hector rebuked him, and all
Of the Trojans cheered, poor childish fools that they were!
For Pallas Athena deprived them of sense. They lauded
Hector and his bad advice, but not one man
Had praise for Polydamas, although his counsel was wise.[6]
Then throughout the host they took their evening meal.

        All night the Achaeans raised the wail for Patroclus.
And among them Achilles led the mournful chant,
Laying his man-killing hands on the breast of his friend
360 And incessantly moaning, with grief as wrathful as that
Of a tawny lioness, one whose cubs some hunter
Of deer has stolen from out a deep wood, and the lioness
Comes back too late and is stricken with furious grief,
And her bitter anguish keeps her trailing the man
Through many a gorge in a frantic effort to find him.
So now Achilles, heavily groaning, spoke
To the Myrmidons:

        "Ah misery! how vain were the words I uttered
That day when at home in the palace I tried to console
370 The noble Menoetius, saying to him that when

We had sacked the city of Troy I would bring back to him
At Opus his splendid son Patroclus and with him
His share of the spoil.* But Zeus does not bring to fulfillment
All of the promises mortals make, and now
Both Patroclus and I are doomed to stain with our blood
The same Trojan soil, since I shall never go back
To be welcomed at home by the knightly old Peleus, nor
By Thetis, my mother, for here the black earth shall hold me.
But now, Patroclus, since I shall go under this ground
After you, I will bring to this place before your body   380
Is burned both the armor and head of Hector, the killer
Of great-hearted you! And in front of your pyre I'll cut
The throats of twelve splendid sons of the Trojans, venting
My wrath because of your killing.† Until that time,
You shall lie here beside my beaked ships, and around you
Day and night shall captive women of Troy
Along with deep-breasted Dardanians cry out in mourning
With shedding of tears, all of the women Patroclus
And I took by force, toiling hard with our spears, when together
We plundered rich cities of mortal men."   390
     So saying,
Royal Achilles told his comrades to set
A great three-legged cauldron over the fire, that they
With all speed might wash the blood and gore from Patroclus.
They set the bath cauldron over the coals and poured in
Water for washing and beneath it heaped wood. Then,
As the flames leaped round the cauldron's belly, the water
Grew warm. And when it boiled in the gleaming bronze,
They washed the corpse and anointed it richly with oil,
Filling the wounds with ointment aged for nine years.   400
Then they laid him out on a bed and covered him over
From head to foot with a thin linen shroud, over which
They draped a lovely white robe. So all night long
About swift Achilles the Myrmidons wailed in their grief
For Patroclus.
     Meanwhile, Zeus spoke these words to Hera,
His sister and wife: "I see you have had your own way,

---

*On the parting scene in Phthia, see endnote 4 to book IX.
†The threat to cut the throats of twelve Trojans is further anticipated at XXI.29–37 and
fulfilled at XXIII.207–210.

O heifer-eyed regal Hera, this time by arousing
Swift-footed Achilles. Truly the long-haired Achaeans
410 Must be your very own children!"
         To which Queen Hera
Replied: "Most dreadful son of Cronos, what
Are you talking about! Why even a mortal, who lacks
The resources we have, will do what he can for a friend.
So how was I, who claim to be best of goddesses
On at least two accounts, in that I am the eldest
And also your wife, you being King of all
The immortals—how, I say, was I not to weave
What evil I could for my hated foes the Trojans?"
420   While thus they were talking, Thetis of the silver feet
Arrived at the house of Hephaestus, a mansion built
By the great limping god himself. It was wrought of immortal
Bronze and shone out among the deities' houses
Bright as a star. At the moment Hephaestus was busily
Turning from bellows to bellows, sweating with toil
As he labored to finish a score of three-legged tables
To stand round the sides of his firm-founded hall. On each
Of the legs he had put a gold wheel, that those magic tables
Might cause all to marvel by going with no other help
430 To the gathering of gods and by likewise returning to his house.
The tables were almost finished, but still he had not
Attached the elaborate handles, which now he was forging
With rivets hammered to fit them. While he worked hard
On these with great skill, the bright-footed goddess approached,
And lovely Charis,* she of the shimmering veil
Whom the famous lame god had married, saw her and came
To the door. Then warmly taking her hand, she said:
         "My lovely-gowned Thetis, to what do we owe this visit?
You are indeed an honored and welcome guest,
440 Though your visits here have not been frequent. But follow me
Further, that I may set some refreshment before you."
         With this, divine Charis led her in and seated
Her in a beautiful chair, all richly wrought
And studded with silver, with a rest below for the feet.
And she called to the famous craftsman her husband, saying:
"Hephaestus, come in here. Thetis has something to ask you."
         Upon which the great ambidextrous deity called:

---

*"Grace" is Hephaestus' consort.

"Surely, then, a reverenced and powerful goddess
Is in our home, the very one who saved me
From anguish that time I had fallen so far on account of   450
My bitch-hearted mother who wished to get rid of me
Because of my lameness.* Then I would surely have suffered
Much more than I did, if Thetis had not been so kind—
Thetis and Eurynome, daughter of circling Oceanus.
I stayed with them for nine years and made a great many
Intricate things, brooches and spiral bracelets,
Cupped earrings and necklaces, all highly wrought by me
Within their high-vaulted cave, while around us flowed
The endless stream of Oceanus, seething with foam.
No man or immortal knew where I was, except   460
Of course Thetis and Eurynome, since they had taken me in.
And now divine Thetis, she of the beautiful braids,
Has come to our house on a visit. Hence I must do all
I can to repay her for rescuing me. Serve her
Something refreshing and fine, while I put my bellows
And tools away."

    So saying, he roused his huge bulk
From the anvil, puffing and limping, though his thin legs
Were nimble enough. He set the bellows away
From the fire, and gathering up his tools he put them   470
Away in a silver chest. With a sponge he wiped
His face and hands, his powerful neck and shaggy
Chest, then put on a tunic, took a strong staff,
And limped toward the door. Quickly, girls of gold,
Exactly resembling living maids, hurried
To help their master—they all have minds of their own,
Speech and strength, and the gods everlasting have given them
Marvelous skill with their hands. When these had assisted
Their master through the door, he limped up to Thetis,
Sat down in a gleaming chair, took her hand warmly,   480
And calling her name, spoke thus:

    "My lovely-gowned Thetis,
To what do we owe this visit? You are indeed
An honored and welcome guest, but your visits here
Have not been frequent. So say what you have in mind,
And if it can be done and done by me
Then my heart says do it."

---

*Compare the account of Hephaestus' laming at I.689–695 with endnote 8 to book I.

And Thetis, weeping, replied:
"O Hephaestus, is there any goddess who lives on Olympus
490 To whom Zeus has given so many sorrows as he has
To me? He made me alone, of all the sea nymphs,
Endure the bed of a mortal, of Peleus, son
Of Aeacus, sorely against my will.* This Peleus
Lies in his palace, worn out with sad old age,
But now I have other troubles. For Zeus gave me
A son to bear and to raise, one who would be
The bravest and best of all warriors. When I had tenderly
Reared him, as one would a seedling he plants in a rich
Orchard plot, and watched him shoot up like a sturdy young tree,
500 I sent him off with the big-beaked ships to Troy,
That he might do battle with Trojans. But never again
Shall I welcome him home to the house of Peleus. Yet
He must suffer so long as he lives in the light of the sun,
Nor can I help him at all by going to him.
Lord Agamemnon snatched from his arms the girl
That the sons of Achaeans picked out for him as a prize.
Then while he was wasting his heart in grief for her,
The Trojans penned the Achaeans up close to the sterns
Of their ships and held them there. So the Argive elders
510 Pleaded with him for his aid, offering him many
Splendid gifts. And though he refused to defend them
From ruin himself, he did lend Patroclus his armor
And sent him forth into battle with many Myrmidons.
All that day they fought round the Scaean Gates
And could on that selfsame day have taken the town,
If Apollo had not slain Patroclus up front mid the champions,
Killing him there after he had done much damage
To Trojans, though Hector received the credit and glory.
Now, then, I've come to your knees to see if you'll give
520 My soon-to-die son new armor—a shield and a helmet,
Bright greaves with ankle-clasps, and a breastplate too.
For the armor he had was lost with his faithful friend
When he was cut down by the Trojans. And now my son
Lies on the ground grieving his sorrowful heart out."
        Then the great ambidextrous god answered her thus:
"Take heart, and try not to worry. I only wish
That I were as able to save him from hateful death,

---

*See endnote 7 to book I for an account of Thetis' marriage.

When the dread hour of doom comes on him, as I am able
To make a bright set of armor for him, a set
So exceedingly fine that all who see it will marvel."   530
     With this, he left her there and went back to his bellows,
Which now he turned toward the fire and told to blow.
And the bellows—all twenty of them—blew on the crucibles,
Sending forth blasts of wind wherever the toiling god
Wished them to make the fire hotter in order to further
His work. And on the fire he put stubborn bronze,
And tin, and precious silver and gold. Then he set
His huge anvil up on the block and took up in one hand
A massive hammer, and fire-seizing tongs in the other.
     First he fashioned a shield both wide and thick,   540
Skillfully forging it all. About it he hammered
A triple-thick rim, to which he attached a baldric
Of silver. The rest of the shield was five layers thick,
And on it he wrought, with cunning skill, many
Elaborate things.
     He made lovely images there
Of earth and heaven,[7] of sea and weariless sun,
Of the moon at full and of all constellations that shine
In the sky—the Pleiads, the Hyads, and mighty Orion,
And the Great Bear, by some called the Wain, which circles   550
In its place, its eyes on Orion the Hunter, and never
Sinks in the baths of Oceanus.
     On it he wrought
Two beautiful cities[8] and filled them with people. In one
There were weddings and banquets, and by the light of high-blazing
Torches, parties were leading the brides from their homes
And through the streets, as the loud bridal song arose.
Young men were whirling about in the dance to the music
Of flutes and lyres, and women stood at their doors
To watch the procession and marvel. The men, though, had gone   560
To the place of assembly, where two of their number were striving
To settle a case concerning a murdered man's blood-price.
The defendant declared his cause to the people and vowed
He was willing to pay the whole price, but the other refused
To accept it, and each was eager to have a judge's
Decision in his behalf. The people were cheering
Both men, some favoring one and some the other,
But heralds held all of them back from where in the sacred
Circle the elders sat on the polished stones,
Each taking the great-lunged herald's staff when it came   570

To him in his turn. With this each elder would come
To the fore and give his opinion. And in the center
Two talents of gold were lying, the fee to be given
To him who uttered the straightest and truest judgment.
      But the other city was shown besieged by two
Shining hosts of bronze-armored men. And they were divided
Between two plans, either to sack and pillage
The lovely town, or to lift the siege in return
For half its possessions. Those within, however,
580 Would not go along with this proposal at all,
And instead they were arming and getting an ambush ready.
Leaving their wives and small children, together with all
The old men, to guard the wall, the others went forth
Behind Ares and Pallas Athena, both wrought of gold
And wearing gold armor, tall and beautiful figures,
Quite as the gods should be, that clearly stood out
Above the men they were leading. When these arrived
At the place where it pleased them to lay their ambush, down
In the bed of a river where all kinds of cattle watered,
590 They posted two guards apart from the rest to keep
A sharp look-out for sheep and shuffling cattle, and then
They sat down to wait in their flashing bronze. Very soon
The herds came, attended by two happy herdsmen, gaily
Playing their pipes and suspecting no treacherous ambush.
But those in hiding sprang out, killed the two herdsmen,
And quickly cut off the many beeves and beautiful
Flocks of silvery white sheep. Now the city's besiegers,
Gathered in council, heard the bawling of cattle,
And leaping up quickly behind their high-stepping horses
600 They rapidly drove to where the attack had occurred.
And there, by the banks of the river, they fought a pitched battle,
Gashing each other with bronze-headed spears. Hatred
And Chaos took part in the struggle, as did the spirit
Of ruinous Death, who was shown laying violent hands
On one man wounded but still alive, on another
Unwounded as yet, while a third who was dead already
She dragged through the gore by the feet, and the cloak on her
                  shoulders
Was crimson with warriors' blood. Thus they all mingled
And fought like living men, and each side was hauling
610 Its dead away from the foe.
           Thereon he set
A wide field of rich fallow land, thrice-plowed and soft.

Here many plowmen were wheeling their teams and cutting
Long furrows. And each time they came to the edge of the field,
A man would step out and place in their hands a cup
Of honey-sweet wine. Then the plowmen would turn and head
Down the furrow, eager to reach the field's edge again.
And behind them the earth, though made of gold, grew black,
Exactly as real earth does when it's plowed. Such
Was the marvelous art of Hephaestus.   620
      And there on the shield
He depicted the huge estate of a king, whereon
His workers were reaping,⁹ wielding their sharp reaping hooks.
All along the swath the handfuls of grain were falling,
And boys would gather them up in their arms and carry them
Over to binders, who tied them up into sheaves.
Among them the king, his royal staff in hand,
Stood quietly rejoicing, while off from them in the shade
Of an oak his heralds were roasting an ox they had slaughtered,
Preparing a meal for the reapers, and women were sprinkling   630
The meat with abundant white barley.
      And on it he made
A fair golden vineyard, where heavy dark clusters of grapes
Were supported by silver poles. About it he ran
A trench of blue lapis and outside of that a tin fence.
Only one path led into the vineyard, and by it
The pickers came and went whenever they gathered
The grapes. Along it girls and young men were gaily
Bearing the honey-sweet fruit in full wicker baskets,
And with them a boy, strumming his lyre, sang sweetly   640
In his fine voice a dirge for the death of Linus,
While all the others kept time to the music, dancing
And chanting together.
      There he also made a herd
Of straight-horned cattle, fashioning them of gold
And tin. With lowing they hurried from farmyard to pasture,
A field by the quivering reeds of a clamorous river.
Four herdsmen of gold were walking beside the cattle,
And with the men nine flashing-swift dogs were shown.
But up at the front of the herd two awesome lions   650
Had seized a loud-lowing bull and dragged him, terribly
Bellowing, off to one side, while the dogs and young men
Came running. The lions, however, ripped open the hide
Of the bull and gulped his entrails, lapping their fill
Of dark blood, as the herdsmen vainly attempted to scare them

By urging on the quick dogs. These shrank from sinking
Their teeth in the lions, but stood up close, barking
And springing away.
      And the great ambidextrous god
660 Wrought on the shield a wide and beautiful valley,
Wherein was a meadow for silvery white sheep with sheepfolds,
Shelters, and pens.
      And on it the famous lame god
Made with great skill a dancing-floor[10] like the one
In wide Knossos which Daedalus built a long time ago
For her of the beautiful braids, the fair Ariadne.
There on the floor young men and bull-bringing maidens
Were holding each other's wrists and dancing, the girls
In sheer linen gowns, the men in close-woven tunics
670 To which a faint gloss had been given with soft olive oil.
And on their heads the girls wore lovely garlands,
While all the men had golden daggers hanging
From belts of silver. First they would spin in the dance,
Their skillful feet whirling around like the wheel of a potter
Who squats to give it a turn and see how it runs.
Then they would form in long lines and dance toward each other.
And all around the exquisite dancers a large
And delighted crowd was standing, as in and out
Among them a pair of performers gaily turned cartwheels.
680   At last, all about the rim of the massive shield
He put the powerful stream of the river Oceanus.[11]
      Next, having finished the shield both wide and thick,
He forged Achilles a breastplate brighter than flame,
Then beat out a weighty helmet, close-fitting, crested
With gold, and beautifully wrought, and finally fashioned him
Greaves of flexible tin.
      Now when the great
Ambidextrous god had made all the armor, he took it
And laid it before the feet of Achilles' mother.
690 And she like a hawk swooped down from snowy Olympus,
Bearing the flashing armor Hephaestus had made.

BOOK XIX

The Reconciliation

As crocus-clad Dawn arose from Oceanus' stream,
That she might bring light to gods and mortal men,
Thetis arrived at the ships with the gifts from Hephaestus.
There she found her dear son embracing Patroclus
And wailing, while round him his comrades stood weeping. At once
The bright goddess stood by his side among them, took
His hand warmly in hers, and spoke to him thus:
    "My child,
In spite of our grief, we must allow this man
To lie as he is, since now he is dead forever   10
By will of the gods. But take from Hephaestus this glorious
War-gear, more exquisite armor than any man yet
Has worn on his shoulders."
    So saying, the goddess set down
The armor in front of Achilles, and all of the pieces
Rang in their intricate splendor. Then trembling seized all
Of the Myrmidons, nor did they dare to so much as look
At the armor, but shrank back in terror. But when Achilles
Saw the armor, his wrath increased, and his eyes
Glared out from beneath his lids with the awesome fury   20
Of flame. He picked up the gear and deeply rejoiced
In the glorious gifts of Hephaestus, and when he had sated
His soul with gazing upon their elaborate art,
He spoke to his mother in these winged words:
    "My mother,
This armor Hephaestus has given is fit indeed
To be the work of an immortal god, nor could any
Mortal achieve it. Now, then, I'll arm for the fight,
Though I am extremely uneasy that while I'm away
Flies will light on the bronze-dealt wounds of Patroclus   30
And breed worms in them, thus defiling his corpse.
No life is left in him now, and all of his flesh
Will rot."

Then silver-shod Thetis replied: "My child,
Don't let such things distress you. I'll do my best
To keep from his corpse the pestilent swarms of flies
That feed on the flesh of men slain in battle. Though he
Should lie where he is throughout a whole year, his flesh
Would be sound as ever, if not indeed sounder. But you
40 Go call to the place of assembly the men of Achaea
And there renounce your wrath against Agamemnon,
The people's shepherd. Then arm yourself with all speed
For the battle, and fill your heart with dauntless courage."

Thus she spoke, and her words inspired Achilles
With truly invincible valor, and into the nostrils
Of dead Patroclus the goddess instilled ambrosia
And ruby nectar, that his firm flesh might still
Continue to be so.

Meanwhile, noble Achilles
50 Strode off along the shore of the sea, terribly
Shouting, and soon he aroused the Achaean warriors.
Even they who had always stayed at the ships—
The helmsmen who wielded the steering-oars, and the stewards
Who dealt out the rations—even these came to the place
Of assembly, since now Achilles, who had for so long
Stayed out of the painful fighting, had come forth again.
Those two squires of Ares, battle-staunch Diomedes
And brilliant Odysseus, limped in and sat down at the front,
Each using his spear for support, since both were still feeling
60 Their recent wounds. Last of all came King Agamemnon,
He too still favoring his wound, the gash that Coön,
Son of Antenor, had made with his bronze-pointed spear.
When all the Achaeans had gathered, swift-footed Achilles
Arose and spoke thus:

"My lord Agamemnon, was this, then,
Better for us, for you and for me, that we
With hearts full of sorrow raged in soul-eating hate
On account of a girl? O how I wish that Artemis
There by the ships had killed her with one of her arrows
70 That day when I leveled Lyrnessus and took her as booty.
Then would far fewer Achaeans have bitten the dust
Of this unspeakable earth beneath the hands
Of their foes, while I wouldn't fight because of resentment.
Our quarrel did much good for the Trojans and Hector,
But long indeed the Achaeans will think of our strife
With miserable sorrow. Well, what's done is done.

Now we must conquer the anger within us—because
We must. Now I at least shall put an end
To my wrath. It would hardly become me to go on this way
Forever.[1] But come, Atrides, quickly command 80
The long-haired Achaeans to get themselves ready for battle,
That I may engage the Trojans and see if they wish
To spend this night out here by the ships. Believe me,
Many a Trojan will be very glad to sit down
And rest anywhere, that is if he escapes
The fury of war and my spear!"
    Thus he spoke,
And the well-greaved Achaeans roared their applause, so glad
Were they that the great-souled son of Peleus had now
Renounced his wrath. Then the king of men Agamemnon 90
Spoke among them, not coming out in the center,
But standing before his seat:
    "Surely, O friends,
Danaan heroes, comrades of Ares, surely
You should pay attention to him who stands up to speak,
And not interrupt him. The world's most gifted speaker
Could never make himself heard above the hubbub
Of an army, no matter how strong his voice might be!
Now I wish to speak to Achilles, but I want every man
Of you other Argives to pay close attention and know 100
What I say. Very often you men of Achaea have had
Your say and spoken against me, though really I am not
To blame.[2] But Zeus and powerful Fate are, and the Fury
That stalks through the mist. For that day here in the place
Of assembly they hurled on my soul harsh blindness and caused me
To take from Achilles the prize that is rightfully his.
But what could I do, since God himself brings all things
To pass? That day God worked through his eldest daughter,
Sweet Folly—a ruinous power that blinds the judgments
Of all. Soft are her feet, for she never goes 110
On the ground, but always she treads the air just over
Men's heads, ensnaring first one, then another, and making
Them err through foolish infatuation. Why once
She blinded Zeus himself, though people say he
Is the greatest of gods and men. But even him
Wily Hera beguiled, using well her female cunning,
On that day when Alcmene was due to give birth
In tower-crowned Thebes to the powerful Heracles. That day
Zeus made this pronouncement to all of the gathered gods:

120   " 'Pay attention to me, all gods and goddesses too,
          That I may say what my heart commands me to speak.
          This day shall the goddess of childbirth, the labor-inducing
          Eileithyia, bring forth to the light a man who shall rule
          Over all of his neighbors, one of those men descended
          From me by blood.'
              "But queenly Hera craftily
          Answered him thus: 'Your failure to do what you say,
          O Olympian, will prove you a liar in this. But come,
          Swear to me now an unbreakable oath that he
130   Who this day shall fall between the feet of a woman,
          Born a child of your blood, shall really rule
          Over all of his neighbors.'
                  "So Hera, but Zeus was oblivious
          Of what she intended, and there he swore a great oath—
          Even Zeus, completely deluded by Folly. Then Hera
          Sprang down from the peak of Olympus and quickly arrived
          In Achaean Argos where, as she well knew,
          The noble wife of Sthenelus, son of Perseus,
          Had carried a son in her womb for some seven months.
140   This child Hera brought quickly forth to the light
          Before his due time, but she held back Alcmene's son
          By restraining the goddess of childbirth.* Then Hera herself
          Went with the news to Cronos' son Zeus, and said:
              " 'O Father Zeus, lord of the dazzling bolt,
          I come to inform you that on this day there has
          Already been born that excellent man who shall
          Be King of the Argives—Eurystheus, son of Sthenelus,
          The son of your own son Perseus. Hence he is worthy
          To be the Argives' ruler.'
150   "At this, sharp pain
          Struck deep in the heart of Zeus, and grabbing a handful
          Of Folly's bright-braided hair, he swore an unbreakable
          Oath in his fury of soul that never again
          Would she, the deluder of all, be allowed on Olympus
          Or anywhere near the star-studded heaven. So swearing,
          He whirled her about by the hair and flung her down
          From the starry sky, so that soon she arrived mid the works

---

*Hera hastens the birth of Eurystheus and retards the birth of Heracles. Eurystheus, the
weaker man, thus becomes the beneficiary of Zeus' preceding oath, rather than Heracles,
the stronger man—and Zeus' intended king.

Of men. But still Zeus would groan whenever he saw
His beloved son Heracles toiling beneath some foul labor
That King Eurystheus laid on him. So also I,   160
When huge bright-helmeted Hector was cutting the Argives
To pieces beside the sterns of their ships, could not
Forget Folly, who blinded me from the first. But since
I surely was blinded, and robbed of all sense by Zeus,
I am eager to make amends and to give in requital
Gifts beyond counting. So get yourself ready for battle,
And rouse all the rest of the army. As for the gifts,
I promise you all that lord Odysseus offered
The other night when he came to your lodge. Or,
If you'd rather, stay out of the battle for just a while longer,   170
Straining to fight though you are, and my men shall bring
These gifts from my ship, that you may see for yourself
What glorious things they are."
        Then fast Achilles:
"Renowned Atrides, king of men Agamemnon,
The gifts are yours to give or withhold,[3] as is right
And you see fit. But now, with no further delay,
Let us call up our lust for battle. It hardly becomes us
To talk time away when there is great work to be done.
Now when once again Achilles is seen by many   180
Up front with his bronze-headed spear depleting the ranks
Of Troy, let each of you think who is back in the battle
And fight with your man in the mood such thinking inspires!"
        To which resourceful Odysseus answered, saying:
"Not quite so fast, O godlike Achilles, great warrior
Though you are. Don't send the sons of Achaeans
Into battle with Trojans before they have eaten,
For once the ranks clash and the War-god breathes his fury
Into both sides, the fight will not soon be over.
So order the men to breakfast beside the swift ships   190
On food and wine, the source of their courage and strength.
Not one of us here could fight all day long till sunset
With nothing to eat. No matter how ardent for battle
He were, his legs would be leaden before he knew it,
As thirst and hunger caught up with him, and soon
His knees would grow weak. But he who has his fill
Of food and wine fights all day long, sustained
By the strength of his heart, and beneath him his legs hold out
Until all are ready to quit. So come, Achilles,
Break up the meeting and bid the men go fix a meal.   200

Regarding the gifts, let King Agamemnon have them
Brought here to the place of assembly, that all the Achaeans
May see them and your own spirit be warmed with delight.
And let him stand up mid the Argives and swear an oath
To you that he has never gone to bed
With the girl and made love with her, as men and women,
O Prince, so naturally do. And let your own heart
Be forgiving and gracious. Then let him make further amends
With a lavish feast in his lodge, that you may lack nothing
210 You have coming to you. And you, Agamemnon, hereafter
Be juster toward others. A king loses nothing who makes
Amends to one he has first unjustly offended."
    To him the commander-in-chief Agamemnon replied:
"Your words, O son of Laertes, have filled me with gladness,
For justly you have explained as well as expounded,
And nothing has been left out. The oath you describe
I am ready and anxious to take, nor shall I be false
Before God in so doing. But let Achilles stay here
For a while, hot though he be for battle, and all
220 Of you others stay too, till the gifts are brought from my lodge
And we swear our oaths of faith with due sacrifice.
And as for you, Odysseus, these are your orders:
Pick out a number of men, the best young princes
Among the Achaeans, and bring from my ship all the gifts
That we promised Achilles the other night, and bring
The women as well. And let Talthybius get
A boar ready, that here in the midst of this huge gathered host
We may make our due sacrifice to Zeus and the Sun."
    Fast-fighting Achilles, however, answered him, saying:
230 "Most famous Atrides, king of men Agamemnon,
It would be much better for you to take care of these things
At some other time, when perhaps there shall come a lull
In the fighting and when my own spirit is somewhat appeased.[4]
But now the mangled dead still lie where Hector
Left them when Zeus gave glory to him, and you
And Odysseus bid us eat breakfast! My orders now
To all the Achaeans would be to fight hard all day
On empty and starving stomachs, and then, when the sun
Goes down and we have avenged our disgrace, to make
240 A huge meal for ourselves. Until that time no food
Or drink shall pass down my throat, at least, since my
Dear friend lies torn in my lodge, his feet toward the door,
While round him our comrades are mourning. Hence I have no interest

At all in food and drink, but only in slaughter
And blood and the agonized groans of mangled men."
     Then Odysseus, always resourceful, answered him thus:
"O Achilles, son of Peleus, strongest by far
Of all the Achaeans, surely you're stronger than I
And more than a little better at hurling the spear,
But I in counsel may very well far surpass you,   250
Since I am older and have experienced more.
So listen to me and let your heart heed what I say.
Men soon get enough of hard fighting, especially when Zeus,
The dispenser of victory, tips his balance against them.
Then with their bronze they reap far more straw than grain,
And soon they're exhausted. Nor can we consider mourning
The dead by denying our bellies, since day after day
So many men die that, believe me, there'd be no more eating
At all! So we have no choice but to bury the dead,
Hardening our hearts and weeping for one day only.   260
For all those still left alive from the hateful tumult
Of battle must make themselves eat and drink, that we
May go on in armor of unyielding bronze to fight
The foe without undue pause and harder than ever.
Now let no man in this army hold back for want
Of orders—these are your orders, and woe to him
Who loiters here at the ships! All together, let us
March out and charge with savagely slashing Ares
Upon the horse-breaking Trojans."
    So saying, Odysseus   270
Went off with the sons of King Nestor, Phyleus' son Meges,
Thoas, Meriones, Creon's son Lycomedes,
And Melanippus, and quickly they strode to the lodge
Of Atreus' son Agamemnon, where each man followed
Instructions. They brought from the shelters the seven tripods
Atrides had promised, twelve horses, and twenty bright cauldrons,
And forth they led seven women, flawless at work
With their hands, and lovely Briseis made eight. Then Odysseus
Weighed out ten talents of gold and led the way back
With the young Achaeans loaded down with the gifts.   280
These they set in the place of assembly, and up rose
Agamemnon, while the god-voiced herald Talthybius stood
By the army's commander-in-chief holding a boar
With both hands. And the son of Atreus drew the knife
That always hung beside his great scabbard and from
The head of the boar he cut the first bristles. Then lifting

His hands in prayer to Father Zeus, with all
The Argives silently sitting, heeding their King
In good order, he looked up at heaven's expanse and prayed:
290   "May Zeus be my witness first, the highest and best
Of gods, then Earth and Sun and the Furies that punish
Men in the nether world for swearing falsely,
That never yet have I laid a hand on Briseis,
Neither to take her to bed nor for anything else.
She has lived in my lodge the whole time quite unmolested.
And if this oath be false in any way,
May the gods everlasting inflict me with countless sorrows,
All that they give to a man who sins against them
By swearing falsely."
300   He prayed, then cut the boar's throat
With the unfeeling bronze, whereupon Talthybius whirled
With the carcass and flung it into the great gray gulf
Of the sea, thus providing a feast for the fish. Then Achilles
Stood up and spoke mid the war-loving Argives, saying:
      "O Father Zeus, how total is that cruel blindness
You cast upon men! Agamemnon would never have filled
My heart with rage, nor ruthlessly taken the girl
In spite of my wrath, if you, O Zeus, had not
Already decreed that many Achaeans should die.
310 But now let all of you go to your meal, that we
May soon clash with the Trojans."
      With this, he quickly broke up
The assembly, and all of the others dispersed to their ships.
But the spirited Myrmidons busied themselves with the gifts
And brought them all to the ship of godlike Achilles.
There they stowed them away in his shelters, leaving
The women there and proudly driving the horses
Off to his herd.
      But when Briseis, gorgeous
320 As sweet Aphrodite the golden, saw Patroclus
Gashed and torn with the mangling bronze, she flung
Herself on him and shrieked in her grief, and with her hands
She tore at her breasts and soft neck and beautiful face.
Wailing, this woman lovely as goddesses cried:
      "Patroclus, most precious to my wretched heart, I left you
Alive when I went from this lodge, but now, O leader
Of many, I come back to find you lying here dead.
Thus misery continues to follow misery for me.
The husband to whom my father and queenly mother

Gave me I saw lying dead before our city, 330
Gashed with the mangling bronze, and my three precious brothers,
All sons of the mother who bore me, were likewise all
Overtaken by their day of doom. But you, when Achilles
Killed my husband and leveled King Mynes' city,
You wouldn't allow me to grieve, but comforted me
With the promise that you would have great Achilles make me
His lawful wife, and have him take me to Phthia
In one of his ships and joyfully celebrate there
With a wedding feast mid the Myrmidons. Hence I weep
For your death without ceasing, for you the forever gentle."⁵ 340
Thus she spoke, constantly sobbing, and all
Of the other women added their tears to hers,
Outwardly mourning Patroclus, but also lamenting
Their own miserable plight. And around Achilles
The Achaean elders gathered, pleading with him
To eat. But he refused, groaning and saying:
"I plead with you, my friends, if only someone
Will listen, not to urge food and drink on me,
Since I am so full of heart-rending grief. I'll go
As I am till sundown, no matter how empty I get." 350
At this the other chiefs left him there, but the two sons
Of Atreus stayed, as did Idomeneus, Nestor,
And the knightly old Phoenix, all trying further to comfort
Their grieving friend. But his heart would not be appeased
At all, till he had hurled himself straight into
The blood-dripping jaws of war. Remembering Patroclus,
He heaved a deep sigh and said:
"Ah how very well,
O my unlucky, most precious friend, how very well
You would set forth a fine meal for us in this lodge 360
And with what dispatch, whenever the Argives were hastening
To hurl a tear-fraught attack on the horse-taming Trojans!
But now you lie here, gashed and torn, and I, so much
Do I miss you, have no wish at all to eat or to drink,
Though there is plenty right here at hand. Nothing
That I could suffer could be more painful than this,
Not even news of my father's death, who now
In Phthia is probably shedding bitter tears for lack
Of the son he lost, while I am here in a land
Of strangers, fighting on horrible Helen's account 370
With men of Troy—nor even news that my own son
Was dead could hurt me more, he who is being

Brought up for me in Scyros, my own Neoptolemus,
If indeed that godlike boy is still alive.[6]
Always before, I hoped in my heart that I
Alone would die far away from horse-pasturing Argos
Here in the land of Troy, but that you, Patroclus,
Would go back to Phthia and take my son with you,* sailing
From Scyros in a fast black ship, then showing him all things
380 At home—my treasures, my slaves, and my great high-roofed house.
For Peleus by now is probably dead and gone,
Or barely alive, worn out with hateful old age
And his miserable waiting for news that I am dead."

Thus he spoke in his weeping, and all of the elders
Still present added their groans, each one of them thinking
Of those he had left at home. And as they wept,
Cronos' son Zeus both saw and pitied their grief,
And at once he spoke these winged words to Pallas Athena:
"My child, you've now completely forsaken your own
390 Favorite fighter. Have you no more concern for Achilles
At all? He sits down there in front of his high-horned
Vessels, weeping for his dead friend. The others
Have gone to their meal, but he will touch nothing to eat
Or to drink. But go, distill into his breast
Delightful ambrosia and nectar, to stave off the pangs
Of hunger later on."

So saying, he prompted
Athena, a goddess who needed no urging, and she
Like a wide-winged, high-screaming hawk shot down from heaven
400 Through the bright air. And while the Achaeans were hurriedly
Arming for battle throughout the camp, she instilled
Delightful ambrosia and nectar into the breast
Of Achilles, that grim pangs of hunger might not undo
His strong limbs. Then she returned to the thick-walled house
Of her almighty Father, just as the Argives came pouring
Out from the ships. As when from Zeus the snowflakes
Come fluttering down thick and fast, driven on by hard blasts
Of the sky-born North Wind, so now from the ships came flashing
Bright helmets, bossed shields, bronze-gleaming breastplates, and
spears
410 Of tough ash. And the brightness of all went up to the sky,
As earth all around seemed to laugh, so radiant was she

---

*See endnote 1 to book XVIII.

Beneath all that flashing of bronze, and the ground resounded
Like thunder beneath the feet of the marching army.
     In the midst of all this, great Achilles put on his war-gear.
He gnashed his teeth, and his eyes glared fierce as fire,
For into his heart unbearable grief had pierced.
Thus in his hatred of Trojans, he put on the gifts
Of the god, the armor Hephaestus had forged for him
With toil and painstaking art. First he covered
His shins with greaves, fair greaves with ankle-clasps of silver.   420
Next, about his chest he put the breastplate,
And from his shoulders he slung the bronze sword with the studs
Of bright silver, and then with one hand he caught up the shield
Both wide and thick, and from it there came a gleam
Like that of the moon. And as when sailors at sea,
Borne by a storm far over the fish-full deep
Far away from their loved ones, glimpse the gleam of a fire
From some lonely hut in the mountains, so now from the beautifully
Intricate shield of Achilles the brightness went far
Through the air. Then lifting the weighty helmet he set it   430
Upon his head, where it sparkled and shone like a star,
And the golden plumes that Hephaestus had fixed in the crest
Of horsehair danced gaily above it. And royal Achilles
Tried himself in the armor to see if it fitted
Him well and allowed his splendid limbs to move freely,
And he, the people's shepherd, felt light as a bird,
As if that armor were wings to lift him aloft.
Then from its stand he took the spear of his father,
A huge spear, heavy and long. No Achaean fighter
Could wield it but mighty Achilles himself, this strong spear   440
Of ash that Cheiron the Centaur had given to Peleus,
Achilles' dear father. It came from the peak of Mount Pelion,
And was meant to bring death to the foe.*
     Automedon and Alcimus
Busily harnessed the horses, putting about them
The beautiful breast-bands, forcing the bits back into
Their jaws, and drawing the reins behind to the sturdy
Rail. Then Automedon seized the bright hand-fitting lash
And mounted the car, and behind him Achilles stepped up,
Fully armed and as dazzling as blazing Hyperion. Then harshly   450
He called to his father's horses:

---

*See XVI.167–172 for the ash spear of Cheiron.

"Xanthus and Balius,
World-famous foals of Podarge, this time take care
To bring your rider back safe to the Danaan host
When the fighting is over, instead of leaving him dead
On the plain as you left Patroclus."
        From under the yoke
The horse Xanthus answered, he of the bright-glancing feet.
He bowed his head so that all of his mane, streaming
460   From under the yoke-pad, swept the ground, and Hera,
The white-armed goddess, gave him a voice:
        "This time,
O gigantic Achilles, we'll bring you back safe enough,
Though surely your day of doom is already near.
Nor shall we be the cause of your death. That will be
Brought about by a very great god and powerful Fate.
It was through no sloth nor slowness of ours that Trojans
Were able to strip the gear from Patroclus' shoulders,
But one of the strongest gods of all, the son
470   Of lovely-haired Leto, slew him among the front fighters
And gave the glory to Hector. We two can run
As fast as the blasting West Wind, which people say
Is the fleetest of winds, but you are already fated
To die, overwhelmed by the force of a god and a mortal."*
        When thus he had spoken, the Furies deprived him of speech,
And Achilles, deeply disturbed, replied: "Xanthus,
What need have you to prophesy death for me?
I am already aware that it is my fate
To die here, far from my much-loved father and mother.
480   Even so, I'll not relax till I've given the Trojans
Their fill of bloody war."
        So saying, he yelled
And drove those solid-hoofed horses up mid the foremost.

---

*Prior to Xanthus' prophecy, Achilles had known only that he would die after Hector.

BOOK XX

The Gods at War

Thus beside the beaked ships and all around you,
O war-starved Achilles, Achaeans armed for the fight,
And up the plain from them the Trojans did likewise.
But powerful Zeus, from the many-ridged peak of Olympus,
Bade Themis call the gods to a meeting,[1] and quickly
She went to them all and summoned them to the assembly
At Zeus's palace. Not one river-god was absent
Except Oceanus, nor any nymph, of all those
Who haunt the lovely groves, the springs where rivers
Rise, and the grassy fields. Once there at the house   10
Of the cloud-gathering god, all the immortals took seats
Within the rows of bright columns which skillful Hephaestus
Had made for Zeus their Father.
⠀⠀⠀⠀⠀Nor did earth-shaking
Poseidon ignore Themis' call, but emerged from the brine
To join them. And now he sat in their midst and inquired
About Zeus's purpose: "Why, O lord of the lightning,
Have you called this meeting of gods? Are you worried about
The Achaeans and Trojans, between whom battle is almost
Ready to blaze?"   20
⠀⠀⠀⠀⠀Then Zeus of the gathering gale
Answered him thus: "You're right, great shaker of shores,
I have indeed called this gathering of the immortals
Because of my deep concern for those warriors, doomed
Though they are. I myself, of course, will stay on a ridge
Of Olympus, from which I may watch the war as I please.
But all of you other immortals go down and help
The Achaeans and Trojans, aiding whichever side
You prefer. For if fast-fighting Achilles attacks
The unaided Trojans, they won't be able to hold out   30
A moment. They've never been able to so much as see him
Without fear and trembling, and now that flaming rage
For the death of his friend is eating his heart, I'm afraid
He will outstrip his fate by leveling the walls of the city."

These words of Cronos' son Zeus awoke stubborn war,
And the gods went down to join their differing favorites.
Hera and Pallas Athena went to the ships
Of the Argives, and with them Poseidon and luck-bringing
           Hermes,
The wiliest god of all. And with these went Hephaestus,
40 Exulting in might, for though he limped, his thin legs
Were nimble enough. But huge bright-helmeted Ares
And Apollo with hair unshorn went down to the Trojans,
Along with arrow-showering Artemis, Leto,
The river-god Xanthus, and Aphrodite, adorer
Of smiles.
      So long as the gods were not there, the Achaeans
Won glorious victory, since now Achilles, who had
For so long stayed out of the painful fighting, had come forth
Again, and there was no Trojan whose legs did not tremble
50 At sight of quick-footed Achilles, flaming in arms
Like the man-maiming War-god himself. But when the Olympians
Entered the tumult, host-harrying Hatred arose
With a vengeance. Athena screamed her great war-cry, now
From beside the deep trench outside the wall, now
From the surf-beaten shore of the sea, and opposite her
Dread Ares, ominous as a dark whirlwind, screamed
From the citadel heights, and again as he charged down the slope
Of Callicolone beside the banks of Simoeis.
      Thus the happy gods greatly augmented the clash
60 Of battle and made bitter strife break out everywhere
Between the two armies fighting in horrible uproar.
Then from on high the Father of gods and men
Awesomely thundered, while down below Poseidon
Caused the limitless earth to rumble and quake
From plain to sheer mountain peaks. Well-watered Ida
Was shaken from bottom to top, as were the city
Of Troy and ships of Achaea. Hades, god
Of ghosts in the world under ground, was filled with panic
And sprang from his throne with a scream, lest Poseidon, shaker
70 Of earth, should split the ground open above him and thus
Reveal to men and immortals the ghastly abodes
Of death, the moldering horrors that even the gods
Would look on with loathing.
           Such was the mighty uproar
When god clashed with god in strife. For against lord Poseidon
Stood Phoebus Apollo, god of the winged shafts,

And opposite Ares stood bright-eyed Athena. Opposing
Hera was Phoebus' sister, the archer Artemis,
Goddess of golden shafts and the echoing shouts
Of the chase, while coming forth against Leto was powerful   80
Luck-bringing Hermes, and there opposing Hephaestus
Came the god of the great deep-swirling river,
Called Xanthus by the immortals, Scamander by men.
    So gods advanced to meet gods.[2] But Achilles had interest
In none but Priam's son Hector, with whose blood
He most lusted to glut the battling Ares, him
Of the tough hide shield. Host-urging Apollo, however,
Inspired great strength in Aeneas and sent him to face
The raging son of Peleus. Assuming the form
And voice of Priam's son Lycaon, Apollo,   90
Son of Zeus, spoke thus to the counselor of Trojans:
    "Aeneas, where now are the brags you made to the princes
Of Troy when you, over wine, declared yourself ready
To fight man to man with Peleus' son Achilles?"
    To which Aeneas: "Lycaon, why would you tell me
This way to fight face to face, against my will,
With haughty Achilles? Not that it would be
My first encounter with him, since once already
He put me to flight with his spear, driving me down
From Mount Ida where he had come for our cattle the time   100
He sacked and laid waste Lyrnessus and Pedasus both.
That time Zeus saved me by giving me strength and putting
Great speed in my legs. Else I would surely have died
At the hands of Achilles and those of Athena, who went
Before him bearing the light of victory and bidding him
Kill with his bronze-headed spear both Trojans and Leleges.*
May no man, then, fight face to face with Achilles,
For always beside him a god goes, warding off death.
And even unaided his spear flies very straight,
Nor does it stop save deep in the flesh of some mortal.   110
Still, were God to give us an equal chance
In man-to-man combat, he would not easily beat me,
Not though he claims to be made of solid bronze!"
    Then lord Apollo, son of Zeus, replied:
"Heroic Aeneas, why don't you also invoke

---

*At XX.200–225, in their upcoming battle, Achilles will taunt Aeneas with the memory
of this same incident.

The gods everlasting? After all, men say Aphrodite,
Daughter of Zeus, is your mother, while surely Achilles
Was born of a lesser goddess. Remember, your mother
Is Zeus's own daughter, his the sea-ancient's child.
120   But on! Charge with your unyielding bronze straight at him,
And don't be turned aside by any insults
Or threats from him."
                So saying, he breathed great power
Into Aeneas, and he, the people's shepherd,
Strode out through the front line of fighters, his bronze helmet flashing.
Nor was the son of Anchises unnoticed by Hera
As out he went through the moil of men to face
The son of Peleus. Calling her friends about her,
The goddess spoke thus:
130   "Poseidon, Athena, you two
Consider what we should do now. Here comes Aeneas,
Flaming in bronze, set on by Phoebus Apollo
To face Achilles in fight. But come, let us
Turn him back at once, or else let one of us stand
By the side of Achilles and give him great power too.
Nor should we allow his spirit to fail at all,
That he may know beyond doubt that we who love him
Are the best of immortals, while those who have hitherto warded
Defeat from the Trojans are deities worthless as wind.
140   Here we have come from Olympus to mix in this melee
And keep Achilles safe all this day long,
Though afterward he shall suffer whatever Fate spun
For him with the thread of his life on the day his mother
Bore him. But if he fails to learn all this
From heaven itself, he may be unduly afraid
When some god confronts him in battle. For hard indeed
Are the gods to look upon when they appear
In their own true forms."
                And Poseidon, creator of earthquakes,
150   Replied: "Hera, don't rage beyond what is wise.
It hardly becomes you. I myself would not wish
To hurl gods together in hate, and anyway we
Are much too strong for those others. Rather, let us
Go apart from the battle to where we can sit down and watch,
And war shall be for mortals. However, if Ares
Or Phoebus Apollo should start anything, or should they
Hold back Achilles and keep him from fighting, then quickly

Fierce war shall come from us too. And very soon then,
I believe, those others shall leave the battle and join
The gods on Olympus, defeated by our forceful hands!"   160
  So saying, Poseidon, god with the blue-black hair,
Led the way straight to the mighty bulwark of earth
That the Trojans and Pallas Athena had heaped up high
For godlike Heracles, that he might retreat behind it
Whenever the huge sea-monster, sent by Poseidon
To lay waste the land of the Trojans, drove him back
From the beach to the plain. There the gods with Poseidon
Sat down and wreathed their shoulders with cloud that could not
Be dispelled, while opposite them the gods backing Trojans
Sat down on the brow of Callicolone round you,   170
O daring Apollo, and Ares, taker of towns.
  Thus both parties sat in council, both uneager
To enter the sorrowful conflict, though high-throned Zeus
Had bidden them to.
  Meanwhile, the whole plain was aflame
With bronze-flashing men and horses, and earth resounded
And rang beneath the tumultuous beat of their feet
As they charged toward each other. But now their two greatest
    champions
Came out in the space between the two armies, spoiling
To battle each other, Aeneas, son of Anchises,   180
And noble Achilles. First came Aeneas, defiantly
Tossing his heavy-helmeted head, gripping
His gallant shield close in front of his chest, and brandishing
Fiercely his bronze-headed spear. Against him Achilles,
Son of Peleus, came charging on like a lion,
A ravenous beast that all the men of a village
Have come out anxious to kill. At first he pays them
No heed, but goes his way till one of the fast
And lusty young spearmen sinks a lance in his flesh.
Then with a jaw-splitting roar he gathers himself   190
To charge, and foam forms all round his fangs, while in him
His great heart groans. Lashing his ribs and flanks
With his tail, he works himself up for the fight, then charges
Straight on in his fiery-eyed fury, careless of whether
He kill or be killed there in the front line of spearmen.
So now Achilles was driven on by his fury
And warrior's pride to go out and face great Aeneas.
And when they had come sufficiently near each other,

Fast-footed royal Achilles spoke to him thus:
200   "Tell me, Aeneas, why have you come out so far
From the ranks to stand and confront me? Can it be
That your heart is ambitious and fills you with hope of soon
Replacing King Priam as lord of the horse-taming Trojans?
What folly! for even if you should kill and strip me,
Priam would not give the kingship to you. King Priam
Has sons of his own, and his mind is sound, not silly!
Or have the Trojans laid out an estate for you
Greater than any other, acres of orchard
And plowland for you to enjoy—if you should happen
210   To kill me, that is. Not easy, I think, you'll find
That assignment. For surely I now recall a day
Some time ago when I routed you with my spear.
Don't you remember, Aeneas, when you were alone
And I made you leave your cattle and hurtle headlong
Down the slopes of Mount Ida? Not so much as one little look
Did you cast behind you that day as you ran. From there
You fled to Lyrnessus, which I attacked with the help
Of Athena and Father Zeus and sacked it completely,
Leading the women off no longer free.
220   Zeus and the other gods saved you that time, but not
This day, I believe, will they save you again, as you
Undoubtedly think they will. So I myself warn you
Not to confront me, but lose yourself in the crowd
Before you suffer disaster. Once it occurs,
It will be too late for you not to play the fool!"

     And Aeneas answered him, saying: "Son of Peleus,
Don't think to scare me with words, as if I were some
Little boy, since I am at least the equal of you
When it comes to hurling insults. We both know who
230   Each other is with regard to parents and lineage,
For though neither one of us ever laid eyes on the other's
Dear parents, we've both heard the stories which mortal men
Have passed down from days gone by. Men say you're the son
Of matchless Peleus and that your mother is Thetis,
She of the beautiful braids, a child of the brine.
But I claim descent from courageous Anchises, my father,
And Aphrodite herself![3] And of these two couples,
One or the other shall this day mourn a dear son,
For I don't think we two shall part and leave this struggle
240   With nothing exchanged but infantile prattle. But if
You really would hear who I am, listen and learn

What many know already. First of all
Cloud-gathering Zeus begot Dardanus, who founded Dardania
Before sacred Ilium ever went up in the plain
As a city for mortals, who lived at that time on the slopes
Of well-watered Ida. And Dardanus too had a son,
King Erichthonius, one who lived to become
The richest man in the world. He had a herd
Of three thousand horses that grazed in the low-lying meadows,
Spirited mares with fine little colts beside them.   250
With these as they grazed the North Wind fell deeply in love,
And changing himself to a glossy-maned black stallion
He sired twelve colts on them. These, when they galloped
The grain-giving earth, could cross in their sport a field
Of ripe barley without so much as disturbing a kernel,
And when they cavorted across the broad back of the brine,
They would skim the high waves that break on the gray salt-sea.
Erichthonius, then, begot Tros, King of the Trojans,
And Tros had three matchless sons—Assaracus, Ilus,
And godlike Ganymede,* the best-looking boy ever born,   260
So handsome the gods caught him up to Olympus, that he
Might live with them there and be the cupbearer of Zeus.
And Ilus in turn begot peerless Laomedon, father
Of Priam, Tithonus, Clytius, Lampus, and Hicetaon,
Scion of Ares. And Assaracus' son was Capys,
Who sired Anchises, who next begot me, and Priam
Begot Prince Hector. Such is my lineage, Achilles,
And the blood I claim to be of.
        "But as for prowess
In battle, Zeus gives it or takes it away as he,   270
The almighty, sees fit. So come, let us no longer
Stand here in the midst of battle prating like two
Little boys. There is surely no lack of insults for either
Of us to mouth, vile things so many they'd sink
A ship of two hundred oars. For the tongue of man
Is a glib and versatile organ, and from it come many
And various words, whose range of expression is wide
In every direction. And the sort of words a man says
Is the sort he hears in return. But what makes the two of us

---

*These are the three lines of Trojan descent: the descendants of Assaracus are Anchises
and Aeneas; the descendants of Ilus are Priam and Hector; Ganymede, Zeus' "cupbearer,"
will have no descendants.

280 Wrangle and nag like a couple of spiteful women,
     Who having aroused in each other heart-eating hatred
     Go out in the street and spit harsh words back and forth,
     As many false as true, since hateful rage
     Does the talking? For since I am eager for combat, you'll not
     Turn me back with mere words before we have battled with bronze
     Man to man. Come then, let us at once have a taste
     Of each other's spear-points!"
            He spoke, and drove his huge lance
     Into Achilles' dread and marvelous shield,
290 Which loudly cried out about the bronze point of the weapon.
     Achilles, gripped with quick terror, shoved the shield out
     With his powerful hand, away from his flesh, for he thought
     The long-shadowing spear of great-hearted Aeneas would easily
     Pierce it—childish fool that he was not to know
     In his mind and heart that the glorious gifts of the gods
     Will not easily break or give way before the onslaught
     Of mortals. Nor did the huge lance of fiery Aeneas
     Tear through the shield, for the gold, the god's gift, held it back.
     Though he drove it clean through the first two layers, there remained
300 Three other folds, for the great limping god had hammered
     Together five layers in all, two bronze, two tin,
     And between them a gold one, in which the ashen spear stopped.
            Then great Achilles let fly his long-shadowing spear
     And struck the round shield of Aeneas not far from the rim
     Where the bronze and backing of bull's-hide were thinnest. And the
            shield
     Gave out a strident shriek as through it tore
     The shaft of Pelian ash. Then Aeneas was gripped
     With panic, and cringing he held the shield up, away
     From his flesh, as the spear shot over his back and stilled
310 Its force in the ground, though it split apart two circles
     Of the Trojan's man-guarding shield. Having thus escaped
     The long lance, Aeneas stood up, and the sight of that shaft
     So close to his flesh filled his bright eyes with measureless
     Panic and pain. But Achilles whipped out his keen blade
     And charged down upon him, ferociously screaming his war-cry,
     And mighty Aeneas picked up a huge stone, one
     That no two men of today could even lift
     But that he picked up with one hand and easily threw.
     Then Aeneas would surely have struck with the stone the helmet
320 Or life-saving shield of charging Achilles, who then

Would have closed with him and taken his life with the sword,
If Poseidon had not been keeping sharp watch. At once
He spoke thus mid the gods everlasting:
        "Truly my grief
Is great for high-souled Aeneas, who soon indeed
Shall go down to Hades' halls, killed by Achilles
For heeding the word of far-working Apollo—childish
Fool that he was! For Apollo will not keep sad death
From him for a moment. But why should that innocent man
Suffer woes that belong to others, he who has always   330
Given such pleasing gifts to the sky-ruling gods?
So come, let us save him from death, for Zeus himself
Will be angry if now Achilles cuts the man down.
It is surely already decreed that Aeneas shall outlive
The war, so that Dardanus' seed may not die and his line
Disappear, since Zeus adored Dardanus more than he did
Any other child he had by a mortal woman.
For now Cronos' son has come to despise the house
Of Priam, and surely the mighty Aeneas shall soon rule
The Trojans, and after him the sons of his sons,   340
Great princes yet to be born."[4]
        Then heifer-eyed Hera,
Queen of the gods, replied: "O shaker of shores,
You must decide for yourself concerning Aeneas,
Whether you wish to save him or let him be killed,
Despite his great prowess, by Peleus' son Achilles.
For we two, Pallas Athena and I, have sworn
Very numerous oaths in the presence of all the immortals
That we would never keep from the Trojans the hard day
Of doom, not even when Troy shall burn with furious   350
Fire lit by the warlike sons of Achaeans."
        When Poseidon heard this, he went alone through the fight
Mid a tumult of hurtling spears till he came to Aeneas
And famous Achilles. Quickly he covered the eyes
Of Peleus' son with mist, then drew from the shield
Of Aeneas the sharp ashen spear. This he laid down
At the feet of Achilles, but Aeneas he swept from the ground
And sent him vaulting high over the heads of numerous
Heroes and horses till finally he came down
Far out on the edge of the charge-churned chaos of battle   360
Just where the Caucones were arming themselves for the fray.
There earthquake-making Poseidon drew close to his side,

And his words came winged with warning:
    "Aeneas, what god
Commands you to fight in such blind rage with the high-hearted
Son of Peleus, who is both stronger than you
And dearer to the immortals? Rather, give ground
Whenever you meet him, or you before your time
Will enter the house of Hades. But after Achilles
370 Collides with his own dark fate and dies, then summon
Your courage to fight their greatest champions, for none
Of the other Achaeans will ever be able to kill you."
    So saying, he left him there, having told him all.
Then at once he dispelled the marvelous mist from the eyes
Of Achilles, who stared hard about him, and much amazed
Spoke thus to his own great heart:
    "A miracle, surely!
This wonder my eyes behold. Here lies my spear
On the ground, yet he at whom I so eagerly hurled it
380 Is nowhere in sight. Truly it seems that Aeneas
Is dear indeed to the immortal gods, though I
Thought his claims were idle and empty. Well, let him go.
He's so glad to be still alive he'll hardly have heart
To try me again. But now I will call to the Danaans,
Lovers of fight, then go forth myself and test
The mettle of other Trojans."
    With this, he ran
Down the ranks calling out to each man: "No longer, O noble
Achaeans, stand off from the Trojans, but come, let man
390 Attack man, and all of you fight like fury! Very hard
It is for me, no matter how mighty, to deal
With so many foes and fight with them all. Even Ares,
Immortal god though he is, could never hurl back
A charge so galloping fierce as this of the Trojans,
Nor could Athena—not that I intend
To be idle, so long as I've hands and feet and the strength
To use them in battle. Straight through their front rank I will charge,
Nor do I believe any Trojan will greatly rejoice
To find himself close to my spear."
400   Thus he encouraged
The Danaan troops, while glorious Hector called out
To the Trojans, saying that he would go face Achilles:
"You high-hearted Trojans, don't let Peleus' son scare you.
With words I too could battle even the gods,
Though with a spear it would be much harder, since they

Are far stronger than we. But Achilles will be doing well
To fulfill half of his boast. The rest he will leave
Undone. Against him now I will go, though his hands
Are like flame—I say though his hands are like flame, and his heart
Like gleaming iron!"   410
      So saying, he urged them on,
And the Trojans faced the Achaeans and raised their spears
To charge. Then both armies clashed in furious fight
And shrill war-cries went up. But Phoebus Apollo
Came close to Hector and said: "Hector, don't think
For a moment of singly facing Achilles, but wait
For him in the ranks in the midst of roaring conflict,
Or surely he'll cut you down with his spear, or close
And use his sword."
      He spoke, and Hector, terrified,   420
Shrank back among his men, having heard the voice
Of a god.
      But Achilles, his heart clad in valor, charged
Mid the Trojans, screaming his awesome war-cry,[5] and first
He cut down Iphition, the excellent son of Otrynteus
And leader of many men. A Naiad nymph
Had borne him to King Otrynteus, taker of towns,
At the foot of Mount Tmolus in the opulent land
Of Hyda. Him, as he charged straight on, Prince Achilles
Caught with his spear full on the head and split   430
His skull in two. He fell with a thunderous crash,
And over his corpse Achilles exulted, crying:
      "How very low you lie now, O son of Otrynteus,
Most terrifying of men. Right here is the place
Of your death, though you were born on the huge estate
Of your fathers by Lake Gygaea near fish-teeming Hyllus
And eddying Hermus."
      Such was his boast, but shadow
Eclipsed the eyes of Iphition, and quickly the rims
Of Achaean chariots cut him to shreds, right   440
Where he fell in the front of the war-clash, and fiercely Achilles
Went on to slaughter Demoleon, son of Antenor.
That excellent bulwark in battle Achilles stabbed
In the temple, easily piercing his bronze-cheeked helmet.
On through the bronze and bone beneath tore the point
And spattered the helmet inside with the warrior's brains,
Thus stopping Demoleon's furious charge. Then,
As Hippodamas sprang from his car and fled before him,

He thrust his spear deep into his back. And as
450 He gasped out his life he roared like a bull that young men
Drag bellowing in as an offering for Helice's lord
Poseidon, for bull's blood pleases the Earthshaker most.
Even so Hippodamas bellowed as his proud spirit
Took leave of his bones. Then Achilles charged on with his spear
In pursuit of Prince Polydorus, son of Priam.
His father had strictly forbidden his entering the battle,
For he was the youngest and dearest of all his sons,
And the fastest of all as a runner. But now, showing off
His fleetness of foot like a child, he dashed here and there
460 Through the front-fighting ranks till he was deprived of his life.
For him Achilles, fast on his feet as any,
Struck with a cast of his spear in the small of the back
As he darted by, squarely striking him where
The gold clasps of his war-belt joined and the halves of his breastplate
Met. The spear-point tore its way through and emerged
By the navel, and round him a cloud of blackness closed in,
As he sank to the ground clutching his guts with both hands.
          But when Prince Hector saw Polydorus his brother
Clutching his guts and sinking to earth, his own eyes
470 Dimmed with tears, nor could he bear any longer
To range apart, but out he strode to encounter
Achilles, brandishing his keen spear that flashed
Like a flame. When Achilles saw him, he poised his own weapon,
Then challenged him thus:
          "Now near is the man who most
Of all men has caused my heart pain, the man who murdered
My cherished comrade, and now no longer shall we two
Shrink from each other down lanes of hard-fighting men."
          He spoke, then savagely scowling at Hector, said:
480 "Come nearer, that all the sooner you may be bound
In the bonds of destruction!"
          But Hector, his bronze helmet flashing,
Boldly answered him thus: "O son of Peleus,
Don't think to scare me with words, as if I were some
Little boy, since I am at least the equal of you
When it comes to hurling insults. Also, I know
Very well how able you are with a spear, and that I
Am not nearly so strong. Yet truly the outcome of this fight
Lies in the lap of the gods eternal, who may
490 Allow me, though weaker, to take your life with a spear-cast,
Since my weapon too has proved killing-keen before!"

So saying, he drew back his spear and threw, but Athena,
Breathing lightly, blew it back from Achilles
So that it returned to Prince Hector and fell on the ground
At his feet. Then savagely Peleus' son sprang at him,
Screaming his terrible war-cry and eager to kill.
But Apollo caught Hector up, with all the ease
Of a god, and wrapped him in cloud.[6] Three times fast Achilles
Charged and thrust his spear into the mist, but when
The fourth time he rushed like a demon upon him, he cried   500
A chilling and awesome cry and spoke to Hector
In these winged words:
            "Again, you dog, you've managed
To get away with your life, though this time just barely!
Once more you have Phoebus Apollo to thank, to whom
You must be careful to pray before you come
Within even the sound of hurtling spears. Well,
Believe me, I'll finish you yet—the next time we meet,
If only some god will also look out for me.
Right now I'll take my rage out on your friends, whomever   510
I happen to come on!"
            So saying, he thrust his spear
Through the neck of Dryops, who fell at his feet. Leaving
Him there, Achilles went on to put out of action
Demuchus, Philetor's son, a big man and brave,
First wounding his knee with a spear-cast, then ending his life
With a slash of his lengthy sword. Next he charged down
On Laogonus and Dardanus, sons of Bias, and knocked them
Both from their chariot, taking one's life with a cast
Of his spear and killing the other in close with his sword.   520
Then Alastor's son Tros—he reached for the knees of Achilles,
Pleading with him to take him alive, to pity
A man the same age as himself and not cut him off
So young, fool that he was not to know that with him
There would be no heeding, that there was nothing sweet-tempered
Or mild in Achilles, but only ferocious heart—
Tros tried to hug the man's knees, jabbering a prayer
To be spared, but Achilles thrust his sword in at the liver,
Which slipped from the wound as the dark blood quickly welled out
And slithered down to drip from his chest. Soon all   530
Became dark and he fainted. And on went Achilles to stab
His bronze spear-point from ear to ear through Mulius' skull,
And then to strike Echeclus full on the head
With his dark-hilted sword, whereat the whole blade was left smoking

With blood, as purple death came down on his eyes
And powerful fate embraced him. Next, he jabbed
His bronze-pointed spear through the arm of Deucalion, right
Where the tendons join at the elbow, and he stood there
With his arm too heavy to lift, awaiting the death
540 Coming on, and Achilles, whipping his sword through the neck
Of the warrior, swept his helmeted head far away,
Causing marrow to spurt from his spine and his corpse to lie
Stretched out on the ground. On he charged in pursuit
Of Peires' flawless son Rhigmus, a warrior there
From fertile Thrace. Him he pierced deep in the belly,
And down he pitched from his car. And as Areïthous,
Driving for Rhigmus, wheeled the horses around,
Achilles thrust his keen lance through his back and hurled him
To earth. At once the horses panicked and ran.
550   As when through the deep ravines of a drought-stricken mountain
A god-sustained blaze wildly sweeps, and the thick forest burns
As the driving wind wreathes all in whirling flame,
So now Achilles raged everywhere with his spear,
Charging on like a demon, constantly pressing hard
On the foe and cutting them down in such numbers that the black
                earth
Ran with Trojan blood. And like a pair
Of broad-browed, loud-lowing bulls that some farmer yokes
To tread out white barley strewn on his firm threshing-floor,
And quickly their hooves do the husking, even so the solid-hoofed
560 Horses of great-souled Achilles trampled on corpses
And shields. And the axle below and handrails above
Were all splashed and bespattered with blood from the battering
                hooves
Of the horses and metal rims of the wheels, as onward
Achilles pressed in pursuit of glory, soiling
His unconquered hands with the filth of horrible slaughter.

BOOK XXI

The Struggle of Achilles and the River

Now when they came to the ford of swirling Xanthus,
The fair-flowing river that immortal Zeus begot,
There Achilles divided the Trojan forces, and part
He drove across the plain toward the city, routing them
Over the same stretch of land where Achaeans had fled
The day before when resplendent Hector was raging,
And Hera, to make their way hard, now drifted dense fog
In front of them. But the other half were trapped
In the silvery swirls of the deep-running river. Into it
They plunged with tremendous confusion and noise, as man   10
After man hit the stream with a splash and the banks re-echoed
The din. Frantically shouting, they thrashed and swam
This way and that, spun about in the powerful whirlpools.
And as when locusts sense the onrush of fire
And fly for a stream to escape the quick-coming flames
Of a weariless blaze, then huddle low in the water,
So now in front of Achilles the clamorous course
Of deep-swirling Xanthus was cluttered with men and horses.
Zeus-sprung Achilles, leaning his spear against
Some tamarisks on the bank, leaped like a demon   20
Into the water armed only with his sharp sword
And the stern resolution to kill. And he laid about him,
Killing men right and left, and from them came grim sounds
Of groaning as they were struck with the sword, and the water
Ran red with their blood. And as small fish flee darting
Before a hungry huge dolphin, cramming the coves
Of some excellent harbor, lest they be devoured by the glutton,
Even so the Trojans cowered beneath the steep banks
Of the terrible river. At last Achilles, his arms
Worn weary with killing, chose twelve young Trojans alive   30
From out the river as blood-price for dead Patroclus,

Son of Menoetius.* These he led up the bank,
Fear-dazed like so many fawns, and tied their hands fast
Behind them with their own well-cut leather belts, which they wore
About their soft woven tunics, and turned them over
To comrades of his for them to lead away
To the hollow ships. Then back he sprang, eager
As ever to cut men asunder.
      There on the bank
40 He met a son of Dardanian Priam, youthful
Lycaon, anxious to flee from the river. This man
He had captured before, at night in his father's orchard,
Where able Achilles, an evil unlooked for, had come
Upon him while he was cutting young branches of fig
To be the handrails of a chariot. That time he had sent him
By ship to well-settled Lemnos and gotten a price
For him from the son of Jason. From there he was ransomed
By a former guest of his, Eëtion of Imbros,
Who paid a much greater price and sent him to splendid
50 Arisbe. Escaping from those protecting him there,
Lycaon returned to the house of his fathers in Troy,
Where he for eleven days enjoyed himself
With his friends, all glad that he had come back from Lemnos.
But on the twelfth day, God brought him again to the hands
Of Achilles, who this time was surely to send him, unwilling
As ever, down to Hades' halls. Now fast-footed,
Noble Achilles knew him at once, for Lycaon
Had gotten so hot and tired struggling his way
From the river and up the bank that he had thrown all
60 Of his bronze to the ground, and now he appeared without helmet
Or shield or spear. Astounded to see him, Achilles
Spoke thus to his own great heart:
      "Who would believe it!
This wonder before my eyes. Truly the spirited
Trojans whom I have destroyed will now arise
From the deep nether gloom, if one is to judge by the flight
Of this man, who though he was sold in sacred Lemnos
Has somehow escaped the ruthless day there, nor has
The gray brine held him back, the fathomless sea that discourages

---

*Achilles had vowed the sacrifice of the twelve Trojans at XVIII.382–384; he fulfills the
promise at XXIII.207–210.

Many anxious to cross it. But now he shall taste 70
The point of my spear, that I may discover for sure
Whether he will also return from below, or whether
The life-giving earth will hold him as fast as she does
Many other strong fellows."
    Thus thinking, he stood where he was
While Lycaon approached him, crazy with fear and frantic
To catch at his knees, his one thought to avoid harsh death
And final black doom. Achilles raised his long spear,
Hot for the kill, but Lycaon ducked and ran under
The cast to clutch his foe's knees, and the spear shot over 80
His back and into the ground, its yearning for man's meat
Thwarted. Lycaon then pleaded, with one hand clasping
Achilles' knees, with the other his sharp-pointed spear.[1]
Holding on for his life, he spoke these fear-winged words:
    "Achilles, here at your knees, I beg you to have
Some regard and pity for me. To you, O Zeus-nurtured
One, I should be a sacred pleader, since you
Were the first with whom I broke Demeter's bread
On the day you captured me in the well-planted orchard
Of Priam and sent me far from my father and friends 90
To be sold in sacred Lemnos, where I was bought
For the worth of a hundred oxen. But I was ransomed
For three times that much, and this is but the twelfth day
Since I arrived back in Troy after many hardships.
And now once more deadly fate has put me in your hands!
Father Zeus must surely despise me to give me to you
Again, and surely my mother Laothoë did not
Bear me to live very long, she the daughter
Of ancient Altes, King of the war-loving Leleges,
Holding steep Pedasus on the Satnioeis River. 100
His daughter was one of King Priam's numerous wives,
And she bore me and another, and you will have butchered
Us both. For him you've already brought down mid the front rank
Of foot-fighting soldiers, my brother, godlike Polydorus,
Whom you transfixed with your keen-bladed spear. And now
Right here evil death shall be mine, for I don't think I'm likely
To get away from your hands now that some demon
Has brought me near you. But let me say one other thing
For you to consider—spare me, since I was not born
From the same womb as Hector, who slaughtered your friend, the strong 110
And the gentle."

So spoke to him splendid Lycaon, begging
For life, but not at all kind was the voice he heard say:
"You fool! offer no ransom, nor argument either,
To me. For until the day Patroclus caught up with
His fate and was killed, I preferred to spare the Trojans,
And many indeed were they whom I took alive
And sold into slavery, but now there is not even one
Who shall escape death, not a single one whom God
120 Brings into my hands before the walls of Ilium—
No Trojan at all, I say, shall escape, much less
The sons of Priam! And you, my friend, you also
Die, but why all this fuming and fuss about it?
Patroclus too died, a man far better than you!
And do you not see what sort of warrior I am,
How handsome, how huge? My father's a man of great worth,
My mother a goddess, yet death and powerful fate
Hang over me too. One morning or evening or noon
Will surely come when some man shall kill me in battle,
130 Either by hurling his spear or shooting a shaft
From the bowstring."[2]
        At this Lycaon's knees shook and he went
To pieces inside. Releasing the spear, he kneeled
Reaching out with both hands. But Achilles drew his sharp
                    sword
And brought it down on his collarbone close by the neck,
And the two-edged blade disappeared in his flesh, stretching him
Out on the earth, where he lay with his dark blood drenching
The ground. Seizing him then by the foot, Achilles
Slung him to drift in the river, shouting these words
140 Winged with vaunting:
        "Float there with the fish that shall clean the blood
From your wound quite without feeling for you, nor shall
Your mother lay you out on a bed and mourn.
But swirling Scamander shall roll you into the broad gulf
Of the brine, and many a wave-hidden fish shall dart up
Beneath the dark ripple to eat the fat of Lycaon.[3]
So may all of you die, till we reach the city
Of holy Troy, you in retreat, and I
Killing men from behind. Not even this beautiful river,
150 Strong swirling with silver eddies, shall be any help
To you, despite the long time you have sacrificed bulls
To the River-god Xanthus and hurled while still alive
Fine solid-hoofed horses into his swirling pools.

Even so, all of you Trojans shall meet a harsh fate
And die, so paying the price for killing Patroclus
And making suffer those other Achaeans whom you
By the fast-running ships cut down while I was inactive."

    At this the River-god Xanthus became very angry
At heart and pondered hard in his mind how he
Might cut short Achilles' war-work and keep the Trojans   160
From ruin. Meanwhile, Achilles gripped his long-shadowing
Spear and rushed upon Asteropaeus, son
Of Pelegon, hot for the kill. This Pelegon claimed
As his father the wide-flowing Axius River, stream
Of deep swirls, who mingled in love with fair Periboea,
The eldest daughter of King Acessamenus, to sire
The father of Asteropaeus, upon whom Achilles
Now charged. And Pelegon's son strode through the water
To face him, holding two spears, and Xanthus, wrathful
For all the young men whom Achilles had ruthlessly killed   170
In his stream, breathed courage into his heart. Now when
They came within range Achilles, fast on his feet,
Shouted first:

    "Who are you and where are you from, that you dare
To confront me? Unhappy indeed are those whose children
Oppose me!"

    To which the glorious son of Pelegon:
"Haughty Achilles, why do you ask who I am?
I come from fertile Paeonia, far away,
Leading my warriors armed with long spears, and this   180
Is now the eleventh day I've been here. I trace
My line from the wide-rippling Axius River, by far
The loveliest river on earth and the father of spear-famous
Pelegon, who, men say, sired me. But now,
O splendid Achilles, do battle!"

    Such was his challenge,
And shining Achilles drew back his Pelian ash,
But Asteropaeus let fly both spears at once,
Since he was quite ambidextrous. One struck the marvelous
Shield, but the layer of gold, the god's gift, held it back,   190
While the other grazed Achilles' right forearm, causing
The cloud-black blood to gush out. But the spear-head went on
To bury itself in the ground, still lusting for man's meat.
Then Achilles in turn hurled his straight-flying ash
At Asteropaeus, eager to kill him, but missed
And struck the high bank so hard that the spear sank in

Full half its length. But Achilles drew his sharp sword
From beside his thigh and rushed toward his foe, who was vainly
Striving to pull the ash of Achilles free
200 From the bank. Three times he strained with his powerful arm,
And three times he did no more than make the shaft quiver.
The fourth time he tried to bend and break it, but now
Achilles charged in and slashed him across the navel,
Thus spilling his guts on the ground and wrapping his eyes
In darkness. Gasping, he died, and Achilles sprang onto
His chest and stripped off his armor, exultantly crying:
     "Lie here where you fell! Very hard it is for the son
Of a river to vie with a child of Cronos' son.[4]
For though you claim as your grandsire the wide-flowing Axius,
210 I trace descent from almighty Zeus himself!
My father Peleus is King of innumerable Myrmidons,
And his father, Aeacus, he was begotten by Zeus.
And just as Zeus is mightier far than all
Of the sea-mingling rivers, so also his seed is stronger
Than that of a stream. Right here, in fact, is a truly
Tremendous river, and what help has he been to you?
For no one can fight with Cronos' son Zeus. With him
Not even powerful Achelous strives, nor even
The still more enormously mighty deep-circling Oceanus,
220 Stream from whom all seas and rivers rise,
All springs and bottomless wells. But even Oceanus
Dreads the bright bolt of great Zeus, and feels deep terror
Whenever it crashes above him!"
     So saying, he jerked
His spear from the bank and left dead Asteropaeus
Prone in the sand, with the dark water lapping his corpse
And the eels and the fish nibbling and ripping the fat
From his kidneys. Achilles then went in pursuit of the well-horsed
Paeonians, who, having seen their best spearman succumb
230 In hard fight to the hands and sword of Peleus' son,
Huddled in panic along the swirling river.
There he slaughtered Thersilochus, Mnesus and Mydon,
Astypylus, Thrasius, Aenius, and Ophelestes.
Nor would swift Achilles have paused in his killing had not
The angry river called out to him in the voice
Of a man, uttering it from out a deep whirlpool:
     "O Achilles, inhuman you are in strength and brutality
Of performance, for always the gods themselves
Assist you. But if Zeus has willed that you are to kill

All the Trojans, then drive them out of my waters and do   240
Your foul work on the plain. Already my exquisite stream
Is jammed with dead men, and so choked with your ruinous killing
That I can no longer pour my wealth of water
Into the bright sea. So now, great commander of men,
Desist! You truly appall me!"
    To which the fast runner
Achilles replied: "So be it, O god-fed Scamander.
The insolent Trojans, however, I'll not stop killing
Till I have penned them up in their city and fought
A contest with Hector, to see just who will kill whom."   250
    With this, he charged at the foe like a demon, but now
The deep-swirling river spoke thus to Apollo: "For shame!
O silver-bowed one. You have not obeyed the strict charge
Of Zeus your Father, who told you to stand by the Trojans
And give them aid till the sun goes down and darkens
The fertile fields."
    So Xanthus spoke, but Achilles
Sprang from the bank into the midst of his current,
And quickly the river rushed on him with surging flood,
And filling his stream with churning water he cleaned   260
His course of the dead men killed by Achilles, roaring
Fierce as a bull as up on the banks he cast
The innumerable corpses, while saving survivors beneath
His fair waters, hiding them well in the huge swirling pools.
Then grimly the foaming wave curled over Achilles,
And striking his shield the current kept shoving him back
And sweeping his feet from beneath him. Desperate, he caught
Overhead a tall and sturdy elm that grew
From the bank, but it fell across the lovely stream,
Completely uprooted, and with its thick branches and roots   270
It dammed the river still further. Achilles, then, gripped
With panic, sprang out of the swirl and started to run
At top speed across the wide plain. But instead of desisting,
The great River-god rolled on in pursuit with a huge
Churning wave of dark and ominous crest, that he
Might cut short Achilles' war-work and keep the Trojans
From ruin. But Peleus' son got a lead as long as
A spear-cast, fleeing with all the speed of a hunting
Black eagle, the strongest and fastest of birds, and as
He shrank from beneath the high wave and fled across land   280
The bronze on his breast rang loud, and on came the river
Behind him, awesomely roaring. And as when a stream

Flows down from a spring of dark water, led mid plants
And garden-plots by a man with a mattock, who clears
All obstructions away from before it, so that as it burbles
And murmurs along down the slope it sweeps all the pebbles
Away and soon gets ahead of him who guides it,
So now the wave of the surging river outstripped
Achilles, fast though he was, for the gods are far stronger
290 Than men. And every time great Achilles would try
To stand and confront the wave, that he might learn
If all the sky-keeping gods had teamed up against him,
The towering wave of the heaven-fed river would crash
On his shoulders, and though he tried desperately to force
His way up through the flood, the strong undertow of the river
Kept tiring his legs and cutting the ground from beneath him.
At last, looking up at broad heaven, the son of Peleus
Cried out in complaint:
     "O Father Zeus, why is it
300 That none of the gods will pity my plight and save me
From this dread river?⁵ Any other fate would be better
Than this—not that I blame you heavenly gods
So much as I do my own mother, who stupefied me
With false words, saying that I should die by the wall
Of the bronze-breasted Trojans, a victim of swift-flying shafts
From the bow of Phoebus Apollo. If only Hector,
The best man bred here, had slain me! Then killer and killed
Would both have been equally noble. But now I seem
To have been allotted a fate most dismal, trapped
310 In this tremendous river and swept away
Like some poor pig-herding boy who fails to make it
Across a rain-swollen torrent."
     In answer Poseidon
And Pallas Athena immediately came to his side
In the form of men, and clasping his hands in theirs
Spoke reassuring words, the Earthshaker first:
"Son of Peleus, be not unduly afraid or anxious,
Since you have such Zeus-approved helpers as Pallas Athena
And I. It is not your lot to be overcome
320 By a river. Far from it, for soon he'll fall back, as you
Shall see for yourself. But we will give you good counsel,
If you will but listen. Let not your hands refrain
From evil, all-leveling war till you have penned up
The Trojan survivors within the famed walls of their city.
Then, when you have taken the life of Prince Hector,

Go back to the ships. Thus we grant the glory to you."
         With this, they went back to the gods, while Achilles, afire
With the word of immortals, charged over the plain, which by now
Was flooded with water, and the splendidly armored corpses
Of many young warriors floated there. But Achilles   330
Raised his knees high as he charged straight against the onrush
Of water, nor could the wide-flooding river restrain him,
So great was the strength Athena put in him. Not
That Scamander gave up, for he became fiercer than ever
Against Achilles, and rearing his mighty surge
To a foam-capped, curling crest, he shouted thus
To Simoeis, god of the stream that joined his:
         "Dear brother,
Let us combine our forces and quench the might
Of this man, or soon he'll sack King Priam's great city,   340
Nor will the Trojans be able to hold out against him.
Come quickly to help me. Flood all your streams with water
From all of your springs and rouse all your torrents, then raise
A huge billow, churning with tree-trunks and boulders, that we
May stop this monstrous savage who now conquers all
And thinks himself equal to gods. For I do not believe
His strength will help him at all, nor his good looks,
Nor even that marvelous armor, which I shall wrap
In slime deep under water, and he himself
I'll cover with tons of sand and silt, until   350
No Achaean shall know where to look for his bones. Right here
I'll heap up his barrow myself, nor shall he have need
Of another when fellow Achaeans give him a funeral!"
         So saying, he sent his towering wave, churning
With foam and blood and corpses, raging down
On Achilles.[6] And the ominous billow curled high above him,
Just at the point of fatally crashing upon him.
But Hera, afraid that the powerful deep-swirling river
Would sweep Achilles away, spoke out at once
To her own dear son Hephaestus: 360
         "Up, my child.
For surely we thought that you, the great limping god,
Were matched in fight with deep-eddying Xanthus. Go fast
As you can to bear aid, and wreathe the whole plain in your flames.
Meanwhile, I'll hurry and send from the sea hard blasts
Of West Wind and the bright-flowing South, that they may constantly
Fan your fierce fire and burn up the many dead Trojans,
War-gear and all. But you attack Xanthus directly—

Burn all the trees on his banks, and boil all his water,
370   And don't be turned aside by any soft words
Or threats from him. Cease not in your fury one whit
Till you hear me shout. Then hold back your untiring flame."
        She spoke, and Hephaestus prepared his god-blazing fire.
First it flared on the plain and burned all the dead,
The numerous corpses strewn there by Achilles, and soon
The bright water was gone and all the plain dry. And as when
In autumn the West Wind soon dries a new-watered orchard,
Much to the gardener's joy, so now the whole plain
Was dried and the dead completely consumed. Then straight
380   On the river himself he turned his all-glaring fire.
Consumed were the tamarisks, elms, and willows, along with
The clover, rushes, and marsh grass that grew by the stream
So abundantly. Greatly tormented were eels and fish
In the eddies, and all along the fair water they leaped
And tumbled this way and that, badly hurt by the blast
Of resourceful Hephaestus. The powerful river himself
Was on fire, and thus he called out to the great artificer:
        "Hephaestus, what god can successfully quarrel with you?
I will not contend with one so awesomely wrapped
390   In blazing fire. Cease the fight now, and as
For the Trojans, Achilles can empty their city of people,
For all I care. For what has a river to do
With strife, or assisting in strife?"
        On fire all the time
He was talking, his lovely stream was boiling and steaming.
And like a cauldron of glistening hog's lard that bubbles
And spurts when sere logs are kindled beneath it and all
Is melted and brought to a boil, even so the fair stream
Of Xanthus flamed and his water seethed, nor did he
400   Desire to flood the plain further, but halted, greatly
Distressed by the blast of cunning Hephaestus. Then
The River-god earnestly prayed these winged words
To Queen Hera:
        "O Hera, why should your son afflict me
More than he does all others? You surely do not
Blame me so much as you do all those other helpers
Of Trojans. I will cease if you say so, O goddess,
But make Hephaestus also refrain. And further,
I'll swear an oath that I will never keep
410   From the Trojans the hard day of doom, not even when Troy
Shall burn with furious fire lit by the warlike

Sons of Achaeans."

  At this the white-armed Hera
Spoke at once to her own dear son: "Hephaestus,
My so splendid child, withdraw. It is hardly right
To hurt an immortal this way on account of mere men."

  She spoke, and the water returned to the bed of the river
And rolled as before, a strong and beautiful stream.

  When the fury of Xanthus was quelled, the fight with Hephaestus
Was over, for Hera, though angry, ended their struggle.   420
But now strife fell on the other immortals, hatred
Both heavy and hard, for the spirit within them was blown
In conflicting directions. As fiercely they clashed with a deafening
Roar, the wide earth re-echoed their din and the huge vault
Of heaven resounded as if with the blasting of trumpets.
And Zeus, from where he sat high up on Olympus,
Heard the clashing and laughed to himself, delighted
To see the immortals at odds with each other.[7] Nor did they
Hold back any longer, once shield-piercing Ares had charged
On Athena, jabbing his spear and yelling these words   430
Of insult:

  "Why you, you bitch's flea, does your
Proud spirit make you so savage that you dare bring
The very immortals together in hatred and strife?
Have you forgotten that time you helped Diomedes
Wound me, seizing his spear in full sight of all
And driving it into my unblemished flesh?* Now,
I think, you'll pay the whole price for that and all
You have done!"

  So saying, he stabbed her fluttering aegis,   440
The awesome aegis against which not even the bolt
Of great Zeus can prevail. But blood-streaming Ares thrust
His lengthy spear hard on it, and Pallas Athena
Fell back and seized from the ground with her powerful hand
A nearby stone, black, jagged, and huge, that men
Long ago had put there to mark the line of a field.
This rugged rock she brought down hard on the neck
Of charging Ares and unstrung his limbs at once.
His armor rang as he fell, and there he lay
With his locks in the dust, the War-god sprawled out over what 450
    seemed

---

*See V.950–952 for the wounding of Ares by Diomedes.

More than an acre. Then Athena laughed loud, and over him
Spoke these proud words, winged with triumph and vaunting:
    "You infantile fool! how long will it take you to learn
The proper respect for my always superior strength?
At this rate, you'll pay the full price demanded by Hera
Your mother, who in her anger at you for deserting
The Argives and helping the insolent Trojans has called out
The Furies against you."
          When she had thus spoken, she turned
460 Her bright eyes away. But the daughter of Zeus, Aphrodite,
Took Ares' hand and tried to revive him, as he
Lay moaning and groaning, so weak he could scarcely move.
Then Hera noticed her effort and quickly spoke
To Athena these winged words:
    "For shame! O invincible
Daughter of aegis-great Zeus. There once again
That bitch's flea Aphrodite is leading Ares,
Maimer of men, out of the blazing chaos
Of battle. But after her, quick!"
470   At this, Athena
Exultantly sped in pursuit, and charging upon her
She struck Aphrodite a terrible blow on the breasts
With her powerful hand. Then her heart and limbs gave way
On the spot, so that both she and Ares lay helplessly stretched
On the all-feeding earth and, vaunting, Athena spoke over them
These winged words:
    "So may all helpers of Trojans
End up when they fight against bronze-breasted Argives. Let
Their courage and stamina be like those of soft
480 Aphrodite, when she came here against me to help Ares.
If all Trojan allies were such as she, then long
Before now this war would have ended and we would have plundered
The populous city of Troy!"
         At this the goddess
White-armed Hera smiled, but earth-shaking Poseidon
Spoke thus to Apollo: "O Phoebus, why do we two
Stand off from each other? It hardly becomes us, now that
The others have started. Surely it would be disgraceful
For us to go back to the brazen-floored palace of Zeus
490 On Olympus without so much as striking a blow.
Begin then, since you are the younger. It would not be fair
For me to, since I am both older and more experienced.
Fool, how little real sense you have! For you

Don't seem to remember the horrors that we two endured
When Zeus sent only us of the gods to labor
A year for haughty Laomedon here at Troy,
To take our orders and get our firm-promised pay
From him. I built round their city a wall, wide
And most imposing, a barrier not to be broken,
While you, O Phoebus, herded their lumbering fat cattle   500
Through all the valleys and woods of many-ridged Ida.
But when the gay seasons ended the year, then loathsome
Laomedon roughly sent us away with threats
As our only reward. He threatened, in fact, to tie
Our hands and our feet and sell us in far-distant islands
As slaves. Oh yes, and he made us believe he was going
To slice off our ears with a sword! So back to Olympus
We went, boiling inside because of the pay
He had promised and then refused. And now it is
To his people that you give your grace, instead of assisting   510
Us in bringing the arrogant Trojans to abject
Ruin, and with them their children and honored wives."

  Then the far-working lord Apollo answered him, saying:
"Earthshaker, you'd hardly consider me sane if I
Should do battle with you for the sake of ephemeral mortals,
Poor wretches that flame with life for a little while
Like flourishing leaves that draw their food from the earth,
Then wither and die forever. Let us, then, cease
This nonsense at once, and leave the fighting to men."*

  So saying, he turned away, for he was ashamed   520
To trade blows with his uncle. But now his sister Artemis,
Wild Queen of savage beasts and the untamed forest,
Fiercely railed at him thus: "Look how the great archer
Runs! yielding the victory all to Poseidon
And giving him glory for nothing. Fool, why carry
A bow worthless as wind? Now never again
Let me hear you boast as of old mid immortal gods
In the halls of our Father that you would fight face to face
With Poseidon."

  So she, but far-striking Apollo had nothing   530
To say in reply. The revered wife of Zeus, however,
Made this wrathful speech, thus chiding with words of insult

---

*See VI.155–159 (with endnote 3) for a use of the same image, but from the perspective of mortals.

The goddess of fast-flying shafts:
"You brazen bitch,
I'll teach you to stand against me! Believe me, I'm no
Easy mark in a fight, regardless of that bow of yours
And the lioness-like disposition Zeus gave you to use
Against women, whom he allows you to slay as you will.
Truly you'd be a great deal better off in the mountains
540 Killing wild deer and other such wilderness creatures
Than here to fight against those who are stronger than you.
However, learn if you wish what fighting is
And how much mightier I am than you, since now
You insist on matching your strength against mine!"
　　So saying,
Queen Hera seized both of Artemis' wrists with her left hand
And snatching the bow off her back with her right, she boxed
The ears of her writhing foe, spilling her arrows
All over and all the while smiling. Then Artemis, weeping,
550 Fled from her like a dove that flies from a hawk
And hides in some cave or hollow rock, since she
Is not fated so to be caught. Even thus, tearful Artemis
Fled from Queen Hera, leaving her bow and arrows.
Then to Artemis' mother Leto the messenger Hermes,
Slayer of Argus, spoke thus:
　　"Leto, I have
No idea of fighting you. No easy thing
It is to trade blows with the wives of cloud-driving Zeus.
You're welcome to go and boast mid the immortal gods
560 That you overcame me with that great power of yours."
　　Such were his words, and Leto picked up the curved bow
And the arrows that lay all around in the swirling dust
And retired, but Artemis came to the brazen-floored palace
Of Zeus on Olympus and all but collapsed at the knees
Of her Father, her fragrant gown quivering with sobs, and he,
The son of Cronos, hugged his daughter, and laughing
Softly, inquired:
　　"Who of the heavenly gods,
Dear child, has badly mistreated you now, as though
570 You had done something wrong where everybody could see?"
　　To which the fair-garlanded Queen of the echoing chase:
"Your own wife it was that beat me, Father—yes,
I mean white-armed Hera, the cause of all this hatred
And strife among the immortals."

    While these two spoke thus
With each other, Apollo entered high-hallowed Troy,
Concerned for the walls of the firm-founded city, lest that
Very day the Danaans go beyond fate and plunder
It all. But the other immortals returned to Olympus,
Some in wrath and some in great exultation,   580
And sat with their Father, lord of the lowering sky.
    Meanwhile, Achilles continued his slaughter of men
And solid-hoofed horses. And as when the angry gods
Cause toil and suffering for men by setting fire
To their city, from which the smoke billows up to dim
The wide sky, so now Achilles brought labor and woe
On the Trojans.
    At this point, ancient Priam mounted
The god-built wall and saw how gigantic Achilles
Drove all the Trojans before him in headlong, helpless   590
Rout. Groaning, he climbed back down to the ground,
Calling out down the wall to the glorious gate-keeping guards:
    "Hold the gates wide with your hands, till the fleeing troops
Can get inside, for here they come with Achilles
Close behind them, and many, I fear, will not make it.
But shut the double doors tight as soon as the men
Are inside, for I am aghast at the thought of that murdering
Monster within these walls!"
    At this they shot back
The bars and swung the gates wide, thus giving the Trojans   600
A light of deliverance. Apollo, moreover, charged out
To meet the stampede, that he might keep ruin away
From the Trojans, who came on fast for the looming wall
Of the city, all of their throats dry and gritty with thirst
And their bodies grimy with dust from the plain. And always
Behind them Achilles came on with his spear, his heart
In the grip of savage rage and the lust to win glory.
    Then indeed would the sons of Achaeans have taken Ilium,
Town of the towering gates, if Phoebus Apollo
Had not inspired noble Agenor, the blameless and stalwart   610
Son of Antenor. Into his heart Apollo
Infused great courage, then stood beside him in person,
Shrouded in mist and leaning against an oak tree,
That he might keep Death's heavy hands away from the man.
Thus, when Agenor looked out at town-taking Achilles,
He stopped and stood still, awaiting his charge, while in him

His heart darkly seethed with many wild thoughts. Deeply troubled,
He spoke to his own great spirit:
    "Ah misery! if now
620 I run with the rest in rout before mighty Achilles,
He'll surely catch up with me and butcher me there
For a coward. But what if I leave the troops to be driven
By Peleus' son, while I make rapid tracks
Away from the wall across the Ileian Plain
And continue till I am concealed mid the woods and valleys
Of Ida? Then in the evening, when I have bathed
In the river and washed off the sweat, I could go back to Troy.
But why do I argue thus with myself? Achilles
Would certainly see me going from city to plain
630 And soon overtake me with his great fleetness of foot.
Nor would it be possible then to escape dark death
And the fates, for he above all men is awesomely strong.
What else then remains but for me to go out and face him
In front of the city? No one thinks him immortal.
He has but one life, and that may be fatally reached
By the keen-cutting bronze. What glory he has is a gift
From Cronos' son Zeus."
    So saying, he gathered his courage
To face the oncoming Achilles, and his brave heart
640 Was on edge for the clashing of combat. As when a leopard
Leaves a dense thicket to spring on a hunter, and goes
With no fear of the baying hounds, and still goes on
In her fury though he be quicker and pierce her through
With his spear—still she advances to grapple with him
Before death: so now proud Antenor's son, goodly
Agenor, refused to retreat till he had clashed
With Achilles, and holding his round shield before him and hefting
His spear, he shouted:
    "I know, O splendid Achilles,
650 That you in your heart have hope of sacking the city
Of god-gifted Trojans this day—fool that you are!
For many and hard are the battles yet to be fought
Over Troy. She still has plenty of battle-bold warriors
Inside her walls, men who stand between you
And their own dear parents, wives, and sons, and who guard
Great Ilium. You, though, shall meet your doom on this spot,
No matter how awesome and bold you are in a fight!"
    So saying, he hurled the sharp spear with his powerful arm,
Nor did it miss, but struck the shin of Achilles

Under the knee, where his greave of new-hammered tin   660
Shrilly grated and rang, as back bounced the point of keen bronze,
Unable to pierce the glorious gift of Hephaestus.
Then Peleus' son charged hard at godlike Agenor,
But Phoebus Apollo would not allow him to win
Any glory there, and snatching Agenor away
He hid him in mist and sent him out of the battle
To go back uninjured. Then, far-working Apollo
Deceitfully kept Peleus' son from the Trojans. He took
The form of Agenor exactly and stood in the path
Of charging Achilles, who hotly pursued him across   670
The wheat-bearing plain, turning him toward deep-swirling
Scamander. But crafty Apollo remained just a little
Ahead, beguiling Achilles with hope of soon
Overtaking his foe. Meanwhile, the rest of the Trojans,
Madly stampeding, rushed with unspeakable joy
Through the gates of the city and swarmed through the town.
Nor did
They dare this time await one another outside
The walls to find out who managed to get away
And who failed to make it. But frantically all of them poured   680
Through the gates, whoever had legs still able to run.

BOOK XXII

The Death of Hector

So throughout the city they rested like panic-worn fawns,
Exhausted from heat and running, slaking their thirst
And cooling off as they leaned on the marvelous battlements.
Meanwhile, the Achaeans, leaving their shields on their shoulders,
Drew near the wall, and Hector, bound fast in the bonds
Of treacherous fate, stood waiting outside the city
In front of the Scaean Gates. Then Phoebus Apollo
Revealed himself to Achilles, spitefully saying:
"What, O son of Peleus, can you possibly think
10   You're achieving, you a mere mortal hotly pursuing
Me, an immortal god? You rage so madly
That still you have not perceived that I'm an immortal.
But have you no interest in further slaughter of Trojans,
Whom you were routing in panic, but who have now
Poured into the city while you were sprinting out here?
You'll never kill me, since I am not fated to die."
       Then greatly enraged, fleet-footed Achilles replied:
"You've duped me, O far-working god, most ruthless of all
The immortals—duped me by leading me here, away
20   From the wall. Else many a Trojan now in the city
Would surely lie out on the plain with a bloody mouthful
Of dirt. You've robbed me of truly great glory and cheaply
Saved those you favor, since you have no fear of revenge
To come. O would that I had the power to wreak
Vengeance on you as I saw fit!"
       So saying, Achilles
Was off for the city, still thinking great deeds, and he ran
With the speed of a prize-winning horse in a chariot-race,
A powerful stallion that stretches himself full length
30   As lightly he gallops across the wide plain. So Achilles
Churned hard his quick feet and knees.
       The ancient Priam
Was first to see him as on he came toward the city,
Brilliantly flashing bright as the star that rises

In autumn to outshine all of the myriad others
That burn in the blackness of night—the star men call
The Dog of Orion, most brilliant of all, but wrought
As a sign of bad days, for he is the bringer of much
Deadly fever upon wretched mortals. So now the bronze flashed
On the chest of charging Achilles. And the old one groaned   40
A great groan and violently beat his gray head with his hands,
As he screamed a plea to his precious son still standing
Before the high gates, determined and anxious to clash
With Achilles. To him old Priam, reaching out both
Of his arms, called pitifully:
          "Hector, I beg you, dear child,
Don't stand there alone and wait for the charge of that man,
Or death at his hands may soon be yours, since he
Is far stronger than you—and a savage! If only the gods
Loved him no better than I do! Then quickly the dogs   50
And vultures would feast on his unburied corpse, thus lifting
Some measure of terrible grief from my heart. For he
Has deprived me of many brave sons, either slaughtering them
Or selling them off as slaves to distant islands.
Right now I miss two more of my sons, Lycaon
And Polydorus, nowhere to be seen mid the Trojans
Gathered within the city, even those two boys
The Princess Laothoë bore me. If they still live
In the Argive camp, we'll do all we can to ransom
Those two with bronze and gold, since there is plenty   60
At home that ancient Altes, a King of high fame,
Sent with his daughter Laothoë. But if already
They're dead and in Hades' halls, great grief shall come
On the hearts of their mother and me, from whom their lives sprang.
The rest of the Trojans will not grieve so long—unless
You also go down at the hands of Achilles! Come then,
My son, put walls between you and him, that you
May yet save the men and women of Troy, instead
Of giving great glory to Peleus' son and losing
Your own sweet life. Moreover, have pity on miserable   70
Me, wretched but still quite able to feel!
Think of the grinding fate Father Zeus is preparing
For me, to kill me in feeble old age, after I
Have seen countless horrors—my sons in the throes of death,
My daughters and daughters-in-law dragged off by loathsome
Achaean hands, their marriage chambers wrecked
And despoiled, and their babies dashed to the ground in the heat

Of horrible war. Myself last of all, with the life
Ripped out of my limbs by slash or thrust of sharp bronze,
80 Shall hungry dogs tear further—my own table hounds
Brought up in my halls to guard the gate of my palace.
Gone mad from lapping their master's blood, they'll loll
In my courts. A young man cut down in battle may
Very well lie exposed, though the mangling bronze has done
Its worst on his body. Dead and naked though such
A young warrior lie, nothing is seen that is not
Noble and fair. But when savage dogs defile
The gray head and beard and the privy parts of an old man
Fallen—surely nothing more foul than this can come upon
90 Wretched mortals!"[1]

      So saying, old Priam tore
Gray hairs from his head, but he could not persuade the heart
Of his son. And then, beside the old King, Hector's mother,
Wailing and shedding hot tears, undid the front
Of her gown and, holding out one of her breasts, spoke these words
Winged with entreaty:

      "Hector, my child, have
Some regard for this, and pity your mother, if ever
I quieted your crying by giving you suck at this breast.
100 Remember all this, my precious child, and fight
Yonder savage from inside the walls. Do not be so heartless
As now to stand there and face him. For if he should kill you,
I'll never be able, my darling, to whom I gave life,
To so much as mourn your dead body laid out on a bed,
Nor shall your rich-gifted wife, but far over there
By the Argive ships fast dogs shall devour you completely!"

      Thus the two wept and called out to their much-loved son,
Beseeching him over and over, but they could do nothing
To change Hector's heart as there he stood and awaited
110 The clash with gigantic Achilles. And as a bright snake
Of the mountains, swollen and fierce from its diet of deadly
Poisons, waits in his lair for a man, balefully
Glaring forth and coiling about within,
So Hector, his courage unquenched, would not give ground,
But leaned his bright shield against the wall's jutting tower
And, deeply troubled, spoke thus to his own great spirit:

      "Ah misery! if now I take cover within the gates
And the walls, Polydamas surely will be the first
To reproach me, since he is the one who urged me to lead
120 The Trojans back into Troy during the dread

Accursed night when great Achilles came forth. But I
Wouldn't listen, much to the sorrow of many, and now
That I've all but destroyed the troops through my own stubborn pride,
I can't face the men and gown-trailing women of Troy,
Lest some low fellow should say: 'Great Hector put all
Of his trust in his own brute strength and destroyed the whole
                    army!'[2]
So they will surely remark, but it were far better
For me to face and slay Achilles and so
Return home in triumph, or now to die bravely myself
In front of the city. But what if I lay my bossed shield   130
And thick helmet down and, leaning my spear on the wall,
Go out unarmed to meet the matchless Achilles
And promise him that we'll give to Atreus' sons
To carry away both Helen and all the shiploads
Of treasure Prince Paris brought home to Troy—thus starting
The war—and say that I'll have the elders of Troy
Swear a strong oath for the Trojans that we will divide
With the Argives all of the treasure that this lovely city
Contains? But why do I argue these things with myself?
Let me not be so foolish as thus to approach him   140
Only to have him completely refuse to pity
Or hear me at all, but kill me instead, unarmed
As some helpless woman, my bronze lying back by the wall.
This, I fear, is hardly the time for a lengthy
Chat with Achilles by oak-tree or rock, such as
A boy and his girl might have with each other—boy
And his girl indeed![3] Much rather, let us now clash
With no further delay, that we may find out to whom
The Olympian wills the high glory."
          As thus he debated,   150
Achilles, peer of the plume-waving War-god, loomed up
Before him hefting his spear of Pelian ash,
That awesome bronze-bladed shaft, above his right shoulder,
While all about him his marvelous armor was flashing
Like leaping flames or the rising sun. Then Hector
Took but one look before trembling seized him all over,
Nor did he dare hold his ground, but leaving the gates
Behind him, he fled in fear with the son of Peleus,
Putting his faith in his speed as a runner, hot
In pursuit. As a hawk of the mountains, fastest of fowls,   160
Darts with shrill screams in pursuit of a trembling dove,
Hungry to kill her, so now Achilles sped on

In his furious wrath, and Hector before him ran swiftly
Beneath the wall of the Trojans. Past the place
Of lookout and the wind-swayed wild fig tree they ran, always
Out from the wall along the wagon-made road,
And came to the two fair-burbling fountains, where those
Two springs jet up that feed deep-swirling Scamander.
Hot water flows from the one, and over its stream
170 Steam rises like smoke from a blazing fire, while even
In summer the other runs cold as hail or chill snow
Or hard-frozen ice itself. And there by those fountains
Are handsome wide washing-troughs where the wives and fair
            daughters
Of Trojans had washed glossy clothes in the days of peace
Before the Achaeans came.
        By these they dashed,
One fleeing, the other pursuing. A good man led
The race, but the one in pursuit was far the stronger
And came swiftly on, for now it was not for any
180 Mere hide or sacrificed bull that they strove, such as men
Most usually race for, but now it was for the life
Of horse-breaking Hector. And as when hard-hoofed, prizewinning
Stallions wheel fast around the turn-posts, and some
Fine prize is put up, a tripod perhaps, or a woman,
In games for a warrior dead, so now these two
Swiftly circled the city of Priam three times, while all
The gods gazed down on their race. Then the Father of men
And immortals was first to speak out among them, saying:
        "Look now, truly a much-cherished man I see
190 Being chased about the high walls, and my heart grieves greatly
For Hector, who often has burned for me the thigh-pieces
Of oxen high on the crags of many-ridged Ida
And on the citadel heights. But now great Achilles
Is chasing him swiftly about Priam's city. Come then,
You gods, think and decide whether we shall save him
From death, or slay him at last, brave man though he is,
At the hands of raging Achilles, Peleus' son."
        Then the goddess Athena, her blue eyes blazing, answered him
Thus: "O Father, lord of the dazzling bolt
200 And darkly ominous cloud, what are you saying!
Can it be that you really wish to deliver a mortal,
One long fore-destined by fate, from dolorous death?
Well do as you like, but don't suppose for one moment
That all of us like what you do!"

Then Zeus, god of gales,
Replied: "Why so grim, my Tritogeneia?
Dear child, I was not altogether in earnest in what
I said, and surely I want to be gentle with you.
Do as you please, and restrain yourself no longer."
So saying, he started Athena, who needed no urging,   210
And down she went darting from high on the peaks of Olympus.
But fast Achilles, ceaselessly running, pressed hard
Upon Hector. And as when a hound in the mountains jumps
The fawn of a deer and chases him hotly through glade
And winding gorge, relentlessly tracking him down
Whenever he cowers in hiding beneath a dense thicket,
So Hector now could not escape Achilles.
As often as he endeavored to make a dash
For the lofty Dardanian Gates, hoping his fellows
Above on the wall might cover his effort with showers   220
Of shafts till he gained the protection of well-built bastions,
Achilles would cut him off and turn him back
Toward the plain, while he himself continued to run
On the city-side of the course. And as in a dream
A man is unable to chase one who wishes to flee,
And both, though struggling to run, remain rooted fast,
So that neither gains on the other, so now Achilles
Could not overtake Hector, nor could swift Hector
Escape. But how did the Trojan manage to keep
Away for so long from the fierce fates of death? Only   230
With help from Apollo, who came for the last and final
Time to inspire him with strength and quicken his knees.
And Achilles signaled his men with shakes of his head
Not to hurl their bitter missiles at Hector, lest someone
Else might win the glory of bringing him down,
And he himself come second. But when for the fourth
Time around they reached the fair fountains, Father Zeus
Lifted his golden scales and set on the pans
Two fates of forever-sad death, one for Achilles
And one for horse-breaking Hector. Then by the middle   240
He took the balance and raised it, and down all the way
To Hades' house sank the death-day of Hector, whereat
Apollo left him.* But bright-eyed Athena came up

---

*Zeus also weighed the fates of Achaeans and Trojans at VIII.72–79, where his plan to
honor Thetis begins to be fulfilled; in both instances, a prior plan becomes irrevocable.

To Achilles and spoke to him these winged words:
    "Now, finally,
Zeus-loved resplendent Achilles, I've hope that we two
Will cut Hector down, no matter how hungry for battle
He is, and bear to the ships great glory for all
The Achaeans. For now he cannot escape us, not even
250 If far-working Phoebus suffers tremendously for him
And grovels in his behalf before Father Zeus
Of the aegis. So take your stand and get back your breath,
While I go persuade your quarry to fight with you
Man to man."
    So spoke Athena, and Peleus' son, gladly
Obeying, stood where he was, leaning upon
His bronze-bladed shaft of ash. Athena left him
And came up to shining Hector, assuming the form
And weariless voice of his brother Deïphobus. Standing
260 Beside him, she spoke to him these words winged with beguilement:
    "Dear brother, surely fleet-footed Achilles has sadly
Abused you, chasing you thus around Priam's city.
But come, let us now stand against him and beat back his charge
Together."
    To which great Hector, his bronze helmet flashing:
"Deïphobus, you've always been my favorite brother
By far, of all the sons that were born to Priam
And Hecuba. Now, though, I'm sure I shall hold you dearer
Than ever, since you have dared to come out and help me,
270 While all the others stay back of the lofty walls."
    To him then the goddess bright-eyed Athena replied:
"Dear brother, believe me, our father and queenly mother
And all of the comrades about me earnestly pleaded
With me to stay where I was, so fearfully do
They all tremble before Achilles. But my heart was deeply
Pained by piercing sorrow for you. So now
Let us charge straight at him and fight, nor let there be
Any sparing of spears, that we may know at once
Whether Peleus' son is going to cut us both down
280 And carry our bloodstained armor back to the ships,
Or whether he shall go down beneath the bronze point
Of your spear."
    With these guileful words Athena induced him
To fight, and when they got within range of each other,
Huge Hector, his bronze helmet flashing, spoke first to Achilles:
"No longer, O Peleus' son, will I flee before you,

As I have done three times around the great city
Of Priam, without the heart to stand up to your charge.
For now my spirit says fight with you face to face,
Whether I kill or be killed. Come then, let us   290
Invoke our gods to sanction this pact between us,
For they will witness and guard our covenant best.
If Zeus allows me to outlast you and rob you
Of life, I'll do to your corpse no foul defilement.
But when I have stripped off your armor, Achilles,
I'll give your dead body back to the host of Achaeans—
And you do the same for me."
                    Then savagely scowling
At him, fast-footed Achilles replied: "Hector,
You madman, don't stand there babbling to me of covenants.   300
There are no faithful oaths between lions and men,
Nor do wolves and lambs have any oneness of heart,
But they are always at fatal odds with each other.[4]
So too it is not to be thought that we can ever
Be friends, nor shall there be any peace between us
Till one or the other has fallen and glutted with blood
The battling Ares, him of the tough hide shield!
Recall every jot of your warrior's prowess, for now
Is the time to show your courage and skill as a spearman.
Escape for you there is none, but Pallas Athena   310
Shall soon bring you down with this long lance of mine.
And now you shall pay all at once for the grief I endured
For my comrades, whom you in your raging killed with the spear."
        So saying, he poised his long-shadowing spear and hurled it,
But shining Hector, looking straight at him, escaped,
For he saw it coming and crouched, so that the bronze point
Flew over his head and embedded itself in the earth.
But Pallas Athena snatched it up, without
Hector's knowledge, and gave it back to Achilles. And Hector,
His people's commander, spoke thus to the great son of Peleus: 320
        "You missed, O godlike Achilles. It seems that Zeus
Has not yet informed you concerning the day of my doom,
Though surely you thought that he had. You thought by your glibness
And cunning of speech to fill me with terror of you
And completely deprive me of courage and strength. But you'll not
Plant your spear in my back as I flee, but as I
Charge down straight upon you, drive it clean through my chest—
If God has granted you that. Look out now and avoid,
If you can, my keen-cutting bronze. Here's hoping you take

330 The whole shaft into your hard flesh! Surely this war
    Would be lighter for Trojans, if you, their greatest scourge,
    Were dead."
            Then poising his shade-making spear, he cast,
    Nor did he miss, but struck full upon the shield
    Of Achilles, from which a long way it rebounded, enraging
    Hector, since his swift shaft had flown from his hand
    In vain. And now, since he had no second ash spear,
    He stood in deep consternation, then shouted to him
    Of the dazzling white shield, Deïphobus, asking a long spear
340 Of him. But he was nowhere around, and Hector,
    Aware now of just what had happened, spoke thus:
        "So be it.
    Surely the gods have summoned me deathward. For I
    Thought sure that the hero Deïphobus stood right behind me,
    Whereas he is safe on the other side of the wall,
    And Athena has tricked me. Now evil death is at hand
    For me, not far off at all, nor is there any
    Way out. Such, I believe, has always been
    Zeus's pleasure, and that of his far-shooting son Apollo,
350 Who have in the past been willing and eager to help me.
    Now, though, my doom is surely upon me. But let me
    Not die without a huge effort, nor let me dishonorably
    Die, but in the brave doing of some great deed
    Let me go, that men yet to be may hear of what happened."
        So saying, he drew the keen blade that hung by his side,
    A sword both heavy and long. Then bracing himself
    He charged at Achilles, plunging upon him like some
    Huge high-flying eagle that dives through dark clouds to seize
    On the plain a tender lamb or cowering hare.
360 Even so, Hector plunged, his sharp sword held high. And Achilles,
    Seething with savage wrath, met the advance
    With one of his own, protecting his chest with his intricate,
    Exquisite shield and tossing his head, so that all
    The gold plumes that Hephaestus had thickly set in the crest
    Of that four-horned helmet shook with a gorgeous glitter.
    And from the bronze point of the spear that Achilles balanced
    In his right hand there went forth a gleam like that
    Which glints amid stars in the blackness of night from Hesperus,
    Fairest of all the stars set in wide heaven.
370 Hefting that powerful spear, he scanned the form
    Of his foe to find the spot where a spear was most likely

To pierce the firm flesh of Hector. He saw that his armor
Of bronze covered him all the way, the beautiful
Gear he had stripped from mighty Patroclus when he
Cut him down.[5] But there where the collarbones separate neck
And shoulders, there at his throat, most fatal of targets,
Appeared a spot unprotected by bronze. So there,
As on him he charged, great Achilles drove in his spear,
And the point went through his soft neck and stuck out behind.
Even so, the ashen shaft, heavy with cleaving bronze,   380
Failed to sever the windpipe. Hence Hector could still say words
And answer his foe. Dying, he sprawled in the dust,
And shining Achilles exulted above him, vaunting:

     "Hector, I dare say you thought while stripping Patroclus
That you would be safe, nor did you have one thought of me,
Since I was not there and since you are a very great fool!
Behind at the hollow ships that man had a helper,
One mightier far than himself to avenge him—me,
The man who unstrung those knees of yours. Now dogs
And birds will ravin on your shredded corpse, defiling   390
You utterly. Meanwhile, Achaeans shall hold for Patroclus
A high and fitting funeral."

     Then Hector, his bronze helmet
Gleaming, his small strength rapidly draining, answered:
"I beg you, Achilles, by your own knees and parents
And life, do not allow me thus to be eaten
By dogs at the ships of Achaeans. Instead, accept
What you want of our plentiful bronze and gold, a ransom
My father and queenly mother will gladly give you,
If only you'll give back my body, that Trojans and wives   400
Of Trojans may give me my due of funeral fire."

     Then blackly scowling at him, fast-footed Achilles
Replied: "Do not beg me by knees or by parents,
You dog! I only wish I were savagely wrathful
Enough to hack up your corpse and eat it raw—
In view of what you have done—but no man alive
Shall keep the dogs from your head, not even if here
They should bring and weigh out a ransom ten or twenty times
What you are worth and promise still more, not even
If Priam, descended of Dardanus, should tell them to pay   410
Your weight in gold—not even then should your
Queenly mother lay you on a bed and mourn you, the son
Whom she herself bore, but dogs and birds shall devour you,

Bones and all!"[6]
     Then noble bright-helmeted Hector,
Rapidly dying, replied: "I know you, Achilles,
All too well, and clearly foresee what you'll do,
Nor was there a chance of my changing your mind. The heart
In your breast is solid iron. But think what you're doing,
420 Or one day I may bring the gods' wrath on you, when Paris
And Phoebus Apollo destroy you there, great valor
And all, at the Scaean Gates."*
     As thus he spoke,
The final moment arrived, and his soul flew forth
From his body and quickly journeyed to Hades, bewailing
Her lot as one too soon bereft of youth
And manly vigor. And now to the corpse of his foe,
God-gifted Achilles spoke thus:
     "Die—and as
430 For my own fate, I'll accept that whenever Zeus wills
To fulfill it, Zeus and the other immortal gods."
     He spoke, and drawing the bronze from Hector's throat,
He laid it aside and started to strip from his shoulders
The armor, sticky with blood. And the other sons
Of Achaeans ran up all around and gazed at the wondrously
Handsome body of Hector, nor did a man
Approach him without inflicting a wound in his flesh,
And many a one, with a glance at his neighbor, would say:
     "Aha! fierce Hector is not even nearly so hard
440 To handle now as when he hurled blazing fire
On the ships!"
     So saying, a man would step in and stab
Hector's body. At last, having stripped him of bronze, swift Achilles
Stood up among the Achaeans and spoke to them, saying:
"O friends, captains and counselors of the Argives,
Now that the gods have enabled us thus to destroy
This man, who has done more damage than all of the others
Together, come, let us make a tour with our weapons
Around Priam's city and see what the Trojans intend
450 To do next, whether they will desert their high town, now that
Their champion is dead, or whether they've made up their minds
To stay on without Hector's help. But what kind of talk
Is this? Back at the ships lies a dead man unwept

---

*See XIX.462–474 and XXI.136–141 for earlier prophecies of Achilles' death.

And unburied, Patroclus, whom I will never forget
So long as my knees are quick and I am one
Of the living. And though all phantoms else in Hades'
House forget their dead, even there will I
Remember my precious comrade. But come, you sons
Of Achaeans, singing our song of triumph, let us
Go back to the hollow ships, bearing this body.   460
Today we have won tremendous renown, for we
Have slain royal Hector, whom Trojans have always lauded
Throughout the city as if the man were a god."
     So saying, he set about foully defiling the body
Of noble Hector. Piercing behind the tendons
Of both of his feet between heel and ankle, he pulled through
And tied leather thongs, and bound them fast to his chariot,
Leaving the head to drag. Then lifting the famous
Armor aboard, he mounted the car himself
And lashed the team on, and they unreluctant took off   470
At a gallop. And dust billowed up on either side
Of the dragging Hector, as his black hair trailed out
In the dirt and the once so handsome head was defiled
With foul dust.[7] For Zeus had now committed the man
To the hands of his foes to suffer disgrace and defilement
There in the land of his fathers.
     Thus was his head
All filthied with dust, and his mother, seeing him so,
Tore at her hair and, screaming, flung wildly off
Her shimmering veil. And his dear father pitifully groaned,   480
While the people around them and those throughout the city
Took up the mournful wail. Nor could they have grieved
Any more had all looming Troy been wreathed in flames
From walls to the citadel heights. And the people had all
They could do to keep old Priam, grief-frenzied, from rushing
Out through the lofty Dardanian Gates. He begged them
All, groveling in dung of horses, and calling
Each man by his name, crying:
     "Release me, my friends,
And though you don't want to, allow me to go from the city   490
Alone to the ships of Achaeans. I'll pray to this unfeeling
Monster, this worker of horrors, to have some regard
For my age and for himself in the eyes of his fellows.
He too, you know, has a father, Peleus, a man
Like myself, who sired and reared him to be a great scourge
To the Trojans, to me most of all, so many have been

My sons cut off by him in the flower of youth.
Yet not for them all do I mourn so much, great
Though my grief surely is, as I now mourn for one only,
500 Keen sorrow for whom will bring me down at last
To Hades' dark house—sorrow, I say, for Hector.
Ah that he might have died in my arms. Then his mother
And I might at least have found some relief in weeping
And wailing, she who bore him ill-fated, and I
His father."
        So spoke old Priam, sobbing, and with him
His grieving people joined in. And Hector's mother,
Old Hecuba, led in their vehement keening the women
Of Troy, crying: "My child, how wretched I am!
510 Why should I go on alive in this terrible anguish
Of mine, now that you're gone forever? You
My constant glory both night and day in the city
And ever a blessing to all of the men and women
Of Troy, who greeted you quite as they would a god,
While you were alive. But now death and fate have finally
Caught up with you."
        Thus Hecuba wailed through her tears.
But Hector's wife knew nothing of what had occurred,
Since no one had gone to tell her that her dear husband
520 Remained outside the gates. She was weaving a web
In an inner room of the high-roofed house, a scarlet
Web of double width through which she artfully
Sprinkled a pattern of flowers.* And now she called
Through the house to her girls with the beautiful braids to set
A large three-legged cauldron over the fire, that there
Should be a hot bath for Hector when he returned
From the fighting—poor innocent one, who had no idea
That far from all baths strong fire-eyed Athena had cut
Hector down by the hand of Achilles.[8] But then she heard
530 The shrieks and groans from the wall, and shaking all over
She dropped the shuttle to earth and spoke once again
To her fair-braided handmaids:
        "Two of you, come go with me,
That I may see what has happened. For that was the voice
Of my husband's reverenced mother, and my heart leaps
To my mouth and my knees are frozen beneath me. Surely

---

*Compare the scene of Helen at her web at III.141–145 (with endnote 1).

Some horror is close at hand for the children of Priam.
O far from my ears may such news always be,
But I am terribly fearful that great Achilles
Has cut brave Hector off from the city and driven him   540
Out on the plain, and most likely ended by now
The fatal pride that has for so long possessed him.
For Hector would never lag back in the throng of fighters,
But always insisted on charging well out in front
And never allowed any man to outdo him in daring."

     So saying, Andromache rushed from the hall like a woman
Gone mad, her heart wildly pounding, and with her went two
Of her handmaids. But when she had joined the crowd on the wall,
She stopped and looked toward the plain, and there she saw Hector
Ruthlessly dragged by fast horses away from the city   550
And toward the hollow ships of Achaea. Then darkness
Night-black came over her eyes and enclosed her, as backward
She fell, flinging far off her shining headdress,
Her fair coronet, her snood and woven fillet,
And with them the veil that Aphrodite the golden
Had given to her on the day that Hector, he
Of the flashing helmet, had led her forth as his bride
From Eëtion's house, having given innumerable gifts
To her father. Now round her crowded her husband's sisters
And sisters-in-law and in her dead faint they held her   560
And tried to revive her. When she came to and her spirit
Returned to her breast, she lifted her voice in lament
Mid the women of Troy, sobbing:
                            "Ah Hector, what misery
Is mine! To one fate, it seems, we were born, you
Here in Troy in Priam's house, I at the foot
Of wooded Mount Placus in Thebe in the house of Eëtion,
Who raised me, the unlucky father of one whose fate
Is even more cruel. I heartily wish he had never
Sired me. Now you are going to Hades' house   570
In the hidden depths of the earth, leaving me here
In bitter anguish, a widow in your spacious halls,
And your son is still just a baby, the son we two
So unluckily had. For now you can be no help to him,
Hector, nor he any pleasure to you. And though
He survives this tear-fraught war with Achaeans, he'll always
Have plenty of labor and woe to endure, for others
Will take all his land. A fatherless son is cut off
From the friends of his childhood. He goes about with his head

580 Hanging down and his cheeks wet with tears, and when in his need
He comes where the friends of his father are feasting and plucks
At one's cloak or another's tunic, someone out of pity
Holds out his cup for a moment, just long enough
To wet the child's lips but leave his palate still dry.
And up comes a boy whose parents are still alive
And beats him away from the feast with his fists, jeering:
'Get out of here fast! You've no father feasting with us.'
Then, crying, back to his widowed mother the little one
Runs—our little Astyanax, who always before
590 On his father's lap ate only rich mutton and marrow,
And who, when he was through playing and sleepy, would lie
On a bed in the arms of his nurse, a lovely soft bed,
Where he would sleep well with his little heart full of good cheer.
Now, though, with no father, he'll suffer innumerable evils—
My precious Astyanax, Lord of the City, so called
By the Trojans because you alone, my husband, protected
Their gates and high walls. But now by beaked ships, far away
From your parents, slick-wriggling worms shall devour you, the dogs
Having eaten their fill, all feasting on your naked body—
600 Though in your halls you've plenty of handsome fine clothes,
Which now I shall burn to ashes, since you'll never lie
In any of them, and such at least I can do
In your honor for all of the men and women of Troy."
        So she through her tears, and the women all added their wails.

BOOK XXIII

The Funeral Games for Patroclus

While the Trojans were grieving throughout the town, the Achaeans
Returned to their ships and the Hellespont stream, where each man
Went off to his vessel. Achilles, however, would not
Allow the Myrmidons thus to be scattered, but spoke out
Among his war-loving comrades, saying:
    "O Myrmidons,
Men of fast horses and my faithful friends, let us
Not loose from the cars our solid-hoofed horses, but let us
Still mounted close in round Patroclus and mourn him, for such
Is the due of the dead. Then when we have found some relief   10
In our grievous lamenting, we will unyoke our horses
And eat supper here all together."
    At this, they all
As one man began a dirge for the dead, led
By Achilles. And thrice round the corpse of Patroclus they drove
Their mane-tossing horses, the men ever mourning, as Thetis
Aroused in their hearts the desire to lament. And their tears
Streamed down the warriors' bronze to sprinkle the sands
Beneath them, so mighty a master of rout was he
Whom they mourned. And Peleus' son led the sorrowful chant,   20
Laying his man-killing hands on the breast of his friend
And incessantly moaning these words, a funeral vaunt:
    "Rejoice, O Patroclus, even in Hades' house,
For I am already fulfilling all that I promised
To you—that I would drag Hector here and give him
Raw to the dogs, and soon at your pyre I'll cut
The throats of twelve splendid sons of the Trojans, venting
My wrath because of your killing."
    He spoke, and further
Foully defiled Prince Hector, flopping him over   30
Face down in the dust before the bier of Patroclus.
And all took off their glittering bronze and loosed
Their high-whinnying horses. Then the countless army sat down
By the ship of Aeacus' grandson Achilles, and he

Provided for them a sumptuous funeral feast.
Many sleek bellowing bulls, lurching, succumbed
To the iron as they were slaughtered, along with great numbers
Of sheep and bleating goats, and numerous swine,
Well-fattened and flashing their tushes, were stretched to singe
40   Above the flame of Hephaestus. And all round the corpse
Many cupfuls of blood were poured out in sacred libation.
      But now the chief, fast-footed Achilles, the other
Great leaders conducted to King Agamemnon, though they
Had all they could do to get him away, so grieved
Was he in his heart because of his friend. And when
They arrived at the lodge of Atrides, they quickly ordered
The high-voiced heralds to set a large three-legged cauldron
Over the fire, in case they were able to get
Peleus' son to wash from his flesh the horrible gore.[1]
50   But he unbendingly said that he would not, and swore
This oath in his fervor:
      "Now truly, by Zeus, the highest
And best of all gods, no water shall rightly come near
My head until I have shorn off my hair in grief
And laid Patroclus high on his pyre and after
His burning heaped up a barrow above him, for no
Second sorrow shall ever strike through to my heart like this,
So long as I live on earth. For now, though, let us
Complete this sorrowful meal, but in the morning,
60   O king of men Agamemnon, order the soldiers
To bring in wood and to make all fit preparations,
That our dead comrade may journey as such a man should
Down to the dark kingdom of gloom, quickly consumed
From our sight by the weariless fire. Then once again
The troops can turn to their tasks."
      He spoke, and the chiefs,
Having heeded, obeyed him, and quickly they got the meal ready
And ate, each man with an equal share of the food.
And when they had eaten and drunk as much as they wished,
70   The others went off to their lodges to sleep, but Achilles
Went out and, heavily groaning, threw himself down
Mid the Myrmidon host on the beach of the crashing sea
In an open spot near which the billows were breaking.
And when sleep took him, deliciously drifted about him,
Dissolving the cares of his heart—for his splendid limbs
Were exhausted from chasing Prince Hector around windy Ilium—
Then appeared to him there the unhappy ghost

Of Patroclus, exactly resembling the man himself
In stature and dress and voice and beautiful eyes,
And he stood at Achilles' head and spoke to him, saying: 80
    "You sleep, Achilles, forgetful of me—which you
Never were so long as I lived. Now that I'm dead,
You neglect me! But bury me soon as you can, that I
May get within Hades' gates.[2] So far the spirits
Have kept me away, mere shadows of men outworn
That will not allow me to join them beyond the river.
Vainly I wander about unable to enter
The wide-gated mansion of Hades. But give me your hand,
I sadly beseech you, for once you have given my corpse
To the fire, I'll never again come back from Hades.   90
Never again in this life shall we two sit down
Apart from our dear companions and make plans together,
For that loathsome fate toward which I have always journeyed
Has now engulfed me forever. Yes, and you too,
O godlike Achilles, are doomed to fall and die
Before the wall of opulent Troy. And one
Other thing I will say and ask you to do, if you
Will but listen. Do not have my bones lie apart from your own,
Achilles, but let them lie always together, as we
Grew up together in your house, from the time I came there   100
With Menoetius when I was just a small boy, fleeing
From Opus to your place because I had miserably killed
A playmate of mine, Amphidamas' son, not meaning
To kill him, but angry and fighting because of a dice game.
Then knightly Peleus received me into his home,
Lovingly reared me, and made me your squire. Hence
Let one urn contain the bones of us both, that golden
Two-handled urn which your goddess mother gave you."
    Achilles, then, fast in the war-charge, answered him thus:
"Why, O more than a brother to me, have you   110
Come here to give these instructions? Of course I will heed you
And do all you say. But now come closer to me,
That though it be for no more than a moment, we two
May embrace each other and find some relief from our sorrow
In grievous lamenting."
    So saying, he reached out his arms,
But found nothing there. For the ghost, insubstantial as smoke,
Was gone beneath earth, gibbering bat-like. At once
Achilles sprang up, amazed, and striking his hands
Together, spoke these mournful words: 120

"Ah now, even
In Hades' house the soul is something, though only
An image utterly empty of any real life.
For here all night long the ghost of unhappy Patroclus
Has stood over me, weeping and moaning and telling me
What I should do in every detail, and the phantom
Looked wonderfully like my dear friend."
      He spoke, and aroused
In them all the desire for further lamenting, and Dawn
130 Of the rosy fingers spilled her sweet light upon them
While they were still grieving about the piteous corpse.
Then quickly King Agamemnon dispatched both men
And mules from all of the lodges to go after wood,
And in charge of them went a man of high prowess, Meriones,
Squire of manly Idomeneus. Off they went
With their tree-felling axes and strong-braided ropes, while the mules
Jogged on ahead. Then uphill and downhill, about
And around they went till they came to the forested foothills
Of well-watered Ida. There they began at once
140 To fell with their keen-bladed bronze the high-foliaged oaks,
And with thunderous crashing the trees kept falling. The Achaeans
Then split up the timber and bound it behind the mules,
That cut up the ground with their hooves as they strained for the
        plain
Through the dense underbrush. And all the woodcutters bore logs,
As they were ordered to do by Meriones, squire
Of kindly Idomeneus. Back on the beach, they cast
Them down, man after man, on the spot where Achilles
Planned a huge mound for Patroclus as well as himself.
      When the countless logs had all been thrown down, there
150 The Achaeans sat down together. But quickly Achilles
Ordered the war-loving Myrmidons to gird on their bronze
And to yoke their horses to shining cars. And they all
Got up and did as he bade, arming themselves
And mounting their chariots, footmen and riders alike.
In front went the horse-drawn fighters, and following them
Came a huge cloud of infantry, mid whom his comrades bore
Dead Patroclus, whose corpse they had covered with locks of their hair
Which they had shorn off and dropped on him. Behind walked royal
Achilles, holding the head of his friend and constantly
160 Mourning, for matchless indeed was the man whom he
Was escorting toward Hades.

When all had arrived at the place
Achilles had chosen, they set down the dead and quickly
Stacked up for him a high pile of wood. But now
Goddess-born swift Achilles remembered another thing
He must do, and standing apart from the pyre he cut off
A tawny lock of his hair, the lock he had let
Grow long for the river Spercheius. Then deeply moved,
He spoke, looking out on the wine-blue sea:
    "Spercheius,   170
In vain did my father Peleus vow to you
That when I came back to my own dear country, I'd cut off
This lock in your honor and offer a holy hecatomb,
Slaughtering there in addition fifty fine rams,
All consecrated to you and your fair springs
Where you have your grove and temple and altar fragrant
With incense. So promised old Peleus, but you have not granted
His wish. Now, then, since I will never go home
To my dear native land again, I will give to the hero
Patroclus this lock of my hair to go with him in death."   180
    So saying, he placed the hair in the hands of his precious
Comrade, arousing in all of them the desire
For further lamenting. And now the sun would have set
On the weeping Achaeans had not Achilles come up
Beside Agamemnon and said: "Atrides, of course
The Achaeans may mourn as much as they wish, but since
They have most respect for your orders, for now dismiss
The army from round the pyre and bid them make ready
Their meal, while we, the close friends of the dead, remain
And take care of these things. And with us let all of the leaders   190
Also remain."
    When the ruler of men Agamemnon
Heard this request, he dismissed the troops at once
To return to their shapely ships, while the dead's dearest friends
Remained and stacked up a pyre of wood a hundred feet
Square at the base. Then sorrowing still they laid
Dead Patroclus up on the peak of the pyre, before which
They flayed and dressed a great many fine sheep and sleek
Long-horned cattle. From these Achilles gathered the fat
And enfolded the dead therein from head to foot   200
And heaped the flayed bodies about him. Against the bier
He leaned large two-handled jars of honey and oil
And, loudly lamenting, drove four fast neck-arching horses

Up on the pyre. The lord Patroclus had kept
Nine table dogs, of which Achilles now cut
The throats of two and flung them up on the pyre.
And killing with bronze twelve valiant sons of the Trojans—
An evil act he had planned in his heart[3]—he lit
The pyre so that the iron fury of flame
210 Might feed on their corpses. Then groaning, he called by name
On his precious friend:
     "Hail, O Patroclus, even
In Hades' halls—hail and farewell! Already
I'm doing for you those things I promised. For twelve
Brave sons of the great-hearted Trojans are being devoured
By the flames along with you, but Priam's son Hector
I'll not give to fire to feed on. Him I will leave
To the dogs!"
     Such was his threat, but no dogs dealt
220 With Prince Hector, for Aphrodite, the daughter of Zeus,
Warded them off day and night, anointing his body
With magic, immortal oil of roses, to keep
His flesh from tearing when savage Achilles dragged him.
And down on his corpse Apollo drew a dark cloud
From sky to plain, obscuring the place where the dead man
Lay, that not too soon the heat of the sun
Might shrivel his flesh around his bones and sinews.
     The pyre of dead Patroclus, however, would not
Begin burning. But quick-footed royal Achilles knew
230 What to do. He stood apart from the pyre and prayed
To two winds, the North and the West, promising exquisite
Gifts and liberally pouring libations of wine
From a golden cup. He besought them to come, that quickly
The wood might be kindled and all of the corpses flame.
His prayer came first to the ears of Iris, who sped
To the winds with his plea. They were all met at a feast
In the house of the stormy West Wind, and when Iris came running
And stopped on the threshold of stone, they all sprang up
At the first sight of her and each invited her over
240 To him. But she would not sit, and spoke to them thus:
     "I may not sit down, for I must return to Oceanus'
Stream and the Ethiopians' land, where they
Are offering whole hecatombs to the immortals,
A sacred feast in which I would share. But Achilles
Prays to the winds, to you O North and to you
O blustering West, offering fine gifts and begging

For you to come, that you may quickly make burn
The pyre of Patroclus, for whom the Achaeans all mourn."
　　　So saying, she left them, and those two roared off with incredible
Noise, driving the clouds in masses before them.   250
Soon they blew on the sea, raising the waves
Into billows beneath their shrill whistling, and so came in haste
To the loamy land of Troy and fell on the pyre,
Causing the god-blazing flame to roar with huge fury.
All night they howled as one gale about the flames
Of the pyre, while throughout the night quick Achilles dipped wine
From a gold mixing-bowl and drenched the earth all around,
Pouring it from a two-handled cup and ceaselessly
Calling upon the spirit of hapless Patroclus.
Just as a father mourns for his son while burning   260
His bones, a bridegroom whose death has brought misery on both
Of his unlucky parents, so now Achilles mourned
As he burned the bones of his friend, wearily dragging
Himself around the high pyre, incessantly moaning.
　　　But at the time when the Morning Star arises,
Foretelling the coming of light on earth—the star
After which comes crocus-clad Dawn, spreading over the sea—
Then the flames died down, the fire flickered out, and the winds
Returned to their home across the Thracian deep,
Causing the waves to roar and run high. And Achilles,   270
Turning away from the smoldering pyre, sank down
Exhausted, and at once sweet sleep was upon him. But now
All those with King Agamemnon approached in a group,
And when the noise of their voices and footsteps awoke him,
He sat upright and spoke to them, saying:
　　　"Atrides,
And you other leaders of our united Achaeans,
First go quench the smoldering pyre with sparkling
Wine, wherever the fury of flame has been,
And then let us gather the bones of Patroclus, son   280
Of Menoetius, carefully singling them out from the rest,
Which shouldn't be hard, since he lay in the midst of the pyre,
While all of the others, both horses and men, were burned
Apart from him on the edges. Then let us enfold
The bones in a double layer of fat and put them
Away in a golden urn, until I myself
Am hidden in Hades. But not at this time do I bid you
Heap up with much toil a huge barrow, but one that is fitting.
Then later, when I am no more, you men who survive me

290 Amid the many-oared ships build it up broad
And high."
        He spoke, and they did as swift Peleus' son bade.
First they put out the pyre with sparkling wine,
Wherever the flame had been and the ashes lay deep,
And weeping they wrapped the white bones of their lovable friend
In a double layer of fat and put them away
In a golden urn, which they veiled with cloth of sheer linen
And placed in his lodge. Then they laid out the barrow's circle
Around the huge pyre and heaped up inside it a mound
300 Of dark earth.
        Having built him this barrow, they started to leave,
But Achilles restrained them and seated the troops in a large
Open space where the funeral games were to be.[4] And from
His ships he brought out the prizes—cauldrons and tripods
And horses and mules, sleek powerful oxen, gray iron,
And women gorgeously sashed.
        For the charioteers
He set forth splendid prizes—for him who should run
In first place, a woman flawless in exquisite handwork
310 Along with a three-legged, handle-eared cauldron holding
Some twenty-two measures. And for the second he put up
An unbroken mare of six years, big with a mule foal
Soon to be born. For the third he offered a basin
Untouched by fire, a lovely glittering piece
That held four measures, and for the fourth he set out
Two talents of gold, and a two-handled urn untouched
By fire for the fifth.
        Then he stood up and spoke
Mid the Argives, saying: "Atreus' son, and you other
320 Bright-greaved Achaeans, these prizes are waiting here
For winning drivers to claim them. Now if we Achaeans
Were holding these games in honor of some other man,
Surely I would take the first prize off to my lodge,
For you know how far my horses surpass all others
In speed, they being immortal, a gift from Poseidon
To Peleus my father, who gave them to me. This time,
However, I and my solid-hoofed horses will not
Compete, so valiant and famous a charioteer
Have they lost, a driver most kind, who so many times
330 Made both of their flowing manes glossy with soft olive oil
After washing them with bright water. For him they stand
Immobile in mourning, their hearts full of sorrow, their manes

Trailing out on the ground, nor will they move. But you others
Throughout the army, get ready to race, whoever
Among you has faith in his horses and well-jointed car."
At this from Peleus' son, the fast drivers assembled.
Far the first to spring up was Admetus' dear son
Eumelus, commander of many, and able indeed
As a horseman. Next to arise was the son of Tydeus,
Strong Diomedes, who yoked to his car the horses   340
Of Tros, the same he had taken away from Aeneas
The time Apollo saved Aeneas himself.*
After him Atrides got up, the tawny Menelaus,
Descended from Zeus, and yoked his fast horses—Aethe,
Agamemnon's mare, and his own horse Podargus. Echepolus,
The son of Anchises of Sicyon, had given the mare
To King Agamemnon instead of following him
To wind-swept Troy, since he much preferred to remain
At home in broad-lawned Sicyon, delightfully living
On great stores of Zeus-bestowed wealth. That mare Menelaus   350
Led under the yoke, a horse champing eager to run.
And fourth Antilochus harnessed his mane-tossing horses,
He the fine son of high-hearted King Nestor, son
Of Neleus, and his horses of Pylian breed. Then his father
Came up and told him what he should do, a wise man
Advising one who had knowledge himself:
      "Antilochus,
Young as you are, Zeus and Poseidon have loved you
And carefully taught you all that there is to teach
About driving horses. Hence I've no need to instruct you.   360
Already you know very well how to wheel your chariot
Close round the turn-post. Your horses, however, are slowest
Of all in the race, which makes me fear a sorry
Outcome for you. The others are faster, true,
But their drivers are not any smarter than you, my boy,
No smarter at all. So recall every trick you have learned,
If you don't want those prizes to slip quickly by you. It's skill,
You know, not strength, that makes a superior woodman,
And skill alone enables a helmsman to keep
A straight course on the wine-dark sea when his ship is beaten   370
By winds. And believe me, it's skill that makes the difference
In charioteers! One driver will put too much faith

---

*For the horses of Tros, see V.246–249, with endnote 2.

In his horses and car and allow them to wheel round the turn-post
Carelessly wide, not trying to keep them close in
With the reins. But the smart driver, although his horses are slower,
Knows how to stretch them out in a run from the first
And keeps his eyes on the man ahead of him
And on the turn-post, about which he wheels close in.
Now listen to this. Out there stands a stump some six feet
380   In height, a dry stump of oak or pine that the rain
Has not rotted, and by it on either side, set firmly
Against it right where the track turns, are two white stones,
And around it is plenty of smooth ground for driving. Perhaps
It's an old monument to one who died long ago,
Or perhaps it was used as a turn-post in races held
By men in those days. At any rate, swift Prince Achilles
Has made it his turn-post now. When you reach it, wheel
Round it close, leaning a bit to the left as you stand
In your strong-braided car, and give your right horse the whip
390   And a shout and plenty of rein. But hold your left horse
Close in, so close that one might suppose you had grazed
The stone with the hub of your finely wrought wheel—but of course
Be wary of really grazing the stone, lest you injure
The horses and wreck your car, which the others would doubtless
Enjoy much more than yourself. I tell you, dear son,
Think fast and stay on your guard, for if at the turn
You pass all the others, no driver here will be able
To catch you, much less spurt ahead of you, coming back,
Not though he drove the mighty Arion, fast horse
400   Of Adrastus, and bred of heavenly stock, or the steeds
Of Laomedon, far the best ever bred here at Troy."
          So saying, Neleus' son Nestor went back and sat down
In his place, having told his son just what he should do.
          The fifth man to ready his mane-tossing team was Meriones.
Then they all mounted their cars and tossed their lots
In a helmet held by Achilles. He shook them, and out leaped
The lot of Antilochus, son of Nestor, who thus
Got the inside lane, and the lot of lordly Eumelus
Was next to come out. Then out leaped that of Atrides,
410   Spear-famed Menelaus, followed by that of Meriones.
Last of all to get a lane for his horses
Was Tydeus' son Diomedes, much the best man
In the race. Then they lined up to start, and Achilles
Showed them the turn-post far off on the level plain,
And by it he set as a judge his father's man,

The godlike Phoenix, to keep a keen eye on the running
And to tell exactly what happened.

    Then all as one man
Brought their whips down on the horses and rattled the reins
On their backs, excitedly urging them off, and quickly   420
They came to a gallop and sped from the drawn-up ships
Across the smooth plain. From beneath their breasts the dust
Rose up in thick swirling clouds, and their manes streamed back
On the wind. And the chariots ran on the all-feeding earth,
Frequently bouncing high in the air, as the drivers
Stood in the cars, the heart of each man throbbing wildly
To win, and each of them shouted to urge his pair on,
As they flew through the dust on the plain.

    It was not, however,
Till they were galloping down the last stretch of the course,   430
Having rounded the turn-post and headed back toward the sea,
That the field strung out and all of the horses showed
What speed they were capable of, stretching themselves
To the utmost. Then quickly the hoof-flashing mares of Eumelus
Pulled out ahead, and following close behind them
Came Diomedes' great stallions, horses of Tros—
Nor far back at all, for they ever seemed just on the verge
Of mounting Eumelus's car, and constantly blew
Their hot breath upon his back and broad shoulders, since all
But over him stretched their heads as they flew. And now   440
Diomedes would surely have passed him or ended the race
Neck and neck, had Phoebus Apollo, still angry at him,
Not struck from his hand the glittering whip. Diomedes
Wept with frustration as he saw the mares of Eumelus
Spurt even more swiftly ahead, while his stallions, missing
The whip, slowed down and fell back. Athena, however,
Was not unaware of what Apollo had done
To cheat the son of Tydeus, and swiftly she went
In pursuit of the people's shepherd and, handing him back
His whip, put new strength into his horses. Then on   450
She sped to Eumelus, son of Admetus, and snapped
The yoke of his horses, causing the mares to swerve
Apart and the shaft to plow up the plain. Eumelus
Himself was thrown from the car down into the dirt
Right next to a wheel, thus stripping the skin from his elbows,
Mouth, and nose, bruising his forehead, filling
His eyes with tears, and stifling his powerful voice.
But strong Diomedes swept round the wreck with his solid-hoofed

Horses and shot out far ahead of the rest,
460 For Athena endowed his stallions with power and granted
The glory to him. And next came Atreus' son,
Tawny-haired Menelaus, but now Antilochus yelled
To his father's horses:

    "Faster! you two. Stretch
Till you burst! With that pair out in first place, the horses
Of Tydeus' flame-hearted son, I do not bid you
Compete, for Athena has given them speed and granted
Glory to him at the reins. But do overtake
Menelaus's horses, and don't let them beat you, lest Aethe,
470 A mare, disgrace you both! But why are you lagging,
Brave steeds? I'll tell you now what's what, and believe me
I mean it! No loving care will ever be yours
Again from King Nestor, if now you're so sorry as not
To win a good prize, and he will not hesitate, either,
To cut you both down with keen bronze! But faster! I say,
And catch them, and I will take care of the rest. I'll slip by
Them there where the track is narrow. Believe me, I will!"

    These urgent words from their master frightened the pair
And caused them to quicken their pace for a time, till soon
480 Antilochus spotted a low narrow place up ahead
Where the road had been partly washed out by rushing water
From hard winter rains. Menelaus held the track there,
Thinking none would dare try to pass at that place. But
        Antilochus
Swung off the track and drove his solid-hoofed horses
Up beside those of Atrides, at which Menelaus,
Terrified, shouted:

    "Antilochus, rein in your team!
You're driving like some stupid fool! The track here is narrow,
490 But soon it widens again. So pass me there,
Or surely you'll foul my car and miserably wreck
Us both!"

    He yelled, but Antilochus drove even faster,
Bringing his whip down hard, as if he had failed
To hear. And far as a discus flies when a young man,
Testing his brawn, swings it hard from the shoulder,
So far they ran side by side. Then the team of Atrides
Fell back, reined by their master, who greatly feared
That the solid-hoofed horses were going to clash on the track
500 And upset the strong-braided cars, thus painfully pitching
The drivers, so eager to win, head over heels

In the dust. But tawny-haired Menelaus yelled
This rebuke at Antilochus drawing away:
    "Go on,
Damn you! Surely no other mortal has fewer scruples
Than you. I know now how wrong we Achaeans were
To think you had any judgment. Nor shall you carry
That prize away without first swearing an oath
That you drove a clean race!"
    So saying he called to his pair: 510
"Don't stop or hold back now, no matter how hurt
Your spirits may be. But after those horses, quick!
Their legs will give out before yours, for both of them carry
More years."
    These urgent words from their master inspired
The pair to quicken their pace, and soon they drew near
The team of Antilochus.
    Meanwhile, the Argives were sitting
Where they had assembled, watching sharp for the horses
To come through the dust hanging over the plain. And the first   520
To see them was royal Idomeneus, leader of Cretans,
For he sat outside the assembly, highest of all
On a place of lookout. Hearing Diomedes' voice,
He knew it at once, despite the great distance between them,
And also he recognized one of his horses, a bay
With a white full moon on his forehead. Rising, he spoke
To the Argives, saying:
    "My friends, captains and counselors
Of the Achaeans, am I the only man here
Who sees the horses, or do you see them as well?   530
Some other pair, it seems, are now in the lead,
And some other driver. The mares of Eumelus, that led
Clear up to the turn, have now come to grief somewhere
On the plain. I'm sure I saw them still in first place
When they rounded the turn-post, but now I can find them nowhere
At all, though I've scanned the whole Trojan plain. Do you think
Eumelus perhaps dropped the reins, or was unable
To hold his pair on the track as he rounded the turn-post?
He must, I suppose, have failed to make it, and there
At the turn been hurled to earth, as his mares in panic   540
Swerved from the track and tore his car all to pieces.
But all of you get up and look, for I'm no longer
Sure what I see, but I think the man now leading
Is of the Aetolian race and a King mid the Argives,

In fact the son of horse-breaking Tydeus, strong
Diomedes himself!"
    Then Ajax, son of Oïleus,
Shamefully spoke in rebuke: "Idomeneus, why
Do you always blabber so much? Those high-stepping mares
550 Are still far off on that great stretch of plain, and you
Are neither the youngest nor most keen-sighted man
Mid the Argives. Always, however, you blabber the loudest!
Such noise scarcely becomes you, especially here
With your betters. The very same mares are still in the lead,
And that is Eumelus himself, firmly keeping his stance
In the car and holding the reins!"
    Then Idomeneus, King
Of the Cretans, angrily answered: "Ajax, you
Are indeed our best when it comes to stupid abuse,
560 But otherwise you are surely the worst of the Argives
Because of your gross and stubborn mind! But come,
Let us wager a tripod or cauldron, and let Agamemnon
Be judge between us and say which team is in front,
That you by losing may learn!"
    Oïleus' son Ajax
Sprang up at this to answer with hateful hard words,
And surely the quarrel would not have stopped there had not
Achilles himself stood up and said: "Enough,
Ajax, and no more, Idomeneus, no more bitter words,
570 So utterly evil and ugly. They hardly become you.
You'd blame severely another who acted this way,
So sit in your places and watch for the horses. Soon now
They'll be here, all of them straining to win. Then each
Man of you may clearly see for himself whose horses
Are first and whose second."
    As thus the Prince spoke, Diomedes
Drew near, frequently lashing his horses with strokes
Brought down hard from the shoulder, and swiftly his light-leaping
        stallions
Came on at a gallop. Their driver was constantly showered
580 With dust, and his chariot, covered with gold and tin,
Ran on behind the rapid-hoofed horses so fast
That only the slightest trace of the wheel rims was left
In the powdery dust, as onward his horses flew.
Then reining up in the midst of the place of assembly,
With sweat streaming off to the ground from the necks and chests
Of his pair, Diomedes leaped down from his all-shining car

And leaned his whip against the tough yoke. Nor did
The strong Sthenelus, Diomedes' dear friend, at all
Hesitate to claim the first prize for his comrade, but quickly
He gave to his spirited fellows the woman to lead   590
Away and the handle-eared tripod to carry.
     Next
To drive in was Antilochus, grandson of Neleus, he
Who had passed Menelaus, not by superior speed,
But by a low trick. Even so, Menelaus held
His fast horses close to the rear of Antilochus' car.
They ran, in fact, no farther behind than a swift horse
Is from the wheel of a car in which he draws
His master over the plain at a gallop, brushing
The metal rim with the tip of his tail, so close   600
Is he to the wheel as he speeds across the wide flat.
That close Menelaus came in behind Prince Antilochus,
Though at first he had been as far back as one
Hurls the discus. Rapidly he was catching his man,
Running him down as the splendid strength of Aethe,
King Agamemnon's mane-tossing mare, increased.
Had the course been longer, he without doubt would have passed him,
Nor would there have been any chance of a neck-and-neck finish.
     Meriones drove in fourth, the noble squire
Of Idomeneus, fully a spear-cast behind Menelaus,   610
Since his fair-maned pair were truly the slowest of all
In the race, and he the least able driver.
     Last
Came Eumelus, son of Admetus, painfully dragging
His exquisite car and driving his horses before him.
Seeing him so, quick-footed noble Achilles
Stood up mid the Argives and spoke, and his words came winged
With compassion:
     "See how in last place the ablest driver
Of all drives in his solid-hoofed horses. But come,   620
Let us give him a prize, as we should. Let him take the second,
Since now the first has gone to the son of Tydeus."
     To this all the others agreed, and Achilles would then
Have given Eumelus the mare, with full approval
From all the spectators, had not Antilochus, son
Of magnanimous Nestor, stood up and challenged the justice
Of Peleus' son Achilles, saying: "Achilles,
Angry indeed will I be with you if now
You do as you say, for thus you will cheat me of what

630 Is rightfully mine, simply because you respect
    The skill of Eumelus in spite of the fact that his horses
    And car came to grief. Well he should have prayed to the gods
    Everlasting, who then would have kept him from coming in last.
    If you, however, pity him so, and care
    So much for him, why you have great store of gold and bronze
    At your lodge, along with hard-hoofed horses, women,
    And cattle. Later, take some of that and give him
    An even more splendid prize, or do it right now,
    That all the Achaeans may warmly applaud you. But I
640 Will not yield the mare. I'll fight in hand-to-hand combat,
    In fact, with anyone here who wishes to claim her."

         At this, fast-footed princely Achilles smiled,
    Hugely delighting in his dear comrade Antilochus.
    Then he replied in these winged words: "Antilochus,
    If you wish me to give Eumelus some other prize
    From my lodge, for you I'll do even that. I'll give him
    The breastplate I took from Asteropaeus, a breastplate
    Of bronze with a brilliant casting of circular tin
    Laid on all around it. He'll value it highly, I know."

650   So saying, he bade his close comrade Automedon bring it
    Out from the lodge, and he went and brought it and placed it
    At once in the hands of Eumelus, who joyfully took it.

         But then Menelaus got up, his heart fairly seething
    With rage at Antilochus. Into his hand a herald
    Placed the orator's staff and called for silence
    Among the Argives. Then godlike Atrides spoke thus:
    "Antilochus, you that once had good sense, what
    Have you done! You've hindered my horses and made me look
    Like a fool, forcing your own much inferior team
660 To the front by a foul. But you captains and counselors
    Of the Argives, come now, and judge without favor between us,
    Impartially please, or surely someone later on
    Will say: 'Menelaus defeated Antilochus only
    By lies. Even so, he got the mare, for though
    His horses were slower by far, he himself was greater
    In rank and power.' But no, I myself will judge,
    Confident quite that none of the Danaans shall
    Have cause to rebuke me, since what I decide shall surely
    Be perfectly just. Zeus-nurtured Antilochus, come
670 Over here and stand, as is our custom, in front of
    Your horses and car, holding the slender whip
    You use when you drive. Then lay a hand on your horses

And swear by Poseidon, who hugs and shakes the whole earth,
That you committed no willing foul to get
My car behind you."
    To which the shrewd Antilochus:
"Bear with me now, my lord Menelaus, for I
Am much younger than you. As an older and better man,
You know very well what sort of rash overreaching
A young man is liable to, for though he thinks faster   680
His judgment is often too little and light. May your heart
Have patience with me, then, and I myself will give you
The mare that I won. Yes, and if you should ask
In addition some finer thing from my lodge, I'd want
To give it at once, that I may not spend all my days
Cast out of your heart, and feel myself a sinner
Before the powers divine."
    So spoke the son
Of magnanimous Nestor, and leading the mare he gave her
To King Menelaus, whose heart was warmed like the heart   690
Of ripening grain when the ears are sparkling with dew
And the fields are all bristling. Even so, Menelaus, your heart
Was made glad. Then his words to Antilochus flew on the wings
Of forgiveness.
    "Antilochus, now I myself feel no more
Anger against you, since you as a rule are not
At all foolish or flighty. But don't try another such trick
On your betters. And truly, no other Achaean could thus
So soon have appeased me. You, though, have suffered much
And toiled a great deal for my sake, you and your brother   700
Along with your excellent father. Hence I will heed
Your request for forgiveness. And as for the mare, though surely
She's rightfully mine, I give her to you, that all
Gathered here may know that my heart is never unyielding
And haughty."
    Such were his words, and giving the mare
To Antilochus' comrade Noëmon, he took for himself
The third prize, the all-shining basin. And Meriones took
The two talents of gold, since he was fourth to come in.
But the two-handled urn, the fifth prize, remained unclaimed.   710
So Achilles gave it to Nestor, bearing it through
The assembly of Argives. Standing beside him, he said:
    "This, ancient sir, is for you. Lay it away
With your treasures to be a reminder of these funeral rites
For Patroclus, whom never again you'll see mid the Argives.

This urn I give you quite freely, for now your days
Of boxing and wrestling are over, nor will you compete
Again in the javelin-throw or foot-race. The weight
Of years lies heavy upon you."

720   So saying, he placed
The urn in his hands, and Nestor receiving it spoke,
His words flying forth on the wings of joyful thanks:
"Yes indeed, child, all that you say is true, and fittingly
Put. My feet and limbs, young friend, are no longer
Steady and strong, nor do my fists any more
Lash lightly out from the shoulder. If only I were
Young again and as sure of my brawn as I was on that day
At Buprasium when the Epeans were holding last rites
For King Amarynceus and his sons put prizes up

730   For games in his honor. That day no man was my peer,
Neither mid the Epeans, nor mid my own people the Pylians,
Nor mid the great-souled Aetolians. In boxing I won
Over Enops' son Clytomedes, and in wrestling over
Ancaeus of Pleuron, who pitted his strength against me.
Iphiclus, fast though he was, I beat in the foot-race,
And in the javelin-throw I defeated Phyleus
And Polydorus. I lost but one event,
The chariot-race in which the two sons of Actor*
Outstripped me, since they were two against one, fiercely

740   Begrudging me victory and forcing their horses ahead,
For the best prize of all was still in the lists. They were twins,
And one of them drove with sure hand, a very sure hand,
While the other laid on the lash. Even such was the man
I once was, but now I leave these endeavors to men
Who are younger, since now I must yield to irksome old age,
But go, and finish these funeral rites and games
For your comrade too. This gift I gladly receive,
And my heart rejoices that always you think of me
As a friend, nor do you neglect to honor me duly

750   Among the Achaeans. May the gods in return give you
Abundant grace to fulfill each desire of your heart."
        Thus he spoke, and Peleus' son, having listened
To old Nestor's thanks, went back through the crowd of Achaeans
And brought out rewards for the painful and difficult boxing.

---

*The two sons of Actor are the Moliones, who appeared in Nestor's autobiographical account of his youthful exploits, at XI.796–803.

First he led out and tied in the place of assembly
A work-hardy mule of six years, one well broken in—
No easy task with a mule—and for him who should lose
He set out a two-handled cup. Then standing there
Mid the Argives, Achilles spoke thus:

"Atrides, and all   760
You other hard-greaved Achaeans, we now invite
The best pair of boxers here to square off and throw punches
Like fury for these two prizes. Let him whom Apollo
Gives strength to outlast the other, as witnessed by all
The Achaeans, go off to his lodge with the work-hardy mule,
While he who loses shall take the two-handled cup."

He spoke, and at once a huge man, courageous and skilled
As a boxer, stood up, one Panopeus' son Epeus,
And laying a hand on the work-hardy mule, he vaunted:
"Now let him come out and fight, whoever covets   770
This two-handled cup. For the mule, I think, will not
Be won by any Achaean who first of all has to
Beat me with his fists, since I claim to be the best boxer
Here. So I'm not so good in battle—one can't be
Expert in every endeavor! But this I say now,
And believe me I'll do what I say—namely, crush
Every bone in my crazy opponent's carcass and pound
His flesh to a pulp! So let his nearest and dearest
Of kin stand by in a body, that they may carry
Him off unconscious when I have finished with him."   780

Such was his challenge, and all for a time sat utterly
Silent. At last one man stood up to face him,
A godlike man, Euryalus, son of the son
Of Talaus, Mecisteus the King, who had journeyed to Thebes
For the funeral and games that followed great Oedipus' downfall,
And in those games had defeated all the Cadmeans.
Quickly, Euryalus' spear-famous kinsman, Tydeus'
Son Diomedes, girded his cousin's loins
With a cloth and bound his knuckles with thongs well cut
From the hide of a range-roaming ox, warmly encouraging   790
Him with words, for greatly he wished him to win.
When the two had been girded, they strode to the midst of the place
Of assembly and, squaring off, began to throw powerful
Punches, awesomely grinding their teeth and streaming
All over with sweat. Then able Epeus brought one
Up from the ground, as it were, as Euryalus peered
For an opening, and caught him crashingly under the jaw.

Nor did he remain after that in an upright position
For long, since there on the spot his splendid limbs
800 Were unstrung. And as when a fish darts up from beneath
The North Wind's ripple and leaps up out of the water
And onto the sea-weedy sand of a shallow, then quickly
Is hidden again beneath a dark wave, so now
Euryalus arched through the air and flopped on his back,
So great was the force of the blow. But gallant Epeus
Took him and set him once more on his feet, and his cherished
Companions crowded about him and helped him off
Through the place of assembly, his feet dragging trails in the dust
As he went, dangling his head to one side and spitting out
810 Clots of blood. And they set him down—still
None too sure where he was—in the midst of his fellows, while they
Went out and claimed the two-handled cup.
          Then Achilles,
Before all the Danaans, put up rewards for the painful
And toilsome wrestling, the third event in the games—
For the winner, a truly tremendous three-legged cauldron
To straddle the fire, one valued as worth twelve oxen
Among the Achaeans, and for the loser he brought out
Among them a woman of many skills, whom they valued
820 As worth four oxen. Then Peleus' son arose
Mid the Argives and said:
          "Up now, whichever two men
Among you intend to compete in this contest."
          He spoke,
And up got huge Telamonian Ajax and with him
Resourceful Odysseus, skilled at tricks and contriving.[5]
Then, having girded themselves, the two men strode out
To the midst of the place of assembly and immediately locked
Their powerful arms, reminding one of the sloping
830 Beams some famous builder connects at the roof
Of a high-gabled house to keep out the blustering winds.
And their backs fairly creaked as they gripped each other hard
With their hands and grappled for all they were worth, streaming
With sweat and raising many a blood-livid welt
On each other's ribs and shoulders, as both of them strained
Every muscle to win the fair-fashioned tripod. Odysseus,
However, could no more win a fall over Ajax
Than Ajax could over him, so firm was his stance.
But when they had grappled so long that the strong-greaved Achaeans
840 Began to get bored and restless, gigantic Ajax,

Telamon's son, grunted thus to Odysseus:
    "O god-sprung
Son of Laertes, resourceful Odysseus, either you
Lift me or let me lift you, and the outcome we'll leave
To Zeus."
        So saying, he lifted Odysseus, but that
Wily man was alertly on guard, and kicking the bend
Of Ajax's knee with his heel, he caused his legs
To buckle at once, so that backward he fell with Odysseus
Riding his chest. Next it was much-bearing, noble   850
Odysseus' turn to lift, and though he could raise him
From earth a few inches only, he crooked his knee
Behind that of Ajax and down the two went again,
Side by side in the man-clinging dust. And now
The two men would have sprung up again to try a third fall,
If Achilles had not stood up and restrained them, saying:
    "Struggle no further, nor wear yourselves out with agonized
Effort. Both of you win. Take equal prizes
And go, that other Achaeans may also compete."
        To this they willingly listened, then did as he said,   860
Wiping the dust from their bodies and putting their tunics
Back on.
        Next came the foot-race, for which Achilles
Set out still more prizes. For first place he put up
A mixing-bowl of silver, richly engraved.
It held six measures and had no equal in beauty
On all the earth, for the gifted Sidonians, master
Craftsmen, had made it with all of their art, and Phoenicians
Had brought it across the misty sea to the harbor
Of Thoas, to whom they had given the bowl as a gift.   870
And later, in ransoming Priam's son Lycaon,
Euneus, son of Jason, had given the bowl
To Patroclus. This exquisite piece Achilles put up
As a prize in honor of his dear comrade, a trophy
For him who should prove to be fleetest of foot in the race.
For the second he offered a well-fattened ox, enormous
And sleek, and half a talent of gold for the last.
Then standing up, he spoke mid the Argives, saying:
"Up now, whoever would like to compete in this race."
        At this, swift Ajax arose, the fast-running son   880
Of Oïleus, as did resourceful Odysseus. Third
To get up was Antilochus, Nestor's son, for in this event,
Too, he was the best of the younger Achaeans.

They lined up to start, and Achilles showed them the turn-post.
Then off they shot, running hard, with Ajax quickly
Taking the lead. But able Odysseus was close
On his heels, as close as the weaving-rod comes to the breast
Of a brightly-sashed woman when deftly she passes the woof
Through the warp and holds the rod close to her bosom. That close

890 Ran Odysseus, and always his feet pounded fast in the footsteps
Of Ajax before the fine dust had a chance to arise,
And the breath of royal Odysseus beat hot on the back
Of that fast runner's head, as all the Achaeans shouted
To urge Ajax on in his all-out effort to win.
But when they began their sprint down the course's last stretch,
Odysseus prayed quick in his heart to blue-eyed Athena:
"O goddess, hear me, and come put more speed in my feet!"
      Such was his prayer, and Pallas Athena, hearing,
Lightened his legs and feet and arms. Then just

900 As they started their final spurt for the rare mixing-bowl,
Ajax slipped up as he ran—undone by Athena—
And fell where the ground was covered with dung from the bellowing
Bulls that fast Achilles had slaughtered in honor
Of gentle Patroclus, and Ajax's mouth and nose
Were chock-full of noisome bull-dung. Then nobly enduring
Odysseus picked up the mixing-bowl, he
Having run in first place, and excellent Ajax laid claim
To the ox. As he stood there holding the beast by one horn
And spitting out dung, he spoke mid the Argives, saying:

910   "Ugh! but wouldn't you know it! Athena made me
Slip up as I ran, though always she goes like a mother
Right by the side of Odysseus and helps him always."
      At this the Achaeans laughed with high glee at Ajax.
Then Antilochus, last to come in but grinning gaily,
Took up the half-talent of gold and said: "I'll say
Something now that all of you already know, that even
In games the immortals favor the older men.
For though Ajax is only a little bit older than I,
Odysseus there is one from an earlier age,

920 A very ancient, but, as all say, his
Is a flourishing green old age. Hard indeed would it be
For any Achaean to race with him and win,
With the single exception of swift Achilles himself."
      He spoke, giving glory to Peleus' son, the fleet-footed,
And Achilles answered him thus: "Antilochus, not

Without due recognition shall these words of praise have been spoken
By you. No indeed, for now I will add to your prize
Another half-talent of gold."
    So saying, he gave it
To him, and Antilochus took it with thanks. Then Achilles   930
Brought out to the contest ring a long-shadowing spear,
And with it a helmet and shield, the war-gear Patroclus
Had stripped from Sarpedon, and standing he spoke mid the Argives,
Saying: "Now to compete for these prizes, we call
For the best two warriors here to put on their armor,
Take up their bright and flesh-cleaving bronze, and try
Each other's mettle before the whole army. Whichever
Shall first get through to the other's firm flesh and pierce
Through armor and blood to the very vitals, to him
I will give this fine Thracian sword, silver-studded, the blade   940
I took from Asteropaeus. The gear of Sarpedon
Let both men equally share, and I shall give
A good dinner to both in my lodge."
    Such were his words,
And huge Telamonian Ajax arose and with him
Strong Diomedes, Tydeus' son. Having armed
Themselves on opposite sides of the crowd, they strode
To the center, awesomely glaring, as gripping suspense
Held all the Achaeans. Then fiercely they charged, clashing
In combat three times. And Ajax pierced the round shield   950
Of his able opponent, but failed to draw blood on account of
The breastplate behind it. Meanwhile, Tydeus' son
Kept trying to reach the neck of Ajax by thrusting
Above his great shield with the glittering point of his spear.
At this the Achaeans were filled with fear for Ajax
And quickly stopped the encounter, bidding them each
Take equal prizes. The mighty sword, however,
Achilles presented to fierce Diomedes, bringing
It to him along with its scabbard and finely cut baldric.
    Next Peleus' son put up a huge discus of pig iron,   960
Which mighty Eëtion used to heave, before
Fast Achilles killed him and took it away in his ships
Along with his other belongings. Rising, he spoke
Mid the Argives, saying: "Come forth, whoever of you
Would like to compete for this prize. Though his fields lie out
Very far, the winner will have all the iron he can use
For five circling years at least. No lack of iron

Will send his shepherd or plowman into the city.
He'll have all he needs right there."
970   He spoke, and up got
Battle-staunch Polypoetes along with his stalwart comrade,
The godlike Leonteus, and Ajax, son of Telamon,
And high-born Epeus. They took their places to throw
And princely Epeus threw first. Gripping the iron,
He spun and wobbled it off a short way, an effort
At which the Achaeans shouted with laughter. Next
Leonteus, scion of Ares, threw, and thirdly
Great Telamonian Ajax sent the weight spinning
From out his brawny huge hand past the marks of both
980 Other men. But then battle-staunch Polypoetes gripped
The thick discus and got it off with tremendous force,
And as far as a herdsman can fling his short throwing-staff,
Whirling it lightly away above grazing cattle,
Even so far beyond all the other marks
Polypoetes threw the large weight, and the army went wild
With applause. Then the comrades of strong Polypoetes got up
And took the fine prize of their King to the hollow ships.
     For the archers, next, Achilles put up as prizes
Gleaming blue iron, this time in the form of twenty
990 Good axes, ten double-bladed, ten single, and tying
A trembling dove by the foot with thin cord to the top
Of the mast from a blue-prowed ship, he set it up
Far off in the sand and bade the men shoot, saying:
     "Whoever hits yonder timorous dove let him take
The ten double axes off to his lodge, but whoever
Hits the cord instead of the bird is the loser!
The single axes are his."
     At this, strong Teucer
Arose and Idomeneus' able squire Meriones.
1000 Then lots were tossed in a helmet of brass and Teucer's
Was first to leap out. Quickly, with marvelous vigor
He got off a shaft, but neglected to promise Apollo
A glorious hecatomb offering of first-born lambs.
So he missed the bird, since Apollo begrudged him a win,
But hit the cord by the foot of his target, and clean
In two the keen arrow cut the thin string. At once
The dove darted skyward, the cord dangled down, and loud
Was the cry that went up from the troops. But Meriones instantly
Snatched the bow from Teucer—he already had
1010 An arrow, since he had been holding one while Teucer

Was aiming—and quickly vowing a glorious hecatomb
Offering of first-born lambs to Apollo, who hits
From afar, he spotted the timorous dove high up
Beneath the clouds, and there, as she circled, he hit her
Beneath the wing, full in the side, and the arrow
Went all the way through and, falling, stuck in the ground
At Meriones' feet. But the dove sank down on top
Of the mast from the blue-prowed ship, dangling her head
And drooping her twitching wings, as swiftly life flew
From her body, and she toppled down from the mast a long way   1020
To the ground. And the gazing Achaeans were gripped with amazement.
Meriones, then, took all ten double axes,
While losing Teucer carried the ten single-bladed
Off to the hollow ships.
        Finally, Peleus'
Son brought out and set in the contest ring
A long-shadowing spear and a basin untouched by fire,
Of an ox's worth and engraved with flowers. And up got
The javelin-throwers—Atreus' son, the high King,
Great Agamemnon, along with Meriones, worthy   1030
Squire of Idomeneus. Thus, then, the swift Prince Achilles
Spoke out among them, saying:
        "Atrides, we all
Know well how far you surpass all others, how far
You're the strongest and how far the best in the javelin-throw.
So the basin is yours without a contest.[6] Take it
And go to the hollow ships. But the spear, if you will,
Let us present to the hero Meriones. Such,
At least, I would like."
        He spoke, and commander-in-chief   1040
Agamemnon did not disagree. In person he gave
The bronze-headed spear to Meriones, then handed the basin,
A truly exquisite piece, to his herald Talthybius.

BOOK XXIV

Priam and Achilles

So ended the games, and now the spectators dispersed,
Each man to his vessel, but whereas the rest looked forward
To supper and then to their fill of delectable sleep,
Achilles continued his weeping, ever recalling
His precious companion, nor could all-conquering sleep
Overcome him, as restless he turned from side to side
On his bed, sorely missing the manhood and noble heart
Of his friend and thinking of all that he had achieved
With him and of all they had been through together, the wars
10 Of men and the punishing waves.
        Thus night after night
He would spill his big tears, now lying upon his side,
Then on his back, and presently prone on his face,
Only to get up at last and roam up and down,
Distraught, on the shore of the sea. Nor did he fail
To notice the coming of Dawn, as she spread her light
Over billows and beach, for then he would yoke to his car
His fast-running horses, and binding Hector behind,
He would drag him three times around dead Patroclus's barrow.
20 Then he would sit in his lodge, while Hector lay stretched
On the ground outside, face down in the dust. Apollo,
However, protected his flesh from defilement, for he
Pitied him even in death, and wrapping him up
In the golden aegis, he kept Achilles from tearing
His corpse as he dragged him.
        Achilles, then, madly raging,
Foully dishonored the body of noble Hector,[1]
But meanwhile the blessed gods, who saw what he did,
Had compassion on Hector and prompted Hermes, the keen-eyed
30 Killer of Argus, to go steal the corpse. And all
Of the gods thought he should, save Hera, Poseidon, and maidenly
Bright-eyed Athena, each of whom kept up the hatred
Which they had felt from the first against holy Troy,
King Priam, and Priam's people, because of the sin

Of Prince Paris, the man who deeply insulted Athena
And Hera, when they had come to his courtyard, by favoring
Sweet Aphrodite, the goddess who furthered his blind
And disastrous lust.* But when the twelfth morning came
Since Hector had lain a corpse, Phoebus Apollo
Spoke thus among the immortals: 40
          "You're ruthlessly cruel,
You gods, and workers of evil! Has Hector, then,
Never burned thigh-pieces for you of bulls and goats
Without flaw? And have you so little concern to save
His mere corpse, for his wife and mother and little boy
To look upon, along with his father Priam
And Priam's people, who soon would burn his dead body
And build him a barrow with all due funeral rites?
Oh yes, you'd rather help monstrous Achilles, whose thought
Is outrageous, whose will too rigid to bend. His heart   50
Is obsessed with savage revenge, a heart as unfeeling
And brutal as that of a lordly lion urged on
By his spirit and might to spring on the flock of some shepherd
And try for a feast. Like him, Achilles is void
Of all pity, nor has his heart any shame, which can help
As well as harm mortal men. A man, after all,
May lose one dearer to him than this man was,
A brother, sprung from the same womb as he, or even
A son. But when he has wept and fittingly mourned
For him, he ends his grieving, for surely the fates   60
Have given to men a tough and patient spirit.[2]
Achilles, though, having taken the life of great Hector,
Binds him in back of his car and drags him daily
About his dear comrade's barrow. Truly, he'll win
Nothing good by so doing. Let him, indeed, beware,
Before we grow really angry at him, brave man
Though he surely is, for now in his stupid fury
He sinfully fouls and defiles insensible clay!"
          Angered by this, white-armed Hera replied:
"Something may come of your words, O silver-bowed one,   70
Providing you gods honor Hector no more than Achilles.
For Hector, you know, is mortal, and to him a mere woman
Gave suck, but Achilles was born of an immortal goddess,
Whom I myself lovingly reared and gave to a man

---

*This is the Iliad's only explicit retelling of the Judgment of Paris.

In marriage, to Peleus, who was very dear to the gods.
And all of you shining immortals were there at her wedding,
Including you, Apollo, you friend of blackguards,
Treacherous always—but there you sat in our midst
With your lyre in hand!"

80   Then Zeus, the gale-gathering god,
Spoke thus in answer: "Do not be so utterly angry,
Hera, against the immortals. Those two shall never
Be honored the same. Even so, of all the mortals
In Troy, Hector was dearest indeed to the gods.
So, at least, I regarded the man, for never once
Did he fail to please me with gifts. Never once was my altar
By him left bare of the ample feast—drink-offering
And savor of burning meat—that we consider
Our due. But let us forget the proposal to steal

90   Brave Hector's body. It surely could not be done
Without Achilles' knowing, since night and day
His mother closely attends him. But I wish some immortal
Would go tell Thetis to come here to me, that I
May advise her in time to get her great son to accept
King Priam's gifts of ransom and give Hector back."

He spoke, and gale-footed Iris hurried to carry
His message. Midway between Samos and craggy Imbros
She dived into the dark sea, and the billows boomed
As they closed above her. Then down she shot, like a sinker

100 Of lead attached to the horn-guarded hook that plummets
Below bearing death to the ravenous fish. And there
In a high-vaulted cave she found Thetis, and all around her
A throng of other sea-goddesses sat, while she
In their midst was bewailing the fate of her matchless son,
Who as she knew was destined to fall and die
In the rich land of Troy, far from his own dear country.
Standing beside her, quick-footed Iris spoke thus:
"Up now, O Thetis. Zeus of the unfailing counsels
Calls you to come."

110   To which the silver-shod goddess:
"Why should that almighty god send summons to me?
I'm ashamed to go mid the gods everlasting, since I
Am now one boundless chaos of grief. Go,
However, I will. Nor shall his counsel, whatever
It is, be useless to me."

So saying, the goddess,
Radiantly fair, took a sea-blue veil, the darkest

Thing she possessed, and started the journey to Zeus,
With wind-footed Iris leading the way, and about them
The billows parted as out they stepped on the beach.   120
Then off they sped to Olympus. There they found Cronos' son,
Far-seeing Zeus, and gathered around him sat all
Of the other undying gods. Then Thetis sat down
Beside Father Zeus—Athena yielded her chair—
And Hera, placing a gorgeous gold cup in her hand,
Welcomed her warmly. When Thetis had drunk and returned
The bright cup, the Father of gods and men was the first
To speak:
        "You came, divine Thetis, up here to Olympus
In spite of the comfortless grief I know you are full of.   130
Let me, then, tell you why I called you to come.
For the last nine days the immortal gods have wrangled
About Hector's corpse and Achilles, taker of towns.
They've even suggested that keen-sighted Hermes, killer
Of Argus, steal noble Hector's body. But I
Would much rather resolve their strife in a way that will honor
Achilles and keep for me in later days
Your worship and love. Go, then, with all speed to the camp
And tell your son what I say. Tell him the gods
Are angry with him, I most of all, because   140
In his madness of heart he still keeps noble Hector
Beside the beaked ships, refusing to give him back.
His awe of me may then overcome him and lead him
To yield the body. Meanwhile, I'll dispatch Iris
To great-hearted Priam to bid him go to the ships
Of Achaea with ransom for his dear son, gifts
That will soften the heart of Achilles."
        Such were his words,
And the goddess silver-shod Thetis did not disobey him,
But down she went darting from high on the peaks of Olympus   150
And came to the lodge of her grieving son. She found him there,
Riddled with groans, while round him his comrades were busy
Preparing the morning meal, having already slaughtered
A huge shaggy ram. Then sitting close by his side,
His goddess mother gently caressed him, called him
By name, and said:
        "My child, how long will you go on
Eating your heart out with grieving and weeping, forgetful
Of food and bed alike. Even that would be
A good thing, for you to make love with some woman, since you,   160

Dear child, have not much longer to live. Already
Death and powerful fate are standing beside you.
But hear, now, this message from Zeus. He says that the gods
Are angry with you, he most of all, because
In your madness of heart you still keep noble Hector
Beside the beaked ships, refusing to give him back.
But come, give up the body, and take in return
A ransom paid for the dead."
　　　　To which swift Achilles:
170 "So be it. Whoever brings ransom here, let him
Bear off the body, if truly such is the purpose
And will of the great Olympian himself."
　　　　Thus,
Mid many ships, mother and son spoke words
Both winged and numerous, each to the other. Meanwhile,
Zeus dispatched Iris to sacred Ilium, saying:
"Up now, swift Iris, and go. Leave your seat
On Olympus and bear these tidings to great-hearted Priam
In Troy, saying that he must go to the ships
180 Of the Argives to ransom his precious son, taking gifts
With him to soften the heart of Achilles. And tell him
To go by himself, save only perhaps one herald,
Some older man, to drive the well-running mule wagon
And bring back to town the body of him cut down
By Achilles. But let him not dwell on death, nor have
Any fear, for he shall be led by the greatest of guides,
Even Hermes, slayer of Argus, and he will take him
Right into the lodge of Achilles, who will not only
Not kill him himself—he'll hold back all of the others.
190 For he is not really stupid or thoughtless, nor is he
An utterly godless sinner. No, he'll treat
A suppliant father with care and every kindness."
　　　　He spoke, and gale-footed Iris hurried to carry
His word. Arriving at Priam's house, she was greeted
By clamorous keening. There in the courtyard his sons
Were seated about their old father, moistening their garments
With tears, while he in their midst sat tightly wrapped
In his shroud-like cloak of mourning, his ancient head
And neck filthily fouled with dung, which he
200 Had smeared on himself with his hands as he rolled in grief
On the dung-laden ground. And throughout the palace his daughters
And daughters-in-law were wailing with sorrow, recalling
The many brave heroes undone at the hands of the Argives.

Coming up close, the bright agent of Zeus addressed him,
And though she spoke softly, his body trembled all over:
    "Be brave, O Priam, descended of Dardanus, and banish
All fear. I have not come to you now with a message
Of evil, but one you'll be glad to hear. I come
Directly from Zeus, who though far away still has
Great care and compassion for you. He, the Olympian   210
Himself, bids you go ransom your precious son,
Taking gifts with you to soften the heart of Achilles.
And you must go by yourself, save only perhaps
One herald, some older man, to drive the well-running
Mule wagon and bring back to town the body of him
Cut down by Achilles. But don't dwell on death, nor have
Any fear, for you shall be led by the greatest of guides,
Even Hermes, slayer of Argus, and he will take you
Right into the lodge of Achilles, who will not only
Not kill you himself—he'll hold back all of the others.   220
For he is not really stupid or thoughtless, nor is he
An utterly godless sinner. No, he'll treat
A suppliant father with care and every kindness."
    So saying, fleet-footed Iris took off, whereupon
Old Priam ordered his sons to harness mules
To a well-running wagon and bind the wicker body
On top. He himself went down to his high-vaulted chamber,
Fragrant with cedar and full of bright treasures, and calling
To him his wife Hecuba, gently he spoke to her, saying:
    "My sorely afflicted lady, a messenger straight   230
From Zeus and Olympus has just come to me, bidding me
Go to the ships of Achaea with adequate ransom
For our dear son, splendid gifts to soften the heart
Of Achilles. But tell me, how do you feel about this?
As for myself, I'm more than anxious to go
To the ships, deep into the widely spread camp of the Argives."
    At this his wife cried out, shrilly protesting:
"O misery! where now is that wisdom for which you have always
Been famous, both here at home and abroad? Why
Would you wish to go unattended into the fiercely   240
Glaring presence of him who has murdered your sons
So many and brave? Surely your heart is of iron!
For once he gets you before him and sees who you are,
He'll have neither care nor compassion for you, believe me.
So now, my husband, let us lament for our son
Right here in the palace. For such is surely the lot

That powerful Fate spun out for him on the day
When I myself bore him, that he should glut the lean guts
Of flashing-swift dogs far from his loving parents,
250   A corpse by the lodge of a violent monster, whose liver
I'd joyfully eat, if only somehow I could sink
My teeth into it!* Only then would I feel that he'd paid
For the life of my son, who died doing nothing unmanly,
But standing out in defense of the men and deep-breasted
Women of Troy, with no thought at all of running
Or taking cover."
          Then answering her, old Priam
The godlike said: "Don't try to restrain me when I
Am so anxious to go, nor be a bird of ill omen
260   Here in the palace. Believe me, you'll not change my mind!
For had any earth-dwelling creature bidden me do this,
Whether some priest or seer or teller of omens,
We might have considered it false and thus ignored it
Completely. But now that I've heard in person the voice
Of the goddess and looked on her face, I'll go, nor shall
Her words have been spoken in vain. And if my fate be
To lie a corpse by the ships of the bronze-clad Achaeans,
Such is my preference. Achilles may quickly kill me
With my dear son held close in my arms, once I
270   Have quenched my desire for tearful grief and lamenting."
          Thus he resolved, and lifting the ornate lids
Of the chests, he took twelve exquisite robes, twelve cloaks
Of single fold, and a dozen each of blankets,
White mantles, and tunics. Then he weighed and bore out
Ten talents of gold, which he followed with two gleaming tripods,
Four bowls, and a marvelous goblet, a gift from the men
Of Thrace when he had gone there on a mission, a truly
Rare treasure, but not even this would the old man spare
In his palace, so deeply desirous was he to ransom
280   His precious son.
          The next thing he did was to drive
All loitering Trojans out of his portico, chiding
Them thus with hard words: "Get out, you disgraceful wretches!
Can it be that you have so little sorrow at home
That you have to come pestering me here? Do you think it nothing,
This grief that Cronos' son Zeus has brought upon me,

---

*Compare Achilles' vaunt over Hector's body at XXII.404–414, and see endnote 6.

This loss of my most valiant and princely son?
But you too shall know very well what I mean, for all
Of you now will fall a much easier prey to Achaeans
With no Hector here to protect you. As for myself,   290
Before I see this city sacked and her people destroyed,
May I go down and enter Hades' dark halls."

    So saying, he rushed at them with his staff, and all of them
Rapidly scattered before the furious old one.
Then he called out to his sons, rebuking them harshly—
To Helenus, Paris, and Agathon, nobly gifted,
To Antiphonus, Pammon, and battle-roaring Polites,
As well as Deïphobus, Hippothous, and haughty Dius.
To these nine their old father shouted harsh orders, crying:

    "Hurry up, my no-account sons, my groveling disgraces!   300
O how I wish that you'd all been killed at the ships
And that Hector was still alive! How utterly luckless
Can one old man be? For I sired excellent sons,
The best by far in the whole wide country of Troy.
But now, I tell you, not one of them is alive,
Not Mestor the godlike, not horse-prizing Troilus, and now
Not Hector, who lived a god among men, for always
He seemed far more like the son of some immortal
Than he did of any mere man. All of them Ares
Has slaughtered, leaving me nothing but you poor excuses   310
For men, a bunch of flattering knaves, champions
Nowhere but on the dance floor, and stealers of lambs
And kids from your own Trojan people! Well why the delay?
Get busy right now! Make ready a wagon, and put
All these things aboard it, that we may get started at once."

    He spoke, and they, gripped with fear at the words of their father,
Hauled out a newly built, beautiful wagon, strong
And smooth-running, and on it they bound the light wicker body.
Then down from its peg they lifted the mule-yoke, a box-wood
Yoke with a knob at the center and well fitted out   320
With rings for the chains to pass through, and with it they brought
The yoke-band some fifteen feet long. Snugly they set
The yoke at the right-angled end of the car's polished shaft
And flipped the yoke-ring over the peg in the pole.
Next with the yoke-band they lashed the knob fast to the upturned
End of the shaft, with three quick turns to the left
And three to the right, and fastened the straps, deftly
Tucking the ends in. Then they brought from the chamber
The treasures of Priam, the boundless ransom for Hector,

330 Which they heaped high on the gleaming wagon, and yoked
     To it the solid-hoofed mules, strong toilers in harness,
     A glorious pair that once the people of Mysia
     Had given to Priam. For Priam himself they yoked
     His own horses, a team reserved for his use and reared
     By himself at the smooth wooden manger.
                    Now while the old King
     And his herald were waiting beneath the high roof for all
     To be ready, both of them anxiously planning ahead
     In silence, old Hecuba, grieving, came with a cup
340 Of honey-sweet wine in her wrinkled right hand, that they
     Might pour a libation before setting out. She stopped
     In front of the horses and said:
                    "Take now this cup
     And pour a libation to Zeus the Father, earnestly
     Praying for your safe return from the midst of our foes,
     Since now your heart is determined to go, in spite of
     My wish that you wouldn't. Then pray to Zeus once again,
     To Cronos' son, god of the lowering gale, who scans
     At a glance the whole country of Troy, and ask him to send
350 His most favorably ominous bird, his own swift bearer
     Of omen, the dearest of birds to him, and the strongest
     Of wing. And let him fly by on the right, that you
     May go on to the ships of the swiftly-drawn Danaans, trusting
     In that mighty sign. But if far-seeing Zeus
     Refuses to send you his own most favorable bird,
     Then I would by no means advise you to go to the ships
     Of the Argives, no matter how strong and deep your resolve."
                    To which old Priam the godlike: "My dear, I'll not
     Disregard this urging of yours, for always it is
360 A good thing to lift up our hands to Zeus, praying
     That he will have mercy."
                    So spoke the old King, and asked
     The handmaid in attendance to rinse his hands with fresh water,
     And soon she came up with basin and pitcher. Then,
     Having washed his hands, he took the cup from his wife,
     And walking out to the midst of the court, he poured
     The libation of wine, looking toward heaven and praying:
                    "O Father Zeus, ruling from Ida, most great
     And glorious lord, grant that I come to the lodge
370 Of Achilles as one to be pitied and cared for. And send
     Your most favorably ominous bird, your own swift bearer
     Of omen, the dearest of birds to you, and the strongest

Of wing. And let him fly by on the right, that I
May go on to the ships of the swiftly-drawn Danaans, trusting
In that mighty sign."

　　　Such was his prayer, and Zeus
The contriver heard him. At once he sent out an eagle,
The surest of all winged omens, the deadly dark hunter
That men call the grape-colored one. From tip to tip
His wings were as wide as the double well-bolted doors   380
Of some wealthy man's high-vaulted chamber, and by he flew
On the right, swooping low through the city. All were made glad
By the sight, and the hearts of all were warmly encouraged.

　　　Then quickly the old one mounted his car and drove
Through the gate and loud colonnade. In front the mules
Drew the four-wheeled wagon, with prudent Idaeus driving,
While rapidly on came old Priam, constantly laying
The lash on and urging his pair through the city. And following
Him came all of his kinsmen and friends, wailing loudly
For him as for one who went to his death. But when   390
They got out of the city and came to the plain, his sons
And sons-in-law turned back to town with the rest, while the herald
And Priam went on toward the ships, nor were they unnoticed
By far-seeing Zeus.[3] Feeling pity at sight of old Priam,
He spoke at once to his dear son Hermes, saying:

　　　"Since you, swift Hermes, who listen to whom you like,
Take most delight in going as guide to a man,
Go down and conduct King Priam to the hollow ships
Of Achaea, and let no Danaan see him at all
Till he comes to Achilles himself."   400

　　　He spoke, and swift Hermes,
Slayer of Argus, obeyed him, putting on his bright sandals
Of magic immortal gold, which bear him always
Swift as the wind over boundless earth and sea.
And he took the wand with which he can lull to sleep
Or wake from the deepest slumber whomever he wishes.
With this in his hand the mighty slayer of Argus
Flew down, and quickly he came to the Hellespont stream
And the Trojan plain. Then he went on afoot in the form
Of a princely young man with the first fine down on his lip,   410
At that age when youth is most charming.

　　　Meanwhile, the old King
And his herald had driven past Ilus' huge barrow and stopped
For the horses and mules to drink from the river. Darkness
Had fallen on earth when the herald looked up and there

Close at hand saw Hermes, whereat he spoke thus to King Priam:
"Look out! Dardanian. Now is the time for quick thinking.
Here comes a man, and soon, I fear, we shall both
Be ripped all to pieces. But come, let us leap in the chariot
420 Now and run for our lives, or else hug his knees
And beg him for mercy!"
      At this the old King was so frightened
He lost all power to think. He stood in a daze,
Struck dumb, and the hair fairly rose on his gnarled old limbs.
But Hermes the helper came up and taking his hand
Inquired: "Where, O father, can you he driving
These horses and mules through the fragrant and immortal night
While other people are sleeping? Have you no fear
At all of the fury-breathing Achaeans, hostile
430 And ruthless men that they are, and so close at hand?
If one of them saw you conveying such huge store of wealth
Through the fast-fallen blackness of night, what would you do then?
You're not young yourself, and he who goes with you is old,
Nor could you defend yourselves against any man
Who chose to attack you. But so far from doing you damage
Myself, I will go against any who tries to. For you
Remind me a lot of my own beloved old father."
      To which ancient Priam the godlike: "Things are, dear child,
Just as you say. But surely some god has stretched out
440 His hand in protection above me, since now he has sent
A man such as you, so splendid in face and physique,
So gifted with keen understanding, and truly a bearer
Of blessings to me. Your parents are happy indeed
To have such a son."
      And again the messenger Hermes,
Slayer of Argus, spoke: "What you say, old sire,
Is well and happily put. But come, tell me frankly.
Are you taking this treasure to some foreign folk
For safe keeping, or have you all started to leave holy Troy
450 In fear, now that your greatest and noblest is dead,
Your own valiant son who never let up for so much
As a moment in waging fierce war against the Achaeans?"
      And the old one, Priam the godlike, replied: "Who are you,
Brave friend, and who are your parents, you that have spoken
So fairly and well of the fate of my unlucky son?"
      And the messenger Hermes, slayer of Argus, said:
"You're trying me now, old sire, to see what I know
Of great Hector. I've seen him a good many times in the fury

Of hero-enhancing battle, including the time
He drove the Argives to the ships and cut many down 460
With sharp bronze. And we just stood there and marveled, forbidden
To fight by Achilles, who seethed with furious wrath
Against Agamemnon. I am Achilles' squire,
And the same sturdy ship brought both of us here. I'm a Myrmidon,
Son of Polyctor, a rich man and old, very much
Like yourself, and I am the youngest of his seven sons.
On me the lot fell to come here and fight, and now
I have left the ships and come to the plain, for at dawn
The quick-eyed Achaeans will once again attack Troy.
They're restless indeed sitting idle, nor can the kings 470
Of Achaea restrain them, so hot are they for the fight."

    And godlike old Priam replied: "If you really are
A squire of Peleus' son Achilles, come now,
And tell me truly all that you know as to whether
My son is yet at the ships or whether by now
Achilles has hacked him apart and thrown his flesh
To the dogs."

    Then the escort Hermes, slayer of Argus:
"Old sire, not yet have dogs and birds devoured him,
But he still lies mid the lodges beside the ship 480
Of Achilles, just as he has from the first. And though
This makes the twelfth day he has lain there, his flesh has not even
Begun to decay, nor do any worms consume him,
Worms such as feast on the bodies of battle-slain men.
It's true that Achilles each day at the coming of bright
Divine Dawn unfeelingly drags him about the barrow
Of his beloved friend, but he does his body no damage
At all. If you were to go and see him yourself,
You'd surely marvel at how he lies, washed clean
Of blood and fresh as the dew, altogether unmarred 490
And unstained. For the numerous wounds he received from the mob
That thrust their bronze in his flesh have all closed up
Completely. Even such is the care the happy gods take
Of your son, though only a corpse, for he was quite dear
To their hearts."

    At this the old one, rejoicing, said:
"My child, what a fine thing it is to give the immortals
Such gifts as are rightfully due them. For never once
Did my son—if ever I had such a son—neglect
In our halls the gods who live on Olympus, which is why 500
They've remembered him now, though his fate was to die as he did.

But come, accept this choice goblet from me and be
My protector, that I by the grace of the gods everlasting
May come to the lodge of Peleus' son Achilles."
        And once again the god who slew Argus answered:
"You're testing me now, old sire, but young though I am
I'll certainly not allow you to bribe me with gifts
Behind the back of Achilles. Were I to accept
What will soon be his own, my heart should be filled with terror
510 And dread at the prospect of what might become of me
Hereafter. But go as your guide I most surely will,
Even all the way to world-famous Argos, if such
Is your wish, very carefully guiding and guarding you always,
Whether on land or aboard a swift ship. Nor would
Any man attack you for want of respect for your escort!"
        So saying, help-bringing Hermes sprang up behind
The car-drawing horses, caught up the whip and the reins
And breathed fresh spirit into the horses and mules.
When they came to the trench and the wall round the ships, the guards
520 Had just begun fixing supper, but Hermes quickly
Put them to sleep and, thrusting the bars back, opened
The gates. Then into the camp he drove the old King,
And with them they brought the wagon of glorious gifts
For Achilles. Soon they arrived at his lodge, the lofty
Shelter the Myrmidon men had built for their chief,
Hewing out beams of pine and roofing it over
With reed-shaggy thatch from the fields. And they had built round it
For him a spacious courtyard high fenced with stakes
Closely set, with a gate strongly locked by means of one bar
530 Across it. This huge beam of pine it took three Achaeans
To move back and forth, though Achilles could handle the thing
By himself. Once there, luck-bringing Hermes opened
The gate for old Priam and drove him inside, and with them
They brought the marvelous gifts for the swift son of Peleus.
Then stepping down, Hermes spoke thus to the King:
        "Old sire, I that have come to you thus am a god
Everlasting—Hermes, sent by the Father to act
As your guide. But now I'll go back without letting Achilles
See me, for it would be wrong for an immortal god
540 To be so openly welcomed by mortal men.
But you yourself go in and, embracing the knees
Of Peleus' son, make your plea in the name of his father,
Lovely-haired mother, and son, that you may stir
The depths of his soul."

　　So saying, Hermes took off
For the heights of Olympus, and Priam sprang down from the car
To the ground and, leaving Idaeus in charge of the horses
And mules, strode straight for the lodge where Zeus-loved Achilles
Sat. And inside he found him, apart from all comrades
But two, the hero Automedon, and Alcimus, scion　　　　　　　　　　550
Of Ares, who busily waited upon him, since he
Had just finished eating and drinking, and still the table
Had not been removed. Great Priam came in unnoticed
By any, till coming up close to Achilles he threw
His arms round his knees and kissed his dread hands, the
　　　　　　murderous
Hands that had killed so many of his precious sons.
And as when thick darkness of soul comes down on a man
And killing another he flees from his own dear country
And comes to some foreign land and the house of a man
Of bountiful wealth, and wonder grips all who see him　　　　　　560
A suppliant there, so now Achilles was seized
With exceeding amazement at sight of sacred Priam,
And those who were with him marveled and looked at each other.[4]
Then Priam made his plea, beseeching him thus:

　　"Remember, Achilles, O godlike mortal, remember
Peleus your father, a man of like years as myself,
Far gone on the path of painful old age. Very likely
His neighbors are grinding him down, nor is there one there
To keep from him ruin and destruction. However, so long
As he hears you're alive, his heart can daily be glad　　　　　　　570
In the hope that he shall yet see his dear son returning
From Troy. But I am without good fortune completely,
Since though I begot the best sons in the whole wide country
Of Troy, yet now not even one is left!
When the sons of Achaeans arrived, I had fifty sons
Of my own, nineteen from the womb of one mother, the rest
Borne to me by women of mine in the palace. But though
They were many, furious Ares has unstrung the knees
Of all, and the only one left me, who all by himself
Protected the city and people, fell to your spear　　　　　　　　580
Some days ago as he was defending his country—
Hector my son, and now I have come to the ships
Of Achaea to pay you a ransom for him, and I bring
With me a load of treasure past counting. Have awe
Of the gods, O Achilles, and pity on me, remembering
Your dear father. I am indeed even more

To be pitied than he, for I have endured what no other
Earth-dwelling mortal has—to reach out my hand
To the face of him who slaughtered my precious sons!"

590   Such was his plea, and he stirred in Achilles a yearning
To weep for Peleus his father, and taking the hand
Of old Priam he gently pushed him away. Then the two of them
Thought of their losses, and Priam sobbed sorely for man-killing
Hector, the old King huddling in front of Achilles,
Whose weeping was now for his father and now for Patroclus,
And throughout the lodge arose the sound of their grief.
But when great Achilles had found some relief in lamenting,
And longing for such had gone out of his body and soul,
He suddenly sprang from his chair, and filled with pity

600 For Priam's gray head and gray beard, he raised the old King
By the hand and spoke to him these winged words:
    "Wretched sire,
Many indeed are the horrors your soul has endured.
But how could you ever have come here alone to the ships
Of the Argives to look in the eyes of the man who has killed
Your many brave sons? Surely your heart is of iron!
But come, sit down in a chair, and we'll both let our grief,
Great though it is, lie quiet in our hearts. Cold crying
Accomplishes little. For thus have the sorrowless gods

610 Spun the web of existence for miserable mortals—with pain
Woven in throughout! There stand by the threshold of Zeus
Two urns, one full of evils, the other of blessings.
To whomever Zeus, the lover of lightning, gives
A portion from each, that man experiences
Both evil and good, but to whomever Zeus gives nothing
But of the grievous, that man is reviled by gods
And men and hounded by horrible hunger all over
The sacred earth. Take Peleus my father for instance.
No man ever had more glorious god-bestowed gifts

620 Than he from the time of his birth, for he surpassed all
In wealth and good fortune, was King of the Myrmidon people,
And though but a mortal himself, the gods gave a goddess
To him for a wife. But even on him the immortals
Brought evil enough, since there in his halls no plentiful
Offspring of princes was born, but only one son,
And he undoubtedly doomed to die young. Nor can I
So much as look after him as he ages, since far,
Very far from home I live in the country of Troy,

A plague to you and your children. And you, old sire,
We hear were once happy, for you, because of your wealth   630
And your sons, were the first of mortals in all the great space
That lies between Lesbos, south in the sea, where Macar
Was King long ago, and Phrygia off to the north
And the free-flowing Hellespont. Since, though, the heavenly gods
Brought on you this baneful war, your city has been
Surrounded by havoc and dying men. But you
Must bear up, nor can you afford to grieve without ceasing.
You'll not thereby do anything good for your son.
Before you bring him back to life, you'll suffer a fate
Little less unhappy yourself!"   640
       To which the old Priam:
"By no means ask me to sit, O god-nourished man,
So long as Hector lies mid the lodges uncared for.
Release him to me at once, that I may see him
Myself, and take the great ransom we bring to you
For his body. May you enjoy it all and come
Even yet to the land of your fathers, since you now have spared me
To live on for a while beholding the light of the sun."
       Then scowling at him, quick-footed Achilles spoke sternly:
"Do nothing else to provoke me, old man! I myself,   650
With no help from you, have already agreed to give
Hector back, for Zeus has sent word to me by the mother
Who bore me, the briny old sea-ancient's daughter. And don't think
I haven't known all along about you—that you
Were guided here by some god to the swift-sailing ships
Of Achaeans. For certainly no mere mortal, no matter
How young and strong, would ever dare enter this camp.
He could not get by the guards, nor could he easily
Push back the bar of my gate. So say nothing else,
Old man, to make me feel any worse, or I   660
May forget to spare even you mid the lodges, and so break
The strict law of Zeus."
       At this the old king was gripped
By a wordless terror and watched as Achilles sprang
Through the door of the lodge like a lion, not by himself,
But accompanied by the two squires, the hero Automedon
Followed by Alcimus, two that Achilles honored
Beyond all his comrades, save only the dead Patroclus.
These then unharnessed the horses and led
The herald inside, the old King's aged town crier,   670

And gave him a seat, and from the wagon they took
The boundless ransom for Hector. They left, however,
Two cloaks and a well-woven tunic, that these Achilles
Might use to wrap up the dead and so give him back
To be borne to his home. Then Achilles called for handmaids
To wash and anoint the dead body, bidding them do it
Where Priam could not see his son, for Achilles feared
That his guest might not be able to hold back his wrath,
And so he might lose his own temper and kill the old man,
680   Thus sinning against Zeus's law. When the handmaids had washed
The body and rubbed it with oil and put about it
A tunic and beautiful cloak, Achilles himself
Lifted it onto a bier and helped his companions
Lift it onto the wagon.⁵ Then groaning, he called
On his precious friend by name:
         "Do not be angry
At me, O Patroclus, if even in Hades' halls
You hear that I've given Prince Hector back to his father,
For not unbefitting at all was the ransom he gave me,
690   And you may be sure of getting your due share of that."
         So spoke great Achilles, then went back inside and sat down
In his richly wrought chair by the opposite wall from old Priam,
To whom he spoke thus: "Your son, old sire, has now
Been released to you as you have requested and lies
On a bier, and you yourself shall see him tomorrow
At daybreak while carrying him away—but let us
Not neglect supper, for even the lovely-haired Niobe
Ate, though her twelve children all died in her palace,
Six daughters and six lusty sons. Shaft-showering Artemis
700   Brought down the daughters, while Phoebus Apollo put arrows
Through all of the sons with his silver bow, both of them
Wrathful with her for comparing herself with their own mother
Leto, Niobe saying that Leto had only
Two children while she herself had borne many. So they,
Though only two, destroyed all twelve of hers.
And there for nine days they lay in their blood unburied,
For Cronos' son Zeus turned all of the people to stones.
On the tenth, however, the heavenly gods held the funeral,
And Niobe, weary of weeping, remembered to eat.
710   And now somewhere mid the crags in the desolate hills
Of Sipylus, where, men say, the nymphs go to bed
When they tire of dancing about the stream Achelous,
Niobe stands and, though solid stone, broods

On her god-sent disasters.* So come, my royal old sire,
And let us likewise remember to eat, and later,
Back in your city, you may lament your dear son
With innumerable tears."

    So saying, Achilles sprang up
And slaughtered a silvery white sheep, which his comrades flayed
And made ready in every detail, skillfully cutting   720
The carcass into small pieces, which meat they spitted
And roasted well, and drew it all from the spits.
Then Automedon served them the bread, setting it forth
In exquisite baskets, while swift Achilles apportioned
The meat, and they reached out and ate of the good things before
        them.
But when they had eaten and drunk as much as they wanted,
Priam, descended of Dardanus, sat there and marveled
At mighty Achilles, thinking how huge and handsome
He was, a man in the image of gods everlasting,
And likewise Achilles marveled at Priam, looking   730
Upon his fine face and listening to what he said.
When both had looked on each other enough, old Priam
The godlike spoke thus:

    "Show me my bed, now, Achilles,
O nobleman nurtured of Zeus, that we may enjoy
A night of sweet sleep. For never once have my lids
Come together in sleep since my son lost his life at your hands,
But always I've mourned, miserably brooding on
My innumerable sorrows and groveling in dung on the ground
Of my high-walled courtyard. Now, though, I've tasted some food   740
And drunk flaming wine. Till now, I had tasted nothing."

    He spoke, and Achilles ordered his comrades and handmaids
To place two beds in the portico and cover them
With fine purple robes, light spreads, and fleecy warm blankets,
And the girls went out with torches and made the beds.
Then Achilles, fast on his feet, spoke to King Priam,
Somewhat bitterly saying:

    "My dear aged friend,
You'll have to sleep outside, since one of the counselors
Of the Achaeans may come to consult me, as often   750
They do, and as they should. But if one of these

---

*In her inconsolable grief, Niobe is petrified; she becomes the rock formation of Mount
Sypylus, whose running waters are her ceaseless tears.

Were to catch sight of you through the fast-flying blackness of night,
He might very well go straight to King Agamemnon,
Commander-in-chief of the army, and so there would be
A delay in my giving back the body. But come,
Tell me frankly. How long would you like for the funeral rites
Of Prince Hector, that I myself may hold back from battle
And keep back the others also?"
      And the godlike old King:
760 "If you really want me to give noble Hector his full
Funeral rites, this, O Achilles, is what you could do
To help me. You know how we're penned in the city and also
How far the terrified Trojans must go for wood
From the mountains. Let us, then, mourn for him in our halls
For nine days, then burn him and hold the funeral feast
On the tenth, and on the eleventh build a barrow
For him. Then on the twelfth we'll fight again,
If we must."
      To which fleet-footed, noble Achilles:
770 "So be it, my ancient Priam, just as you wish.
I'll hold back the battle for all the time you request."
      So saying, he clasped the old King's right wrist, in a gesture
Of friendly assurance. Then there in the porch of the lodge
The old ones retired, the herald and Priam, their hearts
Ever thoughtful. But Achilles slept in one corner of the spacious,
Strongly built lodge, and beside him lay Briseis,
Lovely of face.
      Now all other gods and mortal
Wearers of horsehair-plumed helmets slept soundly all night,
780 Overcome by soft sleep, but not on help-bringing Hermes
Could sleep get a grip, as he pondered within his mind
How he could get King Priam away from the ships
Unseen by the powerful guards at the gate. Standing close
By the head of his bed, he spoke to him, saying:
      "Old sire,
To sleep this way in the midst of your foes, it must be
You have no idea of possible harm, now that
Achilles has spared you. True, you have ransomed your son,
And great was the ransom you paid. Just think what the sons
790 You left in the city would have to pay for your life—
Three times as much at least—if Atreus' son
Agamemnon should find that you're here and the other Achaeans
Get word!"

At this the old King was afraid and awakened
His herald. And Hermes harnessed the horses and mules
For them and drove the two old ones quietly out
Through the slumbering camp, nor did anyone know of their going.
When they came to the ford of the fair-flowing river, the swirling
Xanthus, that immortal Zeus begot, then Hermes
Left for Olympus, just as crocus-clad Dawn   800
Was scattering light over earth. And the King and his herald
With moaning and wailing drove the two horses on
Toward the town, and the mules came on with the dead. Nor were
They noticed by any, no man or brightly-sashed woman,
Until Cassandra, lovely as golden Aphrodite,
Having gone to the heights of Pergamus, stronghold of Troy,
Saw her dear father coming on in the car with his herald,
The aged town crier, beside him. And then she saw
What they brought on the bier in the mule-drawn wagon.
Screaming,   810
She roused the whole town, crying to all in her grief:
"Come, you men and women of Troy, you
That took such delight in welcoming Hector back
From battle alive, since he was the whole city's joy
And pride. Come, I say, and look at him now!"
She called, and soon not one man or woman was left
In the town, for unbearable grief seized all, and close
By the gates they met Priam bringing the corpse of his son.
Hector's dear wife and royal mother rushed up
To the wheel-spinning wagon, and touching the head of the dead   820
They wailed and tore at their hair, while the people crowded
Around them and wept. And now all day long till sunset
They would have stayed outside the gates, lamenting
And weeping for Hector, had not the old King, still
In the chariot, spoken thus to his people:
"Make way
For the mules to pass through. Later, when I've brought him home,
You may weep to your heart's content."
He spoke, and the crowd
Opened up, making way for the wagon. Once at the palace   830
They laid Hector out on a corded bed and seated
Beside him singers to lead in the dirge, and they chanted
The funeral song with the women responding in chorus.
Then white-armed Andromache led their lament, holding
The head of man-killing Hector close in her arms,

And wailing:
    "My husband, early indeed you have left us,
Me a widow in your spacious halls, your son
Still a baby, the son we two so unluckily had,
840 Who now, I think will never live to be grown,
Since long before that this city shall topple in ruins.
For you, my husband, are dead, you that protected
The town and kept from harm its excellent wives
And little children. These, I fear, shall soon
Be riding the hollow ships, and I among them—
And you, my child, must go with me to where you shall toil
For some monstrous master, or have some Achaean seize
Your small arm and hurl you down from the wall to a miserable
Death, being bitter at Hector for killing his brother,
850 Perhaps, or his father, or else his son, since many,
Many Achaeans have bitten the dusty huge earth
At the hands of brave Hector, for your father was not at all gentle
In horrible war—so now the people are mourning
For you, Hector, throughout the city, and grief beyond words
You have brought on your parents, but I far more than all others
Have nothing left but miserable sorrow. For you
As you died neither stretched out your arms to me from the bed,
Nor did you say any word of sweet love that I
Might have kept in my heart through long days and nights of weeping."
860   Thus she spoke in her wailing, and all of the women
Responded, moaning and weeping. Then Hecuba took up
The dirge and led the vehement keening, crying:
"Hector, the dearest by far to my heart of all
My children, you when alive were also dear
To the gods, and so they have cared for you now, though your fate
Was to die as you did. Whenever swift-footed Achilles
Took other children of mine, he sold them as slaves
Beyond the barren and unresting sea, into Samos,
Imbros, and Lemnos, lost in the haze. But when
870 With his tapering bronze he had taken your life, he dragged you
Daily about his comrade Patroclus's barrow—
Patroclus, whom you, my son, slew—though even this
Did not resurrect his friend. But now you lie
Fresh as the dew in our palace, like one merely sleeping,
Or one whom silver-bowed Phoebus Apollo has slain
With his gentle shafts."
      Even so she spoke in her wailing,
And roused the passionate keening. Then Helen was third

To lead the lament, crying: "O Hector, dearest
By far to my heart of all my husband's brothers, 880
My husband is Paris the godlike, who brought me to Troy—
Would I had died first! Now this is the twentieth year
Since I left my own country, but never once have I heard
From you an evil word or an ugly. In fact,
When the others reproached me here in the palace, some brother
Of yours, a sister, or a well-dressed sister-in-law,
Or even your mother—your father was kind to me always,
A father to me as well—at such times you
Would turn them away and restrain them with your gentle spirit
And courteous words. Hence now I weep for you 890
And my own luckless self, grieving at heart, for now
No longer is anyone left in wide Troy that is gentle
Or loving to me. All shudder whenever I pass."

     Such was her wailing lament, and the numberless crowd
Re-echoed her moans. Then the old King Priam spoke
Mid his people, saying: "Bring wood, you men of Troy,
Into the city, and have no dread in your hearts
Of a treacherous Argive ambush, for Achilles truly
Assured me when he sent me forth from the hollow black ships
That he would do us no harm till the twelfth morning came." 900
     Such were his words, and they harnessed their oxen and mules
To wagons and rapidly gathered in front of the city.
Then for nine days they carted in wood, a supply
Unspeakably great, but when the tenth man-lighting morning
Arrived, they carried brave Hector forth, and laying
Him down on top of the pyre threw flame upon it.

     But as soon as young rose-fingered Dawn appeared the next day,
The people gathered about Hector's pyre, and when
They had quenched with sparkling wine whatever still burned,
His grieving brothers and friends, weeping big tears 910
All the while, collected Hector's white bones. These they placed
In a golden box, which they wrapped in soft purple robes
And laid away in a hollowed-out grave. This they closed
With huge stones laid side by side and over it, rapidly
Working, they heaped his high barrow, setting guards round about
To prevent a surprise attack from the well-greaved Achaeans.
When the barrow was done, they returned to the palace of Priam,
The Zeus-nurtured King, where they feasted a glorious feast.
     Even so they buried Prince Hector, tamer of horses.

ENDNOTES

Book I: The Quarrel

1. (p. 1) *Sing, O Goddess . . . godlike Achilles*: The first seven lines of the *Iliad* are called the proem. The performing poet calls upon the immortal Muse to inspire his own voice. The Muses are the daughters of Zeus and Mnemosune, goddess of Memory—an especially evocative genealogy for a poet performing within an oral tradition. The bard's topic is the "wrath of Achilles" and its devastating effect upon Achilles' comrades. The Greek word *menis*, which is conventionally translated as "wrath" (as in line 1 of the *Iliad*), elsewhere in Homer always denotes a specifically divine wrath (for example, V.499, and see Muellner's *Anger of Achilles*; find this and other titles in "For Further Reading"). Achilles' wrath is thus associated with the avenging anger of the gods that is consequent upon a transgression of the proper, divinely sanctioned order of both society and the cosmos. The macabre promise to sing of the heroes' bodies made prey for the beasts (in line 5) is literally unfulfilled within the *Iliad*, but the dehumanization that is implicit in the image is literalized in the murderous fury and vicarious cannibalism of Achilles' eventual return to battle in books XX–XXII (see, for example, XXII.404–414, and Segal's *Theme of the Mutilation of the Corpse in the "Iliad"*).

2. (p. 1) *the two sons of Atreus*: Agamemnon and Menelaus are Atreus' sons. Agamemnon, the older, rules over Mycenae; he is the commander—king of kings—of the entire Achaean army. Agamemnon is married to Clytemnestra (who will murder him upon his eventual return home). Menaelaus' domain is Sparta (often called Lacedaemon). His wife is Helen (the half-sister of Clytemnestra), whose flight to Troy, whether willing or unwilling, precipitates the Trojan War.

3. (p. 2) *"Chryse . . . Cilla . . . Tenedos . . . the tears I have shed"*: Greek prayers often invoke the places where the god's presence is especially potent; and the one praying often reminds the divinity of what deeds he or she has previously performed for the god. Apollo is especially associated with pestilence; see, for example, the opening of Sophocles' *Oedipus Tyrannus*.

4. (p. 5) *"I didn't come . . . because of the Trojan spearmen"*: Achilles' rhetoric contains some truth. All the heroes but Achilles are bound to Agamemnon by the Oath of Tyndareus. At the wedding contest of Helen, Tyndareus,

the nominal father of Helen (her actual father is Zeus), bound all the suitors by oath to honor his choice of a husband for Helen (Tyndareus eventually chooses Menelaus, who brought the most gifts); Tyndareus further obliged Helen's suitors to defend her marriage should it be violated. The Achaean army at Troy is, thus, comprised of her former suitors. Achilles, however, did not participate in the marriage contest for Helen, because he was too young (see Hesiod's *Catalogue of Women* frag. 204.87–89); as the youngest of all the Achaean heroes, he has come to Troy, as he says, to "gratify" the sons of Atreus—and, we might suspect, for the adventure itself.

5. (p. 5) *Briseis*: As with the name Chryseis, the name Briseis is a patronymic: "daughter of Chryses," "daughter of Brises"—the parallelism between the names underscores the status of each as a "prize" within the Achaean camp of warriors. Both Chryseis and Briseis were captured during Achaean raids on other cities in the region of Troy; each was then "redistributed" by the collectivity of the camp, the former to Agamemnon, the latter to Achilles (we might assume that Chryseis was judged best in appearance and in domestic talents, while Briseis was deemed second best). Within the heroic economy, women are the paramount signs of a warrior's honor; the loss of Briseis is, thus, a public diminution of Achilles' status within the camp, of his very social being. In book IX, Achilles will assert that Briseis was more than a sign of honor—indeed, that he loved her. Briseis herself will speak of her own hopes for a marriage with Achilles at XIX.325–340.

6. (p. 6) *"the monstrous mountain Centaurs, and the slaughter they there / Performed was terrible indeed"*: Nestor recalls the battle of the Lapiths and the Centaurs. Perithous, king of the Lapiths, invited the Centaurs (a breed of creatures half-man, half-horse) to the wedding of his daughter Hippodameia. The drunken Centaurs attempted to rape the bride; the ensuing battle is depicted on the frieze of the Athenian Parthenon, where the victory of the Lapiths is presented as a victory of civilization over barbarism, akin to (for the Athenian viewer) the Greek victory over the Persians in the wars of 490 and 480 B.C.E.

7. (p. 11) *his goddess mother / Heard him*: Thetis is a sea-nymph, the daughter of Nereus—the Old Man of the Sea—and the wife of Peleus. From Pindar (*Isthmian Ode* 8.26–57), we learn that Thetis was desired by both Zeus and Poseidon, but Themis—a prophetic goddess—revealed that Thetis was destined to bear a son greater than the father. Thetis is then married off to the mortal Peleus, and their child is Achilles, who will be greatest of mortals, but who will not become a threat to Zeus. Thetis, by "marrying down" (to a mortal) effectively preserves Zeus' order from a son who would overthrow him. Thetis' shaming marriage to a mortal thus explains her hold over Zeus as well as the tormented "semi-divine" status of Achilles (see Slatkin's *Power of Thetis* for a full exploration of the mythic background and thematic centrality of Thetis within the *Iliad*).

8. (p. 17) *"after my fall"*: Hephaestus' lameness is perhaps explained at XV.20–26: Zeus, enraged with Hera for driving his son Heracles to Cos in a threatening storm, had hung her from Olympus with anvils tied to her feet; Zeus then threatened to hurl from Olympus anyone who came to Hera's aid. The ancient commentators attributed Hephaestus' lameness to just such an attempt—punished as threatened by Zeus— to aid Hera. There is, though, a second account of Hephaestus' laming at XVIII.448–452, where Hephaestus is thrown from Olympus by Hera, who wished to conceal having given birth to a lame child; in this account, he is rescued by Thetis.

Book II: Trial of the Army and the Catalogue of Ships

1. (p. 21) *"try them with words and bid them flee"*: Agamemnon abruptly decides to test the troops—a plan not instructed by the Dream and a near-disaster. When Agamemnon has told the Achaean troops to take flight, the other commanders are to then endeavor to check their flight. But only Odysseus—and only with the assistance of Athena—is able to turn the troops back to Troy. Agamemnon persists in his role as a bad king (he is utterly dependant upon the efforts of Odysseus, as indispensable enforcer), even as we see the overwhelming desire of the troops—if left to themselves—for a homecoming.

2. (p. 22) *"great Zeus . . . has bound me now in woeful blindness of spirit"*: It is characteristic of Agamemnon to blame his errors upon the "blindness of spirit"—in Greek, *ate*—that Zeus sends (see also IX.20 and XIX.105). Here, Agamemnon, as part of his deceptive testing of the troops, castigates Zeus for the *ate* he sends, even as he is himself being deceived by Dream: a fine example of Homeric irony.

3. (p. 25) *Thersites*: The name Thersites is derived from the Greek for "boldness" or "rashness." He is the only Homeric character to lack both a patronymic and a homeland, which might indicate that he is a common soldier, here giving voice to the resentment of the people; his ugliness might also be taken as a sign of his lower-class status: The peasants are revolting, as the old joke goes. His base appearance, however, might also place him within a tradition of blame poetry, in which ugly speakers raise a laugh at the expense of the kings; their speech reveals the harm—the "ugliness"—that the kings have done to the community. In Greek poetry, this tradition is represented by the work of Archilochus and Hipponax.

4. (p. 32) *Tell me now, O Muses . . .* : With this new invocation of the Muses, the poet embarks on the Catalog of the Achaeans, in which he sings of the leaders, homelands, and ships of the twenty-nine contingents that comprise the Achaean army. The Catalog has been the subject of much scholarly dispute as to whether it reflects the geographical and political world of the Mycenaean palace-kingdoms (the mid to late thirteenth century B.C.E.) or of the Early Iron Age (c.1025–950 B.C.E.) or of the eighth and even seventh centuries B.C.E. While the Catalog surely does transmit some Mycenaean elements (though largely from sites where there was continuity of habitation from the Mycenaean period to the Archaic period), it is also marked by the inclusion of later historical settlements, as well as by the omission of earlier, Mycenaean elements that would have been anachronistic or incomprehensible to an audience of the early Archaic period. Though daunting to the modern reader, the Catalog's compendium of geographical, political, and mythical lore—delivered with great poetic virtuosity—was of great fascination for its contemporary audiences.

5. (p. 35) *Thamyris the Thracian:* The Homeric bard includes a digression of especial poetic relevance: Thamyris boasts that his own singing would surpass even that of the Muses in a contest, whereupon they "damage" him and take away his memory. An analogy between hero and bard is, perhaps, suggested: Just as the hero, in his battlefield accomplishments, becomes like to a god, and thus tempts their deadly anger, so too, the poet sings himself into a condition like to the immortal Muses, at which point he might likewise tempt their jealous vengeance.

6. (p. 37) *warlike Protesilaus:* As in the case of the entry for Philoctetes immediately below (lines 811–820), the bard gives an account of a well-known figure who set out on the expedition to Troy, but who is now not fighting: Protesilaus was the first Achaean killed at Troy; Philoctetes and his bow will have to be brought to Troy from Lemnos before the city can be conquered. The entries for Protesilaus and Philoctetes might be compared to that for Achilles (lines 779–787), who is now also absent from the fighting.

7. (p. 39) *. . . forty black ships:* The Achaean Catalog is now complete; the grand total is: 44 leaders, 1,186 ships, and 60,000 troops (assuming an average ship-load of 50); these numbers are from the commentary of G. S. Kirk. The poet would surely object to the historian Thucydides' slighting assessment of the troop strength at Troy (*History of the Peloponnesian War*, 1.11–12).

8. (p. 41) *Bright-helmeted Hector led the Trojans:* With Hector, the principal Trojan defender, the poet begins the Catalog of Trojans, which consists of twenty-six leaders and sixteen contingents. For the roughly tripartite political division of the Trojan force, see the note below.

9. (p. 41) *Anchises' brave son Aeneas:* This is the very Aeneas who will escape from Troy to found Rome. Aeneas is the son of Aphrodite and Anchises, whose *liaison dangereuse* is recounted with much charm and wit in the Homeric *Hymn to Aphrodite*, which also foretells Aeneas' escape from the ruins of Troy so that he might re-found Troy in the west (a prophecy that the *Iliad*-poet also knows, XX.334–341). The genealogy of the entire Trojan royal house is recited by Aeneas himself at XX.233–268. Both Aeneas and Hector are descendants of Dardanus (Aeneas through the line of Assaracus, Hector through that of Ilos), but while Hector is the supreme commander, with especial charge over the contingents from Troy and its environs, Aeneas commands the Dardanians, who inhabit the foothills of Ida that lie outside the Troy region proper; the third group at Troy is the allies, who come from farther afield: from the Northern Troad, extending to the Hellespont and the Propontis; and from the south, especially from Maeonia (about Sardis) and Caria.

Book III: The Duel of Paris and Menelaus

1. (p. 46) *Helen she found in the hall, weaving . . . on her account:* The poet introduces Helen with an image of extraordinary metapoetic implication. The web that Helen weaves is the color of "purple" (Greek *porphureos*), which is elsewhere in the *Iliad* associated with blood and with death; the "battles" (Greek *aethla*) that she weaves into her cloth might also be translated as "sufferings" or "contests" (and the latter might include the contests of her suitors). Helen weaves her own epic.

2. (p. 47) *"Yonder Achaean is Atreus' son":* Beginning with the scholar-critics of Alexandria in the late third century B.C.E., Helen's identification and description of the Achaean leaders has been known as the *Teichoskopia*, the "Viewing from the Walls." The scene has often been charged with anachronism, as it would seem that, nine years into the war, Priam would have little need of the information that Helen provides. True enough, but it is preferable to regard the *Teichoskopia* as one of a series of episodes in books III through VIII that serve to fill in the background of the Trojan War and some of the events of the prior nine years. The single combat of Paris and Menelaus—which will soon be narrated—would also "better" belong to the first year of the War; but, again, the poet narrates "past" events so that his audience might better understand the present disposition of his characters and his plot. Other examples of the past-in-the-present include: Paris' recollection of his first night with Helen, which concludes book III (and where we might also ponder the difference, for Helen, between past and present); Agamemnon's mustering and inspection of the troops in book IV, as well as the depiction of Trojan oath-breaking in that same book; the Battle of Champions between Ajax and Hector in book VIII, which might, again, resolve the dispute, followed by the rejected offer of ransom and the building of the Achaean Wall.

3. (p. 51) *Put on his beautiful armor:* This is the first of four arming-scenes in the *Iliad:* Agamemnon also arms at XI.18–47, Patroclus at XVI.156–167, and Achilles at XIX.414–439. In each instance, the armor, weaponry, and order of dress are the same: greaves, corslet, sword, shield, helmet, spear; this is an example of the oral poet's use of a type-scene (as are scenes of sacrifice and of hospitality). Greaves cover the area between the knee and ankle. As a light-armed archer, Paris has no "breastplate" (corslet) of his own and so must borrow one from his brother Lycaon; single-combat is not Paris' métier.

Book IV: *Agamemnon's Inspection of the Army*

1. (p. 57) *"how many horrible / Wrongs . . . level / Their mighty stronghold?":* Zeus' question has some force, as it is only Paris who has offended Hera (and Athena)—though perhaps the entire city of Troy is implicated in the defense of Helen. At the Judgment of Paris, Paris was asked to choose the fairest from among the trio of Hera, Athena, and Aphrodite; he chose Aphrodite, thus gaining the prize of Helen, but also the fierce enmity of the rejected goddesses. Homer, however, does not explicitly recount the Judgment of Paris until XXIV.34–38, at which point the fall of the city is imminent. The poet's immediate emphasis is upon the implacable, savage wrath of Hera: In place of the divine meal of ambrosia, she would eat Priam and his sons raw—a violation, in the realm of humans, of a fundamental boundary between men and beasts; gods and beasts are equally unconstrained by the culture-defining taboos of the Greeks (the gods are, for instance, incestuous).

2. (p. 58) *the Father of gods . . . by no means ignored her:* Hera does succeed in gaining Zeus' assent to her plan to break up the truce that has still held—shakily—from the end of book III. Greeks and Trojans will not be reconciled; moreover, the Trojans will now be re-characterized as oath-breakers.

3. (p. 62) *You would not then have found / The great Agamemnon napping . . . :* After the debacles of leadership that marked books I and II, Agamemnon reasserts himself in an episode that the ancient critics called the *epipolesis,* the "Tour of Inspection." Agamemnon inspects the troops and offers speeches of praise and of blame; this will be the last major episode before the long-delayed outbreak of full combat between Achaeans and Trojans.

4. (p. 66) *Prince Polyneices*: Polyneices is the brother of Eteocles; both are sons of Oedipus, and both have been cursed by their father. The curse is active in the dispute of the two brothers over the rule of Thebes. Polyneices looks for aid to his father-in-law, Adrastus, and assembles five other heroes (and their followers) to march against Thebes: These are the Seven against Thebes; their attack upon the city will fail (see the following note). The story of the failed mission was recounted in an oral tradition know as the *Thebais*, of which only the barest scraps of fragments survive, as well as in a *Thebaid* by the Latin poet Statius (91/92 C.E.). Aeschylus' *Seven Against Thebes* of 467 B.C.E. also tells of the attack upon Thebes; it focuses upon Eteocles and the defense of the city.

5. (p. 67) *"So don't compare our merits / With theirs"*: Sthenelus speaks intemperately but truthfully: Tydeus' generation did fail to capture Thebes, and their failure was a direct consequence of their "reckless folly" and contravention of divine signs. Indeed, Tydeus' death is especially distinguished for its transgressive cannibalism: Tydeus—while writhing in his death throes—attempted to eat the brains of the mortally wounded Theban defender Melanippus. Athena, who had intended to confer immortality upon Tydeus, changes her mind upon seeing Tydeus' final act of blood-thirst. Sthenelus' allusive account of Tydeus' bestiality thus tops Agamemnon's prior account of Tydeus' deeds and, more generally, casts a skeptical light upon the oft-repeated claim that fathers are better than sons.

Book V: The Valiant Deeds of Diomedes

1. (p. 72) . . . *she sent him into / The thickest part of the battle*: Diomedes' *aristeia*— his "excellent deeds" on the battlefield—begins with Athena's kindling of his war-strength. In the absence of Achilles, Diomedes emerges as the single greatest offensive warrior of the Achaeans (Ajax is the greatest defender). Book V narrates his ever-increasing martial successes, which lead him into a state "like to a god" or even "like something more than a god." During this period of heightened physical prowess, Diomedes even wounds Aphrodite and Ares, thus putting himself in great danger of suffering divine vengeance; his martial exultation becomes such that he threatens to overstep the boundary between mortal and divine, to "fight Father Zeus himself," as Aphrodite will later claim (V.400). The *aristeia* of Diomedes provides an interpretative template for the battlefield glories and dangers of the other heroes, including both Patroclus (in book XVI) and Achilles (at the start of book XXII, Achilles is also likened—ominously—to the brightest of late summer stars, which is the dog-star Orion).

2. (p. 77) "*. . . what the horses of Tros are like*": The horses of Tros are of a divine breed, initially a gift of Zeus to Tros (in recompense for Zeus' abduction of his son Ganymede). The horses are particularly valuable booty; as such, they especially command the actions of Diomedes (assisted by Sthenelus) in the following narrative.

3. (p. 83) "*. . . horse-taming Diomedes*": Dione's threat that Diomedes will die for his attack upon Aphrodite is not fulfilled, though it does illustrate the danger into which his *aristeia* has inevitably led him: death-provoking contention with the gods themselves (the preceding example of Heracles, who is not killed by the gods, but himself immortalized, is a strictly one-time exception). Diomedes, upon his safe return home after the fall of Troy, will discover that his wife Aegialeia has been unfaithful—perhaps this is Aphrodite's belated revenge. Diomedes sails from his native Argos and ends his days in northern Apulia, among the Daunians.

4. (p. 89) "*. . . he leveled the city of Troy and plundered / Her streets*": Laomedon (the father of Priam) had promised Heracles a reward of his partly divine horses (from the same breed as those that Diomedes earlier won from Aeneas; see also note 2 above), as Heracles had saved his daughter Hesione from a sea-monster. Laomedon reneged on the deal, and Heracles sacked the city; this is the first Sack of Troy. (The poet tells of a marker of Heracles' battle with the sea-monster at XX.161–167.)

5. (p. 90) "*. . . Zeus who bears the aegis*": The Homeric aegis is a kind of shield, perhaps covered in goat-skin (its etymology connects it to the Greek for "goat": *aig-*), perhaps suspended from the shoulders. In classical art, Athena's aegis is a shawl-like skin wrapped around the shoulders. In addition to its protective function, the aegis, when shaken, can put an army to flight or produce storms.

Book VI: Hector and Andromache

1. (p. 97) *clutching the knees of his captor*: Grasping the knees of the victor while begging for mercy (while also promising a ransom) is the regular gesture of battlefield supplication in the *Iliad*; it is never successful (though we will hear of Achilles' positive response to supplications in

the past—for example, at XI.115–118). Other examples of supplication include the appeals of Dolon (X.427–431), of the sons of Antimachus (XI.145–150), of Lycaon (XXI.95–121), and, finally, of Hector (XXII.395–401). The following threat of Agamemnon to kill even the unborn children of Troy foreshadows the general fate of the city and casts a particularly grievous shadow upon the upcoming scene between Hector and Andromache.

2. (p. 99) *"But if you are some immortal . . . I will not fight you . . . Not even . . . brawny Lycurgus"*: Diomedes, who in the prior book fought with three gods— Aphrodite, Apollo, and Ares—now claims that he would not fight with an immortal. A lesson learned or words of consummate self-satisfaction? Diomedes' negative paradigm is Lycurgus, a Thracian king who attempted to resist the spread of Dionysus (who is both "mad" and "maddening") and his cult; he is punished by the Olympians with blindness and early death (the *exemplum* of Lycurgus is otherwise mentioned at line 955 of Sophocles' *Antigone*, and compare the deeds and punishment of Pentheus in Euripides' *Bacchae*). The nurses of Dionysus received the baby god from his father, Zeus, and nurtured him on Mount Nusa in Thrace.

3. (p. 99) *". . . so one generation of men / Gives way to another"*: The comparison of human generations to leaves is one of the most famous and most imitated of Iliadic similes—see, for example, Mimnermus 2.1–2, Simonides 19, and Aristophanes' *Birds* 685; see also the *Iliad* XXI.526–528, where the simile is recast by Apollo from a divine perspective. Human life is as evanescent (and as unredeemed) as that of the leaf that falls in season; nature cares nothing for the life of the individual, only for the survival of the species. Yet Glaucus proceeds to recite the names and exploits of his ancestors ("listen and hear what many know / Already"); some mortals do, it seems, through their adventures, gain a place within the collective memory, thus rescuing their name from the anonymity and sameness of the leaves—a rescue of meaning all the more valuable for its very uncertainty.

4. (p. 100) *"Anteia . . . lusted madly to lie with Bellerophon"*: The tale of the Queen who longs for her husband's guest-friend and who, upon being rebuffed, makes false and potentially deadly accusations to her husband is a folktale found in many cultures—it is often referred to as the Potiphar's-wife theme, after the story of the false accusation of Joseph (see the Bible, beginning at Genesis 39:7 ff.). The most familiar version in Greek is found in Euripides' *Hippolytus* (where Hippolytus is Phaedra's stepson); see also the story of Peleus and the wife of Acastus (Apollodrus 3.13.3 and Pindar *Nemean* 4.54–58). In the Homeric version, the reluctance of Proetus to kill Bellerophon probably reflects a family connection between Proetus and Glaucus, the father of Bellerophon—a guest-host relation that, if violated, would provoke a blood-curse or a

vendetta or both. Proetus instead sends Bellerophon on the series of death-defying adventures that become the basis of his fame: a vindication of his name against the false charges of Anteia and an immortalization of his name through heroic deeds.

5. (p. 101) ". . . *he roamed alone the Aleian Plain, / Consuming his soul and avoiding all human tracks*": The end of Bellerophon is mysterious and haunting. The poet avoids recounting the most famous (and notorious) of Bellerophon's exploits, which is his attempt to storm Olympus on the back of Pegasus, the immortal winged horse; the gods hurl him from his mount. Rather, the poet emphasizes the final wandering unto death of Bellerophon, who ends his life, apart from men and gods, upon the Plain of Wandering ("Aleian" is a pun on the Greek word for "to wander"). All the heroic deeds and rewards seem insufficient for Bellerophon, whose centripetal wandering leads him onto a plain that might well be an image of his own consciousness. During the Renaissance, Bellerophon became a defining type of the melancholic, the man born under the sign of Saturn; see [Aristotle] *Problem* 30, as reread by Marsilio Ficino in the late fifteenth century.

6. (p. 102) . . . *golden armor / For bronze, or a hundred oxen for nine*: The unequal exchange of armor affects a jolt in ethos and tone following the joyous chivalry of the pact that Diomedes and Glaucus just agreed upon. Ancient and modern critics have expended enormous ingenuity upon explaining the shift in tone; perhaps we should simply acknowledge a (somewhat mystifying) Homeric joke.

7. (p. 107) ". . . *where the city / Is best assaulted and the wall most easily scaled*": Andromache pleads that Hector remain close to the city wall. Andromache's claim that there is a weak spot in the Trojan defense may reflect a tradition that the Wall of Troy was built in its entirety by Apollo and Poseidon except for one section, which was built by the mortal Aeacus and which is, in consequence, vulnerable to attack (Pindar *Olympian* 8.31–46; see also VII.491–494, where Poseidon recollects his part in building the Trojan Wall).

8. (p. 107) "*But how could I face the men of Troy, or their wives . . . if I were to skulk like a coward*": In response to Andromache's plea that he remain near to the Trojan Wall and mindful of wife and child, Hector invokes his sense of *aidos*—of reverence, of respect, of shame. In Homeric Greek, *aidos* is a responsiveness to the ethical judgments of others within the community; it is a social emotion provoked by the perception of one's place in the social structure and of the obligations that accompany that place. Hector's sense of *aidos* before the entirety of his community does not permit him to rank the claims of wife and son above those of his community. In being preeminently responsive to the claims of his community, Hector must set aside the claims of those who are most his own.

(For an illuminating reading of this extraordinarily moving passage, see Redfield, *Nature and Culture in the "Iliad,"* pp. 113–127.)

Book VII: The Duel of Hector and Ajax

1. (p. 113) "*. . . and my glory will not be destroyed*": Hector imagines funeral rites for the defeated man that include the heaping of a great barrow over his grave. The tumulus will itself be a mighty memorial sign to those who pass by of the name of Hector—a visual analog to the "glory forever" provided by epic poetry itself, which Achilles invokes at IX.475.

2. (p. 114) "*. . . if only / I were as young as when . . .*": This is the second of four autobiographical recitations by Nestor: Earlier, at I.303–317, he told of his comradeship with the Lapiths; at XI.653–853, he will tell of his youthful exploits in the battles between Pylians and Epeians; and at XXIII.726–743, he will recall his victories at the funeral games of Amarynceus. In this instance—as also in the example from book XI— Nestor asserts the excellence of his prior deeds as a foundation upon which to base his exhortation to the present generation of heroes— here, to the front-fighters of the Achaeans; in book XI (where Nestor's intervention will be decisive), to Patroclus and, he hopes, Achilles.

3. (p. 119) *So they turned back . . . .* : With this exchange of pledges of friend- ship and gifts, Hector and Ajax bring their strife to an end. The elabo- rate courtesies of the heroic code are enacted for a final time in the *Iliad*; there will be no further peaceable resolutions in the fighting to come.

4. (p. 119) "*. . . land of our fathers*": With the establishment of a truce and the collection of the bones of the dead, the "First Great Day of Battle" comes to an end, as does the first narrative movement of the *Iliad*: The past, in- cluding prior attempts at resolution, has been re-represented; the principal heroes have been richly characterized; the dispositions of the Achaean and Trojan armies have been dramatized. With the building of the Achaean wall and the refusals of Paris to return Helen and of the Achaeans to accept ran- som that immediately follow, the hostilities of the narrative present are set to be rejoined, as is the plan of Zeus (first announced in book I) to honor Achilles by turning the tide of battle against the Achaeans.

Book VIII: The Weakening Achaeans

1. (p. 124) "*That's how much stronger I am than you gods and all mortals*": With this vivid assertion of his own preeminence, Zeus clears the mortal battle- field of the Olympians. Zeus can now—through the martial successes

of Hector—fulfill his promise to Thetis to bring the Achaeans to grief in the absence of Achilles. (For the futility of resistance by the other gods to Zeus, see also the exchange between Hera and Poseidon at VIII. 224–240, as well as Zeus' threatening speech to Hera at VIII.534–553, with note 3 below.)

2. (p. 127) . . . *the old King mounted the car / With Diomedes*: The epic tradition also knows a version of the rescue of Nestor in which the old man is saved by his son Antilochus, who sacrifices his own life for his father's. The poet Pindar (*Pythian* 6.28ff.) makes of that telling a paradigm of filial piety.

3. (p. 137) *"For massive Hector . . . about the corpse of Patroclus"*: Zeus, having dramatically quelled any rebellion against his rule by Hera and Athena, now foretells the fulfillment of his promise of book I to honor Achilles: Hector and the Trojans will continue to have martial success until the death of Patroclus, after which Achilles will rejoin his comrades. As well, we now see that Zeus' honoring of Achilles will bring enormous grief to Achilles himself—the loss of Patroclus.

Book IX: *Agamemnon's Offers to Achilles*

1. (p. 140) *". . . since his is the greatest power"*: Agamemnon urges flight upon the Achaeans with the same words he used in book II, when he was under the influence of the deceptive Dream sent by Zeus (II.19–41, and IX.18–28); here, his words are in earnest (and Zeus is now responsible for his plight), but his counsel of retreat is met not with a rush to the ships (as in book II), but with Achaean resistance and refusal. The reuse of speech-blocks and type-scenes is a technique of the oral poet; here, that technique is in the service of a (rather ironic) characterization of a persistently despondent Agamemnon, as well as of an intensification of the dramatic urgency of the present moment: The deliberations that follow are of the utmost consequence, wholly lacking the dream and comic elements of the "retreat" of book II.

2. (p. 143) *"I acted blindly"*: Agamemnon claims he was struck with a moral blindness or an infatuation of mind that diminished his capacity for reasoned action—what the Greeks call *ate*, and which always leads to disaster. In book XIX (lines 104–167), Agamemnon will offer a lengthy account of *ate* ("Sweet Folly"). Earlier, in book I (lines 478–485), Achilles had asked Thetis to appeal to Zeus for a Trojan victory so that Agamemnon "might know his *ate*" ("that Atreus' son . . . may know how blind he was"). Achilles' appeal to Zeus is now reaching fulfillment.

3. (p. 145) *. . . there they found him / Soothing his soul with a resonant lyre . . . Part of the loot he had taken when he himself sacked / Eëtion's city*: Achilles is reintroduced into the narrative with an extraordinarily suggestive image. He now sits apart, playing the role of the bard, singing of "warriors' fame"; he is no longer the doer of martial deeds but is the commemorator of those deeds. The lyre is itself an object and instrument of beauty, even as it was captured in bloody warfare; so, too, Homeric poetry makes a beauteous song out of carnage.

4. (pp. 146–147) *". . . your father Peleus was talking / To you . . . 'be reconciled quickly / That Argives young and old may respect you still more'"*: The parting of father and son in Phthia is also recalled in book XI (lines 881–884) by Nestor, who recollects the same occasion, though with a somewhat different version of Peleus' words; Nestor will also include the parting words of Menoetius (Patroclus' father) to Patroclus. At XVIII.368–373, Achilles will recall his own final words to Menoetius. In the present passage (and in the book XI passage), Peleus' knowledge of his son's quick temper is evident.

5. (p. 148) *"All of these gifts are yours, if only / You'll stop being angry"*: Up to this point, Odysseus has faithfully reported Agamemnon's offer of gifts, but he now omits Agamemnon's conclusion, which contained an implicit comparison of Achilles to Hades and a command to Achilles to recognize Agamemnon's greater rank and age (IX.179–183). Instead, Odysseus first appeals to Achilles' sense of pity for his comrades, then to his desire for glory by offering up Hector, who now fights in the front-ranks. Achilles, however, will fully (and furiously) understand that an acceptance of Agamemnon's gifts (and especially an acceptance of Agamemnon's offer to make him his son-in-law!) amounts to a recognition of Agamemnon's greater authority; to accept the king's gifts is to acknowledge the (greater) social position that they concretize.

6. (p. 148) *"I, then, will say what seems to me best"*: In book I, Athena stopped Achilles from killing Agamemnon with the promise of receiving "three times as much as what you may lose" (line 248). Achilles has now been offered much more than that (and Agamemnon has acknowledged his *ate*, note 2 above). All expectation is that Achilles will accept the gifts and return to his comrades, yet Achilles refuses. It is at this point that the *Iliad* ventures into previously unexplored thematic terrain; and Achilles, in the emotionally roiling, bitterly sarcastic, and relentlessly reevaluating speech that now follows, is the primary explorer of that new terrain—no longer a hero (only) of deeds, but of consciousness. (See the introduction for further discussion of some aspects of Achilles' great speech.)

7. (p. 151) *"The knightly / Old Peleus made me your guardian . . ."*: In the first part of his response to Achilles' refusal of Agamemnon's gifts and to his threat to depart at sunrise, Phoenix recounts his own youthful autobiography and how he came to be Achilles' tutor (a role that the poetic tradition more often attributes to the kindly centaur Cheiron) and surrogate father. As a young man, Phoenix, too, was embroiled in a potentially deadly dispute over a mistress—in this case, his father's. Amyntor will curse his son with sterility, driving Phoenix to flee his homeland rather than become a parricide. In Phthia, Phoenix, now an exile, receives an act of extraordinary grace: Peleus not only offers him refuge (which is obligatory in the case of exiles), but a kingdom and the nurturance of a son. Peleus, in effect, rectifies the curse that Amyntor had placed upon Phoenix: Peleus loved Phoenix as a "father loves / His only son and heir"; in return for this act of generosity beyond expectation, Phoenix will love Achilles as his own son. (Peleus' Phthia seems to be a notable place of refuge; the homicides Epeigeus and Patroclus also find refuge there—see XVI.651–659, and XXIII.98–104).

8. (p. 153) *"Even the gods can yield . . .":* The second part of Phoenix' speech features the allegory of the Prayers. Following inevitably, if at a slower pace, upon instances of "Sin," which here translates the Greek *ate* (an impaired mental state that leads to moral error and further folly; see above, note 2), the Prayers offer a chance of healing, of brooking disaster before it fully erupts. If the Prayers are rejected, they themselves (as Phoenix presents it) pray to Zeus for vengeance, which takes the form of further and decisive *ate*. Though others in the *Iliad* speak of *ate* (most prominently, Agamemnon at lines 19.104–167), Achilles himself will never explain his own actions in terms of *ate*.

9. (p. 154) *"We've all heard similar stories / About the old heroes . . .":* In the third and final part of his speech, Phoenix recounts the old story of Meleager, a traditional tale that would have been part of the repertoire of the performing bard. Meleager's successful killing of the Calydonian Boar is succeeded by two tales of strife: Fighting breaks out between Curetes and Aetolians (Meleager's people) over the spoils of the Boar, and anger erupts between Meleager and his mother Althaea over Meleager's killing of Althaea's brother, perhaps also in a dispute over the spoils of the Calydonian Boar. Althaea calls upon the Fury to avenge her brother, and Meleager—in anger—withdraws from the battle against the Aetolians to retire with his wife, Cleopatra. In other versions of the Meleager tradition, Althaea takes hold of a magical firebrand that represents Meleager's life and casts it into the fire; as the firebrand diminishes, so too does Meleager's strength (see Bacchylides 5.94–154, Ovid's *Metamorphoses* 8.273–525, and Apollodorus 1.8.1–3). The other tellings of Meleager's story also relate his death in battle at the hands of Apollo, a death similar to that of Achilles (see Hesiod's *Catalog of Women*, frag. 25.11–13 and 280)—a not insignificant part of the story, though not told by Phoenix.

10. (p. 156) *"Her lurid account stirred Meleager's / Soul . . . he went out and donned / His flashing armor"*: Meleager is supplicated first by priests and elders, then by father, mother, and sisters, then by comrades, and finally by his wife, Cleopatra. The order of supplication enacts a traditional scale of ascending affection: fellow citizens, parents and siblings, spouse; into this order, Phoenix inserts the "friends"—the martial companions—between family and spouse. In terms of the embassy to Achilles, we might understand Odysseus to represent the army, Phoenix the father, and Ajax the companions. Crucial to an interpretation of the Meleager paradigm is to note that the name of Meleager's wife is Cleopatra, which simply reverses the two elements that are also found in the name of Patroclus (in Greek, *Kleo-patre* and *Patro-kleos*). In the *Iliad*, it is Patroclus' plea (in book XVI) that will finally move Achilles, though even then Achilles will send—much to his own grievous loss—Patroclus to fight in his place. Finally, the name of Patroclus—so much in play at the climax of Meleager's story—is itself a "speaking name," signifying "the fame of the ancestors" (from Greek *kleos* "poetic fame" and *patre-* "father/ancestor"). Patroclus thus has the exemplary heroic name, as it signifies epic poetry itself, which transmits the fame of the prior generations. Patroclus—as comrade and as concept—thus stands at the summit of Achilles' "scale of affection"—though both meanings cannot finally coexist, and each will experience revaluation.

11. (p. 157) *". . . whether we / Should go back to our own or stay where we are"*: Though Achilles warns Phoenix that his supplication on behalf of Agamemnon risks a permanent alienation of his love, he now makes a first concession: They will consider in the morning whether to stay or to go; compare IX.489–491, where Achilles had asserted that he would definitely sail home on the coming morning.

12. (p. 158) *"But Hector . . . Will stop his advance . . . when he reaches my lodge / And looming black vessel"*: Achilles now makes a second and crucial concession: He will not sail in the morning, and he will fight when Hector brings fire to his ships. Though Ajax' just preceding speech was the shortest of the three, its appeal to the "love of friends" proves to be the most effective. The degree to which Ajax' appeal to the love and respect of the martial collective both succeeds (Achilles will not now return home) and fails (but Achilles will not yet honor the supplications of his friends and return to battle) presents some concluding measure (in book IX) of the volatile state of Achilles' mind. (See the introduction for further discussion of Ajax' speech.)

Book X: The Night Adventure

1. (p. 160) *... no sweet sleep held ... Agamemnon, so worried was he / By the many problems of war*: Book X begins with a sleepless Agamemnon calling a council, as he did in book II; the result, however, will not be a full-scale mobilization of the troops, but the dispatch of Diomedes and Odysseus under cover of night to spy upon the Trojans. Beginning with the first ancient commentators and continuing to present-day scholar-critics, book X has often been judged to be an interpolation within the overall design of the *Iliad*. Nothing in book X advances the overall plot of the poem; it has also been ejected from the monumental *Iliad* for its folkloristic qualities, for its depiction of Odysseus and Diomedes as murderous liars, for its nighttime setting, and for its culmination in an Achaean victory (which is inconsistent with the full activation in book VIII of Zeus' plan to bring honor to Achilles by aiding Hector and the Trojans). Book X has also been scorned for numerous atypical linguistic features (words and phrases found in the *Odyssey* but not otherwise in the *Iliad*), as well as anomalies of religious practice (gilding the horns of sacrificial cattle, X.329) and of heroic headgear (Diomedes' leather helmet, Odysseus' boar-tusk cap, X.288–295). Critics who have retained book X have found respite from the solemnities of book IX in its grim humor and, when humor fails (as in the killing of Dolon and of the sleeping Rhesus and his men), have praised the book for its depiction of the brutality that lurks just beneath the heroic code, ready to erupt under cover of night—and, perhaps most tellingly, in the absence of Achilles. Finally, we might note that the treacherous deceit of Diomedes and Odysseus foreshadows the Fall of Troy itself, which will succumb not to the daytime force of the Achaeans but to nighttime tricks.

2. (p. 169) *Then he put on his head / A ferret-skin cap*: While Diomedes wears the helmet of a bull and Odysseus that of a boar, Dolon wears the helmet of a ferret (or weasel) and the skins of a wolf. While the clothing and caps are disguises (the heroes have shed their conventional attire), they seem also to communicate something essential about the characters of those who put them on.

3. (p. 171) *"... the Thracians, newly arrived, and among them / Their King, Rhesus"*: Dolon, in his terror, discloses more than he was asked; and, at Dolon's revelation of the exceptional horses and chariot of Rhesus, Diomedes and Odysseus set aside their original intent of reconnaissance so that they might capture such rich booty. The epic tradition knew of at least two other versions of the Rhesus story: In one, an oracle foretells that Rhesus and his horses will be invincible if they should drink of the waters of the Scamandrus (see Virgil's *Aeneid* 1.472–473); in another, Rhesus'

actual deeds are so extraordinary that Hera grows alarmed—in both versions, Diomedes and Odysseus are dispatched to kill Rhesus.

Book XI: The Valiant Deeds of Agamemnon

1. (p. 176) *Strife shouted a loud and terrible war-scream, which stirred . . . the Achaeans . . . to fight / Without ceasing:* With the new dawn and the war-cry of Strife, Zeus further enacts his intention to bring honor to Achilles through a defeat of the Achaeans (see VIII.536–544, and note 3 to book VIII above). The Great Day of Battle now begins; the battle itself is in two primary movements—books XI–XII and XIII–XV—and though each movement begins with an Achaean success, each ends with a resounding Achaean defeat. The day itself does not come to a close until book XVIII (lines 254–257), where Achilles' supernatural shriek at the trench (many translators and commentators use the term "ditch") echoes the opening cry of Strife. Achilles' cry will be so disordering that Hera will compel the Sun to set early.

2. (p. 183) *. . . such were the sharp and bitter / Pangs that racked Agamemnon now:* With a startling simile that compares the pain of Agamemnon's wound to that of a woman in labor, Agamemnon's brutal *aristeia* comes to an abrupt end; the great king will now be led off like a woman to her accouchement (Achilles is surely somewhere laughing). Agamemnon's *aristeia* is followed by that of Hector, just as Zeus had earlier promised (XI.212–216); and indeed, the pace of Zeus' plan now accelerates: In short order, Diomedes, Odysseus (neither any longer protected by Athena, as they were in book X), Machaon, and Eurypylus are wounded, and finally, Ajax is forced to retreat (see XI.621–639, where Ajax is compared first to a lion, then—uniquely and rather touchingly—to a donkey being cudgeled by boys).

3. (p. 187) *Deeply troubled, / He spoke to his own great heart:* Odysseus' monologue is the first in the *Iliad*, though two more will follow in this book and ten more in books XVII–XXII (among the most striking are those of Menelaus at XVII.104–123, Agenor at XXI.629–647, and Hector at XXII.117–149). The lone warrior debates with himself the contrary possibilities of fight and retreat. Odysseus' speech moves beyond the now familiar motives of worldly honor and posthumous glory (and the converses of blame and shame) to a consideration of the moral obligations of the "brave" (or "excellent") man as opposed to the coward. Under duress from the wound that he will soon receive from Socus, the pragmatic Odysseus—"insatiably wily"—will reemerge in retreat.

4. (p. 188) *"But carrion birds shall pick the flesh from your bones . . . Whereas . . . The noble Achaeans will surely bury me / With all due funeral rites"*: The threat that the heroes' bodies will be made prey for wild beasts was first expressed in the *Iliad's* proem. Odysseus now makes explicit an opposition that thematically structures the poem: Funeral rites, which serve both to close a wound within the community and to memorialize the name of the dead, are contrasted to a horrific "anti-funeral," in which the body, treated as mere meat (or as mere nature), is consumed by wild beasts—and so made to vanish without trace.

5. (p. 192) *. . . thus marking the start of evil / For him*: This is a crucial turning point: Achilles has been observing the Achaean rout from the stern of his ship, and he now sends forth Patroclus to gather further information. Patroclus' embassy to the Achaeans sets in motion the series of events that will lead to Patroclus' death and to Achilles' return to battle. The referent of "him" is double: The "start of evil" is surely for Patroclus, but it is for Achilles as well. Achilles' call to Patroclus is motivated by a wound to Machaon, who—like Achilles—learned the healing art from Cheiron. Book XI will conclude with Patroclus, who in turn learned his medical skills from Achilles, tending to the wounded Eurypylus (XI.904–913).

6. (p. 194) *"If only I were / As young and my strength as unyielding as once . . ."*: Nestor now uncorks a loquacious reminiscence of his own youth. His tale is one of heroic coming-of-age through cattle-raiding; indeed, it has been convincingly argued that the defining initiatory adventure for an Indo-European hero is the cattle-raid, in which the boy must display the bravery and the stealth that the adult male hero requires. Nestor's adventure takes place in the context of ongoing strife between the Pylians and the Epeans, in which the latter have had by far the greater success; Nestor's eleven older brothers have been killed in the previous battles. Nestor's coming-of-age—in which, crucially, he must also overcome the opposition of Neleus, his father—is both a personal achievement and the revivification of his community. Upon emerging from his disguise among the foot-soldiers with his triumphant leap upon a chariot and now wielding a deadly spear, Nestor is the new ruler of Pylos, surpassing and supplanting his father—and saving his own people by so doing. Nestor offers his tale as a goad to action for Achilles (via Patroclus), but an audience might also sense that the past was a simpler (if already oedipalized) time.

7. (p. 197) *"Let him send you at the head of the Myrmidon host"*: Nestor now formulates the fatal plan that Patroclus should fight in Achilles' stead and in Achilles' armor, and Patroclus, greatly moved, sets off to return to Achilles' shelter. His progress, however, is immediately halted by the wounded Eurypylus, who provokes Patroclus' pity (XI.904–913). Patroclus will not return to Achilles until book XVI.

Book XII: The Storming of the Wall

1. (p. 200) *Where they before had poured their bright-flowing streams*: Book XII begins with an extraordinary reflection upon the destruction of the Achaean Wall, which was proposed and constructed in book VII (lines 367–374 and 472–481), where its destruction was also foretold by Zeus (in response to Poseidon's complaints, VII.482–494). In the proem to book XII, that destruction is now narrated, but—uniquely in the *Iliad*—from the point of view of the poet's historical audience, for whom the epic heroes are half-divines (see line 24), a term used only here in the *Iliad* and a word appropriate to civic cult-practice—that is, to an audience for whom the heroes are now recipients of cult-offerings rather than, or in addition to, the subjects of epic verse. Moreover, the poet's insistence upon the complete disappearance of any sign of the Achaeans from the beach of the Hellespont might itself be understood as responsive to an audience that now wonders about the historical remains of Troy: Where's the evidence? The poet's boldly self-confident answer is to destroy any traces of the Wall; all an audience needs in order to know the story of Troy is the bard's own song. (A quip of Aristotle's well captures the bard's world-creating—and -destroying—power: "The poet who invented it destroyed it," frag. 162.

2. (p. 200) *. . . Polydamas came up / To daring Hector and spoke to him and the others*: Polydamas has the role of counselor to Hector; this is the first of four speeches of advice; see also XII.223–245, XIII.835–860, and XVIII.284–317. All four of Polydamas' speeches are guided by a concern for the collective safety—and not with individual honor or glory; contrast, for example, Odysseus' speech at XI.458–468 (see book XI, note 3 above) or Sarpedon's upcoming speech at XII.330–351. Hector's subsequent rejections of Polydamas' advice (XII.223–268 and, especially, in book XVIII) underline his increasing recklessness, driven by the fatal delusion that Zeus' favor will last.

3. (p. 206) *"Glaucus, why is it that we above all are honored . . . as though we were gods?"*: Sarpedon's speech on the motives of the hero is among the finest in the *Iliad*. In the first part of his speech, Sarpedon speaks of heroism as a social obligation: The hero receives special honors—land grants, prominent places at the communal feast—from his community, for which he must ultimately show himself worthy by fighting in defense of his community; or, as in the case of the Lycian Sarpedon at Troy, the hero must fight elsewhere so as to show himself deserving of the rewards he receives at home; a role that begins in the community's need for defense thus generates a necessity for martial aggression. In the second part of his speech (beginning with "Ah, my friend . . ."), Sarpedon

shifts to individual motives: The hero's heightened sense of death (Sarpedon speaks as if the Death-spirits are right behind his back)— his knowledge that he will not be "deathless and ageless forever"— leads him to venture knowingly into battle, where he might gain the compensatory immortality that epic poetry promises. (See Redfield, *Nature and Culture in the "Iliad,"* pp. 99–101 and Schein, *The Mortal Hero,* pp. 70–72, for two exemplary readings of Sarpedon's speech.)

Book XIII: Fighting Among the Ships

1. (p. 212) *. . . that any immortal would dare come down / To strengthen either the Trojan or Danaan forces:* Following the headlong narrative rush that culminated with Hector's bursting through the gate to the Achaean camp, the opening of book XIII directs Zeus' gaze—and the audience's attention—to regions far to the north of Troy: The milk-drinking Hippemolgi are nomadic Scythians (like Herodotus' Massagetae in his *Histories* 1.216), while the utopic Abii, whose name signifies "without violence" in Greek, inhabit the nether northern regions. Zeus' averted gaze permits the intervention of Poseidon into the battle and a (temporary) revival of Achaean fortunes. The careless ease of Zeus—even as he risks, but never loses, his rule—is not untypical.

2. (p. 216) *Like a ruthless, death-bearing boulder that bounds down the slope . . . and rolls to a stop:* The boulder to which Hector is now compared recalls that with which Hector burst open the gate of the Achaean defenses at the end of book XII (lines 481–497). But the simile of the boulder also suggests the increasing degree to which Hector, caught up in his own momentum, in his own certainty of Zeus' favor, becomes less the agent of his own choices than the object borne along by the now uncontrollable rush of events that he himself has set in motion.

3. (p. 218) *He met . . . Meriones / On his way to fetch a bronze-headed spear:* Idomeneus and Meriones come upon each other in a situation of potential mutual embarrassment, for each discovers the other well behind the fighting line. With relieved good humor, each asserts his own valor and accepts the correspondent claims of the other. With their spears restored, they return to the battlefield.

4. (p. 224) *. . . standing / In back of the battle, for Aeneas was always angry / At royal Priam:* Aeneas' absence from the battle is explained in terms of rivalry between the two branches of the Trojan royal house—one represented by Priam and Hector, the other by Anchises and Aeneas (see note 9 to book II above). The cause of the dispute is an offense to "honor" that goes unexplained, but Aeneas' anger is expressed by a (verbal) form that derives from the word for Achilles' anger (menis); and like Achilles after Patroclus' death, Aeneas ends his withdrawal for the sake of one who is dear to him.

5. (p. 232) ". . . I'll come back as soon as I've given my orders": Polydamas concludes his third speech of advice to Hector with a first Trojan premonition of the return of Achilles. Hector does not acknowledge that point, but he does (for the first and only time) heed Polydamas' advice to call a council of the Trojan leaders. A council, however, is not possible, as it turns out that the principal Trojan fighters are wounded or dead. Polydamas' advice is good, but circumstance has rendered it inapplicable; caution is no longer permitted Hector.

Book XIV: The Tricking of Zeus

1. (p. 236) The cries of battle were not unheard by Nestor, / Though at his wine: This opening scene of Nestor at his wine, accompanied by Machaon and attended by Hecamede, picks up immediately upon the scene where we last saw Nestor (in book XI, immediately before the dispatch of Patroclus). The ancient commentators express some shock at the amount of time that Nestor has been drinking while his fellow Achaeans have been fighting—ever since XI.720, some three books earlier. But at issue is less Nestor's heroic tippling than Homer's narration of simultaneous actions as consecutive. A scene that the poet puts aside is picked up where it was left off, while the intervening actions are conceived of as concurrent with that scene. The battlefield action framed by Nestor's bout of drinking is simultaneous with it—that is, the drinking of book XIV is temporally continuous with the drinking of book XI (no intervening time has elapsed), and the scenes in Nestor's shelter are simultaneous with the fighting of books XII and XIII.

2. (p. 238) "Far better to flee and escape / Than stay and be taken": Agamemnon proposes, now for the third time, a retreat to the ships and a sailing from Troy—though a launching of the ships while under attack risks a total disaster, as Odysseus will point out. When Agamemnon falsely and foolishly proposed a retreat in book II (131–138), it was Odysseus who succeeded in regrouping the army; following Agamemnon's call for retreat in book IX (lines 18–26), it was Diomedes who rallied the leaders with a speech. In the present instance, both Diomedes and Odysseus will intervene to prevent an Achaean retreat.

3. (p. 240) And then she considered, the heifer-eyed / Queenly Hera, how she might best trick the wits / Of aegis-great Zeus: Hera, delighting from afar in Poseidon's aid to the Achaeans, resolves that Zeus should remain indolent for as

long as possible; she will seduce her husband. The ensuing "Deception of Zeus" is an episode of darkly glittering humor that burlesques the tradition of the *hierogamia*, or Sacred Marriage. The holy union of Zeus and Hera was imagined to take place upon a mountaintop and to produce the divine, fertilizing dew upon which the seasonal success of the crops was dependent; this divine marriage was reenacted and celebrated at various festival-rites throughout the Greek world from as early as the Mycenaean period (see lines 394–399 for an eruption of fecund nature at the climax of the *hierogamia* of Zeus and Hera). In the Homeric parody, neither Zeus nor Hera retain much—or any—of their cultic aura and awe. Hera, driven by hatred, perverts her role as protector of the domestic hearth: She must seduce her own husband; her conjugal "duty" is itself a trick. Zeus' role as husband of Hera (and guardian of guest-friendship) is surely vitiated by his catalog of prior seductions (lines 360–370), while his recitation of past amours—each an occasion of strife with Hera—seems calculated to repel rather than attract (though Hera, if her seduction is to succeed, must swallow any of the gall that Zeus' recitation of former lovers surely induces).

4. (p. 241) *And slyly Queen Hera replied: "Give me now, then, / Love and desire . . .":* Hera's seduction of Zeus requires an initial deception of Aphrodite; if Hera is to succeed, she will need the love-charms that Aphrodite can provide. The less-than-astute goddess of love is easily duped by Hera's tale that she is on a mission to restore conjugal relations between the squabbling Oceanus and Tethys (who are here conceived of as primeval, cosmogonic parents), for domestic harmony is, after all, Hera's divine concern. But, of course, the outcome of Hera's seduction will be an increase in strife between her and Zeus, a further sharpening of Olympian divisions. Oceanus and Tethys—whose union might bode a cosmic harmony—will not be reconciled.

5. (p. 243) *"And now / You want me to do this other impossible thing":* Sleep initially refuses Hera's request with a recollection of a prior occasion on which he had aided Hera's plans by charming Zeus to sleep. While Zeus was held under Sleep's dominion, Hera caused Heracles—as he departed from Troy, following the first Sack of the city (V.715–716, and see note 4 on book V above)—to be swept away to the island of Cos (Zeus himself will give further details at XV.28–32); on Cos, Heracles will have to fight several Giants (Pindar's *Nemean* 4.25–27 and *Isthmian* 6.31–33), who are also among the opponents of Zeus' rule. The entire narrative of the "Deception of Zeus" is shot through with allusions to prior cosmic strife (note Zeus' response upon waking up from Sleep's first spell)—and will itself precipitate an intensification of Olympian discord.

6. (p. 247) *And as when a huge oak / Falls . . . Hector crashed to the dusty earth:* The battle of Hector and Ajax has been forestalled from the end of book XIII (lines 956–960). The simile of the felled oak—toughest of trees—leads an audience to think that Hector has been slain. Hector, however, though badly stunned, is carried off the field and revived, if with difficulty, by his comrades. In Hector's absence—and as Zeus slumbers contentedly on—the Trojan rout begins (and is soon accelerated by the gruesome, panic-inducing slaughter of Ilioneus, at XIV.561–573). The battle will not be reversed until Hector's return to battle in book XV (beginning at line 301); the Greeks will respond to Hector as to a man miraculously restored to life (beginning at line 327).

Book XV: The Achaeans Desperate

1. (p. 252) "*. . . how little real good it does you / To . . . Seduce me to lie with you and make love*": Zeus, roused from his post-coital slumber, quickly realizes the implication of Hera's perfidy; she no longer simply resists his will (as she did in books I, II, and VIII) but actively plots against it. In response, Zeus invokes the very same rebellion that Sleep had earlier cited in his initial refusal of Hera's plans: the stormy transport of Heracles to Cos (XIV.281–290, with note 5 to book XIV above); but the emphasis now falls not upon Sleep's fear of punishment, but upon Zeus' extravagant prior punishment of Hera: his hand-to-foot binding of her by a golden chain. Though Zeus' response to Hera retains some of the comic energy of the "Deception of Zeus," his description of lashing and binding Hera likely references an underlying myth of cosmic strife between sky-god and earth-goddess. The "anvils" (Greek *akmones*) attached to Hera's ankles are themselves meteorites, signs of Zeus' punishing thunderbolt.

2. (p. 252) "*. . . it is by no will of mine that Poseidon . . . does damage to Trojans and Hector / And nothing but good for their foes*": Hera once again swears by the Styx (as she did in her persuasion of Sleep), but her words carefully sidestep essentials: Poseidon had intervened on the Achaeans' behalf of his own accord; she says nothing of her own actions to aid Poseidon. Perjury is avoided, and so is the truth.

3. (p. 253) "*. . . Thetis . . . pleading with me to honor her son, / Achilles, taker of towns*": In response to Hera's oath, Zeus foretells his overarching plan in the greatest detail yet—now including the death of Sarpedon, his own son. No longer immobilized by Hera's trick, Zeus reasserts his own authority as he prophecies the progress of his plan to honor Thetis. Zeus' speech, however, is unexpectedly conciliatory: He will not beat Hera or hang her from her ankles but will instead seek to incorporate her into his plans: She is to be the agent of Poseidon's acquiescence to Zeus' plan; the goal is now an Olympian unanimity in Zeus' will. Zeus' inclusion of the death of Sarpedon in his unfolding of events is itself a sacrifice to the cause of Olympian conciliation. All the immortals, Zeus included, must lose someone or something dear to them; thus, we next see that Ares must reconcile himself (under Athena's harsh tutelage) to the loss of his son Ascalaphus (XV.148–166).

4. (p. 257) *". . . then truly the rancorous breach between us / Will not be subject to healing!"*: Poseidon is reconciled to Zeus' rule with more difficulty than was Ares. He acquiesces only after a second reminder from Iris that Zeus is the elder—now given threatening force by an invocation of the Furies, enforcers of familial order and respect. Poseidon's sticking point of contention is the threat that Zeus poses to the balance of divine power. Though younger than Zeus, Poseidon stakes his claim on his brotherly equality with Zeus, as well as with Hades. According to the story of the drawing of lots, each of the three brothers received as their own the respective realms of the Sea, the Heavens, and the Underworld (with earth and Olympus as shared territory). Poseidon claims that he would stay in his realm if only Zeus would remain in his, but Iris' reiteration of the link between primogeniture and power finally prevails, and Poseidon abruptly retires into the sea—in much less grandiose fashion than that with which he emerged at the start of book XIII (lines 49–50).

5. (p. 261) *. . . O powerful Phoebus / You undid the Achaeans' hard toil and filled them with panic*: The Achaeans' hard labor in the building of their wall and the Trojans' grueling campaign against that wall and its defenders in book XII stand in marked contrast to the ease with which Apollo now breaches the wall—like a boy gleefully knocking down his sand castles. The present passage surely recalls the proem of book XII (see endnote 1 to book XII above).

6. (p. 262) *Patroclus . . . groaned aloud and slapped his thighs / With the flat of his hands . . .* : Slapping the thighs expresses extreme and pressing grief. Earlier in the poem, Asius (XII.170), then Ares, in grief for his son Ascalaphus (XV.129–130), used this gesture; this linked series will culminate at XVI.149, when Achilles slaps his thighs at the sight of fire on the Achaean ships. The present scene of Patroclus tending to Eurypylus rejoins that at the end of book XI (lines 902–920), where Patroclus' return to Achilles was interrupted by his pity for the wounded Eurypylus; his concern for the entirety of the Achaeans now sets him back in motion.

7. (pp. 267–268) *Zeus . . . was waiting to see the glare from a flaming ship, / For then . . . he would . . . give the Danaans glorious victory*: The poet prefaces the great and fearful victory of Hector with a recapitulation of Zeus' plan: Even as the poet anticipates Hector's coming triumph, he also reminds

his audience that Hector's glory (coupled with Zeus' favor) will be temporary, subordinate to Zeus' overarching plan to honor forever Thetis and her son.

Book XVI: The Death of Patroclus

1. (p. 272) *... Patroclus / Came up to Achilles ... weeping like a spring / Whose dark streams trickle down the rocky face of a cliff:* Patroclus' interrupted return to Achilles is now complete (see endnote 6 to book XV above). The comparison of Patroclus' tears to a spring of dark water recalls the tears of Agamemnon that began book IX (lines 15–16); and as in book IX, a supplication of Achilles now follows, which itself evokes two examples from Phoenix' book IX speech: First, as Meleager was supplicated by Cleopatra, so Achilles is now supplicated by the one dearest to him, Patroclus (see endnote 10 to book IX above); second, Patroclus' plea to Achilles might well be construed as analogous to the intervention of the Prayers, who (in Phoenix' allegory), if scorned, pray to Zeus for a renewed and decisive *ate* (see endnote 8 to book IX above). But we should also keep in mind that Achilles, in book IX, seems—in his concentrating wrath—to contemplate understandings and actions that, though shaped by the old stories and allegories, are no longer wholly in agreement with, or guided by, those same stories.

2. (p. 273) *"But if your heart is set on escaping some dire word / From Zeus, revealed to you by your goddess mother ..."*: Patroclus, in his concluding appeal to Achilles, takes up the very words of Nestor's exhortation to Patroclus in book XI, which follows upon the old man's account of his youthful exploits (lines 877–884): Is Achilles inhibited by some prophecy? If so, then let Patroclus go forth in Achilles' armor. In place of Nestor's account of boyhood cattle-raids, Patroclus charges Achilles with pitilessness: His parents are not Thetis and Peleus (whom he has just claimed to love), but the sea and the cliffs, so bereft is he of mortal care. Responsiveness to others, which Patroclus has exemplified in his healing and tendance of Eurypylus in books XI and XV (lines 904–913 and 447–451, with notes above), is now also the ground of Patroclus' indictment of Achilles and of his fatal appeal that he himself be permitted to return to the fight.

3. (p. 273) *"... nor has my goddess mother brought to me / Any such word from Zeus"*: This is an interpretative crux: Some readers, ancient and modern, have charged Achilles with a lack of full candor in his denial of any prophetic word from his mother, for at IX.471–478—the "Choice of Achilles," itself one of the most famous of Iliadic passages—Achilles spoke of Thetis' prophecy of alternate fates: a long life without renown in Phthia or a youthful death at Troy recompensed by "glory forever"; other readers, however, have stressed the human motivations of Homer's characters: They do not seek, and are not influenced by, prophetic advice, for such would diminish their mortal responsibility; prophecies are directly referred to only when their recollection is too late (see XVIII.8–12: "O let it not be . . ."); full revelation of Zeus' plan for Achilles does not take place until XVIII.109–111, when Achilles, "greatly moved," acknowledges his coming death.

4. (pp. 273–274) *"I will not, it seems, / Be filled with fierce anger forever, though I said I would not / Change my mind till the fighters were screaming about my own vessels"*: Another interpretative crux: Achilles acknowledges that he cannot remain ceaselessly wrathful, and yet he still does not return to battle but rather assents to Patroclus' plan (which originated with Nestor) to send Patroclus forth in his stead. One interpretation proposes that Achilles is simply holding himself to his word, as he announced it to Ajax and the Embassy at IX.747–759 (and see endnote 12 to book IX): He will not fight until the fire reaches his ships, which has not yet happened; Achilles, then, suffers for his own ethic of honesty. A second interpretation holds that Achilles, even while acknowledging that his wrath cannot be perpetual, clings relentlessly to his hatred of Agamemnon, who treated him as "some lowly contemptible tramp"; the price paid for Achilles' intransigence, his "tragic error," is the death of Patroclus. A final interpretative possibility is that Achilles recognizes that the moment to put aside his wrath has arrived, even as he honors Patroclus' request to aid the Achaeans; Achilles relinquishes his wrath by means of an act of friendship.

5. (pp. 274–275) *". . . Deeply I wish . . . That just myself and Patroclus might live and alone / Succeed in reducing this . . . sacred city / To rubble and dust"*: To Patroclus' earlier question about what profit Achilles might be to men to come (XVI.35–36), Achilles responds with a demonic prayer for the destruction of all Achaeans and Trojans except for himself and Patroclus. And to Patroclus' appeal to the love or comradeship of the army (Greek *philotes*), Achilles responds that the only love that now binds—the only love worthy of existence—is that between himself and Patroclus. In Achilles' prayer, the unconscious—where love and death intertwine, which knows neither yes nor no—erupts.

6. (p. 276) *. . . and Patroclus / Put on the glittering bronze*: For arming scenes, see endnote 3 to book III above. The assemblage of Patroclus' borrowed regalia highlights elements that likely derive from the folktale motif of three magical gifts: invincible armor, a spear that always returns to its hero, and immortal horses. Achilles' armor will have to be knocked from Patroclus before he can be killed (XVI.913–931), while Achilles' mighty ash spear proves too weighty for Patroclus to lift, foretelling Patroclus' doomed effort to take over Achilles' role. To Achilles' immortal horses, Automedon adds, as a trace-horse, the mortal Pedasus, who will be killed by Sarpedon: The mix of mortal with immortal horses surely also bodes ill, even as it also suggests something of Patroclus' own unstable admixture of elements.

7. (p. 279) *"I pray let him come back to these swift ships and me . . . And with him bring back his close-fighting Myrmidon comrades"*: In his solemn prayer, Achilles reminds Zeus of his positive response to Achilles' prayer from book I: The Achaeans have, indeed, been smote (Achilles' present prayer to Zeus follows the model set by Chryses' second prayer to Apollo in book I, following Apollo's striking of the Achaeans with plague [see lines 531–537]). By invoking Zeus' prior favorable response, Achilles hopes again to influence Zeus, to bring Zeus into accord with his own desire. But Zeus' plan no longer aligns with Achilles' desire, nor with the possibilities of the traditional hero's life. Achilles prays that Patroclus might gain, in the fighting, both glory and a safe return—the two poles of Achilles' "choice" in book IX and two elements that cannot both structure a hero's life. In another sense, Achilles prays to Zeus to affirm Achilles' own prior double injunction to Patroclus upon sending him forth to battle (XVI.104–107): "to win great glory," but not to "get carried away / In the heat of conflict and slaughter"; as we will soon see, the two commands cannot coexist.

8. (p. 284) *". . . and you / Will surely stir up fierce resentment among the immortals"*: The death of sons and the grief of fathers has been a recurrent source of pathos in the *Iliad*'s account of fallen warriors; that theme is now enacted on the divine level. In response to Zeus' sorrow and vacillation about the death of Sarpedon (which Zeus himself foretold at XV.71–74; see also V.733–738 and XII.434–435, where Sarpedon is, in each instance, saved for his present fate), Hera invokes the finality of human mortality, and, crucially, she holds Zeus to the divine compromise that was enunciated in book XV: All the gods must lose something beloved; Zeus, as ruler of the gods, must make a paradigmatic sacrifice of his own beloved son. If Zeus should fail to uphold the order of the cosmos, itself predicated upon an irreversible human mortality, chaos would ensue: All the gods would take to the battlefield.

9. (p. 290) *". . . the dead's due rites, a proper / Entombment, with mound and memorial pillar"*: Sarpedon's body was earlier described as unrecognizable, covered by weapons, blood, and dust (XVI.728–730); the befouling of Sarpedon's body anticipates the mutilation with which Patroclus' corpse will be threatened as well as the actual savagery inflicted upon Hector's corpse. Sarpedon's corpse is, however, rescued by Apollo and by Sleep and Death, under orders from Zeus. The terrifying violence of

the battlefield, in which warriors are not only killed but their corpses mutilated, gives way to divine cleansing and to a mysterious transport as gentle (and welcome) as sleep. The "mound and memorial pillar" that Zeus promises foresee the establishment of a heroic tomb in Lycia, at which cult honors will be dedicated to Sarpedon; later literary and epigraphical evidence does, indeed, attest to local honors in Lycia for Sarpedon (and for Glaucus).

10. (p. 291) *Three times Patroclus / Sprang up . . . and three times / Apollo battered him back . . . :* Patroclus' triple attack upon the Wall of Troy, countered by Apollo's triple defense, is a narrative pattern that we first saw at V.482–496, in Diomedes' attack upon Apollo; we will see the same pattern again, at XX.497–498, where Apollo has already swept Hector away. In each instance, the hero is said to be "like a demon"—or, "like something more than a man"—upon his fourth charge. To make the fourth charge is, then, to surpass a mortal limit, to bring oneself into direct conflict with the god—who is, in all three cases, Apollo. In book V, Diomedes retreats following Apollo's warning at the fourth charge (thus barely saving his life); here, in book XVI, Patroclus too retreats after the fourth charge, but only temporarily, for the pattern will soon repeat itself at lines 910–914, where Apollo proceeds to contrive Patroclus' death. Achilles—whose permanent condition is "like something more than a man"—will also be killed through Apollo's machinations (though outside the *Iliad* itself).

11. (p. 292) *"I had no idea they had / Such performers in Troy":* If Patroclus' pity—his healing capacity—has been the leading element of his prior characterization, his cruel taunt over the body of Cebriones, as well as the escalating blood-frenzy of his killings, dramatizes that Patroclus is no less susceptible than his comrades to the berserker aspects of the warrior. Achilles' parting advice to Patroclus—to "come back" once the Trojans have been driven from the ships (XVI.101–102)—proves fatally impossible, for the trajectory of the warrior in his *aristeia* moves inevitably toward a furious transgressive violence that wreaks death even as it pollutes the warrior himself. The warrior who is "like something more than a man" is also like something less than human—defiling and finally defiled: This is the state that epic poetry itself must purify.

12. (p. 295) *". . . while Hector came third in my slaying":* In his death throes, Patroclus knows exactly who his slayers were, which he could not have known at the climax of battle itself, for Apollo was invisible, while Euphorbus struck from behind, then disappeared into the ranks. The nearness of death makes Patroclus prophetic, and the accuracy of his account of his own death vouchsafes his prophecy that Hector will die at Achilles' hands. Hector's victory precipitates Hector's death.

Book XVII: The Valiant Deeds of Menelaus

1. (p. 300) *"So something, at least, would be saved"*: On the form of the warrior's monologue, see Odysseus' speech at XI.459–468, with endnote 3 to book XI above. Menelaus begins with an acknowledgment of his own responsibility for Patroclus' death—beneath which might also lurk a deeper sense of his own responsibility for the war as well as his own ineffectiveness in prosecuting it. He further acknowledges the blame that others would cast upon him for now abandoning Patroclus, but then—extraordinarily, and in marked contrast to the other monologists cited above—he withdraws, seeking the help of Ajax. The general pattern of withdrawal and call for aid will recur throughout book XVII, as will the use of rebuke as a goad to action.

2. (p. 301) *". . . for he is much stronger than you"*: Sarpedon's dying words were an appeal to Glaucus, his comrade from Lycia, to recover his armor (XVI.561–572); following Sarpedon's death (and after being healed by Apollo), Glaucus rallied the Trojan forces. In this speech of rebuke, Glaucus' grief for his lost comrade leads to angry abuse of Hector and to the threat to return home with the remaining Lycians. Glaucus' conviction of the cowardice and ingratitude of Hector and the Trojans, freely developed amid thoughts of the lost beloved, bears comparison to Achilles' response to Odysseus in book IX.

3. (p. 302) *. . . armor he had from his father*: The armor of Achilles was a gift from his father, Peleus, who himself received the panoply (full suit of armor) from the gods. Hector, like Patroclus before him, secures his own doom by donning the immortal armor (as Zeus' immediately following prophecy reiterates). The gifts of the gods are, it seems, intended only for their original recipients (and their descendants); but the divine arms also prove irresistible for those who would "be" Achilles, whether first for Patroclus in his beneficent desire to save the Achaeans and now for Hector, who is driven by a densely compacted set of emotions and motives: resentment at Glaucus' chastening rebuke, the desire to claim (and extend) divine favor, desperate need to save Troy, and heroic vainglory.

4. (p. 304) *Zeus . . . hated to see / His body become the delight of his enemies' dogs*: With this evocation of Zeus' care for Patroclus as well as of the dread fate that threatens the unprotected body, the battle for Patroclus' corpse recommences in earnest; it will not be settled until XVIII.238, by Achilles' intervention. The extraordinary length of the battle for Patroclus' corpse, in its brutality and animal similes, well dramatizes the tendency of Homer's warriors to become the beast—preeminently, the

dog or jackal—that they themselves most fear (the extraordinary simile of the Myrmidons and the wolves at XVI.184–192 anticipates this
theme); as well, an audience remains in prolonged anticipation of
Achilles' response to his comrade's death (Achilles' ignorance of Patroclus' death at lines XVII.474–485).

5. (p. 309) . . . *still / As a pillar of stone on the grave of some dead man or woman, /
Bowing their heads to the ground:* At the very center of book XVII stand
Achilles' immortal horses, as immobile as a grave stele in their mourning for Patroclus (which foreshadows their inevitable mourning for
Achilles). Zeus then proceeds to read (as it were) that central stele in
his following reflections upon the "wretched" condition of humans,
so keenly aware of their own mortality. Zeus' pity, however, is more for
the horses than for the humans, for the immortal horses have permitted themselves to grieve for mortals.

6. (p. 317) *And there was no respite at all from the horrible war:* With the sending-
forth of Antilochus to Achilles and with this final chaotic scene of
fighting, the absence of Achilles is drawing to a close, as is the battle
narrative that has dominated the previous ten books, with the exception of book IX. The impasse evident in the fighting over Patroclus'
corpse is set to be broken by the vengeful return of Achilles.

Book XVIII: The Shield of Achilles

1. (p. 318) *Truly, / Gallant Patroclus must now be dead:* We have not seen Achilles
since his prayer to Zeus for Patroclus' safe return (XVI.274–291, with
endnote 7 to book XVI above). In the monologue that opens book
XVIII, Achilles fears what an audience has long known: Patroclus is
dead. The evident rout of the Achaeans signals to Achilles that Patroclus
must have perished. As well, Achilles now recalls Thetis' prophetic
words that Patroclus would die at Troy before Achilles—a clarification
of the prophecy as reported at XVII.480–483, where it was understood
to mean that Achilles and Patroclus would not take Troy together (and
where Achilles seemed to understand that he himself would die first).
The full recollection and clarification of Thetis' prophecy—namely,
that Patroclus will die first—only comes when it is devastatingly too
late. The confusion and late memory that surrounds Thetis' prophecy
serves to ensure that Achilles' motivations are only human—limited by
partial knowledge and expectant hopes.

2. (p. 319) . . . *Antilochus . . . held / The hands of heart-grieved Achilles, for fear that
he might / Draw a blade and cut his own throat:* Gestures of mourning and in-
timations of Achilles' own death now merge. The befouling of head

and of clothes while rolling in the dust is a sign of mourning, even as
it is also suggestive of the warrior's death. The lamentation of the
Nereid chorus that follows, as well as the particular lament of Thetis at
lines 59–67: ("Here me, O Nereids . . ."), also suggests that it is
Achilles who is now mourned as much as Patroclus. Thetis' cradling of
Achilles' head upon her arrival at the ships is also a gesture of mourning; she holds Achilles as if he were already a corpse.

3. (p. 320) *"Then soon let me die! since I was not there to help / My friend when he died"*:
With these terse lines, among the most moving in the poem, Achilles accepts his own death; the meaning of Thetis' prophecy is now crystalline,
as is Achilles' acceptance of it. He will return to battle not for gifts or
kingships but to avenge the loss of his beloved. As Achilles acknowledges
in his prior exchange with Thetis, Zeus has granted Achilles' prayers, but
only with the sacrifice of the one companion whose love bound Achilles
to the mortal world. Apart from Patroclus—and now forever separated
from Patroclus—Achilles is, as he goes on to assert, "just so much / Useless weight to burden the earth" (lines 116–117).

4. (p. 321) *". . . for I will have made them / Know what it means for me to be present
in battle"*: Achilles speaks of the coming mourning of the Trojan widows
even as he himself lies prostrate, surrounded by the grieving Nereids.
Achilles reasserts his place as warrior—and his image foreshadows the
Fall of Troy—but in his grief for Patroclus he seems also to identify
himself with the inconsolable widow. Our perspective oscillates rapidly
between the heroic battle for glory and the devastation that the battle
wreaks.

5. (p. 321) *Then Zeus-loved Achilles / Got up, and about his shoulders Athena flung /
The bright-tasseled aegis . . .*: As he rises from his prostrate position of
mourning, Achilles' withdrawal comes to an awe-filled end. This is
Achilles' apotheosis, the momentary culmination of his desire for immortality. Athena herself arms the naked Achilles with the divine aegis,
and the goddess wreathes his head with a golden cloud, which is otherwise only associated with divinities; the fire that burns from Achilles'
head is elsewhere used by Zeus to subdue the Titans. The triple-scream
of Achilles (XVIII.254–258) is itself a deadly force, killing twelve Trojans and throwing their army into rout (thus freeing Patroclus' corpse);
and the scream is a response to the loss of the beloved Patroclus—an
intensification of the mourning cries upon the beach. The force that
Achilles' scream unlooses is so daemonic that the cosmos itself is dis-
rupted: Hera, fearful of utter chaos, pushes the Sun down early—and,
at last, the Great Day of Battle comes to a stunning conclusion.

6. (p. 326) *They lauded / Hector and his bad advice, but not one man / Had praise for
Polydamas, although his counsel was wise*: The poet unambiguously signals
Hector's error. Exulting in the victories of the day and still confident of

Zeus' favor, Hector vaunts that he can now defeat even Achilles—if Achilles really has even returned. Borne along by Hector's hopes, the Trojans assent to his counsel to remain on the Trojan plain rather than to retreat behind the safety of the city-wall. And so the Trojans are destroyed by Achilles on the following day.

7. (p. 331) *He made lovely images there / Of earth and heaven . . . :* For Achilles, Hephaestus forges a great round shield upon the model of those that the other heroes have carried: a shield of multiple layers stretched over a lighter frame, fronted by decorated bronze. But the divinely wrought Shield of Achilles quickly leaves its precedents behind so as to become a dazzling display of the poet's own art—now deployed not in the representation of the heroic order, but of a non-heroic world, which we have previously glimpsed only in the similes. On the Shield of Achilles, the disparate abundance of similes scattered throughout the poem is shaped into a coherent and ordered whole. Hephaestus begins his work with the central ring of the Shield, which depicts the heavenly bodies. These are the fixed signs, whose regular, observable progress through the heavens orders the rhythms and regularities of human life and the seasons of the agricultural year.

8. (p. 331) *On it he wrought / Two beautiful cities . . . :* The second ring of the Shield (from the center) depicts a city at peace and a city at war. The emphasis falls upon cultural and political practice and mediation: The wedding and adjudication scenes present the possibility of political unity through, first, the making of kinship, then through the possibility of political adjudication of communal strife. In the city at war, we also see the possibility of collective action in the debates of the council and in the planning and execution of the ambush. For further interpretative suggestions on this ring of the Shield, see the introduction.

9. (p. 333) *And there on the shield / He depicted the huge estate of a king, whereon / His workers were reaping . . . :* On the third and central ring of the concentric design, Hephaestus depicts the farmer's year: ploughing, reaping, vintage, and fallow seasons. While the first ring presented the world of nature and the second the world of human culture (as kinship and as politics), the middle ring displays man's potentially productive relation with the natural world—a relation wholly excluded from the main narrative of the *Iliad*.

10. (p. 334) *And on it the famous lame god / Made with great skill a dancing-floor:* On the fourth and penultimate ring, Hephaestus returns to the depiction of the cultural world, but now as art. The dance is pure motion; the community depicted is a joyous one. It is the genius of the *Iliad*-poet to remind us that if the cultural work depicted on the second ring— the wedding and the court—is what we need to live with each other in something close to peace (in private and in public), we yet also need

artful communion and release; while the second ring depicts the culture that we need, the fourth ring depicts the culture that we want.

11. (p. 334) . . . *all about the rim of the massive shield / He put the powerful stream of the river Oceanus*: The final, encircling ring of the Shield repeats the pure motion of the fourth ring, though now in the realm of nature, and presents a contrast to the first ring, which depicted nature in its fixity and regularity.

Book XIX: The Reconciliation

1. (p. 337) *"Now I . . . shall put an end / To my wrath. It would hardly become me to go on this way / Forever"*: Achilles' language and sentiment is quite close to that at XVI.72–74 (and see endnote 4 to book XVI). In the earlier passage, the recognition that anger cannot be fierce forever led to the sending forth of Patroclus. With Patroclus now dead, and with Achilles suffering for that death, Achilles himself will venture forth. Though Achilles' speech is one of reconciliation with Agamemnon and with the Achaean camp (he does not speak of Patroclus or of the motive of revenge in this speech), his imperiousness remains: It was Achilles who called the Assembly, and it is Achilles who now gives a battle-order to Agamemnon.

2. (p. 337) *"Very often you men of Achaea have had / Your say and spoken against me, though really I am not / To blame"*: Agamemnon, in response to Achilles' expression of remorse to the assembled Achaeans, pronounces himself blameless: Zeus, Fate, the Fury, and, most especially, *Ate* ("Sweet Folly") gained control of him; Agamemnon has blamed *Ate* before, in his false account of Zeus in book II and in his sincere and desperate proposal to flee Troy in book IX (see II.131–132 and IX.132, with endnotes to each passage). In hindsight, a foolish and disastrous act, otherwise inexplicable, is blamed upon an impulse from without. Agamemnon proceeds to offer a lengthy etiology of *Ate*—and why she wanders among mortals—in his retelling of the birth and bondage of Heracles. Throughout his account, Agamemnon draws a parallel, doubtless displeasing to Achilles, between himself and Zeus, but ignores the parallel suggested by the story of Heracles and Eurystheus—the man of better nature enslaved to the man of kingly power.

3. (p. 339) *"Renowned . . . Agamemnon, / The gifts are yours to give or withhold"*: Though *Ate* is to blame, Agamemnon does offer gifts to Achilles; the social practice of compensation—the acceptance of juridical responsibility—needs still to be enacted. Achilles, however, no less than in book IX, is unmoved by the old stories and will not accept Agamemnon's gifts. No less than before, Achilles' acceptance of Agamemnon's compensatory gifts would legitimate Agamemnon's authority, as well as the underlying economy of heroic honor. The desire for revenge drives Achilles' return to the Achaean camp, but he remains resistant to the social forms and obligations that construct and govern that camp.

4. (p. 340) *"It would be much better . . . to take care of these things / At some other time . . . when my own spirit is somewhat appeased"*: Odysseus has diplomatically proposed a transfer of gifts and a swearing of oaths; he has also vigorously and at surprising length asserted the necessity of the feast so as to refresh and fortify the troops for the coming battle; Agamemnon approves. Achilles again defers the gifts and, now, the oaths (when the gifts are brought to his shelter, he makes no acknowledgment of them); as for the feast, whose practical necessity is so passionately described by Odysseus, Achilles will not join in that either. To Odysseus' appeals to the life-sustaining necessity of food, Achilles, now death-bound, is impervious. The feast, for Achilles, is neither an occasion of collective commensality nor even of biological sustenance; what does sustain is the desire for revenge.

5. (p. 343) *"Hence I weep / For your death without ceasing, for you the forever gentle"*: Briseis, the object of the initial dispute between Achilles and Agamemnon, previously a mute sign of the honor of male heroes, now speaks. The history that she recounts is one of escalating loss, including that of her husband. But Patroclus, "forever gentle" in his healing role, had assuaged Briseis' grief with the promise of a wedding in Phthia to Achilles, where she might have recovered a social place and a social world. With the death of Patroclus and, soon, that of Achilles, Briseis' displacement and grief—her suffering of the depredations of war— becomes, again, her fixed fate.

6. (p. 344) *. . . my own Neoptolemus, / If indeed that godlike boy is still alive*: Achilles makes the extraordinary assertion that the death of Patroclus is more grievous to him than that of father or of son. The prior limit of imaginable grief, the loss of male kin, is here surpassed by the loss of the companion in love. To eat would, in Achilles' formulation, be a betrayal of that love, for it would be a tacit admission that life goes on in the absence of the beloved.

Book XX: The Gods at War

1. (p. 347) *But powerful Zeus . . . Bade Themis call the gods to a meeting . . .* : At the end of book XIX, Achilles had armed in his new panoply, had mounted his chariot, and was setting off to lead the Achaeans (who have by now had their feast) into battle. His *aristeia* is now interrupted by a council of the gods, at which Zeus revokes the prohibition that he had established at the divine council that began book VIII: The gods are now free to enter the melee. Zeus' reasons are twofold: Without the gods on the field, Achilles will too soon, earlier than is fated, take Troy; and Zeus, who now watches from the Olympian heights, anticipates a spectacularly entertaining contest: the comedic struggles of the gods; the piteous, tragic struggles of the mortals. We might also suggest that the disordering presence of the gods upon the battlefield—at XX.67–73, Hades itself might burst open—is especially appropriate to the return of Achilles: As the overthrowing son that Zeus avoided by marrying Thetis to Peleus (see endnote 7 to book I above), Achilles, in his return to battle, with its cosmic and potentially chaos-inducing response, evokes the cosmos-overturning battle that Zeus has forever precluded—and that Zeus now manages, as if the artist-director of a private spectacle.

2. (p. 349) *So gods advanced to meet gods:* With the gods now paired off against each other, like boxers awaiting the bell, the poet suddenly returns our attention to Achilles. The narrative of the *Theomachy,* "The Battle of the Gods," will not resume until XXI.431 (where it will take a rather more comic turn). Achilles' *aristeia*—the hero himself is searching relentlessly for Hector—is now rejoined, but only to be interrupted again: Rather than the usual series of successful duels, Achilles is now involved in a lengthy and inconclusive battle with Aeneas (on whom, see endnote 9 to book II and endnote 4 to book XIII above).

3. (p. 352) *"But I claim descent from courageous Anchises, my father, / And Aphrodite herself":* Achilles has just taunted Aeneas for his lack of favor within the Trojan ruling house ("Priam would not give the kingship to you. King Priam / Has sons of his own," lines 205–206). Aeneas, following his complaints about needless verbosity, responds to Achilles with an extended discourse on genealogical themes. He first matches his descent from Aphrodite against Achilles' descent from Thetis (both heroes are "half-divines"), then offers a full recitation of the Trojan genealogical line. Aeneas' recitation, coming at a point in the poem where images of Troy's impending destruction have been cumulating (most impressively in the similes on the fire that shoots from Achilles' head upon his appearance at the trench, XVIII.232–239), serves as a memorial of the entire Trojan line, which is soon to be utterly destroyed—with the exception of Aeneas himself (see note immediately below).

4. (p. 355) *". . . Aeneas shall soon rule / The Trojans, and after him the sons of his sons, / Great princes yet to be born":* Poseidon's prophecy of Aeneas' coming rule over the Trojans reverses the lack of honor in which his line is now held. Though the line that descends from Ilus through Priam and his sons will be destroyed for Paris' abduction of Helen, the descendants of Aphrodite through the blameless line of Anchises and Aeneas will be saved (see, too, the Homeric *Hymn to Aphrodite* 196–197, which likewise prophecies the survival of Aeneas' line). The contrast between the fates of Achilles and Aeneas, both goddess-born, is instructive: Achilles dies as a youthful hero and will be immortalized in the honor—the poetic fame—that the bard bestows; Aeneas, in contrast, will survive Troy's fall so as to be immortalized in the city-founding and cultural work of his own descendants; the former is immortalized in the timelessness of art, the latter in the ongoing works of history. (Virgil's version of Poseidon's prophecy is: hic domus Aeneae cunctis dominabitur oris / et nati natorum et qui nascentur ab illis ("There the house of Aeneas will reign over all lands, even his children's children and those who will be born of them"), *Aeneid* 3.97–98).

5. (p. 357) . . . *Achilles . . . charged / Mid the Trojans, screaming his awesome war-cry:* Achilles' *aristeia*, much interrupted, now begins in earnest with a massacre; the mounting carnage is vividly evoked by the image of the chariot wheel that lacerates the corpse beneath (an image reiterated in greater detail in the final lines of this book). Achilles' killing of the especially youthful, especially beloved Polydorus, son of Priam, draws Hector back to the forefront of the battle.

6. (p. 359) *But Apollo caught Hector up, with all the ease / Of a god, and wrapped him in cloud:* Achilles is, once again, thwarted by divine intervention; even Achilles' power, it seems, is limited by the fated time for the Fall of Troy. On the immediately following triple attack, see endnote 10 to book XVI. While the fourth attack has, in our prior examples, placed the hero in fatal danger, Achilles will emerge from Apollo's mist baffled, but with his killing energy redoubled; "like a demon," he will slaughter the Trojans until, as is prophesied—but deferred—within the *Iliad*, Apollo (and Paris) will kill him before the gates of Troy.

Book XXI: The Struggle of Achilles and the River

1. (p. 363) *Lycaon then pleaded, with one hand clasping / Achilles' knees, with the other his sharp-pointed spear:* For prior scenes of supplication, see endnote 1 to book VI above. Achilles' encounter with Lycaon is the culmination of supplication scenes involving "minor" characters; as well, it prepares the audience for the plea of Hector in book XXII. Lycaon, moreover, has a prior claim upon Achilles' religious scruples: While Lycaon was Achilles' captive (as both Achilles and Lycaon recount, Achilles did—in the time before the death of Patroclus—respect the pleas of suppliants), he received hospitality ("Demeter's bread") from him; the breaking of bread between captor and captive creates a bond of guest-friendship between the

two; this aspect of Lycaon's story perhaps anticipates the shared meal in book XXIV between Achilles and Priam (who is Lycaon's father).

2. (p. 364) *"One morning or evening or noon / Will surely come when some man shall kill me in battle, / Either by hurling his spear or shooting a shaft / From the bowstring"*: Achilles acknowledges Lycaon's claims as suppliant and guest-friend by calling Lycaon "friend" (line 132, Greek *philos*). Yet, in Achilles' present logic, all are preeminently "friend"—or "dear"—to death. Claims of religious scruple, as also claims of rank and status—Achilles, after all, is a goddess' son—are rendered meaningless by the brute fact of death itself: As Patroclus has died, so must Hector; as Hector, so Achilles; as Achilles, so all mortals. Achilles, in his demonic presence upon the battlefield, has himself become death for the Trojans, the agent of their fate as mortals.

3. (p. 364) *". . . and many a wave-hidden fish shall dart up / Beneath the dark ripple to eat the fat of Lycaon"*: Though the haunting threat that the hero's body will be devoured by dogs and birds is never literally fulfilled in the *Iliad*, Achilles does feed the body of Lycaon (and of Asteropaeus, soon to follow) to the eels and the fishes. If death in the river perhaps holds some possibility of purification that might lessen the horror of consumption by the fishes, that possibility is quickly eliminated by the complaint of Xanthus, the river-god, that his waters have been polluted by the slaughter that Achilles has wreaked within it.

4. (p. 366) *"Very hard it is for the son / Of a river to vie with a child of Cronos' son"*: Achilles, vaunting over the corpse of the ambidextrous Asteropaeus, now responds to his opponent's initial boast of being born of a river goddess: Achilles is a son of Zeus, with whom no mere son of a river can contend; even Oceanus, the source of all the world's rivers, is no match for Zeus' lightning. Achilles' attempt to assert Zeus' paternity is, perhaps, motivated by the success of Aeneas' claims of superior descent from Aphrodite, which were acknowledged by Poseidon's rescue. By invoking his grandfather Aeacus' descent from Zeus, Achilles would play a genealogical trump card, though he can do so only by ignoring his mother's association with the element of water and by invoking his grandfather rather than his father.

5. (p. 368) *"O Father Zeus, why is it / That none of the gods will pity my plight and save me / From this dread river?"*: Achilles' boast of genealogical superiority to any river has been put to the test by the enraged Scamander and has been proven false. The river has overwhelmed him, seemingly sweeping away even the possibility of a hero's death before Troy; what awaits is an ignoble death no better than that of "some poor pig-herding boy"—so much for Achilles' genealogical boasts! Likewise, Achilles' prayer to Zeus, of whose paternity he just boasted, will not be answered; rather, Poseidon and Athena, in mortal form, will offer Achilles encouragement. The defeat of Achilles' claims to be the son of Zeus again evokes the underlying mythology of Zeus' avoidance of union with Thetis (on which see endnote 1 to book XX and endnote 7 to book I); if Achilles were the son of Zeus, he would be the ruler of the cosmos. The battle with the river, in all its disordering and polluting force, evokes the possibility of Achilles' descent from Zeus, only so as to reject it decisively.

6. (p. 369) *... he sent his towering wave, churning / With foam and blood and corpses, raging down / On Achilles:* The process begun by Achilles' slaughter-drive of half the Trojans into the river and by his feeding of Lycaon and Asteropaeus to the fishes reaches a pitch of pollution, which then provokes yet more pollution. Only the fire of Hephaestus—which now engages in an elemental battle with the water of the river—can finally succeed in purifying the Scamandrus' streams; the higher purifying element burns the corpses and restores the prior beauty of the river (XXI.427–428).

7. (p. 371) *And Zeus, from where he sat high up on Olympus, / Heard the clashing and laughed to himself, delighted / To see the immortals at odds with each other:* With the laughter of Zeus, the *Theomachy*, which was interrupted at XX.84, where the gods were paired off and champing for action, resumes. The bouts that follow, with the exception of that between Apollo and Poseidon, prove well worthy of Zeus' laughter. The knockabout antics of the gods offer a brief respite from the defilement of Achilles' battle with the river and the upcoming duel with Hector. The essential frivolity of the Homeric gods is contrasted to the heroizing efforts of the mortals (a point acknowledged at the conclusion of the one non-comic encounter, between Poseidon and Apollo, where the brevity of human life becomes the reason for the gods' withdrawal). Finally, the comic battles present a last defeat of the pro-Trojan gods (Ares, Aphrodite, Artemis, Hermes) prior to the Fall of Troy. Only Apollo retains his dignity; he departs to protect the fleeing Trojans, but even his role is limited to assuring that Achilles does not sack Troy before its appointed time (XXI.586–589).

Book XXII: The Death of Hector

1. (p. 380) *"... surely nothing more foul than this can come upon / Wretched mortals":* Priam concludes his appeal to Hector with a vivid description of the very worst death that can befall a Homeric man: to be devoured by his own dogs before his own house, exposed and disgraced among his own people; the proper orders of both house and community are betrayed and overturned. The warrior's role, which finds its origin in the necessity of the community's defense, is also associated with a savagery that reduces humans to predatory dogs and that destroys the constituent values of civilization itself. In his appeal to Hector to return within the walls of Troy rather than to face Achilles, Priam threatens Hector with the guilt of killing a parent; so too—in the following speech—does Hecuba, who, in exposing her breast to her son, makes her appeal in the most literal of ways.

2. (p. 381) "*'Great Hector put all / Of his trust in his own brute strength and destroyed the whole army'*": In the first portion of his soliloquy, Hector recalls his error in rejecting the advice of Polydamas at XVIII.353–355 (on which see endnote 6 to book XVIII): The Trojans did remain on the Trojan plain, where they were then destroyed on the following day by Achilles. Hector's sense of shame before his community causes him now to remain outside the wall. His words also recall his dialogue with Andromache at VI.486–487 (on which, see endnote 8 to book VI). Hector had rejected Andromache's plea that he remain within the wall by invoking his sense of *aidos*—of reverence and shame before the community. He now invokes that same sense of *aidos*—before Polydamas, before the women of Troy, before the nameless inferior man— to explain his inability to return within the walls of Troy; as Andromache had foreseen, Hector's own strength will be his downfall.

3. (p. 381) "*. . . such as / A boy and his girl might have with each other—boy / And his girl indeed*": As Hector feels himself isolated from the community, the preeminent source of his strength and identity, he falls into fantasy: first, of somehow arranging a settlement between Trojans and Achaeans, then—most startlingly—of approaching Achilles as a virgin girl approaches a boy in a scene of courtship. Having lost his social identity as warrior of Troy, he imagines himself to be "some hopeless woman."

4. (p. 386) "*There are no faithful oaths between lions and men . . . But they are always at fatal odds with each other*": To Hector's proposal that each pledge to the other that he will return the vanquished man's corpse, Achilles responds that oaths are not possible between beings of different species; Achilles will treat Hector as the wild animal treats his prey. Hesiod, in his *Works and Days* (275–279), provides one commentary upon Achilles' claims: "Cast these things into your heart / And listen now to justice; forget about force. / This law the son of Cronos set out for people: Fish and beasts and winged birds / eat each other, since they have no justice. / To men he gave justice; it is best by far."

5. (p. 387) *. . . the beautiful / Gear he had stripped from mighty Patroclus when he / Cut him down*: When Achilles looks at Hector, he sees his own armor (which Hector had put on at XVII.225–231, and see endnote 3 to book XVII). He is, thus, reminded of Patroclus, even as he puts the spear to an image

of his former self. Virgil recalls and transforms this scene at the close of the *Aeneid*, when Aeneas kills Turnus upon catching sight of the belt that Turnus had stripped from Pallas (*Aeneid* 12.940–952).

6. (pp. 387–388) *"I only wish I were savagely wrathful / Enough to hack up your corpse and eat it raw . . . but dogs and birds shall devour you, / Bones and all"*: This is perhaps the most horrific speech in the *Iliad*, though one for which we have been well prepared; see Achilles' preceding image of the lion at XXII.301, his treatment of the bodies of Lycaon (XXI.151–156) and Asteropaeus (XXI.234–238), as well as Zeus' ascription to Hera of the desire to eat "old Priam raw / Along with . . . all the rest of the Trojans" at IV.40–41; finally, Hecuba will express a desire to eat Achilles' liver at XXIV.250–251. In Achilles' present speech to Hector, he addresses Hector as "dog"; but note that in a preceding simile, the poet has compared Achilles to a dog (XXII.213–216, "as when a hound . . ."). The relation between predator and prey is continuous and reversible: As the warrior marshals from within himself the predatory energies that his role requires, he becomes himself a beast—and always potential prey to another.

7. (p. 389) *. . . and the once so handsome head was defiled / With foul dust*: The evocation of Hector's prior godlike beauty and status in Troy is immediately followed by Achilles' defiling of Hector's body. For Achilles, it is as if killing Hector is not enough to satisfy his desire for vengeance, but he must again and again enact the conquest of Hector by continually despoiling his body (which the gods will protect). The resolution of this impasse—the release of Hector—is, then, central to the final book of the poem.

8. (p. 390) *. . . far from all baths strong fire-eyed Athena had cut / Hector down by the hand of Achilles*: Andromache was last seen in the final scene of book VI, where Hector had instructed her to return to her loom and to her supervision of the household maids, while he returned to the battle (lines 541–544). These are precisely the activities in which Andromache is now engaged, with the further detail—of excruciating pathos—that she has ordered the water for Hector's bath to be heated. With the casting off of the headdress that she had received at her wedding and with her imagining of the fate of Astyanax, the full desolation of her future is vividly anticipated.

Book XXIII: The Funeral Games for Patroclus

1. (p. 394) *. . . wash from his flesh the horrible gore*: The inconsolable, irresolvable quality of Achilles' grief, even after the slaying of Hector, is suggested by his unwillingness to wash the gore of the battle from his body. Achilles insists, as it were, upon his own impurity, his own distance from the purifying activities of his comrades. Likewise, he remains apart from the feast and its commensalities, even as he now arranges a sacrifice and feast for the other Achaeans. And, finally, he continues in his despoliation of Hector's body, futilely seeking resolution through the repetition of his own violence and anger.

2. (p. 395) *"But bury me soon as you can, that I / May get within Hades' gates"*: In the opening of his speech, Patroclus' ghost states the ancient belief that cremation or burial permitted the ghost to enter Hades; once the body was buried, the ghost could no longer depart Hades. Throughout the speech, Patroclus' ghost recalls, if enigmatically, details that evoke the quality of his former life with Achilles: In life, the two "sat apart" from their comrades, where they made private plans; in death, Patroclus' ghost now asks that that separate unity be maintained: The ashen remains of the two should be mingled in a single urn. Patroclus' ghost concludes his speech with a recollection of his own boyhood arrival in Phthia, as a fugitive from the slaying of a playmate over a game a dice (an ironic commentary on "gentle Patroclus"?). Once in Phthia, Patroclus—like Phoenix before him (see IX.500–508, with endnote 7 to book IX)—received far more from Peleus than the conventions of asylum required: While Phoenix received a surrogate son to love, Patroclus receives a friend who will be beloved.

3. (p. 398) *And killing with bronze twelve valiant sons of the Trojans— / An evil act he had planned in his heart . . .* : Achilles' premeditated sacrifice of the twelve Trojans (prepared for at XVIII.382–384 and XXI.29–30) is an act of exceptional violence, going far beyond anything that Patroclus' ghost instructed and further dramatizing the irremediable quality of Achilles' mourning: The blood-price of Patroclus is paid by the lives of twelve others, yet still Achilles remains without peace, lacking any relation to the world that is not articulated through violence; even after the sacrifice of the twelve Trojans, Achilles continues his boast that he will feed Hector to the dogs.

4. (p. 400) *But Achilles restrained them and seated the troops in a large / Open space where the funeral games were to be*: Following the cremation of Patroclus' body and the heaping up of the grave-barrow, Achilles brings forth the prizes for the funeral games, which will occupy the remainder of book XXIII. The events will be the chariot-race (lines 336–751—by far the longest of the events), boxing (752–812), wrestling (813–861), running (862–928), warrior's duel (929–959), putting the shot (960–987), archery (988–1024), and spear-throwing (1025–1043). The events are themselves imitations of aspects of combat; at the games, the contestants deploy the skills and strengths that also serve them on the battlefield, but the victor is restrained by the rules of the contest, while the loser is not victimized, is not made the victor's prize. In the context of the funeral of Patroclus, the games are an opportunity for a wounded and grieving community to reassert, within a controlled arena, some of its constituent strengths and potential unities. Achilles himself, however, remains remote, a detached, god-like convener of the contests and an arbiter of disputes. The sustaining passion of Achilles remains the dragging and defiling of Hector's body, an action in excess of any mortal rules, yet not beyond mortal capacity.

5. (p. 412) *And up got huge Telamonian Ajax and with him / Resourceful Odysseus, skilled at tricks and contriving*: The wrestling contest of Ajax and Odysseus perhaps foreshadows the contest of the same two heroes, at the post-Iliadic funeral games of Achilles, for the hero's arms—a contest that will be won by Odysseus by treachery and one that will lead to Ajax' suicide. Here, Achilles, with the mediating, strife-dispelling tact that he displays throughout the games precludes such a disaster by declaring both heroes to be the victor (so, too, does the poet of the *Iliad* forestall Odysseus' coming victories over a heroism of strength by one of craft).

6. (p. 417) *"Atrides, we all / Know well how far you surpass all others . . . so the basin is yours without a contest"*: If Agamemnon were to lose the spear-throwing contest, the ability of games to disguise and regulate the harder violence and inequities of the social order would be sorely taxed; it is best not to put Agamemnon's prowess to the actual test, but instead to simply acknowledge his preeminence. Thus, in the realm of games, does Achilles avoid an outbreak of the resentments and angers that ignited the strife of book I.

Book XXIV: Priam and Achilles

1. (p. 418) *Achilles, then, madly raging, / Foully dishonored the body of noble Hector . . .* : For Achilles, nothing has changed. Though he convened and adjudicated the rituals of the games with extraordinary grace, those rituals have accomplished nothing for him: He remains restless and disconsolate in his grief and longing for Patroclus; he continues futilely to wreak his inexhaustible vengeance upon Hector's corpse. We move, then, from the realm of social practice (the games) to divine intervention.

2. (p. 419) *". . . But when he has wept and fittingly mourned / For him, he ends his grieving, for surely the fates / Have given to men a tough and patient spirit"*: Apollo, in his complaint to the other gods about the savage mourning of Achilles (he is like a "lordly lion"), describes Achilles as having destroyed pity and shame (Greek *aidos*, on which see endnote 8 to book VI); he is responsive to his community neither as one recognizing a shared mortal lot nor as one guided by that community's norms. Moreover, Achilles' mourning—claims Apollo—exceeds that appropriate for blood-kin, and even the loss of blood-kin is one that mortals, with their "tough" spirits, are able to bring to an end. Apollo's claim about blood-kin is earlier contradicted by Achilles' claim that Patroclus' death is more painful than that of father or son (XIX.371–374, with endnote 6 to book XIX). Finally, the truth of Apollo's claim about the tough, enduring spirit of mortals remains at issue in the following encounter of Achilles and Priam and, especially, in Achilles' retelling of the story of Niobe.

3. (p. 427) *And Priam went on toward the ships, nor were they unnoticed / By far-seeing Zeus:* Priam's nighttime journey to visit Achilles contains many elements of a *katabasis*, or Journey to the Underworld. Even before setting out, Priam has been bewailed as a dead man by Hecuba and by his kin and household. His crossing of the Trojan plain to the shelter of Achilles is guided by Hermes, who is traditionally a *psychopompos*, a conductor of the souls of the dead to Hades. Together, Priam and Hermes pass by a tomb (that of Ilos) and cross over a river. Night, Hermes, the crossings of tomb and of river—these are four mythical boundaries of Hades. The elaborate and emphatically heavy door of Achilles' shelter is also suggestive of the entrance to Hades' palace. Achilles, then, who has slain so many of Priam's sons, plays the role of King of the Dead (or, perhaps, that of Minos, rich judge of the Underworld).

4. (p. 431) *. . . so now Achilles was seized / With exceeding amazement at the sight of sacred Priam, / And those who were with him marveled and looked at each other:* This is the *Iliad's* final and most magnificent scene of supplication: The familiar gesture of grasping the knees is here followed by Priam's kissing of the man-slaying hands of Achilles; in the crossing of a taboo boundary, there is, perhaps, some new possibility of healing. In the simile that follows, Priam is the murderer, while Achilles is the wealthy man who might offer refuge; for a moment each takes on the role of the other (of refugee and of king, of father and of son)—an occasion of wonder, which opens each to the experience of the other's grief; it remains uncertain whether, as Apollo claims, mortals, with their tough hearts, can put their grief away, but between Achilles and Priam grief can now be shared. So, too, can a meal now be shared, as well as the telling of stories, within which Achilles and Priam might locate and make sense of their common humanity.

5. (p. 434) *. . . Achilles himself / Lifted it onto a bier and helped his companions / Lift it onto the wagon:* Having shared in Priam's grief for Hector, Achilles now supervises the washing of Hector's body and, with his own hands, places the body upon the wagon that will carry it to the bier; this is the traditional task of the mother of the dead. Thus, Achilles inaugurates and participates in the burial of Hector, with which the *Iliad* is complete.

INSPIRED BY THE *ILIAD*
AND THE *ODYSSEY*

The *Iliad* and the *Odyssey* established the underpinnings of all subsequent serious Greek poetry and drama. Important Greek poets who followed—from Aeschylus to Sophocles to Theocritus—borrowed techniques used in the two poems, including elevated language and a distinguished hero in a situation of extremity. The Latin critic Longinus pointed out the *Iliad* and the *Odyssey*'s influence on, among others, Plato and Herodotus, and the works' strong impact on ancient Greece was well documented. In addition to poets, dramatists, philosophers, and historians, the overall culture reflected veneration for "Homer"; the Greeks printed his imagined face on coins, held celebration days in his honor, and often repeated his verse aloud.

Virgil's *Aeneid* (c.29–19 B.C.E.), the great Latin poem of the classical age, is in many ways a sequel to the *Iliad*. Virgil modeled the poem on the Greek narrative in an effort to link ancient Greece with the later flowering of Rome. The *Aeneid* follows the journey of the Trojan hero Aeneas as he flees the smoldering remains of Troy and realizes that his destiny is to found a grand new city in the West. The first six books, patterned after the *Odyssey*, trace his journey to what is modern-day Italy. Borrowing heavily from the *Iliad*, the subsequent six books detail the war between the Trojans and the native Latins, who are wary of the influx of foreigners. The Trojans eventually win the war, and Aeneas marries the daughter of a local ruler and establishes the city of Lavinium; his descendants go on to found Rome.

After the Roman Empire collapsed in the late fifth century C.E., Homeric studies became practically dormant for hundreds of years. In the fourteenth century, Italian poets Giovanni Boccaccio and Francesco Petrarca (Petrarch) commissioned Latin translations of the *Iliad* and the *Odyssey* that helped spread the reputation of the epics during the Renaissance. Though in *The House of Fame* (c.1374–1385) Chaucer cites the two poems as a key influence, their impact was slight in England before the sixteenth century, when the study of Greek became more common in schools. George Chapman's famed English translation of the *Iliad* appeared in 1598. Shakespeare drew from Chapman's *Iliad* for the play *Troilus and Cressida*, a tragic love story set in Troy.

The English language's closest match to the *Iliad* and the *Odyssey* is John Milton's *Paradise Lost* (1667); the preeminent epic poem in English, it reflects Milton's profound understanding of the spirit of the great Greek epics. *Paradise Lost* tells the biblical tale of Adam and Eve's fall from grace, with special emphasis on the role of a magnificently characterized Satan. Besides following the style of the *Iliad*, Milton modeled the opening scene and several other parts of his poem directly on it.

In the eighteenth century, Alexander Pope achieved wealth and renown for his translation of the *Iliad*, the first parts of which appeared in 1715. Owing partly to Chapman and Pope, and the decline of medievalism, the *Iliad* and the *Odyssey* were among the most widely read works in England in the seventeenth and eighteenth centuries. Their influence at the time manifested itself most clearly in an abundance of mock epics that parodied the traditional form's lofty themes and diction. Among these the best remembered today is Pope's poem *The Rape of the Lock* (1714).

John Keats wrote two sonnets about the Greek epics: "On First Looking into Chapman's Homer" (1816) and "To Homer" (1818). In the latter poem, Keats writes of the bard:

> So thou wast blind;—but then the veil was rent,
> For Jove uncurtain'd heaven to let thee live,
> And Neptune made for thee a spumy tent,
> And Pan made sing for thee his forest-hive.

Lord Byron wrote the epic *Don Juan* (1819–1824) in the Homeric style, and several other poets also invoked it, including William Wordsworth, Samuel Taylor Coleridge, and Ralph Waldo Emerson. Among nineteenth-century poets, Alfred, Lord Tennyson, most famous for "The Charge of the Light Brigade" (1854), shows the strongest Homeric influence in style and subject. But in general the nineteenth century was a time of invention in the world of poetry, and most authors steered clear of the epic form.

Several twentieth-century poets and prose stylists reimagined the two great epic Greek works with radical new perspectives. Rupert Brooke's poem "Menelaus and Helen" (1911) cynically sees the couple growing senile in Troy years after the war has ended. Arguably the most innovative stylistic adaptation is James Joyce's *Ulysses* (1922), which mirrors Homeric epic in structure and scope yet takes place in modern Dublin on a single day: June 16, 1904. The title poem in W. H. Auden's *The Shield of Achilles* (1955) is a sober work that debunks the supposed majesty of war, instead exposing its gruesome inhumanity. *Omeros* (1990), an epic poem by Caribbean-born Derek Walcott, winner of the 1992 Nobel Prize in Literature, movingly applies the Homeric template to the lives of fisherman and villagers on the island of Saint Lucia.

The twentieth century's invention on behalf of narrative—the cinema—has made abundant use of the two great Greek epics. Recently, Brad Pitt starred as Achilles in director Wolfgang Petersen's blockbuster *Troy* (2004), which was loosely based on the *Iliad*. Generally, however, film has favored the *Odyssey* over its counterpart; the creative adaptation of Joel and Ethan Cohen's *O Brother, Where Art Thou?* (2000) is a notable example.

COMMENTS & QUESTIONS

In this section, we aim to provide the reader with an array of perspectives on the text, as well as questions that challenge those perspectives. The commentary has been culled from sources as diverse as comments contemporaneous with the work, literary criticism of later generations, and appreciations written throughout the work's history. Following the commentary, a series of questions seeks to filter Homer's Iliad through a variety of points of view and bring about a richer understanding of this enduring work.

Comments

PLATO

Homer intended Achilles to be the bravest of the men who went to Troy, Nestor the wisest, and Odysseus the wiliest.

—from *Lesser Hippias* (c.399 B.C.E.),
translated by Benjamin Jowett (1871)

ARISTOTLE

Besides this, Epic poetry must divide into the same species as Tragedy; it must be either simple or complex, a story of character or one of suffering. Its parts, too, with the exception of Song and Spectacle, must be the same, as it requires Peripeties, Discoveries, and scenes of suffering just like Tragedy. Lastly, the Thought and Diction in it must be good in their way. All these elements appear in Homer first; and he has made due use of them. His two poems are each examples of construction, the *Iliad* simple and a story of suffering, the *Odyssey* complex (there is Discovery throughout it) and a story of character. And they are more than this, since in Diction and Thought too they surpass all other poems.

—from the *Poetics* (c.350 B.C.E.),
translated by Ingram Bywater (1920)

QUINTILIAN

I shall, I think, be right in following the principle laid down by Aratus in the line, "With Jove let us begin," and in beginning with Homer. He is like his own conception of Ocean, which he describes as the source of every stream and river; for he has given us a model and an inspiration for every department of eloquence. It will be generally admitted

489

that no one has ever surpassed him in the sublimity with which he invests great themes or the propriety with which he handles small. He is at once luxuriant and concise, sprightly and serious, remarkable at once for his fullness and his brevity, and supreme not merely for poetic, but for oratorical power as well. For, to say nothing of his eloquence, which he shows in praise, exhortation and consolation, do not the ninth book containing the embassy to Achilles, the first describing the quarrel between the chiefs, or the speeches delivered by the counsellors in the second, display all the rules of art to be followed in forensic or deliberative oratory? As regards the emotions, there can be no one so illeducated as to deny that the poet was the master of all, tender and vehement alike. Again, in the few lines with which he introduces both of his epics, has he not, I will not say observed, but actually established the law which should govern the composition of the exordium? For, by his invocation of the goddesses believed to preside over poetry he wins the goodwill of his audience, by his statement of the greatness of his themes he excites their attention and renders them receptive by the briefness of his summary. Who can narrate more briefly than the hero who brings the news of Patroclus' death, or more vividly than he who describes the battle between the Curetes and the Aetolians? Then consider his similes, his amplifications, his illustrations, digressions, indications of fact, inferences, and all the other methods of proof and refutation which he employs. They are so numerous that the majority of writers on the principles of rhetoric have gone to his works for examples of all these things. And as for perorations, what can ever be equal to the prayers which Priam addresses to Achilles when he comes to beg for the body of his son? Again, does he not transcend the limits of human genius in his choice of words, his reflexions, figures, and the arrangement of his whole work, with the result that it requires a powerful mind, I will not say to imitate, for that is impossible, but even to appreciate his excellences? But he has in truth outdistanced all that have come after him in every department of eloquence; above all, he has outstripped all other writers of epic, the contrast in their case being especially striking owing to the similarity of the material with which they deal.

—from *Institutio Oratoria* (c.96 A.C.E.),
translated by H. E. Butler (1920)

LONGINUS

Was Herodotus alone a devoted imitator of Homer? No, Stesichorus even before his time, and Archilochus, and above all Plato, who from the great Homeric source drew to himself innumerable tributary streams. And perhaps we should have found it necessary to prove this, point by point, had not Ammonius and his followers selected and recorded the particulars.

This proceeding is not plagiarism; it is like taking an impression from beautiful forms or figures or other works of art. And it seems to me that there would not have been so fine a bloom of perfection on Plato's philosophical doctrines, and that he would not in many cases have found his way to poetical subject-matter and modes of expression, unless he had with all his heart and mind struggled with Homer for the primacy, entering the lists like a young champion matched against the man whom all admire, and showing perhaps too much love of contention and breaking a lance with him as it were, but deriving some profit from the contest none the less. For, as Hesiod says, "This strife is good for mortals." And in truth that struggle for the crown of glory is noble and best deserves the victory in which even to be worsted by one's predecessors brings no discredit.

—from *On the Sublime* (approximately first century C.E.),
translated by W. Rhys Roberts (1899)

ALEXANDER POPE

Homer is universally allowed to have had the greatest invention of any writer whatever. The praise of judgment Virgil has justly contested with him, and others may have their pretensions as to particular excellences; but his invention remains yet unrivalled. Nor is it a wonder if he has ever been acknowledged the greatest of poets, who most excelled in that which is the very foundation of poetry. It is the invention that, in different degrees, distinguishes all great geniuses. . . .

Our author's work is a wild paradise, where, if we cannot see all the beauties so distinctly as in an ordered garden, it is only because the number of them is infinitely greater. It is like a copious nursery, which contains the seeds and first productions of every kind, out of which those who followed him have but selected some particular plants, each according to his fancy, to cultivate and beautify. If some things are too luxuriant it is owing to the richness of the soil; and if others are not arrived to perfection or maturity, it is only because they are overrun and oppressed by those of a stronger nature.

It is to the strength of this amazing invention we are to attribute that unequalled fire and rapture which is so forcible in Homer, that no man of a true poetical spirit is master of himself while he reads him. What he writes is of the most animated nature imaginable; every thing moves, every thing lives, and is put in action. If a council be called, or a battle fought, you are not coldly informed of what was said or done as from a third person; the reader is hurried out of himself by the force of the poet's imagination, and turns in one place to a hearer, in another to a spectator. . . .

We come now to the characters of his persons; and here we shall find no author has ever drawn so many, with so visible and surprising a variety, or given us such lively and affecting impressions of them. Every one has something so singularly his own, that no painter could have distinguished them more by their features, than the poet has by their manners. Nothing can be more exact than the distinctions he has observed in the different degrees of virtues and vices. The single quality of courage is wonderfully diversified in the several characters of the Iliad. . . .

If we descend from hence to the expression, we see the bright imagination of Homer shining out in the most enlivened forms of it. We acknowledge him the father of poetical diction; the first who taught that "language of the gods" to men. His expression is like the colouring of some great masters, which discovers itself to be laid on boldly, and executed with rapidity. It is, indeed, the strongest and most glowing imaginable, and touched with the greatest spirit. Aristotle had reason to say, he was the only poet who had found out "living words"; there are in him more daring figures and metaphors than in any good author whatever. An arrow is "impatient" to be on the wing, a weapon "thirsts" to drink the blood of an enemy, and the like, yet his expression is never too big for the sense, but justly great in proportion to it. It is the sentiment that swells and fills out the diction, which rises with it, and forms itself about it, for in the same degree that a thought is warmer, an expression will be brighter, as that is more strong, this will become more perspicuous; like glass in the furnace, which grows to a greater magnitude, and refines to a greater clearness, only as the breath within is more powerful, and the heat more intense.

—from the preface to his translation of the Iliad (1715)

SAMUEL RICHARDSON

I admire you for what you say of the fierce, fighting Iliad. Scholars, judicious scholars, dared they to speak out, against a prejudice of thousands of years in its favour, I am persuaded would find it possible for Homer to nod, at least. I am afraid this poem, noble as it truly is, has done infinite mischief for a series of ages; since to it, and its copy the Eneid, is owing, in a great measure, the savage spirit that has actuated, from the earliest ages to this time, the fighting fellows, that, worse than lions or tigers, have ravaged the earth, and made it a field of blood.

—from a letter to Lady Bradshaigh (1749)

PERCY BYSSHE SHELLEY

I have [been] reading little else but Homer. I am now in the 23rd book; you can imagine the wonders of poetry which I have enjoyed in the five preceding books. Indeed this part of the Iliad, the Patrocleiad, seems to me to surpass all other portions of the Iliad, as that production considered as a whole surpasses any other single production of the human mind. Familiarity with Homer increases our admiration and astonishment— I can never believe that the Odyssey is a work of the same author.

—from a letter to Thomas Jefferson Hogg (July 6, 1817)

HENRY DAVID THOREAU

But in Homer and Chaucer there is more of the innocence and serenity of youth than in the more modern and moral poets. The Iliad is not Sabbath but morning reading, and men cling to this old song, because they still have moments of unbaptized and uncommitted life, which give them an appetite for more. To the innocent there are neither cherubim nor angels. At rare intervals we rise above the necessity of virtue into an unchangeable morning light, in which we have only to live right on and breathe the ambrosial air. The Iliad represents no creed nor opinion, and we read it with a rare sense of freedom and irresponsibility, as if we trod on native ground, and were autochthones of the soil.

—from A Week on the Concord and Merrimack Rivers (1849)

MATTHEW ARNOLD

I think there never yet has been a perfect literature or a perfect art because the energetic nations spoil them by their illusions and their want of taste—and the nations who lose their illusions lose also their energy and creative power. Certainly Goethe had all the negative recommendations for a perfect artist but he wanted the positive—Shakespeare had the positive and wanted the negative. The Iliad and what I know of Raphael's works seem to me to be in a juster measure and a happier vein than anything else.

—from a letter to Arthur Hugh Clough (September 6, 1853)

GEORGE MEREDITH

So you like Ballads. Well, the Iliad, greatest of poems, is a great Ballad. So you choose well.

—from a letter to Mlle. Hilda de Longueuil (April 30, 1887)

EDWARD THOMAS

I am interested in nothing and would for ever sit still and seek nothing if I had to be continually nailing my mind to something with my nice docility. And yet unawares I am lured into interest as when I found my-self today near crying as I read the Iliad to Merfyn.

—from a note found among his wife's letters (October 9, 1907)

G. K. CHESTERTON

One vital mistake is made about this matter by Mr. Carnegie and his kind. They persistently say, and they actually seem to think, that wars arise out of hatred. There may have been wars that arose out of hatred, but at this instant I cannot recollect a single one. In this, as in many other matters, the truest tale in the world is the Iliad or Siege of Troy. Wars never begin in hatred; they either arise out of the honourable af-fection a man has for his own possessions; or else out of the black and furtive affection he has for someone else's possessions. But it is always affection; it is never hate. The Greeks and Trojans did not hate each other in the least; there is scarcely one spark of hatred in the whole of the Iliad, save that great flare that comes out of the hero's love for Patro-clus. The two armies are strewing the plain with corpses and dyeing the very sea with blood from love and not from detestation. It all arises because Paris has conceived an evil affection for Helen, while Menelaus cannot cease to love her. In other words, both hosts are fight-ing, not because fighting is not nasty, but because they have something nice to fight about. . . .

If one may love a tree one may love a forest; if a forest, one may love a valley; if a valley, a whole country or a whole character of civilisation. One may love it rightly, like Menelaus, or wrongly, like Paris. But it is al-ways desire and not repugnance.

—from the Illustrated London News (January 14, 1911)

HENRY BRADLEY

I have got through 13 books of the Iliad, bored a good deal with read-ing how X wounded Y, how Y killed X, and what a lot of blood ran out of X + Y. But the Hector and Andromache passage is not surpassed, if it is equalled, by anything even in the Odyssey; and I stick to my old heresy that the much despised Doloneia is a brilliant piece of work, though it does look like a patch of different colour from the coat.

—from a letter to Robert Bridges (March 16, 1912)

HAROLD LASKI

The Iliad, after all, is great drama; the scene for instance where Priam goes to ask Achilles for the body of Hector, and is refused, would wring the heart of a stone.

—from a letter to Oliver Wendell Holmes (August 29, 1923)

Questions

1. Let's say that Agamemnon can stand for institutional power, although the man is a moral pipsqueak. And Achilles, we could say, stands for individual genius; no one doubts that he is a great warrior. Surrounding them is their community, which has its own kind of authority and power. If you were a soldier on the field of Troy, to which of these three would you lend your support? But remember that sometimes we support a weak ruler for the sake of public order, or to unite a community toward an important goal, such as winning a war. Remember also that sometimes charismatic geniuses, people we admire and even love, make ruinous mistakes. And remember that majority opinion can be wrong, as when almost everybody everywhere thought that the institution of slavery was perfectly acceptable.

2. What would you say is the function of Thersites, Odysseus, or Diomedes within the *Iliad* as a whole?

3. Which would you choose: a long life celebrated by no one but your immediate circle, or a short life of dramatic accomplishment and unwithering fame?

4. Does the *Iliad* in your eyes have any relevance to events occurring now?

FOR FURTHER READING

General Reference, Historical Works, and Collections of Essays

Cairns, D. L. Oxford Readings in Homer's "Iliad." Oxford and New York: Oxford University Press, 2001.

Fowler, R. The Cambridge Companion to Homer. Cambridge: Cambridge University Press, 2004.

Kirk, G. S., general editor. The "Iliad:" A Commentary. 6 vols. Cambridge: Cambridge University Press, 1985–1993. These volumes have been near at hand in the preparation of the endnotes for this edition.

Morris, I., and B. Powell. A New Companion to Homer. Leiden and New York: Brill, 1997.

Snodgrass, A. Archaic Greece: The Age of Experiment. Berkeley and Los Angeles: University of California Press, 1981.

Vernant, J.-P. The Origins of Greek Thought. Ithaca, NY: Cornell University Press, 1982.

See also www.stoa.org/chs for recent state-of-the-art work in Homeric studies.

Introductions to the Iliad

Edwards, M. Homer: Poet of the "Iliad." Baltimore, MD: Johns Hopkins University Press, 1987.

Owen, E. T. 1946. The Story of the "Iliad." Ann Arbor, MI: University of Michigan Press, 1966.

Schein, S. L. The Mortal Hero: An Introduction to Homer's "Iliad." Berkeley and Los Angeles: University of California Press, 1984.

Books on the Iliad: The Traditional Background

Foley, J. M. Homer's Traditional Art. University Park, PA: Pennsylvania State University Press, 1999.

Graziosi, B. Inventing Homer: The Early Reception of Epic. Cambridge: Cambridge University Press, 2002.

Lord, A. B. 1960. The Singer of Tales. Second edition, with an introduction by the editors, S. Mitchell and G. Nagy. Cambridge, MA, and London: Harvard University Press, 2000.

Muellner, L. C. *The Anger of Achilles: Mênis in Greek Epic*. Ithaca, NY: Cornell University Press, 1996.

Nagler, M. N. *Spontaneity and Tradition: A Study in the Oral Art of Homer*. Berkeley and Los Angeles: University of California Press, 1974.

Nagy, G. 1979. *The Best of the Achaeans: Concepts of the Hero in Archaic Greek Poetry*. Revised edition. Baltimore and London: Johns Hopkins University Press, 1999.

————. *Greek Mythology and Poetics*. Ithaca, NY: Cornell University Press, 1990.

————. *Pindar's Homer: The Lyric Possession of an Epic Past*. Baltimore: Johns Hopkins University Press, 1990.

Parry, M. *The Making of Homeric Verse: The Collected Papers of Milman Parry*. Edited by A. Parry. Oxford: Clarendon Press, 1971.

Slatkin, L. M. *The Power of Thetis: Allusion and Interpretation in the "Iliad."* Berkeley and Los Angeles: University of California Press, 1991.

Books on the Iliad: Historical and Anthropological Views

Detienne, M. *The Masters of Truth in Archaic Greece*. Translated by J. Lloyd. New York: Zone Books (distributed by MIT Press), 1996.

Dodds, E. R. *The Greeks and the Irrational*. 1951. Berkeley: University of California Press, 2004.

Finley, M. I. 1954. *The World of Odysseus*. Revised second edition. London: Chatto and Windus, 1977.

Haubold, J. *Homer's People: Epic Poetry and Social Formation*. Cambridge: Cambridge University Press, 2000.

Loraux, N. *The Experiences of Tiresias: The Feminine and the Greek Man*. Translated by P. Wissing. Princeton, NJ: Princeton University Press, 1995.

Redfield, J. M. 1975. *Nature and Culture in the "Iliad": The Tragedy of Hector*. Expanded edition. Durham, NC: Duke University Press, 1994.

Seaford, R. *Reciprocity and Ritual: Homer and Tragedy in the Developing City-State*. Oxford and New York: Oxford University Press, 1994.

Shay, J. *Achilles in Vietnam: Combat Trauma and the Undoing of Character*. New York: Atheneum, 1994.

Tatum, J. *The Mourner's Song: War and Remembrance from the "Iliad" to Vietnam*. Chicago: University of Chicago Press, 2003.

Vernant, J.-P. *Mortals and Immortals: Collected Essays*. Edited by F. I. Zeitlin. Princeton, NJ: Princeton University Press, 1991.

Wilson, D. F. *Ransom, Revenge, and Heroic Identity in the "Iliad."* Cambridge and New York: Cambridge University Press, 2002.

Books on the Iliad: Literary and Artistic Perspectives

Basset, S. E. *The Poetry of Homer.* Berkeley and Los Angeles: University of California Press, 1938.

Ford, A. *Homer: The Poetry of the Past.* Ithaca, NY: Cornell University Press, 1992.

Friis Johansen, K. *The "Iliad" in Early Greek Art.* Copenhagen: Munksgaard, 1967.

King, K. C. *Achilles: Paradigms of the War Hero from Homer to the Middle Ages.* Berkeley and Los Angeles: University of California Press, 1987.

Lynn-George, M. *Epos: Word, Narrative, and the "Iliad."* Atlantic Highlands, NJ: Humanities Press International, 1988.

Segal, C. *The Theme of the Mutilation of the Corpse in the "Iliad."* Leiden, The Netherlands: Brill, 1971.

Snodgrass, A. *Homer and the Artists: Text and Picture in Early Greek Art.* Cambridge and New York: Cambridge University Press, 1998.

Stanley, K. *The Shield of Homer: Narrative Structure in the "Iliad."* Princeton: Princeton University Press, 1993.

Taplin, O. *Homeric Soundings: The Shaping of the "Iliad."* Oxford: Oxford University Press, 1992.

Weil, S. *Simone Weil's "The Iliad"; or, The Poem of Force.* Edited and translated by J. P. Holoka. New York: P. Lang, 2003.

Whitman, C. H. *Homer and the Heroic Tradition.* Cambridge, MA: Harvard University Press, 1958.

INDEX

The following index shows syllabic accent for most of the proper names in this book and gives selected page numbers for their occurrence.

501

Look for the following titles, available now and forthcoming from
BARNES & NOBLE CLASSICS.

Visit your local bookstore for these and more fine titles.
Or to order online go to: WWW.BN.COM/CLASSICS

Title	Author	ISBN	Price
Aesop's Fables	Aesop	1-59308-062-X	$5.95
The Age of Innocence	Edith Wharton	1-59308-143-X	$5.95
Agnes Grey	Anne Brontë	1-59308-323-8	$5.95
Alice's Adventures in Wonderland and Through the Looking-Glass	Lewis Carroll	1-59308-015-8	$5.95
Anna Karenina	Leo Tolstoy	1-59308-027-1	$8.95
The Art of War	Sun Tzu	1-59308-017-4	$7.95
The Awakening and Selected Short Fiction	Kate Chopin	1-59308-113-8	$6.95
Babbitt	Sinclair Lewis	1-59308-267-3	$7.95
Barchester Towers	Anthony Trollope	1-59308-337-8	$7.95
The Beautiful and Damned	F. Scott Fitzgerald	1-59308-245-2	$7.95
Beowulf	Anonymous	1-59308-266-5	$4.95
Bleak House	Charles Dickens	1-59308-311-4	$9.95
The Bostonians	Henry James	1-59308-297-5	$7.95
The Brothers Karamazov	Fyodor Dostoevsky	1-59308-045-X	$9.95
The Call of the Wild and White Fang	Jack London	1-59308-200-2	$5.95
Candide	Voltaire	1-59308-028-X	$4.95
A Christmas Carol, The Chimes and The Cricket on the Hearth	Charles Dickens	1-59308-033-6	$5.95
The Collected Poems of Emily Dickinson	Emily Dickinson	1-59308-050-6	$5.95
Common Sense and Other Writings	Thomas Paine	1-59308-209-6	$6.95
The Communist Manifesto and Other Writings	Karl Marx and Friedrich Engels	1-59308-100-6	$5.95
The Complete Sherlock Holmes, Vol. I	Sir Arthur Conan Doyle	1-59308-034-4	$7.95
The Complete Sherlock Holmes, Vol. II	Sir Arthur Conan Doyle	1-59308-040-9	$7.95
A Connecticut Yankee in King Arthur's Court	Mark Twain	1-59308-210-X	$7.95
The Count of Monte Cristo	Alexandre Dumas	1-59308-151-0	$7.95
The Country of the Pointed Firs and Selected Short Fiction	Sarah Orne Jewett	1-59308-262-2	$6.95
Daisy Miller and Washington Square	Henry James	1-59308-105-7	$4.95
Daniel Deronda	George Eliot	1-59308-290-8	$8.95
David Copperfield	Charles Dickens	1-59308-063-8	$7.95
Dead Souls	Nikolai Gogol	1-59308-092-1	$7.95
The Death of Ivan Ilych and Other Stories	Leo Tolstoy	1-59308-069-7	$7.95
The Deerslayer	James Fenimore Cooper	1-59308-211-8	$7.95
Don Quixote	Miguel de Cervantes	1-59308-046-8	$9.95
Dracula	Bram Stoker	1-59308-114-6	$6.95
Emma	Jane Austen	1-59308-152-9	$6.95
The Enchanted Castle and Five Children and It	Edith Nesbit	1-59308-274-6	$6.95
Essays and Poems by Ralph Waldo Emerson		1-59308-076-X	$6.95
Essential Dialogues of Plato		1-59308-269-X	$9.95
The Essential Tales and Poems of Edgar Allan Poe		1-59308-064-6	$7.95
Ethan Frome and Selected Stories	Edith Wharton	1-59308-090-5	$5.95

(continued)

(continued)

Sister Carrie	Theodore Dreiser	1-59308-226-6	$7.95
Six Plays by Henrik Ibsen		1-59308-061-1	$8.95
Sons and Lovers	D. H. Lawrence	1-59308-013-1	$7.95
The Souls of Black Folk	W. E. B. Du Bois	1-59308-014-X	$5.95
The Strange Case of Dr. Jekyll and Mr. Hyde and Other Stories	Robert Louis Stevenson	1-59308-131-6	$4.95
Swann's Way	Marcel Proust	1-59308-295-9	$8.95
A Tale of Two Cities	Charles Dickens	1-59308-138-3	$5.95
Tao Te Ching	Lao Tzu	1-59308-256-8	$5.95
Tess of d'Urbervilles	Thomas Hardy	1-59308-228-2	$7.95
This Side of Paradise	F. Scott Fitzgerald	1-59308-243-6	$6.95
Three Lives	Gertrude Stein	1-59308-320-3	$6.95
The Three Musketeers	Alexandre Dumas	1-59308-148-0	$8.95
Thus Spoke Zarathustra	Friedrich Nietzsche	1-59308-278-9	$7.95
Tom Jones	Henry Fielding	1-59308-070-0	$8.95
Treasure Island	Robert Louis Stevenson	1-59308-247-9	$4.95
The Turn of the Screw, The Aspern Papers and Two Stories	Henry James	1-59308-043-3	$5.95
Twenty Thousand Leagues Under the Sea	Jules Verne	1-59308-302-5	$5.95
Uncle Tom's Cabin	Harriet Beecher Stowe	1-59308-121-9	$7.95
Utopia	Sir Thomas More	1-59308-244-4	$5.95
Vanity Fair	William Makepeace Thackeray	1-59308-071-9	$7.95
The Varieties of Religious Experience	William James	1-59308-072-7	$7.95
Villette	Charlotte Brontë	1-59308-316-5	$7.95
The Virginian	Owen Wister	1-59308-236-3	$7.95
The Voyage Out	Virginia Woolf	1-59308-229-0	$6.95
Walden and Civil Disobedience	Henry David Thoreau	1-59308-208-8	$5.95
War and Peace	Leo Tolstoy	1-59308-073-5	$12.95
Ward No. 6 and Other Stories	Anton Chekhov	1-59308-003-4	$7.95
The Waste Land and Other Poems	T. S. Eliot	1-59308-279-7	$4.95
The Way We Live Now	Anthony Trollope	1-59308-304-1	$9.95
The Wind in the Willows	Kenneth Grahame	1-59308-265-7	$4.95
The Wings of the Dove	Henry James	1-59308-296-7	$7.95
Wives and Daughters	Elizabeth Gaskell	1-59308-257-6	$7.95
The Woman in White	Wilkie Collins	1-59308-280-0	$7.95
Women in Love	D. H. Lawrence	1-59308-258-4	$8.95
The Wonderful Wizard of Oz	L. Frank Baum	1-59308-221-5	$6.95
Wuthering Heights	Emily Brontë	1-59308-128-6	$5.95